# The Immortals

# Other Books by Tamora Pierce

## Song of the Lioness

*Alanna: The First Adventure*
*In the Hand of the Goddess*
*The Woman Who Rides Like a Man*
*Lioness Rampant*

## Protector of the Small

*First Test*
*Page*
*Squire*
*Lady Knight*

## Circle of Magic

*Sandry's Book*
*Tris's Book*
*Daja's Book*
*Briar's Book*

## The Circle Opens

*Magic Steps*
*Street Magic*
*Cold Fire*
*Shatterglass*

## Daughter of the Lioness

*Trickster's Choice*
*Trickster's Bet* (coming in 2004)

# The Immortals

### Wild Magic
### Wolf-Speaker
### Emperor Mage
### The Realms of the Gods

# Tamora Pierce

50 YEARS
SFBC
SCIENCE
FICTION

WILD MAGIC Copyright © 1992 by Tamora Pierce
WOLF-SPEAKER Copyright © 1994 by Tamora Pierce
EMPEROR MAGE Copyright © 1995 by Tamora Pierce
THE REALMS OF THE GODS Copyright © 1996 by Tamora Pierce

First SFBC Science Fiction Printing: November 2003.

Published by arrangement with Atheneum Books for Young Readers,
a division of Simon & Schuster Children's Publishing
1230 Avenue of the Americas
New York, NY 10020

Visit The SFBC at http://www.sfbc.com

ISBN # 0-7394-3803-4

Printed in the United States of America.

# Contents

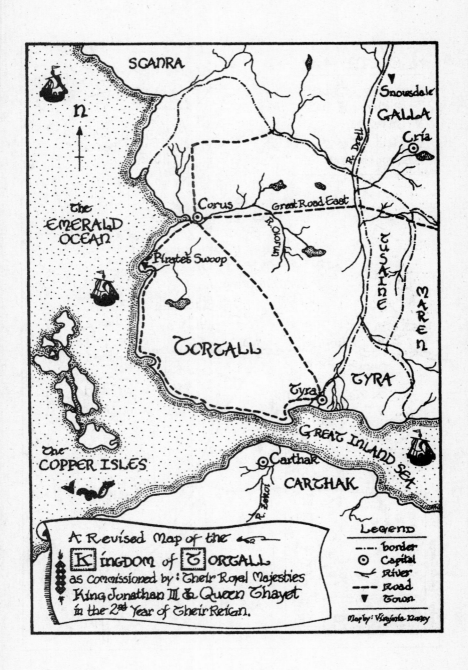

SCANRA

the
EMERALD
OCEAN

Snowsdale
GALLA
Cria

R. Drell

Corus

Great Road East

TUSAINE

MAREN

Pirate's Swoop

R. Olorun

TORTALL

the
COPPER ISLES

Tyra

TYRA

GREAT INLAND SEA

Carthak

CARTHAK

R. Zekoi

A Revised Map of the
Kingdom of Tortall
as commissioned by: Their Royal Majesties
King Jonathan III & Queen Thayet
in the 2nd Year of Their Reign.

Legend
---- border
⊙ Capital
~ River
---- Road
▼ Town

Map by: Virginia Norey

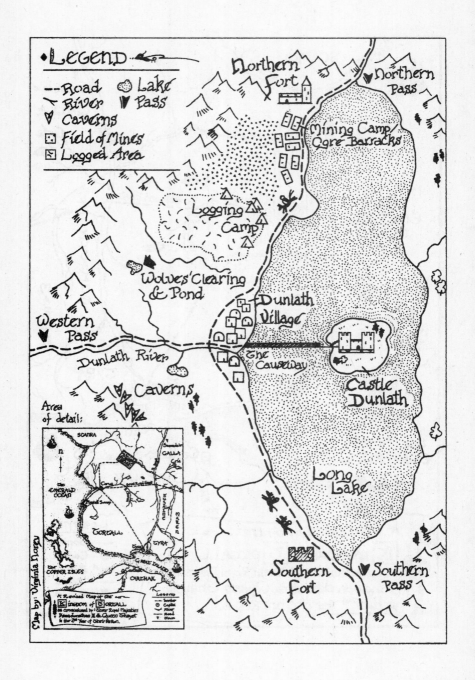

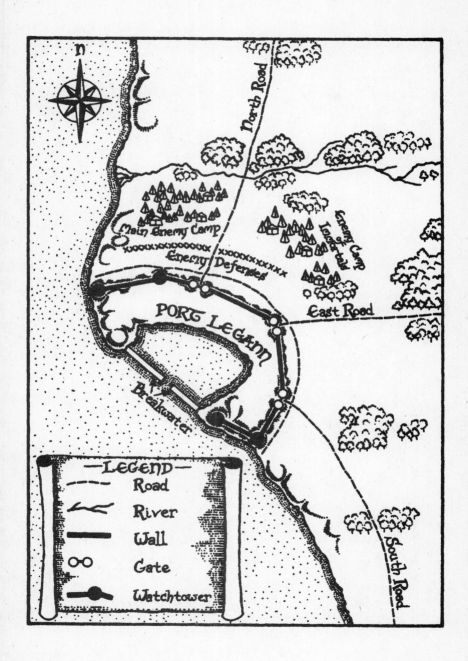

n

North Road

Main Enemy Camp
xxxxxxxxxxxxxx  xxxxxxxxxx
Enemy Defenses

Enemy Camp
Longtrails

East Road

PORT LEGANN

Breakwater

South Road

-LEGEND-
--- Road
River
Wall
∞ Gate
Watchtower

# WILD MAGIC

To Raquel Wolf—Sister

and

Tas horse—hearted

Who opened my heart to the songs of all beasts

# Contents

# Contents

# ➤➤ ONE ◀◀

# GIRL WITH A PONY

Each year, at the end of March, a great fair was held in Cría, the capital of Galla. Like thousands of others in the Eastern Lands, Onua Chamtong went there to do business: buying ponies, in her case. This year she had another transaction to make and was having no luck with it. By the end of her fifth day at the fair, it seemed she would never find the assistant she required. The prospect of taking her animals south, with no one to help, was an unpleasant one.

"Excuse me—Trader Onua?" The speaker was a girl, shy and country bred. "I heard you was hiring. I'm"—she paused, then went on—"a fair hand with animals, all kinds." She waited as Onua looked her over: a girl in a green wool dress, skirts short enough to show leggings and boots. Brown curls tamed by a head-scarf fell to thin shoulders. A soft, full mouth said she was vulnerable; her chin was entirely stubborn. A quiver filled with long arrows hung on her back, a bow rested in her hand, unstrung.

"Is that yours?" the trader asked, pointing.

Blue-gray eyes flashed. "I'd not have the nerve to carry it otherwise."

"Hmph. String it." The girl hesitated. "Just what I thought," Onua jibed. "Whose is it, really?"

The girl brought a coiled string out of her sash. With ease she fitted it to one end of the bow and set it against her foot. Raising the free end of the string, she brought the other end of the bow down, hooking them together neatly. The bow strung and in her grip, she turned sideways to it, caught the string in two fingers, and drew it back to her ear in a smooth, practiced gesture. Now Onua could see she wore an archer's wrist- and armguards.

"I'd put an arrow up," the girl said, gently releasing the string, "but I'd hit someone, surely."

Onua grinned. "I'm impressed. I can't draw a bow that big."

The girl took the string off the bow, coiled it, and put it away. "Nor did I, at first. I keep this one limber, or I *still* couldn't draw it."

"Crossbow?" The question was out before Onua remembered, I don't want to hire her—I want to send her home to her mama. She's a runaway for sure.

"Yes'm. We have—" Something flickered in her eyes. She looked down. "We *had* bandits at home. I stood watch with the sheep, so I learned crossbow and longbow. And sling"—a half smile appeared—"not that I'm bragging."

We *had*, Onua thought. Did she change it 'cause she wants me to think she's been gone from home awhile? Or hasn't she *got* a home?

Something looked around the girl, inspecting Onua with a large brown eye. It was a shaggy mountain pony, a steel gray mare. She was plump and well combed, and bore two packs easily.

"Yours?" The girl nodded. "How much would you ask for her?" Onua motioned to a pen filled with ponies at her back. "I'm in the market."

"I can't sell Cloud. She's family—all the family I got." Again Onua saw a flash of sorrow that was pushed aside.

"What's your name?" The K'mir stuck her fingers into a pouch filled with a powder known as "eyebright."

"Daine, mum," came the soft reply. "Veralidaine Sarrasri."

The eyebright made her fingers itch when Onua called on her magical Gift. "How old are you, Daine?"

"Fifteen." An aura of red fire, visible only to Onua, flared around the girl's face. The lie was a good one—she must have practiced on the way, the trader thought wryly—but a lie nevertheless. She looked about thirteen.

"Where are you from?"

"Snowsdale, up north. About two weeks' walk."

There was no flare of red—she had told the truth. Onua sighed. "Are you a runaway? From home, or a bad master—"

"No, mum." The soft mouth trembled. "I got no family—just Cloud."

No red fire this time. Onua dusted the powder from her hand. "I'm Onua Chamtong, of the K'miri Raadeh."

Daine looked puzzled. "The k-k—the what?"

"The K'mir are a people to the east. Raadeh is the name of one of the K'miri tribes." Daine looked only slightly less baffled. "Never mind.

You say you're good with animals. C'mere." She led the girl to her pen. Inside, twenty-seven shaggy ponies in all colors and sizes milled around.

"I buy horses. I had an assistant, but he got offered a better job working for a horse merchant here, and I wasn't about to hold him back. *If* you hire on—and I didn't say I'd hire you—you'll help me take these south. It's three weeks' drive—*if* we don't bog down in mud, *if* we aren't hit by raiders, and *if* we go before all these people take the road to the next fair. It'll be just you and me, and my dog, Tahoi. Why don't you climb in and look 'em over? I want to see how you manage 'em."

Daine glanced back at her mare, Cloud. "Stay put, and *no biting*," she ordered sternly, and clambered over the fence and into the pen.

Poor thing must have been alone a long time, to be talking to a mare as if she could answer back, Onua thought. She sat on the fence rail to watch.

The ponies watched as Daine passed among them. Ears went back. Those close to her appeared to wonder which would do better: a bite or a kick.

When a yellow stallion, the king of the small herd, minced into place at her back, the girl spun and put both hands under his muzzle, lifting his head to stare into his face. "No, sir," she told him firmly. "I'll not stand for any tricks. I may be human, but I'm not stupid." The stallion tried to rear. She forced him down, then blew gently in his nostrils, to teach him her scent. He shuffled, then fidgeted—then bowed his head in submission.

Horse Lords, Onua thought. She's establishing domination over him and the entire herd!

In years of managing horses, she'd never seen the like. This particular breed was famous for its fiery nature (one of the reasons she purchased them for her employers). She had achieved peace—of a sort— with them using her strength, her wits, and bribes. All horse folk handled their animals that way. Only this child was different: Daine treated the stallion as if she were a pony herself, a dominant one.

She isn't lying about her folks or running away—just about her age. If I let her go, she might get into trouble. There are too many predators around, looking for a pretty like this one. The road isn't too safe—but what is?

She watched the girl move among the ponies, running her hands over each one. She was giving them bits of apple and sugar from her pockets. Onua was glad to see she *could* deal with the animals in a normal way. One display like that with the stallion was more than enough.

"D'you ride?" she called.

Daine came over to the fence. "Some. Mostly bareback, but I can use a saddle, and I know how to look after tack."

"What about hunting, fishing, tracking?"

The grin lit a face that was too thin and eyes that were too weary. "I do all that—had to, to get this far. I couldn't trust folks on the road. Some looked like—bandits."

As Daine climbed over the rail, the shadow was back in her eyes: grief, Onua decided, but anger too. "Tired of them already?"

The girl shook her head. "I'm getting an oil I have, and a swab. The strawberry has ear mites. They're not too bad—if I get them now, he won't spread them to the herd." She went to the gray mare, who was plainly sulking, and opened one of her packs.

"How do you know you can trust me?"

Daine shrugged. "I don't. How do you know you can trust *me*?"

"Was that a joke?" Onua's voice was stern, but her eyes laughed. Her last two assistants had possessed no sense of humor.

Daine gave her a quick smile and climbed into the pen, a clay bottle and swabs in one hand. Onua watched, amazed, as the strawberry gelding trotted up to the girl. If someone had said that morning she'd see one of her charges willingly submit to an ear cleaning, she would have laughed herself sick.

*I shouldn't do it. She's a baby. There're all those rumors—no smoke without fire. Still, my magic will keep us safe at night, and she can handle a bow.* "Daine!" she called.

The girl had finished the gelding's ears. She came over. "Yes?"

"I'll tell you right now—I've heard a lot of weird stories lately, about monsters in the wild, attacking travelers. Things out of legend, so folk say. I haven't seen any myself, but that doesn't mean I won't. Are you sure you want to hire on?"

Daine shrugged. "I hear tales. I need work, mum. If I see monsters, I see monsters. My family was killed and my home burned by human ones."

"All right, then—here's the job," said the K'mir. "You, me, and my dog take the herd south, like I said. I have the Gift, and I can shield our camp at night. It's two coppers a day, two silver nobles as a bonus at the end. I pay all expenses, and we share chores. No drinking, no drugs. If you leave me on the trail, you'll wish you died as a child." Daine giggled. "At the end of the road—we'll see. We're bound for the capital of Tortall—"

The girl's face lit up. "Where a lady knight is the king's champion, right? And they let girls in the army? *That* Tortall?"

"You heard those stories too," the K'mir murmured. "Well they don't let girls in the regular army, mind—just the Queen's Riders. Why—have you a fancy to be a soldier?"

Daine shook her head. "Not me. But if they take girls for that, maybe they'll let a girl be a hostler, or work around the camp, or some such." Her eyes were filled with painful hope.

"As it happens, they *do* let girls work as hostlers—or at least, they let me. I'm in charge of the horses for the Riders."

"Oh, glory," the girl whispered. "I'll do whatever you want, if you'll take me on—"

Onua put a hand on Daine's shoulder, touched by her eagerness. "We'll see. If we don't get on, I'll make sure you have some kind of work. I won't leave you stranded. Sound fair?"

Daine nodded vigorously. "Yes, Mistress Onua."

Onua offered a callused hand. "Then shake on it. And stop calling me 'Mistress.' My name's Onua."

Daine returned the woman's firm grip. "Onua Chamtong, of the K'miri Raadeh," she said. "I remember."

Onua smiled. "Very good. Now, will your Cloud mix in with the others?"

"No reason not to." Daine removed packs and saddle from Cloud's back.

"Stow your things with mine." Onua pointed to a canvas-covered mound in one corner. "They'll be safe—these ponies are better than guard dogs."

Daine ushered Cloud into the pen and stored her packs with Onua's. She finished in time to stop Cloud from biting the yellow stallion, and then from kicking a blood bay mare. "You behave," she ordered her pony. "I mean it."

Cloud flicked an ear back, and lifted a hind foot experimentally. Daine leaned down and whispered in her ear. The mare snorted, then stood on all fours, looking as innocent as a summer sky.

"What did you tell her?" Onua asked, letting the girl out of the pen.

"I said I'd sell her to the man that makes dumplings down the way."

Onua chuckled. "That's the threat my mother used on *me*. Look— I want you to meet my dog, Tahoi." She put her fingers to her lips and whistled two short notes. A large form surged over the rear wall of the pen and wound through the ponies, ducking hooves and teeth with the ease of long practice. Coming over the fence in another easy jump, he sat panting at Onua's feet. He was as tall as his owner's hip, and covered with curling gray fur.

"He's near big enough to be a pony himself." Daine offered her open palm. The dog rumbled in displeasure, and warily sniffed her fingers.

"*Tahoi* means 'ox' in K'mir. Careful—he's a one-woman dog—" Onua shut up. Tahoi's plumed tail had begun to wave. The wary guardian of her stock turned into an eager-to-please pup that licked Daine's hand, then stood to sniff her face. "He's *supposed* to be a guard dog," Onua continued, frowning. "*Not* a pet. *Not* a dog who believes every human's his friend."

"Don't blame him." Daine looked up at Onua apologetically. Her fingers scratched Tahoi in a place he couldn't reach, while his tail thudded in the dust on the ground. "Animals just take to me, is all."

"Hmph. Can you spare her, Majesty?" the woman said to Tahoi. "I'd like to get some grub, saving your presence. And your new friend is coming with me. Guard!" She steered Daine away from the pen.

At one of the cook tents littering the fairgrounds, Onua ordered a rich meal for them both. When it was over, they explored. After a while Daine's eyes hurt from staring so much. Coming from a poor mountain village, she couldn't believe the variety they found at every turn.

"How are you fixed for gear?" her new employer asked. She was eyeing a pair of boots in a leather-worker's stall.

"I'm fine," Daine assured her. Meeting the K'mir's warning look, she insisted, "Really. It was too wet"—she swallowed, trying to speak as if it were someone else's farm that was attacked—"too wet for our place to burn much, so I saved a lot. Clothes, boots, my sleeping gear. I really don't need anything." Seeing the woman's gray green eyes remained suspicious, she raised a hand. "Swear by the Goddess."

"All right, then. Just remember, it's my responsibility to keep you decently clothed and outfitted. I don't want people saying I'm a skinflint."

Daine thought of the huge meal she had consumed. "Just point them out to me, and I'll set them straight," she offered.

Onua chuckled. "Good enough."

On their return, the K'mir raised a sleeping platform outside the pen. "We'd best turn in," she advised. "We leave an hour before dawn."

Daine laid the bedrolls out, wriggled into hers, and took off everything but her shift under the sheltering blankets. "Onua?"

The woman was nearly asleep already. "Yeah?"

"Thanks."

They had a cold breakfast: fruit, cheese, and bread. Onua said little as they ate and packed. She split a pile of lead reins with Daine, indicating she was to connect half of the ponies into a string, while she did the same with the others. They worked quickly as the fair came to life and the air filled with breakfast smells. When the ponies were ready, Onua placed their packs on the first animal in each string.

"Aren't you going to put her on a lead?" Onua pointed to Cloud, who stood free of the others, wearing only a halter and a cross expression. The mare snorted and shook her head.

"She'll be fine," Daine assured the K'mir. "She's as good as a guard dog, that way."

"You know best," Onua said, dubious. "Let's move 'em out."

The K'mir led them away from the fairgrounds and the traffic coming in. They had reached open road when she called for a midmorning break. Digging apples out of her pocket, she gave Daine one. "*You* eat this," she ordered. "I've more in a basket for the ponies. I should've warned you, by the way—I'm a real bear in the morning. It's no good talking to me—I'll only bite your head off. You didn't take it personally, did you?"

Daine *had* begun to wonder if the K'mir regretted hiring her. She smiled her relief. "It's all right. Ma always says"—her lips tightened— "Ma always said there was no living with me until lunchtime."

"You miss her," Onua said gently.

Daine twisted the stem off her apple. "Her, Grandda, our farm—" Her face was grim. "They took my life, those bandits. I saved _things_, like clothes and food, but all my family was gone except Cloud. They wouldn't even have left her, except she was with me and we weren't there." She got to her feet. "I'm sorry. I didn't mean—"

"To speak of it?" asked the K'mir. Daine nodded. "You have to, just to bleed off the poison from the memory." The girl shrugged. "Well, it doesn't have to be today." She peered at the sun. "We'll be at Coolspring by noon—a village, good-sized. Let's pass that before we stop again."

If Onua and Daine were now well awake, so were their charges. They fussed at every turn. Luckily, many who passed them were traders who knew mountain ponies: they kept a respectful distance. Only Cloud, who seemed to realize she would go into a string the moment she misbehaved, walked meekly beside Daine. The only time she offered violence to a bystander was when he, or she, was too interested in how well the strings were tied together.

Daine worked on the ponies one by one, talking, pleading, cajoling. Repeatedly she explained why she wanted them to follow Onua, *without* making a fuss. One after another the ponies listened as she appealed to their better natures. Some people would have said these creatures had no better nature, but—as Daine told Onua—she had found most animals listened, if things were properly set out for them.

Onua had explained things to ponies and horses for twenty-eight years without the success this thirteen-year-old was having. How does she do it? the K'mir wondered, fascinated. They're *ponies*, by all the gods. They're wonderfully clever animals, but they don't *think*, not the way people do.

Past the village of Coolspring lay a rest stop, one of the springs that gave the town its name, sheltered by elms. Picketing the animals, the two women sat down to share a meal of bread and cheese.

"Tell me if you get tired," the K'mir ordered. "I can go for hours, once I get moving."

"I'm fine," Daine said. It was the truth. It was good to be in fresh air, headed away from the city. "It's easier than it was coming all the way here. The roads were muddy, you know—with the spring floods."

"Ever been to Cría before?"

Daine shook her head. "Never saw a village bigger than Snowsdale, till yesterday." She sighed. "How can folk live like that, all mashed together?"

Onua shrugged. "City people. They're different, is all. They look down their noses if you didn't grow up penned in." Getting to her feet, she stretched. "Unless something goes wrong, we'll make Wishing Hollow by dark—we'll camp there. We're making wonderful time, thanks to you."

Daine looked at her, baffled. "Me?"

"This is the fastest I've gotten clear of the fair in six years of trade. That's *your* doing. You must have the Gift—though I never heard of it being put to such a use."

Daine laughed. "Oh, please! I've a *knack* with animals, but no Gift. Ma—" She stopped, then made herself go on. "She tried to teach me, but I never learned. I can't even start a fire, and Gifted *babies* manage that. She was so disappointed. Wanted me to follow her path, I s'pose."

Onua touched the girl's hair. "Your mother will be proud no matter what path you take, Daine. I don't know you well, but anyone can see that."

Daine smiled at her. "Thanks."

They sat quietly for a few moments, until Onua remembered something. "I saw you draw that bow of yours, but I don't know what kind of shot you are."

Daine shrugged. "I'm good."

"Mind giving me a demonstration?"

Daine got up and took her longbow from her packs. "Name your target." The wood was warm from the sun and bent willingly for the string. She drew it a couple of times back to her ear, loosening her muscles.

Looking around, Onua spotted a fence that would serve. It lay well within the range of such a powerful bow, but it wasn't so close that Daine would feel insulted. Walking out to it, she fixed her handkerchief to a post with her belt-knife and returned. "How about three arrows?"

"Fair enough." Daine had already fitted one arrow to the string, and her quiver was on her back. Carefully she set her feet, and gently she brought the string back as she focused on her target. The arrow, when she loosed, flew straight and true. Two more followed it.

Onua gaped. All three arrows clustered neatly at the center of her handkerchief. Their heads were buried so deeply she had to cut them loose.

"I take it this is something else you have a 'knack' for," she said when Daine came to help.

"Grandda thought so." The girl shrugged. "It worked out for the best. His bones got to hurting him so bad he couldn't even string a bow, so I brought in all our game."

The yellow stallion screamed a challenge to a passing draft horse and reared, pawing the air. "Odd's bobs!" Daine yelled, exasperated. "Can't a person take her eye off you for a moment without you acting up?" She ran to the stallion's head and dragged him back down to all fours, holding him until the draft horse walked calmly past.

Onua came up to them, smiling. "Time to get back to work."

Well before dark, Onua led them out of sight of the road and into a grassy hollow sheltered by trees. It was plain other travelers stopped here: the fire pit was lined with stones, and a lean-to kept stacks of firewood dry.

"Toss you to give the ponies a going-over," Onua suggested. "For ticks, stones, whatever. Winner gets to dig the latrine trench and catch fish."

Daine considered. "I druther check the ponies."

Onua grinned. "Wonderful—I feel like a bit of fishing just now."

Smiling, Daine went to work. It made no sense to give the ponies a thorough grooming while they were on the road, but she got rid of the worst tangles and checked the animals' hooves. The strawberry's ear mites had to be treated again, and Cloud and Tahoi had picked up ticks in forays off the road.

The girl was finished when Onua returned with two fat trout. "Think this'll feed us?" the K'mir asked, holding them up.

"More than. I'm so tired I couldn't eat but a mouthful." Daine saw that Onua's hair was wet and her face pink from scrubbing. "It's safe to wash?"

"If you make it fast."

"It's too cold to be slow." She hesitated. "Need my help with supper?"

Onua waved her away. "Tahoi'll keep watch for you."

The water was *very* cold. Daine scrubbed quickly and jumped out, feeling deep respect for Onua's courage. Supper—fish and a pot of spiced white cereal grains Onua called "rice"—was hot and filling. They ate without talking, but the silence was a comfortable one.

After the meal, Daine washed up. The fire was banked; their beds lay on the ground, ready for slumber, when she finished. She got into hers with a sigh. It was warm, and the heavy pad underneath eased the day's aches. As she watched, Onua got several pouches out and tied them to her belt.

"I told you I had the Gift, right? Well, I'm going to place the wards now. Last call for the latrine."

Daine yawned. "I'm set, thanks." She watched as Onua drew a circle around the camp, ponies and all, first in salt, then in water. Soft chanting came from the woman as she walked the circle a third time, calling on magic powers to guard its contents. Red fire spilled from her hand to follow the circle and complete it.

"Ma did that," Daine commented sleepily when Onua finished. "She wasn't very good with it, though." It was easier to speak of her mother when she was so tired. "Maybe she'd be alive now if she'd'a been better."

"Or not," Onua said, sliding between her blankets. "There's always somebody with stronger magic. Lots of raiders have their own witch or mage. That's why every Rider group has at least one member with the Gift."

"Tell me about the Riders. I only know they take girls. Aren't they like the regular soldiers?"

"Not exactly. The fancy name is 'irregulars.' Tortall has a bad time with bandits, and the army's too big and too slow. Bandits hit and run. To fight 'em you need to move the same way. The queen, Thayet, she started the Riders seven years back. The groups run six or eight Riders each, male and female, mounted on ponies. Right now there are six groups, posted all over Tortall. They live off the land, protecting the small villages from raiders."

"Who runs it?"

"Queen Thayet is commander in chief. Her guard, Buri, handles day-to-day affairs, so she has the title 'Commander.' A black man, Sarge, comes just under them. The king's champion you heard of, Alanna, she helps out." Onua looked over and saw that the girl was fast asleep. Smiling, she pulled up her covers and closed her own eyes.

The badger crawled in with Daine soon after that. Although he was big, he didn't wake her: she was used to nighttime visitors. Without waking, she caressed the animal's head. He sighed gratefully and slept too, his muzzle pressed into her palm.

She did notice him when she woke later and was careful as she sat up.

"I tell ye, I saw 'em. Two strings of ponies—gold on the hoof down in Tortall." The speaker's voice was rough and country bred.

Reaching for the crossbow beside her, Daine saw that Onua and Tahoi were also awake. The dog's hackles were up, his teeth bared in a snarl, but he made no sound. Seeing her, the K'mir put a finger to her lips. Daine nodded, easing the bow onto her lap. Inside her bed her guest shifted nervously, quieting only when she rested a hand on his head.

"If ye saw 'em, then where'd they go?" Leaves rustled as men prowled the hollow around their campsite.

"I'm no witch, to guess such things! It's like they vanished off the face of the world."

"Shut up. They prob'ly found a farm, or kept movin'. Let's get back t' the rest." The new voice held authority; the others grumbled, but obeyed.

They had been gone some minutes before Daine relaxed enough to put down her weapon. Tahoi licked Onua's face, his tail wagging.

"It's all right," Onua whispered. "Nobody can hear us if we're quiet."

"That's some protection," Daine breathed. "With Ma's circles, you couldn't get in, but you knew it was there."

The K'mir grinned. "Now you know how I can take the road with, just my assistant and Tahoi." She curled up in her blankets. " 'Night."

The badger grumbled as Daine settled, and walked in her dreams.

*"It's about time I found you," he said. "Do you know how long I've been looking? I actually had to come into the Human Realms to get a scent of you!"*

*"I don't wish to seem rude," she apologized, "but why were you looking for me? I don't believe we've met—have we?"*

*"Not exactly," he admitted with an embarrassed snort. "You see, I promised your father I'd keep an eye on you. So I looked in on you*

*when you were a kit, pink and noisy. Then when I looked for you again,*
*you were gone. I forgot time passes differently in the Human Realms."*

*If she had been her waking self, his saying he knew her father would*
*have made her unbearably excited. Now, though, her dream self asked—*
*as if it weren't too important—"Have you met my da, then?"*

*"Yes, yes, of course. Now, see here—I'm not coming to the Human*
*Realms any more than I have to. If you're going to wander, we must*
*be connected in some way." He looked at a paw and sighed. "I know*
*it barely hurts and it grows back and all, but I still hate it. So messy."*
*He began to chew at the base of one of his claws.*

*"No, don't—please!" she protested. "I can't think—"*

*The claw came off. He spat it into her lap. "There. Hang on to it*
*no matter what. This way I won't lose track of time, and I'll be able to*
*find you. Understand?"*

*She nodded, then gulped. A silvery mist gathered around his paw,*
*and vanished. A new claw had appeared in the bed of the old one.*

*"Now go back to sleep."*

Cold air on her feet woke Daine in the morning. Her guest, working
earlier to leave the bedroll, had pulled it apart entirely. She sat up with
a yawn and a smile. To think she'd dreamed of a badger who knew her
father . . .

Her hand was locked around something—a large animal's claw, or
a semblance of one. Complete and perfect, it was made of shiny silver.

"Goddess," she whispered.

"Daine?" Onua was dressed and cooking breakfast. "Let's go."

No time to think about it now, she told herself, and scrambled out
of her bedroll. Because if I do, I won't know *what* to think.

Later that day, she wove a thong to grip the base of the claw tightly,
and hung it around her neck. Just because she wasn't entirely sure of
where it came from was no reason not to keep it close by—just in case.

# TWO

# THE HAWK

ᗡᑕ A week later they crossed the River Drell into Tortall on a ferryboat. Watching the Gallan shore pull away, Daine searched her soul. I should tell Onua all the truth, she thought. (By then she had given her new friend the less painful details of her life, and had come to see Onua was right—it felt better to talk.) I should tell the rest—but won't she turn on me, like they did? Maybe it's best to keep shut. The madness, the scandal—it's all back there. Maybe that's where it should stay.

She went forward to took at Tortall as it moved closer. I could start fresh. It can't be worse than home, with folk calling me "bastard" and scorning me. Nobody here knows I've no father, and they don't know about the other thing—the bad thing. They don't need to know.

"You worry too much." Onua ruffled the girl's hair. "It'll work out. You'll see."

Cloud butted Daine's shoulder; Tahoi pawed her leg. Their concern and Onua's gave her comfort. I'll manage, she told herself as the ferry bumped the landing dock on the Tortallan shore. Silence is best.

The country beyond the crossing was a mixture of hills and wide valleys, some of it farmed and grazed, but most left to the woods. Towns here were back from the road, and traffic this early in the spring was thin. There was little to keep them from their usual routine of camp and march, riding the ponies, hunting for game birds or fishing for their supper.

The third day from the river brought rain, slowing them and the animals down before the sky cleared at day's end. Both women were up late, getting mud out of shaggy coats and off their own skins and clothes.

It was the first time on that trip that no animal crawled in with Daine overnight. She slept badly, flipping back and forth, never quite waking or sleeping. Her dreams were thin and worrisome. She remembered only one:

*The badger was in his lair, neatening up. "There you are. I'm glad to see the claw works so well."*

*"Excuse me, sir—" she began.*

*"No questions. Kits must listen, not ask. Pay attention." He squinted at her to make sure she was listening. "If you* look *hard and long, you can find us. If you* listen *hard and long, you can hear any of us, call any of us, that you want." Rolling onto his back, he added, "The madness was to teach you something. You should mind the lesson."*

She woke a little before dawn. The sky was gray and damp, the air sour.

"Onua." When the woman only stirred and muttered, she went over and shook her. "I think trouble's coming. Last time I felt this way, a rabid bear came out of the woods and killed the blacksmith."

"A rabid *bear*?" The K'mir yanked on her clothes and Daine followed suit. "Goddess, how many of *those* do you see in a lifetime?"

"One's more than enough." She rolled up her bed and fixed it to her pack. The animals were restless and ill tempered. Tahoi paced the camp, his hackles up. He stopped often to look down the road, only to resume pacing.

"Maybe it's another storm?" Onua suggested over breakfast.

"I don't think so." Daine gave her barely touched porridge to Cloud. "My head aches—not *aches*, exactly. It's—itchy." She sniffed the breeze, but picked up only the scent of water and plants. "The wind's not right, either."

Onua looked at her thoughtfully, then doused the fire. "Let's go." She hitched the ponies to lead reins while Daine secured the packs. "There's a fief on the other side of this next valley, near a marsh. If need be, we'll ask for shelter. I'd prefer not to." She strung her curved bow. "Lord Sinthya doesn't like the queen; he loathes the Riders. Still, we can wait a storm out in his barns, particularly if no one tells him we're there. If we're caught in the marsh, we're in trouble. I don't have any marsh craft."

Daine warmed her longbow and strung it. The quiver's weight on her back made her feel better as they took the road. Past the next ridge she saw a wide, shallow valley filled with reeds and water, with nowhere to hide.

By the time they reached the center of the green expanse, the hair was standing straight out on the back of her neck. Where are the frogs, and the birds? she wondered when they stopped for a breather. I don't even see dragonflies.

Something made her glance at the wood that bordered the far edge of the marsh. "Onua!" She pointed as a bird shot from the cover of the trees. It was black and hawk-shaped, flying crazily, as if drunk.

Shrieks, metallic and shrill, tore the air. Eight giant things—they looked like birds at first—chased the hawk out of the cover of the trees. Immense wings beat the air that reached the women and ponies, filling their noses with a stink so foul it made Daine retch. The ponies screamed in panic.

Daine tried to soothe them, though she wanted to scream too. These were *monsters*. No animal combined a human head and chest with a bird's legs and wings. Sunlight bounded off talons and feathers that shone like steel. She counted five males, three females: one female wore a crown of black glass.

Onua gave a two-fingered whistle that could be heard the length of the valley. When the monsters turned to find the source of the noise, their quarry dropped into the cover of the reeds and vanished. The monsters swept the area, over and over, trying to find the black hawk, without success.

"Look at them," Onua whispered. "They use a grid pattern to search by—they're working that part of the marsh in squares. They're *intelligent*."

"And they can't land easy on level ground," Daine pointed out. "Those claws aren't meant to flatten out. They have to fly—they can't walk."

When the creatures gave up, they turned on the women.

Daine watched them come, her bow—like Onua's—ready to fire. The attackers were smeared with filth. When they spoke or smiled, she saw razor-sharp teeth caked with what she knew was old blood. Halting over the road, they fanned their wings to stay aloft. Their smell was suffocating.

"We almost had the motherless spy," one of them snarled.

"But *you* had to interfere," another said. "*Never* interfere with us." It lifted its wings above its head and stooped. The others followed.

"Daine, *fire!*" Onua shot: her arrow struck the first, hitting a wing with a sound of metal on metal, and bounced off. Daine struck a man-thing square in the throat. He dropped with a cry that brought sweat to her face.

Onua and Daine fired steadily, aiming for the flesh of heads and chests. A female almost grabbed Daine by the hair before Onua killed her. Cloud got one by a leg, and Tahoi seized its other foot. Together pony and dog tore the monster apart. Birds—herons, bitterns, plovers, larks—rose from hiding places to fight the creatures, blinding some, pecking others, clogging the air so the enemy couldn't see. Many paid for their help with their lives.

The glass-crowned one was finally the only monster alive. She hovered just out of Onua's range, one of the K'mir's arrows lodged in her shoulder.

"Pink *pigs*!" she snarled. "How dare you defy me, maggots! You *filth*!"

"Look who's talking," Daine shouted, sliding an arrow onto her string. She lowered her bow, wanting the creature to think she was done. "Your ma was a leech with bad teeth," she taunted. Onua laughed in spite of herself. "Your da was a peahen. I know chickens with more brains than you!"

The queen screamed and dropped, claws extended. Daine brought the bow up, loosing as she reached the best point in her swing. Her arrow buried itself in the queen's eye as Onua cheered.

Daine had another arrow on the string and in the air, but the queen pulled away. Blood dripped from her ruined eye. If she felt pain, she ignored it, hovering well out of bow-shot, her good eye furious.

"Ohhh, I'll remember *you*, girlie." The hate in her voice forced Daine back a step. "Your name on my heart." She looked at Onua. "I'll return for you two ground crawlers. You belong to Zhaneh Bitterclaws now." She launched herself into higher air and was gone.

"I can't believe it." Onua sounded as if she were talking to herself. "The rumors said there were monsters abroad, but *these*? Where did they come from?" She went to examine the body of one of the creatures, the stink so bad she had to cover her nose to get close to it.

Limping, Daine followed. She was unhurt, but she *felt* battered and cut and torn in a thousand places.

A chickadee lay in the road. She picked it up, to find a wing was attached by only a bit of skin. Tears rolled down her cheeks to fall on the dying bird. All around her, birds lay in the rushes, bleeding, dead.

"I'm sorry, little ones," she whispered. "You should've stayed hid." Her temples pounded. Stripes of black-and-yellow fire crossed her vision. Her ears filled with a roaring sound, and she fainted.

Onua saw her fall. The bird that had been in Daine's hand jumped into the air and zipped past, nearly missing the K'mir's nose. In the marsh, she heard a rush of song. Birds took off, clumsily at first, as if they were stiff. An owl that lay in the road moved, then flew away as she stared. She was positive that the bird's head had been cut half off.

Shaking her head, she went to the fallen girl. As far as she could tell, Daine was unhurt. With a grunt the K'mir levered her onto a shoulder, surprised by how light she was. "You need to eat more," she told her burden as she carried her to the ponies. Cloud trotted over to nuzzle Daine, worry in every line of the pony's body.

"I don't suppose you know a place where we can get off the road," Onua asked, half jesting, never thinking these animals would understand her as they did the girl. Cloud trotted into a nearby stand of reeds. Just beyond her Onua saw a clearing, floored in solid ground.

This was food for thought. Onua followed Cloud. The remainder of the ponies followed her, Tahoi bringing up the rear.

Coarse hairs tickled Daine's face. Opening her eyes, she saw nothing but Cloud's nose.

"Let me up." Her voice emerged as a croak. "I'm fine." She wasn't really—her whole body ached—but the pain that had knocked her out was over.

"Swallow this." Onua brought over a cup of water. Drinking it, Daine tasted herbs. A tingling filled her veins and left her feeling much improved. The only sign of the pain that had knocked her down was mild stiffness.

"I didn't faint 'cause I'm a baby or anything—" she began, afraid the K'mir would be disgusted by her weakness. She struggled to sit up, and finished the water.

"Don't be silly." Onua gave her a silvery feather. "Don't touch the edges," she warned. "They're razor sharp."

It was metal, etched and shaped like a feather. If it was steel, as it seemed to be, it was paper thin, impossible to bend. Moreover, it *felt* wrong, as the sight of the creatures had felt wrong. If she knew nothing else, she knew nature. Such creations did not belong in the world: seeing them made her feel wobbly and sick. "What *were* those things? Do you know?"

"I've heard tales, but—they aren't supposed to exist, not here. They're called Stormwings." She heard awe and fear in Onua's voice.

"What are Stormwings?"

"The Eaters." Onua wrapped the feather and put it away. "But they're *legends*. No one's seen them for three, four centuries. They lived on battlefields, desecrating bodies—eating them, fouling them, scattering the pieces." She crouched beside Daine again. "Listen—I need to leave you and the ponies for a while—I hope not too long. I can't tell you why."

"Then I'll follow." Daine was comfortable enough with her now to be blunt. "This is a marsh, remember? Quicksand, mud bogs, snakes—you told me you don't know anything about marshes."

"I can't help that. What I must do is important. You stay put—"

A picture of the Stormwings as they'd first seen them flashed into Daine's mind. "It's that hawk, isn't it?" she asked, and Onua looked away. "That black one. You tried to call him, but he couldn't make it, so he hid in the reeds. Now you want to go after him. Why is a *bird* so important?"

Onua's eyes glittered with annoyance. "Never you mind. He is, that's all—he's more important than you could imagine. If something happens to me, take the ponies to the Riders. Tell Buri or Sarge what happened—"

Daine saw how she might repay some of what she owed this woman for taking her in. "I'll go."

"Out of the question."

She retrieved her crossbow and quiver from the packs. "Don't be silly. It's only a few hundred yards out. How much trouble can I get into? Besides, I know about bogs. And I can find lost animals." If she waited, the K'mir would find a good reason to keep her back. She saw a game trail leading into the reeds and took it. "I'll yell for Tahoi if I get stuck," she called.

"Daine!" There was no answer. "When *I* was that age, *I* listened to my elders," Onua muttered, conveniently forgetting she had done no such thing. She grabbed Cloud's rein as the pony tried to follow her mistress. "No, you stay here. And don't try to argue." She tied the mare's rein into a string for the first time since they'd left the fair, and settled down to wait.

The trail took Daine to a pond. She skirted it, always making for the spot where the monsters had left the wood. A grouse darted out of the brush. Following it, she walked a trail that lay on firm ground to reach the trees at the marsh's edge. There she sat on a rock, wondering what to do next. If the bird was alive, it had come down somewhere nearby to hide from the Stormwings.

It was nice, this green wilderness. The scents of growing things filled her nostrils; the sounds of animals and plants waking from their winter sleep filled her ears. What had the badger said, in her dream? *If you* listen *hard and long, you can hear any of us, call any of us, that you want.*

Surely *listening* wouldn't bring on the madness. She wasn't trying to *be* an animal; she just wanted to *hear* them. Definitely she'd taken advice from worse people than badgers in her time.

Besides, if the hawk was alive and hurt, it might be thrashing or crying its pain. She'd hear it, if she listened.

She'd have to be very quiet, then.

She settled herself and slowed her breathing. Her blouse itched; she eased it. A burn throbbed on a finger; she put it out of her mind.

A breeze fanned the tips of the reeds, making them sigh.

Two plops ahead: a pair of mating frogs. She had no interest in *that*.

A rustle on her left, some feet behind: a pair of nesting ducks. Didn't people think of *anything* else?

A gritty noise at her side was a grass snake, coming up to sun. It was nice on the rock, the warmth just perfect on her face and on the snake.

There—left, closer to the trees. She frowned. It didn't sound like a bird—like the hawks and falcons back home. She felt dizzy and befuddled, almost like the time she had swiped a drink of her mother's home-brewed mead.

That yip was a fox, who had found a black bird. A large one.

Daine headed in his direction. The fox yipped again when she almost made a wrong turn. She found him next to a large, hollow log. The hawk had concealed itself inside.

"Thank you," she said. The fox grinned at her and vanished into the reeds while Daine looked at her new patient. "Clever lad, to think of hiding there," she murmured. (And since when did hawks ever think of concealing themselves?) "Come on out—they're gone." She put her hands into the log's opening, praying she wasn't about to get slashed.

The bird waddled forward, easing himself onto her palms. Moving very slowly, she lifted him out and placed him on top of his hiding place.

He stared at her, beak open as he panted. One outspread wing seemed broken in two places, maybe even three. Her hair prickled at the back of her neck. Anyone less familiar with hawks might have taken this bird for one: she could not. He was too big, and hawks were not solid black. His color was dull, like velvet—there was no gloss to his feathers at all. He wasn't wrong as those Stormwings were wrong, but he was not right, either.

She cut reeds for splints. "I'm from Onua—Onua Chamtong of the K'miri Raadeh," she told him. "You recognize the name?" She didn't expect an answer, but she knew a kind voice was something any hurt creature responded to. "I have to splint that wing. It's broken." She cursed herself for not having bandages of any kind, and cut strips out of a petticoat.

"It'll hurt," she warned. "Try not to peck me, or we'll never get you fixed." Ignoring his gaze, she gently spread the wing. The hawk cried out only once. That was *another* strange thing, she thought; other birds had savaged her for less pain than she was giving this one. She secured the outspread limb onto its reed framework, feeling him shake under her hands. "You're being a fine, brave lad," she crooned, securing the last cotton ties. "Your ma'd be fair proud of you—wherever she is. *Whatever* she is."

Repairs made, she slung the crossbow on her back. "I've got to carry you," she explained. "Try to keep still." When she gathered him up, taking care not to bump the wing, he trembled but didn't bite or slash. "You're the oddest bird I've met in my life," she murmured as she followed the trail back to the road. "Heavy too." She was sweating by the time she found Onua. "His wing's busted."

"Horse Lords be praised, you found him!" The relief on the K'mir's face was scary, as if he's a friend or something, Daine thought. Onua lifted the hawk from Daine's arms, examining him with delicate fingers. Somehow Daine wasn't surprised to see that he was as calm with Onua as he'd been with her.

"If we move the packs onto one of the gentler ponies, he can ride on them," Onua suggested. "We have to get well away before we camp." Daine nodded and shifted the packs to a mild-mannered chestnut gelding. On the road, the bird rode quietly, panting without making any other sound.

They left the marshy valley and entered the wood, moving on after dark. Onua lit the way ahead with her magic. They had walked for hours before she took them off the road, onto a small path.

Here she lit a torch and gave it to Daine.

"Farther up there's an open shed for drying wood. It's big enough to shelter us and the ponies." She dug out the materials she used to work her magic. "Get a fire going. I'll be there as soon as I can." She went back to the road, a bag of powder in her hand. Tahoi started to follow: she ordered him to go with Daine.

"I think she wants to hide our trail," Daine told the dog. She led the pack pony, and the others followed obediently. "But why? The monster—what's her name? Zhaneh Bitterclaws—can she see in the dark? Apart from revenge, why follow us?" She glanced at the hawk. Meeting his eyes directly still made her head spin. "Not for you, surely."

The bird shuddered.

The shed was big, with three walls to keep out the wind. Moreover, it had a fire pit inside, and a well outside. With relief she freed the ponies, watered them, and fed them grain from the extra stores.

Tahoi had brought in three rabbits that afternoon. As soon as the fire was going, Daine skinned and gutted them. Two went on the spit for her and Onua; Tahoi got half of the third. Cutting strips from the remaining half, she offered it to her patient. He turned his head away.

Perhaps he hadn't gotten the scent. Daine waved it in front of him. Again he turned his head aside.

She sniffed the meat: it was no different from what Tahoi crunched so happily nearby. She laid it on the pack in front of the bird, having moved his travel arrangements to the floor of the shed. The hawk picked the morsel up in his beak and threw it away.

Getting the rejected meat, she offered it to Tahoi. The dog ate it and returned to his bones. Planting her hands on her hips, Daine scowled at the bird. She'd heard of captive animals refusing to eat, but such a thing had never happened to *her*.

"There's many a hawk would be happy for a nice bit of rabbit," she told him, not even realizing she sounded like her ma. "Now, I'll give you another piece. Don't you go throwing that away, for I won't give you any more." She offered a fresh strip to the bird, who sniffed it— and turned his head. She placed it before him, and he threw it to Tahoi.

"He won't eat," she told Onua when the K'mir joined them. "What's the matter with him? I never had an animal that wouldn't eat for me."

The woman crouched near the hawk, her gray green eyes puzzled. "Let me try, Maybe it's 'cause he doesn't know you."

"I've fed plenty of animals that never met me first," Daine snapped, cutting another strip of meat for Onua. The hawk refused it as well.

Onua scratched her head. "Try cooked meat. I have to ward this place. There're armed men all over the road, searching." She walked outside the shed.

"For us?" Daine asked. Onua shook her head and began the now-familiar spell. "Not for you, surely," the girl whispered to the hawk. Cutting meat off the spit, she cooled it with water and offered it to her patient. He sniffed it for a while, but refused it in the end.

"Maybe he's sick," Onua suggested as she ate. "I broke my collarbone once, and I was queasy for a day or two."

"That's shock." Daine rested her chin on her knees. "I s'pose that might be it."

"He's not just any creature." Onua finished her meal. "He may be a little strange to care for, Daine. Just do your best—please?"

The girl awoke in the night to hear a quiet murmur. Peeking with a half-closed eye, she saw that Onua sat with the hawk, talking softly to him. *And Ma said I was fair foolish with animals,* she thought. Rolling over, she went back to sleep.

They moved on in the morning. Searchers passed them on the road, men on horseback and men afoot, but none appeared to see the bird riding in state on ponyback. "I can't throw fire or heal," Onua told Daine, "but when I hide a thing, it stays hidden."

For three days they pushed on. The hawk's eyes still would not focus, and his balance was poor. After some debate with herself, Daine lightly bound his claws to the pack he rested on. He didn't seem to mind, which bothered her still more. Even the mildest sparrow would have fought the ties.

Her patient worsened. He refused any and all meat, raw or cooked. Their third day together she offered him raw egg and then cheese. He ate both, to her joy, but vomited it up later. That night she woke to hear Onua chanting a spell over him, but it didn't seem to help. The K'mir still talked to him about human things—road conditions, the fair in Cría, the doings of the Queen's Riders.

Once, after meeting the bird's eyes, Daine walked into a ditch. Another time she fell over her own feet. After that, she avoided his gaze and resented it. Why *couldn't* she look at this bird? And why did she not feel connected to him, as she felt with other creatures?

His wing did not heal. The fourth night she stayed up with him, coaxing water mixed with honey into his beak. It did no good. The fever she had fought to prevent set in and began to climb.

She woke Onua sometime after midnight. "He's going to die. Not today—tomorrow, maybe. I *hate* losing one I've nursed!" To her shame, she felt tears on her cheeks, and wiped them away with an impatient hand. "He's not right! He's not like any bird I ever met, and *I can't fix him*! Can we stop at a village or town, and find a sorcerer who might—"

Onua shook her head. "Out of the question." When Daine opened her mouth to argue, the woman said, "There are *reasons*. Important ones." She tugged at her lip, and came to a decision. "All right. Get some rest—I'm calling for help. Horse Lords willing, somebody will be in range."

Daine was too exhausted to protest or ask questions. It was hard even to crawl into her bedroll. The last thing she saw was Onua, kneeling before a fire that now burned scarlet, hands palm up in a summoning.

She slept until dawn, and Onua greeted her cheerfully. "I got lucky—help is closer than I thought. Eat something, and you might want to wash up. There's a bathing pool behind that hill. They'll be here around noon."

"They who?" Daine's voice came from her throat as a croak.

Onua shook her head.

"Wonderful. More secrets. My favorite," Daine muttered grumpily as she found towels and soap. Since the day was warm, she washed her hair and took extra time to scrub every inch of her skin. Why hurry? she thought, still feeling grouchy. *They* won't get here till noon—whoever *they* are.

The hawk's eyes were closed when she returned, and he was shivering. She warmed small rocks and wrapped them in cloths—towels, scarves, handkerchiefs. Carefully, talking to him the whole time, she cocooned bird and rocks in a blanket, hoping to sweat the fever out. After an hour of the extra warmth, he took some heated water and honey when she coaxed.

Onua had worn herself out with her magical efforts, and slept all morning. Daine had to content herself with frequent trips to the road, looking for the promised help. Cloud and Tahoi followed her, as worried as she was.

The sun was at its height, covered by thickening clouds, when she saw movement to the east. She raced back to camp. "Onua, there are people coming."

The K'mir grabbed her bow and arrows; Daine got hers. They went to the road to wait. It wasn't long before Onua said, "It's my friends. The ones in white are in the King's Own. They answer directly to King Jonathan."

Daine gaped at the company that approached. Mail-clad warriors on beautiful horses rode in four rows, their white, hooded capes flapping grandly at their backs. The earth shook with the pounding of their steeds' hooves. Before them came a standard-bearer, his flag a silver blade and crown on a royal blue field.

Beside him was a full knight in gold-washed mail, his gold helm mirror bright. He bore a lance; on his left arm was a red shield with a device like a gold cat rearing on its hind paws. The knight's horse was larger than those of the white-caped warriors, though not as large as the chargers normally used by those who wore full mail or plate armor. It was as gold as the cat on the knight's shield, with a black mane and tail.

Together the company made a picture out of legends. "Oh, glory," whispered Daine.

Reaching Onua, the knight halted the warriors with a raised hand. His horse refused to stop and walked up to butt his head against Daine's chest.

"You beauty," she whispered, running her hand along his mane. "Oh, you pretty, pretty thing."

Laughing, Onua went to the war-horse's head and gently made him back up. The knight peered down at the K'mir through his open visor. "Are you camped here?" Onua nodded, and he turned to his company. "Hakim, this is it."

A brown man in the front rank of the white-caped riders nodded and called out instructions. The result was instant activity: men dismounted, giving their reins over to a few of their number while others removed packs from their mounts and from the spares. Within seconds they were off the road, erecting tents to share the clearing with the ponies and Tahoi.

The knight secured shield and helm to his saddle. Dismounting, he gave the reins to one of the others, then stripped amethyst-decorated gauntlets from his hands. "I should've changed to leather," he complained. "My back has been one whole itch the last mile." He grinned at Daine. "The outfit looks nice, but it's not very comfortable."

Daine was *very* confused. Out of the saddle, the knight was two whole inches shorter than she was, and built on stocky, not muscular, lines. His cropped, coppery hair was tousled from being inside a helmet. Amethysts winked at his earlobes, stones that matched the color of his eyes.

"My wits have gone begging," Onua said. "Daine, this is Sir Alanna of Pirate's Swoop and Olau—the king's champion. Alanna, this is Daine. Wait till you see what she can do with animals."

Daine stared at the hand offered her, then into purple eyes. "The *champion*? The knight they call 'the Lioness'?"

"Don't tell me," Alanna said. "You expected someone bigger."

Daine took the offered hand. Remembering her patient, she asked, "Can you help? I can't fix 'im at all."

Onua took the champion's elbow. "Alanna's a healer and a sorceress—if she can't come up with something, no one can."

"Aren't you going to be sorry if I can't?" the knight asked as Onua steered her toward the ailing hawk.

Daine unwound the bird from his wraps. "He won't eat anything but a little honey and water," she explained. "Not meat or fish. And he's dizzy all the time."

The purple eyes looked at her sharply. "How would you know that?"

Daine met that gaze squarely. "I just do. I've—"

" 'A knack with animals,' " Onua chorused along with her, and grinned.

Alanna lifted the bird with a care for the splinted wing. The hawk blinked, looked at her—and buried his head against her chest. "He knows me. Good." She carried him to a tent the warriors had set up, and went inside.

"Wait here," Onua told Daine. "Don't let these men bully Tahoi or the ponies." She followed the knight inside.

Daine realized she ought to picket the strings so the smaller horses wouldn't disturb the big ones. Tahoi stuck close to her as she worked, and Cloud was on her best behavior. The warriors smiled at her as they set up more tents and built cook fires. A handful went to the nearby river with fishing lines in their hands. She would have liked to go too, but she couldn't bring herself to ask these businesslike Tortallans.

"Great merciful Goddess!" The shout came from the tent where Alanna and Onua had taken the hawk. "Of all the gods-cursed, simple-minded—"

Daine gaped. The man the knight had called Hakim smiled. "The Lioness has a temper," he told the girl. "Sometimes it gets the better of her."

The knight stamped out of the tent. She had discarded mail for breeches and a white shirt. At her throat a red gem burned like a coal in the fire. "I can't see—" Her purple eyes lit on Daine. "You, girl—come here!"

Tahoi growled, bristling. He didn't like the knight's tone.

Alanna stared at the dog, and then smiled. "I'm sorry. Daine, would you come here, please? I think I need your help." Steering the girl into the tent, she said, "Onua says you found him under—unusual conditions." The hawk lay on a man-size cot, his eyes wide and frightened. "How?"

There was something here that pounded on her ears, making her nervous. "Honest, Your Ladyship—"

"Alanna," was the firm interruption.

She thought of calling the champion, the only lady knight in living memory, by her first name, and winced. "I listened for him, is all. I sat down and just—listened."

"Would you do it for me now, please?"

Daine swallowed. "But he's right there, mum. Lioness."

"Turn your back to him, if that helps." Alanna fiddled with the red gem at her throat. "Listen for him *exactly* as you listened back then."

Listening's fine, Daine thought nervously. You only listened before, and had no trouble. And the badger said it was all right. Well, then!

Closing her eyes, she emptied her mind, letting her breath slow until she couldn't hear it. She concentrated on her ears. Outside, Cloud chewed on a clump of grass, thinking she ought to check on Daine, alone with strangers. The gold war-horse shifted; he wanted to run some more.

There! A strange and distant voice, one that sounded like no animal she knew. That had to be the hawk. Was he *muttering* to himself?

"I hear him." That sleepy voice was hers. "He's a prisoner. He can't get out. But he's just on the bed—"

"Hush." Purple fires played inside her eyelids. "Call him, Daine—with your *mind*. His name is Numair Salmalín."

"Alanna—maybe Arram's better." That was Onua, sounding distant. "He's only been Numair for eight years—he's been Arram all his life."

"True. Call to him as Arram, Daine." The fires evened into a steady purple light, warming her face like the sun.

"Why—"

"Call him." The knight's voice was gentle, but firm.

Daine sighed. "Arram Salmalín? Arram—come on. You're too far off. It's all right, Arram—it's safe—"

Something behind her snapped, breaking her concentration. She opened her eyes as wooden sticks hit the tent wall in front of her: the hawk's splints. "Now look at this," she scolded, picking them up. "His wing won't get any better that way." She turned to show them the evidence.

The hawk was gone. Onua pulled a sheet up to cover a large, naked man.

He smiled drowsily at the three of them. "Can I have something to eat?"

Daine's jaw fell open. "Where did *he* come from?"

Alanna bent over the newcomer, peering into his eyes. Onua grabbed the girl's elbow and steered her out of the tent. "Explanations later," the K'mir said. "There's a lot to be done for him still."

"Onua, where's my hawk? Where'd that man come from?" Her knees shook.

Onua put a hand on Daine's mouth. "Hush. No more questions. I'll explain everything—later." She went back into the tent, pulling the flap tightly shut behind her.

"Later," Daine muttered to herself. "Wonderful. Hawks disappearing, men appearing—why not? Later." She stamped off to look after the ponies, who at least would tell her things and not wait for any "laters."

# ⤁ THREE ⤀

# SPIDRENS AND MEDITATION

Hedgehogs woke Daine as they wriggled into her bedroll, shaking in terror. It wasn't the controlled fear they felt around hunters, but the wild panic that made them run before a fire. She eased out of the covers. "It's all right," she whispered. "Stay here."

She dragged on her clothes and boots. She felt it now, heaviness in the air and in her mind—not like the Stormwings or the rabid bear, but there was a flavor in it that reminded her of the winged monsters. In the camp around her, the men slept quietly—no snorers like Grandda. Onua was mumbling in her sleep. Tahoi was not with her or the ponies.

"Stay," Daine told Cloud, who wanted to follow. She fitted the string to her bow and checked its draw as she looked around. A light burned in the Lioness's tent. The other one, where the man who'd been a hawk lay, was dark.

The wood outside their camp was thick with fear. Tiny beasts dug as far into burrows as they could. The big ones were gone. An owl sitting overhead was almost mindless with terror. That was bad: owls didn't scare.

Tahoi sat at the edge of the trees, nose to the wind. When Daine rested a hand on his shoulder, the dog flinched. "What is it?"

He knew only that it was bad, and it was coming.

"Stay with the ponies. Guard them." Tahoi whimpered a protest. Waiting for trouble to reach him was hard; better to hunt it out. "Go on." He obeyed, reluctantly.

A sentry nearby raised a hand in greeting. Looking past him, Daine saw another. "Do you hear anything?" she asked. "I think something bad is coming. Something *wrong*."

"I hear nothing." It was Hakim. He didn't take his eyes off the woods beyond. "Go back to your sleep."

There was no sleeping, not now. Checking the ponies, Daine found they were afraid too. Beyond them the horses were alert, watching the trees like sentries. The war-horse pawed the air: he *knew* danger was close. Wanting to fight it, he pulled his tether to see if it could be yanked from the ground.

"Not yet," she said, patting his withers. "Watch. Wait." She walked toward the forest.

"Don't go alone."

Daine wrenched around and lost her balance. A strong hand grabbed her elbow and raised her to her feet. It was the Lioness, wearing a shirt, breeches, and boots. The red gem at her throat glowed steadily; a naked sword lay in her right hand.

"Easy," the knight cautioned. "What brings you out here?" They walked to a small clearing almost thirty feet away.

Daine took a deep breath and made herself calm down. "There's something close by that isn't right. I can't explain better'n that."

The Lioness scanned the trees all around them. "I feel it too." She tapped her gem. "This warns me of trouble, sometimes."

"Look." Her ma had said she had an owl's nightsight. That was how she saw the rabbit in the clearing, when someone else would miss it. Kneeling to lift the body, she found it was still warm.

White light—Alanna's magic—appeared over her hands. The knight touched the body with a palm and felt its warmth, then touched the red drops at the rabbit's nose. She sniffed her fingers. *"Blood?* Its heart burst—"

"It was scared to death." Daine was sure of it. Gently she lay the dead creature atop a nearby stump. "There's something else, Lioness. The big animals—there isn't a one within a mile of this place right now. Listen."

The knight doused her light and obeyed. "Nothing's moving out—"

A bat darted between them, chittering a warning. Startled, the knight and the girl jumped back—and a rope that glowed a sickly yellow green dropped into the space where Alanna had been standing.

Noise overhead made Daine look up as she put an arrow on the string. A monstrous spider hurtled down at them. She shot it before she even knew what she fired at. A man screamed above; black fluid fell onto her hand, burning like acid. She put two more arrows into the thing and jumped aside when it hit the ground.

Alanna was shouting a warning to the camp. Daine was about to wipe her hand on a leaf when something moved on the edge of her vision. She leaped out of the way and the Lioness moved in, as smoothly as butter. Her sword flashed once—a powerful cut sliced two of the near legs off a new attacker—then twice, beheading the thing. It happened so fast Daine wasn't quite sure it happened, till Alanna dragged her out of the way of the monster's death throes. Knight and girl waited, breathless, for a moment or two, to see if another giant spider would appear.

"I don't think there are more," Daine said at last. "It felt—*wrong*—out here, before. That's almost gone now."

Many-jointed legs moved, and she knew the one she'd shot was alive. Gulping down nausea, she drew her dagger and walked around front to kill the thing—cutting off its head was best.

She had thought they were spiders, almost as big as she was, with bodies dressed in dull black fur. That was bad enough, until she saw this one from the front. Head and neck were human—its teeth as sharp and pointed as a giant cat's. It screamed with a man's voice, enraged at seeing the knife.

Her mouth dropped open; a cry of fright and repulsion came out as a strangled croak. Her knife dropped from numb fingers. No wonder these had felt like Stormwings in the night. They were just as wrong, an eerie mating of animal and human that had no reason to exist.

"Great merciful Goddess." Alanna came up behind her. It made Daine feel better to know the paleness of the knight's face wasn't due entirely to the light she had called so they could see. "Have you ever heard, or—"

"Never." She turned her back on it—let it die slowly—and found a log where she could sit, shuddering in horror. Grandda had told her stories about monsters, human-headed and spider-bodied, named spidrens. A brave man hunted them best at night, he'd said: their webs glowed in the dark.

A hand rested on her shoulder. "Little girl, your ancestors are proud tonight." It was the sentry, the man Hakim. "You are the best archer I have ever seen—better even than the Lioness."

Alanna nodded. She knelt beside the thing, examining it with a stick rather than touching it herself. "We're lucky you sensed them coming, Daine."

The girl swallowed, thinking, You couldn't *pay* me to touch that, even with a stick. "The hedgehogs woke me. They didn't know what was out there. I could feel something wrong was close, but I didn't think it'd look like—like this." Wincing as the knight pulled the thing's head back by the hair—it was dead now—she added, "Grandda told me stories about spidrens, but he said they were killed, ages and ages ago."

"Not killed." Hakim's voice was steady, but his face glowed with sweat. "They were imprisoned in the Divine Realms four hundred years ago, by the greatest of shamans."

"You mean they're *gods*?" Daine asked, horrified.

"Immortals and gods aren't the same. They just live in the same place." Alanna dusted her hands. "Like the Stormwings, Daine. They were shut into the Divine Realms at the same time, along with a great many other creatures. Griffins, dragons, and so on."

Daine swallowed: there were *more* of these? What if they were loose too, escaped from the prison where they'd been locked for so long?

"Horse Lords." Onua had found them. "Lioness, what—"

"They're called spidrens." The knight's voice was almost matter-of-fact. "Goddess knows how many of us they would have killed and dragged off to munch on if your Daine hadn't been alert."

"You killed one too," Daine reminded her. She went to the clearing's edge and listened to the woods beyond, just in case. All around she heard creatures stirring, large and small, as they resumed their night's business. I don't know if I'd ever come out of my burrow again, she thought.

Remembering an obligation, she glanced behind her. Hakim and Onua were going over the spidren, using sticks. Most of the camp had come to watch, and to marvel. One of the soldiers was vomiting at the edge of the clearing, which made her feel better. At least *she* hadn't thrown up.

She faced the trees where the bat had fled after warning them. "Thanks, wing-friend," she whispered. "Thank you for both of us." In the darkness ahead, a bat squeaked in reply. Daine smiled and went back to the humans.

"It's over," she told Alanna. "The animals are coming out." She felt suddenly exhausted; the burn on her hand throbbed.

Onua put an arm around her. "We've *both* had enough excitement. Come on." She steered her to their fire. "Are you all right?" She hissed in sympathy when Daine showed her the burn, and got her medicines. Daine barely remembered having the burn cleansed and bandaged, she was so tired. The pain gone, she got into bed.

"You're *certain* you're all right?" The woman was plainly concerned.

Daine smiled at her. "I think so." The hedgehogs snuggled in around her once more. "I'll have nightmares, for sure."

"Me too," Onua sighed. "At least we're alive to have them." She eased into her own bed.

"What of him? The hawk—the man?" Daine pointed at the patient's tent.

Onua smiled. "Master Salmalín slept through the whole thing. He'll be mad as fire when he hears too. Spidrens are more *his* line than ours."

Daine said shyly, "Why didn't you tell me the truth? About the hawk?"

A sigh came from the other bedroll. "His shape-shifting—it's a secret. Only a few people know, and we're not supposed to tell. It isn't that I don't trust you—I do."

"He's a spy?"

"Only sometimes, when the king's spymaster can't send anyone else."

"He was just supposed to get well and fly off, and I'd never know."

"That was the plan." There was a rueful note in Onua's voice.

"I know now."

"Yes. You planning to tell somebody?"

Daine thought about that. "You just said it's a secret, didn't you? I won't tell."

"Good. Now go to sleep."

No one left the camp by the river the next day. The men of the King's Own burned the dead monsters and searched the woods for more. The Lioness and Onua sat with their patient all morning. In the afternoon they summoned Hakim and another soldier who carried a writing desk.

Daine kept out of the way of the men. She wasn't used to being noticed and greeted by so many people. Her caution did not extend to their mounts, of course. Once she'd cared for her ponies, she looked at the big horses. Her favorite was Alanna's mount, the young stallion who had greeted her so happily the day before. She examined every inch of him, crooning praises into his ear.

"I think the feeling's mutual."

Daine jumped—once again the Lioness had come up unheard. She grinned at the knight. "He's a beauty."

"His name is Darkmoon." The stallion lipped Alanna's breech pockets. "He's spoiled rotten." Fishing a lump of sugar out, she fed it to him. "His grandam was my first horse—a fine mare, true to the bone." Giving Darkmoon another sugar lump, she added, "You saved my life last night."

Daine blushed. "You saved mine." Purple eyes are very discomforting when they look at you, she thought. Or is it that she's got so much Gift it leaks over to all she does?

"Where did you learn to shoot like that?"

"My grandda taught me. Carved me that bow too."

"You'd think, your size, you'd only be able to manage a smaller one."

Daine shrugged. "I've always been a fair shot."

The woman snorted, but her eyes never left Daine's face. She toyed with the gem around her neck. "Three times you shot overhead and hit a mark that moved, in the dark. That's more than 'fair' shooting."

Daine shrugged again. "I practice a lot."

Alanna grinned. "I'll stop. I didn't mean to interrogate you. I've been so busy getting Arram's story out of him that I forgot I just wanted to say thanks. You saved my life, and the life of one of my best friends. Arram wouldn't be here if you hadn't nursed him. I'll remember it."

Daine swallowed. "It was no trouble—"

Alanna took her hand. "If you need anything, come to me. A place to stay, money, work—I don't care. If I'm not around, go to my husband." Startled, Daine looked at Alanna's ring finger and saw a wide silver band. "He's the baron of Pirate's Swoop. He'll do anything for you I would."

Daine gulped. A king's champion in debt to *her*? An offer with no limits, and she to apply to the lady or her baron husband? People like her had no business bothering the great and wealthy! And if Alanna knew the truth about her, about what she'd done once, she'd hate Daine. She'd have to.

The knight must have seen refusal in her face. "Promise me."

Daine wondered if there was any way to get out of it. Alanna had the look of someone who wouldn't let this go, however. "I promise, Lioness."

"Alanna," Onua called from the tent. "We need you for a minute."

"Coming," the knight replied. "By the way—can you wield a sword?"

"*Me?* Gods, no!" she said, shocked. A sword was a weapon for nobles!

The Lioness grinned. "I shouldn't be glad, but I am." Seeing Daine's puzzlement, she explained, "If you were as good with the sword as you are with a bow, I couldn't take the competition." She clapped Daine on the shoulder and returned to her patient.

The next day everyone rose at first light, Onua and Daine from habit, the others from necessity. "You're staying here?" Alanna wanted to know.

Onua spooned porridge into a bowl and gave it to her. "Just for today—give Arram a little more time before we go west. How about you?"

"I'll see the local magistrate, now I have Arram's information," Alanna explained, drizzling honey into her bowl. "Once I get a writ of arrest from him, Sinthya's mine."

"So *that's* why you were so near when I called for help," said Onua. "Springtime you're usually at Pirate's Swoop. You were waiting for Arram?"

Alanna nodded. "He has proof now that Sinthya is dealing with Carthak."

Onua smiled grimly. "I knew it!"

The knight frowned. "I'm sending word to the king, to tell him about our visitors last night, and the Stormwings." She shook her head. "I can't understand why these immortals are reappearing *now*. We've had reports from all over Tortall, and from our neighbors as well. Also, I don't like it that they were on hand to chase our friend when he escaped."

"You don't think it was a coincidence?" Onua asked. "Or does Sinthya have an arrangement with those—things?"

Daine winced. The idea of humans welcoming such creatures was chilling.

Alanna sighed. "I don't know. That's one of the questions I'll ask His Lordship—when I arrest him. In the meantime, I leave you to your travels. Don't let Arram overdo things. And it might be best if he kept from shape-shifting for a while, not that I think he'll have the strength to try." The knight finished her breakfast and got to her feet. "Time to ride."

With the consent of the man who tended Darkmoon, Daine brought the saddled horse to his mistress and held him as the Lioness mounted. This time the knight wore a leather jerkin studded with metal rings, instead of her mail. Seeing Daine look at it, she said, "I drew it from our spares. They always bring one in my size. It doesn't look as nice as the mail, but it's more comfortable." She offered Daine a gloved hand to shake. "I'll see you again—if not at the palace, then later on. Take care of my friends, and take care of yourself."

Daine returned the woman's firm grip. "Safe journey, Lioness. Give that Sinthya man a few lumps for me."

Alanna laughed. "I hope to do just that." She looked back: the men of the King's Own were in the saddle. "Forward!"

Daine, in awe, watched them go. *This* was what she'd dreamed when Onua said they were going to Tortall. Well, *some* things are different, she thought as the riders retreated from view. Pulling the badger's claw out of her shirt, she polished it with a thumb. She's shorter than I expected. And I never thought she'd swear, or make jokes. She's a legend, sure enough, but she's so *human*.

An idea made her jaw drop: if *she's* a legend, and a hero, then *anyone* could be a hero. Tucking the claw back into her shirt, she ran back to camp. If anyone might be a hero—could I? she asked herself, and smiled. No, not me.

Still, she mulled it over as she started on a pile of reins that needed mending. Onua joined her at their fire with leatherwork of her own. They worked quietly until she heard her friend say, "Look who's up."

Their patient stood in front of his tent. Someone—Daine assumed one of the men—had given him a shirt and breeches, as well as a pair of boots.

She stared up at him. He was five inches over six feet in height, with broad shoulders and a well-muscled body. His mass of coal black hair was combed back and tied into a horse tail to show a face that was dark and sensitive. He moved with the ease of a giant cat as he sat on a log beside Onua, but Daine suspected that he hadn't always been so graceful. As a boy he must have resembled a stork, all elbows and knees. In his late twenties now, he had grown into his looks, and he seemed completely at home with himself.

"How'd you find a pair that fits?" Onua pointed at his feet with the awl she'd been using on her tack. "There's tea in the kettle, and a clean mug right there."

His lips parted to reveal white teeth in a shy smile. "Thanks." He poured and blew gently on his tea to cool it. "Alanna witched them so they'd fit." He regarded his boots with a wistful grin. "Nobody else had a pair even near big enough."

"What about your own magic?" Onua asked.

"I'm dry for the moment. Tapped out." His voice was midrange for a man's, warm and a little hesitant—nice to listen to, Daine thought. She kept her eyes away from him as she wrestled with her leatherwork.

A pair of large hands came into her field of vision to hold the strap while she set the final stitches.

"Thanks," she whispered, blushing.

"You look different."

Startled, she looked up into long, shadowy eyes. "What?"

He smiled. "You were a *lot* bigger."

She grinned in spite of her shyness. "Seems to me *you* was a bit smaller, now I think of it."

The strap was fixed. He gave it back and returned to his seat on the log. "I'd be dead if it weren't for you. You're called Daine?"

She nodded.

"I'm glad to meet you, Daine. I'm Numair Salmalín."

"I thought it was Arram."

His eyes flicked to Onua and back to her. "Arram's my boyhood name. I go by Numair now."

Daine took the hint. "The honor's mine, Master Numair." Then, because she *had* to know, she asked, "Why didn't you change back?"

"I was stuck."

*"Stuck?"*

"When Sinthya caught me, his mage fed me drugs. I panicked, and shape-shifted. I didn't remember I was full of all the drugs it takes to knock out somebody my size."

"You're lucky they didn't kill you," Onua pointed out.

"You're right. By the time you found me, I couldn't tell ground from air anymore. The food you offered? I didn't know it was food. Not that I was able to keep anything down." He sipped the tea. "It'll be a long time before I take hawk shape again."

*"That's* why you had funny eyes," breathed Daine. "And that's why you made me dizzy."

"I wanted to ask you about that. Onua says you got sick, disoriented. I can't understand *how*. She says you don't have the Gift—"

"Odd's bobs!" Daine snapped. Would all her new friends harp on that one thing, like Ma? "I don't see why this *Gift* is so grand. It comes and goes. You can't do too much at once, and you need all kinds of rules. It's more trouble than it's worth." She got up. "But whenever I turn 'round, somebody asks if I have it. I'm good with animals—isn't that enough?" Furious, not knowing there were tears on her cheeks, she stamped off into the woods.

Numair looked at Onua. "What did I say?"

The K'mir sighed and put down her work. "Her mother was a hedgewitch." (She meant someone with basic Gifts, taught by other hedgewitches, never hoping to be more than village healer-midwives.) "She and Daine's grandfather were killed by raiders in January. She wanted Daine to have the Gift, not just whatever she has with animals. Fool woman kept testing her, as if she thought the girl would develop it overnight. I'd better go after her."

"No—when she cools off, I'll go. You and Alanna were right. She has real power. Not the Gift, though." He tapped a pair of twigs together, looking thoughtful. "It's wild magic, pure and simple. She's brimming with it. I've never seen a human with so much."

"You felt it then."

He smiled. "I felt it when I was a bird, half-crazy and dying."

Onua sighed. "Be careful with her, Arram. She's hurting."

"I will." He rose, unfolding his length with a groan. "Use Numair, will you? I know you trust Daine, but there's no telling who else might overhear. I still have enemies in Carthak who'd like to know where I am."

Onua made a face. "You're right—Numair."

He grinned. "Come on—what great sorcerer has a name like Arram Draper? I have to have a name to fit my calling, don't you think?"

"All you mages are Players at heart, I swear. Can't do the magic unless you have all kinds of robes and props and a big audience to cheer you." She waved him off and returned to her work, smiling.

Numair found Daine greeting a woodchuck, and stayed in the trees to watch. The girl lay on the ground, her eyes on a level with the chuck's. The animal stood on his hind legs, chattering to her. She giggled, then offered a hand: the chuck snuggled against it for a moment. Then he chirped a farewell and trotted off into the brush.

Numair came forward slowly. "He seemed to have a lot to say."

Daine was thinking about the chuck, how *nice* he was after the monsters two nights before. "Oh, it's the usual spring talk. Freshening up the burrow, getting nice-smelling leaves. I told him where to find some wild mint." Her memory returned, and she felt her cheeks get hot. "Master Numair. I—"

He smiled. "No offense taken—if you stop calling me 'Master.' If I'm to help with the ponies the rest of the way, we may as well use first names."

"Is Onua mad at me? For losing my temper?"

He shook his head. The motion popped open the tie that held his black locks, and it fell. "Gods bless it. . . ."

Daine came to help him look. By the time they found the tie, she'd forgotten to be nervous with him. "It's easier if you wet it before using it on your hair," she explained as they returned to camp. "When it dries, then it shrinks."

"Good advice. Your hair gives you trouble?"

"Oh, Goddess, my hair's so dratted thick I don't even bother with ties." She giggled suddenly. "This is a very strange talk we're having."

He grinned down at her. "Boys worry just as much about their looks as girls do. We only *hide* it better."

"Seriously?" she asked, delighted. Living with only Grandda and Ma, away from the males of the village, she'd begun to think young men were totally alien.

"Seriously," he assured her. "You should see the lotions I put on my hair to get it to behave." He winked at Onua when they reached the campfire.

Onua and Daine spent the next day exercising the ponies and practicing hand-to-hand combat, something Onua said a woman alone should know. Numair dozed, mended his spare shirt, or did exercises with the arm that had been broken. "Is he up to the road?" Daine asked during one of his naps. She kept her voice low—he was stretched out under a nearby tree. "He maybe should ride, but he's too big for the ponies."

"We'll take it easy," the K'mir replied. "Alanna laid a slow healing on him, to fix the arm and build his strength. She said in two or three days he'll be fine."

"Did you know him, from before?"

"We're old friends." Seeing the look on Daine's face, Onua said, "Not *that* kind of friend! He goes for shapely blondes, and I like a man that likes horses. No, our hawk took pity on me when I didn't know anyone but the queen and Buri. If he likes you, he's the best of friends. Horse Lords help you if you get on his bad side." Seeing that Daine looked puzzled, she explained, "He *is* the most powerful sorcerer in Tortall."

Daine stared. A boyish man who talked hair-ties? Looking over, she saw a butterfly hovering over Numair's long nose. *"Him?"*

Onua chuckled. "Yes, him. It takes a powerful Gift to shape-change."

Numair opened his eyes. "You're talking about me. I can tell."

"He's vain too," Onua said loudly. "He takes as much time to dress for court functions as any lady. Which is bad enough, but then he ruins his clothes sitting on the grass to watch meteor showers."

"But that's my good side," protested Numair. "You really should tell her some of my faults." He paused then added, "Then again—please don't. I forgot you actually *know* my faults."

Daine laughed. She could see the rest of the trip would be fun.

The adults were arguing about protective circles when she began to think of supper. It wasn't fair to let Onua hunt all the time. Like her predator friends, Daine ate meat, taking care to make her kills swift and clean. Now she got hooks and line, and told the adults where she would be. There was a big tree on the riverbank where she could sit and mind her lines in comfort, and Onua had a very good way of preparing trout.

It wasn't long before her lines were baited and set in the deep pool under the tree. With the hard part done, she watched the sky and day-dreamed, rousing herself only to greet the animals who came to say hello. Cloud found a nearby patch of clover and grazed, keeping her company.

Tahoi joined them, looking disgusted. He lay down where Daine could easily scratch his ears. Onua and Numair were doing the sitting thing, not talking or working or paying attention to him. It bored him silly.

"What's the sitting thing?" Daine asked.

The dog showed her an image in his mind: Onua, seated with her legs crossed, hands resting on her knees, eyes closed. To that picture he added Numair, doing the same thing. A shimmering, pearly light gleamed around each of them, rippling over their faces.

"What's that?" Daine asked him. "That light, there?"

Tahoi didn't know. It was a thing some humans had and others didn't.

Magic, Cloud said. Your dam had it, and some of the others back home. Not so bright as these two—more like a glitter. But it's magic, all right.

Onua only does the sitting thing with humans that have the light, Tahoi commented, and sighed.

The girl smiled. "Find a stick—I'll play with you. Not here, though—I don't want to scare the fish." Tahoi wagged his tail and hunted for a stick that wouldn't hurt his mouth. "Cloud? Do *I* have the light inside?"

No, the mare replied. The light's only for humans. You may look like a human, but you aren't. You're of the People: the folk of claw and fur, wing and scale.

"Impossible," the girl said flatly. "Look at me. I'm pink, my fur's patchy, I walk on two legs. I'm human, human all over."

On the outside, the pony insisted. Not inside. Inside you're People.

Tahoi brought a stick, and Daine went to play with him. Cloud was joking, of course. She was human. Ma would have told her, if she weren't.

They left their camp the next day. Onua set an easy pace, stopping twice in the morning to rest. Numair kept up without appearing to tire. Catching Daine's eye on him once, he thumped himself on the chest and said, "When the Lioness puts a healing on a man, he stays *healed*!"

"Does your ma know you're this silly?" she demanded tartly.

He nodded, comically sad. "The few gray hairs she has on her head are my doing. *But*"—with an exaggerated change of mood—"I send her plenty of money, so she can pay to have them dyed!"

"I hope she beat you as a child," Onua grumbled.

The day passed quickly. Numair and Onua told stories about the people they knew at the palace. The man even juggled for her, a most unmagelike feat. By the time they made camp, she felt she had known him for years.

Building their fire, she ran into trouble. No matter what she did with flint and steel, the wood was too damp to catch. At last she coaxed it into a tiny flame and held her breath.

"How does it go?" he asked over her shoulder, and the flame went out.

"Gods bless it!" she snapped.

"What's the matter?"

"Oh, they must've had rain here yesterday. Everything's damp."

"Sit back."

She did as she was told, and the tinder burst into flame. She had to put large sticks of wood on it fast, before the fire used up the tinder. "But you didn't point, or make circles, or chant anything—"

He shrugged. "Some people need those things. I don't."

She gasped at his arrogance. "Well, excuse me for breathing!"

His laugh was full throated and made her grin. "What—did they have to enact fire-making rituals before anything would burn, where you came from?"

Her spirits dropped. "Things burned easy back home," she said flatly. "*Real* easy." She'd been having a good time while her family lay in the ground. Grabbing the shovel, she went to dig the latrine.

Teeth dug into the mage's elbow, making him yelp. He looked down at his attacker, Cloud. "Stop that, or I'll light a fire under your tail." The mare squeezed a little harder and released his arm.

"It was going so well." Onua was grooming the ponies. "She *laughed*."

Numair rubbed his elbow. He'd gotten off lightly—Cloud had only barely nicked the skin. "She'll laugh again."

Daine kept to herself, and the adults left her alone, talking quietly. When cleanup was done, they did the sitting thing. It was as Tahoi had shown her: with eyes closed and legs crossed they sat, hands on their knees, breathing as if they were asleep. In fact, Daine went to sleep watching them.

That night it came to her that Ma and Grandda probably wouldn't mind if she had fun now and then. They'd been partial to fun, making berry strings or playing catch with the bread dough. In her packs were two of the dancing puppets Grandda had made for her birthdays: the horse and one that looked just like Ma. The others had been ruined, but she had saved these.

She got up in the morning with caution and sent the raccoon and the marten who had spent that night with her on their way. She hated apologies, but if Onua and Numair were angry, she would make some.

Luck was on her side. Their grouchiness seemed to be normal morning grouchiness; all they wanted to do was drink their tea, eat their food, and get moving. Daine let it go at that. If they weren't angry about how she'd behaved, why remind them?

They made good progress that day. Once supper and cleanup were done, Numair stretched. "Let's go, Onua. You won't improve without practice."

Daine knew what came next. "What's the sitting thing?" They looked at her blankly. "You know—what you're going to do now."

"Meditation," Numair said. "It clears the mind, and rests it. If you have the Gift, meditation helps your discipline." His eyes were thoughtful as they rested on her. "Would you like to learn?"

"I don't have the Gift." Was he going to start on that?

He shrugged. "It's not only for the Gifted. I told you, it rests the mind. It helps you get a—a grip on the way you think."

"It helps you decide what you want," Onua added. "And how to get it."

Daine scuffed her foot in the dust. "Is it hard?"

Both of them smiled. "You won't know till you try," Numair pointed out.

Daine shrugged and sat as they did, tailor-style. "Now what?"

"Hands on your knees. Sit straight. Close your eyes. Let the thoughts empty out. For tonight, that's enough. Just let your thoughts go."

Daine heard Tahoi sigh. Now he had no one to play with.

The next morning they weren't far from their camp when riders overtook them on the road: Alanna and the men of the King's Own. Daine was startled to see that the Lioness, so friendly before, was now pale with fury. Darkmoon was as angry as his mistress. He pranced and fidgeted until Daine went to his head. He calmed slowly under her hands.

"He's gone," the knight told them. "From the looks of it, he fled the minute he knew you were safe. Curse him! Those dungeons of his—"

"I know," whispered Numair. He looked suddenly tired.

"I don't understand," Onua protested. "You searched?"

"We did." Alanna rubbed her neck. "His servants claimed Stormwings came, with a box, like a sedan chair. They flew off with him in it."

"Then they can be talked to," Numair said. "They're intelligent."

"Sure they are," Daine said. "They talked to Onua and me in the marsh."

"She's right," the K'mir told them. "And they searched for Numair in patterns after they lost him."

The Lioness sighed. "Lovely. More fun. All right—we have to see the king. Come along as soon as you can now. Be sure to ward your camp at night!"

"We'll do fine," Numair told her. "See you at the palace."

The knight and Hakim nodded, and within a few moments the company was galloping out of sight.

Four mornings later Onua and her companions topped a rise, and Daine thought her eyes would fall from her head. Before them a river halved a valley that cupped a walled city and more houses than she could count. At the heart of the valley three bridges linked the northern and southern banks, and roads entered the city from every angle. In the west, the city broke through its wall to climb a long slope dotted with estates and temples.

Above everything stood a huge castle shielded by high walls. Its towers, flying bright-colored flags, shone in the early sun. A small dome placed among them glowed silver like a giant pearl. Black dots like ants climbed a broad, white-paved road from the city below, to scatter before the walls and stream in through several gates.

"That's the palace," Numair said. "Home of the most unusual royal couple in all history and their peculiar court."

"I don't think 'unusual' and 'peculiar' are the right words," protested Onua, and Tahoi barked agreement.

"Do you live there?" Daine asked the man.

He shook his head. "I live south, along the coast. They have rooms for me here, though." He looked at Onua. "Press on?" She nodded.

Their road took them around the city until they reached a bridge over a deep moat. Here the palace wall was only ten feet high; the gate was a simple affair of wood and iron. Inside lay a small town, its air scented with molten copper, pine, cows, and baking. All this, Numair said, supported the palace. Daine shook her head in awe.

Guards in maroon and beige waved them across the bridge. Inside the gate, Numair pointed at the palace. "I go that way—I need to report in."

Tears stung Daine's eyes. You knew he'd leave sometime, she scolded herself. This is it. Don't be a baby. He's got important things to do!

A big hand patted her shoulder. "Just for now," the man said quietly. "I'll see you again soon."

Onua grinned when he kissed her cheek. "You just can't wait to lay hands on your books again. *I* know that look in your eye."

"She does too," Numair admitted. "Take care of our Daine." He waved and headed toward the palace, hands in his pockets.

"Come on," Onua told her. "It's this way."

Following her out of the gate's inner yard, Daine saw more wonders. Around them soared the levels of the palace, with wings and turrets in many styles telling of additions over time. She saw more glass in a look than she'd seen in her life. Her nose smelled flowers, both plain and exotic; her ears were filled with creaking wagons, shouting people, and the clang of metal.

Onua led them downhill. Chief among the buildings they passed were large stables, rich with horse smells. Daine would have stopped there, but Onua walked on. Before them lay meadows dotted with grazing animals. Behind the herds were masses of trees—the Royal Forest, said the K'mir.

The road ended at the meadows, where two long, wooden buildings had been built. One was a stable, a neat and quiet one. The other, connected to the stable by a covered walk, was a two-story barracks. Before it was a tall pole, a flag at its tip. As if showing the banner off, the wind lifted it up with a pop. A red horse reared on a gold brown field.

"The Queen's Riders," said Onua. "Home, or at least as much of one as *I* need. Let's put the ponies in the meadow, and then we'll talk."

# ⤞ FOUR ⤝

# THE QUEEN'S RIDERS

᭍  Unloading the packs, they shooed the ponies into the meadow, and Daine followed Onua into the barracks. Climbing stairs, Onua led them through a door painted a bright red. Inside was a big room with two rows of beds, six in each row.

Taking a key from her belt-purse, the K'mir unlocked a room near the door to reveal a single bed, several chests, a desk, and a shelf of books. With a sigh, she dropped her packs on the floor and motioned for Daine to do the same. "I'm not here often, but I'm always glad to see it." She opened the shutters and flopped onto the bed. "Pull up a chair." Daine obeyed.

The woman smiled at her. "As to your future. I'd like you to stay with me—you're the best assistant I've ever had. If you don't want that, you have other opportunities. Alanna would give you work, here or at Pirate's Swoop. Numair could do the same. Both of them say they'll mention you to the king."

Daine shook her head. The road was one thing; people might forget their station in life there. Here they'd go on with their real lives. Exalted persons like Alanna would not bother their heads over a homeless Gallan. Surrounded by wealth and magic, Numair would have better things to think of.

Onua drew a leather bag out of her purse and gave it to Daine. "There's your pay, and the bonus. You can sleep here till you decide what you want."

"Don't be silly," Daine informed her. "I'll work for you."

Onua's face lit, and she grinned. "Don't you want to know the terms?"

Daine had opened the bag and was gaping at the contents: a handful of silver coins and two gold ones. "Did you overpay me?" she accused.

Onua laughed. "You earned every penny, girl-child." She ticked points off on her fingers. "You fought Stormwings and spider-monsters. You found Numair and nursed him. That's *besides* what I said I'd pay you for. No, don't argue. Listen. The job's two coppers a day, plus room and board and bonuses for unusual duty. You help me with the trainees—selecting mounts, handling 'em, grooming 'em, and so on. They get two, so they have a spare ready all the time. But you know these ponies—if *one's* a handful for most people, think what *two* are like!"

Daine giggled. "I feel sorry for your trainees."

"Don't. They learn—or they wash out. You and I take care of the rest of the herd. In a few weeks we all go to the field training camp, and we make sure the recruits don't abuse their ponies. You have lots of free time. Socially, you're as good as a trainee—better, 'cause *you're* trusted to know what to do with a horse, and they aren't. Don't let them order you around. Most of the bad apples will go home crying after a week or so, anyway." Onua grinned. "What d'you think?"

Her head spun. Take today as it is, she thought, making herself calm down. Tomorrow I'll deal with tomorrow. "I'll stay." They shook hands.

"You're back!" Two people came in. One was a short K'mir, her face broader, less friendly, than Onua's, her eyes black instead of gray green. The other was a big man, taller even than Numair and powerfully built. His skin was dark brown; his close-cut hair looked like black wire. Pink, shiny skin like old scars wrapped around his wrists.

Onua hugged the visitors. "Daine, this is Buriram Tourakom—Buri, the commander of the Riders. And this is Sarge." To the adults she said, "Daine is my assistant. She's young, but she's worth her weight in gold."

Blushing, Daine looked at the floor. "Onua!"

"She isn't free with praise," Buri told her. A smile lit her face and made her less forbidding. "If Onua says good things about you, then they're true. Welcome." She offered a hand for Daine to shake, and Sarge did the same. Daine was relieved to find both had the palm calluses of those who worked, and worked hard. "Actually," Buri told Onua, "we just saw Numair. Sounds like you had a rough time coming home."

"It wasn't so bad," Onua replied. "Pretty uneventful, in fact, after Numair reached us. How are things?"

"Same-same." Buri leaned against the wall. "The new class is ready.

We'll start after lunch. There's the usual lot of soft-hands merchanters and farmers' babies. A Player—George recommended him. He's pretty solid, though he's tall for ponyback. We may have to give him a horse."

"We lost two from the Third Rider Group, one from the Fifth," Sarge added. Sitting on the floor, he still came up to Daine's waist. "Half of the First Rider Group is on the casualty list, but nothing permanent."

Plainly these people had a lot to catch up on. Daine got up. "Excuse me," she said. "Onua, I'm going to look at the herd."

Her friend smiled. "Don't stray far."

"It's good to meet you, Daine," Sarge told her. "We'll get acquainted later. It's just—"

Daine smiled and waved good-bye. She was a *little* envious of Onua, with her home and friends, but she forced that envy down. For certain she didn't want Onua to be alone in the world as she was.

Leaving the barracks, she climbed the fence into the horse meadow. The animals she and Onua had brought hung back. Strange ponies, who had never met anyone like her, crowded around. Heads were thrust under her hands. Colors passed before her eyes: cream, dun, roan, chestnut, gray, odd-colors. She saw stars, blazes and masks, stockings and the spine-long stripe called a list; mares, geldings, stallions. All were the shaggy-coated mountain breed.

Now the ponies who knew her mixed with the strangers, bragging that she was *their* herdmaster. Daine giggled as they butted her with their heads and flicked her with their tails. There was no need to be envious of Onua, not with friends like these.

Time passed—she wasn't sure how much. When a great bell chimed, she jumped.

"It's the noon bell." Daine hadn't seen the woman on the fence. "Lunchtime." She smiled. "Or will you just graze with the herd?" Her voice was low and clear.

Daine grinned and disentangled herself from her friends. Nearing the stranger, she had a good look at her and stopped. The woman was dressed simply in breeches and a shirt, but she turned them into the richest garments ever worn. Masses of coal black hair had been woven into a braid and coiled around her head. She had green hazel eyes set beneath level brows, ivory skin, and a full, red mouth. Her proudly arched nose was strong for classic beauty, but it fit her. Her only ornaments were a diamond on her gold marriage band and diamonds on her earlobes, but she didn't need any more decoration. She was the most beautiful female Daine had seen, lovelier even than Ma.

The woman had said something. Daine wiped her hands nervously on her skirts and went to the fence. "I'm sorry, mum—I didn't hear."

"You look like Chavi West-wind." She mistook Daine's surprise and explained, "Chavi is known for horse magic. She's a goddess, where I come from, one of the four—"

"Horse Lords. Onua told me. Bian North-wind, Shai South-wind, Vau East-wind, and Chavi. But they're K'miri gods. Excuse my saying so, but you don't look K'miri!"

The woman fingered the arch of her nose. "There's bad blood in my family. I'm half K'mir, anyway. You're a friend of Onua's?"

"I work for her."

The hazel eyes sharpened. "You're Daine." With a smile she explained, "Word travels fast here. You'll get used to it." She offered a small, delicate hand. Shaking it, Daine found calluses on the soft palm and smiled with relief. For a moment she'd been afraid she was talking to some kind of noble. She had never met a noble, apart from the Lioness, and she wasn't sure she wanted to. What would she say to one?

"Let's go eat," the woman told her. "I'm starving—you must be too."

Daine climbed the fence. "I think the whole city knows my name," she grumbled as they set off toward the barracks. "Did you tell me yours?"

"No. It's Thayet."

"The *queen*?"

"Only when I can't avoid it," said Thayet of Tortall. "Please don't get all formal on me now. We were having such a nice talk."

Daine scowled. "Odds bobs, this is a strange place! Knights who say call 'em by their first name and wizards that light tinder and queens that run around dressed like real people—"

Thayet laughed. "No wonder Alanna and Numair like you. You have a very unusual way of looking at things!"

Daine blushed. "I'm sorry. I'm just so—confused, here."

"That's normal," the queen assured her. "I felt the same, once." They entered the barracks. "Some lunch will make you feel better." She steered Daine through a door and into chaos. This room was filled with long wooden tables and benches. A third of them were occupied by men and women in their late teens and early twenties, who created enough noise to fill the place.

Daine copied Thayet as the queen picked up a wooden tray and went to the servers at the back of the room. These people confirmed the woman's identity: each bobbed respectfully and called her "Majesty" as they put bread, cheese, bowls of stew, fruit, and mugs of cider on her tray and Daine's.

"Thayet, there you are!" Buri came up as they left the servers. "We've been looking for you. Onua says she and Daine here met up with Stormwings, and some kind of spiders with human heads—" Talking, she led the queen to a table at the head of the room, where Onua and Sarge waited.

Onua beckoned to Daine, but the girl didn't want to be there, under the eyes of everyone. Shaking her head, she went to the corner of an unoccupied table and sat with her lunch. I'm younger'n anyone here, she thought, buttering a roll. How can I make them mind what I say about the horses?

A girl sat down across from her. "Hello!" She had dark hair cut boyishly short, and a pair of dancing green eyes. With a tip-tilted nose, a cleft chin, and a dusting of freckles, she looked like pure mischief. "I'm Miri. Are you a new trainee?"

Daine shook her head. "I work for Onua, the horsemistress. I'll be helping you with the ponies, I guess."

"Good—we need more girls. There are too many boys." Miri stuck her tongue out at the tall, blond youth who settled his tray beside Daine.

He smiled. "Do you mind if I sit here?"

She shook her head. He had a very kind smile and bright blue eyes.

"Evin Larse." He sat and offered a hand.

Daine accepted it. "Daine Sarrasri."

He reached for her ear and seemed to pull a roll out of it. "Didn't wash this morning, did you?" He smeared cheese on the roll and grinned at Daine's openmouthed surprise. "My family's Player folk," he explained. "I have all sorts of useless talents."

"She's going to help us with the ponies," Miri said. "I need all the help I can get," she informed Daine. "Up till two weeks ago I could count on one hand the times I've been on a horse."

"You're doing fine," Evin told her soothingly. He looked at Daine. "She's been grooming and riding up at the palace stables."

"But these ponies are different," Miri protested. "You heard Sarge—they're picked to be fussy and mean, and they bite."

Daine grinned. "They're not so bad. Me'n Onua brought some down from Galla, and I've been with the herd. There's nice ones. You'll see." Looking around, she thought that the last time she'd seen such a mixed herd of humans was at the fair in Cría. There were two other blacks, three very brown youths, and five more as blond, pale skinned, and blue eyed as Scanrans. The rest could have come from any of the realms around the River Drell.

"You look overwhelmed," Evin told her. "They're just trainees, like Miri and me."

"Yes, but what does it take to be a trainee?" she asked. "How did you two join up, if you don't mind my asking?"

"Oh, joining's the easy part," Miri said. "They post the rules in all the schools and at recruiting stations in the towns."

"You have to be fifteen or more," Evin said. "Healthy, with all your body parts still attached—no missing hands or eyes."

"Single," added Miri. "No spouse and children. It helps if you ride, but it's not required—they took me, and the only thing I ever rode in my life was a fishing boat. That's what my people do, fish."

"You need good reflexes," Evin went on. "You have to read and write. For Tortallans that's no problem—schools have been open to everyone for nine years now. For the ones that can't read, the Riders'll give you work in the palace till you learn. I think that's all. Oh, and you have to be here by the March full moon. That's when training starts every year."

"That's *all*?" Daine asked, shocked. "That doesn't seem like much!"

"It isn't," said Evin. "The problem isn't getting *into* the Riders— it's *staying*. We've lost ten in the last two weeks—sick, wouldn't take orders, couldn't handle the schedule. We'll lose more by summer's end."

Sarge rose and thundered, "Listen up, darlings! Today is your last day of fun at the king's expense." ("He calls running us around the meadow every day 'fun,' " Miri whispered to Daine.) "Here's Onua, our horsemistress." Onua stood and nodded to everyone. "Daine—stand up, girl"—she obeyed—"is her assistant." Daine sat when Onua did. "They brought the rest of the ponies we need," Sarge went on, "so we're ready to start the *real* work. You have till the bells chime one stroke to do what needs doing. At the bell, come to the horse meadow." He clapped his hands. "Don't sit there gawping, children—you pick your mounts today. Get those trays to the kitchen and get out of here!"

Onua took Daine aside. "What about sleeping arrangements? I can put a cot for you in my room or a storeroom, or you can sleep with the trainee girls. Your choice."

"Please, Horsemistress—" It was Miri. "If nobody minds, Daine could bunk with me—if you want to, Daine."

Daine thought it over and nodded.

"Fine," Onua said. "After supper you can show Daine the bed. Would you excuse us now, though? I want to ask her something."

The girl nodded and raced upstairs. Onua and Daine followed at a slower pace. "I'm glad you're making friends," the K'mir said. "It's

good for you to meet people your own age. Listen—I have to ask"—
she pointed to Daine's skirts—"doesn't that outfit get hot?"

She'd hit on the burden of Daine's life. The girl scowled: the litany
she'd given Ma and Grandda for years bubbled to her lips. "Hot in
summer, cold in winter, always getting tangled and ripped and soaked,
clumsy, *heavy*—"

Onua smiled. She knew an old grievance when she heard one. "Then
why wear 'em? Get yourself breeches and a shirt like me."

Daine gaped at her. "*Men's* gear? With folk talking about me all
the time as is?"

Onua shook her head. "You're not home now. The rules have
changed."

Daine opened her mouth to object—then closed it. She looked at
her skirts. To be rid of them, and the petticoats . . . it hit her, *really* hit
her, that she was free of Snowsdale. What could they do to her now?

From what Evin and Miri said, Riders came from all walks of life.
In Galla she was strange. Here, *everyone* was different. These people
wouldn't care if Ma was a hedgewitch. Maybe they wouldn't even care
that her father was unknown, someone her ma met one Beltane night
and never saw again.

But they'll care if they know you went mad, a tiny voice inside her
cautioned. Best keep shut about that!

Onua let her think, and was rewarded when Daine's blue-gray eyes
shone like lanterns. "I'd *love* to put on breeches."

"Come on, then." Onua took her out of the girls' dormitory and
down the hall. "That's men's country," she said, pointing to a bright
yellow door. "Off-limits to females, like we're off-limits to them."

In the supply room, a tall woman with red-bronze hair and great
kindness in her face looked up from her desk. "Onua, welcome!" She
came over to hug the K'mir. "Your assistant?" she asked.

"Daine, this is Kuri Tailor—she's in charge of the girls. If there's
anything you need, Kuri's the woman to ask." Onua hugged Daine
around the shoulders. "Kuri, she needs breeches and shirts. Daine, I hate
to rush, but I need to talk with Sarge. You'll be all right?" The girl
nodded. "When you're done, come out to the meadow and we'll get
these two-leggers mounted." She left the room.

"The first day or so is crazy," explained Kuri. "They always start
as soon as Onua comes, so she has to move fast. You'll be rushing too,
once the Riders see how much work they can get from you—my word
on it." She measured Daine quickly and wrote down her findings. "I'll
have others tonight, but take these for now." From stacks of homespun
garments on one side of the room, she chose a pair of worn breeches

and a patched white shirt. "No use wearing good clothes when you're with the horses," she explained. "Step behind that screen and try these on—let's see how they fit."

Behind the screen, Daine drew the shirt and breeches on with trembling hands. Doubtless the trainee girls were used to such things. She had seen they all wore breeches. But she was a little scared. Dressed, she stepped out into the open.

"What the matter?" Kuri walked over to tug and adjust the garments.

"It's—men's gear," she explained shyly. "At home, the priests and the headman—they'd never approve."

"Forget them." Kuri turned her, checking the clothes. "You're ours, now. I'm not saying there won't be people to carp and pinch at you. That's human nature, alas." Daine nodded. *She* knew. "But here life's what you make it. Who you *used* to be doesn't matter. Look at Sarge— he was a slave, once. Onua was beaten by her husband and left to die. Her Majesty and Commander Buri had to flee Saraine. Do you catch my drift?"

It was a lot to digest. Onua? It was impossible to think of Onua as beaten and abandoned by anyone. And Sarge? "I—I think so."

Palace bells chimed one stroke, making Daine jump. "The bells take getting used to," the woman informed her with a sigh.

"How often do they ring?" the girl asked, pulling on her boots.

"Every hour until late in the evening." Kuri smiled. "All set?"

"Yes'm." Daine grinned at her. "Thank you."

"Welcome to Corus, dear," the woman said as Daine ran out the door.

Onua, Buri, and Sarge waited at the fence with a barrel of apples. Daine arrived just as Onua stuffed fruit into every pocket Miri had. "Bribe them," she said, and shooed the reluctant girl through the gate Sarge held open.

"What do I do?" Daine asked.

"Use your instincts." Onua watched the field as she spoke. "You have to make your own authority with the trainees. Not that I think that will be a problem. Just keep an eye out. Remember they have to pick two."

"One for morning, one for afternoon," Sarge added with a grin.

It was one thing to say "Make your own authority," another to start doing it. For the moment Daine watched. Most trainees met the ponies cautiously or easily, depending on their natures. A mouse-gray mare twined about Evin as if she were a cat.

Looking for Miri, she saw trouble. Some of the more wicked animals had gone to torment the girl, who was plainly scared. Stopping an arm's reach from her, they frolicked, showing more tooth and hoof than was necessary.

This won't do! Daine thought, jumping into the meadow. She bore down on the mischief-makers with a scowl, Cloud following like a lonely dog. "Stop that!" she ordered. "What would your mas say if they saw you acting bad? Shame on you! Scat—and don't come back till you've learnt manners!" The ponies shook their heads, looking properly ashamed, and fled.

"If she wanted to be a Rider, she *ought* to know how to *ride*," a female voice muttered. Daine looked for the source, but none of the nearby trainees met her eyes.

"At home only lords or couriers ride," Miri explained, shamefaced. "I've *been* practicing. It's just—there's so many, and they're so *frisky*."

Daine put a hand on her shoulder. Her new friend was solid, muscular, with a love of life she could almost feel. "Look—there's some you'll like." She pointed to a cluster of ponies milling around a tree in the open meadow.

"I'd have to go through the herd," the older girl whispered.

Daine stuck her hands in her pockets. "See how you kept to the fence, because you're shy?"

"I didn't think 'shy' was the right word," Miri confessed.

"Hush. Those ponies are nice, but they're shy too. If you want to meet them, *you* have to do the walking. They're just animals. They can't know you've kept to the fence because you're shy."

"It can't be worse than sailing through a storm," Evin said from nearby.

"I only did that *once*." Miri looked at the herd and the shy ponies, swallowed—and walked forward. Daine and Cloud followed her to the tree.

"Here, boy." The pony Daine beckoned forward was a gelding, his body hairs a mixture of black and white, his mane, tail, face, and socks black. "I want you to meet someone." The pony sidled around until he was behind Daine, peering at her human friend. "This fellow is what we call a blue roan. We came south together." Daine looked over her shoulder. "Come out here and meet Miri. If you ask nice, she might give you an apple."

The roan's ears pricked forward at the word *apple*. Carefully he emerged from behind Daine to approach the older girl.

"He's beautiful." Timidly Miri offered him a fruit. Within seconds it was gone and he was inspecting her pockets for more. Daine instructed, "Now blow in his nostrils, gentle like. It's how you get acquainted."

"It seems rude to me." Miri obeyed, and giggled when the blue returned the courtesy. "You know, they aren't as scary as I thought."

"Animals are easy to understand," Daine told her. "You just have to know how to talk to them."

"*You* talk to them like they really *are* people." Miri smiled as the roan leaned into her hands.

"Don't say it's like I have magic," Daine said. "I hear it all the time, and it makes me crazy."

"Depends on what you mean," Miri commented. "The sea's full of magic, but we can't use it like the Gift. It isn't the same. My uncle is a wave-speaker—he swims with dolphins. He talks to them, whole conversations. Have an apple," she told a tan mare who had come near. The pony took one daintily. Soon they were breathing into each other's faces.

"Walk with them a bit," Evin suggested, joining them. The reins he held belonged to the mouse-gray mare and to a tall stallion, a cream-colored beauty with a white mane and tail. "Daine, what do you think?"

She went over both. Evin had chosen well: they were tall for ponies, which meant they would suit his long legs. The stallion was a showy, life-loving fellow, reflecting the Player's extravagance of character. The mare was smitten with him, matching the sweetness that lay close to Evin's bones.

"You got lucky," she said when she was done. "This pair will do anything for you, if you handle them right."

Evin grinned. "I'm glad you approve."

Another trainee called her for help, a redheaded youth named Padrach. She gave it to him, then to another. Before she knew it the afternoon was done, and the trainees were taking their new mounts to the stables for grooming. Daine, Onua, Buri, and Sarge helped then too, though Daine couldn't see how *she* could ever be comfortable telling a twenty-year-old man he was missing spots on the pony he was grooming.

She did try it: "Excuse me, trainee—what did you say your name was?"

Blue gray eyes twinkled at her over his cream-colored mare's back. "I didn't. It's Farant." His blond hair curled thickly over his head, almost matching the pony's in color.

"Thank you. Trainee Farant, you're missing spots."

"Not at all, sweetheart. I'm just combing too fast for you to see."

*"Trainee Farant, you're missing spots!"* Sarge boomed just behind Daine. She thought later she actually might have levitated at that mo-

ment—certainly Farant had. *"Next time the assistant horsemistress tells you something, don't flirt—correct it!"*

He moved on, and Daine pressed her hands against her burning cheeks. Farant leaned on his mare and sighed. "Yes, Assistant Horsemistress. Right away." He winked at her and went back to work.

Daine went to Sarge as the trainees were finishing up. "Sarge, I—"

He shook his head. Daine thought if he leaned against the stable wall any harder, it would collapse. How did a human, without bear blood in him, get to be so *large*? "Not your fault. These city boys see you, you're young, sweet-lookin' "—he winked at her—"they're gonna try to take advantage. If they can't keep their minds on the job after I've had them two weeks already in my patty-paws, then I ain't been doing *my* job right." His grin was wolfish. "But that can be fixed." Seeing her openmouthed stare, he asked, "Something the matter, my lamb?"

She closed her jaw. "No, sir. I just never met nobody like you."

"And if you're lucky, you won't again," muttered Buri, passing by.

After the stables there was a bath, a hot one. Bathing with other females in a tub as large as a pond would take getting used to, Daine thought, but at least she had plenty of soap and shampoo.

Dressed in clean clothes, she went to the mess hall, where Evin and Miri waved for her to join them. She noticed there was much less talk than at lunch. Afterward, the trainees cleared and scrubbed the tables, and Kuri went to the head of the room. Buri and Sarge were moving a map of Tortall into place behind her as she laid bundles of plants onto the table before her.

"Tonight it's medicinal herbs," she told them, and the trainees groaned. She smiled. "That's not so bad. Remember, last week I was teaching you how to sew your own cuts—without anything to numb the pain."

Daine saw Onua slip out the back, and followed. "Do I have to stay?"

"No, indeed not. *You* aren't a trainee. You can help me unpack."

That sounded like something she could get her exhausted muscles and brain to do. She followed Onua up the stairs to her room. "Do they have to study *all* the time?"

She sat on the bed while the K'mir opened her packs. "Clothes in a pile by the door. Don't get up—just throw them. Packages on the bed next to you. Hand me scrolls and papers." Daine hoisted a pack onto her lap and went to work. "Well, they have to get their book learning now, while they're here. They won't have much time, once we head for the summer training site. You'll like the one this year: Pirate's Swoop."

Daine's face lit. "Lady Alanna's home?"

"The very same."

Returning to the subject on her mind, she asked, "What do they study? The trainees?"

Onua numbered the topics on her fingers. "Poisons, medicines, edible plants. Tracking and hunting, all terrains. Reading maps, drawing them—maps here are a lot more accurate, now that Riders help draw them. Battle tactics. Weapons and hand-to-hand combat. Teaching combat and tactics—they show villagers how to protect themselves. The ones with the Gift have to learn all they can do with it. Veterinary medicine. I think that's most of it."

"And they learn *all* this?" the girl asked, shocked.

The K'mir laughed. "They do their best. They have to. At the end of fall they go to groups in the field to start their trial year. If they survive, and most do these days, they're assigned a permanent group. Why? Were you thinking of going for a Rider after all?"

"Not anymore!" Daine said emphatically.

Onua grinned. "I have trouble seeing you play soldier, even so odd a soldier as the Riders turn out."

Later, tucked into a bed next to Miri's, Daine thought Onua was probably right. It must be hard, having to account for every minute of the day as the trainees did. Why, she'd never get to meet any new animals!

Dozing off, she woke abruptly, feeling trapped. At first she didn't even remember where she was. Sitting up, she looked around: the five girl trainees were in their beds, asleep. The barracks were silent.

If she didn't get some air, she'd suffocate.

A window opened over her bed. She pried the shutters apart in time to hear a watchman's distant cry: "The midnight hour, and all is well!"

Her bed was too soft after so much sleeping on the ground. She cursed under her breath and took blankets and pillow to the floor. That at least was firm, and the air was cooler too. She waited for sleep again.

Miri turned over and said clearly, "But I *love* to ride." Daine sat up to peer at her. The girl was fast asleep.

She lay back. The badger's claw weighed heavy on her chest. When she turned onto her side, the thong half-choked her. She eased it and closed her eyes. Sheets and blankets rustled. A blond girl who had snubbed her in the baths snored. Another tossed and turned for what seemed like hours before she settled. Outside, Daine heard a dog's bark.

A headache grew in her temples. She missed having animals close by. At home, she'd had a ground-floor room. Even in winter she left the shutters open a crack, and never slept cold. Her friends always kept her warm.

Disgusted, she grabbed her breeches from the chest in front of her bed. Her traveling gear was there, including her bedroll. It was the work of a second to dress and stuff her feet into boots. With her bedroll under her arm, she slipped downstairs and outside.

The night air was a relief. She inhaled the scents of field and forest happily, feeling sleepy and content as she crossed the open pasture. The tree that had sheltered the shy ponies that afternoon was there, the ground underneath mercifully free of manure. She spread out her bedroll and, already half-asleep, crawled in. Cloud lay down to support her back. Someone—a pony she didn't know—lipped the foot of her covers.

"This is *much* better," Daine said. "Good night, everybody." Falling asleep, she knew the free ponies had come to stand nearby and keep her company.

*In her dream, she walked down the road with Onua. Instead of ponies, they led people—the trainees—in chains. The night air was thick and sour, and marsh creatures made an incredible noise.*

*The noise stopped abruptly, cut off. Onua halted. "What's that?"*

*A stench fell on them in waves. "Stormwings!" Daine cried.*

She was awake and sitting up. Dawn shone between clouds in the east. The ponies milled nearby, restless and afraid. She drew a deep breath, feeling air pour into her chest like soup. Lurching to her feet, she peered overhead. The sky was empty, but that meant nothing. They were coming.

She dragged her boots on and ran for the building; the ponies ran with her. "Ho, the barracks!" she yelled, knowing she was too far away. "Riders!" On the second floor a window was open—her own. "Miri! Onua, wake up!"

A tousled head appeared. "Daine, what's wrong?" Kuri yelled.

"Get Onua!" Daine screamed. "Tell her Stormwings are coming!" She gasped for breath. At her back she felt wrongness surge.

Kuri vanished from the window. The girl turned, knowing she could never reach the barracks in time. They rose from the trees, the sun's first thin rays striking off metal wings. The familiar stink fell over her.

Zhaneh Bitterclaws led her flock, homing in on Daine. "Kill it!" she screeched. Her left eye was a black and oozing ruin. "Kill this beast!"

More than fifty Stormwings stooped to the attack. Cold with terror, Daine crouched against the ground. Cloud reared, ordering the Stormwing queen to come down and fight like a horse. Steel claws groped for her as the mare struck at the creature with her hooves. The ponies crowded around Daine, lunging at the Stormwings when they came too close.

Goddess, Horse Lords, get me out of this and I will never, *ever* sleep without a bow again, she promised.

Tahoi raced onto the field with a pack of hounds, all of them as big as he was. More dogs followed, baying. Seeing rocks nearby, three of them as big as her fist, Daine grabbed them. Her first struck Zhaneh Bitterclaws square on the nose.

"There, you monster!" she yelled, shaking her fist at the Stormwings. "Come close, so I can do it again!" A little dog that came with the hounds wove in and out of the ponies' hooves to bring her more ammunition.

Black fire filled with silver lights wrapped around a Stormwing. The creature struggled, trying to throw it off: the fire crept into its mouth and blew it apart. More clouds of black fire chased Stormwings to kill them.

Darkmoon came, saddled and trailing his reins. He leaped to seize a Stormwing by the leg. Shaking his prize like a terrier, he snapped its neck.

Other war-horses followed. Behind them ran Sarge in only a breech-clout, armed with a fistful of javelins. He threw the first with a yell. Daine gaped when a Stormwing dropped, trying to drag the weapon from its chest. The black man fixed on a new target and waited for his best shot, as calm as he'd been at lunch. Each time he threw, a Stormwing went down.

Onua raced onto the field in her nightgown, her small bow and quiver in her hands. She had an arrow on the string: lining up her shot, she dropped the Stormwing that was her target. Zhaneh Bitterclaws saw the K'mir and screeched her triumph as she attacked.

Daine yelled. Half of the animals went to Onua, ringing her as the others ringed Daine. More horses and dogs leaped the fence to cover Sarge.

Purple fire—Alanna's magic—appeared, weaving a net around a pair of attackers. They screamed and beat at it uselessly: it dragged them to earth and the hounds. Thunder that was more than thunder pealed. The dogs howled—Daine clapped her hands over smarting ears. The Stormwings shrieked, trying to do the same thing with their steel feathers. Blue lightning darted from the top of the field, consuming each Stormwing it struck.

Near the fence a bearded man in shirt and breeches was the source of the blue fire. It shone around him, and pooled in his hands. Beside him was Alanna, dressed as he was, for riding. Numair was there too, in what looked like a nightshirt. Fire lashed from their hands—purple for the Lioness, black for Numair—to cut the enemy in two.

Zhaneh spoke in her odd language and began to climb; those that were able followed. A wall of their own fire wrapped around them, coloring them scarlet with an edge of gold light.

The bearded man threw a fistful of blue. The red shield consumed it, but the man continued to hurl bolts until the monsters were specks in the sky.

Daine's knees buckled from exhaustion and shock. Numair came down the rise, looking as tired as when she had first seen him as a man. "I said I'd see you again," he joked, leaning on the tree.

She grinned at him. "You timed it perfect."

Darkmoon and the other horses, ponies, and hounds sat where they were, trembling with nerves. Many were cut and bleeding, but—miraculously—none were dead.

The bearded man crouched beside a Stormwing corpse. He must have discovered their smell: he sneezed and put a hand over his nose. Alanna and Onua went to him, Onua leaning on Tahoi for support. A liver chestnut and an iron gray horse nuzzled Sarge, making sure he was in one piece. Daine giggled, and found she was getting the same treatment from Cloud.

Numair offered Daine his hand. Cloud supported her on her free side, and a stranger mare let Numair prop himself on her. "The trainees usually wait till they're *away* from the palace before starting any wars," Numair told her. "The nobles will complain you got them out of bed."

Daine looked up at him, worried. "Will I get in trouble?"

Sarge had heard. He laughed. "Let 'em complain. It's good for them to be up in time for breakfast."

When she was calmer, she thanked the dogs, horses, and ponies who had come to her rescue. Only when the men who worked in the palace stables and kennels arrived to retrieve their charges did she return to the Rider barracks.

"Should I go help them?" she asked Onua as she cleaned up. "Some of the animals were hurt. They'll need stitching and bandaging—"

"Calm down," the woman said. "There's a sorcerer attached to each of the stables and kennels, to do any healing. Your animals will be fine."

Daine followed her to breakfast, envious. Wouldn't that be a wonderful thing, to be able to wave her hands and put an end to a creature's hurts?

Evin and Miri besieged her with questions as she joined them. Why was she in the field? Hadn't she been scared? Why did the animals fight for her and Onua? She answered as well as she could, but when Padrach and Farant came to ask the same things, she felt embarrassed.

After breakfast, Sarge ordered the trainees to report to the horse meadow for cleanup. Daine helped Kuri to clear a ground-floor store-room, freeing it to serve as her bedroom. Its best feature was a door to the outside she could leave open. Other than that, it was tiny, just big enough to hold a bed, a storage chest, a chair, and a small table.

That afternoon she helped the trainees saddle and ride their new mounts. By the time everyone took their day's-end bath, she was exhausted. She was content, at supper, just to listen to her new friends talk. Afterward, as the trainees got ready for their night's lessons, Onua beckoned.

"What's up?" Daine asked.

The K'mir led her to a room across the hall from the mess. "There's somebody who'd like to meet you." She opened the door. "I brought her," she announced, following Daine inside. "Are we late?"

## ➤➤ FIVE ◄◄

# WILD MAGIC

∞ Seated at the table was the bearded man Daine had seen that morning. "I just got here," he said in a deep, gentle voice. "I took the liberty of ordering refreshments from the cooks, by the way."

Close up, he was a sight to wring any female heart. His close-cropped hair and beard were blue black, his eyes sapphire blue, his teeth white against the blackness of his beard. Daine gulped. She felt ten feet tall and clumsy. Her face was probably breaking out in pimples as she looked at him.

He got to his feet and smiled down at her. "You must be Daine. You may not remember me from before—you were busy."

Looking up into those eyes, the girl felt her heart melt like butter in the sun. "No, sir, I remember. You threw blue lightning."

He held a chair out for her. "Sit down, please." She obeyed and was glad when he sat again. Having him behind her was wonderful but terrifying. What if she had forgotten to scrub the back of her neck?

A cook entered with a tray loaded with cakes, fruit, and a pitcher of juice. Placing it on the table, he bowed to the man. "Your Majesty."

"Exactly what we need," the stranger told him. "My thanks." The cook bowed again and made his escape.

Daine gaped at her host. "You're the *king*!" she cried. Belatedly remembering she ought to bow, or kneel, or something, she jumped to her feet.

Jonathan—*King* Jonathan—grinned. "It's all right. Please sit. Otherwise good manners say I have to get up again, and I'm tired."

She sat, trembling. This is a *very* strange country, she told herself, not for the first time. Back home, you couldn't *pay* a noble to speak to a commoner!

The king selected a cake and bit into it. "Wonderful," he said with his mouth full. "The Riders eat better than I do."

"It just *seems* as if we do. We don't have six footmen asking if you're *sure* you don't want a taster," Onua teased. She poured juice for all of them.

King Jonathan snorted. "Don't remind me." He looked at Daine. "Seers can tell, sometimes, if the immortals will attack a place. You, however, are the first I know of to sense them nearby. Are there seers or fortune-tellers in your family?" He smiled at her, *just* at her.

She'd tell him anything for another smile. "Ma was a hedgewitch, Your Honor. She had the Gift for birthing, healing. Protection spells— not as good as Onua's. She was best with plants. She never could see any future things, though."

"Did she have the Gift from her family?" he asked.

She nodded, fiddling with the lacing of her shirt. "All the girls in her family was healers but me." She swallowed a throat-lump, remembering how disappointed Ma had been that Daine couldn't follow in her steps.

"What of your father?" His voice was kind, but the question hurt. The king saw it in her face and said gently, "I'm sorry, but I must know. If your father was a peddler or a vagabond, perhaps he sired other children with your ability. We can use more people like you."

"Why? Sir—Your Majesty, that is?"

"Winged horses were seen in Saraine this winter." The grimness in his eyes caught and held her. "Griffins nest in the cliffs of the Copper Isles. There are spidrens throughout the hill country this spring."

Winged horses? Griffins? "Where do they come from, do you know?"

"The Divine Realms—the home of the gods. Four hundred years ago, powerful mages locked the immortals into them. Only the greatest gods have been able to leave—until now."

An arm crossed Daine's vision to pick up a cake. Numair took an empty seat, and the king went on. "Our neighbors—Galla, Scanra, Tusaine—report unicorns, giant birds, even winged people as small as wrens. *We* are plagued by monsters, ogres, and trolls." He drummed his fingers on the table. "It's interesting that a weak mage like Sinthya could send rare creatures like Stormwings after you. Where did he get such power? As far as we know, he had only one secret worth protecting: he was dealing with Carthak."

"Carthak's another country?" Daine asked, blushing for her ignorance.

"Across the Inland Sea," Numair said. "They're desperate. Their crops failed two years in a row—not enough rain, and tornadoes that ripped up the fields. There were food riots in the capital last winter. The emperor needs good farmland, and we're the closest target."

"Carthak has the university, its school for mages, and its library— the same library used by the mages who sealed the Divine Realms." The king looked at Numair. "I think the Carthaki mages found those spells."

Numair was rolling a cake into a ball. "*And* spells to compel immortals to obey humans. How else could Sinthya get Stormwings to chase me?"

"We have nothing like those spells," Jonathan told Daine. "Sinthya's papers vanished. We're searching our own libraries, but it might take months. In the meantime, the warnings foretellers give us aren't enough. If we could send those with your ability to sense immortals to our villages and towns, we could better protect our people. If we can find your father—"

It had come back to that. She shook her head, humiliated.

"Daine?" It was Onua, who had given her trust and work that she loved. She owed this woman, at least, an answer.

She looked down. "I don't know who he is. It's in my name. Sarrasri—Sarra's daughter. Only *bastards* are named for their mothers." She spat out the hated word, but its taste stayed on her tongue.

"Why don't you know?"

She didn't look up to see who had asked. "Ma never told me. She never told anybody. She kept saying 'someday, someday.' "

"Do you know *anything*?" Onua rested a hand on Daine's shoulder.

She fought to get herself under control. "It was Beltane. They light fires, and couples jump over the embers when they burn down." So they'll have babies in the coming year, she thought, but she wasn't going to say *that*.

"We do the same thing," the king remarked.

Daine looked at him, startled. "*You* never jumped over no embers," she accused before she knew what she was saying.

The others laughed. She ducked her head to hide her blush.

"The ruler takes part in all great feasts, to show respect for the gods," Jonathan told her gravely. His eyes danced. "Thayet and I do it every year."

"I didn't mean—I wasn't trying to be—disrespectful—"

He patted her knee. "I didn't think you were. Go on."

"Ma wasn't sweet on anybody, so she went walking in the wood alone. She met someone. I used to think it was a man that was already married, but when I asked last year, she said no. And I don't look like anyone from Snowsdale. Most of 'em are blond and blue eyed, being's we're so near Scanra and all."

The king sat back with a sigh. "Well, it was an idea," he said to no one in particular.

"I'll help if I can," she said, knowing that she had disappointed them. "I just don't know what I could do. And the warnings aren't that, exactly. I know something *wrong's* coming, but I knew that much about the rabid bear."

"A rabid *bear*?" the king asked in horror and awe. "Mithros—that's not something *I'd* ever want to see!"

Daine smiled. "I didn't want to see him, either, sir. I just got to."

"Did you get the identical sensation from the bear as you got with the Stormwings or the spidrens?" asked Numair.

"Oh, no. It was different. Bad, but in a brown kind of way."

"In a *what*?" Onua asked.

"Well, animals—I think of 'em in colors, sometimes." She tapped her head. "To me, bears feel brown, only this one had red and black lights. *Very* sick, he was. I get the monsters as colors too, but they're gold with black and green lights in them. I *never* felt any real creature as gold."

"I *told* you she has magic," the mage told the king triumphantly.

"No!" she retorted, jumping to her feet. "Didn't Ma test me and test me? Don't you think I'd've grabbed at magic, if I had it, just to please Ma?"

"Easy, little one." The king put a hand on her arm, guiding her back into her chair. "Numair believes—and I agree—you have magic. You may have no *Gift*, but there are other magics, 'wild magics.' The Bazhir tribes use one kind to unite their people. The Doi read the future with another. There are creatures we call 'elementals,' whose very nature is composed of wild magic."

Daine frowned. "Miri told me the sea people know about it. Some of them use it to talk to fish and dolphins."

"Exactly. From what your friends say"—the king nodded to Onua and Numair—"your wild magic gives you a bond with animals. Your mother might not have recognized it. Only a few people know it even exists."

Daine frowned. "Can't you see it on someone, like them with the Gift can see it on other folk that have it?"

"I can," Numair said. "And you do." Daine stared at him.

Jonathan said, "He's perhaps the only living expert on wild magic."

Daine scowled at Numair. "You never mentioned this on the road."

He smiled. "If you were trying to get a deer to come to you, would you make any sudden noises?"

Her scowl deepened. "That's different. I'm no deer."

Jonathan took Daine's hands. "Will you let Numair help you study wild magic? It may help expand your awareness of the immortals, for one thing."

"Wouldn't it be easier to *tell* creatures to obey you?" Onua added. "All the way here you coaxed the ponies to mind you. You're dominant—you proved that on the stallion, the day you and I met. Why prove it to each pony in the herd, if you could do it just once and never again?"

"Daine." Something in Numair's voice made her look at him, and only him. At the expression in his dark eyes, she even forgot that the king still held her hands. "I can teach you to heal."

"Animals?" It came out as a squeak. "You mean—like Ma did humans? But how do you know if I can?"

"Because I saw you do it once." That wasn't Numair; it was Onua. "At the marsh, after the fight. You were holding a bird, and you fainted, remember?" Daine nodded. "I was looking right at an owl with its head cut almost off. The wound healed; he flew away. So did a lot of birds that shouldn't have been able to fly. I think it happened because their need just *pulled* the healing out of you." The K'mir nodded to Numair. "He can teach you to heal of your own will, without burning yourself up so you faint."

All her life she had splinted, sewed, bandaged. Most of her patients had mended, but some had not. She felt the badger's claw heavy on her chest. To *fix* her friends, like he'd fixed himself after giving the claw to her . . .

She looked at the king. "I still think it sounds crazy, but I'll try."

He squeezed her hands. "You will?" he asked quietly.

I'm in love, she thought, and nodded. "Oh, wait, I hired on with Onua for the summer."

"That isn't a problem," said Numair. "The trainees will be going to Pirate's Swoop. I live near there. Why don't I just go along?" When the king frowned, he added, "Hag's bones, Jon, there's nothing I can do here right now that you don't have a hundred other mages doing already. If I work with Daine, maybe I can devise a spell to warn people that immortals are coming."

The king made a face. "You just say that so I'll let you go."

"You have too many mages eating their heads off around here as is," Onua pointed out. "It's not as if you can't contact him if something comes up."

"Whose side are you on?" the king asked. The woman grinned. He sighed and looked at Daine once more. Squeezing her hands, he let them go. "Thank you." He got up. "Onua, Numair, keep me posted?" They nodded. "I'd best go then. I have to dance with the Carthaki ambassador's wife."

Numair grinned at him. "Wear iron shoes, Your Majesty."

Daine said, "Excuse me—Your Majesty?"

The king looked back at her. "Yes, my dear?"

No one had *ever* called her that. She blushed, and managed to say, "I'm sorry I can't help more. With the sensing, and my da, and all."

Jonathan of Conté smiled at her. "If I've learned anything as a king, it's been I never know when someone will be able to help me. I have a feeling you'll be most welcome in this realm, Veralidaine Sarrasri."

And he was gone, which was really just as well, because it was suddenly hard for her to breathe.

Onua patted her back. "He has this effect on most of us, if it helps."

Numair rose, nibbling on one last cake. "No time like the present to begin. Daine, will you get Cloud, please? We'll meet you by the stables."

Dazed, she went out and called her mare. With the nights so fine, Cloud had asked to stay with the free ponies instead of being stabled with the trainees' mounts. She came racing over at Daine's summons and leaped the fence rather than wait for the girl to open the gate.

Overwhelmed by the day's events, Daine buried her face in Cloud's mane: it smelled of night air, ferns, and horse. "Things are so *weird* here," she whispered. "You ever hear of 'wild magic'? They say I have it."

You have something, and you know it. Who cares what name it has? Or did you really think the wild creatures visit because they like humans?

"But *magic*?"

Did you call me to worry about the names of things? If you did, I'm going back. There's a salt lick over by that big rock I want to taste.

"Daine?" Numair and Onua were coming. "Good, you have her," Numair said. "If you can persuade her to come with me, I'd like to check your range with an animal you know well."

"What do you mean, my 'range'?" she asked.

"I've observed that when you say you 'hear' an animal, you actually mean hearing in your mind—not with your ears. I want to see how far I can walk with Cloud before you stop hearing her."

"But how will you know?" the girl asked reasonably. "Should I have her tell you when we lose touch or something?"

"No!" Onua said, and laughed. "Daine, knowing Cloud, she'd do it by kicking him. Numair will do a speech spell with me. You and I will sit here, and you tell me what you hear from Cloud, and when you stop hearing her."

"*If* Cloud will do it," amended Numair.

"Of course she will." Won't you? the girl asked Cloud silently. The mare switched her tail, thinking it over. Daine didn't rush her. Sometimes, if she was too eager, Cloud would refuse just to keep her in her place.

Very well. The pony trotted off down the fence, away from the palace.

"I think you're to follow her," Daine told the mage with a grin.

Numair sighed and trotted off after the pony. "Only one of us can lead here, and that has to be me," he called.

Onua and Daine hoisted themselves to the top rail of the fence, and Onua held her palm out between them. In it glowed a ball of ruby-colored fire. "Numair will take a moment to set up his end of the spell."

"Onua—if the king's on the bad side of these Carthaks, why does he have to dance with the ambassador's wife?"

"Politics," Onua said. "We don't have to mess with that, thanks be to Father Storm and Mother Rain. It means you sit down to dinner with enemies and ask how their children are."

"Aren't we at war, then?"

"Nah," the woman replied. "We aren't at war till both sides sign a paper *saying* it's a war. The Carthaki emperor can raid us and send monsters against us, but there's no war. Yet."

"That's crazy," Daine said, and Onua nodded. They waited, enjoying the night. Uphill the palace glittered, its lights blurring the stars overhead. Downhill lay the forest, dark, moist, and quiet. The free ponies had come to graze near the two women, their soft movements a comforting sound.

In the distance the girl heard the callings of a pack of wolves. Did I hear them on the road? she wondered. Not so close, that's for certain. I wonder if they miss me, Brokefang and Rattail and the others.

Listen to these wolves. Is it hunt-song? No, pack-song. They're just singing to be doing it, not to celebrate the kill.

If I could just run . . . dive into the forest. Go to them, be hunt-sister and one with the pack—

"Daine? *Daine!*" Onua was shaking her with one hand.

"Onua? What's wrong?" Numair's voice came from the fire in the K'mir's other hand.

Great Goddess—I almost forgot who I am! "I'm fine," she told Onua, forcing herself to sound calm. "Can you hear them?"

"The wolves? Of course," Onua replied.

The pack had sensed her—their voices were approaching through the trees. The ponies snorted anxiously, huddling near the women and the fence. "I'll be right back," Daine said, and jumped into the meadow. "Calm down and stay put," she ordered the herd. She walked until she was halfway between trees and fence, knowing the ponies would not come closer to the wolves.

"Go away!" she yelled. "There are hunters here, and dogs! Go!" There was that other way to speak to them, but she didn't dare try it. Not after she had almost forgotten, just listening to them!

Their calling stopped: they'd heard a human and run. It was against their own better judgment to approach human dwellings in the first place.

Daine returned to Onua, glad that the night hid the sparkle of tears on her cheeks. "I'm too tired for this—I'm sorry. It hit me all of a sudden."

Onua spoke into the red fire on her hand, then closed her fingers on it. The globe vanished. "Go to bed, then. Numair will let Cloud back into the meadow. I'll get someone to come watch the herds, in case the wolves return."

Daine watched her go. "I'm sorry," she whispered though only the ponies could hear. They crowded around, needing reassurance after hearing wolves. She couldn't leave them scared. It took her several minutes to pat and soothe them into calmness once more. It wasn't their fault the wolves thought they'd heard a wolf-sister in the night.

She was climbing the fence out of the meadow when Numair and Cloud arrived. Cloud came right up to her, sniffing Daine all over for wolf smell.

"Are you all right?" the man asked, panting as he rested a hand on Daine's shoulder. "I should have remembered you might be tired after this morning. I get carried away sometimes. I forget that not everyone has my academic enthusiasm."

She stared at him, patting Cloud. He was a sorcerer. He'd cut his eyeteeth on the impossible. He'd understand if anyone did, she thought, and opened her mouth to tell him.

" 'Evenin', sir, miss." A burly man climbed over the fence, holding a crossbow out of harm's way. Two big dogs wriggled through the rails and came over, tails wagging, to sniff Daine. "Mistress Onua tells me wolves are near the forest rim tonight. Must be a new pack. Most of 'em know t' stay clear of the palace. Me'n my lads'll keep watch for a bit, to discourage 'em, like."

Daine scratched the ears of both "lads," dogs almost as big as Tahoi. *Run, pack-brothers!* she called to the wolves, under her breath, hoping they'd somehow hear her. *Run and keep running—there are hunters here!*

She and Numair said good night to the man, and Numair walked her to her new room in the barracks. She let herself in, waving to him as he climbed the hill to the palace. The chance to tell him the truth had gone.

*Just as well*, she told herself as she changed into her nightshirt. *What he don't know won't hurt him—or me.*

As she was crawling under the covers, three palace cats entered through the partly open door and climbed in with her. Daine smiled as they made themselves comfortable. It would have been nice, talking with Miri after lights-out, but this was better. Miri didn't know how to purr.

She didn't realize her new room was beneath the boys' dorm until thunder the next morning crashed through the ceiling overhead: "Trainees, *turn out!*" She sat up, tumbling cats right and left and scaring an owl out the door. That thunder had been Sarge's voice. It must have had an equally powerful effect on the male trainees. They were dressed and stumbling blindly on their way to the stable by the time Daine had pulled on her breeches. Neither Onua nor Buri, who slept in the girls' dorm, could roar, but whatever they did seemed just as effective. The female trainees were just as quick down the stairs.

Once the stabled ponies were groomed and fed, the humans performed the same chores for themselves. "You'll work afoot," Onua told Daine as they ate. "Keep an eye on what's low, hooves to hocks, but if you see a trainee misusing an animal or a problem with the tack, don't be afraid to sing out. The rest of us will be mounted, so you'll see things we miss." She clapped Daine on the shoulder with a grin as she got up. "We'll have some fun."

Going to the meadow while everyone else saddled up, Daine was startled to find the queen already there, patting a savage-looking yellow dun mare. Soon the trainees, Onua, and Buri arrived on ponies, and Sarge joined them on a horse, a strongly built liver chestnut gelding. The four mounted officers put the trainees through a morning's hard work, trying the ponies at different gaits—walk, trot, canter, gallop— with and without saddles. After lunch, everyone switched to his spare mount and went through it all over again.

Daine soon learned a polite "excuse me" went unheard. She also learned she wasn't shy if she thought a pony had picked up a stone or had strained a muscle. By morning's end she had developed a bellow—not as shattering as Sarge's, perhaps, but loud enough for her purposes.

Numair found her after lunch. "How's it going?" he asked, leaning on the meadow fence next to her.

When she opened her mouth, a croak emerged. She cleared her throat and tried again. "Fine. It's all fine."

"I was wondering—about that range-finding experiment"—he squinted up at the sky—"you're too busy to try it now, I suppose."

Cloud trotted over to them. Tell the stork-man *I* will go with him.

Numair looked oddly at Daine as the girl laughed at the pony's name for him. When she caught her breath, she said, "No, don't ask me. You really don't want to know!" To the pony she said, "But there's no hearing spell for me to talk to him with. I can't ask Onua, not now. I shouldn't even really try it myself, not if I'm to earn my pay with these people."

The pony stamped impatiently. You act as if you're the only clever one. I will tell the stork-man when I can no longer hear *you*.

Daine relayed the pony's offer to Numair.

"You mean *she'll* undertake the test situation without dealing through you? Can she do that?" he asked, fascinated.

"She says she can. I know she always finds me if one of us wanders off."

"All right, then." He bowed to the pony. "Lead on." As they walked off, Daine heard Numair say, "And no biting."

The trainees left the stable with their spare ponies, followed by the queen and the other officers. Soon Daine was busy: she forgot about Cloud and Numair. The afternoon followed the morning's pattern, with one difference: the officers were still fresh, but the pace had begun to tell on the trainees.

"Come on, Evin!" yelled the queen, circling the Player at a gallop. "Raiders won't give you a break for lunch, laddy!"

"I don't want to see air between butt and saddle, trainee!" Sarge roared at Miri's heels. "You ride that gelding like he's a separate creature! He ain't! He's part of you, so connect the parts again!"

Onua swooped down on a brunette, Selda, and scooped the bow out of her hand. Circling back, she told the girl, "An enemy might do that with an ax. Every time you have to concentrate on your mount you give a foe a chance."

"Your stirrup's too long!" Daine yelled at one of the men. "Stop and fix it!" He didn't seem to hear. Within seconds Buri, slung low on her pony's side, came up unwatched to grab the stirrup in question. The trainee's pony wheeled away from the K'mir; her rider, Tarrus, slipped off and down.

Buri righted herself on her pony's back and looked at Tarrus. "Your stirrup was too long, trainee. Fix it." She rode off calmly.

"I'm sorry," Daine said as the young man struggled out of the mud. She gave him a hand. "I tried to warn you—"

He grinned at her, his small, pointed nose quivering like a rabbit's. "I figured I'd fix it the next break. Next time I'll do it right off." He looked at his behind and the backs of his legs, where he sported a coat of mud. "It's an ill wind that blows no good. With a mudpack like this, my skin will be lily soft." He fixed the stirrup and mounted up again.

Daine was tired when it came time to stable the trainees' mounts at day's end, but she knew she couldn't be as tired as the others. They moved stiffly as they groomed and fed their ponies, without joking or arguing as the officers and Daine corrected them. Only when each pony had been tended and the trainees had retreated to the baths did the queen say farewell and trudge up the long slope to the palace. She had groomed her mounts while the trainees groomed theirs, still finishing with enough time to criticize their work.

"She does this every day?" Daine asked Buri as she followed the Rider officers to the barracks.

The stocky K'mir nodded. "In the fall and winter she can't be out in the field. That's the social season. She has to travel around being queen. She works with the trainees to make up for when she can't be with the groups."

"But there's times she'll leave a ball or dinner to go to a Rider group in trouble," Onua remarked. "Remember the pink tissue dress?"

Buri rolled her eyes. "Three hundred gold nobles that thing cost, just for cloth and sewing. That's not counting pearls in the collar and cuffs—gray ones, almost perfectly matched in size."

Daine whistled in awe. She couldn't imagine a garment that cost so much. She couldn't even imagine what such a dress would look like. "What happened?"

"Two years ago," Buri said, "the Fifth Rider Group chased outlaws into a swamp and got bogged down. Thayet was visiting some earl nearby."

Daine winced. "And the dress?"

The two K'mir shook their heads as they led the way into the baths. "What happened to the group and the outlaws?" Daine asked as they undressed.

"The Rider group lost two. The outlaws didn't make it, but Thayet and the Riders saved the village girls they'd kidnapped." Buri plunged into the heated pool, and the girl trainees yelped as a wave almost swamped them. Onua and Daine entered more decorously. Buri surfaced and gasped, "Thayet always said it was worth losing the dress."

"And the king wasn't mad?" Daine wanted to know.

Onua replied, "He just told her next time, try to change clothes."

It wasn't until supper was almost over and the mage had come to the mess hall door that Daine remembered he'd gone off to experiment with Cloud. "Ready for lessons?" he asked, sitting next to her.

"How was it this afternoon?" she asked.

"We determined that your range, with Cloud at least, is a mile and a half. It may be more or less than that with animals who haven't been exposed to you for a prolonged period of time."

"You make her sound like a disease," Evin commented with a laugh. "Are we going to need healers or something?"

Numair smiled. "No. But Daine, have you found that animals you spend a lot of time with are, well, smarter than others? Smarter in a human sense?"

She played with her spoon. A friend of Ma's had said as much, when she had nursed one of his falcons. Some of the local herdsmen had liked her to train their dogs for that reason. "Is it bad?"

"No, how could it be? It doesn't make your animals less able to survive in the wild; quite the opposite." Numair took her food tray and stood. "Come on. We're going for a walk." He took her tray to the servants who cleaned up.

Daine rose with a sigh, tired muscles creaking. Miri winked. "If you don't want lessons, I'll take them," the girl offered. "He's cute!"

Daine followed her teacher, shaking her head. Numair was well enough, as men went, but he wasn't the king.

The mage steered her out of the barracks and through the horse meadow gate. In silence they crossed the wide swath of green, letting their eyes get accustomed to the night. They had to stop every few feet while Daine greeted the grazing ponies and horses. Each time she patted them and excused herself, saying she would visit with them another time.

The horses stayed back as the man and the girl went into the forest along a trail. There was just enough light to follow it without stumbling into trees. Here, away from the torches of the palace, the dark-clad mage turned into a large shadow, a slightly ominous one.

The trail opened onto a grassy clearing. The animals who normally would have been drinking from the large pond in its center had fled on hearing them, but Daine could feel their eyes. Overhead a bat squeaked.

"Have a seat." Numair motioned to a rock near the pond. She obeyed a little nervously. He came up behind her to rest his hands on her shoulders. "I'm going to use my Gift, but through *you*. You must understand that. If I did this with the king or Alanna, they wouldn't see what you will."

"If you say so." The hair on the back of her neck was standing up, and she was quivering. It wasn't fear, exactly, because she wasn't afraid of him. On the other hand, the dark was filled with strange currents that flowed into and out of the presence at her back.

He put his fingers on her temples. "Now, do just as we do when we're meditating," the soft voice over her head commanded. "Slow, deep breath—inhale." He inhaled with her. "Hold it. Let it go, carefully. Again, in . . . and . . . out . . ." Eyes closed, she breathed at his command.

Her mind filled with vines of sparkling light wrapped in darkness— or was it the other way around? When the space behind her eyes was full, the magic spilled out of her. She felt it ripple through the clearing, soaking grass and trees. It dripped into the pond, following the water into the ground.

"Open your eyes." His whisper seemed to come from inside her head.

She obeyed. The clearing, so dark before, was veined with shimmering fibers. All that was green by day grew from emerald threads now. Awed, she reached down and plucked a blade of grass. The needle of green fire that formed its spine flared, and went dark.

She gasped, remorseful. "I didn't mean to—"

"Hush," Numair said quietly. "Look at the earth."

A pale bronze mist lay on the piles of dead matter under the trees. When she let the blade of grass fall, its spine turned the same dim bronze as it touched the ground. "It returns to the Goddess," she whispered.

The stone beneath her and the other rocks she could see were veined with dark silver. An owl on a nearby branch gleamed with a tracery of copper fire. A vole grubbed beneath a bush near the spring, a point of copper light.

Daine looked at her hands. They were laced through with strands of reddish light, almost as if her veins had the power to glow. Intertwined with the red were strands of copper fire. She looked at the owl, at the vole, and at her hands—all the same shade of copper.

Half twisting, she managed to see part of Numair. He too was laced with red fire. In addition a white, pearly glow flickered over his skin like a veil. She recognized the light Tahoi had shown her once.

"Sit straight," the mage ordered her quietly. "I have to remain in contact with you to keep the spell going."

She obeyed. "I wish I could see this by myself."

"You can learn. The vision is in your mind, like the power to heal. Just remember what your magic feels like, and practice reaching for it."

"Reaching for it _how?_"

Something between them shifted, and she knew she looked into herself. At her center, deep inside, welled a spring of copper fire.

She called, and a slender thread rose from it to her. She caught it, opened her eyes, and threw it out to the owl.

"You don't need the hand motion," Numair said. "In magic, the thought is the deed."

"If you _want_ it bad enough," she added. "That's what Ma said."

"She was right."

The owl glided down through the air. She held out her arm, and it perched, looking her over with solemn eyes. He was a barn owl a little more than a foot tall, with the white ghost-face of his kind and a powerful grip.

You called to me, night-sister?

His voice was cold and precise. It was also clearer than the voice of any animal she'd ever spoken to, except Cloud's.

"Only to greet you, silent one," she replied with respect.

"You don't need to say it aloud," Numair commented.

Daine shook her head. "Can we do this a little bit at a time?" she asked, not looking away from the owl. "Please?"

She _felt_ him smile. "Whatever you say."

The owl ruffled his feathers in disapproval. It is not for the nestling to decide the proper time for lessons, he said, and flew off.

"I heard that," Numair remarked. "He's right. And it's time to stop." The ending of the spell felt to Daine as if she were a waterskin and the water was trickling out. She opened her eyes.

"How do you feel?" he asked.

She didn't reply. She felt a tickling in her mind—a feeling similar to the one caused by Stormwings, only faint and far more pleasant—and looked around for its source. It came from the pond. A tiny figure not much bigger than the owl, glittering with scales, was levering itself out of the water.

Numair saw what she was looking at. He spoke a word Daine couldn't understand, and the clearing filled with bright light. The little female creature in the pond whistled shrilly and vanished into the water again.

"Her hair was blue." Daine said it calmly. She had used up her excitement for the day. "She was all over scales and her hair was blue."

"Undine," Numair whispered. His dark face glowed with awe. "I *think* we just saw an undine—a water sprite." He walked over to the pond and knelt beside it. "I'm sorry, little one. Won't you come up again?"

"Maybe if you doused the light," Daine recommended. She sat back down on her rock. Her knees felt a little weak.

"Oh—of course." He said something, and the clearing was dark once more.

They waited until Daine was half-asleep, but the undine did not return. Finally Numair gave up his vigil and roused the girl. "I'll have to tell the king," he said as she stretched. "Or maybe not. She won't harm anyone. They're said to be incredibly shy of humans."

"I noticed," she said dryly.

He produced a globe of light so they could see the trail: they both were tired and needed the help. "To see a water sprite," he murmured, steering her down the path. "We live in marvelous times, my little magelet."

"What's a magelet?" she asked, and yawned.

"Nothing, really. Well, 'little mage.' Isn't that what you are?"

As they left the clearing, Daine saw movement out of the corner of her eye. Another tiny person, a green female, watched them go from the branch of a tall oak. She decided not to mention tree sprites to Numair just now. She wasn't sure that she liked being called "magelet."

The next day passed in the same manner—driving the trainees morning and afternoon—with one difference. As if her time in the undine's clearing had opened a door in her mind, Daine saw glimpses of copper fire in every furred and feathered creature to come near her. It was very distracting until she got used to it. Most alarming were the flashes at the corner of her eye, the ones that made her turn to look.

"Why do you keep twitching?" the brunette Selda wanted to know. "You look like you have a palsy."

Daine glared at Selda but held her tongue. The older girl was like some people back home, never happy unless she had something to complain about. Still, the comment was enough to make her guard herself so she wouldn't jump at the hint of copper light. She came to like seeing it. Her only regret was that copper was the only magical glitter she saw—no blue or green threads, no bronze mists and pearly shimmers.

She had a fresh shock that day: when she saw Onua with the ponies, the same copper color threaded the K'mir's head and hands.

"Why so surprised?" Numair asked that night, when Daine told him. They were on their way to the horse meadow once more. "She's— what's the K'miri term?—horse-hearted. Did you think Thayet would commission just *anyone* to obtain mounts? The Riders depend on horses more than any other military company. Onua ensures they have the best."

"Does she know?" Daine asked.

"Of course." He boosted himself up to sit on the top rail of the fence. "She doesn't have it enough that she needed training in it, like you. There are a few people here with it: a man and his grandson in the palace mews, two sisters at the kennels, some of the hostlers. Stefan, the chief hostler, has a lot of it. He breeds great-horses—the extra-large mounts many knights need to ride in combat. I trained him."

Shaking her head, Daine sat on the rail beside him, looking at the animals grazing in the meadow. "And I only heard of all this two days ago."

He tweaked her nose. "Being all of thirteen, of course you should be omniscient," he teased. "Now, magelet—to work." He pointed to a pony grazing by itself nearly three hundred yards away. "Call to it."

She opened her mouth, and he clapped his hand over it. "*Without* sound."

She glared at him. "Then how'm I supposed to call her?" she asked, his palm tickling her moving lips.

"With your mind. One thing I've noticed is that you tend to be confused about how you speak to and hear animals. We're going to break you of the habit of assigning concrete manifestation to magical phenomena."

"What?"

"Believing you *actually* hear or speak with your body when all of it is done with your mind. Call that pony."

" 'That pony' is a mare. Why can't I just talk to her?"

He sighed. "A time may come when being heard will get you killed. Also, your mind needs discipline. If your thinking is more direct, what you can *do* with your thoughts will happen more directly. Learn to focus your mind: focus creates strength. Meditation helps you reach the same end.

"We're doing spring cleaning up here." He tapped her forehead with a long finger. "Once you put everything into its proper place—once you organize your mind—you'll be able to find what you want quickly. Now call her, please."

Daine clenched her teeth and thought, as loudly as she could, *Come here, please*! The mare continued to graze peacefully.

"Think of the magic," Numair said calmly. "Try again."

An hour or so later they gave it up and went inside. Daine's head ached fiercely, and the pony had not come closer by so much as a step.

"We'll keep practicing," Numair said calmly.

"Lucky me," she muttered, following him into her room. A large book lay on her writing table. "What's this?" She opened it to a colored page and gasped in awe: it was a precise drawing of the bones of a wild pig.

"It's a book on mammalian anatomy," he said, sitting down on her bed.

"A book on what?"

He sighed. "I keep forgetting you're not a scholar—sorry. Anatomy is what's inside a body: muscles, veins, organs, and so on. 'Mammalian' refers to mammals. You know what they are; you just don't know the fancy term. Warm-blooded animals with hair-covered bodies that suckle their young are mammals."

"That's most of my friends." She said it quietly, turning page after page of drawings with fingers she had scrubbed on her shirt.

"Exactly. If you're to learn healing, you need to understand how animals are put together."

"I already know some." Here was a bear's skeleton; here the veins and organs of a cat. Every drawing was done with an eye to the finest detail.

"This book will help you to *organize* what you know and add to your present knowledge."

She made a face. "Why? My friends don't organize their minds. Everything they think about is all tumbled together, willy-nilly."

"For them that's enough," he said patiently. "As animals they remember the past only vaguely. They are unable to visualize a future, apart from the change of seasons. They have no comprehension of mortality—of their deaths. They don't learn from books or teachers, so they have no need to structure their minds in order to find what they learn. You, however, are human and different. If you do *not* find a way to organize your mind, at worst you might go mad. At best, you'll be stupid."

She made a face—she didn't like the sound of either fate. With a sigh she looked at the page before her. The artist had drawn a bat, its frame spread so she saw how bones fitted together. "You'd best take this when you go. My friends come in every night. I wouldn't want it soiled."

"The book is spelled against dirt and tearing. It's yours. I want you to use it, not admire it."

It took a moment for her to realize what he'd said. "Mine!" she gasped. "No! It's—it's too valuable. The likes of me don't keep such things!" Her fingers shook, she wanted it so much, but peasant girls didn't own books.

He caught her hand, his eyes earnest. "Daine, listen to me." He pulled her down to sit beside him. "You're a student mage. You need books like this to do your work. I am your master. It's my duty—in this case it's my pleasure—to give you whatever books and scrolls I believe you require to learn. Unless you don't want to learn?"

"Odd's bobs, of course I do!"

"Good. Then get your book. We'll start at page one."

They ended some time later, when Onua knocked and stuck her head in. "We're about to meditate. Come on, if you're coming."

"Do we have to?" Daine asked, closing the wonderful book.

"Spring cleaning," he replied, getting to his feet.

She followed him to the Rider mess. She'd been surprised to learn that meditation was required of all trainees, not just Gifted ones. They worked at it every night before they went to bed, along with all their officers, Daine, and Numair, "whether we need it or not," Evin commented once, in a whisper.

That day set the pattern for the next three weeks. It took Daine six days to learn how to deliberately call the nearest pony without using words. Numair then had her summon a pony farther away but still within sight, until she could do that. Next she had to call an animal from inside the barracks or stables, where she couldn't see it: often that was Tahoi or one of the cats that slept in her room. She worked hard. Each task took less time to master.

Anatomy lessons she swallowed in gulps. Every spare moment she had went into studying her beloved book and memorizing its contents.

Meditation was the hardest. She did her best, wanting to control the copper fire that was her kind of wild magic, but clearing her mind was *hard*. Stray thoughts popped into her head; something would itch; a muscle would cramp, and she would have to start over. Often she fell asleep. The best thing about meditating with the trainees was the knowledge that she wasn't the only one who was easily distracted or who dozed off.

Slowly they all grew used to their work. She saw it in the trainees before noticing it in herself, as their bodies hardened and the hard routine became habit. After two weeks she was taken off watching them on foot and put to teaching archery, something even the officers had to work to beat her at. It wasn't until she saw that few trainees were falling asleep in meditation that she realized she no longer fell asleep, either. With practice it got easier to learn to think of nothing at all. The deep breaths emptied her thoughts and quieted her body rhythms. Her mind learned to drift. She began to feel as she had in the marsh, when she had listened for the hawk.

Is *that* what it is? she thought one night, lying awake in bed. She grasped the badger's claw. "I wish you'd come and tell me," she whispered, earning a curious look from the pine marten who had arranged herself and her kits on the girl's blanket-covered legs.

If the badger heard, he did not answer the summons. "Typical," Daine told the martens, and went to sleep.

## ⤙ SIX ⤚

# MAGELET

⤷⤶ The next day, a month after her arrival, she was waiting for the trainees to finish their morning workout when she heard a low persistent rumble. For a week the hill above the barracks had swarmed with men loading empty wagons. Now draft horses had been hitched to the wagons; one by one, they towed the laden vehicles up the hill.

Sarge clapped Daine on the shoulder. "This is it," he said cheerfully. "The king is on his way, so *we* can be on ours. I'm ready!"

"I'm confused," she said, craning to see his face. "He's on *what* way?"

"See, my lamb, in summer the king goes on progress, to see how fares the kingdom. Soon as he goes, the queen takes the trainees to our summer camp—"

"Pirate's Swoop this year," Alanna put in. She'd been training with the Riders for the last week. "We set out tomorrow."

"That isn't much notice," remarked Farant, who had overheard.

"How much notice do you *need*, trainee?" Sarge asked. "You *have* half a day to prepare. One day you'll have to roll out of *bed* ready for a long ride. Then you'll appreciate this leisurely pace."

Technically, Daine thought that night, the trainees didn't have even half a day to get ready. They'd put in their usual afternoon's work with their spare mounts. The only change in their routine was that they were excused from their lessons before meditation to pack. She hadn't been excused from her lessons, but she had little packing to do.

Meditation was held, as always, in the mess hall, and everyone attended. When Numair gave the word to begin, she decided to try her idea from the night before. Instead of thinking of nothing, she closed her eyes and *listened*.

How could breathing be so *loud*? She concentrated, putting the sound of her lungs aside. As the noise lessened, her nerves calmed. Her neck itched, but it was a distant feeling, not a distracting one. She scratched, lazily, and let her hand settle into her lap. A drumlike thud in her ears was her own heart. Easy, she told it in her mind, and the sound retreated.

Something bumped steadily at the front of the mess: Tahoi, lying near Onua, was wagging his tail. Daine peeked and saw the dog shining with copper fire. She looked at Onua—the K'mir was veined with fine copper threads.

Taking a deep breath, she looked inside. The wellspring of her own power was there, just as it had been the night by the undine's pool.

Remembering Numair's lectures, she trapped how it had felt just now, to listen and to find her power, and memorized it. When she placed the feeling in her mind, she knew exactly where it was and how to find it again, quickly. It's *organized*, she thought with an inner smile.

She let the excitement fade and listened again. In the closed and dark kitchen at her back, mice hunted for scraps. She directed them to a rind of cheese she'd hidden for them beneath the long table, then sent her hearing out of the mess hall, into the night. Sounds crashed into her skull: bats seeking insects, cats on the hunt, kenneled dogs settling for sleep, horses relaxing, the hawks in the palace mews. It was too much to hear all at once: she almost lost her inner silence in panic. Stopping, she pushed the animal sounds back with her mind until they didn't overpower her. Only when she was sure they were under control did she send her hearing out to the horse meadow once more.

A herd of ponies, including Cloud, grazed there. All of them knew her by now, from the silent-calling lessons. She joined with them, entering the herd. A breeze filled the air, bringing lush scents: ripe grass, leaves, the heady, rich smell of the earth. Around her were the others, her brothers and sisters. A king stallion watched over their family, ready to lead them to safety at the smallest hint of danger.

Spring made them all coltish. With a snort, the king horse broke into a run, just to be running. The herd and Daine followed, racing, black earth thudding under their hooves, the night air in their nostrils. With the herd she was safe; with the herd she had all she could need of comrades and family . . .

Cloud knew the instant Daine came into the herd. She'd seen this coming, as the stork-man encouraged the girl to venture farther and farther from herself. Tonight the feel of Daine's presence was stronger than it had been since they came to this giant human stable, making

Cloud edgy. When Daine's spirit began to change, to take on the scent of the herd, the mare knew they were in trouble again.

She ran for the fence and jumped it. From the meadow she felt the herd call her to go with them. She wavered, wanting to follow. Then, with an angry neigh at the part of her that made her think unhorselike things, she broke free of the call and ran to the stable where Daine's body was.

The gate was barred. She flung herself at it, flailing with her hooves. Putting her hindquarters to it she kicked the gate once, and again, until the large human, the wood brown man, yanked it open. She shoved past him—no, time to be polite—and looked around this room that smelled of human food.

Sure enough, there Daine sat on the ground, front hooves limp in her lap, eyes closed. Cloud went to the girl and knocked her over.

A warm force slammed into Daine's body. Suddenly she was free of the herd, safe inside her own mind. Opening her eyes, she saw Cloud standing over her. People around them were talking.

"I did it again, didn't I?" she whispered.

Numair knelt beside her, dark eyes worried. "What happened? She nearly kicked down the door to get at you—"

Daine was shaking. They didn't know. They didn't know what Cloud had prevented. Thank you, she told the mare.

Don't run with the People again until you remember to hold on to yourself, the mare ordered. I won't always be here to wake you up!

Daine fumbled in her pocket and produced two lumps of sugar. "You'd best go outside now," she whispered, and Cloud obeyed.

Numair helped the girl to her feet. "It's all right," he told everyone. "We were just trying an experiment. I didn't realize it would work so well." Shielding her from the stares of the trainees, he guided Daine out of the mess and into her own room. "What happened?" he asked, closing the door.

"I felt sick," she lied. "Just a headache, that's all."

"Cloud wouldn't come here for that," he retorted. "She was in a panic. What went wrong? And what's this?" The badger's token had fallen outside her shirt. He picked it up, squinting at it. "From its appearance, it's a claw."

"It's mine," she retorted, yanking it away from him. "It's *private*. Can't I have anything *private* anymore?"

"Daine—"

Her voice rose. She knew she was about to cry. "Would you *please* go away? I'm tired and my head hurts! Can't you leave me alone for once?"

"Very well." His face was grave and sad. "But I wish you would trust me." He left, quietly shutting the door.

Daine sat on her bed, tears on her cheeks. What could she do? If she went too deep in meditation, she risked madness. If she *didn't* go deep—He said I might learn to heal, she thought desperately, squeezing the claw tight. But I have to master this first—or I'll *never* be able to heal.

Caught between fear of losing control and wanting the power Numair said she could have, the girl tossed and turned all night. She would doze off, only to dream of running down a forest trail on all fours. Behind her would be the trainees, or the King's Own, or Stormwings, tracking her so they could tear her to pieces.

Habit woke her at dawn, the hour Sarge usually bellowed for everyone to turn out. That morning the trainees had been given an extra hour to sleep, which meant if she hurried, she'd have the stable to herself. Soundlessly she called Cloud in for a thorough grooming and breakfast: there'd be no time for it later on. Onua had asked her to handle the supply wagon, and Daine expected her time before they left would be spent looking over the cart horse and making sure any last-minute additions to her load were safely stowed away.

A stranger was in the stable, a potbellied man the ponies greeted with enthusiasm from their stalls. Copper fire shone inside his red face. When he saw her, his head flew up as if he were a surprised horse.

Suddenly shy, Daine halted just inside the door. "Excuse me—might you be Stefan? The chief hostler?"

"Maybe. Who're you?"

He can't see it in me, she realized. I can see his magic, but he can't see mine. "Daine, sir. Master Numair said you have wild magic. So do I."

The man relaxed—slightly. "You're the one, then. I brung ye a cart horse." He led her to a newcomer, a sturdy bay cob. "This be Mangle."

Daine offered the gelding her hands to sniff. *"Mangle?"* she asked with a grin. The cob felt like a calm well-behaved sort of horse to her.

Stefan smiled and ducked his head. "Oh, well," he muttered by way of explanation. "Anyways, he's good for whatever ye need in th' way of work." Daine leaned down to blow in Mangle's nostrils. "He likes ye. Onua said I needn't worry if *you* was in charge of 'im." Cloud butted him from behind. "Who's this fine lady?" He bent to the task of greeting the mare, while Daine finished getting acquainted with the cob. When she finished, Stefan was looking at her oddly. "You know this little beauty's changed, 'cause of you."

She couldn't tell what the emotion in his pale blue eyes was. "Me'n Cloud have been through a lot together."

He gave the mare a last pat. "It shows." With a wave to Daine, he walked to the stable door.

"Master Stefan?" He turned to look at her. "D'you ever want to run with the herd? To just—be a horse? Do what the herd does?" She sweated, waiting for an answer. It had cost a lot to ask.

" 'Course I do," was the mild reply. "Don't everybody?"

She gripped the badger's claw hidden under her shirt. "What keeps you from doing it?"

He rubbed his strawlike hair. "I'm a man. I can't be runnin' with the herd, now can I?" He left, closing the door behind him.

He makes it sound easy, but it's not. There's something wrong with me, she decided. It's the madness, just waiting for me to drop my guard so it can take me again. That's how he can protect himself—he never forgets what he really is. And I can't remember.

Taking Cloud into an empty stall, the girl swore she would never let her guard down again. Better to disappoint Numair in her studies than to run wild and lose the friendships and respect she had found in this new country.

She was almost done with Cloud when Onua came into the stable. "There you are. Did Stefan bring our cart horse?"

Daine jerked a thumb at him. "His name's Mangle."

Onua grinned as the bay sniffed her pockets. "Is that so?" Looking at Daine as she fed the cob an apple, she asked, "Did you meet Stefan?"

The girl nodded. "Onua—about last night—I'm sorry."

"For what?" The K'mir gave Mangle a last pat and went to see to her own two ponies. "Daine, your magic is taking you down a different road from most folk. Your friends understand that, if you don't. Stop worrying so much."

"Thank you," she whispered.

"Don't thank me—get moving. We want to be assembled and ready to go when the first morning bell rings."

Once she'd eaten a quick breakfast, Daine finished stowing the officers' packs in the wagon, harnessed Mangle to it, and drove it to the flat area in front of the horse meadow gate where the Riders would assemble. The queen, Buri, Onua, and Sarge turned their spare mounts over to her to lead, so they would be free to range along the trainee column during the ride. The girl considered roping the three ponies and Sarge's horse together for appearances' sake and decided not to: all four mounts knew her well and promised to walk in their own column on one side of the wagon.

Alanna waved as she rode past on Darkmoon, going to wait with the queen. Daine grinned, knowing the Lioness would be more talkative after lunch.

She had started to wonder about Numair when several packs thudded into the back of the wagon. The mage rode up on a black-and-white gelding, looking tired. As if to prove it, once he stopped, he lay along his horse's neck. "Wake me when we stop for lunch," he said, and—to all appearances—went to sleep.

Daine looked at him, smiling. Dressed in a brown tunic, white shirt, and green breeches, he looked like the man she had known on the road to Corus, not the silk-clad friend of kings who'd been giving her lessons. The jeweled pins and rings he'd worn since his return to court were nowhere to be seen. The only hint of his apparent wealth was a large amber drop dangling from one earlobe.

Slowly twenty-three trainees assembled ahead of Daine in two columns, leading their spares on the outside. Each was inspected by the queen, Buri, Sarge, or Onua; some, including Farant and Selda, were sent to the barracks to lighten their packs. Four trainees, again including Selda, were sent back twice, this time with Sarge to harry them. Daine could hear his bellowed "Riders travel *light!*" when he was inside the barracks with his victims.

At last everyone was ready. Alanna and Buri took places on the left, Sarge and Onua on the right, outside the columns. Thayet rode to the head of the company, and Daine nudged Numair. He opened a bloodshot eye. "I think this is it," she whispered. He nodded and straightened in the saddle.

It was. Thayet unsheathed her slightly curved blade and held it aloft. "Riders, *move out!*" she cried, her clear voice rippling through the columns, and started forward. The trainees followed, keeping the prescribed distance between their mounts as they took a well-marked road into the Royal Forest.

Daine's skin quivered with goose bumps. "That's fair beautiful," she said to no one in particular. "Gi' up, Mangle!" His ears pointing forward with eagerness, the cob obeyed.

The company stopped at noon for lunch. After cleanup, the trainees and officers switched mounts. Daine, her shame about the previous night put aside, tried not to smile when Numair asked if she minded if he rode with her. She agreed instantly. It was hard to be aloof from a man whose seat on a horse was so bad that he had to feel every bump in the road. Making friends with his patient gelding, Spots, she told the horse he deserved a carrot for bearing with such an ungraceful rider, and gave it to him.

Things went better during the afternoon: they picked up speed, covering some distance before camping for the night. Supper came from kettles that had been stowed in her wagon, their contents gently reheated over that night's fires.

"Tomorrow you *hunt* for your meal," Sarge warned as they filled their bowls with stew. "You'd best make less noise, my lambs, or you won't eat." Daine, settling between Miri and Evin, fought to hide a smile.

Returning to the fires after she had cleaned and put away her things, she was intercepted by Numair and led away from the trainees to an isolated clearing. "Lessons," he said firmly. "As long as you and I are within riding distance of each other, my magelet, we will have lessons."

She couldn't protest, really. She knew the trainees were having lessons and, unlike them, she didn't have the excuse of having fought two spirited ponies all day. With a sigh she took a seat on a nearby rock.

Numair put her book on another rock, where Cloud—who'd joined them—couldn't nibble on it, and took a tailor's seat next to Daine. He rubbed his large hands together. "Tonight we'll try something a bit different. While you were washing up, I untethered Mangle and Spots. I want you to call them *both* to us, at the same time."

"Why can't I call them one at a time?"

"You're being difficult," was the forbidding reply.

"It don't make sense."

"Remember the Stormwing attack in the horse meadow? You called quite a few animals to you, all at once. You might need to do something like that again one day. Wouldn't it be nice if—instead of calling entire herds—you only called enough horses to keep you safe?"

He had her there.

She found the copper thread in her mind, the one she wrapped around a call to an animal, and held it.

Mangle—Spots, she called. Would you come here, please?

They crashed through the brush, coming up to nuzzle her and Numair.

"See? That wasn't so bad," he told her. "Send them back, please."

With an apology and a short explanation to the horses, Daine obeyed.

Numair held up thumb and forefinger: between them sparkled a tiny ball of his magic. "Onua, now, if you please," he said calmly. Putting thumb and forefinger together, he snuffed the ball out. "Our friend is releasing some of the other mounts," he told Daine. "How many has she loosed?"

Daine listened—*not* with my ears, she reminded herself. "Spots and

Mangle are still free. Onua's loosed—let's see, Ox and General, Sarge's two horses, and her pair, Whisper and Silk, and also Darkmoon."

"Call them," Numair said.

She struggled with the calling magic. It only worked for one creature, or two at best, because all she did was focus the magic on an easy-to-hear mind. To call several minds, she had to open her mind to her surroundings. She tried it, and lost her concentration when an owl screeched overhead.

"Relax," Numair said, his voice pitched low. "It gets easier with practice. Find them, and call them—softly. You don't need too much."

She nodded, wiped her face on her sleeve, and tried again. Closing her eyes, she listened for the ones who were free of their ropes. That was easy—a tethered horse was always aware of the thing that kept him from getting that extra-juicy clump of grass just out of reach. There— she had them. She opened the cupboard in her mind where she'd put all her calling skill. . . .

A scent of deer on the breeze; a frog croaking in the distance; the soft patter of bats hunting overhead. The herd was around her, contentedly browsing on lush, fat grasses that had been amazingly overlooked by the deer. Ox and General were with her, then Whisper, Silk, Spots, Mangle. Darkmoon, young and blood-proud, fought her command. She'd teach him to obey with teeth and hooves if need be, to give way to *her* domination—

She gasped and threw herself out of the magic. The herd had caught her up so much *easier* than last night! "I can't," she told Numair, her voice shaking. "My head aches."

"You *must* learn this." For the first time since he started her lessons, his voice was stern. "You didn't have a headache before. Try again."

I can't, she thought, but there was no sense in telling him that— not unless she wanted to tell him everything. Desperate, she cheated, and hated herself for cheating. She wrinkled her face, clenched her teeth, shut her eyes, all so he'd think she was trying—but she kept her mind blank. She did this over and over, until he sighed.

"Perhaps I push too hard. You've done well—too well, perhaps. Most apprentice mages take over a year to make the progress you have in a month."

She stared at him. "But I thought I wasn't—How can you tell?" Scared, she added, "Can you see in my mind?"

"No. I wouldn't if I could. We all have secrets." Sadness moved over his face, making her wonder what his secrets were. Then he smiled. "I'm a mage, a well-educated one. When I wish, I can see things hidden from normal vision—like a person's magical aura. See mine?" He lifted his hands. White fire laced with shadows outlined his fingers. "The first day I was strong enough to do it, I examined your aura." He let the brilliance fade. "Your magic was like a tangle of vines around you, going in a hundred directions. You've been getting that tangle under control, pulling it inside your skin, and you're doing it faster than anyone I've ever known. Well, perhaps you've earned a night of rest. Come on—let's go back to the others. We'll meditate and stop there for the night."

She started to protest the meditation, and kept her silence. I'll just pretend, like with the calling, she told herself.

When they stepped into the clearing where the Riders were camped, Padrach was saying in his mountain burr, "Why won't he declare war, then?"

"It's true Carthak has the largest standing army in the world," the Lioness replied. Sarge was rolling up a large map that had been spread out on the ground. "But to attack us they have to cross water at every turn—the Inland Sea, or come up our coast on the Emerald Ocean. We have the advantage, being firmly on land when they have to come ashore to engage us."

"The navy's grown since my lord came to the throne," Thayet put in. The queen was dressed like the others in homespun breeches and tunic and a plain white shirt. Her glorious hair was severely pinned down, but nothing could dim the beauty of her face and clear, level eyes. "The emperor's policy of coastal raiding and paying bandits to attack in the mountains and hills has made the people in those areas determined to fight. Also, since His Majesty built his university outside Corus, we've brought a lot of mages to Tortall—enough even to make Emperor Ozorne's trained sorcerers think twice about taking us on."

"And only a fool would want to attack King Jonathan without some kind of real advantage," Numair said. "Not on Tortallan soil."

"Why's that, Master Numair?" asked Miri.

"Jonathan's magic, and the magic of the crown, are tied into every grain of soil in this land," explained the mage. "Unless an enemy has some kind of advantage that will hurt the king, or keep him from calling on his magic, it's possible that every tree, stream, and rock would form death traps for an enemy." Daine could see it in the trainees' faces, the fear a warrior would live with when the land itself fought him. The thought gave *her* goose bumps.

"Very well, my doves, it's that time again," Sarge barked after giving the trainees a moment to reflect on such warfare. "Seat yourselves comfortably, but not *too* comfortably."

Daine settled near the edge of trees around the clearing. Within a few moments the only sound to be heard was the breathing of the others. She watched them, envious. In the month she'd been with the Riders, she'd come to see that meditation supplied them with something they got nowhere else: a time to be calm, a time to find quiet inside themselves. It would be useful when they were living in the wilderness, hunting raiders and being hunted, she realized. Tonight especially she envied them that serenity. She wished *she* could find some measure of quiet in herself.

Carefully, gingerly, she closed her eyes and drew a breath. It was all right; she was safe. She released the breath, took another. Peace wrapped her like her mother's arms. She opened her ears to the night.

In the distance, a wolf howled, and got no answer.

Poor wind-brother, she thought sadly. No one to sing with, no brothers and sisters to hunt with . . . like me. It's so lonely, outside the pack.

As she breathed, her body fell into the habit she'd been making for it. Her mind cleared, her heartbeat slowed. Forgetting her danger, she opened herself to the music of the forest:

The swish of tails, the shifting of feet, the crunch of grass under broad teeth. A sense of peace and solidity flowed out from the humans to infect their mounts. The herd was content . . .

Once again she forced herself awake, to find she'd sweated her clothes through. What am I going to do? she asked Cloud as the mare nuzzled her. I can't even close my eyes without it happening!

It doesn't happen when you sleep, Cloud reminded her. It's only when you use that fire-stuff—the thing that makes you People—or when you do the sitting thing. Leave the fire-stuff and the sitting thing alone, and you'll be fine.

Daine shook her head. It seems like I can't win for losing, she told Cloud silently. Sometimes I think I never should have left home.

The next day the Riders picked up the pace. There were fewer stops as they headed through the coastal hills; those that were made were shorter.

Daine faked her lessons that night, as she faked her meditation. She thought she'd handled it well too, until Numair stopped her just before she climbed into her bedroll.

"Are you all right?" he asked, feeling her forehead. "Is something wrong?"

Looking up at him, she swallowed hard. "What's wrong, except for me being worked to death?" she asked, trying to put him off by being rude. "Honestly, can't you stop fussing at me for one *day*?"

Tahoi whined from his spot near Onua's bed, worried by Daine's tone. Glancing over at him, Daine saw that Onua, Evin, Miri, and the

Lioness had heard her as well and were staring at her as if she'd just grown horns. "I'm tired of being watched all the time too!" She struggled into her blankets and wrapped herself in them, not wanting to see how they reacted to that.

She heard Numair sigh. He patted her shoulder. "Sleep well, magelet." He walked away as Tahoi came to lie down next to her.

Tears rolled down her cheeks as she hid her face in her covers. *I'm afraid,* she wanted to tell her human friends. *I'm afraid if I go any deeper in my magic, I'll forget who I am.*

She woke in the morning to a campsite draped in fog. Without speaking to anyone, she groomed and fed Mangle and Cloud, and hitched Mangle to the wagon. She drove in silence all day, ignoring the worry she saw on Onua's and Numair's faces. The fog burned off by midmorning, leaving the air crisp. By afternoon the breeze coming out of the west bore a new scent to it, tangy and strange. She sniffed it often, wondering what it was.

"That's the sea," Miri told her when she saw Daine lift her nose to the air. Her cheeks were flushed; her green eyes sparkled. "It's close. That's brine you smell, and seaweed. I can't believe how much I missed it!"

"If she starts to talk nautical, plug your ears," Evin advised. "She's just showing off." Miri stuck her tongue out at him.

Their road topped a rise, and a new world spread itself before them. Daine dropped her reins. "Goddess and glory," she breathed.

Miri beamed with pride. "I told you."

Nothing had prepared her for this. Endless blue-gray water stretched north to south, and waves pounded the rocky coast. Salt winds nearly plucked off her head-scarf before she retied it. In the distance a toy with a dab of sail bobbed along—a boat, she realized, but far off.

Soon they reached the coast road, crossing it to pitch camp in a sandy cove. Automatically she cared for Mangle and Cloud, barely able to take her eyes off the water that smashed against the sand. Every time she blinked, something new appeared. Even Cloud's accusation that she looked like a cow, standing about with her jaw open, had no impact. She was entranced.

As soon as archery practice was done, Miri and Alanna took the trainees to find supper in the rock pools of the northern curve of the beach, leaving the officers and Daine to entertain themselves. Thayet removed her boots and stockings, rolling up the legs of her breeches. "Come on," she told Daine. "We'll go for a walk."

She ran to join the queen, trying to shed her boots at the same time. The woman laughed and steadied her as Daine wrestled her footgear off. "It won't go away," she said. "Slow down. Onua says you never saw it before?"

"No, mum." She made sure her breeches, rolled above the knee like the queen's, were tucked in securely.

"Then look. See how steep the beach is? It means waves pound it hard. They create a force called 'undertow' that grabs you and drags you out if you aren't careful. The easier a beach slopes into the water, the less undertow you'll find. Never forget it's there, Daine." Thayet's low voice was stern. "Plenty of good swimmers drown because they can't fight that drag."

Daine nodded soberly. This place had dangers, like any other part of the world—that made sense.

"Then, let's go." The queen stepped down as a wave hit the shore, and let foaming water surround her ankles.

Daine took a breath and followed. The water was icy. When it met her skin, she heard singing. Gasping, she jumped back.

Thayet stood ankle deep in the retreating waves, fighting to keep her balance as they ate the sand under her feet. "Too cold?" she asked, grinning.

She doesn't hear it, Daine thought.

"Come on," the queen urged. "You'll be numb before long." She walked forward, stopping when the water swirled around her knees. Lifting her face to the sun, she gave a loud, bloodcurdling war cry.

"Thayet, stop that," Numair called. His breeches rolled up, he had gone to explore a lumpy and pitted block of stone at the northern edge of the beach. He held up something. "Come look at this."

Thayet went to him. Daine walked forward, immersing her feet to the ankles as a wave overtook her. A few steps more: she was far enough in the water that a wave's backward crawl didn't leave her dry.

"Singing" was not right, but she had no idea of what the proper term might be. Part of it was a croon, the speech of a wolf mother to her cubs, but held past a wolf's ability to hang on to a note. A moaning whistle followed, then a series of short, high notes. The quality of the eerie calls was something like sound carried inside a cave—almost, but not entirely.

Hello? she cried silently (all she needed was for Numair to ask why she was talking to the ocean). Who are you?

There was no answer, not even the shift of attention she felt in most animals. Were these monsters? No—there was no gold fire in her mind. She gripped a thread of her magic, as much as she dared use, and tried again. Is anyone there? It's me—it's Daine! Can you hear me?

The songs—there were many, all beautiful and different—faltered.

—*Call?*—The voice was faint and alien, unlike any animal voice she'd heard in her life.

She strained to hear without using her power to help her listen. Yes! I'm calling! Me, here by the rocks—

—*No call*—

I called! I did! Where are you? *Who* are you?

—*Calf-call?*—

—*No call*—

I'm not loud enough, she realized. If I used my magic, maybe they could hear me, but I don't dare.

Thayet yelled, trying to get Daine's attention. Daine turned, but before she could answer a heavy form slammed into her. Down she went, mouth filling with brine. Trying to rise, she was slammed again and thrust deeper in the water by the animal's impact.

She opened her mouth to scream, and breathed seawater.

Miri and Evin said later she popped into the air to hang upside down from an unseen hand, pouring water as she fought. She only knew she was free to cough and vomit out the liquid that had nearly killed her. Looking down, she shrieked, clawing at the invisible grip on her ankles. Then the hands that weren't there whisked her to the beach, where Onua waited with a blanket. Daine was put gently on her feet, but her knees gave. Onua caught her before she fell.

Numair strode down the beach toward them, his face like a thundercloud. Black fire shot with white light gathered around his outstretched hand. Sarge grabbed up a quiver of javelins, Buri her double-curved bow. Both raced to attack the brown creature lumbering up onto shore.

Daine saw them just in time. "No, don't!" She threw herself in front of the animal. "Don't!" she screeched when fire left Numair's fingers, flying at them. He twisted his hand, and it vanished.

Clutching the blanket around her, she faced the one who had tried to kill her. He returned her look with huge, liquid brown eyes set in a pointed face capped by a small crest. His body was wide in the center and pointed at both ends. Covered with slick, blond brown fur that went light and shaggy around his head, he waddled toward her on fins that ended in claws. Curiously she touched his chin and lifted his head, the better to see his slitlike nostrils and small, curled-leaf ears.

Like most of the big predators she had met, he chose to speak in sounds. He chattered away in sharp, varied barks. He was confused: he'd thought she was a rival male, come to take his harem. She looked where he did: twelve furry lumps, all a fourth to a third smaller than the male, watched her from the most southern arm of the cove.

"Why did you think I was another male?" she asked, curious.

She *felt* like one, a king bull. He'd been terrified. He was young, and the power of her mind had convinced him she could easily take his females.

"Well, I'm no king bull," Daine assured him, tickling his curving whiskers until he calmed down. "I'm just me—whatever that is."

He was relieved. His harem was safe.

"May I visit after supper?" she asked.

Food? Pictures of fat, juicy fish were in his mind, and the knowledge he couldn't leave the females to hunt.

She promised to bring something. It seemed the least she could do, after giving him such a scare. He barked his thanks and slipped into the water, anxious to return to his mates before another male sneaked up on them.

"I forgot to ask what he was," Daine muttered to herself.

"Sea lion." Miri had come to stand beside her. "They're touchy in the breeding season. The way he went for you, it looked like he thought you were another male, coming to steal his wives."

"Do they eat in the breeding season?" Daine asked, curious.

"Not the beachmasters. If they hunt, another male will take their harems. They can go two months without food—Wave-walker defend us—look!"

A huge shape, far bigger than the sea lions, shot out of the water at the mouth of the cove: a great, lumpy gray thing that cleared the water and plunged back in with a tremendous splash.

"I can't believe they came so close to the land," Miri whispered.

"They who?" Daine's heart was thudding. "Is that a fish?"

Miri shook her head. "They suckle their young, like furred animals."

"Mammals," Daine supplied, from what Numair had taught her.

"Oh. That was a humpback whale—whales are the biggest things in the sea. They sing, you know."

Daine grabbed her friend's arm. "What d'you mean, *sing*?"

"Well, not singing, not like us. They talk in sounds—whistles, some of them, and moans—eerie noises. You should hear them from a boat in the middle of the ocean. It comes right through the wood, and fills the air."

Supper was ready by the time Daine had washed in a freshwater creek and put on dry clothes. She ate little, pondering the whale songs and her failure to reach the singers. After chores, she gathered up extra food and her bedroll.

"No lessons?" Numair asked quietly.

"I promised I'd bring him something to eat. And I do need a holiday." She looked away, rather than meet his eyes and see the disappointment in them.

"If that's what you want. Good night, then." But he watched her all the way as she walked down to the sea lions.

The beachmaster greeted her—and her food—with enthusiasm, and let one of his wives show the girl the first of that spring's new pups. When she slept, it was with her cheek pillowed on a yearling's flank, and with heavy, fishy-smelling bodies ranged all around her.

*The badger came. His fur was puffed out; he was very, very angry.*

*"I have lost patience with you," he snarled. "If you were my kit, I'd knock you tail over snout. When will you stop being stubborn? I didn't guide you all this way so you could fail to learn what you must! Tell these people what happened at that town of yours. Tell them what you're afraid of! Did you think I would send you to more hunters?"*

*"Predators," she told him.*

*With a smack of one heavy paw he knocked her onto her behind and jumped onto her chest. "Don't talk back, youngster. Have you no sense?* Your time is running out! *Soon the storm will be here. Lives depend on learning your lessons. I realize you are only a kit, but even you must see more is at stake than your fear of the hunt. Now, promise me you will tell them." She hesitated, and the badger snarled. "Promise me!"*

*He bore down on her with his will, thrusting his face into hers. She wondered later if it was the force of his mind, or the overpowering reek of his supper (decayed rabbit and a few worms), that made her surrender. "I promise."*

*"Tomorrow, and not one day later." He climbed off her chest, and she could breathe. She sat up, pulling air into her squashed lungs.*

*"Well, you're a good enough girl," he grumbled. It was as much of an apology from him as she would get. "I just worry about you, and things are moving so fast." He lifted his nose and sniffed. "Phew—these friends of yours stink of fish!"*

She woke to fog, dense and wet, beading in the sea lions' fur. Sitting up, she winced. She felt like one large bruise. Luck had been with her the day before. If she hadn't been in shallow water, she would have died, smashed by four hundred and fifty pounds of fast-moving sea lion. On top of the bruised ache were new, sharp pains. Peering inside her shirt, she found deep gouges, four on each shoulder—as if a badger had rested his weight there.

The morning fog turned into rain, and Thayet announced they would remain in their present camp. Steeling herself, Daine approached Onua and Numair as breakfast was being served. "Can I talk to you later?" she asked. "Alone?" She swallowed. "There's something about me you ought to know."

A few words to Thayet and Buri were all that was needed. Numair and Onua followed her to the south end of the cove, where a rock overhang kept a strip of sand dry. Numair built a fire. Tahoi sprawled between him and Onua, head on Onua's lap, his belly to the warmth of the flames. Cloud lay down so Daine could lean against her, encouraging the girl silently.

"Is it so hard to begin?" Onua asked.

Daine looked at the high waves, feeling her chin quiver. She gripped the badger's claw for reassurance. "Oh, yes. Don't interrupt me. If I'm stopped, I don't know if I'd have the courage to go on." Drawing a breath through a chest that had gone all tight, she began, "When the thaw came, end of January, nothing would do for Ma but I go to the next valley over, and visit her friend that married a shepherd there. She heard that Lory—her friend—was coughing a lot, and Ma had a syrup to give her. She made me promise not to come home in the dark, but stay over till morning. Sometimes I wonder if she just knew . . . but prob'ly not. As a foreteller, Ma always made a good cook.

"So, I saddled Cloud and went. Lory was glad to see me. Her 'n' Rand, her husband, always treat me nice. There was a new baby she let me play with. They're sweet when they're that little. And Rand wanted me to take a look at his best ewe. Good thing I did. She was getting set to give him twin lambs, only breech birth, which might've killed them and their ma. So I was up late, and Lory let me sleep till noon.

"Coming out of their place, I couldn't see anything anywhere but fog, couldn't smell, couldn't hear. I was clear to our village before I knew.

"They hit around dawn. The mill was burned, the miller dead. They took the wheelwright's oldest girl and the headman's wife. Really, they mighta passed my house by, Ma having the Gift, but they remembered she was pretty too, see.

"They fought—all of them. Ma, Grandda, dogs, ponies, horses— even the stupid chickens. Even Ma's geese. Not the rabbits. They left. Well, they never fight, and you can't ask them to go against their nature. But the rest fought. They killed some of the bandits.

"The bandits went crazy. They killed everything on the farm and didn't carry any of it away, Mammoth told me. Mammoth was my boss dog. He said they was too scared of animals who fought like that.

"Mammoth told me what happened, and died.

"So we buried them, me and Cloud, every last one of our family. Cloud's dam and sire, her brothers are in those graves.

"I straightened up the house, what was left. The raiders had tried to burn it, but only the upper story and the roof were gone. Ma had a bunch of charms against fire in the kitchen, so most of the downstairs was saved.

"It was two days before anyone came to see. After Ma helped them birth their children, and nursed them when they was sick. *Two days*! She could've been alive and hurt all that time! If the bandits had passed us by, Ma would have been at the village with medicines and bandages, making me and Grandda help.

"When I saw them, I just—popped. I said get out. I threw rocks, and they ran. You got to understand, there was all this mad inside me, all this hate and wildness. I couldn't hold it. My animal friends, they're the only ones who came right off to see if *I* was alive. I was going to them when I found the blood trail the bandits left.

"I knew where the pack of wolves was. The boss male and female thought I was smart, for a two-legger. It took explaining—they don't hunt their own kind. It's one thing to run another pack off your territory, but to hunt each *other* like they're prey, that makes them sick. When I showed them our farm, well, it made them crazy. We picked up the bandit trail and found them, in some caves.

"It was hard, keeping the pack from taking the bandits all at once, but I didn't want the wolves to get killed. We picked off three shifts of sentries, 'cause nobody was awake or sober enough to remember if the old sentries came back. When the other bandits came out in the morning, we took them. I remembered enough to let the women taken from the village loose, and kept my pack-brothers from killing them too.

"By then I was gone wild entirely. I went to all fours, and me and the pack denned in the bandit caves. I was safe with the pack. Cloud couldn't even talk to me. It scared her silly, being around the wolves, but I remembered she was family and I wouldn't let them get her. There was plenty of meat, anyway, from all the bandits stole.

"We heard the humans coming. I told the pack to go to the old den. I waited to see what was what. Maybe I was getting human again, a little.

"I hid in the brush. They sent Hakkon Falconer ahead to talk to me. He used to visit Ma and stay over, before he married again. He'd've wed Ma, but I heard her tell him my da wouldn't like it. She always spoke of my da that way, as if he was just around the corner. Anyway, Hakkon treated me all right, even after he married, because I helped with the birds.

"He said the women we set loose made it home and told what we did. He said I'd best come in now, before I took sick. He said he'd put me up, and I could earn my keep with him. He trained falcons for our lord.

"I came out onto the road. They'd've had me, but Cloud snuck up on one of the archers and kicked him. He shot too soon, and I ran.

"Hakkon said I was crazy, it was for my own good. He said I was like the rabid bear. I had to be put down merciful. If I'd come out, it'd be over in a minute—wouldn't hurt at all. The rest of them were calling me a monster.

"Then they tried to set the dogs on me, but the dogs wouldn't go. When them with ponies tried to come after me, the ponies threw them and lit out for home. The men should've known they couldn't get their animals to come after me.

"Me and Cloud headed up into the rocks. Trouble was, they were mountain men, fair trackers even without dogs. I wasn't thinking like a human, so I didn't remember to hide my trail. The weather didn't help, either.

"I don't know how long they hunted me. I think it was most of a week. I got pretty tired and cold and hungry. Cloud saved me. She started to nip and bite my arms. See—this one left a scar, above my elbow. She only left me alone when I got on my hind feet. When I got used to walking like that, I remembered I was human, and I knew I had to get out of Snowsdale. I snuck back home, got the things I had left, and came south.

"That's why I've been scared with the lessons. It never happened before my folks got killed, but now when I go deep in my magic or the meditating, when I'm by myself, I start thinking like the closest group of animals—like a herd of horses, or a pack. I forget I'm human. I forget I'm *me*.

"I was afraid to tell the truth. You don't know what it's like, having them you knew all your life hunt you like you was a deer. Hearing them on your trail and knowing if you don't start running, your hide'll get stretched on a frame and the rest of you goes into someone's stewpot. And I *was* crazy, running on all fours, hunting with a pack. I wanted to forget all that, if I could. I wanted to be all new here, all normal, just like everyone else.

"Only I guess I can't. The badger says I have to learn."

## ✈ SEVEN ✦

# BUZZARD ROCKS

She hadn't watched them as she talked, and she was afraid to look now. Suddenly Onua hugged her tight. The tears that had stopped coming when she buried her family came again, in a hot and silent flood.

"What about the badger?" asked Numair, when she was calm again.

Daine shrugged. "He comes in my dreams, sort of." She described the badger's visits, showing the silver claw and the marks in her shoulders as evidence. Onua shook her head over the wounds and fetched her medicines.

As she tended Daine's scratches, Numair thought. Finally he said, " 'Time is running out'—'the storm will be here.' What time? What storm?" He sighed. "I hate omens. They depend on translation, and I never was good at it. If he tells you anything more solid, let me know." Daine nodded. "As for the rest . . . I never heard of a human with wild magic losing contact with his essence—the part that tells us we *are* human.

"On the other hand, I've never met anyone with wild magic as powerful as yours. It *is* conceivable that your bond to animals overwhelms your humanity." He rubbed his hands together. "Well, *that's* easy enough to fix."

She gaped at him. "It *is*? All this time I've been afraid of joining a herd or a pack or a flock or whatever, and I could've *fixed* it?"

"With help from your humble servant." He stretched his arms. "Are you up to meditating now? I won't let you swim off with the sea lions." He smiled warmly at the girl, and she smiled back.

Onua patted her knee. "I leave you mages to it. I'm going to camp and torture some trainees." Quietly she added, "Thanks for trusting me, Daine."

"I wish I'd told before," Daine replied guiltily. "Only I was scared—"

The K'mir stood and dusted sand off her bottom. "After your village hunting you, I'm surprised you made yourself talk to another human again. Don't worry about it. And don't let him work you too hard." With a wave, she set off down the beach. Tahoi watched her go: he refused to leave the warmth of the fire to be drenched by the rain.

"She's quite a woman," said Numair. "You have a good friend in her."

"I know," Daine admitted.

"Now—just like meditation." She nodded and closed her eyes, feeling his fingers come to rest on her temples. His hands were warm. Carefully she breathed, pushing the sounds of her heart and lungs out of her mind until she barely heard them. Her muscles relaxed one by one.

Now she heard a thundering—Numair's heart. She pushed the sound back and let her hearing spread. Tahoi slept, dreaming of rabbits. A sea lion cow had started labor nearby, bringing a new pup into the world. Another pup, already born, suckled at his mother's teat. She heard doubled heartbeats in some of the other cows, signs of pups to come.

*Inside*, Numair said. Obediently she looked for her wellspring of copper fire. She dropped in and they fell through it, until she saw a white core to the fire. It bled into the copper as the wild magic bled tendrils into it. Suddenly she was inside the white column, looking out.

A shadow glittering with bits of light came between her and the magic. In its tracks flowed a glass wall, its surface etched with odd runes. When the shadow had circled her, the beginning and end of the glass connected.

Her head was clear: for the first time in weeks she felt sure of herself. Examining the white fire around her, she found it untainted by her magic, just as the magic was entirely apart now from her inner self. She also knew that she was alone—Numair had gone. She followed him to the real world and opened her eyes.

"How do you feel?" asked the mage.

She tried to stand and nearly fell over. She was stiff! "A bit rusty, but aside from that, wonderful. Am I fixed? Am I all right?"

"You tell me," he said. "Try the listening again. Sea lions live in groups like wolves and horses. If you're going to lose yourself, you should be able to with them. If not, the Rider ponies are just down the beach."

Daine closed her eyes, took a breath—and she was among the females of the harem, hearing their sleepy talk of fish and weather. The cow in labor had given birth: her new pup suckled contentedly. The mother barked at him, teaching him the sound of her voice so he'd always know which female she was.

Daine opened her eyes and grinned at Numair.

The mage smiled back. "Did you forget who Daine is?"

"Nope," she said gleefully.

"Sure you don't want to plunge into salty water and eat live octopi? That's what they eat, among other things."

She looked at him suspiciously. "What's an octopi?"

"One octopus is an octopus. Two octopuses or more are octopi."

"So what's an octopus?"

"I take it what all this means is you were able to stay Daine."

"It does. What's an octopus?"

He laughed. "All right, magelet. Let's go to sea."

She worked the day through, learning about ocean animals (no whales were within range, she was disappointed to learn) and about calling groups of sea animals to her. Afterward, it was a pleasure just to eat, clean, and mend tack with the others, and listen to Sarge talk about daily life in Carthak. Onua had to wake her up to get her into her bedroll.

The sea otter found her in the night, hobbling on three paws. The fourth dangled uselessly. She told Daine she'd been hunting in a tidal pool when a wave slammed into her, jamming her into a rock crevice. A second wave had yanked her free, but the paw got caught and broke. Cradling her patient and whispering reassurances, the girl eased out of the tent where she'd been sleeping. Sticking her head into the small tent the trainees had pitched for the mage, she said, "Numair?"

He sat up in his bedroll. "Daine? Is something the matter?"

"I've an otter with a broken leg here. I hate to disturb you, but— now I'm doing better with the magic, I thought there might be a chance I could—"

"Of course. Come in." Light filled the inside of the tent, making Daine and the otter blink. "Sit."

She obeyed, cradling the otter in her lap with a care to the broken leg. "You'll go deep, but into your patient instead of yourself. You need to see her bones from the inside—do you understand?"

"I understand right enough. I'm just not sure I can do it."

"I can help with that part. What you must do on your own is apply your magic to the break and *will* it to heal. You need to burn out any infection. Make sure the muscles, veins, and nerves knit together, not just the bone.

"The strength of your desire is what will complete the task. You must *want* this to work more than anything, and keep on wanting it, no matter how weary you become. *That's* the hard part—maintaining the concentration to finish. As it tires, your mind will want to attend to something else, just as it does in meditation. You'll get a muscle spasm or an itch, and you'll want to see to it. You can't—not unless you plan to resume splinting your friends and hoping you can keep them quiet long enough for an injury to mend."

Daine looked at her patient. The otter gazed up at her calmly. She had sensed that Daine could help her, and she was content.

"I'll do it," the girl said grimly. "Let's go."

The magic came swiftly into her hold. Numair guided her into the copper-laced animal in her lap and to the broken limb. Gently he shaped the grip of her mind around the injury and showed her an extra-bright strand of copper fire from the deepest part of her magic. She grabbed it and brought it to bear on the shattered bone.

It *was* hard work. She was tired; her head began to ache. It required patience. For a while it seemed nothing was happening. Once she almost gave up, but she remembered the otter's wholehearted trust and the promise to heal her. Ma had always said, Never break a promise to an animal. They're like babies—they won't understand. Daine hung on.

At last she saw movement. Tiny bone spurs grew across the break, slowly at first, then quicker. Marrow formed, building itself inside the protection of the spurs. Bruising in the muscles around the break began to vanish.

She got sleepy. Her back cramped almost unbearably. Nuh-uh, she thought fiercely. No quitting—not ever. If I'd known this, I could've saved Mammoth. If I learn it, I can save others.

She did not allow herself to think of anything else until marrow, bone, nerve, vein, and muscles were whole and healthy.

When she opened her eyes, she was cocooned in blankets and fiercely hungry. The otter was gone; so was Numair. She crawled out of the tent to see the trainees practicing hand-to-hand combat in the rain. Day had come.

"How do you feel?" Numair was sitting under a canvas awning, writing in a fat notebook. He capped his ink bottle and put his quill aside.

"How is she?" Daine asked.

"She's fine. I saw her swim off a while ago. We had lunch. I kept some for you." He passed a small bag to her.

She fell on the contents—chunks of smoked ham, bread, cheese, dried figs, an orange—and polished them off in record time. "I can't believe how *hungry* I was," she said when she finished at last.

"You worked hard. Of course you're hungry."

"How long did it take?" she asked, running her fingers through her hair.

"Some hours—that's to be expected. Healing in wild magic is more difficult than it is with the Gift. Wild magic depends on the body's own power to mend what's damaged. The Gift simply restores health that was lost."

"One thing I don't understand. Onua said I must've healed the birds in the marsh—remember? But I didn't know how to heal then, and it took me hours to do it now." She bit back a yawn. "I'm also worn out. Maybe I fainted in the marsh, but I never felt like this."

"Hmm." Numair fingered the bridge of his nose. "Several possible theories exist, but only one fits both of the limitations you just described. I'd have to say the birds' *need* to be healed pulled the magic out of you in raw form. You didn't force it to work within the limits of *your* strength then—you served only as a channel. The magnitude of the power transfer made you lose consciousness, but your overall health and reserves of strength were unaffected. That *is* the problem with wild magic—it has been known to act without the cooperation of the bearer."

"You mean it could happen again, and I couldn't stop it."

"I'm afraid so. If it's any help, I imagine the need in those connected to you by wild magic would have to be overwhelming. It's only happened once that you know of? No fainting spells as a child?" She shook her head. "Once in thirteen years, then. I wouldn't worry, if I were you." He smiled when she yawned outright. "Go back to sleep. I'll wake you for supper."

He was as good as his word. She was still tired, but forced herself to bathe in the stream and visit with the ponies. By the time the trainees had begun their meditation, she was in her bedroll, asleep.

The otter's return awoke her late that night. She had brought Daine a sea urchin shell, one that was cleaned of its original inhabitant and dried.

"Thank you," Daine whispered, touched. "I'll treasure it." The otter chirped her own thanks, and squirmed out through the gap in the tent wall. Daine smiled and snuggled into her covers, feeling the bumps of the shell with her fingers. I can *heal*, she thought. Ma, I wish you were here to see!

☙☙☙

They moved out in the morning under a clear sky. Daine's studies went on. Slowly, she honed her ability to speak with groups of animals so no other creatures might hear. She learned to put her will on four, then five, then six animals, to make them obey. She used whoever was closest: a flock of gulls, dogs in a village where the company stopped for eggs, harbor seals. Her greatest success came when a herd of mule deer came down to graze near their camp one morning. When Daine rose, she saw them. She watched, keeping Tahoi with her, simply enjoying the sight of deer so close to humans.

At Sarge's *"Turn out!"* the flock prepared to flee.

"Stop!" Daine called, throwing up her arm.

The deer stopped and did not move until she said, "What'm I doing? Go on, scat!" She took her will off them, and they ran. Feeling pleased with herself, she turned around, to find the trainees out of their beds and staring at her oddly.

"It's a good idea not to say anything out loud," Numair murmured, coming up beside her. She looked up at him and was rewarded with a smile. "It keeps the uninitiated from noticing. Just a little professional advice."

The Lioness walked over to them. "Congratulations, Numair. Your student learns fast."

"I have a good teacher," Daine said, and the mage tousled her hair.

"Come on, children, you aren't paid to gawp like a bunch of yokels!" Sarge's training voice could cut through stone, Daine was sure.

Evin was so close that she heard his soft: "We aren't paid at *all*, yet."

Sarge's eyes flicked his way, and a corner of his mouth twitched. "Let's move it or lose it, people!"

They pushed hard that day, stopping only once, to change mounts. By noon Daine felt as if her teeth would never stop rattling from the wagon, even though she'd switched to riding Cloud twice. About then she found a brush rabbit by the road: he'd been slashed by a goshawk and was dying. Daine took him into her lap, giving Mangle control of the wagon, and went to work.

The healing was harder than before, partly because concentration in a wagon traveling over a rutted road was more difficult than it had been in Numair's tent, late at night. Several times Daine was banged out of her meditation. Finally she switched places with Numair, asking Spots to give her as easy a ride as possible. On a large and placid horse, her luck was better than it would have been on a pony, or than it had been in the wagon. Still, by the time she finished, she had drenched her clothes in sweat, and she had been working throughout the early afternoon.

Weary to the bone, she freed the rabbit. He thanked her and fled, promising to keep a better eye out for predator birds in the future. She watched him go, elated in spite of her exhaustion.

They camped on a wide, open space that ended in a bluff over a tumble of rocks. "Daine, look!" Miri said as they were caring for the horses. She pointed out to sea. Three long, sleek, gray shapes broke from the waves and plunged in again, then four shapes, then two. "Dolphins!"

Once her chores were over, she went to the edge of the bluff. This was her first sighting of dolphins, and she wanted to talk to them. Sitting on the grass, she reached for her magic—and felt it slip from her grip. Working on the rabbit had tired her to the point of being unable to bear down with her mind. She closed her eyes and tried again. Tahoi barked. One of the trainees loosed an ear-piercing whistle. *"Concentrate,"* she ordered herself through gritted teeth. "You can do this!"

Slowly she discarded every sound nearby, until the only one left was her own heartbeat. Bearing down, she pushed it away, and farther. Perversely, it hammered in her ears louder than ever. She forced it back one more time.

Numair saw her collapse.

"Alanna!" he roared. "Come quick!"

A wide, smooth path sloped ahead, bordered in wildflowers. At the top of the hill two people waited in the shade of an old and gnarled oak.

"Ma?" she whispered, her eyes filling, and the woman held out open arms. Daine floated up the path toward her. The man was unfamiliar: he stood by Ma lazily, wearing only a loincloth. He was very brown, heavily muscled, and carried an unstrung bow like a man born with it in his hand. With so much of his skin bare, she could see that there were streaks of green in his tan, a deep green that gleamed in his eyes. Strangest of all, she could see what looked like antlers planted firmly in his curling brown hair.

"New friend, Ma?" she asked dryly.

The woman laughed. "Still mothering me, Daine?"

A bolt of lightning shot through her chest once, twice.

Her mother's face saddened. "No!" she cried. Daine fought, but a force was pulling her away.

"Ma!" she yelled.

"Sarra!" The man's voice was commanding. "It isn't time. Let her go."

Suddenly she felt reality shatter. Now she hung in open air, high over a rocky bluff where ants gathered around a purple fire. She looked back toward the hill, and a Stormwing dropped between her and her mother.

He looked her over, a nasty grin showing filthy teeth. "Well, well— what a surprise. What brings you here, little pigeon? Aren't you the darling Queen Zhaneh has offered so much to have brought to her *alive*?"

"Your queen can eat my arrows!" she screamed. "I want my ma!"

"Kiss my claws and say 'pretty please,' " he taunted, and vanished. Daine fell to earth and back into her body.

Numair shook Daine as he held her. "You fiend!" he yelled. "What on earth *possessed* you? You were *dead*! I ought to kill you myself!"

"Numair, calm down." The Lioness bent over Daine, looking white and drawn. "How are you, youngling? You gave us a scare."

Daine grabbed her hand. "You're the purple fire. You brought me back?"

"I gave you a direct jolt to the heart. We thought we'd lost you."

"My heart?" She frowned, remembering. "It made too much noise. I wanted it to quiet down so I could talk with the dolphins."

"Do you *hear* her?" Numair asked the clouds. "She wanted to talk to dolphins, so she stopped her own blessed *heart*! Mithros, Mynoss, and Shakith!"

Daine sat up. "I never."

Numair opened his mouth and Onua, behind him, covered it. "Not until you can talk without screaming," she said firmly.

"Daine, meditation is done for control over body responses, and thus over the mind." Alanna's purple eyes were amused, but serious as well. "In cutting back the sound of your heart, you were cutting the heartbeat itself."

"Well, I won't do *that* again," Daine promised, sitting up. "I feel like a mule kicked me in the ribs."

The knight chuckled. "In a way, one did. I gave you quite a shot, youngster." She reached a hand to Evin, who helped her get to her feet.

"Will you behave now?" Onua asked Numair. He nodded, and sighed as she took her hands from his mouth. "And men say *we're* emotional," the K'mir told Daine. "Don't do that again. I'd hate to find another assistant at this time of year." Wiping her hands on her breeches, she went back to the trainees.

"May I ask why you couldn't hear dolphins in the *usual* way?" Numair's voice was dangerously pleasant.

Daine rubbed her eyes with her fists. "I was tired."

"You were tired—ah. That makes it much clearer. Listen, magelet. The *next* time you're tired, try *resting* for a while. If you simply *can't* rest, go where you'll get nice and chilled, or step into salt water." He indicated the ocean below. "As you can see, there is quite a bit of it down there."

"I don't get it."

He sighed. "Reductions in temperature or contact with salt water can act as amplifiers for magic."

"So that's why the whale songs are so loud in the water!"

"Yes, that's why they're loud. Daine, you must realize—these things you're doing when you meditate are *real*. When you reduce the inner sound of your breathing, you are reducing your *breath*. When you quiet your heart, you're slowing it *down*. Your body will react—understand?"

"Yes, sir." She got to her feet with a groan. "Do people have visions when they think they're dead?"

His control vanished. "I don't *know*! I've never *tried* it!"

"Oh, well, I can see there's no talking to *you* the rest of the night," she said wisely. "Not till you're out of this pet you're in."

"The pet *I'm* in?" he bellowed.

Definitely time to go groom the horses, she thought.

She fell asleep during supper, and slept through the night. She felt rested when she woke, an hour before dawn, with something already on her mind.

It was the Stormwing. He had been nastily real, in a way Ma and her friend had not been. Even now she could smell that thing's reek, fouling the salt air—

Salt air.

There had been no scent to the hill in her vision. She had a good nose, and she would have remembered. There had been flowers. Ma always wore wood's lily or sweet pea sachets, and Daine had smelled nothing at all. But the Stormwing had come when she was in the air over *this* place. She had smelled him.

Standing outside the tent, in a cold wind, she reached out.

She was too tired to go far—less than a mile, only part of her usual range. She brushed the mind of an albatross that wheeled just over the rocks, but that was as far as her senses went. At that distance, she could trust her eyes as much as her magic, and they told her there were no Stormwings about.

Cloud followed her to the ocean, as cross as Numair had been.

Haven't you had enough fun? she asked, gracefully picking her way down the bluff while her mistress slid and scrambled.

"Not near," Daine replied. She sighed in relief when she reached the strip of sand between cliff and water. "Don't distract me, either."

I wouldn't dream of it, the mare retorted.

If I think about it, I'll only chicken out, Daine told herself firmly. Like as not it isn't near as cold as it looks, either. Yanking off boots and stockings, she plunged into the waves up to her knees. Once her feet were numb she tried again, gripping a rock to keep from being knocked off balance.

There—far overhead, hovering behind a long cloud, a tiny dot of wrongness. The hackles went up on the back of her neck.

Why so far up? she wondered. He just hangs there, waiting. Watching?

She sat down. "Cloud, keep me from being sucked under!"

I will do no such thing, the mare replied. Come out this instant.

Daine turned and fixed her eyes on Cloud. "Now, please." She used her will—just a touch of it. "It's important."

Grumbling, the pony waded in and gripped the back of Daine's shirt in her teeth. I hope it rips, she grumbled.

Daine reached behind herself to grab the pony's mane. If I go, you go, she retorted. Numb to the waist, she closed her eyes and sent her magic out.

There was her nasty friend, a jarring note in the sky. He was far from a single note, however. He was part of a thin, jangling chord that reached north and south where the waves boomed, as far as her hearing could go.

She dragged herself out of the water. "Get me to the others? Please?" she gasped, crawling onto Cloud's back. "Not the trainees. Umm—"

To Numair's tent? The mare sounded worried in spite of herself.

"Good. Yes. Have Tahoi bring Onua. It's important."

Just hang on and be quiet.

Daine collapsed over her friend's neck. "Of course." Cloud's mane was delightfully warm on her face.

"I'm sure," she repeated. All the adults were gathered around Numair's small fire. "They're up and down the coast as far as I can hear."

"How can they stay in one place like that?" Buri asked.

"They have their own magic," Numair replied, drying his feet from his own seawater dip, taken once he'd heard what Daine had to say.

"Can they see everything?" Alanna wanted to know. "Can they look through walls or stone?"

"I think they see like hawks," Daine guessed. "I don't know what they can do with their magic."

"They can use only a little without being noticed." Numair was still shivering. "If a sorcerer knows where to look, he can see the aura of their magic for miles. All they dare risk is the bit that holds them aloft." He made a face. "Once I thought to *look* that far, of course."

"Don't blame yourself," Alanna said tartly. "I see magic too, and *I* never spotted them." She patted Daine's shoulder. "Good work." She got to her feet. "I have to let Jonathan know. He won't be pleased." She walked away, far from the noise made by the trainees getting up. Within minutes a small fire blazed where she had gone, burning first orange, then purple.

Buri fed their fire more wood. "What now?" she asked the queen.

Thayet sighed. "I *wanted* to stay a few days at Buzzard Rocks, but maybe that's not a good idea. We'll move them along today, camp early at the Rocks, and go before dawn. Onua can ward the camp. There's not much else *we* can do, once my lord gets Alanna's message."

"We've seen fishing boats and villages," Onua said thoughtfully. "They aren't raiding. They aren't raiding, and they aren't killing."

"You sound almost sorry," Buri commented.

"In a way I am. That would make sense." Onua got to her feet. "They're watching the coast like cats at mouseholes, but who's the mouse?"

The Riders moved out briskly, and kept up the pace of the day before. Numair, apparently over his bad temper of the previous night, taught and questioned Daine on the habits of dolphins and whales.

Late in the day, when they took a side road to the village of Buzzard Rocks, Daine picked up a growing hum. With it came a feeling of *other*ness, though not that of monsters, or even of the water and tree sprites of the Royal Forest. She intended to tell Numair once they had pitched camp.

Their talk was postponed. When they reached the cluster of huts and sheds that marked the town, they found it was deserted. Thayet broke the trainees up into groups, and they fanned out to search the cluster of buildings. Daine and Cloud followed Numair, who did a search of his own.

"It happened fast, whatever it was," he said, almost to himself, as he peered into barns, wells, and chicken coops. "Yet they did have a chance to pack and gather livestock." Then turning he asked, "What's the matter with your ears?"

She blushed and stopped rubbing them. "I keep hearing this— *sound*."

"Oh?" His look was skeptical. "Hearing with your ears, or your mind?"

She listened for a moment. "With my mind. Sorry."

"Is it like the Stormwings?"

"No—more like the undine, but not *like* her exactly. And I have this feeling, as if—I don't know—when I see a juggler or something marvelous." She looked up at him miserably. "I'm sorry—I can't tell you anything else."

"Don't worry. Come on—maybe the others have learned something. Tell me right away if anything changes."

They joined the Riders in the village square. No one had found any clues. "They had time to pack," Alanna said. "It wasn't a raid or disease—"

The hum turned into a roaring chime in Daine's head. Selda shrieked.

They came in low over the beach where the fishing boats lay, giant things too large for birds. The mounts went crazy with fear, needing all their riders' attention. Spots, Cloud, and Tahoi shrank close to Daine and Numair, who were frozen with awe. Selda's ponies broke from her hold and ran into the rocks—five other ponies and Sarge's General did the same.

Daine realized poor Mangle was having hysterics, and went to grip his bridle. "Shush," she told him absently. "Calm down." Trembling, he obeyed.

"Weapons!" barked Thayet. Those who could do so grabbed their bows.

The birds—if they were birds—banked and came for another pass, giant wings shining like dim gold in the sun. This time they gave voice to shuddering, screaming roars. One of them raked the cart's roof with its claws, slicing the canvas as neatly as butter.

Daine saw what was about to happen. "Stop!" she called, to attackers and defenders.

Buri got in the first shot, Thayet the second. The great creatures were out of range, but already they were curving around again. *"No!"* Daine yelled now to the humans. "Leave them be!"

"We're under *attack*!" Buri yelled.

"Don't shoot! They don't understand. If you'll *give* me a second—"

But she could see fifteen arrows were fitted to strings. She screamed her fury.

Ponies and horses grabbed for the arrows, breaking them in their teeth. Sarge's Ox actually knocked him over. Daine wasted no time watching something she knew she could catch trouble for later. She ran toward the sea and the incoming creatures, waving her arms. "No! *Stop!* It's not what you think! It's not what *they* think!" Closing her eyes, she grabbed her power and threw it out like a net, pleading, *Listen to me!*

They broke off their attack two wingbeats in front of her, curving to each side. Rising above the lapping waves, the female flew out to a rock at the foot of a nearby cliff and perched. The male stalled with his wings and came down, scant yards away from Daine. He cocked his head, predator's eyes glittering down at her, and waited. Sitting on his haunches, he was as tall at the shoulder as Numair; each of his claws as large as a small sword. His body was that of a giant, feathered cat, blending harmoniously into the head, beak, and wings of an eagle. His eyes spoke of a nature that was alien to hers, but intelligent. His voice in her mind was deafening.

"It's all right to put down the weapons?" Numair asked.

The griffin—it had to be a griffin—nodded regally.

The mage's eyes lit with wonder. "You can understand me?"

The great haunches rippled.

"A little, he says," Daine translated. "It's ideas he gets, like 'weapons' and 'safety.'"

"Thank you," Numair told the griffin. He went to the Riders as Daine examined the two creatures. The female was gray silver in color, her mate brown threaded in gold. Both gleamed and shimmered in the dying light of the sun. In her magical vision, they blazed copper.

"I don't suppose you could tone down your voice? No," she said when the griffin looked at her arrogantly.

Footsteps crunched in the sand. Alanna came up on Darkmoon, shield on her arm, bared sword in hand. The great horse stopped a few feet away, his sides streaked with sweat. Daine knew the knight had brought him so close to a creature that scared him witless because she would need the advantage of Darkmoon's height if the griffin attacked; but she wished Alanna had tried for less advantage and the horse's peace of mind. She went to the stallion and stroked his muzzle, assuring him he was safe. He believed her—barely.

"Ask him where the village is," Alanna told Daine, her voice hard.

The great head cocked, and the griffin examined the knight. Daine swallowed as the chiming in her head broke into a handful of notes. "What?" she whispered. "Please, sir, I'm very new at this. You have to—" He chimed again, impatient. From the fire that was his presence in her mind, she picked out an image: Alanna's shield. She shook her head, and the griffin repeated the question/image. "Lioness, I—I *think* he wants you to explain the device on your shield. He won't talk about anything else till you do."

The woman's eyes were hard jewels in the light. "It's a lioness, my own sign. A female lion."

The male stretched his wings, and settled. Could you speak more gently? Daine asked him. Your voice hurts—I feel your answers in my bones. It makes translation difficult.

Pressure—a broad hand—settled at the nape of her neck. Suddenly she was inside a circle of light, shielded from the worst noise of the griffin's speech. "Calm down," Numair said gently. "Relax. I'm shielding you. Take a deep breath—good girl. You can manage this—just go easily."

She ordered her mind, sorting out what was griffin and what came from other animals. Focusing on the griffin, she reached more directly into his mind until each ringing note became a symbol or an idea. Once she could manage what her mind heard, Numair carefully freed her from his shield. Now she had control of the translation.

The griffin spoke again.

"He says there're too many griffins held captive on human shields," Daine told Alanna. "That's why they attacked the village—no, 'attack' isn't right. They flew over, like they did with us, to warn the people not to raid the nest and steal the little ones for shields. They're nesting atop that large spire of rock." She pointed to where the female sat at its base.

"How many villagers did they kill in this 'warning'?" Alanna wanted to know. "And Daine, you'd best not lie to protect them."

She listened to something the griffin was telling her. "I couldn't lie if I wanted to, Lioness. He won't let us." His correction boomed in her mind, and she sighed. "That's not right. Lies can't be *told* near a griffin. He's surprised we didn't know. That's why they were captured for shields."

"There haven't been griffins here in centuries," Numair put in. "We've forgotten the lore. Does he know how long it's been since they were seen in human lands?"

Daine struggled with the answer. "He—sorry, Numair—he doesn't know what you mean. I *think* he doesn't understand time as we use it. He *does* say they killed no one. The villagers screamed a lot, then they ran. They're at a great stone house about a day's ride down the coast."

"Pirate's Swoop," Alanna said, relaxing. "That's easy enough to check. Is it true, about lying around them, Numair?"

"I'd heard it. You could try."

Alanna opened her mouth—and no sound came out. Her throat worked, but nothing happened. At last she smiled. "I can't."

"How do they live?" Thayet came to stand with them. "What do they eat?"

That at least was easy to understand. "Fish," Daine said. "Dolphins if they can get them, seals, sea lions—but mostly fish. He says there're big ones in the open ocean."

"No cattle? No sheep or pigs?" the queen wanted to know.

Another easy one. "No, mum. They think grass-eaters taste nasty."

The queen hooked her hands in her sword belt, thinking. "Will he agree to let the villagers come back and not harass them?"

The griffin's reply was emphatic.

"Ouch! As long as they keep away from their nest, he doesn't care what people do." Daine smiled weakly at the queen. "Their voices—our voices—discomfort their ears. They don't want to come any closer to us than they must, to protect the little ones."

Alanna sighed, leaning on the pommel of her saddle. "It'd be a shame to destroy such magnificence," she said, admiring the great creatures.

The griffin preened his chest feathers and stood a little straighter.

Thayet laughed. "All right. I'll talk to the locals when we see them. Tell your friend we *will* fight them if they harm a human or any livestock."

The griffin's reply was so loud that Daine's temples throbbed. "He says don't insult him by calling me his friend. His kind has better things to do than associate with humans." She knew she was blushing. "He says at least my voice doesn't hurt his ears."

Alanna saluted the griffin with her sword. "Your point is taken, sir. Return to your nest, and we won't inflict our voices on you again."

Opening his beak, the male loosed a great, ringing cry. Before the echoes had faded he and his mate were in the air, spiraling up to their nest.

The humans made camp in the village square. Once the trainees were busy, the officers and Numair took Daine aside. "You shouldn't have turned our mounts against us." Thayet's green hazel eyes were serious.

She gulped. "I didn't—honest. They did it without me asking. If you don't believe me, maybe we could bring the griffins back—"

"No," Alanna said firmly. "We just got the ponies calmed down."

The queen pursed her lips. "You had best study control, mistress," she warned Daine. "If *we* can't trust our mounts, we're in trouble."

"There's only so much she can do," Numair put in. "This is wild magic, Your Majesty—not the Gift. She can't help animals knowing her feelings any more than she can help breathing. I've tested her control. It's as good as she can make it. Wild magic is unpredictable—thus the name."

Onua slung an arm around Daine's shoulders. "It's got to be harder on her than on us, Majesty. She's a good girl."

Daine bit her lip, glad she had friends—human ones, not just animals.

Thayet rubbed her neck. "I'll be so glad when we reach Pirate's Swoop," she said. "A hot bath and a night's sleep in a bed, and I'll be a new woman." She smiled at Daine. "I'm not going to bite you, youngster. I'm not even angry, not really. I will say this—riding with you has been an eye-opener!"

"Welcome to the club," muttered Numair.

"You know," Alanna remarked, "I have a feeling, if the people come back, this is going to be a *very* honest village from now on."

Onua said, "If so, a lot of husbands will be sleeping in the barn."

In the morning the road swung away from the coast. Daine watched with disappointment as trees blocked her view of the sea. Her sadness grew when Numair left them after noon. He lived in a tower visible to the west; it would take him an extra three hours to reach it if he followed the Riders. He promised that he'd see her soon. She had to be content with that.

By midafternoon the trees thinned and vanished. The main road sloped downhill from there to pass a large, prosperous-looking village on the shore. The road they followed left the main one to approach a strong-looking fortress built around three towers, one much thicker than the others.

"Pirate's Swoop," Evin said. He had fallen back to keep Daine company. "You'll like this place. I think you'll like the baron too. He and my father have been friends for years. He's—different."

The gates ahead opened to reveal the baron's—and Alanna's—domain.

## ⇢ EIGHT ⇠

# PIRATE'S SWOOP

They climbed a tall mound to enter the castle. Daine was impressed by the thickness of the walls around the outer court and by the alert and well-armed guardsmen. The baron of Pirate's Swoop kept his home in fighting order.

A man in gold-trimmed brown ran up to Thayet, bowing repeatedly as he talked to her. The queen signaled Buri, and the second-in-command turned in her saddle. "Riders, this way!" She and Sarge led the trainees to long, low buildings along the wall: stables, by the look of one, and the guard barracks.

Onua came up beside Daine. "Wait here. I want them to stable their mounts so they can unload the cart." She grinned. "A bit of advice, for what it's worth. Never do anything you can order a recruit to do for you."

Daine grinned. "I'll remember that." Movement caught her eye: a flag was being run up on one of the three towers. When the breeze caught it, she grinned: it was a gold lioness rampant on a red field, the same as Alanna's shield. On the tower next to it was a brown flag decorated with a gold key.

"The baron's flag," Onua said, noticing the direction of her gaze. "Those flags mean the baron and the lady knight are both in residence."

"No flag for the queen?" she asked.

Onua shuddered. "Gods, no! It's bad enough the whole palace knows where the summer training camp is, without crying it from the towers. George has made this place strong, but why ask for trouble if you don't need it?"

Grooms took Thayet's and Alanna's mounts as the women stretched. Suddenly shrieks filled the air. It took Daine a moment to realize the sound was not birds but children screaming, "Mama, Mama!" A pack of them dashed through the inner court's gate and separated: three to Alanna, two to the queen. Thayet's pair—both dark haired, a boy and a girl—bowed when they were a foot away from their mother, then threw themselves at her.

"The prince is nine, the princess eight," Onua explained. "They asked to watch the training this year instead of staying with the younger children in the summer palace."

Alanna's three—the tallest a true redhead, the younger two blondes with a touch of red in their locks—didn't even stop to bow. She laughed and knelt to return their hugs, disappearing for a moment under their bodies.

"You'd think they'd been brought up in a barn, wouldn't you?" a lilting voice asked nearby. "Climbin' on their ma like she was a hobbyhorse." Daine looked down from her seat on the wagon. The speaker was a tall, broad-shouldered man with brown hair lightened by the sun. His nose was too big for good looks, but there was a wicked twinkle in his large, green hazel eyes, and his grin was catching. He wore a shirt and breeches, and had come from watching the sea, to judge from his tousled hair and the spyglass in his hand.

She had to return his smile. "They must love her very much."

"She's easy to love," he replied.

"For you, maybe," Onua said, dismounting. "I know threescore offenders against the king's law who don't find her at all lovable. Hello, Baron."

"Onua, every time I see you, gods be my witness, you make me wish I wasn't married." They hugged vigorously, slapping each other on the back.

"You'd never pull in my harness, George. Daine, this gentleman—"

"Don't call me 'gentleman.' I *work* for a livin'," he interrupted. Daine grinned. Sarge often said the same thing.

"This *noble*man is Baron George of Pirate's Swoop. George, this is Daine, my assistant."

A large hand was offered. Daine shook it. Like all the nobles she'd met in this strange country, his palm was callused. "Welcome to Pirate's Swoop, Mistress Daine. How did you fall into such bad company?"

She blushed, not knowing how to take this charming man.

"Stop flirting with her, George—you'll only break her heart." Onua winked at Daine, who winked back, thankful for the rescue. "How long have the prince and the princess been here?"

"A week only," the baron replied, taking his sharp eyes off Daine.

In a quieter tone, Onua asked, "Any trouble?" George's eyes flicked to Daine. "You can trust her," the K'mir assured him. "We all do."

Daine blushed again when George raised his eyebrows. "That's quite a recommendation, young lady. I didn't think Onua even *liked* two-leggers." Looking around, he said, "Bless me—so you did take on Evin Larse."

Seeing them, Evin waved and loped over, his long legs taking him across the outer ward court in seconds. "George, I made it," he said, panting as he offered his hand. "I told you I would. Wait till you hear about the trip we've had! Did you know you have *griffins* nesting up the coast?"

"I've got the whole village quartered here," George said, making a face. "Eatin' our food and beggin' me to send soldiers after them. Tell me true—is it really griffins, or just a pair of mean albatrosses?"

"It's griffins, and you don't have to send a company," Evin assured him. "Daine here got them to make peace."

"I didn't 'get' them to do anything," Daine retorted. With the charming baron she might be tongue-tied, but never with Evin. "They don't do anything they don't want to. But they promised the queen not to attack people or livestock," she told George. "And they can't lie, so I believe them."

"Wait," he ordered. "You've had speech with them, *and* made a treaty—"

"This is a fine welcome you've given me, laddy-buck," Alanna said, trying to imitate her husband's speech as she approached. She bore a gold-haired child on each hip. "Here I am, home from the wars, and you let me be swarmed over by barbarians whilst *you* flirt with my friends."

"Excuse me," George said gravely to the adults, and to the children he plucked from his wife's hold. Gripping the Lioness firmly, he bent her back in a prolonged kiss that looked like a romantic scene in a play. Everyone, even the men-at-arms posted along the walls, clapped, whistled, and cheered.

"Does anyone in this land act like they're supposed to?" muttered Daine.

Onua heard her question. "They do in lots of places," she said, eyes twinkling. "But this isn't 'lots of places,' it's Pirate's Swoop. And if you think *this* is strange, just wait till you've been here a couple of days."

Exploring after the evening meal in the castle's great hall, Daine got directions to the observation deck on top of the third, largest tower. Here the wall rose out of stone cliffs. Looking down, she saw rocks, a thread of beach, and heavy waves. Relaxed, she watched the sun dip itself into the ocean as a cool breeze blew across her face. She liked the Swoop, she decided. If she had to live within stone walls all her days, this would be the kind of place she'd want.

"Beautiful, isn't it?" The Lioness relaxed against the stone wall at Daine's side. "I'm so glad to be home."

You have a home to go to, the girl thought, and was immediately ashamed of herself. How could she begrudge the knight a place of her own? "I don't see how you could ever leave this," she admitted.

"I don't, either, except I took an oath as a knight, then as champion, long before I came here. And I keep my oaths."

They fell silent again. It's odd to see her in a dress, Daine thought. Wearing perfume—it's pretty, whatever it is—and pearl earbobs and silk. And yet she fits here. She sighed. I wish this were *my* place, she thought wistfully. I bet I could fit here too.

A distant cry fell upon her ears. She and Alanna looked north and saw a bird shape wheeling over the ocean. "Griffins," the Lioness remarked. "It's like a story, or a bard's tale."

So are lady knights, thought Daine, but she kept that to herself. "If only the griffins were all of it."

They looked up. Only a handful of clouds were in the sky, but they knew there was a Stormwing behind one, and that more waited up and down the coast.

"My father is a scholar." The woman's voice was soft. "The king asked him to report on what he could learn about Stormwings. He says they live for destruction and the fear that destruction provides. They eat only the products of war, famine, and disease—the bodies of the dead. They drink only the energy of human suffering and fury. They've had a long fast—four hundred years' worth, in the Divine Realms. I have the feeling they won't be as easy to send back as they were to set free."

"Send back?" Daine had a thought, and she didn't like it. "If they *had* to be locked in the Divine Realms, maybe they were never supposed to be there. Maybe they're *our* predators."

"*Our* predators?"

"Surely." She tugged one of her curls. "You speak of locking them up again as if it can be done. What if the gods don't allow it, because the Stormwings are supposed to be here, not there?"

Alanna winced. "That's a very cheerful thought. I wish you hadn't come up with it. If you're right, we have a lot of battles ahead."

Daine slept in the stable loft, cushioned by the bodies of the castle's many dogs and cats. At breakfast, she listened as the trainees were given a day off (except from caring for their mounts). That meant a day off for her as well, and she could use one. All her shirts needed mending, and a wash wouldn't hurt any of her clothes.

Getting directions to the castle laundry, she returned to her loft and gathered her clothes. On the way back from the laundry, she found Selda checking the saddlebags that had been issued to each trainee for the trip south.

"Smile," the brunette said, shoving her belongings into a pack. "I'm quitting. I've had enough fun in the wilderness."

Daine glanced away. She wouldn't miss the girl at all.

"Don't look so pleased." Selda folded the bags and hung them next to her tack. "One of these days you'll be packing yourself."

"Me? Whatever for?"

The older girl's smile was bitter as she looked Daine over. "Are you blind? How long can they afford to keep you on, do you suppose? After that thing with the griffins, I figured it was all over for you."

Daine felt cold. "I've no notion what you mean."

"What happens if they're in a battle and you get hurt? You think they can risk their mounts coming to *your* rescue? I don't." The girl shouldered her pack as Onua came in. "Don't say I didn't warn you."

Onua looked at her suspiciously. "You'd best get to the wharf. That boat won't wait."

Selda gave both of them an ironic salute, and was gone.

Onua rolled up her sleeves. "This is a surprise inspection. Let's see how the trainees' mounts look while they're off relaxing. You start on that side; I'll start here," she ordered. "We can talk while we work. Look at everything, mind—nose to tail. What poison was she dripping in your ear?"

Daine stroked the muzzle of the first pony with a hand that shook. "She said the Riders can't afford to keep me. She's right, isn't she? If animals know I'm in trouble, they *will* come to me. Numair himself said I couldn't shield all my wild magic."

"Maybe that's so." Onua ran a brush over Padrach's Minchi to see if extra hair fell out after a morning grooming. "But it wasn't the Riders that hired you. It was *me*. As long as I say so, you work for me, not them."

"How can you do that?" she whispered. "You're a Rider."

"No, I'm a civilian expert. I deal with whatever concerns horses, and that's *all*. I'm no soldier." Onua pointed at her with a brush. "You saved my life in the marsh and at the palace, when the Stormwings hit. You saved Numair—he was the first person here I knew liked me for myself. I won't let you down." She reached over and dabbed at a tear rolling down Daine's cheek. Those of us that's horse-hearted have to stick together, all right?"

Daine nodded. "But you'd tell me if I wasn't giving satisfaction?"

Onua grinned. "If we spend more than the morning checking these mounts, I will be *most* unhappy. I was planning to take the afternoon off."

Daine went to work, smiling. They had just finished when hoofbeats rang outside and a voice yelled, "Daine? They said you were in here."

She ran outside as Numair climbed off his sweat stained gelding. "Come with me," he ordered. "We have to find the Stormwings."

She shaded her eyes to look up at him. "What d'you mean? Aren't they behind their little clouds, being sneaky?"

He shook his head. "They're gone. Vanished."

She spent the afternoon on the observation deck with Numair and Alanna, searching as far out as she could drive her magic for any sign of the immortals. The Gifted ones applied themselves to scrying, or looking. Numair used a round crystal he carried in a pouch, Alanna a mirror with (Daine was tickled to see) roses painted on the back.

"It's not *my* taste," the knight said dryly. "This is from Thom—my oldest. A birthday gift. It's the thought that matters." She glanced at the back of the mirror, winced, and turned it to the reflecting side. "That's what I keep telling myself, anyway. And it makes a very good scrying tool."

For herself, Daine sank deep into meditation, listening up and down the coast. She heard the griffin female return to the nest with food: griffin males, it seemed, helped to brood eggs. Her friends among the sea lions were prospering, as were other seals and sea lions. A number of whales had come to swim in the waters around the Swoop, but she didn't have time to attempt to speak with them. Crossing her fingers, she hoped they'd stay close long enough for her to get a chance. Other sounds she identified as two groups—Miri called them "pods"—of dolphins.

At last she drew her senses back to the castle. "Nothing."

Alanna grimaced. "No luck for us, either."

"So our friends have given us the bag." The baron had joined them at some point. Seeing Daine's puzzled look, he said, "They've escaped us. It's thieves' cant, meanin' a delightful trick whereby you wait for your pursuer and slip a large bag over his head to blind him."

Daine scowled. "Well, I'm not blinded, and they aren't there."

George smiled at her. "I believe you." He looked at Numair. "Is there a way to nab one of these beasties for questionin'?"

Numair frowned. "I'm not really sure. If we can kill them, I assume we can capture them. . . . You know, it's moments like this that I really miss the university library."

"We're working on ours," Alanna pointed out. "Maybe the king has the proper books already. And wait—what about the Golden Net?"

Numair's face lit. "You know, with a few adjustments—"

"My lords and ladies." A proper man in the livery of a castle servant had come up to the deck. "We dine in half an hour."

"I think I have the basic spell in a book I've been reading," Alanna told Numair. "If you want to come take a look—" They followed the servant down into the tower, talking about spells and their variations.

Daine looked at the sun; it was low. "No wonder I'm hungry."

"If you hear one of those nasties again, let's catch it," George said.

"I don't think we'll get anywhere talking to one," she pointed out.

The baron's grin was neither warm nor friendly. "You leave that to me." They studied the ocean together. "It's strange how folk look at a thing. Numair sees what's comin' to us—he thinks of the return of old magic, magic that's controlled by none and understood only by a few. My wife sees a threat to her kingdom. Me, I'm a commoner born and bred, title or no. You know what I think of? Omens and portents—like the red star that blazed over us when the emperor Ozorne was crowned, seven years back."

"Then maybe we're lucky the Stormwings are giving us so much time to think about them before they do something really nasty," Daine said.

George laughed. "Now *there's* a practical way to look at it, and I thank you. It does no good to brood about what might come." He offered his arm with a bow. "Let's go to supper and drink to the confusion of our enemies."

Numair kept her at her lessons until the midnight hour was called. She trudged back to the stable the Riders used, yawning heartily as she climbed to her loft bed. Her mind spinning with new animal groups, she kept her eyes open barely long enough to pull on her nightshirt.

She awoke to a stable cat giving birth near her ear and three children—a girl and two boys—watching her solemnly.

"I s'pose you're fair proud of yourself," Daine told the cat. "My wondrous book says you're a feline, and a carnivore, and a vertebrate, and a mammal. I wish them that wrote it could smell around here right now and maybe they wouldn't call you all those pretty names." The girl wriggled out from between her blankets and grabbed her clothes. The feline was busy cleaning the last of the new kittens and refused to reply. "It's too early to be paying social calls," she told the children.

"Our mamas said you're a mage." That was Thayet's daughter, Kalasin. She took after her handsome father, sharing his blue eyes and coal black hair.

Daine sat on her bed. "I'm no mage." She grinned. "Numair calls me a magelet, but that's just for fun. It's too early to be answering questions."

"Ma says you help animals." Thom's hair was redder than Alanna's, and he had George's green hazel eyes. "We brung you him. He was on the wall."

The two older children lifted a basket and offered it to Daine. Inside lay an osprey, a fishing hawk, glaring at her over a broken leg. If the cat hadn't been giving birth close by, she would have known about him already.

She sighed and took the basket. "It's all right, then. You can go now." Turning her attention to the bird, she carefully took him from the basket. "How'd you manage this, sir?"

He shrieked and slashed at her when she joggled his leg. "I'm sorry," she murmured, gentling him with her mind. "I'll make it better—I hope."

She went to work, unaware that the children watched her, fascinated. Bird bone was easier than otter bone to mend: it was thinner and hollow. Better still, it wasn't a clean break, but one of the greenstick kind, which meant the bone simply had to be fused together again.

Opening her eyes, she saw that the break was healed, the bird's pain gone. She was dripping sweat onto him. "Sorry," she murmured as he shook himself.

He cocked his head, looking at the mended leg. He was impressed, and intrigued by what she had done. At the moment, however, what he was most interested in was a nap.

She smiled. "Just, when you wake up, obey the rules—no hunting or teasing any other creatures in this castle. They're all my friends too."

The osprey understood. She settled him on a wooden rail and brought water from the stables below. Promising she'd see him later, she gathered her things again and left.

Her early visitors waited for her by the stable door. "You missed breakfast," Prince Roald said. "We brought you some." He handed over a napkin wrapped around sweet rolls.

"Thank you," Daine said. "That was very kind." She wolfed two of the rolls, knowing her manners were terrible and not caring.

"Papa gets hungry when he's been using his Gift," remarked the princess.

Daine wiped her mouth. "It was good of you to bring the osprey, and the food. I thank you. Now, I think you should go back to the nursery, please. Won't the servants be missing you?"

"We're too old for the nursery," replied Thom, with all the dignity of his six years. "Only the twins have to stay there. They're four."

"Poor things. Listen—I have to bathe, and then I work for the Riders, which means I've no time to chat. Good-bye."

They looked at her hopefully.

What was she supposed to say? At home she'd never spoken with a child. Parents had always kept them from her. If I ignore them, they'll go away, she decided, and went to the baths.

When she came out, they were waiting. They trailed her to the stable, admiring the new kittens while she stowed her gear. They followed her back down to the ponies and helped as she looked after Selda's old pair as well as Mangle and Cloud, holding brushes, pails, and rakes for her. They were still with Daine as the trainees, subdued after a morning conference with their officers, came to look after their mounts.

Thayet broke out laughing when she saw what was going on. "I'm sorry, Daine," she said, giggling, "but it's like ducklings. No offense, children."

"You said we ought to learn more about the stables, Mama." Kalasin was more outspoken than her brother. "You said if we wanted to come with you and the Riders when we're older, we'd have to take care of our gear and all."

"Daine has to decide if you can stay, however," the queen said.

The girl wished the children wouldn't look at her piteously. Thayet was right—it *was* like ducklings. She could have shot them easier than resist those eyes. "Onua? Sarge?" she asked, hoping. They shook their heads.

"Look at it this way," Buri said. "You'll need help with the new extras—Jacy and Kenelm handed in resignations a little while ago. Starting tomorrow we're taking groups outside the castle walls for days at a stretch. You won't even have Onua then."

Selda had been right, Daine thought, looking at Buri and the queen. They know I won't be helpful in the field, not if the ponies obey me first.

A gentle hand rested on her shoulder—Onua's. "Somebody *does* have to care for the washouts' horses," the K'mir whispered. "It's real work, not just something to do because we haven't the heart to throw you out. And you need to stay close and study with Numair, remember?"

"Once you start, no quitting," Thayet told her children. "If you agree to help Daine, that's what you do. It's a responsibility. You can't stop just because you're tired of it." The two coal black heads nodded seriously.

"Thom?" the Lioness asked.

I don't think he's old enough to bind him, Daine thought, but Thom was already promising. She recognized the expression on his face. He might be only six, but he would keep up with Roald and Kalasin or die trying.

Which means I'll have to watch him, she thought with a sigh. Ducklings.

A week passed. It was easier to manage them than she expected. Being able to meet wild animals was a powerful attraction, one the "ducklings" did not tire of and would not risk losing. Though she incurred the wrath of all the nursery helpers but the chief one, Maude, by introducing their charges to savage beasts, she presented her friends to weasels, crows, bats, and deer. She let them watch as she worked to heal one of the dogs, who'd had a paw smashed by a passing wagon.

She was surprised to find Roald and Kalasin *did* help in the stable, and that only Thom's size kept him from doing as much. She knew from her meetings with the twins that his maturity came from the possession of two appallingly lively younger siblings. Roald and Kalasin also had younger sibs, but their maturity seemed to result from what people expected Tortallan royalty to do. She was surprised, and a bit shocked, to learn that they fed and groomed their ponies at home. She had never heard of princes and princesses who had chores.

"I'll be a page in a year," Roald pointed out one day as they helped with the constant chore of mending tack. They had settled on the flat area in front of Daine's stable (as she had come to think of it) as a place for such chores. "I'd have to learn then, anyway. It's best to know as much as I can ahead of time. Papa says later the other lessons will keep me busy."

"I'll be a page too." Kalasin had insisted Daine call her "Kally" as the children did. "Papa said girls can be knights, so that's what I'll do."

Daine was about to ask Thom if he wanted his shield when a messenger came through the gate at full gallop. Covered with dust, the man slid from his horse as hostlers came to take it.

"Lioness," he gasped. "Message for the Lioness."

A servant bowed. "This way."

Thom, the princess, and the prince watched, all looking grim. "Great," Thom said. "She has to go away again."

Kally sighed. "It's like Mama in raiding season," she told him. "We're lucky to have mothers who fight. Our fathers must stay home and protect their people."

"Da fights when they hit the village." Thom was a stickler for fact.

"Papa fights if he can," Roald tried to smile and failed.

Poor things, Daine thought. They miss their folks, coming and going all the time. At least while Ma and Grandda were alive, they were *there*.

"How about a run to the beach?" she asked. "The seals aren't that far out. If we ask nice, maybe they'll come in."

"Maybe I should wait," replied the redheaded boy.

"I'll have Gimpy keep watch," Daine wheedled. Usually the bloodhound's name made Thom smile, but not now. "He'll fetch us if they saddle Darkmoon."

"I'm not a *baby*. I won't *cry* or anything. It's just—I keep having bad dreams anymore." Thom looked down, biting his lip.

"Let's go look at the seals," Daine urged gently.

Gimpy was coming for them when the Lioness and Darkmoon passed him on the slope to the beach. The minute she stopped they knew it was serious: she wore full mail. A company of the Swoop's guards waited by the gate, wearing combat gear. One of them carried a banner, crimson silk with a gold lioness rampant—the personal flag of the king's champion.

The knight slid from the saddle, hanging shield and sword from the pommel before kneeling to embrace her son. Thom fought tears.

"You know Fief Mandash?" She spoke to all three. Roald and Kally liked her and didn't look any happier than her son. "They've got ogres—three of them. They killed the lord and his son and have the rest of the family trapped in the keep. I have to go. We're the closest king's representatives."

Thom swallowed. "Ma, ogres are *buge*."

"Not *buge*, huge. The messenger says the male is eight feet or so. That's not bad, and he's the biggest." Alanna smiled, but her eyes spoke of worry and watchfulness. "I'm taking some men, all right?" That seemed to reassure the children. "Thom, mind your father and Maude, and don't get under people's feet. A hug and a kiss"—she took them—"and you be good." She tousled his hair and shook hands with Roald and Kally. "Tell your seal guests good night," she advised. "You need to clean up before supper."

All of them went to obey. The knight watched them pat the seals, pulling on an amethyst-stitched glove.

"Should I go with you, Lioness?" offered Daine. "If it's immortals?"

"No, with twenty men I should be fine. What gets me angry is I *told* Mandash to arm his people, if he was too cheap to hire soldiers. But *no*, we can't teach peasants to use weapons—what if they decide they don't like their overlords?" She sighed. "I shouldn't speak ill of

the dead. I just don't like the timing, and I don't like it being immortals."
She took one of Daine's hands in both of hers. Her grip was powerful.
"Will you and Numair look after my family? Don't let anything happen
to them."

Chills crept up the girl's spine. "We won't, Lioness."

Alanna smiled. "Thank you." She drew a deep breath and went to
bid good-bye to the children once more.

The Lioness had been gone for two days. Daine had collapsed early
into her loft bed, worn out from her evening's lessons.

*She dreamed: it was a pleasant night in her badger set. With her
belly full, she listened to the kits play. She was about to go for a cool
drink of water when her dreams changed. Trees and a moonlit sky
tumbled around her. Boats filled with men came onto the beaches, and
men crept among the trees. Speaking softly and fast, they lit fires,
scorching the roosts and blinding her. Into flight she tumbled, over the
roaring cold and salty place with panic in her throat. There was the
light ahead, the one the forest bats had sung about, a beacon of safety.
She was the greatest of the People—she could protect them when
strange men broke the night rituals*!

Daine gasped and sat up. "Odd's bobs, what was *that* about?"

With her excellent night vision and the light of the full moon that
came in the windows under the eaves, she saw that the rafters overhead
were thick with bats. A good thirty of them, mixed breeds, watched her
with nervous eyes. Three were hoary bats, named for the frost on their
brown fur. By themselves they would not have been a surprise: they
weren't sociable bats, not like the clusters of big and little brown bats
that hung with them, or the handful of pipistrelles.

"Wing-friends, what's amiss?" she asked softly. "Come and tell
me."

Within seconds she was a bat tree, with little bodies festooned on
her curls and parts of her nightshirt. All of them trembled in terror.

"Hush," she told them. Closing her eyes, she thought of deep and
even breaths, of safety in caves, of the drip and echo of water in high
chambers. Slowly the bats took her calm into themselves. Small talons
changed their grip, this time so flesh was not caught along with the
cloth. The trembling eased and became a thin vibration. Some of the
bolder ones returned to the rafters, to give her air. She sent the calm
out with them, enticing more of those who clung to her to take the
perches they were used to, hanging from wood. The ones left were the
hoary bats and the leaders of each group.

Daine opened her eyes. "Now. Let's hear it—one at a time."

It was all she could do to stay calm when they described what they had seen. It was her dream: men, strangers, coming from the woods and from boats on the water, hiding under the trees. She had to clamp down on her witnesses a little to make sure of the numbers they were describing. Bats tended to count by the way they roosted: their idea of numbers was flexible, and depended on the breed of bat. Daine knew she couldn't tell the baron or the Riders her friends had seen six quarter-colonies or whatever the total was. Not only would that not be helpful, but they would think she was crazy.

To the hoary bats, who roosted alone, the men had arrived in flocks, like deer they saw grazing at night. Moreover, each bat had come from a different part of the wood that ran along the coast. After scribbling with a stick of charcoal on her drawing pad and squinting to read her own marks, she concluded that each hoary bat had seen nearly fifty men.

The big brown bats had seen at least two colonies—sixty men or so. Most of the pipistrelles were from one place and had seen less than half of one of their colonies—almost fifty. One lone pipistrelle from the wood north of the Swoop identified another half-colony. The little brown bats had come from the east and south. Each of their sightings came to two tenth-colonies; for them that meant two hundred men, all told.

All the bats assured her their counts had not overlapped, and that she took as truth. Their concepts of numbers might be odd, but a bat's knowledge of territory was precise to a pin.

Daine looked at the numbers, her skin tingling in shock. If the bats were right, they had seen more than five hundred strange men coming overland or by sea and landing near the cove. The bats were more familiar with the locals than those humans might have believed possible. The little animals insisted the strangers were not *their* humans. Moreover, the strangers all wore metal over some parts of their bodies, and all carried or wore wood tipped with metal, and bars of metal. Daine could see their faces in the bats' minds: they were the hard faces of warriors.

Carefully, without frightening the animals, she eased into her breeches and boots. In the process she talked two of the hoary bats into staying behind. The others, the head of each colony, the lone pipistrelle and one particularly scared hoary, clung to her nightshirt and hair. They would go with her, they said.

Sarge, who ran the trainees on night watch, and Kally sat in front of the stable, talking. From the look of things, the princess had been unable to sleep. "Daine?" Sarge asked when she emerged. The girl's blue eyes widened.

Abruptly Daine saw herself as they—as humans—must see her: small, wriggling animals swarming on her, clinging to hair and clothes. They tried their best to be clean, but a couple of them had lost control of their bowels.

I must look like a monster. Daine swallowed a lump in her throat. She hadn't realized how much Kally's opinion—or Sarge's—had come to mean to her.

"I have to talk to the baron," she whispered without looking at them.

Kally walked over hesitantly. She stopped, then reached out to touch a furry body. The little brown bat transferred his affections to her in a leap. She squeaked, then let him snuggle into her collar. "He smells you on me." Her tiny smile trembled and held.

Sarge got up, his brown eyes kind. "Come on, girls."

The master of the Swoop was in his study. The queen and Josua, the captain of the Swoop's guards, were there as well, seated in comfortable chairs, while Numair stared out one of the windows.

"What's all this?" George asked. His sharp eyes took in Daine's riders as well as Kally's small hanger-on. Thayet yelped when she saw Daine; Josua was on his feet, dagger half-drawn. Numair looked around, frowning.

"Please—don't startle them." The bats caught the surge of her own fears. She made herself take a deep breath and get under control. Don't open your eyes, she cautioned the bats. The room was cozily lit from a human standpoint, but not from theirs. "They won't hurt anyone."

"It's only bats, Mama." Sarge's mouth twitched: it was impossible to tell that Kally herself had been upset by them only a few minutes ago.

Thayet and Josua stared at Daine.

"It's important, sir," she told the baron. "I wouldn't have brought them if it wasn't."

"May I?" Numair asked, pointing to the hoary bat.

The animal's nose was already questing, having located interesting smells on the sorcerer's clothes. Gently Daine handed him over: in one of Numair's gigantic palms, the bat was dwarfed.

"What news have your friends brought for me?" George asked. Daine looked at his face, but saw no trace of mockery or disbelief.

Either he's the world's finest Player or he believes in me, she thought. "Have you a map?"

He gestured behind her. She turned and saw a table covered with sheets of parchment: on top was a map of Pirate's Swoop. Holding down a corner of it was a box of small, colored pebbles. Consulting with her friends, she put one at each location where strangers had been seen, explaining to the adults as she worked. "All this since twilight," she said when she finished. "We think it's more'n five hundred, all told." She looked at the picture she'd made, and blanched. The stones formed a half circle a mile away from the castle and village of Pirate's Swoop. They had been surrounded in the dark.

## ⇥ NINE ⇤

# SIEGE

ᔕᓍ Things moved so fast Daine's head spun: Pirate's Swoop was more than prepared for night attacks. Within minutes Captain Josua, Thayet, and Sarge had left to quietly wake the village and bring the people back to the castle.

With them they took Daine's promise the livestock would move quietly. Once she had explained things to them, the village animals were eager to help. She felt ashamed of herself for showing them images of the raiders' imaginary stewpots in such gruesome detail, but told herself the cause was a good one. Even the geese and chickens had been willing to go along after that.

Next she asked the bats to return to their friends in her stable. You won't like the people I'm going to talk to now, she assured them, and they believed her. George had asked her for spies who would spook less easily than the bats, and that meant only one thing: owls. Daine had to admit owls were unnerving to deal with, and she *liked* them— the bats did not. While they weren't natural enemies, there was always a chance an owl could make a mistake, and apologies meant nothing to a dead bat.

With the bats gone, she went to the limits of her range, contacting owls and explaining her problem. She wasn't surprised to find that the silent predators were already angry about the invasion: the strangers had chased all the game worth hunting into burrows in earth and tree.

Waiting for the owls' report, she and Numair went to the observation deck. From there they watched as the Swoop's gates quietly opened and guards and Riders headed for the village, to help the people pack and move. Daine noted with approval that the hooves of all the horses and ponies were muffled. With the moon full and the night clear, they didn't need torches—a small blessing, since the invaders also had used moonlight to keep their arrival secret.

The owls reported, and Daine wrote their information on her paper. When they finished, she added the total with fingers that shook. She checked her numbers and came up with the same total. A third check bore the same result.

Her voice emerged as a squeak. "Lord Baron?" He had come while she was working. "I have the whole thing."

He raised his eyebrows. "So soon?"

"Owls are fast." She pointed out the total—a little more than six hundred men had infiltrated the woods. "The owls say they aren't moving. They're camped. No fires, but they've settled."

"Waitin' for dawn," the baron said. "Waitin' for *that*." He nodded at the sea. Two miles out a fog bank lay on the ocean, its top as high as the tower on which they stood. It took her a minute of looking before she saw what was wrong: the curved dome was clean, as if the thing were shaped by a sculptor. It was also dead on the water. Fog was neither tidy nor slow. It moved fast and overwhelmed everything in its way. This close, she should not have been able to see the sky, and she ought to have seen it move by now.

"Numair?" George asked. The sorcerer was leaning on the wall, his eyes closed. A transparent black cloud surrounded him; bits of light flickered in it like fireflies.

He shook his head. "It's opaque. I can't even feel the weather-working spells that are holding it in place, and there *have* to be spells. Fog is defined by natural law like any atmospheric creation. In the absence of those laws, we have to assume magic, which I *should* be able to detect. Since I *can't* detect it, that argues the presence of damp-ening spells in the fog."

"Dampenin' spells." George's face was tight. "We're boxed in, then—like rats in a trap. Whatever's in that fog will hit us in the mornin', sure as the Crooked God cheats. Why'd we have no idea this was comin'?"

The mage looked at his friend. "George, there are more illusion spells and diffusion spells than there are stars. Scrying is an inexact magic: I have to know what to look for. All right, I'm good, but even I can be overwhelmed or outflanked. Alanna and Jon would tell you the same thing."

George put a hand on Numair's shoulder. "I'm sorry. I didn't mean you failed at your job. It's just been a long time since I've been sucker-punched. I don't like it." His face had taken on harsh new lines. "They'll crush us, between what's out there and those six hundred at our backs."

"And the army won't come before we're bruised at least," Numair said.

"Aye."

"How many warriors here?"

"Eighty—not countin' the Riders." George drew a deep breath and looked at Daine. "What can your friends do to help?"

She swallowed. "Don't ask me to make them fight," she pleaded. "They're not—this isn't *about* them. I can't ask them to fight and die for humans." Shivering, the girl remembered the marsh and the slaughtered birds. "Please say you understand."

George's silence drew out for a long moment and it was impossible to read what was in his face. At last he smiled and patted her arm. "I don't, entirely, but then I'm all too human. Will you ask them to watch, then? To let us know if more soldiers come, or if the ones out there start to move?"

She nodded, and whispered, "Thanks." Sending out her request, Daine settled to wait for her friends' reports from the woods. As she listened, guards and Riders began to return with the villagers. Never before had an evacuation gone so well. The livestock had been waiting for their owners to come out. There were no problems with catching animals, not even chickens. The trainees, at least, had a good idea of why this was so. The villagers did not, and fled to the castle as if their own animals had turned to ghosts.

Dawn. The first raiders came into sight, to find the village empty and the castle gates closed. The battlements were lined with warriors who did not look surprised in the least to see raiders outside their walls.

When the sun rose above the horizon, fog rolled over Pirate's Swoop.

A gentle hand was shaking her, and a wet tongue was bathing her face. Daine looked up and saw Onua, Kalasin, and Tahoi. "I'm sorry, I must've gone to sleep." She turned scarlet with embarrassment and tried to get up. Her knees buckled. "Goddess! How long have I been here?"

Onua caught her on one side, Kally on the other. "Since the middle of the night. The baron says we owe the warning to you and your friends."

"Thank my friends. I just passed the word on." She massaged the cramps from her legs. Kally gave her a roll stuffed with fruit and held a jug full of juice to go with it. Daine was still hungry when she finished. "What's going on now?" she asked, accepting a sausage roll from her young friend.

"We're in trouble. This"—Onua's wave took in the fog surrounding them—"isn't just fog. It carries dampening spells for the Gift—plenty of 'em. We're not sure how many sorcerers are out there holding it, but there have to be a lot of them. Whoever engineered this planned for everything."

Daine looked at the two humans. "That hurts you both, right? You're both Gifted."

Onua nodded. "Lucky for us, there's no need for magic just yet. Numair got word out to the palace and to the king before the fog came in."

Daine looked at the woman, wondering if the mage had found anyone nearby who could help. Reading her, Onua shook her head.

"I'd best put on clean clothes, then, and get my bow." She caught an angry call from below. "And let Cloud know I'm alive. She's upset with me."

"Can I go with her?" asked Kally.

Onua smiled. "Of course. Just make sure you *stay* with Daine. If you run into your brother, have him report to me."

Daine glanced around to see who was there, and saw the queen, Numair, and the baron, with trainees and guardsmen armed and keeping watch. "Where should *I* report to?"

"Here. Take your time. Nothing can happen as long as this mess hangs over us."

She nodded. "Let's go, Kally. I need to clean up."

Roald and Thom were waiting for Daine in her loft. She shooed them downstairs while she changed, combed her hair, got her weapons, and comforted the frightened bats. In the stable below she soothed the ponies, all of whom knew something bad was going on. She was uneasy, herself. She'd been fogged in before at the Swoop, but it wasn't the same. The mist felt dirty, and the hackles were up on the back of her neck. The two boys, both Gifted, were in worse condition than Onua and Kally, and clung to Daine's hands as she walked them back to the inner court.

On her trip down she hadn't looked at the new arrangements: now she did. Long tents were set up for healers. Water barrels were stacked everywhere. Temporary corrals held the village animals. Seeing them, Daine went to thank them, assure them they were safe, and reinforce the need for their good behavior. It was the first time anyone had explained that raider attacks were the reason why they were so often dragged up to the castle without warning. Understanding that, they were more than eager to help.

"Honestly, you'd think people would have *told* them before now and saved everyone trouble," Daine growled. "Speaking of people, where's their masters?"

"Some are on the wall," Thom said. Looking up, Daine saw villagers armed with bows, shields, and metal caps among the guards and Riders. "The rest are in the lower levels. We're dug into the rock. There's plenty of room down below."

She was startled. She'd never dreamed there might be more to the castle than what she saw. "How many more surprises does your da have up his sleeve?"

Thom grinned. "A *lot*."

Sarge waved to her from the wall. She waved back, hoping her face didn't reveal her thoughts. She had human friends here too—friends who might be hurt, or die. With Ma and Grandda gone, she'd thought she was free of that kind of pain, but she was less free than ever. She'd never love anyone as she had her family, but others had come to be important to her: Evin and Miri, who gave her acceptance; Onua, an elder sister; the Rider officers, respect for her judgment. Each of those people now was a potential wound.

Thinking grim thoughts, she climbed the outside stair to the deck, the children following her. I should've stayed wild, she told herself. I never should've got back up on my hind legs.

Never? another part of her asked. Never means not meeting sea lions and griffins. Never means not hearing whales sing. Never means not learning how to heal. She sighed.

On deck once more, she saw two guards and two trainees, Elnore and Padrach, on duty with bows strung and ready. The queen and Onua were armed as well. Buri, like Sarge, was elsewhere on the walls, keeping an eye on the other trainees. Baron George was talking quietly to one of the guards.

Thayet smiled at her and crooked a finger at her son and daughter. "Come talk to me," she ordered, and they obeyed. Thom went to stand with his father, and Daine sought out Numair.

"Are you all right?"

He looked tired and strained. His mouth was tight, as if he were afraid he might say too much if he opened it. He barely managed a smile for her. "I'm scared," he said quietly.

She looked up at him. I'm the only one who understands, she thought. If the Lioness were here, he'd've said it to her, but she's not and I am. There's magic in the air, lots of it, and everyone looks to him for a miracle. Right now he can't even tell if his magic is the right kind, and he's afraid.

She put her hand in his, and he squeezed it tight. "I hate to theorize without information, but I need a working plan," he told her softly. "As it is, I either hold the spells off the Swoop so the others can function, or I leave the dampeners on them and punch through myself, to fight with what *I* have. The problem is that as a warrior-mage my talents are limited, and I have no healing magic at all. If Alanna were here, we could work off each other, but—" His face tightened again.

"That's it, then," she said, trying to think aloud as he did. "They lured the Lioness off and put an army between her and us just for that."

He nodded.

"Which means they've been watchin' us all along." Daine and Numair both jumped when George spoke behind them. "They know we've the queen here, and the next two in line for the throne."

Daine and Numair looked at each other and chorused, "The Stormwings."

"*That's* why they were spying out the seacoast," Numair went on. "They were waiting for us to arrive and get settled. I'll bet they also made sure none of our army or navy was close enough to help." Something occurred to him, and his eyes lit. "Daine—your magic. How is it?"

She was surprised he even asked. "It's the same as ever. You told me, yourself, I couldn't turn it off."

"Wild magic," Numair breathed. "It's in everything. No matter how many dampeners they lay on us, *you'll* be able to function!"

Something tugged at the back of her eyes—something ugly and sour. "I can't send my friends to die," she warned, but already her attention had shifted. "Bows!" she yelled, getting hers off her back and putting an arrow to the string. "Bows! Stormwing in the air!"

George shoved Thom down between the wall and the floor of the deck, grabbed the prince and princess and did the same with them. Thayet and Onua had their weapons in hand. The trainees and guards were armed and ready. The baron had drawn his sword and dagger.

Numair swore so vividly that the children looked at him in awe and delight and added, "The wind's shifting. They don't need the fog anymore."

"The dampeners?" George asked hopefully.

The mage shook his head. "Still there. The fog laid them down. Now the spells will stick to all that the fog touched."

Within minutes the fog was gone, and the world around them was lit by a midmorning sun. Daine gasped at the scene that lay before them. A fleet lay in the cove: five long boats, or galleys, rowed by chained men belowdecks, and seven smaller vessels, all bristling with warriors and their arms. Behind them lay four barges, huge, flat-bottomed boats with no apparent way to move. Large wooden structures sat in the middle of each, things that were wood, rawhide, and rope knit together. Each barge carried a stock of round stone balls, and a complement of barrels. Around their rims, and around the weird structures, were huge bags of sand.

"Such a big siege for such a little castle," Thayet murmured. "Where could they have sailed from?"

"Copper Isles," George replied quietly. "They're Carthak's allies now."

"What are the big, flat ones?" Daine asked, searching the air for the Stormwing she had felt.

The queen raised a spyglass to her eye. "War barges—the terror of the Carthaki navy." She offered the glass so Daine could see clearly. "The things in the middle are catapults. Each barge is counterbalanced with magic and ballast so the catapults can hurl stone balls or liquid fire. They can pound the walls of a place like this to rubble in the space of a day."

"So this emperor has declared war?" Daine asked. She had found the Stormwing, high above. He stooped, dropping onto the deck of the largest of the galleys, laughing as humans scrambled away from him.

"No Carthaki flags," Onua said. "This isn't official."

Daine stared at her. "Surely that makes no difference. A flag's only a bit of cloth, after all."

"A war's not a war until an official declaration is made and the armies march under flags." Onua pursed her mouth cynically. "None of those men or our friends in the woods are wearing uniforms, either."

"And he can *do* that?" Daine asked, outraged. "It's not a war till this emperor fellow *says* it is?"

"Or until His Majesty does," Numair remarked.

Onua said, "We can't expect *any* help from our navy?"

"A week ago Scanran wolf-boats hit all along the north coast," George told them. "Most of the navy is up there, or on our part of the Inland Sea."

"How nice," Prince Roald muttered.

"Heads up, darlin's," George said. "I think we're about to hear terms." The Stormwing was taking flight again, an elegant white flag in one claw and something much smaller in the other.

"This is not good." Numair too had a spyglass. "See the red robes at the bow of each ship? And there are at least four yellow robes per barge?" He lowered his glass. "A scarlet robe from the university in Carthak means you have your mastery—the same level as the Mithran

black-and-gold robe. University yellow robes are adepts. They brought
the barges here, and their spells keep them afloat and working."

"What robe are you?" Daine asked, watching the Stormwing's approach.

"None," he replied. "Ever put one of those things on? They're *hot*."

"He's a black robe," Onua said, hands tight on her bow as she
watched the monster. "There are only seven of them in the world."

The Stormwing was a hundred feet away.

"Bows," Thayet said quietly. In the same movement she and all the
archers on the deck raised their weapons, sighting on the messenger.

He hovered in the air before them, smirking. "Now, is that nice?"

Daine clenched her teeth. This was the one who'd come between
her and her ma. This close, she could put an arrow clean through him.

The creature dropped a scroll onto the stone between Thayet and
George. The queen didn't blink; it was the baron who picked it up and
opened it. " 'To Queen Thayet of Tortall and Baron George Cooper of
Pirate's Swoop, from the Lord of the Free Corsairs, Mahil Eddace,
greetings. By virtue of superior numbers and armament, I claim the
castle, village, point, and waters of Pirate's Swoop for the League of
Free Corsairs. Should you prove obdurate—' "

"Obdurate?" Daine whispered without taking her eyes from her target.

"Stubborn," supplied Numair.

George continued to read, " '—I shall have no choice but to reduce
the castle, enslave the survivors, kill all beasts, and sow its fields with
salt. You have one chance only to avoid death, capture, or enslavement:
surrender to me the person and effects of Thayet of Tortall and her
children, Prince Roald and Princess Kalasin. You have what remains of
this day and tonight to reflect. If the three persons named are not given
over to us by such time as the dawn sun will clear the horizon, we will
commence bombardment by catapult. If you wish to signify acceptance
of these terms, you may do so by runnin' up three white pennants.' "
Calmly he rolled the message up again, and as calmly ripped it to pieces
and tossed them over the wall.

"Looks like Ozorne decided what advantage he needs against the
king," muttered Onua.

"There was a time when your folk were no one's errand boys," the
baron told the Stormwing. His voice was even and almost friendly.

"We don't mind helping out," the Stormwing told him, baring his
filthy teeth in a grin. "In a good cause, you understand." He looked at
Daine. "Hello, pink pig. Zhaneh Bitterclaws will be here to see you

soon." He nodded at Onua. "*Both* of you." Turning back to George and Thayet, he said, "Well? Your answer?"

The baron spat on the stone near his feet. "Get out, before I let them make you into a pin cushion."

The Stormwing's giggle was high and grating. "Oh, good. We *hoped* you'd say that." He pumped his wings, pulling away from them fast.

A hunter's screech split the air, and Daine's osprey friend shot past the humans. He tangled his feet in the monster's hair and hung on, pecking for the monster's eyes. The Stormwing shrieked in fury and tried to dislodge the bird from his head, but lacked the arms with which to do it.

"Daine, call him off," Numair said, his voice suddenly tight.

"I didn't call him on—"

"*Do* it!" her friend yelled. Before them gold fire was stretching above the galleys to form a great square, anchored by the red robes below.

"Come back," Daine yelled, putting her will behind it. "It's not worth it, come back!" Something was pounding through the air, making her ears hurt.

The osprey broke off the attack and returned. Onua grabbed the children and hustled them off the deck.

I almost had his eyes, the bird complained. Just one more wing-beat—

The gold fire in the square exploded, knocking everyone down. Like a nightmare, a horde of Stormwings blasted through, led by Zhaneh Bitterclaws. They filled the air with a degree of stench and evil that had not been felt in the world in four centuries. To that they added pure fear in a weight that crushed the humans before them. Something—something huge and red in color—almost seemed to shove the gigantic flock through the gate, but it vanished. It had only been an impression; Daine was too busy trying to breathe with a full pack of terror on her mind to think about it for more than a second.

She straightened: an act of will that took all the courage she had. At the palace she'd had a taste of what a flock of the monsters could be like, but it was nothing like this. She brought up her longbow. At the edge of her vision she saw Numair, then the baron, struggle to their feet. She smiled, blinked the sweat from her eyes, and loosed her arrow.

The messenger had chosen to attack with the flock. As she suspected, her arrow went clean through him. Before he had struck the rocks below she had another arrow on the string and loosed. It flew in a volley as the other humans released their arrows.

Battle raged. Archers, Daine included, fired bolt after bolt, making sure of the target before they loosed. Numair made a hard decision fast: sitting against the wall, where he'd trip no one up, he lifted the dampener spells. The people with lesser Gifts, including those who knew fire- and war-spells, got to work. Onua quickly drew a protective circle around the mage to hide him from the Stormwings.

Daine fought two wars. Her animal friends wanted to rescue her, but she refused to let them. She soon learned that keeping her will on so many species, in the woods, the castle, and the air, was impossible. Pain shot through her head: twice she lost control of the gulls and ospreys. With triumphant screams the birds leaped into the air to harry the Stormwings. With claws and beaks they attacked, trying to drive the monsters onto the rocks or into each other.

Tears rolled down Daine's cheeks. Mechanically she fired as birds fought and died, cut by steel wings or torn to pieces by steel claws and teeth. There was no chance that her power to heal would be pulled from her in this battle as it had been in the marsh: a wound here was death on the rocks below.

When the Stormwings attacked, so did the land raiders, reinforced by the fleet once the fog lifted. For the rest of the morning and into the long afternoon they tried to bring rams and ladders up to the castle walls, and were driven back.

Eventually the Stormwings lost interest in the battle and went to feast on the enemy dead outside the walls. They had what they wanted, no matter who won. They left the air over the deck first, not wanting to go on defending themselves against the archers and the birds.

When the deck had been quiet for a while, George ordered Daine to rest. She found some shade close to Numair and sat, leaning her throbbing head on her updrawn knees. No! she told the animals, who wanted to fight. No, no, *no!* With her last refusal she tightened her grip, until they gave in.

"Look at you." While she'd battled her friends, Miri had come to the deck with Kalasin and one of the maids. All three carried laden trays and wineskins. The fisher-girl came to Daine, frowning. "Your skin's a nice lobster red. You landlubbers don't think about reflected glare—" She rubbed a cool salve into Daine's hot face and arms. "Kally, where's the tonic?"

The princess filled a tankard from her wineskin and handed it over.

"Drink, or you'll be sick." Miri put the tankard to Daine's lips. She took a gulp and choked—it was tomato juice laden with salt and other things. "Drink it all."

"Goddess, that's nasty!" she croaked. She had the Smith-god's own headache. Her hands throbbed, and her fingers refused to close. The muscles of both arms were screaming. She had never shot so much in her life.

"Nasty it may be, but it'll keep you from collapsing on us. Have some more. Maude brewed it up special for you. Only think how her feelings would be hurt if you refused it."

She sat up, wincing as her head pounded. Maude?—the old woman in charge of the nursery. "That's right—she's a healer, isn't she?" From her cradle Daine had been taught to do as a healer said. She drew a deep breath and drank what was in the tankard as fast as possible. For a moment her stomach surged and her head screamed; then most of the pain and sickness were gone. "Goddess bless all healers," Daine whispered. Even her hands had improved a little.

She sat up, and the maid gave her a bowl of stew and a roll. Daine took them and began to eat as Miri and the servant looked at Numair. "Should you even be out here?" she asked Kally.

"Onua put a protective circle around this place," Miri said over her shoulder.

Daine smiled at Kally, then looked at Miri. "How's it going?"

"Not bad." That came from Numair. He sat with his head tilted back against the wall, his eyes closed, his face pouring sweat. Pillows had been put around his sides to make him comfortable. Someone—a redheaded six-year-old, Daine suspected—had tucked his prize stuffed bear under one of the mage's big hands. "They can't breach the walls—can't even get near them. They're having a *horrible* time with the archers. We're holding our own."

"Can you drink or eat?" Kally asked. "Maude says you should if it won't distract you from the spells."

He nodded. The girl fetched a cup of water from a nearby barrel and held it to his lips. He drank without opening his eyes. "How are you doing, Your Highness?"

"Please don't call me that." The girl's voice cracked. "It's 'cause of me being a princess that all this is happening. It's my fault and I hate it!"

Daine rolled to her knees and went to the child. "Here, now—stop that," she said, patting Kally's shoulder. The girl turned and buried her head in Daine's shirt. She was crying, and fighting hard to keep from making any sound. She's only eight, Daine thought sadly. "You got it all wrong, sweetling. Those men would do this no matter who they're after. They could have asked for Numair, here, who's in trouble in that Carthak place, or Sarge, that's a runaway slave. It isn't 'cause of you

or Roald or anybody. You're just the excuse. If you must blame somebody, blame them Carthaks."

"Carthakis," Numair corrected. He was smiling a little. "Daine's
right, Kalasin. The person who commits an action is the one responsible
for it, not the people he commits the action upon."

"But they *said* it was 'cause of Mama and Roald and me." Kally
blew her nose and wiped her face.

"So they would." Daine burned with fury. The Riders, the guards—
even she had put herself in spots where a fight might sometimes be the
only answer. They all knew the risks. But to twist a little girl's mind
so she blamed herself for the fight—that was horrible. "Evil people say
evil things to make good people cry and doubt. Don't let them get that
hold on you. It's because they're too cheap to buy food. They druther
steal it if they can. That's *really* what it's about."

"Kalasin?" Maude was at the stair, calling. "I need you below.
There's healing to be done."

Kally sniffed and wiped her face again. "Coming."

Daine watched her go. "But she's only a child."

"That child is a strong, natural healer." Numair hadn't once opened
his eyes. "She's partly untrained, still, but Maude can talk her through
whatever has to be done. How are you managing?"

Daine looked at him warily. "What d'you mean?"

"I mean your friends out there must be dying to go after the raiders,
and I definitely recall you saying you won't let them fight. The birds
got away from you this morning, didn't they?"

Daine clenched her fists and immediately regretted it. "I'm all
right."

"Liar." He said it almost with amusement. "Is it a strain?"

The air was singing to her. "What?" She got to her feet. Where was
it coming from? "Numair, do you hear it?"

"Hear what?"

It was like the griffins, only different, a singing coming from the
north, low and close. It filled her eyes and ears and beat against the sore
palms of her hands.

Onua was with George and Captain Josua, trying to talk Thayet into
going below, when she felt her circle of protection on the deck evaporate. "Down!" She pushed the queen to the floor. George and Josua had
their swords out as the source of the music came thundering up from
below to surge over their heads. Numair was on his feet instantly, his
watch over the castle shattered.

The dragon shrieked its fury and broke away, to head out to sea;
she turned and came back. Everyone was on the floor but Daine. She

stood on the wall, scant inches between her toes and empty air, awed by the glory before her. Scarlet wings and scales glittered like rubies along that long and graceful form. The wings, fashioned like a bat's, were huge, delicate structures of deep red, lit from within by silver bones. As the dragon passed inches over her head, almost knocking her onto the deck, she could see orange and yellow scales decorating the great creature's belly. Like the Stormwings, her claws and teeth were silver, but not the hard silver of metal.

Her song almost deafened the girl. She struggled to force the notes into a form she could understand, until she heard:—*Kidnappers! Filthy kidnappers! Rend them, take the raven-haired one to a cage on the ships!*—

Daine shook her aching head. What was she hearing?

The dragon came in low and almost seized Thayet before having to reverse her flight.—*Bring me here? You will send me home with your human tricks!*—

The girl closed her eyes. What tricks? she shouted with her magic, as loudly as she could. Tahoi yelped. Below the horses screamed, their delicate ears in pain.

The dragon came in again and yanked the sword from Josua's fist. The man was flung to the stone, where he lay stunned.

"Stop!" Daine yelled. "Stop! What kidnappers? What lies?"

The dragon was coming again.—*Send me home! I demand it!*—

Numair threw fire at her, fire that settled on her like a cloak and blew away. The long head twisted around to focus on him.—*Human mage, you will pay for stealing me!*—

Daine threw herself at Numair and knocked him down. The long shadow fell over them, and stayed. The stone beneath them quivered. Somewhere distant a number of people screamed.

The deck was sixty feet across. The dragon had taken twenty of those feet for her person, forefeet to hind legs, and cluttered a good twenty feet more with her tail and wings. Everyone but Daine and Numair, between her forepaws, was pressed to the wall or had made it to the stairs.

Daine jumped to her feet and raised her hands. I *think* I have the knack of it now, she thought, or please Goddess I *hope* I do. . . . Putting her hands on that scarlet breast, she called,—*Listen, wing-sister!*—

Information flooded into her mind as the dragon let out an ear-rending screech. Daine's nose began to bleed; the intensity of her contact with the dragon's mind had overloaded her body's limits.

—*Who speaks?*—

Daine drew a breath, forcing her heart and lungs to slow down.—*Me.*—

—*Joking.*—Disbelief was loud in the dragon's mind and in hers.

—*No joke,*—Daine said.—*What did they tell you, the red robes on the ships?*—

Why did she feel as if she were healing something? A quick look inside showed her copper fire streaming through her hands, being pulled out of her and into the dragon. When she tugged, she realized she couldn't yank away. Her palms were locked against the dragon's scales.

The dragon was hesitant now.—*They say—they say, raven-haired one and her kits stole me from home, brought me here to destroy boats.*—

—*Can't you smell a lie?*—Daine asked. She was getting a sense of the mind behind the huge, catlike eyes. This dragon was not much older than a human of Miri's age, say, and very frightened: panic-stricken, in fact.

—*Only smell on red robes was Eaters.*—The Stormwings were vivid in the dragon's mind.

—*They brought you, the robes. They brought you with the Eaters.*—

—*Do not understand . . .*—The dragon was confused and scared. She was quivering under Daine's hands.—*Tired. Sick. Little one . . .*—

Daine felt the dragon's hide ripple. It was like a convulsion—or a contraction! Ma's daughter realized.

—*You're having a baby*!—she cried.

Suddenly the dragon's mind filled with a hot excitement that shattered Daine's magical hearing. Her hands dropped free of the dragon, and she clapped them to her ears.

The dragon screeched and launched herself into the air. Before Daine realized she was leaving, she had gone, flying north along the cliffs. Her image blurred, then vanished.

She can do magic, the girl realized with awe.

Numair got to his feet and jerked her into his arms. "You little idiot," he whispered, hugging her so tightly she squeaked.

"She was in labor and on her way home," Daine told him, feeling mashed. "They opened the gate nearby, and it pulled her in. I think it killed her baby. Maybe it would've killed her—but it was just what you said, the wild magic was just sucked right out of me, so I think she's healing. And she's been educated, Numair, from books! Her mind—it's all organized, like you've been after *me* to do—"

Around them the others were coming forward. In Josua's and the guards' eyes she saw an emotion that looked like fear.

Someone ran up to the deck—Farant. "Master Numair? The healers are asking if something's wrong. If you don't shield them now, we'll lose Sarge."

"Oh no," Thayet whispered.

Numair released Daine and sat against the wall once more. His eyes closed, and the quality of air around him changed.

Daine decided she might like to sit down for a while herself. Her legs folded before she told them to, and she never remembered hitting the ground.

# TEN

# LISTENING FAR ENOUGH

Someone had carried her below and put her on a cot in what she realized was the baron's study. Tahoi lay nearby, worried; a couple of the bats clung discreetly to the hangings. The osprey—missing an eye, but miraculously alive—sat on the perch, letting Onua feed him raw fish. Daine sat up. Her head pounded worse than ever, and she felt her stomach heave. "I think I'm going to be sick," she whispered.

Onua got a basin to her just in time. "What's the matter?" she asked when Daine finished vomiting. "Was it the dragon?"

"No," she croaked. "How long've I been out?"

"Not too long. It's just after sunset."

Looking at her shirt, Daine saw it was a gory mess. "What happened?"

"You had a nosebleed. What's wrong with your head? Can you tell?" Onua smoothed her hair. "It's important. *You're* important."

They knew she was awake and their struggle to get free increased. She didn't even know she'd stopped answering the K'mir until coolness entered her veins, driving back the hot fire of the headache. She opened her eyes. Kally held one of her hands, Thom another. The coolness had been theirs.

"Hello," she said. Her voice sounded like a rusty gate. "Thank you."

"You're wearing yourself out." Maude stood behind the children, looking stern. "You have to let some spells go. I know your magic is different, but your body's just like anybody else's. You're doing too much. Release some of your spells, or we can't answer for the consequences."

Daine looked at Onua as the old woman steered Kally and Thom out. "Easy for her to say," she muttered when the door was safely closed.

Onua brought over a tray of food and put it on the table beside her cot. "Eat. What magic do you have going, anyway?"

Hotcakes, drenched in butter and syrup, fruit juice, hot cocoa. The sugar cleared her head as she ate. "I can't let them fight," she said, her mouth full.

"Let who fight?" Onua scratched Tahoi's ears, and patiently allowed the bats to settle on her shoulders as they listened to Daine.

There was cold water, to cut the sweetness. She drank half a tankard in a gulp. "Them." She waved her fork in the direction of the woods outside the castle. "The wild creatures—they won't let me be. They want to fight the raiders—they've been wanting to all day."

Onua moved her fingers to Tahoi's spine, and the great dog sighed. "I don't understand. Is it so bad if they fight? It's their home too."

Daine glared at her. "They'll get *killed*! They're animals. It's not for them to get tangled in human stupidness!"

"You won't like any of that," Onua told the bat that sniffed the tray. To the girl she said, "It seems to me we tangle them in our stupidity all the time. At least if you tell them *how* to fight, they have a chance."

Daine got up and paced. "You don't understand! Once I meet them or talk to them, I *know* them. They're my friends; they're part of me. When they get hurt and die, it hurts *me*." She pounded her chest to make her point.

"You think it doesn't hurt me, when one of my horses dies?"

Daine blushed, embarrassed. "I forgot. I'm sorry."

The older woman sighed. "We share this world, Daine. We can't hold apart from each other—humans and animals are meant to be partners. Aren't we, Tahoi?" The dog wagged his tail. "He knows. He saved my life, when my husband left me to die. I've saved his life since. He can't cook or sing, and I can't chase rabbits, but we're partners all the same. The Riders' ponies are full partners with their master. They have to be, and that's what I train them to be, so everyone has a better chance of surviving.

"The Swoop's animals are in the same trap we are. Men broke into their homes, killed their families, threatened you—and you won't let them *do* anything for fear *you*'ll be hurt. That's selfish. How would you like it if I took your bow and said I cared too much about you to let you fight?"

Daine winced. "I see your point."

"You've made your friends helpless, just like bandits made you helpless when they killed your family. Of course the animals fight you."

Onua sighed. "We have no choice in being hunted—not animals, not humans. That's how the world is. The choice we *do* have is to take it— or fight. Why don't you show them how not to get killed, and let *them* decide?" She studied her nails and added, "I'll be honest with you. We need all the help we can get."

Daine went to the window, fingering her badger's claw. I know what she means, she realized. They'll start with the catapults in the morning and smash our walls. Then they'll come take Thayet and the children if they're alive. And the rest—Thom, the twins, Gimpy and Cloud and Mangle . . .

There's got to be something my friends can do to help.

Suddenly she remembered a talk she'd heard Buri give the trainees. "If your numbers are small—a Rider Group, say—it's idiotic to attack face-on when the enemy has superior numbers. *But*, enemies are only men, and men scare easy. Use booby traps: snares, pits covered with branches, pebbles strewn across the road to cripple them and their mounts. Foul their water sources. Sneak into camp and ruin their food, if you can. Keep up a racket all night so nobody gets any rest, and you've got the sentries shooting at ghosts. Do they buy or steal food from the locals? Make sure the food they get their mitts on is moldy, stale, or wet.

"An enemy that's tired, ill fed, and scared is an enemy who's half beat."

We could do that, Daine thought now. If the soldiers here on land are crippled, Thayet and everybody else might be able to fight their way through and escape before the ships get their warriors to the castle.

Closing her eyes, she opened her mind to the extent of her range. The countless animals in the woods around Pirate's Swoop began to clamor. They wanted her to release them. They wanted to tear, and gnaw, and leap—

*Quiet!* she yelled.

They obeyed.

She reached first for minks, weasels, and martens—clever, small animals with sharp claws and teeth. They were quick to grasp the images of leather wrappings, rope, and bowstrings. They must not be seen, she said over and over, with all her will behind it; they mustn't be caught. She pressed the image of bows, knives, and swords into their minds, until they knew to run or hide if they saw a human with a weapon in his hand.

Bears, wild boars, and woodchucks went after supplies, once she'd made them promise to run at any signs of human attack. She left them pulling apart sacks and boxes of grain, cheese, salted meat, and vegetables. Shrews and voles offered to take care of the tea and coffee supplies. If there was an edible or drinkable scrap in the camp by morning, she would be surprised.

Foxes she asked to free the picketed horses and mules. Once she had explained things, the strangers' mounts were happy to leave their masters and run for the woods. Some of the enemy's mules, once they were freed, came back to give water barrels a kick or a roll downhill. Owls and bats volunteered to keep the guards busy. Sentry after sentry had the unpleasant experience of an owl dropping on him silently from above, or of a bat flying directly into his face. Raccoons walked away with arrows and knives. Wolves howled on the fringes of the camp, to be answered by wildcats of all sizes.

*Gods go with all of you,* she thought sadly, and broke off the contact.

The room was empty. Surprisingly, it hadn't taken long to muster her army at all: the candle that marked the time had burned down one hour's mark and half of another. *I guess it's easier to get them to do what they want than it is keeping them from doing it,* she thought.

*Please Goddess, don't let my friends be hurt.*

She put on the clean clothes that lay on the cot, and let herself out.

Numair was right down the hall, in a room filled with books. The skin around his face was slack and gray; his nose thrust out like the prow of a sinking ship. His crisp mane was matted with sweat, his face drenched with it. Checking the water jug on the table beside him, she saw it was empty. She went back and brought her own water to him. This time, when she came in, his eyes were open. They were dull and tired.

"Thanks," he whispered as she poured water for him. His hands shook when she gave him the tankard.

"Wait." She supported his head and shoulders, steadying his grip on the tankard with her free hand. "You're still keeping those dampeners off?"

He nodded as he drank, and gasped when he was done.

It hurt to talk casually when he looked half-dead. *You won't help him if you turn into a baby,* she told herself sternly. "Can I get you some food?"

"I'll just throw up." He smiled. "How do you like your first siege?"

"That's very funny," she told him sourly. "I'm so glad you've hung on to your sense of humor. Only think how scared I'd be if you hadn't."

He closed his eyes and smiled. "That's my magelet."

"Can't you let up awhile?"

He shook his head. "The healers. They're still going. Daine—this afternoon. You said the dragon can *think*? It's educated?"

"She. *She's* educated. Even the griffins are like my animals, with all that's in their heads jumbled together higgledy-piggledy. Not her. She's read things in scrolls—I saw them in her mind."

"Amazing," he whispered. "I'd heard stories—just never believed them."

"What stories?"

"They're mages. Well, we saw that. She came right up on us. Even you didn't hear her until she was close. And she vanished. Do you hear her now?"

Daine listened, hard. "No, sir. But like you said—I didn't hear her until the last." She pulled off his boots and put a cushion under his feet. More cushions went behind his head. She noticed that he still clung to the toy Thom had put in his hand. "There's got to be something else I can try. I let the land animals go. They'll do some damage. There's not enough creatures on the ships to work with, though. It's mostly rats out there. I can't work with rats. I've tried, but they don't even want to listen to me."

"Whales? Ask them to swim up under the barges—capsize them. The catapults are the biggest danger. Then the red robes on the galleys."

She thought it over. "If whales're out there, I can't hear 'em. They're not in range." She chewed on a thumbnail until he knocked her hand away. "I'm fair tired too. The dragon sucked me almost dry." This time she didn't even get the thumbnail to her mouth before he grabbed her wrist. "Pity I can't reach the sea. If there's a cold spot in the cellars—"

"Find George. He'll figure out a way to get you to the water."

She saw another danger. "What if the mages on the ships catch me?"

"It's a risk, but you stand a better chance than anyone with the Gift. Only a very few can detect wild magic. It's a skill mages in Carthak are discouraged from acquiring. Remember, *they* think it's old wives' tales. If someone out there *could* sense it, he'd have a difficult time convincing the others. If you're detected, you can escape among the seals and sea lions." He sighed. "I know it's dangerous, and I hate to drive you this way, but—we need a miracle. I'm hoping you can come up with one."

She got up. "Wish me luck." She hesitated, then kissed his cheek.

He gave her a feeble hug. "Luck, magelet."

Daine looked down the length of rock at the castle's rear. George and Evin stood by with ropes and a sling. "You sent folk down this way before?"

"It's a better ride than it looks," the baron assured her. "They won't see you from the water, because you're goin' down a rock chimney. When you return, just get in the sling and give the rope three big tugs"—he showed her what he meant—"and three little tugs. I'll have someone I trust on watch here for you. Got it?"

She nodded and fitted herself into the rope sling between the two men. "Good thing I grew up in the mountains and I'm not afraid of heights," she said with false cheerfulness, easing herself out over the edge of the wall. "I told you this is a long shot, didn't I?"

"Several times," the baron assured her. "Don't worry, I'm expert in long shots, youngling. Been takin' them all my life."

"What will you do for light?" asked Evin.

She looked at him in surprise. "I don't need any. There's the moon, after all. And I see well in the dark."

George nodded. "Try to be topside when the fun starts in the mornin'."

She smiled up at him. "Wouldn't miss it for the world."

The trip down the rock chimney seemed over almost before it started. At the bottom she found herself on the beach. Here she climbed out of the sling, pulled off her boots, and rolled up her breeches. At a brisk walk, she followed a strip of beach north, along the cliff face. She needed a place where she could anchor herself among the rocks. It wasn't her intention to be washed out to sea.

Finally she reached a spot that looked good. The cliffs were at her back. To the north lay more rock. The castle bluff shielded her from all sight of the enemy fleet, riding at anchor in the mouth of the Swoop's cove.

Gripping her badger's claw for luck, she wedged herself between two boulders and lowered herself into the ocean. She had to bite a lip to keep from shrieking at the cold wetness. Within seconds she was numb to the waist. For good measure she immersed her hands and sent her magic out.

The salt water made her feel as if the dragon had never drained her magic. Her mind raced past tumbles of rocks and kelp, past quite a few sunken ships. So *that's* why this is Pirate's Swoop, she thought. They swooped out from the cove.

She found the seals first and called a greeting. They wanted to play, but she explained she hadn't the time just now. On she went, beyond her normal range and into deep water.

Whale songs rose all around her to fill the sea with their magic. She had found a pod of nearly forty blue whales. Three quarters of them were adults, each at least eighty feet long and weighing over one hundred and forty tons. Daine faltered, awed by their magnificence, then called,—*Hello!*—

In a cave high over Daine's head, the dragon stopped nuzzling her little one. It was the mage-child, the one who had restored her baby to life when she had thought it dead in her body. The dragon couldn't mistake that atrocious accent.

Whales came into Daine's mind, huge shadows staring at a girl-shadow. One—a hundred feet if he's an inch, Daine thought, a bit frightened—moved ahead of the others with grace and majesty.

—*Who calls!*—

This was nothing like talking with land animals, seals, or fish. Whales seemed wise, in their own fashion, and words only partly conveyed the things they said. To their question she gave them what she was, or how she saw herself, and image embroidered with feeling and ideas.

They were amused.—*Why do you seek us out, tiny human calf?*—

With images and ideas she explained the siege, the Carthakis, the release of the Stormwings and the dragon.—*They want to take our freedom and they're hurting my friends. I came to ask your help. If four or five of you came up under the barges and overset them, and maybe one or two of the large boats, we'd have a chance. I know it's a big favor to ask. I can't say they won't hurt you—maybe they can. But you're my best hope, you see.*—

The chief whale heard her out politely. His answer, when it came, blasted into her mind and ears.—*No.*—

She barely remembered that she was out in the open in time to choke back a scream. She bit deep into her own wrist to smother it.

—*You don't understand!*—How could she explain so they would care? She gave them Onua's wry humor, Thayet's leadership, Miri's love of the sea, George's intelligence, Numair's curiosity.—*The enemy kills humans and animals who never hurt* anyone. *They brought monsters here.* (She gave them spidrens as well as Stormwings—it never occurred to her to add the griffins or the dragon.) *We have calves there— little ones who depend on us to keep them safe.* (Roald, Kally, and Thom were as fresh in her mind as if they stood with her. She offered them to these distant, cold judges.) *You wouldn't let your calves die. Grown humans may hunt you, but not these. Help me save them!—*

The dragon looked at her newborn. Knowing the kit was dead in her belly had sent her in a rage to attack the humans. She had blamed them for stealing her from home at the start of her labor, had blamed them for the magic voyage that had killed the life in her. Her kit, her first, had been dead—until this girl-child had put her hands on her breast. The pangs had begun again—her kit had been born. Dragons do not give birth lightly, do not face the loss of young lightly.

*—You do not understand, mortal calf,—*said the whale leader.

*—Explain it to me, please?—*She struggled to be polite. There had to be a way she could talk them around.

*—We will not fight or kill. Not for your cause—not for any cause. Violence against higher life-forms is disgusting. For centuries the People have vowed that the taking of a higher life is an abomination.—*

*—But Miri told me, you've attacked ships that kill your kind. . . . —*

*—No.—*Once again the force of the reply hurt.

*—There have been accidents. There are times when one will go insane. Always, when the one who has fought understands what took place, that one starves himself, herself to death, to pay for the sin. We will not fight. We will not kill.—*

She had never heard such absolute refusal. It sounded in the marrow of her bones and through her nerve endings. Under its pressure her head began to pound again.—*We'll die, then. Their machines will break our walls—they'll have us out as an octopus has a hermit crab out of its shell. My friends, in the air, on the land—they'll have died for nothing.—*

*—You should not have asked them to fight.—*

*—I didn't ask them! They wanted to—because they're my friends!—*

*—There is no good reason to fight. There is no good reason to kill.—*The whales' voices were growing faint.

*—Where are you going?—*Tears rolled down her cheeks. They were her last chance, and they wouldn't even listen.

*—If ships are here, there is a chance of an accident. We cannot accept that risk. We go, far from this place where you make a killing-ground.—*

*—I didn't make it!—*she yelled, furious.—*They came to me!—*

The whales were gone. The only sound in her mind and ears was the lapping of waves. It would happen again, just like at home. The queen would die before she'd let Carthakis take her or her children.

Numair would burn out. The raiders would win. If she'd learned her lessons better, if she'd explained things at the palace instead of waiting till the badger came to her at the beach . . . She put her face in her hands and sobbed.

*If you* listen *hard and long, you can hear any of us, call any of us, that you want*. It sounded now, so clearly that she looked up, trying to find the badger. He was nowhere to be seen.

*If you* listen *hard and long, you can hear any of us, call any of us, that you want*. That's what he had told her. Maybe she could catch up to the whales, convince them. Maybe she could bring them under her will. Surely that was like calling anyone she wanted to, wasn't it?

It's wrong to force the whales to fight, a small voice in her mind argued. Not when they hate it so.

I won't let my people die, she told the voice. I *can't*.

She took a deep breath, and another. She let go of herself, opening her mind entirely to wild magic. Grabbing her up, the copper fire took her west.

She rolled along the ocean's bottom like a wave, hearing each click and gurgle the sea creatures made. Her awareness spread in a half circle, hearing the fleet, finding the departing whales. She would have talked to them, but the copper fire wrapped tighter around her mind and kept moving. Deeper and deeper the ocean floor sank. With dreamy surprise she slid around a patch of islands—where had they come from?

She dropped into ice water that was black as ink in her mind. In the west, past the islands, he lay—ship killer, man-eater, old as time. The mages had missed him when they sealed the Divine Realms, centuries ago. He had lain on the bottom, the ultimate predator, dining on whales and human ships. His immense tentacles, each a mile long, stirred with interest.

The kraken had never seen a little fish like her.

Daine stared at him, aghast. His was the body of an octopus with far too many arms, his mantle a mile and a half across.

—*I will kill any fleet you like, little fish.*—His voice was filled with soft, deadly good humor.—*You were talking to the whales. Pacifists, all of them—enough to make me vomit. Just show me where those nasty raiders are. I can guarantee they won't trouble you for long.*—

—*You'd never make it on time*,—she said, to cover her real thought: I could never get rid of him!

—*Leave that to me. Come, my dear—this is no time to be squeamish.*—

Deals with demons, she thought nervously. It's a deal with a demon. . . . Wait—what about Numair? Once he returns to full strength, he'll be a match for this monster. I hope he will, anyway, because this kraken is the only hope I have left.

Please Goddess and Horse Lords, let this be a good choice!

Daine thrust what she knew of the fleet at the giant thing, and fled as his laugh echoed all around her. She flashed through the water faster than she would have believed possible. It was hard to say what she was doing: running from the kraken or racing to get to the Swoop before sunrise.

It was too late. When she opened her eyes, the incoming tide was up to her chin, and the sky overhead was pink.

She struggled, fighting to get her tightly wedged body out from between the rocks. Everything was numb; her hands couldn't get a purchase anywhere. How can I reach the castle, let alone the deck? she wondered, panting as she tried to free herself. And what can I tell them, anyway? If those islands are what I *think* they are, they're the Copper Isles, four days' sail out. *If* I didn't dream that whatsits, that kraken, there won't be anything here in four days for him to eat—

Curved silver bars closed around her middle, gently. She looked up into the dragon's catlike eyes.

—*I will take you to your friends, little mage.*—

The dragon wrapped her other forepaw around the one that gripped Daine. The girl held on to those silver claws, running her hands over them in awe. There was a tremendous jolt, and they were airborne. She screamed in delight to see the earth fall away below them, forgetting briefly all she had been through, and all that was coming, in the joy of flight. Behind her she could feel the surge of the dragon's wings as they soared higher and higher. To their left she saw the enemy, and the Stormwing that dropped to Mahil Eddace's ship. The red robes in the galleys and transports sat or lay at the prows of their ships, many clutching their heads in their hands. Slaves, bare but for a loincloth and a collar, ministered to the red robes.

Her appearance—the dragon's appearance—had dramatic results. Men pointed and screamed; archers scrambled for their weapons. One red robe got up and did something that involved waving hands. It resulted in a yellowish cloud that boiled their way.

—*Amateurs,*—the dragon said coldly. When the cloud reached them, she blew on it, and it vanished. She banked gracefully, heading for the Swoop. Tiny figures on the deck pointed at them, while any of the archers who might be in range had their bows up. Someone on the deck recognized Daine and called an order. Slowly the weapons came down.

She peered at one of the dragon's toes, examining the bone structure and the violet scales. (She picked up several tiny cuts on the scale edges, which were razor sharp.) "Excuse me—weren't you red yesterday?"

—*I was angry. We may change color, to suit our wills—or to reflect strong emotion.*—The great creature hesitated, then went on,—*I heard you speak to the whales.*—

She swiveled to face her bearer. "You did? But these days nobody else hears when I'm talking to just one species."

—*That may be so, among* mortal *creatures.*—(It occurred to Daine her rescuer was a snob.)—*We are mages of the air.*—Sounding anxious, she added,—*Could you send me home? I do not understand how I came to be here, and I wish to be with my family.*—

"We don't know how," Daine replied sadly as they descended. "We're trying to learn, though. If you stay with us, we'll find a way to send you home—if we survive, that is."

The dragon touched down, more gracefully than she had the day before, and released Daine. Onua, Roald, Kally, and Thom ran to hold her up as the great creature rose into the air and flew back along the cliff. Once more she vanished in midair.

"Any luck?" the baron asked as he and Thayet came over, their faces worn and exhausted. Daine looked around and saw Numair, seated on the wall. He waved a shaky hand.

"No," she told her audience quietly. "The whales said no." She couldn't even bring herself to look at Numair again. "There—there might be something, but—I don't know. I don't think it can be here in time. I'm sorry."

The queen patted her arm. "You tried. You've done so much already. I don't think the men from the camp outside the walls are fit to go into battle today, thanks to your friends."

"The dragon?" George asked Daine.

"I don't know. She's not very strong. I could try and call her back—"

"Well, well. All the little pigs tidy in one pen." Zhaneh Bitterclaws hovered overhead, just out of bow-shot for the deck's guards. The Stormwing queen's looks had not improved: her eye socket continued to ooze. Whatever other magic they've got, Daine thought to herself, healing isn't part of it.

Daine glanced around for her own bow and quiver: they were in Numair's lap. Thom sidled away from their group, backing up toward the mage with his hands open behind him. "What's the answer, mortals? Will you surrender the three we want?"

"We surrender nothing to you and your *handlers*," Thayet spat.

"Tell them they've just bought my husband's eternal enmity—*and* mine."

"You won't live long enough to care about enmity!" Bitterclaws snarled.

Something hard and something leathery pressed against Daine's cold fingers. Thom had brought her bow, already strung, and her quiver. The girl's numb muscles couldn't respond fast enough. The Stormwing laughed and climbed away when she tried to get her bow into a firing position. Daine swore, flexing her hands to get them limber again.

"Children, get below!" Thayet snapped. They wavered, and the queen roared, *"Now!"* They obeyed at a run.

The girl looked seaward to find what had made the woman raise her voice so uncharacteristically. In the night, the four barges had been moved to the front, ahead of the ships, and each catapult was assembled and loaded with a stone ball. Two of them fired; the balls struck the cliff face below the tower with an earsplitting boom. The stone beneath their feet shook.

The two remaining barges shifted. Must be the sorcerers that move them, Daine thought, since there were no oars and no sails. Their catapults let fly. The first stone ball smashed into one of the other towers; the second hit the curtain wall. Already men were reloading the first two catapults.

The dragon, her scales flaming gold, dropped on them from what had looked like empty sky. She immediately put flight to the stories that her kind spat flame from their mouths. The fire came from her forepaws, and devoured the sails on Eddace's flagship. Banking hard, she cut directly across the face of one of the catapults to seize the stone ball loaded in it. Her flight sagged from the weight of the stone, but only momentarily. She dropped it on the next barge. The flat boat immediately listed to the side.

Numair propped himself on Daine's shoulder. "Wasn't she red yesterday?"

"They change color. Numair, she's not big enough."

"Maybe she's big enough to stop them. And it's justice, my magelet. They're the ones who brought her here in the first place."

Archers shot at the dragon uselessly. The red robes tried their magic, but like Numair's it washed off her. She hurled fire at a transport, burning it entirely, before heading back to the catapults.

Stormwings broke out of the woods on land and streaked to defend the ships. Daine watched, sobbing, as their claws cut deep into the dragon's sides. "Can't you help?" she demanded, forgetting the state he was in.

"I wish I could. Call her back this way, if you can. Our archers can swat the Stormwings away from her."

Daine called, hard. The dragon ignored her to fall on the red robe at the prow of Eddace's vessel. With him in her grip, she rose into the air and dropped him among a knot of Stormwings.

They exploded. Scared for the lovely creature though she was, Daine cheered as the other red robes fled to more protected parts of their ships.

Another catapult fired. Moving fast, the dragon was on the missile and had it in her talons. This time, when she dropped it onto a barge, she waited until she was much higher over it. When the stone hit, it went straight through the wooden bottom. With the other stone balls off-balance and rolling everywhere, the barge began to sink.

"Oh, gods," Numair whispered. "Call her in, Daine. Quick!"

"She won't listen! What's wrong?"

"They're loading the slings with liquid fire. Call her in fast!"

Daine *screamed* with all the wild magic she could find.

The dragon's only reply was a vision of a cave, high above the sea, with light coming out of its mouth.

"She won't come," Daine whispered, and tried again.

The Stormwings gathered before the dragon, forcing her back. She fought to rise above them or fall below, but they blocked her. At the right moment, the two remaining catapults fired—not stones this time, but balls of a clear, jellylike substance. They splattered over the dragon, and burst into flames.

She uttered an ear-tearing shriek that none who saw the battle would ever forget, and dropped. Her flaming body crashed into a barge, and sank it.

Daine wailed her grief. "I'll kill them!" she screamed, putting an arrow to her bow with fingers that shook. "Let 'em get near enough and I'll kill them!"

The catapult that remained in action fired. Its stone thudded into the wall at the base of the tower. "Fall back!" George ordered their guards, who obeyed. "Onua, Daine, Numair—let's go!"

Numair looked out to sea and froze, his hand locked tight on Daine's shoulder. His eyes opened so wide they started to bulge. "What dice did the Graveyard Hag roll?"

Someone on the wall below screamed as a huge, black tentacle darted out of the water to grip the catapult that had just fired. Clutching it as a baby might hold a rattle, the tentacle yanked the catapult and the barge it was fastened to onto its side.

Another tentacle shot out of the water beside Eddace's flagship. Up and up it soared, until it reached the crow's nest. Delicately, with precision, it gripped the nest—and the man inside—and snapped it off the mast.

"Friend of yours?" Numair asked. His voice was very quiet, but she could hear him perfectly. No one at the castle was making a sound.

"Not exactly," she whispered. "I guess he moves faster than I thought."

A third tentacle crawled over the rim of the last barge, the one the dragon had knocked off-balance. It snaked all the way across the bed, gripped the opposite rim, and flipped the entire thing over.

Daine gulped. "Oh, dear—I think he's going to be nasty."

"How big did you say it was?" George had come to stand with them, his face white under its tan.

"I didn't," she replied.

Tentacles sprang up around the fleet like a forest of snakes, hemming it in. More tentacles groped into the boats, to begin a systematic destruction.

Numair straightened, blinking. "The dampening spells are breaking up."

Thayet had run to the opposite side of the deck, the part that looked out over the rest of the castle. "Listen!" she yelled.

Horn calls split the air. From the woods to the east came a company of the King's Own and the rest of the Swoop's guards, the Lioness at their head. From the northern woods came another company of the King's Own. They fell on the raiders outside the wall, as the Stormwings converged on that battle.

Onua, Thayet, and George raced down the stairs to reach the curtain wall, where they'd have a better view. Numair sagged to the floor of the deck. "I'm all used up," he told Daine, smiling at her. His eyes fluttered shut.

"Rest quick," she told him. "You and Lady Alanna are going to have to get rid of Himself, out there."

He fluttered his hand at her—of course, of course—and let it fall. Within seconds he was out cold.

To her surprise, she heard the sound of hooves on stone. Cloud emerged from the stair, her withers streaked with sweat. *I have been looking all over for you,* the pony told her crossly, coming to sniff Daine from top to toe. *First they tell me you got sick, then they tell me you went down to the ocean, then—uh-oh.*

Daine looked up. Zhaneh Bitterclaws had returned.

"I suppose you think very well of yourself, girlie. I suppose you think you did something wonderful, calling up *that* greedy-guts." She jerked her head in the direction of the kraken, who continued his breakfast of ships.

The girl shook with fury. She hadn't taken her arrow off the string, but it would do no good. Even supposing she could aim her bow, she had lost the strength to draw it. Numair wasn't the only one to be all used up.

The Stormwing queen knew it too. She fluttered closer. "You're mine," she said with a grin. "I'll be on you before you make the stair. And maybe I'll cut up your long friend here too, before I go. You think about that a moment—it'll be your fault that he dies."

"Liar," Daine spat. "Folk like you always lay the blame on somebody else. If I'd listened to talk like that, I'd've let myself get killed by my own people months ago."

"They *should* have killed you, girlie." The Stormwing drew in closer yet. "You call me a monster—what are you? My gods made me. You're just a freak. All you do is get your friends killed, like that poor dragon. They'd be better off if you just threw yourself off the cliff right now."

Cloud leaned against Daine's thigh. Suddenly the girl was filled with energy; she was as fresh and strong as if she'd had a full night's sleep. Lightning fast, she swung her bow up and loosed.

The arrow went clean through Zhaneh Bitterclaws' neck as the creature gave voice to a choked scream. She dropped, trying to claw the arrow out of her flesh, until her body smashed to the rocks below. As she tumbled end over end to the sea, her own wing feathers cut her to pieces.

Daine and Cloud stuck their heads over the low wall, watching the Stormwing die in silence. Finally the girl straightened. Her newfound strength was gone. "Is she right?" Daine asked her pony.

She isn't, Cloud said firmly. Your friends all make their own choices to live or die for you. I've yet to see you force death on a friend.

Carefully, muscles aching, Daine unstrung her bow and coiled the string, tucking it into her pocket. "Did *I* know you could do that?" she asked. "Give me strength like you did?"

Of course not, was the pony's smug reply. We People don't have to give you *all* our secrets.

"*Now* she tells me." Daine sat with Numair and curled up against him. "Wake me in time for supper," she told Cloud tiredly.

Of course, the mare said, knowing her human was already asleep. There was a blanket where Numair had been sitting when the dragon returned Daine to the castle. Cloud dragged it over, covering the man and the girl. She assumed a guard stance near the two of them and waited for the rest of the fighting to end.

# ➤➤ EPILOGUE ◄◄

Her dreams were filled with the vision, the one the dragon had given her of a hole in the cliff. At first, the silvery light from the cave had been strong, almost enough to read by. As she dreamed the same thing, over and over, the light dimmed. Just before she awoke, it was almost gone.

"How long?" Her voice emerged in a whispering croak. Her throat was so dry she began to cough.

Numair hauled her into a sitting position and put a canteen to her lips. "Drink!"

Daine gasped, swallowed a mouthful of liquid, gasped again, and drank some more. Finally she drained the canteen. "How long?" she asked again.

"The rest of the day the kraken arrived, then yesterday and today." He gave her a cake, sweet with honey and filled with raisins and nuts.

Daine ate it and took another. "I have to go out."

"Don't be silly," he told her. "You're weak. You're staying here."

"That's where you're wrong," she replied. She swung her feet off the bed and stood. For a moment the room spun, then settled into place.

She was in the stable. They had placed her cot in an empty stall, where the ponies could watch her. Her bat friends hung in the rafters overhead, where the loft ended, leaving plenty of room for the one-eyed osprey to perch. None of the animals were pleased when Daine started to pull on her clothes. Cloud in particular glared at her over the partition.

Remembering something, she froze. "My friends—the woods creatures—"

"Some were killed," Numair said gently. "Once the enemy was driven off, we found the injured ones. They've been cared for. There weren't as many casualties as you'd think. You gave them the right advice."

"Good," she said, a weight off her mind. She went on dressing.

"You *need* to rest and eat. I'm still weak on my pins myself."

"There's something I have to take care of," Daine said. *"Now."* She stuffed her feet into her boots.

Her friend sighed. "Then wait a moment. We need an armed escort. There may still be enemies out there. And let's get horses. Where are we going?"

She closed her eyes and recalled the vision. "Northwest," she said finally. "Along the cliff. We have to hurry."

He smiled at her. "Then we'll hurry."

She couldn't even manage Cloud's tack. Soon after the mage had left, Miri raced in. "Master Numair says you need someone to help you saddle up." She gave Cloud a wary look. "You behave," she told the mare, "or Wave-walker help me, I'll singe your tail."

Cloud stood meekly and did as she was told.

Daine was glad to sit on her cot and watch. "What time is it?"

"Afternoon," the older girl said. "You beat Master Numair by half a day. He got up this morning."

"He looks a lot better." She gasped. "I forgot—the kraken!"

Miri grinned. "Don't worry about *that* one," she said, tightening cinches. "Once Master Numair was up, him and Lady Alanna had a talk with that old ship killer. You should have *seen* him scuttle out of the cove! He sucked the water after him and left the bottom dry. The Lioness had to pull it back in!" She patted Cloud's withers. "There you are—all set."

Daine rose and took the reins. "You've come a long way since we met."

Miri grinned shyly. "Thanks. It means a lot to hear you say so."

They waited in the courtyard as castle hostlers brought out Darkmoon, Spots, and horses belonging to the King's Own. Here, shading her eyes from the sun, the girl saw the first repercussions of what she had done. The stable hands had liked to talk to her, before the enemy invasion. Now they avoided her glance and kept well away from her.

A small explosion struck her back and almost knocked her off her feet. It was followed by a second, and a third. Whatever the hostlers might think, Roald, Kally, and Thom were glad to see her up. Her eyes stinging, Daine knelt to return the hug. "There, there," she whispered, more to herself than the children. "It's all right. It's over."

"Can we go too, Ma?" Thom asked the Lioness as she approached.

"No, my dears. Some other time. We're not sure the enemy is completely gone." The knight grinned at Daine. "You've been a busy girl."

Daine grinned back. "So have you." Looking at the men of the King's Own who followed Alanna, she recognized Hakim and his companions. "It's good to see you," she told them.

"The honor is ours," Hakim replied gravely.

"You said it was urgent?" Numair reminded her.

The group left the castle at a trot, following Daine. The vision's lure was powerful in her mind. Following it, she guided Cloud onto a road that ran along the cliff face, high above the sea. Gulls followed them, filling the air with their cries.

Alanna drew level with the girl. "I've yet to thank you," she said quietly. "I never thought you'd have to keep your promise in such a way."

She smiled at the knight. "What happened? They lured you off, didn't they?"

Alanna nodded. "The ogres were real enough. They kept us busy for more than a day. By the time we felt we could return, there was a small army between us and home. Lucky for me Hakim rode in with two companies of the Own. They were still in Corus when Numair sent word you were up to your eyeballs in trouble."

Daine held up a hand: they were close. Listening, she dismounted. "Stay put," she ordered Cloud.

Numair came after her on foot. "What are we looking for, exactly?"

She was about to say she wasn't sure when the ground dropped under her. For a second time she had the doubtful pleasure of being picked up to hang in midair—this time, at least, she wasn't half-drowned. Looking down, she saw she had almost gone through the roof of a cave that opened in the cliff face.

"Can you set me down in there?" She wasn't sure who had her, Alanna or Numair. "I found it."

The Lioness chuckled. "You have a unique way of finding things." Gently Daine was lowered through the hole she had made, until she was on the stone floor of the cave below.

There was a rustle nearby, and a chirp. A silver shape, no bigger than a large cat, came over on legs that hadn't yet mastered the skill of walking.

She knelt. The little creature stared at her with slit-pupiled blue eyes. Tiny, scaled forepaws gripped her breeches: the baby dragon pulled herself up onto her hind legs.

Daine's eyes brimmed with tears. "I'm sorry," she told the dragonet. "I guess I'm your ma now." She scooped up the armful of kit and looked up at the hole she'd made in the roof. Alanna, Numair, and Hakim stared down at her. "The dragon had a little one," she explained. "She's hungry."

Carefully the Lioness raised her and the dragonet up through the hole, to stand them on solid ground.

Daine managed to construct a bottle that would hold up under the kit's small, but sharp, teeth. After consulting with the healer Maude, she warmed goat's milk and loaded it with butter, to make it even richer. The dragonet gulped a pint of the mess, burped, and fell asleep in Daine's lap.

The entire operation was watched, in awe and fascination, by the queen, Alanna, George, Numair, Buri, Onua, Maude, and the children.

Gently Kally ran a finger along the sleeping animal's flank. "She so *soft*," the girl whispered. "What's her name?"

"Skysong," Daine said. She frowned—where had that knowledge come from? "I guess her ma passed that on to me too, before she— died." Coming to a decision, she looked at Onua. "I don't think I can stay with the Riders past the summer. My duty's to this little one, now."

"You can still make your home with us," Thayet told her. "That is, if you wish. I know my lord and I would prefer to have you in the palace."

Daine stared at her. *"Me?"*

"You." Thayet took her hand. "Veralidaine Sarrasri, you saved my life and the lives of my children. A home is the *very* least we can offer you."

Daine lowered her head, to hide her beet red face.

"But we want her to live here," objected George. "Surely we're more suited as a home, bein' on the sea and near Master Numair and all." He grinned. "And bein's how our girl's made so many friends in our woods."

"I don't see why she can't live in my tower," Numair protested. "She *is* my apprentice, after all."

"A girl's got to have females to talk to," Alanna informed him. "You haven't even gotten a new housekeeper since the last one interrupted one of your experiments."

"Come live in the palace," Kally and Roald begged, tugging her arm. "We'll be good forever and ever if you will."

Skysong sneezed and shifted in Daine's lap.

"Shh," Maude ordered. "You'll wake the baby." The children hushed, guilty faced.

"You don't have to decide now," Onua pointed out. "I don't see why rearing Skysong should interfere with helping me this summer."

Daine looked at these unusual people who had become friends, and laughed. "It's fair funny," she explained. "I've gone from having no home to having too many!"

The Lioness smiled and put a hand on her shoulder. "Welcome to Tortall," she said.

# WOLF-SPEAKER

To Raquel Wolf–Sister,

once again,

To Thomas,

who has taught and still teaches me
to keep my mind flexible and
my creativity from stiffening up,

And to Tim,

always, each and every book,
whether I say so or not.

# Acknowledgments

Normally I prefer not to write acknowledgments until the completion of a series, but this book entailed so much work above and beyond what my nearest and dearest are used to and so much real-life research that I would like to take a moment to express my appreciation.

First of all, I thank my good friend and fellow writer Raquel Starace. This book would never have been written if she had not inspired me with her own interest in and love of wolves. She lent me texts, tapes, and videos; she accompanied me on zoo safaris and bore with equanimity all those weird-hour phone calls with questions like, "Is brown the only eye color they have?" *Muchas gracias*, Rock—you can collect from me at will.

I also thank my writer-husband, Tim, who bails me out of the literary cul-de-sac to which I am prone, and who has lived for more than year with wolves singing from our tape player, hunting on our TV, and watching him from my bulletin board. See, Tim—I *told* you they wouldn't eat you.

Thanks also are due to Robert E. J. Cripps, armsmaster and craftsman of the Celtic Wolf Medieval and Renaissance Style Crossbows, for last minute information on the proper name for the place where one places the bolt (the notch, where it is then secured by a clip!).

Most of all, I wish to thank those researchers and wolf experts whose work I plundered so freely for ideas, behaviors, and scents:

L. David Mech, for all his works, but in particular for *The Wolf: The Ecology and Behavior of an Endangered Species*;

Farley Mowat, whose *Never Cry Wolf* introduced me to that peculiar brand of lupine humor;

Martin Stouffer and his *Wild America* television program, particularly the "Wolf and the Whitetail" segment;

The Nature Conservancy;

The National Wildlife Federation;

NYSZ Wildlife Conservation Society;

The International Wolf Center of Ely, Minnesota, which works so hard for the preservation of this fascinating, endangered species.

Contents

# Contents

# → ONE ←

# ENCOUNTERS

∞ The wolves of the Long Lake Pack, gorged on a careless mountain sheep, slept as they digested their meal. Only Brokefang, their chieftain, was awake to see the moon rise. He sat on a stone outcrop, thinking—an odd pastime for a wolf. In the last full moon of summer, on the advice of Old White, the wolf god, he had sent his best travelers, Fleetfoot and Russet, in search of a two-legger who once belonged to his pack. Their orders were to bring her to him, to speak to the local humans on his behalf. The sight of that night's full autumn moon reminded him that winter was coming. What if his messengers couldn't find Daine? What if something had happened to them?

He did not like "what if" thoughts. Until he'd met Daine two winters before, he had worried about nothing but eating, mating, ruling his pack, and scratching fleas. Now he had complex thoughts all the time, whether he wanted them or not.

Soft chatter overhead made him look up. Two bats had met a stranger. Clinging to a branch over his head, the three traded gossip in the manner of their kind. The newcomer brought word of a two-legger on the other side of the mountains, one who was human outside and Beast-People inside. She carried news from bats in the southwest, and if a Long Lake bat was hurt, she could heal him with her magic. She traveled in odd company: two horses, a pony, an extremely tall human male, a big lizard, and two wolves.

The local bats exclaimed over the news. Their colony should hear this, they decided. Would the visitor come and tell them in their cave-home? Along with their guest, the bats took to the air.

Brokefang stretched. One new thought had been that he could learn much if he listened to the talk of nonwolves. Now he could see it was a good thought, so perhaps the others were good, too. He was interested to hear that Daine also had learned new things since leaving the pack. Before, she could not talk directly with bats. Her healing was done with stinging liquids, needles, thread, and splints, not magic.

He stopped in midstretch as he remembered something. When Fleet-foot and Russet had gone, the pack was laired near the valley's southern entrance, where a river flowed from the lake. While they eventually could find the new den in the valley's western mountains, it might take them days to locate the pack.

He would take his wolves south and guide his visitors home.

Two days later, the girl called Daine watched rain fall outside the cave where she and her friends had taken refuge. For someone Brokefang regarded as Pack, she looked quite human. She was five foot five, slim for her fourteen and a half years, with blue-gray eyes the color of the clouds overhead. Her curly brown hair was tightly pinned up, her clothes as practical as her hairstyle: a blue cotton shirt, tan breeches, and soft-soled boots. Around her neck a heavy silver claw hung on a leather thong.

She played with the claw, thinking. She had been born in mountains like these, in a town called Snowsdale over the border in Galla. The first twelve years of her life were spent there, before she lost her family. When she left Galla to serve the king and queen of Tortall, she had hoped that she might never see the mountains again. And here she was, in a place that could be Snowsdale's twin.

Soon she would be with the wolves that had hunted in her old home. They had left soon after she did: Fleetfoot and Russet, her guides, had told of fleeing human hunters to find their new home by the Long Lake. What would it be like to see them again? To be with them again?

"What are you thinking of?" a light male voice asked from deeper inside the cave. "You look grim."

Daine turned around. Seated cross-legged by the fire, a traveling desk on his knees, was her teacher, the wizard Numair Salmalín. He wore his springy mass of black hair tied into a horsetail, away from his dark face and out of his brown eyes. His ink brush was dwarfed by the hand that held it, an exceptionally large hand that was graceful in spite of its size.

"I'm just wondering if Onua is managing the Rider horses all right without me. I know the king told her he needed us to come here, but I still feel as if I should be helping her."

The man raised his eyebrows. "You know very well Onua managed the Rider horses for years before you came to work there. What's *really* bothering you?"

She made a face. She never could distract him when he wanted to know something. "I'm scared."

He put down his brush and gave her his full attention. "What of?"

She looked at her hands. They were chapped from cold, and this was only the third week of September. "Remember what I told you? That I went crazy and hunted with wolves after bandits killed Ma and Grandda and our animals?"

He nodded. "They helped you to avenge the deaths."

"What if it happens again? When I see them, what if I forget I'm human and start thinking I'm a wolf again? I'm s'posed to have control of my wild magic now, but what if it isn't enough?" She rubbed her arms, shivering.

"May I remind you that the spell that keeps your human self apart from your magic self is one I created?" he teased, white teeth flashing in a grin. "How can you imply a working performed by your obedient servant"—he bowed, an odd contortion in a sitting man—"might be anything but perfect?" More seriously he added, "Daine, the spell covers all your contacts. You won't lose control."

"What if it wasn't the magic? What if I simply went mad?"

Strong teeth gripped her elbow hard. Daine looked around into the bright eyes of her pony, Cloud. If I have to bite you to stop you feeling sorry for yourself, I will, the mare informed her. You are being silly.

Numair, used to these silent exchanges, asked, "What does she say?"

"She says I'm feeling sorry for myself. I don't think she understands."

I understand that you fidget over stupid things. Cloud released Daine's elbow. The stork-man will tell you.

"Don't fret," said the mage. "Remember, you allowed me into your mind when you first came to Tortall. If there was a seed of genuine madness there, I would have found it."

Daine smiled. "There's folk who would say you're the *last* man to know who's crazy and who's not. I know a cook who won't let you in his kitchen, a palace quartermaster who says he'll lock you up if you raid his supplies again—"

"Enough!" Numair held up his hands in surrender.

"Just so you know." Feeling better, she asked, "What are you writing?"

He picked up his ink brush once more. "A report to King Jonathan."

"Another one?" she asked, startled. "But we sent one off a week ago."

"He said *regular* reports, magelet. That means weekly. It's a small price to pay for being allowed to come to the rescue of your wolf friends. I just wish I had better news to send."

"I don't think we'll find those missing people." In March a group of the Queen's Riders—seven young men and women—had disappeared in this general area. In July twenty soldiers from the Tortallan army had also vanished. "They could've been anywhere inside a hundred or two hundred miles of us."

"All we can do is look," Numair said as he wrote. "As wanderers we have seen far more than soldiers will. Even so, it's a shame the whole northeastern border is opaque to magical vision. I hadn't realized that a search by foot would be so chancy."

"Why can't you wizards see this place with your magic?" Daine wanted to know. "When I asked the king, he said something about the City of the Gods, and an aura, but then we got interrupted and he never did explain."

"It has to do with the City of the Gods being the oldest center for the teaching of magic. Over the centuries magic seeped into the very rock of the city itself, and then spread. The result is a magical aura that blanks out the city and the lands around it for something like a five-hundred-mile radius."

Daine whistled appreciation of the distance involved. "So the only way to look at all this mountain rock is by eye. That's going to be a job and a half."

"Precisely. Tell me, how far do you think we are from our destination?"

Fleetfoot and Russet had measured distance in the miles a wolf travels in a day. Daine had to divide that in half to figure how far humans might go on horseback. "Half a day's ride to the south entrance to the valley, where the Dunlath River flows out of the Long Lake. From—" She stopped as something whispered in her mind. Animals were coming, looking for her. She ran to the mouth of the cave as their horses bolted past.

Here they came up the trail, wolves, three in the lead and four behind. Two of the leaders were her guides to the Long Lake: the small, reddish white male known as Russet and the brown-and-gray female called Fleetfoot. Between them trotted a huge, black-and-gray timber wolf, plumed tail boldly erect.

"Brokefang!" Daine yelled. "Numair, it's the pack!" She ran to them and vanished in a crowd of yelping, tail-wagging animals. Delighted to see her, they proceeded to wash her with their long tongues.

Standing at the cave entrance, waiting for the reunion to end, the man saw that the rain was coming down harder. "Why don't we move the celebration inside?" he called. "You're getting drenched."

Daine stood. "Come on," she told the pack, speaking aloud for Numair's benefit. "And no eating my friends. The man is Numair. He's my pack now." Two wolves—Numair was touched to see they were Fleetfoot and Russet, his companions on their journey here—left the others to sit by him, grinning and sprinkling him with drops from their waving tails.

Once out of the rain, the newcomers greeted Cloud, sniffing the gray mare politely. Brokefang gave the mare a few licks, which she delicately returned. The pony, the sole survivor of the bandit raid on Daine's farm, had stayed with Daine in the weeks the girl had run with the pack. In that time, wolves and pony had come to a truce of sorts.

Next Daine introduced her pack to Spots, the easygoing piebald gelding who was Numair's mount, and Mangle, a gentle bay cob who carried their packs. The horses quivered, whites showing all the way around their eyes, as the wolves sniffed them. They trusted Daine to keep the wolves from hurting them, but their belief in her couldn't banish natural fear entirely. Once the greetings were over, they retreated to the rear of the large cave and stayed there.

"Kitten," Daine called, looking for her charge. "Come meet the wolves."

Knowing she often scared mortal animals, the dragon had kept to the shadows. Now she walked into the light. She was pale blue, almost two feet long from nose to hip, with another twelve inches' worth of tail, a slender muzzle, and silver claws. The wings that one day would carry her in flight were, at this stage, tiny and useless. Her blue, reptilian eyes followed everything with sharp attention. She was far more intelligent than a mortal animal, but her way of knowing and doing things was a puzzle Daine tried to unravel on a daily basis.

"This is Skysong," Daine told the pack. "That's the name her ma gave her, anyway. Mostly we call her Kitten."

The dragon eyed their guests. The newcomers stared, ears flicking back and forth in uncertainty, tails half-tucked between their legs. Slowly she rose up onto her hindquarters, a favorite position, and chirped.

Brokefang was the first to walk forward, stiff-legged, to sniff her. Only when his tail gave the smallest possible wag did the others come near.

Once the animals were done, Daine said, "Numair, the gray-and-black male is Brokefang." When the wolf came to smell Numair's hands, the mage saw that his right canine tooth had the point broken off. "He's the first male of the pack, the boss male." Numair crouched to allow Brokefang to sniff his face and hair as well. The wolf gave a brief wag of the tail to show he liked Numair's scent.

"The brown-and-gray male with the black ring around his nose is Short Snout," Daine said. "The tawny female is Battle. She fought a mountain lion when she was watching pups in Snowsdale—that's how she got her name." Short Snout lipped Numair's hand in greeting. Battle sniffed the mage and sneezed. "The brown-and-red male is Sharp Nose. The gray-and-tawny female is Frolic." The girl sat on the floor, and most of the wolves curled up around her. "Frostfur, the boss female, and Longwind stayed in the valley with the pups."

Greetings done, Numair sat by the fire and added new wood. "Has Brokefang said why he needs you?" he asked. "His call for help was somewhat vague."

Daine nodded. "Brokefang, what's going on? All you told Fleetfoot and Russet was that humans are ruining the valley." As the wolf replied, she translated, "He says this spring men started cutting trees and digging holes without planting anything. He says they brought monsters and more humans there, and they are killing off the game. Between that and the tree cutting and hole digging, they're driving the deer and elk from the valley. If it isn't stopped, the pack will starve when the Big Cold comes."

"The Big Cold?" asked Numair.

"It's what the People—animals—call winter."

The man frowned. "I'm not as expert as you in wolf behavior, but—didn't you tell me that if wolves find an area is too lively for them, they flee it? Isn't that why they left Snowsdale, because humans there were hunting them?"

Yes, said Brokefang. They wanted to hurt us, because we helped Daine hunt the humans who killed her dam. They killed Rattail, Longeye, Treelicker, and the pups.

Daine nodded sadly: Fleetfoot and Russet had told her of the pack's losses. The older wolves had been her friends. The pups she hadn't met, but every pack valued its young ones. To lose them all was a disaster.

Brokefang went on. We left Snowsdale. It was a hard journey in the hot months, seeking a home. We found places, but there was little game, or other packs lived there, or there were too many humans. Then just before the last Big Cold we found the Long Lake. This valley is so big we could go for days without seeing humans. There is plenty of game, no rival pack to claim it, and caves in the mountains for dens in the snows.

Scratching a flea, Brokefang continued. The Long Lake was good—now humans make it bad. They drove us from the valley where I was born, and my sire, and his sire before him. Before, it was our way to run from two-leggers. Yet I do not run if another pack challenges mine—I fight, and the Pack fights with me. Are humans better than another pack? I do not believe they are.

Will you help us? Will you tell the humans to stop their tree cutting and noisemaking? If they do not stop, the Long Lake Pack will stop it for them, but I prefer that they *agree* to stop. I know very well that if the Pack has to interfere, there will be bloodshed.

Daine looked at the other wolves of the pack. They nodded, like humans, in agreement. They would support Brokefang in the most un-wolflike plan she had ever heard in her life. Where had they gotten such ideas?

Will you help us? asked Brokefang again.

Daine took a deep breath. "You're my Pack, aren't you? I'll do my best. I can't promise they'll listen to me, but I'll try."

Good, Brokefang replied. He padded to the cave's mouth and gave the air a sniff. The breeze smelled of grazing deer just over the hill. Looking at Daine, he said, Now we must hunt. We will come back when we have fed.

They left as Daine was translating his words. She followed them to the cave mouth, to watch as they vanished into the rain. It was getting dark. Behind her was a clatter as Numair unpacked the cooking things. Thinking about the pack and about her time with them, she was caught up in a surge of memory.

*The bandit guard was upwind of a wolf once called Daine. The night air carried his reek to her: unwashed man, old blood, sour wine. Her nose flared at the stench. She covered it with her free hand. The other clutched a dagger, the last human item she remembered how to use.*

*He did something with his hands as he stood with his back toward her. She slunk closer, ignoring the snow under her bare feet and the freezing air on her bare arms. Forest sounds covered the little noise she made, though he would not have heard if she'd shouted. He was drunk. They all were, too drunk to remember the first two shifts of guards had not returned.*

*She tensed to jump. Something made him turn. Now she saw what he'd been doing: there was a wheel of cheese in one*

*hand, a dagger in the other, and a wedge of cheese in his*
*mouth. She also saw his necklace, the amber beads her mother*
*had worn every day of her life. She leaped, and felt a white-*
*hot line of pain along her ribs. He'd stabbed her with his knife.*

*Brokefang found her. She had dragged herself under a bush*
*and was trying to lick the cut in her side. The wolf performed*
*this office for her.*

*It is dawn, he said. What must be done now?*

*We finish them, she told him, fists clenched tight. We finish*
*them all.*

"I think I know why Brokefang changed so much," she said. "I
mean, animals learn things from me, and probably that's how most of
the pack got so smart, but Brokefang's even smarter. I got hurt, when
we were after those bandits, and he licked the cut clean."

"It's a valid assumption," agreed Numair. "There are cases of magically gifted humans who were able to impart their abilities to nonhuman
companions. For example, there is Boazan the Sun Dancer, who eagle
Thati could speak ten languages after she drank his tears. And—"

"Numair," she said warningly. Experience had taught her that if she
let him begin to list examples, he would not return to the real world for
hours.

He grinned, for all the world like one of her stableboy or Rider
friends instead of the greatest wizard in Tortall. He had begun to cook
supper: a pot of cut-up roots already simmered on the fire. Daine sat
next to him and began to slice chunks from a ham they had brought in
their packs. Kitten waddled over to help, or at least to eat the rind that
Daine cut from the meat.

*—This is very nice,*—a rough voice said in their minds.—*Cozy,*
*especially on a rainy afternoon.—*

They twisted to look at the cave entrance. It shone with a silvery
light that appeared to come from the animal standing there. The badger
waddled in, the light fading around his body. He stopped at a polite
distance from their fire and shook himself, water flying everywhere from
his long, heavy coat.

Daine fingered the silver claw he had once given her. She liked
badgers, and her mysterious adviser was a very handsome one. Big for
his kind, he was over a yard in length, with a tail a foot long. He
weighed at least fifty pounds, and it appeared he could stow a tremendous amount of water in his fur.

When he finished shaking, he trundled over to the fire, standing
between Daine and Numair. Seated as Daine was, she and the badger

were nearly eye to eye. She was so close that she couldn't escape his thick, musky odor.

"Daine, is this—?" Numair sounded nervous.

The badger looked at him, eyes coldly intelligent.—*I told her father I would keep an eye on her. So you are her teacher. She tells me a great deal about you, when I visit her.*—

"May I ask you something?" the mage inquired.

—*I am an immortal, the first male creature of my kind. The male badger god, if you like. That is what you wished to ask, is it not?*—

"Yes, and I thank you," Numair said hesitantly. "I—thought I had shielded my mind from any kind of magical reading or probe—"

—*Perhaps that works with* mortal *wizards,*—the badger replied.—*Perhaps it works with lesser immortals, such as Stormwings. I am neither.*—

Numair blushed deeply, and Daine hid a grin behind one hand. She doubted that anyone had spoken that way to Numair in a long time. She was used to it. The badger had first appeared in a dream to give her advice sixteen months ago, on her journey to Tortall, and she had dreamed of him often since.

"Another question, then," the mage said doggedly. "Since I have the opportunity to ask. You can resolve a number of academic debates, actually."

—*Ask.*—There was studied patience in the badger's voice.

"The inhabitants of the Divine Realms are called by men 'immortals,' but the term itself isn't entirely accurate. I know that unless they are killed in some accident or by deliberate intent, creatures such as Stormwings, spidrens, and so on will live forever. They don't age, either. But how are they 'lesser immortals' compared to you, or to the other gods?"

—*They are "lesser" because they can be slain,*—was the reply.—*I can no more be killed than can Mithros, or the Goddess, or the other gods worshiped by two-leggers. "Immortals" is the most fitting term to use. It is not particularly correct, but it is the best you two-leggers can manage.*—

Having made Numair speechless, the badger went on.—*Now, on to your teaching. It is well enough, but you have not shown her where to take her next step. I am surprised. For a mortal, your grasp of wild magic normally is good.*—

Numair looked down his long nose at the guest who called his learning into question. "If you feel I have omitted something, by all means, enlighten us."

The badger sneezed. It seemed to be his way of laughing.—*Daine, if you try, you can learn to enter the mind of a mortal animal. You can use their eyes as you would your own, or their ears, or their noses.—*

Daine frowned, trying to understand. "How? When you said I could hear and call animals, it was part of something I knew how to do. This isn't."

*—Make your mind like that of the animal you join,—*he told her.—*Think like that animal does, until you become one. You may be quite surprised by what results in the end.—*

It sounded odd, but she knew better than to say as much. She had questioned him once, and he had flattened her with one swipe of his paw. "I'll try."

*—Do better than try. Where is the young dragon?—*

Kitten had been watching from the other side of the fire. Now she came to sit with the badger, holding a clump of his fur in one small paw. She had a great deal to say in her vocabulary of chirps, whistles, clicks, and trills. He listened as if it meant something, and when she was done, waddled over to talk with Cloud and the horses. At last he returned to the fire, where Daine and Numair had waited politely for him to end his private conversations.

*—I must go back to my home sett,—*he announced.—*Things in the Divine Realms have been hectic since the protective wall was breached and the lesser immortals were released into your world.—*

"Do you know who did it?" asked Numair quickly. "We've been searching for the culprit for two years now."

*—Why in the name of the Lady of Beasts would I know something like that?—*was the growled reply.—*I have more than enough to do in mortal realms simply with keeping an eye on her.—*

"Don't be angry," Daine pleaded. "He thought you might know, since you know so much already."

*—You are a good kit.—*The badger rubbed his head against her knee. Touched by this sign of affection, Daine hugged him, burying her fingers in his shaggy coat. To Numair he added,—*And I am not angry with you, mortal. I cannot be angry with one who has guarded my young friend so well. Let me go, Daine. I have to return to my sett.—*

She obeyed. He walked toward the cave's mouth, silver light enclosing him in a globe. At its brightest, the light flared, then vanished. He was gone.

"Well," said Numair. She thought he might add something, but instead he busied himself with stirring the vegetables.

Suddenly she remembered a question she had wanted to ask. "I think he puts a magic on me," she complained.

"How so?"

"Every time I see him, I mean to ask who my da is, and every time I forget! And he's the only one who can tell me, too, drat him."

Kitten gave a trill, her slit-pupiled eyes concerned.

"I'm all right, Kit," the girl said, and sighed. "It's not fair, though."

Numair chuckled. "Somehow I doubt the badger is interested in what's fair."

She had to smile, even if her smile was one-sided. She knew he was right.

"Speaking of what is fair, what do you think of the advice he gave you, about becoming a magical symbiote?"

Most of the time she was glad that he spoke to her as he would to a fellow scholar, instead of talking down to her. Just now, though, her head was reeling from Brokefang's news and the badger's arrival. "A magical sym—sym—whatsits?"

"Symbiote," he replied. "They are creatures that live off other creatures, but not destructively, as parasites do. An example might be the bird who rides on a bison, picking insects from the beast's coat."

"Oh. I don't know what I think of it. I never tried it."

"Now would be a good time," he said helpfully. "The vegetables will take a while to cook. Why not try it with Cloud?"

Daine looked around until she saw the mare, still at the rear of the cave with Mangle and Spots. "Cloud, can I?"

"Cloud, *may* I," the man corrected.

You can or you may. I don't know if it will help, said the mare.

The girl went to sit near the pony, while Mangle and Spots ventured outside to graze again. Numair began to get out the ingredients for campfire bread as Kitten watched with interest.

"Don't let him stir the dough too long," Daine ordered the dragon. "It cooks up hard when he forgets." Kitten chirped as Numair glared across the cave at his young pupil.

The girl closed her eyes. Breathing slowly, she reached deep inside to find the pool of copper light that was her wild magic. Calling a thread of fire from that pool, she reached for Cloud, and tried to bind their minds with it.

Cloud whinnied, breaking the girl's concentration. That *hurt*, the mare snapped. If it's going to hurt, I won't do it! Try it with less magic.

Shutting her eyes, Daine obeyed. This time she used a drop of copper fire, thinking to glue her mind to Cloud's. The mare broke contact the minute Daine's fire touched hers. Daine tried it a second, and a third time, without success.

It's the same kind of magic, she told Cloud, frustrated. It's not any different from what's in you.

It hurts, retorted the pony. If that badger knew this would hurt and told you to try it anyway, I will tell *him* a few things the next time he visits.

I don't do it a-purpose, argued Daine. How can I do it without paining you?

*Without* the fire, Cloud suggested. You don't need it to talk to us, or to listen. Why should you need it now?

Daine bit a thumbnail. Cloud was right. She only used the fire of her magic when she was tired, or when she had to do something hard. She was tired now, and the smell of cooking ham had filled her nostrils. "Let's try again tomorrow," she said aloud. "My head aches."

"Come eat," called Numair. "You've been at it nearly an hour."

Daine went to the fire, Cloud following. Digging in her pack, the girl handed the pony a carrot before she sat. Numair handed over a bowl of mildly spiced vegetables and cooked ham. Kitten climbed into the girl's lap, forcing Daine to arrange her arms around the dragon as she ate. Between mouthfuls she explained what had taken place.

Cloud listened, nibbling the carrot as her ears flicked back and forth. When Daine finished, the mare suggested, Perhaps I am the wrong one to try with.

"Who, then, Cloud?" Daine asked. "I've known you longer than anybody." She yawned. The experiment, even though it hadn't worked, had worn her out.

But I am a grazer—you are a hunter. Why not try with a hunter? It may be easier to do this first with wolves. You are practically a wolf as it is.

"And if I forget I'm human?"

("I wish I could hear both sides of this conversation," Numair confided softly to Kitten. "I feel so left out, sometimes.")

The man said you won't, replied Cloud. He should know. Brokefang is part of you already. Ask the stork-man. He will tell you I am right.

Daine relayed this to Numair. "She has a point," he said. "I hadn't thought the predator-prey differential would constitute a barrier, but she knows you better than I." He watched Daine yawn again, hugely, and smiled. "It *can* wait until tomorrow. Don't worry about cleanup. I'll do it."

"But it's my turn," she protested. "You cooked, so I have to clean."

"Go to bed," her teacher said quietly. "The moon will not stop its monthly journey simply because I cooked *and* cleaned on the same meal."

She climbed into her bedroll and was asleep the moment she pulled the blankets up. When the wolves returned much later, she woke just enough to see them group around her. With Kitten curled up on one side and Brokefang sprawled on the other, Daine finished her night's rest smiling.

It was damp and chilly the next morning, the cold a taste of the months to come. Breakfast was a quiet meal, since neither Daine nor Numair was a morning person. They cleaned up together and readied the horses for the day's journey.

The wolves had gone to finish the previous night's kill. They were returning when Numair handed Daine a small tube of paper tied with plain ribbon. "Can we send this on to the king today?" he asked.

Daine nodded, and reached with her magic. Not far from their camp-site was the nest of a golden eagle named Sunclaw. Daine approached her politely and explained what she wanted. She could have made the bird do as she wished, but that was not the act of a friend. The eagle listened with interest, and agreed. When she came, Daine thanked her, and made sure the instructions for delivering Numair's report were fixed in Sunclaw's mind. Numair, who had excellent manners, thanked Sun-claw as well, handing the letter to her with a bow.

Brokefang had watched all of this with great interest. You have changed, he commented when Sunclaw had gone. You know so much more now. You will make the two-leggers stop ruining the valley.

Daine frowned. I don't know if I can, she told the wolf. Humans aren't like the People. Animals are sensible. Humans aren't.

You will help us, Brokefang repeated, his faith in her shining in his eyes. You said that you would. Now, are you and the man ready? It is time to go.

Daine put Kitten atop the packs on Mangle's back. Numair mounted Spots, and the girl mounted Cloud. "Lead on," the mage told Brokefang.

The wolves trotted down the trail away from the cave, followed by the horses and their riders. When the path forked, one end leading to the nearby river and the other into the mountains, Brokefang led them uphill.

"If we follow the river, won't that take us into the valley?" Daine called. "It won't be so hard on us."

Brokefang halted. It is easier, he agreed, as Daine translated for Numair. Humans go that way all the time. So also do soldiers, and men with magic fires. It is best to avoid them. Men kill wolves on sight, remember, Pack-Sister?

"Men with magic fires?" Numair asked, frowning.

Men like you, said Brokefang, with the Light Inside.

"We call them mages," Daine told him. "Or sorcerers, or wizards, or witches. What we call them depends on what they do."

Numair thought for a moment. "Lead on," he said at last. "I prefer to avoid human notice for as long as possible. And thank you for the warning."

The humans, Kitten, and the horses followed the wolves up along the side of the mountains that rimmed the valley of the Long Lake. By noon they had come to a section of trail that was bare of trees. The wolves didn't slow, but trotted into the open. Daine halted, listening. Something nasty was tickling at the back of her mind, a familiar sense that had nothing to do with mortal animals. Getting her crossbow, she put an arrow in the notch and fixed it in place with the clip.

Numair took a step forward, and Cloud grabbed his tunic in her teeth.

"Stormwings," Daine whispered. Numair drew back from the bare ground. Under the tree cover, they watched the sky.

High overhead glided three creatures with human heads and chests, and great, spreading wings and claws. Daine knew from bitter experience that their birdlike limbs were steel, wrought to look like genuine feathers and claws. In sunlight they could angle those feathers to blind their enemies. They were battlefield creatures, living in human legend as monsters who dishonored the dead. Eyes cold, she aimed at the largest of the three.

Numair put a hand on her arm. "Try to keep an open mind, magelet," he whispered. "They haven't attacked us."

"Yet," she hissed.

Brokefang looked back to see what was wrong, and saw what they were looking at. These are harriers, he said. They help the soldiers and the mages.

Daine relayed this to Numair as the wolves moved on, to wait for them in the trees on the other side of the clearing.

"Stormwings that work in conjunction with humans," the man commented softly. "That sounds like Emperor Ozorne's work." The emperor of the southern kingdom of Carthak was a mage who seemed to have a special relationship with minor immortals, and with Stormwings in particular. Some, Numair included, thought it was Ozorne's doing that had freed so many immortals from the Divine Realms in the first place. He had his eye on Tortall's wealth, and many thought he meant to attack when the country's defenders were worn out from battling immortals.

"Now can I shoot them?" Daine wanted to know.

"You may not. They still have done nothing to harm us."

The Stormwings flew off. Vexed with her friend, Daine fumed and waited until she could no longer sense the immortals before leading the way onto the trail once more. They were halfway across the open space when Numair stopped, frowning at a large, blackened crater down the slope from them. "That's not a natural occurrence," he remarked, and walked toward it.

"This isn't the time to explore!" Daine hissed. If he heard, he gave no sign of it. With a sigh the girl told the horses to move on. "The wolves won't touch you," she said when Spots wavered. "Now go!"

Follow me, Cloud told the horses; they obeyed. Daine, with Kitten peering wide-eyed over her shoulder, followed Numair.

Blackened earth sprayed from the crater's center. Other things were charred as well: bones, round metal circles that had been shields before the leather covers burned, trees, axheads, arrowheads, swords. The heat that had done this must have been intense. The clay of the mountainside had glazed in spots, coating the ground with a hard surface that captured what was left of this battle scene.

Numair bent over a blackened lump and pulled it apart. Daine looked at a mass of bone close to her, and saw it was a pony's skeleton. Metal pieces from the dead mount's tack had fallen in among the bones. Looking around, she counted other dead mounts. The smaller bone heaps belonged to human beings.

Grimly Numair faced her and held up his find. Blackened, half-burned, in tatters, it was a piece of cloth with a red horse rearing on a gold-brown field. "Now we know what happened to the Ninth Rider Group."

Daine's hands trembled with fury. She had a great many ties to the Queen's Riders, and the sight of that charred flag was enough to break her heart. "And you stopped me from shooting those Stormwings."

"They don't kill with blasting fire like this," Numair replied. "This is battle magic. I have yet to hear of a Stormwing being a war mage."

"I bet they knew about this, though."

Numair put a hand on her shoulder. "You're too young to be so closed-minded," he told her. "A little tolerance wouldn't come amiss." Folding the remains of the flag, he climbed back up to the trail.

## ⇥ TWO ⇤

# THE VALLEY OF THE LONG LAKE

**ᴄᴏᴄᴏ** Three days after leaving the cave, the wolf pack led the humans and their ponies through a gap in the mountains. At its deepest point they found a spring, where they ate lunch; from there they followed a stream downhill, until Brokefang stopped.

You must look at something, he told Daine. Leave the horses by that rock—they will be safe there, with the rest of the pack to guard them.

Daine, with Kitten on her back in a sling, and Numair followed him up a long tumble of rock slabs. When they came to the top, they could see for miles. Far below was the Long Lake. Daine noticed a village where a small river—part of the stream they had followed—met the lake. Not far offshore, linked to the village by a bridge, was an island capped by a large, well-built castle.

Numair drew his spyglass from its case. Stretching it to full length, he put it to his eye and surveyed the valley.

What is that? asked the wolf, watching him.

"It's a glass in a tube," Daine replied. "It makes things that are far away seem closer."

"This is Fief Dunlath, without a doubt." Numair offered the spyglass to Daine. "I can't see the northern reaches of the lake from here. Is that where the damage is being done? The holes and the tree cutting?"

Most of it, Brokefang replied. That and dens for the soldiers, like those they have at the south gate.

"Soldiers at the northern *and* southern ends of the valley?" asked Daine. "Then why not here, if they want to put watchdogs at the passes?"

Most two-leggers follow the river in and out, answered Brokefang.

Few come here as we did. When they do, usually the harriers catch them outside, as they did those Riders you spoke of.

Numair listened as Daine translated. "This is not good," he muttered, squinting at Dunlath Castle. "There is no reason for this fief to be heavily guarded. Under law they're only entitled to a force of forty men-at-arms. . . . May I see that again?" He held out a hand, and Daine returned the glass.

They continued to examine the valley until Brokefang said, Come. We have a way to go still. Let us find the meeting place, and my mate.

Daine and Numair followed the wolf back to the spot where they had left the horses. A strange wolf had joined the others, a gray-and-white female with a boldly marked face. Brokefang raced to meet her, tail erect and wagging gaily.

"Well, he's glad to see this one," Numair remarked as they followed more slowly. "Who's the stranger?"

"His mate, Frostfur. The boss female."

Where were you? Frostfur was demanding of Brokefang. What took so long? You said you were going only to the other side of the mountain and you have been gone four nights.

Daine sighed. She'd forgotten how much she disliked Frostfur. During her time with the pack, Rattail had been Brokefang's mate. A sweeter, gentler wolf Daine had never met. After her death, Brokefang had chosen her sister. The new female pack leader was a cross, fidgety animal who had never accepted Daine.

We were traveling with two-leggers and horses, Brokefang told his mate. They can't run as fast as we can.

The only two-legger you need is *her*. Why didn't you leave those others behind? We can hunt if we are hungry. We don't need food brought to us, like the humans' dogs.

At this Cloud, who stood between Frostfur and the horses, laid back her ears. Kitten reared up in her sling, bracing her forepaws on Daine's shoulder, and screeched at the she-wolf. Daine was shocked to hear her friend voice something that sounded so rude. Frostfur looked at them and bared her teeth.

"Enough!" the girl ordered. "We're friends. That means you, Frostfur, and these horses. If you disobey, you'll be sorry."

Frostfur met her eyes, then looked away. You are different, the wolf said. You and the pony both. I suppose you don't even realize it. The pack never was the same after you left it. How much will you change us this time?

Brokefang nuzzled his mate. It will be good, he told Frostfur. You'll see. Take us to the pups. You'll feel better when the pack is one again.

Without reply, Frostfur ran down a trail that led north. The wolves and their guests followed. The path took them on a line that ran parallel to the lake. For a game trail it was wide and, if the tracks and marks on the trees and shrubs were to be believed, used by many animals, not only wolves.

"Mountain sheep," Daine commented, showing Numair a tuft of white fur that had caught on a bramble. "A wolverine, too—keep an eye out for that one. They're nasty when they're crossed." Looking up the trail, she saw each of the wolves stop to lift a leg on a pile of meat. Even the females did so, which was odd. Marking territory was normally done only by males. "Graveyard Hag, what are they doing?" she asked, naming one of Numair's gods. She trotted to the head of the line. "What is this?" she asked. "What's wrong with the meat?"

Brokefang replied, One of the two-leggers is a hunter of wolves. He leaves poisoned meat on our trails. We are telling him what we think of this. When he comes to check the meat, he will curse and throw things. It is fun to watch.

Daine laughed, and went to explain it to Numair.

They made several stops to express such opinions: twice at snares, once at a trap, and once at a pit covered with leaves and branches. Each time the wolves marked the spot with urine and dung, leaving a smelly mess for the hunter. At the last two stops, the horses and Cloud also left tokens of contempt.

"That should *really* confuse him," Daine told Numair and Kitten. "He'll never figure out how horses came to mark a wolf scent post."

A lesser trail split from the one they walked; the wolves followed it into a cuplike valley set deep in the mountainside, hidden by tangles of rock. There the woods opened onto a clearing around a pond. At the water's edge trails crossed and recrossed, and large, flattened areas in the brush marked wolf beds.

A challenge-bark came from a bunch of reeds, and five half-grown wolves, their colors ranging from brown to frosted gray, tumbled out. They still bore remnants of soft baby fur, and were in the process of trading milk teeth for meat teeth. Eyeing the strangers, they whined and growled nervously, until the pack surrounded them and shut the newcomers off from view.

Another grown wolf, a black, gray, and brown male, pranced over to say hello. "He's Longwind," Daine informed Numair. "He was baby-sitting." To the wolf she said, "Say hello to my friends. Cloud you know." As Longwind obeyed, the girl walked up to the pack. The moment the pups noticed her they backed away.

Frostfur said with grim satisfaction, I knew bringing strangers was a mistake. Brokefang nuzzled his mate, trying to sweeten her temper.

Fleetfoot stuck her nose under the belly of one of the male pups and scooted him forward. We know this isn't what you're used to, she told him, but you may as well learn now as later.

Russet gripped a female pup by the scruff of the neck and dragged her to the girl, adding, Daine is Pack, and if she is Pack, so are these others.

The female was the one to walk forward, still clumsy on her feet, to sniff Daine's palm. She is Leaper, Russet said, and Leaper wagged her tail. The male pup trotted over. He is Chaser, commented Russet. These others are too silly to have names. At that the remaining three pups approached timidly, whining.

Daine introduced the young wolves to her friends. The pups came to accept Numair, the horses, and Cloud, but nothing could make them like the young dragon. When she went near them, they would run to hide behind an adult wolf. At last Kitten turned gray, the color that meant she was sulking, and waddled over to the pond. There she played with stones, pretending to ignore everyone.

Why is she sad? asked Russet. They are pups. They don't know any better.

"She's no more than a pup herself," Daine replied. "I can't even talk to her as I could to her ma. She looks big, but as dragons go she's a baby."

I see. Getting up, the red-coated wolf trotted over to the dragon and began to paw at her rocks. Soon they were playing, and Kitten's scales regained their normal, gold-tinged blue color.

Daine was wrestling a stick out of the jaws of a pup she had decided to call Silly when Brokefang came to say, We hunt. Since the pups accept you and Numair and the horses, will you guard them?

"We'll be honored to guard your pups," Daine told him.

The pack left, and Numair began to cook as Daine groomed the horses. The smell of frying bacon called the pups to the fire, their noses twitching. The new scent canceled some of their fear of Kitten: as long as she kept to one side of the fire and they to the other, the young wolves didn't object. When the first pan of bacon was done, Numair gave in to the pleading in five pairs of brown eyes and one pair of slit-pupiled blue, and doled it out to his audience.

After Numair, the pups, and the horses went to bed, Daine lay awake, listening to the chatter of owls and bats. At the fringe of her magic she felt immortals pass overhead. They weren't Stormwings, or griffins, or any of the others she had met before. She sensed she would not like these if they did meet. There was a nasty undertone to them in her mind, like the taint of old blood.

The pack returned not long after the creatures' presence faded in her mind. Was it good hunting? she asked Brokefang silently, so she wouldn't disturb Numair.

He came to sit with her. An old and stringy elk. He gave us a good run, though, he replied. Cloud says you are trying to fit into her skull. It sounds like an interesting thing.

I tried it once, said Daine. Cloud thinks I might do better with wolves. I would have asked before, but I needed to rest first.

Are you rested now? he wanted to know. I would like you to try it with me.

She smiled and said, All right. And thank you.

Must I do anything in particular?

No. Just wait.

She closed her eyes, took a breath, let it out. Sounds pressed on her: Numair's snore, Short Snout's moan as he dreamed of rabbits, the pups chewing, Battle washing a paw. Beyond those noises she heard others belonging to the forest and air around them.

She concentrated on Brokefang until she heard fleas moving in his pelt. He yawned, so close that it felt as if he yawned inside her ears. She listened for his thoughts and found them: the odor of blood from his kill, the drip of water from the trees overhead, the joy of being one with the pack. Brokefang sighed—

Daine was sleepy; her belly was overly full and rumbling as it broke the elk meat down. She could see young Silly from where she lay; he was asleep on his back with his paws in the air. She crinkled her whiskers in a silent laugh.

The *smells*, the *sounds*. She had never been so aware of them in her life. There was the wind through pine needles, singing of rocks and open sky. Below, a mole was digging. Her nostrils flared. Here was wolf musk, the perfume of her packmates. There was the hay-and-hide scent of the horses-who-are-*not*-prey, enticing but untouchable. A whiff of flowers, animal musk, and cotton was the girl-who-is-Pack. She looked at the girl, and realized she looked at herself.

It was a jolt to see her own face from the outside, one that sent her back into herself. Daine opened her eyes. "I did it!"

Numair stirred as the pack got up. "You did what?" he asked sleepily.

Brokefang washed Daine's ear as she explained, "I was Brokefang. I mean, we were both in Brokefang's mind. We were wolves—*I* was a wolf. It was only for a few minutes, but it happened!"

The man sat up, hugging his knees. "Good. Next time you can do it longer." He looked at Brokefang. "Did it hurt you the way it hurt Cloud?"

No, the wolf replied as Daine translated. We will do it again.

The girl yawned and nodded. At last she was sleepy. "Tomorrow," she promised, wriggling down into her bedroll.

Brokefang yawned when she did. Tomorrow, he agreed, as sleepy as she was.

When she woke, it was well past dawn. Numair crouched beside the pond, with Kitten and the pack behind him, watching what he did with interest. Faint black fire dotted with white sparks spilled from his hands to the water's surface, forming a circle there. At last he sighed. The fire vanished.

"What was that?" Daine asked, dressing under the cover of her blankets.

"There's an occult net over the valley," he said, grimacing as he got to his feet. "It's subtle—I doubt many would even sense it—and it serves to detect the use of magic. It also would block all messages I might send to the king. To anyone, for that matter. And since this valley is hidden beneath the aura cast by the City of the Gods, no one outside can even tell the net is here."

"Wonderful," she said dryly. "So Dunlath is a secret within a secret."

Numair beamed at her. "Precisely. I couldn't have put it better."

"And this net—will it pick up *any* magic?" she asked, putting her bed to rights. "Will them that set it know you just looked at it?"

"No. A scrying spell is passive, not active. It shows what exists without influencing it."

"What's here that's so important?" Daine asked. "Stormwing patrols, two forts, a magical net—what has Fief Dunlath got that needs so much protecting?"

"We need to find out," Numair said. "As soon as you've had breakfast, I think we should see the northern part of the valley."

She ate as Numair set the camp in order and saddled Cloud and Spots. Mangle agreed to stay with the pack after Daine convinced them—and him—that he was to be left alone. The girl then offered the carry-sling to Kitten. The young dragon looked at it, then at the still-nervous Mangle. She shook her head and trotted over to the packhorse, clearly choosing to stay and keep him company. With the small dragon by his feet, Mangle relaxed. Daine, who knew Kitten was well able to protect herself, relaxed as well, and mounted Cloud. Brokefang, Fleet-foot, and Short Snout led the way as she and Numair followed.

The group used a trail high on the mountainside, one that was broad enough for the horses, and kept moving all morning, headed north. Daine listened hard for immortals, and called a halt twice as Stormwings passed overhead.

*Stop*, Brokefang ordered at last. We must leave the trail here.

We will hide, Cloud told her, with Spots's agreement. Don't worry about us.

Afoot, Daine and Numair trailed the wolves through a cut in the ground that led up into tumbled rock. Brokefang crawled up to the edge of a cliff, Fleetfoot and Short Snout behind. The two humans kept low and joined them. Lying on their bellies next to their guides, they looked over the edge of the cliff.

Few trees stood in the upper ten miles of the lake's western edge: most lay in a wood between the fort structure and the river that flowed into the north end of the lake. Much of the ground between that fort and their vantage point was heaped into mounds of dirt and rock, some of them small hills in their own right. The only greenery to speak of was patches of scraggly weed.

Roads were cut into the dirt, leading down to deep pits that lay between the mounds. Men and ogres alike toiled here, dressed in loin-cloths and little else. Some pulled dirt-filled carts out of the pits. When they returned with empty carts, they vanished into the black, yawning holes of the mines.

Wherever she looked she saw ogres, aquaskinned beings that varied in size from her own height to ten or twelve feet. Their usually straggly hair was chopped to a rough stubble that went as low as their necks and shoulders. They had pointed ears that swiveled to catch any sound, bulging eyes, and yellowing, peglike teeth. She was no stranger to their kind, but most of her meetings with them had been fights of one sort or another. This was the first time she had seen any used as beasts of burden, or as slaves. All of them appeared to be at the mercy of the armed humans who patrolled the entire area. One ogre, a sad and skinny creature, slumped to his knees. Three humans came after him, their whips raised.

Daine looked away. On her right was the lake. Barracklike build-ings, some big enough to house ogres, had been erected of raw wood on the near shore. Between them, human and ogre children played under the watchful eye of an ogre female. The fort on the town's north side was well built and, to judge from the many tiny human figures that came and went, well manned. Boats lay at docks on the lake between town and fort, guarded by men.

She closed her eyes, listening for animals. In the pits she heard only a few rats and mice. Every other animal had fled the zone of destruction, and its fringes were loud with battles fought over every bit of food. In the lake she heard death. Filth lay in the water: garbage from the town and fort, waste dirt from the mines. The fish gasped for air in the lake's northern waters. Their kinfolk in cleaner water went hungry as food sources died.

Brokefang stuck his cold nose into the girl's ear. *I told you,* he said.

"Those are mines," Numair commented, his voice low. He unhooked his spyglass from his belt, opened it, and put it to his eye. "But what are they for? The opal mines around here were emptied nearly half a century ago."

"What are opals?" asked Daine.

"They are used in magic, like other gemstones. Mages will do anything to get opals, particularly black opals."

Daine was puzzled. Since her arrival in Tortall she had seen all kinds of precious stones, but not those. "What do they look like?"

Numair lifted a chain that lay around his neck, under his shirt. From it hung a single oval gem that shimmered with blue, green, orange, and gold fires. "Opals are power stones. Black ones like this are the best. They store magic, or you may use the stone to increase the strength of a spell. I saved for *years* to purchase this. Emperor Ozorne has a collar made of them—six rows, threaded on gold wire. He has a mine somewhere, but he guards the location even more carefully than he guards his power." He glared at the mines. "Surely we would know if opal dirt were found here once more. Dunlath *is* a Tortallan fief."

*The ground shook last fall,* Brokefang said. *See the raw earth on the mountains, behind the fort? Cliffs fell there. In spring, when the pups were new and still blind, a mage came and exploded holes where the pits are now.*

"Let us speculate," Numair said when Daine finished translating. "Something of value—opal dirt, for example, or even gold—was seen in the fallen cliffs, after the earthquake. The lord of Dunlath sent for a mage with blasting expertise, doubtless a war mage, on the chance he would uncover more—and he did. It may be the same mage who destroyed the Ninth Riders. But who buys what is taken from the land? It isn't the king, or he would have told us."

Daine looked back at the mines. The ogre who had fallen was on his feet again, blue liquid—his blood—coursing down his back in stripes. "I don't care if they *are* ogres," she said quietly. "That's slavery down there, and we aren't a slave country."

"It appears they are expanding, too." Numair pointed over Daine's shoulder. Here, in a direction she had not looked before, humans and ogres with axes were hard at work, cutting down trees and dragging the stumps from the ground.

Now you see why we need you, Brokefang said, baring his teeth as he watched the tree cutting. This must stop. It *will* stop. Soon there will be no game, and everyone here will starve, even the ones who ordered this.

"We need to learn more," Numair replied. "We need to speak with those in charge, in the fief village and the castle. Then I want to get word to King Jonathan. Something is badly amiss." He inched back into the cover of the trees, Daine, Fleetfoot, and Short Snout following.

Realizing Brokefang had not come with them, Daine looked back. The chief wolf stood on the cliff, his fur bristling, his ears forward and his tail up as he growled defiance at the ruin below.

On their return to the campsite, Daine let the others go ahead as she took her crossbow and went hunting. She was in luck, finding and bagging two plump rabbits soon after leaving the trail.

Human friends often exclaimed to see her hunt. They seemed to think, because she shared a bond with animals, that she ought to go meatless.

"That's fair daft," she had said when Princess Kalasin mentioned it. "Some of my best friends are hunters. *I'm* a hunter. You eat what you're made to eat. I just make sure I don't use my power to bring game to me, and I stop listening for animal voices with my magic. I close it all off."

"You can *do* that?" Kally had asked, eyes wide.

"I must," Daine had replied. "Otherwise my hunting would be— dirty. Vile. When I go, I hunt like any other two-legger, looking for tracks and following trails. And I'll tell you something else. I kill fast and clean, so my game doesn't suffer. You know I can, too. I almost never miss a shot."

"I suppose, if that's how you do it, it's all right," the girl had said, though she still looked puzzled.

Daine had snorted. "Fairer than them that kill an animal for its horns or skin, so they can tack it on their wall. I hunt to eat, and *only* to eat."

When she reached the camp, it was nearly dark. The pack had gone, leaving Russet, Numair, and Kitten with the pups and horses. Once Daine appeared, Russet left to hunt for himself. Numair, who had started a pot of rice, smiled when he saw her, but he looked preoccupied. From experience she knew it did no good to talk when something was on his mind, so she let him be.

Once her rabbits were cleaned, spitted, and cooking, she groomed the horses and Cloud, oiled rough patches in Kitten's hide, and wrestled with the pups. She ate quickly when supper was done, and cleaned up without bothering Numair. He wandered to the opposite side of the pond, where he stretched out on the ground and lay staring at the trees overhead.

Russet came back, grinning. All that was left of a pheasant who had not seen him in the brush was a handful of bright feathers in his fur. He panted as Daine pulled them out, then licked her face.

"Would you help me do something?" Daine asked, and explained the badger's lesson.

It sounds interesting, the young wolf answered. What must I do?

"Nothing," the girl said. "I have to come into you." Closing her eyes, she took a deep breath and let it go. All around she heard familiar noises. Numair had gone to sleep. Cloud drowsed where she stood, dreaming of galloping along an endless plain. Kitten sorted through a collection of pebbles, muttering to herself. Daine closed out everything but Russet's sounds: his powerful lungs taking air in and letting it go, the twitch of an ear, the pulse of his heart.

She drew closer and closer until his thoughts crept into her mind. On the surface were simple things, like the shred of pheasant caught on a back tooth, the coolness of the packed earth under his body, his enjoyment of being with her. Below that was the powerful sense of Pack that was part of any wolf, the feeling of being one with a group where everything was shared.

The change from her mind to his was gradual this time. It felt as if she were water sinking into earth, becoming part of him in slow bits. When he blinked, vision came in blacks, whites, and grays, and she knew she saw through his eyes. Her ears picked up the tiniest movement, from the scratch of Kitten's claws on her pebbles to the grubbing of a mouse in the reeds. He inhaled, and a rich bouquet of odors came to her: the individual scents of everyone in the clearing, wet earth, pines, the fire, moss, traces of cooked rabbit and plants.

He sniffed again, and caught a whiff of scent from the trench Daine and Numair used as a privy. The girl was amazed. She disliked that smell, and had dug the trench far from the clearing where they ate and slept on purpose. She certainly couldn't detect it with her own nose. Not only could Russet smell it clearly, but he didn't think the trench odor was bad—just interesting.

Silly galloped over to leap on Russet's back, and Daine was back within her own mind. "Thank you," she told Russet in a whisper.

Thank *you*, he replied, and trotted off to romp with the pups.

She stretched, not quite comfortable yet in her skin. The change to her own senses was a letdown. As good as her ears were, they were not nearly as sharp as the wolf's, and her nose was a poor substitute for his. While she was glad not to be able to smell the trench once more, there had been plenty of good scents available to Russet.

"At least I see colors," she told Kitten. "That's *something*."

The pack returned with full bellies as she was banking the fire. They had fed on a sheep that had strayed from its flock, reducing it to little more than a handful of well-gnawed bones.

Daine frowned when she heard this. "But that's one of the things that make two-leggers hunt you, when you eat their animals."

They will not find out, Brokefang said calmly. When you ran with the pack before, you warned us about human herds. We cannot stop eating them. They are slow, and soft, without hard feet or sharp horns to protect them. What we *can* do is hide signs of the kill. We sank what was left in a marsh, and we dragged leafy branches over the place where we killed, to hide the blood.

Instead of reassuring her, his answer made her uneasy. Here was more unwolflike behavior, a result of the pack's involvement with her. Where would it end? She couldn't even say the change was only in Brokefang, because the rest of the pack helped him. She had to think of a way to protect them, or to change them back to normal beasts, before humans decided the Long Lake Pack was too unusual—too dangerous—to live.

That plan would have to wait. The badger's lesson had tired her again. She went to bed, and dreamed of men slaughtering wolves.

In the morning Daine and Numair rode to the town of Fief Dunlath, leaving the wolves behind. Reaching the village at noon, they entered the stable yard of the town's small, tidy inn. Hostlers came to take their horses. Dismounting from Cloud, Daine took the pack in which Kitten was hidden and slung it over her shoulder, then followed Numair indoors. They stood inside, blinking as their eyes adjusted from the sunny yard to the dark common room. In the back someone was yelling, "Master Parlan! We've guests!"

The innkeeper came out and bowed to Numair. "Good day to you, sir. Ye require service?" he asked with a brisk mountain accent.

"Yes, please. I'd like adjoining rooms for my student and me."

"Forgive me, mistress," Parlan said, bowing to Daine. "I dinna see ye." He looked her over, then asked Numair, "Ye said—adjoinin' rooms, sir?"

"Yes," Numair replied. "If there's a connecting door, it must be locked."

The innkeeper bowed, but his eyes were on Daine. "Forgive me, sir—*locked*?"

Daine blushed, and Numair looked down his nose at the man. "People have sordid minds, Master Parlan." Despite his travel-worn clothes, he spoke like a man used to the obedience of servants. "I would like my student to be spared idle gossip, if you please."

Parlan bowed low. "We've two very nice rooms, sir, overlooking the kitchen garden. Very quiet—not that we've much excitement in these parts."

"Excellent. We will take hot baths, as soon as you are able to manage, please." A gold coin appeared in Numair's hand and disappeared in Parlan's. "And lunch, I think, after the baths," added the mage.

"Very good, sir," the man said. "Follow me." He led the way upstairs.

Kitten wriggled in the pack, and chirped. "Hush," Daine whispered as Parlan opened their rooms. "I'll let you out in a moment."

The room was a small one, but clean and neatly kept, and the bath was all Daine could hope for after weeks of river and stream bathing. The food brought by the maid was plain and good. Daine felt renewed afterward, enough so that she took a short nap. She was awakened by a scratching noise. When she opened her eyes, the dragon was picking at the lock on the door between the two rooms.

"Leave it be, Kit," Daine ordered, yawning. "You've seen locks back home."

The young immortal sat on her haunches, stretching so that her eye was on a level with the keyhole, and gave a soft trill. The door swung open to reveal Numair in a clean shirt and breeches. He was holding a piece of paper.

"Did I know she could do that?" he asked with a frown.

"No more did I," retorted Daine.

Numair glared at the dragon, who was investigating his room as thoroughly as she had her own. "That door was locked for a *reason*," he told her sternly. To Daine he added, "Though actually I *do* need to speak with you. We've been invited to dine tonight at the castle."

"Why?" the girl asked, rubbing her eyes.

"It's typical of nobles who live out of the way. A newcomer is worth some attention—it's how they get news. I don't suppose you packed a dress."

Since her arrival in Tortall, when her Rider friends had introduced her to breeches, she had worn skirts rarely, and always under protest. When the village seamstress showed her the only gown that would be ready in time, Daine balked. The dress was pink muslin, with lace at collar and cuffs—a lady's garment, in a color she hated. She announced she would go in breeches or not at all.

Numair, usually easygoing, sometimes showed an obstinate streak to rival Cloud's. By the time their escort came, Daine wore lace-trimmed petticoats, leather shoes, and the pink dress under a wool cloak to ward off the nighttime chill. A maid had done up her stubborn curls, pinning them into a knot at the back of her neck. Kitten's mood was no better than Daine's: told she could *not* go with them, the dragon turned gray and hid under the bed.

Their escort came after dark to guide them across the causeway to the island and its castle. Hostlers took charge of Spots and Cloud, and servants took their cloaks, all in well-trained silence. A footman led them across the entrance hall to a pair of half-open doors.

Behind those doors a man was saying, ". . . know wolves like th' back of m'hand. I tell ye, these have *got* to be werewolves or sommat from th' Divine Realms. They don't act as wolves should act! See this? An' *this*? *Laughin'* at me, that's what they're doin'!"

"My lord, my ladies," the footman said, breaking in, "your guests are here." He bowed to Numair and Daine and ushered them in ahead of him. "I present Master Numair Salmalín, of Corus, and his student, called Daine."

They were in an elegant sitting room, being looked over by its occupants. The footman announced, "My lord Belden, master of Fief Dunlath. My lady Yolane of Dunlath, Lord Belden's wife and heiress of Dunlath. Lady Maura of Dunlath, my lady's sister."

Numair bowed; Daine attempted a curtsy. Yolane, in her thirties, and Maura, a girl of ten, were seated by the hearth fire. Though introduced as sisters, there was little resemblance between them. Yolane was beautiful, with ivory-and-rose skin, large brown eyes, a tumble of reddish brown curls, and a soft mouth. Her crimson silk gown hugged a trim body and narrow waist; deep falls of lace at her wrists drew the eye to long, elegant hands. Diamonds glittered around her neck and at her earlobes. Maura was painfully plain, a stocky child with straight brown hair, attired in a blue dress that fit badly.

Lord Belden was of an age with his wife, a lean, bearded man who showed more interest in his wineglass than in his guests. His brown hair and beard were clipped short. His clothing was equally businesslike, though his maroon brocade tunic and white silk shirt and hose were of the finest quality.

Before the nobles stood a man in rough leather. He bristled with weapons, and held a pair of wolf traps. Yolane fanned herself, trying to disperse the aroma that came from the traps; Maura held her nose. The wolfhounds that sat or sprawled at the hunter's feet rose when they saw Daine. Slowly they went to her, their wire-haired faces eager. She offered her hands for them to sniff.

"Here!" barked the hunter. "Them ain't ladies' dogs! They're fierce hunters, and no' t' be cosseted!"

Daine snickered as the hunters crowded around her, tails wagging. "Yes, you're fine dogs," she whispered, returning their welcome. "You're *lovely* dogs, even if you do hunt wolves."

We *try* to hunt them, the chief of the wolfhounds said. The man would like us to succeed, but how can we, when wolves do such strange things?

"Tait, take those brutes away," commanded Yolane. "This is a civilized gathering."

The huntsman stalked out, whistling to his dogs. They followed obediently, with an apology to Daine.

As they went, they brushed past another man who entered, smiling wryly. He was broad-shouldered and handsome, dressed neatly in a white shirt, brown silk tunic and hose, and polished boots. His brown-blond hair was clipped short over a clean and open face. Coming up behind Numair, he said, "I hope you forgive my—"

Numair turned to look at him, and the stranger's jaw dropped. His hazel eyes opened wide in shock. "Mithros, Mynoss, and Shakith," he whispered.

Daine frowned. Until now, the only one she'd ever heard use that particular oath was Numair himself.

"Arram?" the man asked in a melodic voice. "Is that Arram *Draper*?"

Numair gaped at him. "Tristan Staghorn? They told me you were still in Carthak, with Ozorne."

# THREE

# FUGITIVES

ᗧᗣ "Oh, Ozorne," the newcomer scoffed. "No, I felt too—restricted, serving him. I'm my own man now—have been for a year." He and Numair shook hands.

"Tristan, you know our guest?" The lady rose from her chair and walked toward Numair, as graceful as a dancer.

"*Know* him?" replied Tristan. "My lady, this is Master Numair Salmalín, once of the university at Carthak, now resident at the court of Tortall."

Yolane offered Numair a hand, which he kissed. "How wonderful to find such beauty in an out-of-the-way place," he said gallantly. "Does King Jonathan know the finest jewel in Tortall does not adorn his court?"

The lady smiled. "Only a man who lives at court could turn a compliment so well, Master Salmalín."

"But Tristan didn't call you that," Lord Belden said coolly. "He called you Arram something."

"I was known as Arram Draper in my boyhood," explained Numair.

Tristan grinned. "Oh, yes—you wanted a majestic, *sorcerous* name when you got Master status. Then you *had* to change it, when Ozorne ordered your arrest."

Yolane and Belden looked sharply at Numair. "Wanted by the emperor of Carthak?" the woman asked. "You must have done something serious."

Numair blushed. "The emperor is very proprietary, Lady Yolane. He feels that if a mage studies at his university, the mage belongs to him." He looked at Tristan. "I'm rather surprised to see *you* here. You were the best war mage in your class."

War mage, Daine thought, startled. That's who Numair said blasted the mines and killed the Riders.

"I brought the emperor to see reason," Tristan replied, looking at Daine. "I'm sorry, little one—I didn't mean to be rude. Who might you be?"

"May I present my student?" Numair asked. "Master Tristan Staghorn, this is Daine—Veralidaine Sarrasri, once of Galla."

Yolane's lips twisted in a smirk. "*Sarra*sri?"

Daine turned beet red. The lady knew it meant "Sarra's daughter," and that only children born out of wedlock used a mother's name. She lifted her head. She was *proud* she was named after Ma.

"Are you a wizard?"

Maura's question startled Daine: she'd forgotten the girl was even in the room. "No," she replied. "Not exactly."

A manservant entered and bowed. "Ladies and lords, if it pleases you, your meal awaits."

Numair offered his arm to Yolane. She accepted it and guided him toward a door in the back of the room. "Would you explain something? We heard you were at the attack on Pirate's Swoop last year. Wasn't it from an imperial fleet? I was surprised His Majesty didn't declare war on Carthak."

"He nearly did," replied Numair. "They used Carthaki war barges, but the emperor claimed they were sold to pirates. As the king was unable to prove we were attacked by anyone other than pirates, he was forced to drop it."

Tristan offered Maura his arm with a mocking bow. The younger girl sniffed and took it. Belden, who appeared to spend much of his time in a brown study, followed them and left Daine to bring up the rear alone. For the first time in many, many months, she felt like a complete outsider. She did not like the feeling.

The dining hall was large enough to seat a household. Daine had been in many homes in the last year where servants and lords ate together, but tonight, at least, Dunlath's nobles dined alone. Four other guests were already seated at a table placed lower and at an angle to the main board. They rose and bowed when the nobles entered. Daine saw Numair halt, dark brows knit in surprise.

Tristan said, "Numair, I think you know Alamid Mokhlos, and perhaps Gissa of Rachne?" A man in a silk robe and a dark, striking woman bowed to Numair, who hesitated, then bowed in return. "They were on their way to the City of the Gods and stopped to pay me a visit."

"My lord's hospitality is so good, we fear we shall be here forever," the woman said in a heavily accented voice. "It is good to see you again, Arram."

"Not Arram anymore," Tristan corrected her. "Numair Salmalín."

"That's right." Alamid had a high, cutting voice. "We'd heard you were the Tortallan king's pet mage."

Tristan introduced the remaining two men in plain tunics as Hasse Redfern and Tolon Gardiner, merchants. Yolane and Belden had taken their places at the main board, and waited with polite impatience for the introductions to end. A maid gave Daine a seat beside Maura, at a table across the room and opposite the four less important guests. Tristan steered Numair to a place next to Yolane. Daine was interested to see that Numair's seat was so far from Alamid, Gissa, and the others that he wouldn't be able to talk to them during the meal.

Her own place beside Maura was entirely out of the stream of conversation. If they strained, they could just hear what was said by the adults on the dais.

"If you're waiting for them to talk to us, you have a long wait," Maura informed her at last.

Daine came to herself with a jerk. It occurred to her that she was being rude. "I'm sorry," she apologized, and tasted her soup. It was cold.

Maura correctly interpreted the face she made. "My sister doesn't want servants eating here, as they did when our father was alive. She says the king doesn't eat with his servants, so we won't, either. That made the servants angry, so they take their time bringing meals."

A mouse was exploring Daine's shoe. She broke off a scrap of bread and fed it to him. When he finished, he whisked out of sight. "Why should the way the king eats decide how you take your meals here?"

"We're his closest relatives—third cousins or something like that," replied Maura, eating her soup. "Yolane says if he hadn't married and had children, she might be queen today. If you're from Galla, why do you live here? And what was your name again?"

Daine looked at her dinner companion, *really* looked at her, and smiled. The girl's brown eyes were large and frank under limp bangs, and freckles adorned her cheeks and pug nose. Perhaps to preserve her ivory skin Lady Yolane never went into the sun, but her sister was a different kind of female.

"I'm called Daine, for short," she replied. "And it's a fair long story, how I came to Tortall."

"It's to be a fair long meal," said Maura. "*She* insists on having all the courses, just like at court."

The mouse had returned, with friends. The feel of their cold noses on her stockinged legs made Daine smother a giggle.

"I keep telling her, if she likes court so much, why doesn't she live there all year, like some nobles. She doesn't take the hint. Uh—Daine, don't jump or screech or anything, but there's a mouse in your sleeve."

Daine looked. A pair of black button eyes peered up at her. "That's hardly a safe place," she commented.

The mouse replied he liked it there.

"Who are you talking to?" asked Maura.

Daine blushed. "The mouse," she explained. "I understand what animals say, and they understand me. Oftentimes I forget that we aren't speaking as humans do, and I talk to them as I might to you or Numair." To the mouse she added, "Well, if a cat sees you, there will be all sorts of trouble."

"No cats in the dining hall," interrupted Maura. "Yolane hates 'em."

"I knew there was something about her I didn't like," muttered Daine.

Servants took the soup bowls, replacing them with plates laden with meat and vegetables. Daine was glad to see steam rise from her food, although none came from those that went to the head table. She mentioned it to Maura as she coaxed her mouse friend to sit beside her, rather than in her sleeve.

"The servants like me, so they try to keep my food hot. It's just hard with soup—it cools fast."

Daine hesitated, trying to decide how to ask her next question. While she thought, she continued to feed bread to the mice. "You two don't seem like sisters," she commented at last.

"Half sisters," Maura said. "Her mother came from one of the oldest families in the realm. She died a long time ago, and Father remarried when Yolane got engaged to Belden. She tells everyone my mother was a country nobody."

Daine frowned. "Forgive my saying so, Lady Maura, but your sister doesn't sound like a nice person."

"She isn't," was the matter-of-fact reply. "She cares about how old our family is and how close to the throne we are, not about taking care of Dunlath and looking after our people. And Belden's as bad as she is. Father said he's just a younger son, so he has a lot to prove."

Daine shook her head, thinking you could never tell with nobles. Sometimes they were normal humans, and sometimes they worried about the silliest things.

Maura watched the mice for a moment. "I don't understand. Do they all come up to you that way?"

"Yes. They like me," Daine replied. "I like them."

Maura sighed. "I wish they liked *me*. I get lonesome. *She* won't let me play with commoners. All my friends in the village think I'm stuck-up now."

"Why should it matter who you play with?" asked Daine. Go sit with her, she urged the mice silently, so Maura wouldn't think Daine felt sorry for her. She's perfectly nice, you'll see.

"I don't think it should matter to anyone, but *she* says I have to think of our house and our honor." The girl turned a dangerous shade of pink. "I care more than *she* does. *She* thinks it's a big secret, but I know what's going on with her and Tristan. Oh!" She stared at her lap. A mouse stood there on his hind feet, looking her over. "Can I pet him? Will he mind?"

"Gently," Daine said. She felt sorry for Maura. From the look of things, no one seemed to care what happened to her or what she wanted. "They're shy. If you feed him, he should stay with you." Won't you? she asked the mouse.

If she feeds me, he replied. Please tell her I am partial to fruit. Humans seem to think all we eat is cheese. That's boring after a while.

Hiding a smile, Daine relayed his words to Maura, who proceeded to stuff him, and his friends. They had gone to sleep in her lap by the time the servants cleared the plates and a bard came in, carrying a lap harp. Taking a seat in front of the nobles, he tuned his instrument as the servants returned to find places around the walls. The bard played traditional songs for an hour or more. Long before he was done, Maura had gone to sleep.

Daine barely listened. Watching the adults at the main table, she realized that here was the opportunity to do what Brokefang expected her to do, deliver his request for a halt to the mining and lumber efforts. She cringed at the thought of giving such a message to these polished, self-assured humans. She also knew Brokefang wouldn't understand if she held back. Mockery and shame meant nothing to wolves.

I wish they meant nothing to me, either, she thought, making up her mind as the bard ended his last song and left the room. Forcing herself to get up, she walked out into the open space in front of the dais.

Numair looked at her, clearly puzzled. Then he guessed why she was there. He shook his head, trying to signal for her to return to her seat, but Daine fixed her eyes on Dunlath's lord and lady and ignored him.

Yolane and Belden were deep in conversation. It was Tristan who saw Daine first. Breaking off his talk with Alamid and Gissa, he looked at Daine with a raised eyebrow, then smirked. Gently he tapped Belden on the shoulder. Numair was now pointing at Daine's seat, giving her a clear order, but she shook her head. He did not have to answer to the pack; she did.

Belden called his wife's attention to the girl in pink before them. Yolane's brows snapped together. "What is it?" she asked impatiently.

Daine clenched her hands in the folds of her skirt. "Excuse me, my lord. My lady. I've been asked to speak to you by the wolves of this valley."

"*Wolves?*" asked Belden, looking haughty. "What can they say to anything?"

"Plenty," the girl said. "They live here, too, you see. They take food out of these forests, and they drink from the streams. They told me when they came, this place was near perfect." She knew her face was red by now. The huge room had gone completely silent. She'd never felt so small, or so alone, in her life. "Then *you* began digging and cutting down trees. Mine trash has started to poison the northern end of the Long Lake, did you know that? And the digging and the lumbering is scaring the game out of the valley."

To her surprise, a rough voice in the rear of the hall called, "She's right, about th' game, at least. I tried to tell ye m'self, three weeks back."

Daine looked over her shoulder. She had forgotten that the huntsman, Tait, had come to hear the bard. She ventured a smile, and he winked. Drawing her breath, feeling better, she went on. "The Long Lake Pack asked me to tell you they want you to stop. If you don't, they'll do something drastic."

"How do you know this?" Tristan's voice was too even and sincere. His eyes danced with amusement. "Did the wolves come to you in a dream, perhaps, or—"

"She has wild magic, Tristan." Numair came to stand with Daine, resting a hand on her shoulder and squeezing gently. She smiled up at him in gratitude.

"Surely you do not yet insist 'wild magic' is real," scoffed Gissa. "You are too old to pursue fables."

"It is no fable," Numair replied. "You and the Carthaki university people are like the blind man who claims sight cannot exist, because he lacks it."

"We lose sight of the point of Mistress *Sarrasri's* argument." There was a strangled note in Yolane's voice. "A pack of four-legged beasts wants us to stop mining. And cutting down trees."

"That's right," Daine said, bracing herself for what she knew was coming.

"And—if we don't"—the choked sound was thicker than ever in the woman's throat—"they'll do something—drastic. Do you know what? No, of course you don't. Perhaps—perhaps"—the strangling began to escape her now, as giggles—"they will piddle on the castle walls, or—or—"

"Howl at the sentries," Tristan suggested, grinning.

"Has she been mad for long?" Yolane asked Numair.

"You laugh at your peril," Numair warned. "This is a very different breed of wolf you're dealing with, Lady Yolane."

Yolane began to laugh, and laugh hard. Briefly she fought to get herself under control. "Maybe they'll bury their bones in my wardrobe!" she said, and began to laugh again.

Tristan smirked. "Suppose for a moment—just a moment—that you are right. Do you think we can't deal with a pack of wolves? Brute creation is in this world to serve man—not the other way around. This valley is ruled by humans."

Daine couldn't believe what she had heard. "Is that what you *really* think animals are here for?"

"No. That's what I *know* they are for. Men do not shape their concerns for the benefit of wild beasts, my dear."

Yolane had gotten herself in hand. "You are a foolish child. Master Salmalín has indulged you too much. Why, in Mithros's name, should I care in the least about the tender feelings of a pack of mangy, flea-bitten curs?"

"Think selfishly," Daine said, trying to make these arrogant two-leggers see what she meant. "You can't go on this way. Soon you will have no forests to get wood from or to hunt game in. You poison water you drink and bathe and fish in. Even if you keep the farms, they won't be enough to feed you if the rest of the valley's laid waste. You'll starve. Your people will starve—unless you buy from outside the valley, and that's fair expensive. You'll ruin Dunlath."

Yolane's eyes glittered. "Who are you to judge me in my own castle?"

"Daine," Numair said quietly.

Daine looked at Yolane, Belden, and Tristan. They stared back at her, sure of themselves and their right to do as they wished. "Well, I tried," she muttered.

Numair bowed. "My lord, my lady—with your good will, we take our leave."

As they walked out, Daine glanced at Maura. The girl had awakened and now watched Daine with a worried frown. Daine smiled, but her lips trembled a little. She hoped Maura wouldn't think she was crazy.

Servants left the dining hall ahead of them to fetch their cloaks and to bring their horses. Within minutes they were trotting across the causeway.

"I'm sorry I didn't keep my mouth shut when you wanted," she said, trying to keep a pleading note out of her voice. "I had to speak. Brokefang wouldn't understand if we came back and said we didn't say anything to them."

He reached over to pat her back. "I know. Please calm down. You aren't the kind of girl who plunges without thinking. I wish I were more like you."

She was glad the darkness covered her blush. It was the highest compliment he had ever paid her. "But you don't plunge without thinking," she protested.

"You mean you haven't *seen* me do so. What, pray, was entering that castle tonight? If I were more cautious—Enough. What's done is done." Reaching the innyard, they gave their mounts to the only hostler still up, then went to their rooms. "Good night," he said cheerfully. "I'll see you in the morning."

Her door closed behind her, Daine used a glowstone from her belt-purse to find her candle, which she lit. Kitten, sprawled on the bed, peeped drowsily.

"You prob'ly would've hated it," Daine told her, shedding her clothes. Hanging them up instead of leaving them on the floor, a habit she'd learned in months of living in the Riders' barracks, she then slipped into her nightshirt. "The little girl is nice—Maura. But the grown-ups—" Daine shook her head as she climbed under the blanket.

Kitten, listening, chirped a question. Though she was too young to hear or to answer in mind-speech as older immortals did, talking to her was never a problem. Kitten understood Common better than some humans they had met. Daine was glad this was so, since from all she had learned in months of study, Kitten would be an infant for thirty years.

"Well, they look nice, but they're cold and proud. And something's wrong. Maura says the mage from Carthak is canoodling with her sister—Lady Yolane, she is." Daine yawned. "If Lord Belden knows, he doesn't seem to care. Put out the light, Kit, there's a girl."

Kitten whistled, and the candle went out. Muttering softly, she curled up with her back against Daine. Within seconds they were asleep.

She was dreaming that she ran with the pack, the scent of elk full and savory in her nostrils, when a voice boomed in her long skull: "Daine. Daine."

Wolf body whirling, jaws ready to snap, she realized she was in bed, waking up. A gentle hand on her shoulder tugged her upright. For a brief moment she saw as a wolf saw, with grays and blacks and white the sole colors of her vision. The shadowy figure over her, lit by pale fire, doubled, then steadied back into one form. It was Numair. He had lit no candles; instead, the shimmer of his magic filled the room with a dim glow.

She felt as if she hadn't slept. "What's the hour?" she asked, yawning.

"Just after the midnight watch." His voice was so quiet it wasn't even a whisper, but she heard it clearly. "Pack. We're leaving."

She blinked, wondering if she still dreamed. "*Leaving?* But—"

"Not here," he ordered. "I'll explain on the road. Pack."

She tumbled out of bed and did as she was told. Within minutes her saddlebags were ready and she was dressed. Numair poked his head through the inner door, which stood open once more, and beckoned for her and Kitten to follow.

He left the saddling of Spots, Mangle, and Cloud to her. She did it quietly, not wanting to rouse the hostlers. Kitten went into her carrypack, an open saddlebag on Mangle that allowed her to see everything as she rode. At the last minute Numair gave Daine a handful of rags, and motioned for her to cover their mounts' feet, to muffle the sound of their shoes on the streets. "Did you leave money for our host?" she asked as she held Spots for Numair to mount.

"With a good tip over that, and a note of apology." He got himself into the saddle, a process she could never watch without gritting her teeth, and motioned for her to mount up. She did so without effort.

Go, she told Spots. He wants silence over speed, I think.

It is just as well, the patient gelding replied, passing the inn's gate with Daine and Cloud close behind. He is so tense, I think if I trotted, he would fall off. What's the matter?

He'll tell us, the girl promised. Do what you can to make him less tense.

I am a riding horse, not a god, was Spots's answer.

When they reached the trees where the road along the lakeshore crossed the river that flowed down from the western pass, Numair dismounted. Kneeling on the northern side of the crossing, he scratched a hole in the road, put something in it, and covered it over, patting the earth down firmly. Walking to the southern branch of the road, he performed the same curious rite.

"If you're leaving an offering to the crossroad god, his shrine is over there." Daine pointed to the little niche where the god's statue rested.

"I'm not," he replied, dusting his hands. He bowed to the small shrine. "No offense meant." Remounting, he guided Spots onto the track that led west, and beckoned for Daine to ride beside him.

"What's all this?" she asked. "Usually you give warning if we have to skip out in the middle of the night."

"I wanted things to seem normal when we got back to the inn, in case someone was listening. We have to get out of here and warn King Jonathan, but I can't send a message from under this shield. Even if I were to succeed, Tristan and his friends would know of it."

"And I guess you don't want them running off before we can get help."

"Exactly. Whatever is going on at Dunlath is big. Anything in which Tristan Staghorn is involved is a danger to the kingdom."

"But he said he didn't work for the emperor anymore."

"In addition to his other talents, he is an accomplished liar."

Hearing iron control in his voice, Daine shivered. It took a great deal to anger Numair Salmalín. She would not give a half copper for the well-being of someone who *did* make him angry. "Then why let us go? Surely he knew when he saw you that there'd be trouble."

"He let us go because he dumped enough nightbloom powder in my wine to keep me asleep for a century. As far as he knows, I drank it."

"Did you?"

He smiled mockingly. "Of course not. Those years of working sleight-of-hand tricks in every common room and village square between Carthak and Corus weren't wasted. The wine ended up on the floor, under the table."

"He should've known you'd see the potion."

"Not particularly. When we were students, I had no skill in the detection of drugs or poisons. I knew *nothing* practical. People are impressed that I am a black robe mage from the Imperial University, but black robe studies cover esoterica and not much else. Yes, I can change a stone to a loaf of bread, *if* I want to be ill for days and *if* I don't care that there will be a corresponding upheaval elsewhere in the world. Much of the practical magic I have learned I acquired here, in Tortall. From the king, in fact."

"But if it's just Tristan shielding this place, can't you break through? Oh, wait—you think those other two wizards are helping him."

He smiled. "There were *five* mages in that banquet hall. Tristan called Masters Redfern and Gardiner merchants, but if they are, it is only as a cover occupation. They have the Gift, too."

Daine guessed, "Another thing Tristan doesn't know you can tell?"

The man nodded. "From the way the others defer to him, he is in charge of what is transpiring here. That means this affair is the emperor's business. Tristan has been his dog for years—only Ozorne can tell him where to bite."

"Nice," growled Daine. "Then Tristan did for the Ninth Riders?"

"I'm afraid so, magelet. It is probable those missing soldiers met the same fate as well."

"He's got a lot to answer for," she snapped. "*And* that emperor. But why here? Why take an interest in Dunlath, of all places?"

"That's an excellent question. I would like to have it answered. Ozorne does *nothing* unless there is something in it for him. What could Dunlath offer the Emperor Mage?"

A half-familiar whisper made Daine look around, then up. Suddenly she felt exposed on the riverbank. "Where can we get under cover?"

"I see trees over there—"

Mangle, Spots, the trees, she ordered silently. Fast!

The horses leaped forward. Numair almost fell before he grabbed his saddle horn. I thought we broke him of not holding onto the reins when he rides, Daine said to his mount as their group hid under the trees.

I thought so, too, replied Spots.

Dismounting, the girl went forward until she could see the sky. A pair of odd shapes reeled overhead, outlined by moonlight, their presence an unpleasant shadow in her mind. It took a moment to identify what she saw: bat wings, spread wide to lift a body not made for flight. Long, wedge-shaped heads craned, searching the ground below. Only when the great creatures gave up and flew north did she see them clearly against the just-past-full moon. They were horses, and something was wrong with their feet.

She had met winged horses. They were shy creatures who tended to keep out of human sight. She sensed them as she could other immortals, and their presence in her mind was never unpleasant.

Returning to Numair and the horses, she asked softly, "If a winged horse is an evil immortal—if something's *wrong* with one—would it have a special name?"

"Hurrok," Numair said. "The name is a slurring of 'horse-hawk.' They have a carnivore's fangs, and claws, not hooves. Their eyes are set forward in their skulls, as a predator's are."

"Goddess bless," she whispered, her skin prickling. "That's *awful*."

"Is that what you sensed? Hurroks?"

"Yes," she said, remounting Cloud. "And I did once before, too. I think it was the first night we were at the wolves' meeting place." Listening to the animal voices all around, she heard familiar ones. She called to them, and they agreed to come. "Let's wait a moment," she suggested. "The pack's near."

"Daine, I want to be out of this valley by dawn."

"Don't worry," she told him. "I said they're close, didn't I? We can ride a little more if it will make you happy."

"It—stop." He held up a hand, as if he listened for something. "They know we're gone," he said at last. "They're searching along the net."

A lump formed in her throat. "What do we do?"

He smiled. "Unveil our insurance." He raised his hands. Black fire that sparkled with points of white spilled out of his palms, arching up and around him and Spots, who shook his head.

*I wish he wouldn't do this when he's on me,* the gelding said nervously. *It's really very upsetting.*

Daine could see his point, but told him, *If you're a wizard's horse, you should be used to it. And you are a wonderful mount for him— patient, willing, gentle. I know he couldn't manage without you.*

Spots blew through his nose, pleased by the compliments.

Wrapped in a shroud of glittering fire, Numair pointed to the northern road below. Black fire shot from his finger like a lightning bolt, crackling as it flew downhill. Shifting his aim to the south, he loosed a second bolt.

"What was that?" Daine asked, startled.

"Those things I buried at the crossroads? Once activated, as I just did, they release simulacra of a man shrouded in my Gift, riding hard on the road. Now Tristan has three of me to chase, and the ones that ride north and south will appear much more like the real me than I do."

*But they will see Daine with only one of you,* Cloud pointed out. The girl passed it on.

The look on Numair's face was one of smug satisfaction. "The magical cloak on my simulacra is very large, and very sloppy, enough to cover more than one person. *Just* the thing a sheltered academic like me would have for concealment, since I'm unused to fieldwork."

"But they *know* you," Daine argued. "They know you handle immortals for the king. Wouldn't they see you *must* have learned something practical by now?"

"Magelet, one thing I have learned is that humans cling to their first knowledge of you, particularly if they have no experience of you once you've changed. Tristan, Alamid, and Gissa knew me in Carthak, when I was a book-bound idiot."

Daine shook her head. She thought her friend placed too much trust in the enemy mages' stupidity.

There was a yip nearby, and the pack streamed out of the trees, Brokefang in the lead. They gathered around the horses, tails wagging. Kitten stuck her head out of her pack and chirped to Russet. Mangle held still unhappily as the wolf braced himself against the cob's withers to lick Kitten's nose.

Where are you going? Brokefang asked. Why are the horses' feet covered?

"The humans are up to no good," Daine told her friend, speaking aloud for Numair's benefit. "We have to warn the king, and for that we must get out from under the magic they put over the valley."

Brokefang backed up so he could see both Daine and Numair. You are leaving?

"To alert the king," Daine reassured him. "He will stop the mining and the tree cutting."

I do not know your king. I know only you. You said that you would help us.

"But I *am* helping," Daine protested. The other wolves, looking worried, sat down to listen. "We're going to get help."

That is help for two-leggers. You are needed here.

"Daine, we have to go," said the man quietly.

She hesitated. There was something odd in Brokefang's eyes. Dismounting, she knelt before the chief wolf, tangling her hands in his ruff. Eyes closed, she opened up her mind to his, and his alone, listening hard to the tumble of ideas and images in his skull.

Brokefang was afraid. New thoughts came thick and fast now, more every day, and he did not understand them all. It had taken him this way before, after the girl-who-is-Pack left, in the time when men drove them from their home. Then he had no one to turn to, no one in the pack who would understand and explain these thoughts. He had borne them alone for months, until they slowed to a trickle. The trickle he could bear. Then the girl had come again, and new thoughts roared through his brain like a flash flood.

"Poor Brokefang," she whispered, rubbing her friend's ears. "I don't s'pose wolves get headaches, but if they did, you'd have a grand one."

"Daine, those simulacra won't last after dawn!" hissed Numair.

She looked at him. He was keeping an eye on the road to the village and trying not to grip Spots's reins too tightly. She had to make a decision, and make it fast. He didn't need her to do what was necessary—she would only distract him. On the other hand, she was the only one who could help this wolf.

Going to Mangle, she undid Kitten's pack and the pack that held her things. "I can't go with you," she said as she worked. "Brokefang needs me."

"This is no time for sentiment! Here you're in *danger* until help comes!"

"And they aren't?" she asked, indicating the pack. "They're changed because of *me*, Numair. Me. I didn't even know I *had* magic when this pack saved my life, but my head must have been wide open, and all the magic spilled out. Now they need help to deal with what happened to them when I didn't know anything. I can't let them down, Numair. I'm sorry."

"So you'll let *me* down?" He was so worked up that Spots was shifting position nervously. "What if something delays my return?"

She smiled at him. "You know I can fend for myself in the woods better'n most anybody. I've my crossbow. I'll be fine."

He drew a deep breath. "I could *make* you come with me."

She knew only grave concern for her would make him voice a threat, so she bore him no grudge. "Maybe you could and maybe you couldn't, but while we found out, Tristan would see you doing something your whatchumacallems weren't."

"Simulacra," he corrected automatically.

"Whatever."

He stared down at her, eyes shadowed. "You are too stubborn for your own good," he said at last.

"That's what Ma told me, all the time." Smiling, she added, "If it was you in my shoes, you'd say the same."

He sighed. "Very well. Stay on the mountainsides. Keep moving. Leave the forts alone, the castle, the village—*everything*, understand? Otherwise I will chain you in the worst dungeon I can find when I get my hands on you again."

"Yes, yes," she told him. "Now scoot. The sooner you leave, the sooner you can return." Mangle, go with him, she added. It will get you away from the wolves for a day or two.

*Thank you*, the cob said gratefully. He trotted off, heading for the western pass, and Spots turned to follow.

"Wait," Numair said. "How *will* I find you, when I return?"

"Spots will know. Please leave. You still have a ride to the pass."

The man reached a hand down, and she gave him hers. He squeezed it gently. "Be careful. Stay out of sight."

"I'll be fine," she assured him.

Spots trotted quickly after Mangle, muffled hooves thudding on the ground. Daine watched them go, feeling a bit forlorn.

## ⤙ FOUR ⤚

# BROKEFANG ACTS

ℭ He mustn't worry, Brokefang said. The pack will keep you safe.
"I know," she whispered. "Besides, who needs humans?" she added more cheerfully, looking at the wolves' faces. "All they do is slow me down and screech when they see my friends. Most humans, anyway."

I like the stork-man, protested Brokefang.

So do I, added Short Snout. Fleetfoot, Russet, and Battle yipped agreement.

He is a good pack leader for you, Brokefang went on. Humans are like wolves. We all need a pack. He looked at Cloud, and added, Or a herd.

"Not me," the girl said, fastening her things to Cloud's saddle. "I can hunt alone."

No, Brokefang said. It is not just for food that you need a pack. It is for warmth, and the pack song. The wolf who sings alone is not happy.

We could chat all night, Cloud put in tartly. Or we can get away from here. The first thing the humans will do when they cannot find Numair is send hunters.

We will move faster if you ride, Russet said. Kitten can ride on me, if she promises not to scratch.

The young dragon chirped and tried to climb out of her carry-sack. Daine helped her, and placed her on Russet. Gently Kitten gripped his fur in all four paws, balancing herself comfortably. Daine looked at the odd picture they made, shook her head, and mounted Cloud. Brokefang trotted to the head of the line. The pack followed in single file, with Daine and Cloud bringing up the rear.

They reached the wolves' meeting place shortly before dawn. Frost-fur and the pups were there to greet them. As the wolves celebrated the reunion of the pack, Daine unsaddled Cloud and rubbed her down. The girl noticed that Kitten, still on Russet's back, ended up as part of the ceremony by accident. To her amusement, and Kitten's pleasure, the pups waved their tails slightly at the dragon this time, even if they still would not approach her.

Once Cloud was tended, Daine removed her boots and crawled into her bedroll, though she wasn't drowsy yet. Sharp Nose and Frolic took the pups for a hunt. Most of the others settled around Daine, while Frostfur lay at the pond's edge, within earshot. Kitten stretched out by the girl and went promptly to sleep.

Now, Brokefang said, did you speak to the two-leggers?

"Yes. They won't do anything. They laughed at me. I told you they would."

Why? Longwind wanted to know. What is there about you that is funny?

"They don't see me the same way you do. To them I'm only a girl-child. They think they know all there is to know," Daine told them. "They think they don't have to listen to me. Would you try to tell an eagle how to hunt?"

No more than eagles would tell a wolf how to hunt, replied Battle.

"To the castle lords and Tristan, I *am* a wolf telling an eagle how to hunt."

Did you *try*? inquired Russet. Did you say they are driving off game and killing fish?

"Yes. They don't care. They say they can use the valley as they please."

I didn't think you would be much help, Frostfur said tartly. What are you good for, except to talk to?

That stung. Daine glared at Brokefang's mate. "I'd like to see you do any better, Mistress Know-it-all."

Frostfur bit a flea that was nibbling her backside and did not answer.

"The king will help," Daine said to Brokefang, wanting him to believe and wait for aid, not try something on his own. "The two-leggers are up to something bad here, and he will set it right."

I do not know of kings, the wolf replied. To me they are just two-leggers.

Exactly, Fleetfoot said. We have yet to see two-leggers fix the harm they do. To Daine she added, You are not a two-legger to me—you are People.

Longwind sighed. Brokefang's uncle, he was the oldest of the pack, with gray hairs in the black fur of his muzzle. You were right to act, Brokefang. I questioned you, until you made me submit. I was wrong. At least now we have made a beginning.

Daine sat up, suddenly wary. "What d'you mean, you've made a beginning?"

It was fun. That was Russet, whose eyes shone with delight. You should have been with us. Can I show her? he asked Brokefang. Please?

Short Snout yipped agreement; Longwind stirred the dust with his tail. Frostfur sat up, watching Daine with an odd, smug look in her amber eyes.

Very well, Brokefang consented.

Russet yapped gleefully and trotted into the reeds. He returned dragging something that looked like a big stick.

Do not worry, Brokefang told Daine as Russet approached her bedroll. We did the same thing as with the sheep we ate, the tricks to hide our trail.

Reaching Daine, Russet dropped the "stick" on the ground, tail waving. His trophy was an ax—one of the big ones used by woodsmen to cut down trees. Daine touched the handle, just to confirm it was real. "How—" she croaked, her throat dry. Grabbing the water bag, she drank, then put it aside. "How many of these do you have? Just this?"

Oh, no, Battle replied. We took all the ones we could find in the tree cutters' camp.

It was safe, Fleetfoot assured the girl. Having traveled with Daine and Numair, she knew the odd things these friends insisted be done in the name of safety. The humans don't den where they cut trees. They den with other two-leggers, by the lake. Only the forest People saw us— they wouldn't interfere.

Daine lurched to her feet. "Where's the rest?"

Russet led her to the spot in the reeds. The girl counted, not believing her eyes. Since Numair and she had gone to the castle, the wolves had stolen fourteen big axes, and five two-man saws.

"Goddess bless," she squeaked, and sat down hard. In all the years she had associated with animals, before and after she got control of her wild magic, she had never seen an animal do something like this. This was thinking about the future. This was knowing tools were separate from the men who wielded them.

We stopped the cutting, Brokefang said. Without these, humans won't destroy more trees. They won't make the noise that frightens deer and elk.

"You don't understand. They'll come after you, just as they did back home."

Only the hunter, the one with the dog pack, can track wolves, Long-wind said.

"Tait," mumbled Daine. "His name is Tait."

None of the others can track us, Longwind went on. And Brokefang has a plan for Tait.

Short Snout grinned. I *like* the plan, he said.

Suddenly the night caught up with Daine. It was dawn; she was exhausted. Getting to her feet, she dusted her bottom and went to her bedroll. "Don't do *anything* until I wake," she ordered as she crawled into it. "Not one thing, understand? We'll talk later."

Don't be upset, Fleetfoot advised, curling up on the girl's free side. Brokefang knows what to do.

"That's what frightens me," Daine muttered, and her eyes closed.

As she slept, she dreamed. Ma tended flowers, golden hair pinned up, out of the way. A man with antlers rooted in his curly brown hair watched. Leaning on the garden wall, he was a handsome, muscular creature dressed in a loincloth and nothing else. When he moved, hints of green showed in his tan skin. Her mother looked at him, shading her eyes against the sun as her lips moved. The man laughed silently, white teeth flashing. Except for the lack of sound, she could have been some-place real, watching from the garden gate.

A bluejay screamed, *Thief, thief!* The dream ended and Daine opened her eyes, feeling *very* confused. A year before she'd had a sim-ilar vision of her mother and the stranger. What did it mean? Were the vision, and this dream, Ma's way of saying she was at peace in the Realms of the Dead? What part did the horned man play? From all Daine had heard, the Black God's domain was reserved for humans, and he was no human. For that matter, what she had just experienced was too vivid for a dream—her dreams were bits and pieces of tales that seldom made sense and never felt real.

*I* say she ought to do it, if she is Pack. The snarling voice was Frostfur's. Why leave the pups to search and fail to bring down game four times out of five when *she* is here?

Daine sat up. The pack stood around the chief wolves, in the middle of the lead-the-hunt ceremony.

Call the game to us, Frostfur ordered, coming over to Daine, ears forward and tail up, to force the girl to submit to her as other females of the pack did. Bring us a nice, fat buck. Why must we take chances when you are here, getting your smell all over our camp? Either you are Pack, and that means you obey me, or you are not. *Obey!*

"No," Daine said, meeting the female's eyes squarely.

Frostfur's hackles rose. She drew her upper lip back, baring strong teeth.

Daine crouched. "Do I tell you how to deal with the pack females?" she demanded. "I let you rule your way, and *you* do not tell *me* how to handle other People. If you weren't a wicked, nasty vixen, you never would've mentioned it."

Frostfur growled, a low, grating noise that started at the bottom of her deep chest and forced its way through her throat.

"Don't make me show you what else I learned while I was away," Daine warned. "You won't like it." Her eyes locked onto the wolf's, and held them.

The moment stretched out like the tension on a bowstring. Frostfur broke the staring contest first. She wheeled and plunged into the reeds. Hidden, she called to Brokefang. She will turn on us!

The pups whined, looking from Brokefang to the plants that hid their mother. It's all right, the pack leader said. Go on. We will bring you meat.

Leaper yipped in apology/agreement, and followed her mother. The other pups and the pack females did the same. Fleetfoot was last. She turned in front of the reeds, looked at Daine, and whined.

The girl smiled. "It's all right," she told the brown-and-gray female. "We've just never gotten along." Fleetfoot yipped in sad agreement, and vanished into the reeds. "I'm sorry, Brokefang."

He came over and licked her cheek. Will you hunt with us?

Daine smiled. "No, thanks. I have provisions."

Is there cheese? Short Snout wanted to know. Russet says it tastes good.

"I'll give you some when you return," Daine promised. "And you'll get round and fat, like a sheep." Short Snout bared his teeth in a silent wolf laugh.

We hunt, Brokefang said, and trotted off, the other males behind him. Soon the adult females, with the exception of Frostfur and Battle, left the reeds and followed. They had been gone only a moment when Frostfur went after them. Daine smiled. It seemed that a new skill, like sulking, couldn't stand up to the demands of Frostfur's stomach.

Kitten tugged at Daine's belt-pouch. The girl kept flint and steel there, and this was Kitten's way to say it was breakfast time. "I s'pose you're right," she told the dragon. "We'd all feel better for some food."

Working quickly, she built a mound of tinder and wood in the fire pit and set it to blazing. Looking up, she saw that the pups, Battle, Cloud, and Kitten had each brought a good-sized branch for her fire.

"You're learning new things too quick for me," she said. "Thank you. I think there's a sausage in my packs that might feed us."

You don't have to give me any, Cloud said with a shudder. I don't know what meat eaters see in that stuff.

Once she had fed everyone, Daine went to clean up. Not wanting to bathe in the pond, where soap would linger in water drunk by the wolves, she used a stream nearby. On her return to the clearing she found the pups, Cloud, and Kitten fast asleep. It was warm for autumn. Battle was cooling off, lying belly-down on the damp earth by the pond.

"You know the thing I've been trying?" she asked the tawny-pelted female. "I did it with Brokefang and Russet."

When you ride inside them, Battle answered. Russet said it was fun. Do you want to try it with me?

"If you don't mind," the girl said.

Very well. Battle closed her eyes and rested her chin on her feet. All I ask is that we not run around. It is too hot.

Daine grinned. "Fair enough." Sitting next to Battle, she first listened around her, checking for any sense that enemies were close. All she heard was the normal chatter of forest dwellers: squirrels, birds, and the like. Feeling safe, she focused on Battle. The joining happened faster than ever. Settling into the female's mind, she felt as if she belonged there. Perhaps Cloud had been right, and she was practically a wolf.

Battle checked the pups with one drowsy eye. They were hardly pups anymore. Soon they would hunt with the pack. She was sorry they had grown so fast. Watching over them was more fun when they were small and fuzzy.

Gazing at each of the young ones through Battle's eyes, Daine realized that even in daylight the wolf had no color vision. On the other hand, she hardly needed it. The marks on each pup's face and body were clearer to Battle's eyes than Daine's, and she could tell each pup's scent from the others with the wolf's vivid sense of smell. Battle inhaled and identified the scents that came into her nose for Daine. She inhaled again, enjoying Daine's fascination with odors as if she too smelled them for the first time.

Eventually the girl returned to her own body. Heavy-eyed, she crawled on all fours to her bedroll, turned three times against her rumpled blankets, and went to sleep curled up in a tight knot. When she woke, the late sun shone through treetops as shadows collected below. She had slept through the wolves' return. Brokefang was sprawled beside her, gorged on deer meat and fast asleep.

She touched him to ask, May I join with you?

Brokefang opened one sleepy eye. Do I have to wake up?

I don't think so.

The eye closed. Then go ahead.

She was learning how to listen, to bring herself speedily into his mind. Now, as with Battle, she made the changeover quickly. With Battle fresh in her memory, she saw how different the pack leader's mind was, not in terms of size, but of space. Numair had said, in an anatomy lesson, that humans used little of their brains. She knew that animals were the same, though they used more of what lay between their ears than humans did. For Brokefang the difference was that each nook and cranny in his skull was packed with information and ideas. He knew he would die, as would his packmates and children. He saw humans not as simple threats, but as creatures in their own right, living in packs, with thoughts and plans and reasons for what they did. He understood the animals he preyed on had lives and customs of their own, different from wolves' but with meaning for the creatures involved. It was a rushing-in of knowledge that he frantically tried to keep up with in his waking hours, with only limited degrees of success.

She withdrew hastily, and found her cheeks were damp with tears. Sitting up—wincing because she had gone stiff—she wiped her eyes on her sleeve. For a moment she thought there was something longer and hairier where her nose should be, but when she touched her face, it was gone, if it had even existed.

What's wrong? asked Cloud. Why were you crying?

Daine jumped. She hadn't known the pony was watching. I feel *terrible*, she confessed to her oldest friend. I feel as if I took something from him. As if I ruined his innocence, and yours, and it looks as if I'm ruining the rest of the pack, too. Maybe they won't be as bad as you or Brokefang, but none of you will be happy doing normal People things anymore.

So you picked up that stupid human habit of blaming yourself for things you didn't or couldn't control, retorted Cloud dryly. You did not force Brokefang to care for your wounds that night, any more than you forced me to bite you and get your blood on my teeth all those times. Just be careful who you bleed on in future. Now, come and get these burrs out of my tail. That will give you something *useful* to do.

Daine blew her nose. Cloud's horse sense spoke to her own common sense, as it always had. You aren't a god, she told herself sternly, rubbing the tip of her itchy nose until it was pink. Coarse, dark hairs fell off it into her lap. Where had they come from?

She looked at her pony and smiled. If you're so smart, then you don't need me, she told the mare.

Cloud glared and stamped. Biting back a groan, Daine lurched to her feet. "I'm coming, I'm coming," she said, picking her way through the slumbering wolves. Kitten, with a chortle, came to help as well.

Daine hunted in the gathering twilight, bringing down a pair of pheasants. As she cooked them, the pack, including the pups, revisited the carcass of the deer they had slain to finish it off. When they returned, they slept again. After a few games of stone, paper, knife with Kitten, Daine joined them.

It was a bad night. She tossed and turned, dreaming she heard a low, nasty hum in the sky overhead. When she woke and listened she heard nothing, and her clothes were sweat-soaked. The hum began once more when she went back to sleep.

Fireballs exploded without warning inside her eyelids, startling her awake. Once her eyes were open, she saw nothing. If hurroks or Stormwings passed overhead in the dark, she couldn't sense them.

She wasn't alone. Kitten woke several times, cheeping plaintively. After the third wake-up, she crawled in with Daine, something she hadn't done for months. She slept better afterward, but the girl could feel her shiver all night long. The wolves moaned and twitched with disagreeable dreams. Twice they woke Daine with their growling and snapping at invisible enemies.

Daine gave up at dawn and went to bathe and dress. When she came back, the wolves were assembling for another hunt. They ate often when they could, and a single deer was not enough for nine adults and five rapidly growing youngsters.

*We do not need to leave one of the pack behind,* Brokefang was telling his mate. *Daine can look after the pups. She is not a wolf, but her weapons serve her as claws and fangs do us. And you know yourself that Cloud will fight. Let all the adults hunt today.*

Frostfur's head drooped. She was tired and didn't want to argue with him. To Daine she said, *Old White help you if any harm comes to my pups.*

"Old White?" she asked, trying to remember if she'd heard the name.

*Old White and Night Black are the first wolf and his mate,* Brokefang said. *They lead the First Pack. And it is unwise to threaten Daine with Old White,* he told his mate. *If he comes, he will nip you for using his name lightly.*

Frostfur bared a fang in wolf disdain, and the pack left the clearing. The pups whined. They were too big to enjoy being left behind.

"You'll get your chance," Daine told them. "You have to build up your strength and your wind before you can keep up with the pack."

Her listeners were not cheered. They remained edgy, constantly fighting with one another. They teased Cloud, nipping at her flanks, until she placed a gentle, but still firm, kick on Silly's ribs. Chaser bit Kitten a little too hard, and got a scratch on the nose as his reward.

"If I have to tell you to stop it once more—" Daine warned.

Leaper yapped crossly and raced through a trail that led east, out of the clearing. The other pups followed.

"Goddess bless!" Daine went after them, tracking them down the path and planning dreadful things to do when she caught them. "I should have known any pups of Frostfur's would be a pain," she muttered, coming to open ground. Here the rocks that hid the wolf camp ended. Between them and the forest below was a meadow with grass so tall that any young wolves could play hide and pounce.

The stream where Daine bathed was near: she went to it and scrubbed her cheeks. As she did, she heard a sour note among the animal voices around her: someone nearby was dying.

Looking around, she found her patient in a tree on the far edge of the open grass. He sat in a knot-hole, shivering. Walking down the gentle slope of the meadow, she sent love and reassurance ahead until she stood below him. "Come, tree brother," she called, holding up her hands. "Let me look at you."

The squirrel opened runny eyes. He was too sick to talk. The source of his illness was plain: deep gashes on his back oozed fluid. He was far gone in fever, and his breathing was wet and difficult. As he ventured from his perch he missed his grip, his claws too weak to hang on. Daine caught him as he fell.

She sat, cradling the animal against her shirt. "You pups stay right here," she called. "And play quiet for a minute or two. Poor little man," she whispered.

She leaned back, using the squirrel's tree as support, and closed her eyes. With her magic she looked deep into the body cradled in her arms. The copper light that was the squirrel's life force flickered. Goddess, don't let me fail, she thought, and went to work.

The lungs were first. She made her power into liquid fire and poured it in to dry them. The animal's breathing cleared. Next she tended his blood, scorching out illness as she wove through his veins. Turning to his wounds, she burned off all the infection. The flesh was laid open down to the bone, the edges as clean as if cut by a knife.

Stormwing? she asked the squirrel, picturing one for him.

Yes, he replied. One landed on my branch, without any warning at all.

She nodded, unsurprised. Why would a being that fed on human misery care if it hurt an animal? Just a little more, she told her patient, and concentrated, knitting sliced muscle together. Next came the fat layer, dangerously thin in this squirrel because fever had burned much of it off. Coaxing and pushing with her power, she built it up until it covered the newly healed muscle. Last came new skin to seal his body again.

Finished, she relaxed, enjoying the fresh air and the sun on her face. When she opened her eyes, the squirrel was searching her pockets for edibles. I'm *hungry*, he explained.

Sunflower seeds in my jacket pocket, she told him. The squirrel thrust his head in and began to eat. Looking for her charges, Daine found them seated nearby, watching her and the squirrel with interest.

"Where's Kit?" she asked.

The pups looked past her, and the girl craned around the edge of the tree that supported her back. Several yards away Kitten sat on her hindquarters, staring down the slope of the ground under the trees. Her skin was changing from pale blue to a brilliant, hard-edged silver. It brightened until she actually began to glow. Opening her mouth, she *shrieked*.

Terrified, the squirrel raced up into the safety of his tree. Daine lurched to her feet. Never had she heard Kitten make such a sound, and she was afraid she knew why the dragon did so now. Ignored during her concentration on healing, a warning drone balanced against a high, singing note in her magical ear. The deep sound was so ugly it made her teeth ache.

"Back to the meadow!" she yelled at the pups. *"Hide!"* She ran for Kitten, who had yet to stop screeching. Stooping to grab the dragon, she saw what Kitten was looking at, and froze.

Over a dip in the ground appeared one clawed hand. Another hand followed. The claws were bright silver, the mark of an immortal. They groped for a hold on the flat of the ground; finding one, they gripped, digging into the earth.

The creature's head topped the rise. It was reptilian, pointed, with slits for nostrils and deep-set, shadowed eyes. It swung to the right, quiet slowly, then to the left. At last it returned to the center of its field of vision: Daine and Kitten.

Daine was cold—very cold. Her breath, and Kitten's, formed small clouds in the air. Neither of them could move. Frost grew everywhere between them and the stranger, as if an entire winter night had been crushed into a few moments.

The monster dragged its long, heavy body over the ridge, taking its time. Its skin was beaded in colors that ranged from emerald to fiery gold, passing through bronze and jade green on the way. Daine shuddered: in mortal animals, such bright markings usually meant the wearer was poisonous.

Slowly it advanced, moving right fore and left hind foot, then left fore and right hind, in a gait that was half skip, half waddle. The tail that dragged behind it bore a knobbed bone rattle, like that of certain desert snakes.

When it had crossed nearly half the distance between them, the creature opened its mouth and hissed. Its teeth were silver, curved and sharp, predator teeth. Worse, when it hissed, two fangs dropped down on bone hinges. At the tip of one a small drop of silvery liquid formed, grew large, fell.

A shaggy body flew out of the brush to fasten on the green creature's wrist, but jaws that could make quick work of elk bone barely dimpled the green creature's flesh. The pup she'd named Runt snarled defiance as he hung on. Leaper grabbed the creature's other forepaw. Chaser and the pup named Berry darted at the immortal's sides, yapping furiously, while Silly went for the rattle on its tail.

Silly went flying, the rattle broken off in his mouth. Now the immortal used its tail for balance as it rose onto its hind legs. Upright it was barely taller than Daine, though powerfully built. With quick, efficient blows of its head it knocked away the four who attacked from the front.

Kitten darted forward when the creature's eyes left hers. When it swung at her, she seized its paw and bit down, hard. The wolves' jaws had not marked the thing, but the bite of another immortal had more effect. Dark blood welled up to drip on the leaves, hissing where it struck the ground. With a snarl, the thing hurled Kitten into a clump of mountain laurel ten yards away.

*That* gave Daine the angry strength to break its hold on her mind. She flung herself to one side and yanked a large rock from the earth. "Pick on someone your own size!" she yelled, and threw.

The stone hit the creature's muzzle and shattered. Daine rolled, scrabbling for another rock, but the immortal was on her. Seizing her by the back of her shirt, it lifted her clear of the ground. She had no way to avoid its eyes. Its power caught and held her again. Details fixed themselves in her mind as her captor opened its jaws: dark blood welling from the cut left by her rock, the greens-and-spice scent of its breath, the high, singing note that cut through the harsh jangle in her mind.

Then she heard a sound such as she had never before heard in her life, a rumbling, ear-bursting shriek that make her think of rocky avalanches. Her captor released her; she crashed to the ground. Free, she scrambled away without understanding *any* of what was taking place.

The jangling sound of the fierce immortal was gone, leaving only high singing in her mind. Gasping, she turned to find the enemy. It hadn't moved from where it had dropped her, and it was no longer green. It had turned gray and dull, looking for all the world like a statue. It was not breathing.

"Horse Lords," she whispered in awe.

Seeing movement in the corner of her eye, she spun. A new immortal walked by, intent on the statue. Taking him in, the girl decided she must be dreaming. She had seen many strange creatures since coming to Tortall—ogres, trolls, winged horses, unicorns, griffins, and more—but the green thing and this one were entirely outside her experience.

Like her attacker, this immortal was similar to a lizard. Walking on its hind legs, it held its long tail off the ground, reminding her of ladies raising their little fingers as they sipped tea. It was taller than Daine's sixty-five inches, taller even than Numair's six and a half feet. Slender and graceful, it had long, delicate paws, fragile-looking bones, and silver talons. Its beaded hide was the pearly dark gray of a thunderhead, with paler gray belly scales.

Stopping at the newly made statue, the stranger broke off a finger, sniffed it, then nibbled. The finger crunched like gravel in its jaws.— *Too raw.*—The voice sounded like a whisper of flutes.—*They really must weather for a decade or so before they lose that acrid aftertaste.*—

Kitten had recovered from her unexpected flight. Chattering frantically, she galloped to the newcomer on all fours and halted by its knee.

"Kit, *no!*" Daine called, but her voice emerged only as a squeak.

The immortal cocked its head.—*Little one, you are far from home.*—Something about that sounded male, and fatherly.—*Where is your mother?*—

Kitten rose onto her haunches, gripping the stranger's leg as she peered up into his eyes. From her throat spilled a variety of sounds Daine had never heard her voice before, in tones that rose and fell like genuine speech.

The immortal looked at Daine. His eyes were deep gray with slit pupils, impossible to read. Neither was there any emotion in the voice that spoke in her mind:—*The little one says you are her mother. You have not the appearance of a dragon. Did an experiment go wrong, to trap you in a mortal shape?*—

Daine knelt to cuddle Berry, who had crept to her with ears down, whining. "You're a brave wolf," she told the pup. To the immortal she said, "Kit's real ma was killed defending my friends and me soon after she gave birth. I've been looking after Kitten—Skysong, her name is really—ever since."

The immortal looked at Kitten as the remaining pups joined Daine.—*What did you take from the humans, Skysong? Or is it this mortal who stole?*—

Kitten squawked indignantly; Daine's fading blush returned in full strength. "We didn't steal anything!"

—*Then you were foolish to stand between a Coldfang and thieves.*—The immortal's tone was one of cool interest, not anger or scorn.

Hearing that, Daine calmed down. She pointed to the statue. "What did you call it again?"

—*Coldfang. They track thieves in all realms, divine, mortal, or dead, and will guard a thing until the end of time. Men brought this one to the camp where they cut trees, last night. I followed her to see what is going on. She picked up a trail there and kept to it since dawn.*—

Daine was about to protest the new hint of theft when she remembered the pack's way to put a stop to lumbering. She took a deep breath and said, "You saved our lives. Thank you."

—*I did not act for you, but for my young cousin.*—The creature reached down to tickle Kitten's nose. She rubbed it against his paw.

"You're family?" Daine asked, alarmed. The thought of losing Kitten was scarier than the Coldfang.

This time she felt a patient sigh behind the response.—*Only in a remote sense are basilisks and dragons kindred, yet both acknowledge a bond.*—

She gulped. While Coldfangs were new, she had heard of basilisks, immortals who turned their enemies to stone.

A whine made Daine look for her charges. The pups were huddled together nearby, anxiously watching the basilisk. "Are you going to attack us?"

Kitten shook her head vigorously. A wrinkle in the basilisk's face might have been a frown.—*I am a traveler and an observer, not a killer.*—

Daine looked at the Coldfang statue: it seemed dead enough to her. Still, she knew she could trust Kitten's judgment. She went to check the pups. Silly was worst hurt, his head cut to the bone and one eye out of focus. Runt limped on a sprained paw, and several back molars were loose. Leaper, Berry, and Chaser had only bruises to show for their tussle with the Coldfang.

Daine knelt in front of Silly. "No more tail grabbing," she ordered, calling up her magic. "He almost knocked you sillier, if that's possible."

The young wolf whined and licked her face. "Enough," she told him as she cupped his head in her hands. "We'll have you fixed in no time."

This was quicker work than the squirrel had been. Infection barely had touched the open wound. She seared it in an eye-blink, and brushed through his brain to heal the inner bruises that had put his eye out of focus. The knitting of cut muscle and skin took less than a deep breath, and she was done. She touched the new scar. "I'll let you keep this," she teased. "The young lady wolves will think you're dashing. C'mere, Runt."

The sprained paw was easy, the loose molars less so. She had never rerooted teeth before, so she worked slowly and carefully to avoid mistakes.

—*Is this a new thing, this relationship of humans and wolves?*— the basilisk inquired when she was done.—*I would not have expected men's dealings with the People to improve.*—

Daine smiled. In many ways he sounded like Numair. "No, sir. I've just had a fair knack with animals since I was a pup myself, and then it turned to magic. Well, my teacher says it was magic all along, but I only learned to use it just a little while ago."

—*I have heard of wild magic.*—The basilisk looked down at Leaper, who had crept around until she was a few yards downwind. Her nose was up, nostrils flaring as she breathed in the immortal's scent. Her tail waved.—*Except for bird-folk, most of the People fear me. Your wolf friends are unusual.*—

Daine smiled wryly. "You should meet their folks."

—*I would like to do so, if you will permit it,*—was his reply.—*I would enjoy meeting the parents of such brave offspring, if they will not run away.*—

"They won't," the girl assured him. "They're fair unusual themselves."

—*Have you a name, wolf-girl?*—

"Daine. My full one's Veralidaine Sarrasri, but that's too much of a mouthful for everyday use."

The basilisk looked at her, large eyes cool and unblinking. Not for the first time and not, she was sure, for the last, Daine wished she could read an immortal's thoughts as she could an animal's.—*My full name you could not pronounce, either. You may call me Tkaa.*—

Silly raced off, followed by three of the other wolves, as Leaper continued to watch the basilisk. Her litter mates soon returned. Silly, ears and tail proudly erect, bore the Coldfang's rattle, broken off when the monster sent him flying. He dropped it in front of Daine and barked.

"For me?" she asked, picking up the rattle. "You shouldn't have."

She wiped it on her breeches. It was silvery and cold, shaped in knobs like the rattle of a mortal snake. She gave it a shake and jumped when the thing buzzed. "Tkaa, you say these things hunt thieves? How much of a trail do they need?"

—*None. They know where a thief has passed, and follow that awareness.*—

Daine shuddered. "We'd best return to camp, then. I must warn the pack."

The wolves raced through the trees and over the meadow, playfully nipping each other's hindquarters. Kitten followed at a swift, ground-eating gallop on all fours, while Daine and Tkaa brought up the rear.

## ➤➤ FIVE ◅◅

# THE TRAP

ΣꙘʓ In the clearing by the pond, the girl introduced Tkaa to Cloud. As the pups took a nap, she groomed the mare and packed. Tkaa occupied himself with Kitten, speaking in the chattering tongue she used to address him, and listening gravely to her replies. The girl fought to understand what was said, with no success.

—*Is something wrong?*—Tkaa wanted to know.—*You are frowning.*—

"I just don't see how Kit can have a language, and actually talk in it, but I can't understand. I almost never have trouble talking to immortals."

—*Your magic permits you to speak mind to mind. Skysong is not old enough for that. On the other hand, the* spoken *dragon language is one they are born knowing. My people are renowned for knowledge of all languages, mortal and immortal. Before humans forced us into the Divine Realms, we walked everywhere and spoke to all.*—He looked around—*Now I wander the mortal realm again, the first basilisk to do so in four centuries, thanks to that yellow mage.*—

"What yellow mage?"

—*The one who brought me here. He did* not *mean* to *bring me, of course, I sneaked through in the wake of the Stormwings he had summoned.*—

Daine stared at him. "Where was this?"

—*Here. He lives on the castle island. I can see the aura of his power there, brighter than that of the other mages who live inside those walls.*—

More than ever, Daine wished Numair had not left so abruptly. Goddess, let him return soon, she thought. He needs to hear what Tkaa can tell us. She also wanted Brokefang to come, so they could leave the area of the pond. The thought of another Coldfang making its slow, relentless way up from the lumber camp made her skin prickle and her stomach knot.

—*Calm yourself,*—advised Tkaa when she cut her palm slicing cheese for lunch.—*I doubt that the mortals who sent the Coldfang to hunt even know that that one is dead.*—

"But the men who sent him have scrying crystals," she protested. "They'll look for him in those—"

—*They may* try.—The thought was reassuringly firm.—*Did I not say Coldfangs are thief catchers? Too many thieves rely on magic. A Coldfang cannot be seen by magic, nor can one be stopped by it. They may be slain by human weapons, but—as you know—that can be difficult.*—

She made a note of that as, in the distance, she felt the pack's approach. "The wolves are here. They may be upset when they see you. Be patient, please."

Kitten added a chirp, and the basilisk tickled her behind the ears.—*I am always patient,*—he said.

The wolves trotted out of the rocks and stopped, looking from Daine to Tkaa. Ears went flat; hackles came up. "No!" she cried. "He saved the pups! There was a monster coming, and he saved all our lives!" Quickly she explained the morning's events. Tkaa held still as Brokefang gave him a cautious sniff.

The Long Lake Pack thanks you, the chief wolf said at last. We thank you for the lives of our young, and the lives of our friends Daine and Kitten. Looking at Daine, he said, It sounds as if it is time for the pack to move.

"Please," she said, thinking of immortals who could trace thieves. "I would feel *so* much better if we did."

—*I told you they would not soon place another Coldfang on your trail,*—Tkaa reminded her.

"No, but them that sent it might come looking for the beastie," replied Daine, forgetting months of grammar lessons. "If they find that statue, they might be smart enough to keep looking uphill."

I know a place we may live in for a time, Brokefang announced. There are caves by the western pass where we can den. You will like it. There are plenty of bats for you to talk with. We will go now, if you are ready. The big wolf hesitated, then added, looking at Tkaa, You are welcome to come there, too.

—*I look forward to seeing your caves.*—

Then let us go, Cloud said. I will feel better when we leave here.

Wait, Brokefang commanded. The tools. The saws and the axes. If we leave them here, and men come, they will find them and go back to cutting trees.

—You *are* the thieves?—There was surprise in Tkaa's cool voice.—*You stole men's tools?*—

They were scaring the game, Brokefang replied calmly. We made them stop.

Tkaa looked at Daine. His tone was coldly stern when he said,—*This was a bad thing you told them to do. Men will hunt them and kill them for this.*—

Stung by the unfairness of it, she cried, "It wasn't *my* fault!"

It was Brokefang's plan, Fleetfoot explained.

Short Snout yipped in approval.

Battle said, Brokefang makes *good* plans.

—*Show me*,—ordered the immortal. Russet led him into the reeds. Daine shook her head and loaded her things onto Cloud. She had finished when she heard that noise again, a screech with a deeper sound of tumbling rock underneath. It lasted for only a breath. When it stopped, Tkaa emerged from the reeds. Russet danced around the basilisk, leaping like a pup with joy.

He did a good thing, the wolf said. He made the tools into rock. Now *no* one can lift them or use them to cut trees!

Kitten whistled in glee; Brokefang grinned broadly. The younger adults—Battle, Sharp Nose, Fleetfoot, and Short Snout—yipped happily, tails wagging. Longwind grumbled under his breath, not liking this newest change in his world.

Frostfur sneezed in irritation. If everyone is happy, may we please *leave*? she demanded. I would like to be far from here before men come!

Brokefang led the way through the rocks. The pack followed in single file, as Tkaa, Daine, and Cloud brought up the rear. Kitten viewed the line of march from her seat atop Cloud's saddle, talking nonstop to Tkaa.

They had gone nearly half a mile when Daine sensed immortals. *Stormwings!* she cried silently to the pack as Cloud bolted for the nearby trees. Hide!

Longwind looked back at Daine. Wolves have nothing to fear from harriers, he said in his dignified way. They have no interest in the People.

Daine, joining Cloud and Kitten under branches that hid them from fliers overhead, yanked out her crossbow, and fitted a bolt into the notch. She thrust extra arrows point-first into the ground by her knee, ready to be fired.

The wolves continued their leisurely trot down the trail. Tkaa dropped back so the Stormwings wouldn't think he was with them, but he stayed in the open. When the four winged immortals saw him, they circled overhead.

"Basilisk! We seek two-leggers," called a filthy-haired brunette. What looked like old blood was streaked across her bare breasts. "A man, tall for a human, with lots of magic, and a young female with dark hair. Seen 'em?"

Tkaa walked on, pretending not to hear.

One Stormwing, whose human parts were the almond-shaped black eyes, black hair, and golden brown skin of a K'miri tribesman, dropped until he could hover a few feet away from Tkaa. His back was to Daine as the girl raised her bow. If he saw her, she would kill him before he could take word of her to Tristan.

Cloud gently clamped her teeth on the elbow supporting the bow stock. Don't, the mare warned. He hasn't done anything to you.

Yet, Daine replied silently. They're evil, Cloud. You *know* they're evil.

There's no such thing as a being who's pure evil, retorted the mare. Just as no creature is all good. They live according to their natures, just like you.

And their natures are *evil*, insisted the girl.

No. Their natures are opposed to yours, that's all. A wolf's nature is opposed to mine, but that does not make wolves evil. Until these creatures do you harm, leave them be. It is as the stork-man told you— learn tolerance!

Unaware of his danger, the K'miri Stormwing spoke to Tkaa. "You want to watch that girl, gravelguts. She kills immortals. She *likes* it. She stole an infant dragon, you know, and sent the dragon mother to her death." Daine went cold with rage, hearing this version of Kitten's adoption. "You see her, make her stone before she puts an arrow in one of those sheep's eyes of yours."

—Flapper,—replied Tkaa with gentle patience,—*your cawing begins to vex me. I am interested in neither your affairs nor those of mortals.*—

"Remember what I said." With a surge of his wings, the Stormwing rejoined his fellows. They circled one last time, jeering, then flew off.

Only when they were gone did Cloud release Daine. Trembling in anger, the girl collected her arrows and put all but the one already loaded back in the quiver. The bow remained in her hand as she and Cloud rejoined Tkaa.

Twice more on the walk to the western pass, Daine and Cloud were forced to take cover to avoid Stormwing searchers. Watching them, the girl realized there was something funny about the sky. She kept glimpsing odd sparkles of colored light winking against the clouds. At least it wasn't in her own mind: Tkaa admitted to seeing it when she asked him, and the wolves, though they were unable to see color, said they noticed light-sparks overhead.

They were about to cross the stream that flowed down from the gap in the mountains when Brokefang halted, nostrils flaring. The wind had brought some odd scent to his nose. Abruptly he turned right, heading along the stream bank, following the path Numair had taken the day before out of the valley.

"Now what?" Daine asked tiredly as the pack followed him. "There aren't any caves that way!" she called. She could hear the distant bat colony in her mind. To reach them her group would have to cross the stream and follow the path Brokefang had taken to show her and Numair the view of the Long Lake.

The wolves disappeared from view. "Maybe they smell game or something," she grumbled, sitting on a boulder to rest her tired feet.

A scream—a human scream, high and terrified—split the air. Seizing bow and quiver, Daine went after the wolves at a dead run. A horse galloped by, white showing around his eyes as he raced toward the distant lake. Daine was reaching with her magic to stop him when she heard another scream. She let the horse go, and ran in the direction from which he had come. The horse would be all right. She could tell he wouldn't stop until he reached his stable.

Rounding a bend in the rocky pass, she found the wolves in a clearing. They were in a circle, attention fixed on the small human at the center.

"It's all right," Daine called. "They won't hurt you!"

The human whirled. Huge brown eyes stared at Daine from a face so white its freckles stood out like ink marks. The mouth dropped open in shock. *"Daine?"*

It was Maura of Dunlath.

"Horse Lords," Daine said prayerfully. She didn't think those K'miri gods could help at a time like this, but all the same, it couldn't hurt to ask.

Maura gulped. "If they're going to eat me, can they get it over with?"

Daine sighed. She could feel a headache coming on. How was she to keep out of sight, as Numair had commanded, when trouble dropped into her lap? "They won't eat you, Maura. That's just stories. Wolves never eat humans."

They taste bad, Short Snout added. You know by the way they smell.

"*Everyone* says wolves eat people!" The girl wiped her eyes on her sleeve.

Daine walked through the circle of wolves, pausing to scratch Battle's ears and Fleetfoot's ruff as she passed. "*Everyone* is wrong. They say wolves kill to be cruel, and no wolf kills unless he's hungry." She put a hand on the ten-year-old's shoulder. "Do I look eaten to you?"

Maura stared up at her. "Well—no."

"These wolves are friends of mine, just like the castle mice."

Maura looked at the pack; they looked up at her. "They're a lot bigger than mice," she said fretfully.

Who is she? asked Brokefang. Why is she here?

"Good question," replied Daine. "Maura, what *are* you doing here?"

The girl's face went from scared to scared and mulish. "It's personal."

Daine looked around. The ground nearby was trampled, as if Maura had let her horse graze for a while before it smelled wolves and fled. Saddlebags and a bedroll lay under a nearby tree. The bags showed every sign of hasty packing: they bulged with lumps, and a doll's arm stuck out from under a flap, as if the doll pleaded to be set free. Maura's eyes were red and puffy. Her clothes—a plain white blouse, faded blue skirt, and collection of petticoats—looked as if they had been put on in the dark.

"You ran away."

Maura clenched her fists. "I'm not going back. You can't make me."

A starling flew by on her way through the pass. She called to Daine, who smiled and waved back. Returning her attention to Maura, she asked sternly, "Just how did you think you were going to live, miss? Where would you go?"

"My aunt, Lady Anys of the Minch, said I can visit anytime." Obviously making it up, the girl went on, "I even got a letter from her a week ago—"

"Lady Maura," Daine began, "I may be human, but I am *not* stupid. That is the most—" Agony flared nearby; a life went out. It felt like the starling. Frowning, she went to investigate.

Fifty yards away, the bird's crumpled form lay in the road. She picked the body up, smoothing feathers with a hand that shook. The head hung at a loose angle. When she had first visited Numair's tower, she had seen that birds couldn't tell that the windows on top of the building were made of clear glass. Many killed themselves flying into the panes before Daine warned them of the danger. The starling looked as if she had met the same end, but there was no glass here.

Instead Daine saw something else. The sparkles she had glimpsed against the sky were thick ahead of her. Near the ground, they formed a visible wall of yellow air flecked with pink, brown, orange, and red fire.

Gently she put the dead bird on a rock, trying not to cry. Starlings died all the time, but this one need not have died here and now.

Be careful, Brokefang warned as she approached the wall.

She put her hand out. The yellowish air was stone hard. It also stung a bit, like the shocks she got from the rugs in Numair's room on dry winter days. When she pulled her hand back, her palm went numb. She looked north. The colored air stretched as far as she could see, forming an unnaturally straight line along the spine of the mountains. Toward the south, her view was the same.

Behind her, Maura screamed. Daine turned to see what was wrong. The rest of her company had arrived, Tkaa bearing a sleepy Kitten in his arms, Cloud walking behind the basilisk.

"Stop it," Daine ordered Maura crossly. "Those are my friends. If you don't quit yelling when you get upset, you'll bring Stormwings down on us."

"I don't see giant lizards every day," complained Maura.

—I am no lizard.—Tkaa's voice was frosty.

"He's no lizard," Daine said, looking at the barrier again. "He's a basilisk. His name's Tkaa." With her back to the girl, she didn't see Maura gather her nerve and curtsy, wobbling, to Tkaa. Brokefang did, and approved.

The little one has courage, he said, showing Daine an image of what Maura had done. You could be nicer to her. She is your own kind, after all.

Daine bent, picked up a rock, and hurled it at the barrier. She had to duck to save herself from a braining when the rock bounced back. Picking up her bow, she checked that an arrow was secured in the notch. "Everyone get back," she warned. She sighted and loosed. The arrow shattered.

"It's no good." The gloomy voice was Maura's. "You can't get through it. Nothing can. I would've ridden right into it, but my horse saw it and balked."

"But where did it come from? When did it come? Was it here when Numair tried to leave the valley, or did it appear after?"

—It was done last night,—Tkaa said.—You must have felt some-

*thing going on. The little one did; she told me so.*—Kitten chirped her agreement.

Brokefang trotted up to sniff the barrier. He jerked back with a snarl when the air stung his nose.

"Shh," Daine whispered, kneeling to wrap an arm around his shoulders. She looked up at the basilisk. "Tkaa? Can you pass it?"

—*Yes,*—he replied. He thrust a paw through the barrier. It moved slowly, as if in syrup, but it went.—*It is only human magic.*—He withdrew the paw.

"Could you carry me through?"

The immortal shook his head.—*I would not advise you even to try.*—

Daine stared at the barrier. Would Numair be able to cross it on his return? He was a powerful mage, but even *his* Gift had limits.

On a nearby bush, a sparrow peeped a greeting, and took off in flight. *"No!"* Daine cried with both her voice and magic. Stunned without striking the barrier, the little bird dropped. She picked him up. She touched him with a bit of her fire, to bring him around and to erase that ache that would result from her overreaction. "I'm sorry," she explained as he roused. "But keep away from the colored stuff, all right?"

Puzzled but obedient, the sparrow cheeped agreement and flew away. The girl turned to her oddly assorted audience. "First things first. I have to warn the birds about this, before any more are killed. Then we'd best get under cover. Maura, we can talk then. Cloud, will you carry Her Ladyship's packs?"

The mare nodded. "Load her," Daine told the younger girl. "This won't take but a moment." Sitting, she closed her eyes. Her studies had included shields to keep her from distraction by animal voices: now she let her shields fall. The common talk of every vertebrate creature within range poured into her mind, then quieted when she asked for their attention. Daine showed them the barrier's image, the many-colored lights within it, and its terrible solidity. To that she added the image of the dead starling.

The People acknowledged her warning: they would know the barrier when they saw it and would avoid it. They would pass her warning on to those outside her ten-mile range, and keep sending it along, until all Dunlath knew the danger.

Finished, Daine rose. "Let's find those caves."

The wolves led the way from the pass until they descended into a fold of rock. It was an entrance to a small cave, which in turn opened up onto a much larger one. A pond inside provided water, though it was bone-chillingly cold and tasted strongly of stone. Passages in the rear led to other caves: escape routes, if the pack ever need them.

The company settled in. Daine relieved Cloud of her burdens and groomed her. Maura built a fire pit around a dip in the stone floor. The pack adults explored or napped; the pups were nowhere to be seen. Tkaa wandered about with Kitten in tow, gouging chunks from different stones with his talons. He tasted each sample carefully, discarding most and stowing the rest near Daine's packs.

"What are they for?" she asked.

—*Supper*,—replied the basilisk.

"Weapons?" suggested Maura, who couldn't hear Tkaa speak.

"He eats them, he says," replied Daine, thinking, This could be complicated, if I'm forever translating when I should listen to animals. She conveniently forgot that she often did such translations for the king's staff and the Riders. A full day and a restless night had combined to make her grumpy.

Maura yelped. Daine spun to glare at her, and the younger girl clapped her hands over her mouth, looking guilty. The cause of her yelp had been the pups, who had come to the fire pit, each carrying a good-sized piece of dead wood. They dropped their finds and went racing outside for more.

"I don't need help," Maura called after them, voice shaking. Avoiding Daine's eyes, she knelt to arrange tinder and kindling in the pit. "I guess they're chewing on logs because they can't eat me." She frowned: a fuchsia-colored puff of sparks flew up from the tinder. Within seconds a small fire burned in the kindling, and she was feeding it larger pieces of wood.

"I didn't know you had the Gift," commented Daine, getting supplies and pans from her gear.

"Not much of a one," replied the ten-year-old. She built up the fire as the pups returned with more wood. This time she actually took a branch from Leaper, though her hand trembled as she did so. "I can light fires and candles and torches. Yolane hates it when I do that. We get the magic from the Conté side of the family, same as the king, but she doesn't have any. It's no good telling her lots of people from Gifted families don't have the Gift themselves. She thinks she'd look like a queen if she could light the candles with magic."

Daine found a cloth ball and smiled. It was a basic soup mixture of dried barley, noodles, mushrooms, and herbs. With the addition of water and salt pork, it would make a good meal for two humans. Taking a pot to the spring, she filled it and brought it to the fire to heat.

As she cut open the ball and poured its contents into the water, she said, "It seems daft, your sister worrying about what a queen looks like. Tortall *has* a queen, after all, a young, strong, healthy one. Unless Thayet catches an arrow or a dagger somewhere, she's going to be queen a long time."

Maura looked away. "It's just one of those things people worry about, even if it doesn't make sense. Don't mind me. I talk too much; Yolane says so all the time. Tell me how you got your dragon. Did you catch her in a net, or with magic, or how?"

Daine was so upset at the suggestion of trickery that she launched into the tale of Kitten's mother dying to defend the queen at Pirate's Swoop. It wasn't until she was dishing up the soup that she realized Maura had changed the subject, and quite effectively, too.

Tkaa read this in her thoughts.—*She is no fool, the little one. There is something quite serious on her mind.*—

She's only *ten*, Daine pointed out silently. How serious can it be?

—*And how old are you, Grandmother?*—

She blushed and replied, Fourteen.

—*Ah. A vast difference of years and experience. Certainly no one could believe her affairs are as vital as yours.*—

"How's the soup?" she asked Maura hastily, before the tall immortal could make her feel even younger and sillier than she did just then.

"Ungerfoll." Maura swallowed her mouthful of noodles, coughed, and said, "It's really good. And clever, how you had most of it in that cloth ball."

"The Riders use them for trail rations," Daine said, hearing voices in search of her. She put her bowl aside and got up facing the rear entrances to the cave. The wolves gathered near her, ears pointed in the same direction.

The bats streamed in from the lower caves to whirl around Daine in a dance of welcome. She laughed as the leaders came to rest on her clothes and hair, landing with the precision they used to find roosting spots among hundreds of comrades. These were little brown bats, an inch and a half to two inches from crown to paw, with a wingspan of three to four inches. Clinging to her, they looked like brown cotton bolls. Though the whole colony, nearly three thousand animals, had come to greet her, most hung overhead rather than chance a welcome from Daine's other companions.

They greeted her in high, chittering voices, introducing themselves as the Song Hollow Colony of bats. She asked if they minded that she and her friends were in their home.

They didn't mind at all, they replied. All they asked was that her friends not try to make a meal of them.

"I think I can promise that," she assured them with a smile.

But what if they taste good? asked Short Snout wistfully. It's true, one wouldn't be more than a mouthful, but there are plenty of them here—

"He's *joking*," Daine said when the bats screeched in alarm, their voices sending jolts of pain through her teeth.

Not about food, retorted Short Snout. Meals aren't funny.

Daine pointed to the entrance. "Out," she commanded.

I probably wouldn't eat *many*, he said as he obeyed. It would be too much like work to catch them, anyway.

Brokefang stretched. We go to hunt, he told Daine. Tonight, the pups come, too. It is time, he added as the young wolves, deliriously happy, frolicked around him. Whatever we see, we will tell you.

"Good hunting," Daine called.

—*Good hunting*,—added Tkaa.

Startled by the basilisk's remark, Brokefang asked, Do you wish to come?

—*I thank you, but no*,—Tkaa replied. Daine heard pleasure at the offer in his voice.—*I will remain with Skysong and the small two-legger.*—

If Tkaa was willing to keep an eye on Maura, that left her free to try something. "Would you do me a favor?" Daine asked the bats. "You prob'ly know, from my sending before, that the pass is cut off by some kind of barrier."

We had heard, one of the leaders replied.

"As you hunt, would you explore the barrier and find its limits? You're the best ones to do it. You won't hit it, and if you all go, you can map the whole thing before dawn. And may I ride along with one of you?"

After a short conference, the bats agreed. One of the leaders clambered from her perch on Daine's boot top to her collar. I am Wisewing, she said, tiny black eyes sparkling. You may try this magic with me.

"Give me a moment," she said, tickling the bat's chin with a fingertip. "I have to sit." The other bats clinging to her took flight. Daine went to Maura, who was covering her head with her hands. "I need to go with them," she told the younger girl. "Why are you doing that?"

"They'll get in my hair."

Daine planted her fists on her hips. "Odd's bobs," she said crossly. The brown eyes that looked pleadingly at her filled. She sighed. "Don't cry. I'm sorry. But Maura—they got in *my* hair because I *invited* them. Bats don't fly into hair. They never bump into anything they don't want to."

"But everybody says—"

"*Everybody's* wrong. See, they squeak at things, and listen to the squeak." She pointed to Wisewing's ears. The long, sensitive flaps wriggled to and fro, hearing every bit of sound in the air. "If the noise comes funny into their ears, they know something's there, and they fly around it. They don't smash into glass, or even that barrier, like birds do. Nothing's invisible to bats."

Maura's hands left her hair. "How can you go with them? You can't fly. Can you?"

Daine shook her head. "Just with my magic, inside this lady." She patted Wisewing. Going to where her packs rested against the wall, she sat, using them as a cushion for her back. "Don't leave this cave," she cautioned Maura. "And you'd best go to bed soon. I have a feeling tomorrow's going to be a long day." Closing her eyes, she fitted herself into Wisewing instantly.

Sounds poured into her ears, echoes from the cavern walls, each scratch of Tkaa's or Kitten's talons, Cloud's munching, wind blowing through the caves. Wisewing leaped into the air, reaching forward with her leathery wings and scooping air back with easy grace. They were in flight.

The voices of the Song Hollow bats rippled ahead of them, a river of sound that Wisewing followed eagerly. Cooler air brushed her face, and they were in the open. Daine could hear the rest of the colony flying along the barrier, heading north, south, and east in waves. Wisewing flew straight ahead, soaring until she skimmed the underside of the barrier's highest arch.

Please stop trying to see it, she protested. You're making my eyes hurt. I don't use them that much. *Listen* for it. You can hear it everywhere.

She was right. The barrier was a constant soft crackle of sound, reflecting the voices of the bats. Wisewing herself struck it constantly with her voice, and the returning echoes not only told her how far off it was, but that its underside was unnaturally smooth, like the inside of a bowl.

Daine just had time to register a different, softer echo when Wisewing scooped the moth that had caused it into her waiting jaws. The taste reminded Daine of roasted, honey-glazed duck. The bat's next victim was a tangy mosquito, followed by a moth that tasted more like fish. She'd always known that bats ate insects by the pound on their hunts, but it was one thing to know this in her mind, another to taste flavor after flavor on her tongue.

I don't want to slow you down by eating, but the Big Cold is soon, said Wisewing. I must be as fat as possible by then, or I won't wake up.

I know, Daine replied. You don't have to apologize.

On they flew, the barrier solidly above them. From all around, other bats sang out information, comparing notes about the magic, the insect supply, and the weather. The crispness of the air made Daine feel giddy and silly.

Then she heard something unpleasant in the distance. The bat's voices came to their ears from something big, something with leathery wings and claws. Her bat darted at the giant, squeaking at it from all angles, building a picture of the great creature in her mind. She had filled in little more than the huge wings and four sets of talons when Daine guessed what it was.

Hurrok, she said nervously. We don't need to hear more. Please let's go!

—*Little squeaker, get away from me.*—The immortal's voice was much deeper than the chorus of bat voices surrounding him.—*I don't like squeakers.*—

Wisewing dove in, settling between the hurrok's wings. Chittering across the immortal's withers, mane, and ears, she picked up the sound of metal. It hummed with a sound the bat recognized as that of human magic. Interested in this new object, Wisewing fluttered across the immortal's chest, to find that a metal band or collar went all the way around the hurrok's throat.

I would have to pick a nosy bat, Daine thought, sick with nerves.

—*It's a slave collar, squeaker,*—the hurrok said.—*It means I must obey a human, a mortal wizard whose power makes it burn into my flesh with only a word. And do you know what that pain, and that knowing, and this collar, do to me? They make me feel like tearing up every living creature I see.*—

She heard a roar of air as something large snapped right over her head: the hurrok had tried to catch them in its teeth. Please Goddess, prayed Daine, let me get through this without losing my life and I will be good forever.

Scolding, Wisewing dropped down, letting the hurrok go its way. Don't let it scare you, she told Daine. It's much too big and slow to catch us. An *owl*, now—an owl is dangerous. You want to stay away from them, particularly barn owls.

I shall keep that in mind, Daine replied.

See that you do, the bat said firmly, and scooped up a fly.

She didn't know how long she flew with the bats, but it must have been for hours. When she opened her own, human eyes and lurched to the cave's entrance, false dawn had turned the eastern horizon pearly gray. She still heard the Song Hollow bats as they returned to their home, greeting her as they flew by. Her mind full of Wisewing's memories, she identified each by his or her particular squeak: Singwing, Chitter, Eatsmoths, Whistle, Flutter. Reunited in the cave where they roosted, they sang their news. From their combined voices Daine built a picture of the barrier's shape. By true dawn her worst fears were confirmed. The wizards' barrier sealed off the entire valley, with no crack or cranny left for a determined girl to wriggle through.

Mission done and bellies full, the bats went to sleep. Daine stayed at the entrance, listening to the shift of hooves on stone as Cloud changed position in her sleep, a soft munch that was Tkaa as he nibbled on a piece of rock, the bustle of voles in the grass. Her ears were tired and sore, the muscles around them cramped from use. Reaching up to rub them, Daine touched a long flap of leathery skin that flicked to and fro, catching each quiver of sound in the air.

Her hand shook. Slowly, praying to the Goddess, the Horse Lords, Mithros, and any other god who might be listening, she felt the other ear. It too was long, and twitching independently of its mate, gathering every sound from that side of her head. She knew without looking that the stone of the cave entrance was six and a half inches behind her, that Kitten lapped water from the spring, and that a raccoon on the mountainside twelve feet and eight inches above her head was finishing a late-night supper of something crunchy, probably acorns.

What *is* this? she thought, her skin prickling. Why is my body changing? It's staying right where I left it. *I* don't change when I do this, I just send my mind someplace else. So how could I have bats' ears?

Unless I'm just imagining that part of me changes. If I am, it means I'm going mad after all, she thought, strangely calm. Surely someone would have told me that it's possible to change part of yourself into something else.

If I ignore these ears, they'll go away, or my mind will let go of them, or whatever. Maybe if I sleep, I'll wake up and be normal again.

That seemed like a good idea. Returning to the large cave, she found her bedroll. When I wake up, the ears will be gone, and I won't be crazy, she told herself firmly as she slid into her blankets. She pulled the covers over her head, just in case. If the ears were still there, she didn't want Maura to wake her with a scream.

## ➤➤ SIX ◂◂

# REBELLION

෨ She awoke slowly, leaving dreams in which she clung to the cavern with the other Song Hollow bats, becoming her normal self in the cave that she shared with her motley group of friends. For a moment she thought she was deaf, the sounds she heard were so few and so dim. She clapped a hand to one ear and found a small, curved shell where the long, ribbed flap had been. Feeling relief mixed with sadness, she knew she was not deaf. Her ears were human once more.

"You're up," said Maura. "I wanted to wake you for breakfast—I was afraid you'd sleep all day—but Tkaa said leave you be." She came over with a steaming mug and set it on the ground as Daine sat up. "I hope you don't mind me'n Kitten getting in your things. I didn't bring any food, and we were *starving*. I found your tea, and the wolves found a beehive, so me'n Kitten had honey for our porridge, and I made tea with honey for you."

"Thanks." Half-awake, Daine asked the first question that came to mind, the one she ought to have asked more firmly the day before. "Why'd you run off?"

The younger girl looked down. "I can't say."

Daine sniffed her tea: it smelled wonderful. "You must. If you had a spat with Yolane, or if you think it's fun to live out in the woods like me, that's no good. You'll have to go home."

"What if she wants to send me to school to be a lady, and I want to go to court and be a knight?"

Under Daine's sharp look the girl reddened. "You've heard too many tales about the King's Champion. I'm not here for fun, Maura, and it's wrong to run off for fun. Leaving home's serious." Remembering the wreck of her own home, she added, "You're lucky to have a place that's yours. You don't just throw that away." She grinned. "And I doubt you'd have any luck as a knight. You screech whenever you see something odd."

Maura smiled, then looked at her hands. "I *have* to see the king. I can't say why. I know girls my age aren't supposed to know important stuff, but I do, and he has to know."

"If it's that Tristan is making trouble for Tortall, you're behind the fair," Daine replied. "We know he's in the Carthaki emperor's service. Numair went out of the valley so he could report to the king and get help. As soon as he does, he'll be back."

Maura looked at Daine with a frown. "Is that all you know? About Tristan?"

"I know for a fact he brought Tkaa here."

"For which I am grateful," a whispery voice said from the entrance. Daine squeaked and lunged for her crossbow. Maura rescued the endangered mug of tea. When Daine brought the cocked and loaded bow to bear on the entrance, she saw only Tkaa and Kitten. "Who said that?" she demanded.

The basilisk stared at her. "I *told* you my people speak all tongues." The whispery voice did come from his mouth. "The only reason I did not address Lady Maura in this wise from the first was that my skills were rusty. In the Divine Realms and with you it is easier to speak mind-to-mind."

"Mithros, Mynoss, and Shakith," Daine breathed. "I don't know what to say."

"Then say nothing," advised Tkaa as he put Kitten down. "That is best."

Still unnerved by hearing him speak human, Daine got clothing out of her packs and took it into her bedroll to dress. As she did, wriggling under the covers, she heard Maura tell the basilisk, "We need to think about laundry and supplies. I can't eat all Daine's food."

If Tkaa answered, his voice was drowned out by a sound. Once Daine had heard a great bell, its sides as thick as her hand, clang as it was struck with a mallet. This noise was similar, but so loud it made her teeth and ears ache. Hundreds of yards away, cushioned from the outer air by tons of rock, the Song Hollow bats heard it and were startled into flight. Cloud neighed in protest outside; Kitten dived into Daine's blankets, pulling them over her tender ears. Tkaa clapped his forepaws over his earholes and shut his eyes in pain.

"What was that?" cried Maura.

It came again, so loud it pressed on Daine's eardrums. Where? she asked the bats, knowing they could pinpoint it. Confused and frightened, they sent an image of the western pass as it would appear to them, painted in sound at night.

She grabbed her crossbow and quiver. Barefoot, shirt half-tucked into her breeches, she ran outside. Cloud followed at a gallop, and when she drew alongside, Daine leaped onto the pony's back in a trick learned from the Riders. As the mare raced for the barrier, Daine counted the bolts in her quiver with her fingers: ten. She hoped that would be enough if Stormwings caught her in the open.

When they reached the barrier, they saw no one. Daine could hear a marmot scolding on the other side of the magical wall. "If you see any danger, nip me or something," she ordered her mare, and sat down. Closing her eyes, she listened for the marmot.

She found her quarry instantly. The marmot, a female, was on the sloping ground that was the southern wall of the pass, guarding the entrance to the burrow she shared with her large family. Shocked, frightened, and irate, she was calling the man below names that Daine hadn't thought a marmot would use.

You must have learned that from squirrels, she commented. None of the marmots *I* know ever said such things.

They weren't scared out of their wits, retorted the chubby rodent. I was minding my own business, standing watch, and the two-legger made that noise. He scared me out of a month's fat! I'll have to eat *twice* as much now to be ready for the Big Cold and—Look at him! He's going to do it again!

If you do I will bite you! she screamed at the man. I don't care if you kill me, I will take a big chunk out of you before I'm dead!

May I? asked Daine, and slipped into the marmot so she could see with her hostess's eyes. At the spot where the barrier closed the way into the pass stood two horses and a tall, lanky human. He was raising his hands again. Sweat trickled down his face as black fire gathered around his palms. He shouted something and hurled the fire at the barricade.

The noise was so loud that Daine was jolted back into her own body. "Tkaa!" she called.

—*I am here.*—The basilisk had caught up with her while Daine was speaking with the marmot. He looked a bit odd: someone, probably Maura, had wrapped cloth around his head to protect his earholes.

"It's Numair—my teacher."

—*A mortal is doing that?*—

"Would you cross and tell him to stop? Oh, wait—perhaps he's doing it to break down the barrier. If he is, would you ask him how long it will take, so I can warn my friends? I suppose he'll want to know about the Coldfang, and you should tell him Maura's with us."

—*Let me go*,—said Tkaa, sounding faintly amused.—*You may think of other things for me to tell him while I am gone.*—He walked over to the barrier and was halfway through when Daine remembered something else.

"Tkaa, wait!"

He looked at her.—*Quickly, if you please. This is not comfortable.*—

"If you can go through, Stormwings can go through. Warn him, please. They might be on their way now, if Tristan heard all this racket."

The basilisk walked through the barrier. Daine looked at Cloud. "I need my writing kit. Tkaa doesn't know all I've learned, and Numair has to be warned." She stopped. In her mind she heard approaching Stormwings. "We've got trouble," she said, and mounted the pony. "What did Tkaa call them? Flappers?"

Just what we need, replied the mare.

In the distance she heard Maura say pleadingly, "Go away! *Please!*"

Cloud picked up her pace, and they rounded a bend. Maura stood where the trail to the caves met the pass road. Above her was a flock of Stormwings.

"Maura, get *down!*" shouted Daine. Cloud stopped as she brought the crossbow to bear on one of the monsters.

"*No!*" Maura lunged at Daine, grabbing for the bow. Her weight dragged Daine's arm down. For one perilous moment the crossbow was aimed point-blank at the ten-year-old's chest. Cloud reared. Maura lost her grip on the bow, and Daine swung it away from her. She was trembling in fear and anger.

"Don't *ever* do that again!" she cried. "I could have *killed* you!"

"I'm sorry," Maura said, looking down. "But I couldn't let you hurt them."

Stormwings were landing on the ground in front of them. Three moved out of Daine's sight. Turning, she saw them settle on the road behind her, cutting off any escape. Coldly she leveled her weapon at the nearest Stormwing, a male who wore a collection of bones braided into his long blond hair.

He stared back at her, contempt in his eyes, then looked at the younger girl. "Tell her we mean you no harm, Lady Maura."

"You're on speaking terms with *them?*" Daine asked.

Maura shrugged. "They visit Yolane and Belden a lot. He is Lord Rikash."

"And *she* is a Stormwing killer," barked the snarl-haired brunette who had spoken to Tkaa the day before. "She slew one of our queens last year!"

"She tried to kill me," Daine snapped. "It was a fair fight—a lot fairer than she deserved."

Rikash hopped around Maura and stopped near Cloud, looking her and her rider over with chilly green eyes. The mare had seen his kind before. While their scent of rotten meat and bad death hurt her nose, she had learned to stand fast when they were near. She eyed Rikash, small ears flat against her skull. Daine knew what was in the pony's mind: one more hop and he'd be in range for a bite.

Don't hit the feathers, warned Daine silently. They'll cut your mouth.

Don't teach your dam to nurse a foal, Cloud retorted.

"You are quick to judge us, Stormwing killer," Rikash snarled. "Too quick, for a *human*. You come from a race that spends more time murdering your *own* kind than do all the immortals put together, yet you insist you are better than us." He spat on the ground, and looked at Maura. "You cannot leave Dunlath, and you must not stay here. Come home. Yolane doesn't need to know you were away."

"You mean she hasn't noticed I'm gone," Maura said bitterly. "Has anyone?"

"That is unjust," the Stormwing replied, firmly and gently. "You know very well that the cook and your nurse are frantic that you've vanished."

"I left them notes. I told them not to worry."

There was something odd between these two, Daine realized. The immortal spoke to Maura with affection. That was impossible. Stormwings were cruel, heartless: she had enough experience of them to know that. Worse, Maura addressed Rikash as she might an older brother or an uncle.

Watching the immortals, Daine saw that she needed help. Starlings gathered with the coming of fall, to gossip and to migrate. Nearby she found three such flocks, each with over fifty birds, and called them to the trees and rocks around her before she looked again at Maura and Rikash. "Do you know what *his* sort do?" she asked the younger girl. "They befoul the dead who fall in battle. They live on human fear and anger. They're monsters!"

Maura shrugged thin shoulders. "They can't help how they're *made*, Daine."

"Maura"—Rikash shook his head—"you can't just run away from home. And *you* shouldn't encourage her," he told Daine. "You're old enough to know better."

"I already know better," retorted Maura.

Daine glared at the Stormwing. "I *haven't* been encouraging her. I *tried* to make her go back. *You're* the one with the wings—*you* take her."

Maura sat on the ground, chin sticking out. "I won't go back, and you can't make me. They're traitors. I won't stay under the same roof with them. My father would haunt me all my life if I did."

"Let us talk of this away from prying ears," Rikash said, an eye on Daine.

"We can speak of it now. Daine can't tell anyone. She's stuck here, too!"

"Quiet!" ordered the Stormwing. "You're a *child*. You do not understand what is taking place, and you must not speak of matters you cannot comprehend."

Her sense of humor overpowering her hatred of Stormwings, Daine looked down so Rikash wouldn't see her smile. Obviously he liked Maura, or he would have bullied rather than debated her. She also could see debate was useless. Maura had the bit between her teeth and would not obey orders. "Go on," she urged the fuming immortal. "Shut her up. I never thought to see you stinkers balked by anyone, let alone a ten-year-old."

Rikash turned red under his dirt, and a few of his own flock cackled. "It is hard for us to bear young," he said, a hint of gritted teeth in his voice. "That being the case, we value others' young, particularly when they are neglected. Affection has led me to indulge Lady Maura more than is wise."

Maura sighed. "All right, Lord Rikash. I'll hush. Only, I'm not coming back with you. You don't have to tell them you saw me."

Rikash shook his head. "If you were mine, I would beat you," he said with grim resignation. He looked up at Daine, eyes sharp. "As for *you*—"

Daine grinned, and made a silent request of the starlings. They set up a clamor, flapping their wings and voicing painfully shrill, *loud* whistles. "Go on," she told Rikash, raising her voice to be heard. "Take me in. You might last two or three minutes in the air with my friends going for your eyes."

The Stormwings looked at the birds with alarm. Starlings, cowards and clowns alone or in small groups, were bullies in a flock. Their whistles alone made the immortals try unsuccessfully to cover their ears.

"The gods help you if I catch you in the open," Rikash snarled, flapping his wings. "Maura, you had better rethink your choice of friends!" The Stormwings took to the air as the starlings jeered and insulted them. Wheeling, the immortals flew straight at the barrier and passed through.

"But what about your friend?" Maura cried, grabbing Daine's arm. "It was him making the noise, wasn't it? They might hurt him!"

"I don't think so," said Daine, watching the barrier. There was a sound like a thunderclap. The Stormwings returned, covered with soot from claws to crown and reeking of onions. "They *hate* onions," Daine told Maura as they flew by, tears running down their faces as they sneezed frantically. "We found out last fall, when we helped mop up after pirates raided Port Legann."

"Goddess bless," the younger girl breathed, watching the retreat until the Stormwings were no longer in view.

Dismounting from Cloud, Daine let the pony go ahead of them on the trail to the caverns. "I can't believe you *like* them," she muttered.

Maura glared at her. "Well, *I* can't believe you like wolves."

There was little Daine could say to that. She didn't try, knowing Maura would disagree with whatever arguments she made.

When they entered the caves, Kitten greeted her with joyful chirps and whistles. Smiling, Daine held and petted her for a little while. "Sorry, Kit," she said at last, and put her friend down. "I have plenty to do." Locating her writing tools, she stowed them in a pack.

"You're going back there?" Maura asked.

"I must. There's things Numair has to know."

The younger girl took a deep breath. "Then you'd better tell him Belden and Yolane are going to rebel against the king, and soon."

Daine, stunned, let her pack slip to the floor. "A *rebellion*?"

Maura nodded, red with shame. Kitten, chirping in concern, rubbed her head against the girl's knee. "I didn't know anything for sure until the day after you left," Maura explained. "It was after lunch sometime, because my nurse wanted to put me on the backboard, and I didn't want her to catch me."

"A backboard?" asked Daine.

"It's so old-fashioned. Nobody uses it anymore. You're strapped with your shoulders against it for *hours*—it's supposed to teach girls to sit up straight. Nurse says I'm round-shouldered, and she puts me on it whenever she can."

Daine shuddered. "It sounds horrible. I've never heard Kally—Princess Kalasin—mention such a thing."

"Good. If we get out of all this, please tell my nurse the princess doesn't have one. Anyway, I left through the secret passage in the family wing. I was behind Yolane's study when I heard Belden yell, 'What do you mean, he's *gone*?' I heard Tristan and Yolane say be quiet, and I stopped. There's spy holes in all the rooms, so I could see and hear everything. It was them and the others, Alamid and Gissa and Redfern and Gardiner. Tristan lied, you know. They weren't going to the City of the Gods. He wrote and invited them."

Daine's stomach growled. She dug out cheese and a sausage, cutting off portions for herself and for Maura. "So what did you hear?"

"Tristan told Belden it's all under control. And Belden said Tristan told him Master Numair would pass out from the nightbloom in his wine and when *that* didn't work, Tristan said there was no way Master Numair could leave the valley. Yolane said they're in trouble if Numair warns the king, and Tristan said he only knows Tristan and Alamid and Gissa are here. He said they'll warn the other con—conspirators, and speed up the rebellion. They'll strike with the next full moon, not at Midwinter like they planned."

Daine dug her brushes, paper, and ink out of the pack. "Wait—let me write this down." Shaking the bottle of ready-made ink, she unstoppered it and wet her brush. Swiftly, using Rider code symbols to speed up note taking, she wrote the main points of what Maura had said thus far. "Go on."

Maura drank some water. "Belden said he didn't like how this is going, and Tristan told the mages to show Belden how they'd ward the valley, and they left. After that Yolane said she hoped this would work. Tristan said as long as she keeps up her end, she'll be queen by the first snows. And Yolane said how can she keep her bargain when the next shipment is sealed in with us? Tristan said they'll handle that when the shipment's ready. Then he started kissing her and saying what a fine queen she'd make, and I left. I snuck out of the castle that night—I hoped I could get out of Dunlath before they closed it off."

"Can you remember anything else?"

Maura shook her head. "I told you everything. I kept going over it in my head so I could tell the king without leaving anything important out."

"What's this shipment they talked about?"

"Whatever they mine up in the north part of the valley. They've been sending that out of Dunlath all summer."

Daine put her things away and tucked her notes into the waistband of her breeches. "Numair has to know all this. He can warn the king."

"He can speak over distances with his Gift?" The younger girl sighed. "I wish I could do that. It would make things a lot easier."

"Is there anyone in the valley who can?"

Maura shook her head. "Just Tristan and his friends. Some villagers have the Gift, but it's like mine. Just good for a couple of things, and nobody can far-speak. Anyone who has a strong Gift leaves to get better training."

Daine sighed. "That's typical. One last thing—didn't you sort of promise Rikash you wouldn't tell me any of this?"

"I know he probably thinks I did, but I didn't. Maybe Yolane forgot her duty to the Crown, but I haven't." She rubbed her sleeve over her eyes.

Touched, Daine gave her friend a quick hug. "All right. I have to take this to Numair. Look after Kitten while I'm gone, won't you?"

Cloud also stayed behind as Daine returned to the barrier. On a slope nearby, the girl found a tumble of rock, one huge slab of which formed a lean-to against its fellows. She hid there, out of the open, and began to write, using the notes she had taken from Maura. To that she added the news that the barrier enclosed the entire valley. She was finishing when she heard the high, singing note that was Tkaa's presence in her mind. Peering out of her shelter, she saw the basilisk step through the barrier, and waved him up to her hiding place.

*—He says he cannot break this spell,—the immortal told her.—He says he must summon more help.—*

Daine rewet her brush and added a further note to her letter: "Can't you use one of those words of power on it?"

*—He is unusual,—Tkaa remarked as Daine waited for her ink to dry.—When I crossed the barrier, he thought I meant to attack. He threw fire at me. I sang the rock spell without blinking—I am not at my best when I am rushed.—A note that might have been amusement entered his soft mental voice.—He became stone, of course. The spell never fails. It lasted for a breath, and then he shattered it, as if all I had done was pour clay on him and bake it. And then he asked me to do it again, to see if he could break the spell twice.—*

Daine rubbed her aching head. "He would," she said dryly. "And did you?"

*—I suggested that the time to conduct experiments will be when all of us have the leisure to enact them properly. If you encounter dragons, you will find the same excuse works with them. More than anything, dragons and mages like to take time with their studies.—*

"Well, thank Mithros for that," replied the girl. "Will you take this to him? It's important."

*—To become a messenger at my age,—Tkaa remarked, shaking his head.*

Daine smiled up at him. "Thank you. I am grateful for your help."

There was affection in his voice when he replied.—*It is I who must thank you. In four hundred years in the Divine Realms, I have not enjoyed myself as much as I have in the last two days. Life is more vivid here, much headier.*—The message in his hand, he returned to the glowing barrier and passed through.

She waited for a moment and then decided she wanted to hear Numair's comments as he read her note. Reaching, she found the marmot and asked again for permission to become part of her. The chubby creature, named Quickmunch, agreed. Daine had the knack of it so well by now that it took only an eye-blink to enter the marmot. It took a bit longer to convince Quickmunch to leave the safety of the burrow and her family, and to approach Numair and Tkaa so Daine could hear them.

If he makes that noise again, I *will* bite him, Quickmunch said as she made her cautious way down the rock slope, with frequent checks overhead for eagles. Humans never stop to think of the People when they are up to their tricks.

He doesn't mean to be rude, Daine said as they stepped onto the road. From here, Spots and Mangle were as big as houses. Quickmunch's first reaction was to run. Daine persuaded her that the horses were peaceful, but Quickmunch still passed them in a wide arc. When she saw Tkaa with Numair, she barked in alarm.

As the immortal bent to examine the rodent, Numair looked up from Daine's note and saw what Tkaa was doing. "Daine, is that you? Can you understand me?"

Nod, Daine told the marmot, and Quickmunch nodded stiffly. This means something to him? she asked.

It means yes, the girl said. It means we understand human speech. Now let me hear what he has to say.

Numair held up Daine's letter. "Your news is serious, but not surprising. Dunlath is too well guarded simply to be a country backwater. When we're done talking, I'll get under cover and speak to the king again." He shook his head. "As to the barrier—did you notice the mixture of colors? It's hard to break a joined spell like this, in which several mages take part." His mouth tightened. "Also, there is an added dimension to this working. The mages Tristan has are disciplined; Alamid and Gissa are both Masters. I believe Redfern may be, as well. All the same, I should have produced a reflection of some kind, from the power I just threw at the barrier." A blush rose in his dark cheeks. "I shouldn't have done that, of course. I'm afraid I lost my temper.

"The fact remains, the barrier absorbed my Gift and didn't reflect it. That means it is fueled with more power than the combined Gifts of Tristan's group can produce. They must be using gemstones that act as power sources to anchor it. If that's the case, I may have to wait for mages to come from the City of the Gods and the Royal University to break it."

She pointed to the paper in his hand.

"Remember what I told you of the words of power." He rubbed his face. "For each one used properly, there is a reaction elsewhere of similar magnitude. The word that *may* break this spell will cause an earthquake somewhere else. I will not kill untold numbers of people to get through, not when other mages will soon come to aid me. I do have some good news. King Jonathan said that two Rider groups and a company of the King's Own are nearby, on border patrol. They're to be sent here. The Sixth Rider Group will arrive in two days, the Twelfth in four, and the men of the King's Own in three days. The mages may take as long as a week to reach us, but that can't be helped."

Daine shivered. She did *not* like the idea of days passing before Numair got help. True, he could defend himself, but there was no telling what unpleasant surprises were tucked into Tristan's sleeve.

"You said each word of power 'used properly,' " remarked Tkaa in Common. He had been listening intently. "What if a word of power is used improperly?"

Numair grimaced. "The magic backfires. It's one reason there are so few of my rank. The others who tried to reach it are dead." He looked at Daine. "Are you comfortable, shifting into your friends' minds? Is it difficult?"

The marmot nodded yes to the first question and shook her head to the second. For a moment Numair sank deep into thought, pulling his long nose idly.

"Daine, I have a tremendous favor to ask," he said finally, coming out of his brown study. "We need more precise information. Is there a way, *without putting yourself in danger,* that you can enter the northern and southern forts and count the men posted there?"

Daine nodded, through Quickmunch. It *was* the next logical step.

"You can do it from within an animal's mind, and your human self will be at a safe distance?"

Again the marmot nodded.

"And you'll be able to return to your own body without mishap?"
Another nod.

"The sooner you can do it, the better. And be careful, or I will *not* put you in the deepest, darkest dungeon I find, understand? I will take you to the glaciers in northern Scanra and drop you in the deepest crevasse known to man."

Quickmunch turned her back to Numair and flipped her tail up, then faced him again. *I like this way of talking,* the marmot confided to Daine.

The mage was grinning. "How are you fixed for supplies?" He glanced at the horses' packs. "I can share what I have, particularly since you are feeding Maura as well as yourself."

Quickmunch shook her head and began to climb to her burrow. *He's being silly,* Daine told her. *I'm a lot better able to supply myself than he is.*

*I know where there are good roots, if you'd like to dig them up,* the marmot offered. *They're really very nourishing.*

*That's sweet,* Daine replied. *But I can find enough food. You eat them. After all, you can't take chances when the Big Cold is on the way.*

*Now you sound like one of the People,* Quickmunch said. *Good-bye, and if you want to do this again, please let me know. It was interesting.*

Smiling, Daine returned to herself. The opening of the stones that hid her was blocked by a large, dark shape. She nearly panicked before she saw it was Maura and Kitten, peering at her with the strangest expression on their faces.

"What's the matter?" she asked, and frowned. Long hairs stuck out on both sides of her nose, and her front teeth felt odd. "And what are you doing here?"

"Why did you do that to your face?" asked the ten-year-old. "You look like a mummer at Midwinter Festival."

"Do what?" No, she was not mistaken. Something was very wrong with her front teeth. "What do you mean, a mummer?"

"You know—they play the parts of the animals, asking Mithros to bring back the sun, so they glue whiskers and furry noses to their faces."

Daine explored with her hands. Her nose had gone flat and—there was no way to get around it—furred, and she had long whiskers curving from either side of her mouth. Her top and bottom incisors were long and extremely sharp, sharp enough to cut her skin. "You can see all this?" It was hard to talk around rodent teeth. Kitten trotted over and touched the new parts with gentle claws.

"Of course," Maura replied scornfully. "It's as plain as the nose—" She stopped just in time. The rest, "on your face," didn't seem tactful.

Daine whooped and stood up, nearly braining herself on the rock overhead. Going outside, she grabbed Maura by the hands and danced her around, laughing.

"I'm not crazy!" she cried. "I'm not mad! It's real! The changes are real!" She skidded to a halt, realizing something. "I think the badger *knew* this would happen. He *said* I'd be surprised." She touched her face, but it was human again. "Odd's bobs. Could I make the whole change? Change entirely into an animal? That would be *wondrous*."

"Don't ask me," replied Maura. "Do you know how it happens?"

"No, but I'll find out." There was a screech overhead. Daine looked up in alarm, but the caller was only a hawk. " 'And here we are, dancing in the open like idiots. Let's get under cover, and decide how we'll eat tonight." She trotted back toward the caves, Maura and Kitten behind her.

"I should have brought food and stuff," Maura complained, panting as she ran. "I didn't stop to think about anything like that. I just wanted to get out of there and get word to the king."

"Are you sure you can't go home now?" asked Daine. "You know that help is on the way, and you'll get proper food." She glanced at her friend. Maura's face was set. "I can't be attending you, you know. Numair wants me to count the soldiers in the forts—unless *you* know how many there are."

Maura shook her head. "They never talked about anything like that around me. If they had, I'd've gotten help a long time ago."

"But wouldn't you rather be sleeping on a soft bed under warm blankets? Not to mention your servants being afeared for you." They had reached the entrance cave. Once inside, they slowed to a walk.

"You don't understand," Maura said, catching her breath. "If you're noble and you find treason, and you live with the plotters or go to their parties or marry into their family or *anything*, then you are just as guilty as they are."

"You're only *ten*," Daine argued, taking all of her remaining supplies from her packs. "Surely no one's going to haul a child up before the Lord Provost."

Maura sat by the fire pit. "My father said the laws were written long ago, when times were simpler. They used to hang children for stealing bread, did you know that? Some things have changed, but not chivalry and the nobles' duties. That's what makes me mad. Yolane was raised the same as me. She *knows* what's right and wrong, but she doesn't care. By law Dunlath can be plowed up and sown with salt, and our people made to leave, but does she care? No. She'd rather risk lives and our home so she can wear a crown and order people around."

Daine patted her friend's arm. "She won't get that chance, and nothing's going to happen to Dunlath. You trust Master Numair. He'll fix it."

Maura smiled crookedly. "It isn't him—I don't know him at all. *You're* the one I trust."

Daine hunted and fished until dark, gathering enough food to ensure that Maura would eat properly. Fish would do for that night, with rice from her supplies. The game birds could be baked in clay for Maura to have later. Kitten found mushrooms and blueberries, which would make pleasant additions. When they returned to the caves, Tkaa was there.

"He is under cover, natural and magical, for the night," the basilisk said as the girls began to cook. "I promised him that I would stay with Lady Maura."

The ten-year-old grinned. "I'd like that." Seeing the pleasure in her face, it was hard to believe that one day ago she had screamed upon seeing him. "The wolves still make me nervous." When Daine glanced at her, she shrugged. "I'm sorry, they just do. Speaking of them, where have they been all day?"

"Hunting, I s'pose," Daine replied. "Some days it takes longer than others." She tried to remember when she last saw the pack, and realized it had been the evening before. "They'll be back when they've fed."

She was dishing up the rice and fish when she saw Tkaa reach into a pouch in the skin of his belly. "Did I know you had that?" she asked, curious.

"One does not expect the very young to know a great deal," he replied. He drew several chunks of rock from the pouch and placed them near the small pile of stones that was to be his own meal. "Dessert," he explained in his soft voice, when he saw that the girls, Kitten, and Cloud watched him intently.

"The birds and the rice and the rest of my supplies will hold you whilst I'm gone," Daine told Maura as they ate, wincing as Tkaa crunched his meal. "You'll be fine here. Tkaa will be with you, and Kitten." The young dragon, wrinkling her muzzle at Tkaa's idea of food, nibbled daintily on a trout.

"Wolves—?" Maura started to ask, voice quivering. "I'm sorry. I don't mean to whine. Only, all my life I was told wolves will eat me. It's hard to forget."

"But you think Stormwings are fine." Daine knew she kept returning to that point, but she couldn't help herself. She had battled them for so long that it was well-nigh impossible to see them as anything but foul.

"Not *all* of them. The one that called you a Stormwing killer and some of the others can be nasty. But Lord Rikash takes me flying sometimes."

Daine gaped. *"Flying?"*

"Yes. They made a rope sling for me, and they carry me in their claws. It's fun! They're a lot stronger than you think."

"Smell?" Daine's voice came out as a strangled squeak.

"Oh, I dab perfume under my nose, and I breathe through my mouth. Once I was getting over a cold, and I couldn't smell a thing. That was the best time. And when you're up in the air over everything, who cares about smells?"

The rest of his meal eaten, Tkaa put a dessert rock in his mouth and hummed his satisfaction. Daine, glad to change the subject, asked, "Is it good, then?"

Tkaa nodded. "The best I've ever had. They are well aged, and I am most partial to this dark variant."

Maura shook her head. "Wouldn't you rather have real candy? I have spice drops. You just reminded me." She fished a crumpled paper from a pocket and offered its contents to Daine and Kitten, who accepted with pleasure, then to Tkaa. The basilisk thanked her politely, but it was easy to see he was not tempted to trade his "candy" for hers.

"What is it, the stone you're eating?" Daine asked.

The basilisk chose a rock and made a sound that was half whistle, half croak. The rock flared with a multitude of lights colored blue, violet, and green, with tiny sparks of red and amber. Slowly the lights faded. "Black opals," the immortal announced with pleasure. "The finest I have ever eaten."

Kitten sat up and whistle-croaked. The pile of stones shone with the same rainbow of colors, and went dark. "Very good, Skysong," approved Tkaa.

Daine frowned. Here was the answer to the mines and the emperor's interest. "Yolane ships opals to Carthak," she said. "And Ozorne gives her mages, gold, maybe even soldiers, for when she rebels against King Jon."

"This just gets worse and worse." Maura's voice was tight. "It's illegal to mine precious metals and stones without telling the Crown."

"Prob'ly for just this reason," Daine pointed out. "So folk won't sell them and use the money, or the magic, to make trouble." She put a hand on Maura's shoulder. "We'll stop them, Lady Maura. You'll see."

# ➤➤ SEVEN ◄◄

# COUNTING SOLDIERS

**ᔕᓏᓂ** Tkaa promised to tell Numair of the opals in the morning, then entertained Maura and Kitten with tales of the Divine Realms. Daine put out the food and made sure Maura knew how to cook it. She was impressed by the girl's camplore: few ten-year-olds could build a fire, let alone cook on it. Maura gave the huntsman Tait the credit.

"You're lucky in your friends," Daine said as she tucked Maura in.

"If not my family," agreed Maura, yawning. "The wolves really won't eat me?"

Daine took a breath and counted to ten, so she wouldn't give an angry reply. It worked, simply because Maura was asleep by the time she finished counting.

"I leave to go south at dawn," she told Kitten, Tkaa, and Cloud later.

Tkaa switched to thought-speech, confiding that so much spoken talk that day had made his jaw muscles ache.—*Have you decided how you will go in?*—

"I'll see who's about," replied Daine. "Oh, listen—the pack's coming."

—*We must take your word for that,*—remarked the basilisk, amused.—*In this, your magic is more powerful than ours.*—Kitten nodded.

Daine went to the cave entrance to greet the wolves. The moment she saw them, she wished she had remained seated. Brokefang, in the lead, bore a ham in his jaws. Frostfur was next with a rope of sausages. Each wolf had something: small bags of grain, meat, sacks of potatoes. Each pup proudly, and gently, bore an egg in his or her mouth. Also,

enthroned on Sharp Nose's back, nagging the wolf to trot slower, was
the squirrel she had healed two days ago.

Brokefang put the ham at her feet as the rest of the pack carried
their burdens into the cave. *The squirrel asked to come,* the chief wolf
told Daine, panting happily. *He wants to help.*

"Help with *what!*" Daine whisper-screamed. Tkaa, Kitten, and
Cloud came out to see why she was so excited. "Are you *crazy*? Why
did you steal all this food? *Where* did you steal it? Mithros above, *how*
did you steal it?"

*Easily,* Battle replied. *We visited the tree cutter den. They had more
food than they could use. We ate some ourselves, and we spoiled the
rest.*

Frolic added, *We knew you and the human pup would soon eat all
you have. Besides, if the men have no food, they will not have the
strength to cut trees.*

"I *told* you, the Coldfang was set on your trail because you stole
the axes! It'll be a lot easier to track you when you stole hams and
onions! They smell!"

*If they follow, we are ready,* said Brokefang coolly. *There is a
rockfall up the slope. When pushed, it will bury a Coldfang, and we
can use other ways out of the cave.*

*It will do no good to moan, 'What have I done?' as you have been.*
(Only Frostfur can be that charming, thought Daine.) *It is time for us
to think this way. Men bully us all our lives. It is time for some revenge.*

*Only a little,* Brokefang cautioned. *Avoiding two-leggers is still
best.*

"What of you?" Daine asked the squirrel, knowing there was nothing she could say to change the wolves' minds. "How did you get pulled
into this madness?"

*You told me to listen to nonwolves,* Brokefang reminded her. *Surely
listening means speaking, too.*

*The big fellow here told me they fight tree cutters,* the little rodent
said. *If* anyone *fights them, I will help. Do you know how many of my
kind lost homes and feeding grounds this year? The Highbranch family
starved, in the growing season, because their nesting places were cut
down! And the big fellow—*

*My name is Brokefang,* the wolf said, looking up at the squirrel.

*I am Flicker,* replied the squirrel. *My family is Round Meadow.*

*—It is useless to get excited,—*Tkaa said to Daine, not unkindly.—
*As you told me, you did not ask them to do this. They thought of it
themselves, and perhaps it is not such a bad thing to think.—*

Daine sighed. Tkaa was right. Also, there was nothing she could say to the pack that she had not said before, clearly with little effect. Instead she looked at Flicker. Squirrels had nimble forepaws, as good as hands in their way, and quick reflexes. They had keen eyes and ears, and a great deal of curiosity. Flicker was perfect for her needs.

"How would you like to go for a walk in the morning?" she asked him.

Often during her ride south Daine cursed the need for secrecy that kept her, Cloud, and Flicker high on the mountainsides, rather than on the road by the lakeshore. They stopped often to rest Cloud, although the mare argued that she was not a soft valley pony, to be coddled every step of the way. By the time they reached the woods near the southern fort, the afternoon was half gone.

Daine cared for Cloud before taking a seat under an old willow. Its long branches swept the earth, screening her and her friends from view. With the mare to stand guard, she was as safe here as anywhere in Dunlath. Making herself comfortable against the bole of the tree, she asked Flicker, "Ready?"

The squirrel finished the nut he was eating and launched himself into the willow's branches. Ready! he replied.

Daine closed her eyes. Before she could draw an entire breath, she was in Flicker's mind. Swiftly they climbed high on the bole, then leaped for the next tree. He seized what looked like a clump of leaves and little more, and fell.

Daine opened her eyes. She was in her own body again, shaking. Flicker dropped to the next branch down and scolded. How are we to do *anything* if you go away on the easiest jumps? Come back at once, and don't be such a baby. I thought you went flying with a bat just the other night.

The bat was *flying,* not falling and missing his grip! she retorted silently.

I did *not* miss my grip. That was a controlled drop. Now are you coming?

Just a moment, Daine replied. Finding her water bottle, she had a drink.

Back so soon? asked Cloud, wickedly.

"Very funny. I'd like to see you leap through trees."

But I don't try. That is why *my* kind has horse sense, and yours does not.

Daine made a face at the mare and settled back against the willow. This time all she did was close her eyes, and she was inside Flicker.

You can trust me, he said as he set out once more. I've done this all my life.

The rest of the trip was a blur. Flicker used jumps as she might use large steps over puddles, whipping his tail for balance, then racing to the next leap.

The trees were cut for a hundred yards around the fort, but the grass was tall enough to screen a gray squirrel. The fort's long walls were easy to climb. At the top Daine made Flicker check for guards. The two they saw were distant and not looking their way: she urged him over. He dropped onto the walk and climbed headfirst to the ground as Daine cringed. You won't make a good squirrel at this rate, he informed her when they were safely on the ground.

They checked the inner enclosure: it was nearly empty. Horses were picketed in front of a low wooden building Daine guessed to be the commander's office. A horse-boy dozed near his charges under the single tree allowed to grow inside the wall. He was the only human in view, though they heard others in the buildings.

Everything was fairly new, built from raw wood. As well as the mess and command post, she identified a stable, a building that had to be a barracks, and the privy. One other building had only a roof, three walls, and a long, low railing. Straw was scattered on the floor; the rail was scarred with what looked like knife cuts.

What's that? asked Flicker. It looks strange.

I *think* it's a Stormwing roost. They're the only creatures big enough to need a rail that large to sit on.

Flicker's teeth chattered angrily. If they have their own perches like this, they had no business landing on *my* branch and almost killing me!

Too right. Now, let's try the command post, she suggested.

The squirrel raced to the closest building, the stable, and ran up the side. One leap: they were on the roof of the Stormwing mews. Even the wood between them couldn't keep the reek from Flicker's sensitive nose. He sneezed, then jumped onto the command post roof. Trotting to the edge, he swung down under the eaves and saw a broad window.

They climbed in and looked around. On the wall by the door, a large slate was mounted. Written across the top in white chalk was Duty Roster—Troops.

Daine examined it. Thirty privates were listed, as well as three sergeants, three corporals, and a captain, making a total of thirty-seven. She counted twice, to be sure, then noticed papers in a stack on the desk.

Let's have a peek at those, she suggested to the squirrel.

Flicker jumped onto the desk and picked up documents one at a time for Daine to read. The first two were supply orders; the third was not. At its foot was a heavy wax seal that bore an image of a crossed sword and wand, topped by a crown and wrapped in a jagged circle. It was the seal of the emperor of Carthak: she knew it from histories and official papers Numair had shown her. The writing was bold and easy to read.

> *The criminal Arram Draper, also known as Numair Salmalín, is to be taken alive and transported to Carthak by Stormwings.*
> *Try also to capture the young dragon. If this immortal is shipped to Us live for inclusion in Our menagerie, there will be a reward of 500 gold thaks. As to the dragon's handler, she is not required. Kill her.*

The girl was so absorbed in her reading that she didn't notice something had darkened the window. When a wave of stench reached Flicker's nostrils, he sneezed and turned.

Rikash had landed on the rail outside and was looking in. "Well. A tree-rat. I think it's odd, a tree-rat going through papers. It's not the kind of thing you little crawlers usually do, is it?"

Flicker's tail whipped savagely in anger and fear. Come here, he cried. I'll show you what a "crawler" can do!

Rikash slid until he could block the window if he raised his wings. "Only magic would let a tree-rat read." He yelled, "Humans to the command post! *Now*, ground pounders, *now!*" Raising a claw, he pointed at Flicker.

The floor! Daine ordered. Flicker jumped as gold fire smacked into the spot where they had been standing.

What was *that*? asked the squirrel, breath coming fast.

Magic. They don't use it much, but when they do . . . *jump!*

Flicker leaped atop a cabinet as another fire bolt struck his last position. I'm getting angry, Smelly, he scolded. How would you like your nose bit off?

This is *not* the time to insult him, Daine warned, looking for an escape. She heard feet pounding: humans were answering Rikash's summons.

Their location had the Stormwing in a bind. His feathers got in the way as he tried to aim. What's wrong? taunted Flicker. Can't work yourself around to point? But one of you was limber enough when it came to *landing* on me!

Someone banged on the door. "Hello? Is anyone there?"

"Yes, you dolts!" snarled Rikash. "Get in here now!"

"It's locked!" yelled the man outside.

"Out of the way!" the immortal cried. He *could* point at the door, and did, to loose a bolt of fire at the lock. Flicker jumped to the floor and ran over just as the door swung open.

Three men, two of them cooks to judge from their aprons, dashed in.

*"Get that squirrel!"* shrieked Rikash as Flicker bolted past.

The cooks gaped at him. "Get the *what*?"

The exit was open. Flicker darted though and raced for the fort's wall.

"Don't argue with me! *It's getting away!*" Rikash's voice was clear even through the command post walls.

The squirrel didn't even pause. By the time a search party could leave the fort, he had reached the woods and was scrambling through the trees.

Daine returned to herself. She tried to get up, but something was not right with her feet or hands. They were squirrel paws. "Oh, no," she whispered. "Not now." Looking up, she said, "Flicker, are you all right?"

The squirrel climbed down the willow. You should have let me bite the Great Stinky, he snapped. Then *he'd* know what it's like! Looking her over, he remarked in a milder voice, You know, parts of you are almost normal.

"Funny," mumbled Daine. "Cloud, we have to go. I think Rikash will search for us. But—" She looked at her hands and feet. They were still paws. "Please change back," she said wistfully.

Why? asked the squirrel. You don't have claws of your own—keep these.

If they are hunting you, it might be wise to warn the local squirrels, Cloud remarked. They'll just kill anyone they see, hoping it's you.

Daine winced. "You're right." She called to the nearby tree folk, whether they were red, gray, or the shy black breed. When she finished, all were finding places to hide, and her hands were human. Teetering on human-size, clawed feet supported by her boots, she saddled Cloud and mounted, with Flicker on her lap.

They halted some hours south of the western pass when the light had gone. Stormwings had forced them under cover several times on the way: she dared not start a fire they might see. Instead she gnawed on waybread and jerky, trying to ignore a pounding headache. To complete her happiness, fog rose from the lake to cover the valley in a clammy shroud.

Flicker cleaned out her supply of sunflower seeds, dug up and ate all the nuts other squirrels had cached within sight of their camp, and curled up in one of Daine's packs to sleep. Daine shoved herself under a rock ledge to get out of the damp, and gingerly removed her boots. Her ankles looked human, but the rest still looked squirrelish. "When will I get my toes back?" she asked Cloud.

The mare liked fog no better than her rider. I am a pony, she snapped. You have to ask that question of someone who understands magic. I do not.

—So.—Daine jumped, and banged her head on the rock over her. How the badger had crept up on her she could not begin to guess.—I see you have learned the wider applications of the lesson I mentioned to you.—

"You could have warned me," she snapped, rubbing her scalp. "I thought I was losing my mind."

—After the man said there was no madness in you? If you cannot trust your own instincts, you could at least trust his.—

"He has no instincts, only things learned from books," she grumbled.

—Why do you say that?—

The question brought her to a sudden boil. "He walked us into a mess of traitors." She knew she was being unfair, but couldn't stop. "And evil mages. He got stuck on one side of a magic wall with me on the other. He won't use a word of power on it 'cause the word might cause a mess somewhere, which I don't believe it will. Now I have to count soldiers at opposite ends of the valley. He thinks I'm safe because I'm inside Flicker. He didn't think of folk who'd see a squirrel looking at papers and know something was amiss!"

Her toes hurt, sending darts of pain up her legs that did nothing to help her thinking. She rubbed them. "I'm saddled with a two-legger who won't go home when she's only in the way. I'm running from Stormwings, hurroks, Coldfangs, and the Horse Lords know what else. I'm cold and hungry and tired and I have squirrel feet!"

The badger breathed on the afflicted parts. His breath was warm and soothing. Hair and claws melted, turned pale and smooth: Daine's toes were back. They cramped, and she winced. The badger breathed on them again. The cramps eased, and stopped. So did her headache.

—You have been a foolish kit,—he informed her.—To return to your original state, you must do the same thing you did to begin to change, only in reverse. You have to think yourself into your two-legger form.—

"Oh." She drew on stockings and boots, feeling ridiculous. The badger sighed, and lay beside her. The weight and warmth of his furred body against hers was pleasant, and the heavy badger aroma was comforting. "No matter what I say, the wolves are doing terrible things, things that will get them hurt if they're caught! How can I help when they won't *listen* to me?"

—*You don't grasp why you were brought here. Haven't you seen, in your travels, that you alone speak to all three kindreds: humans, immortals, and beasts?*—

"No. Is that important?"

—*In other places, perhaps not. But* here . . . *What do you think of this valley?*—he asked, appearing to change the subject.

She blinked. "Dunlath?" He nodded regally. "Well, it's—*nice*. Lots of farmland, the lake for fishing, good forests—or they would be, if Yolane and Belden didn't rip the covering off to get at every drop of what's under it. Except for mountain winters, Dunlath is almost perfect, not only for the People, but two-leggers." She remembered the ogre falling at the mines, blood rolling down his back. "Maybe even immortals, too, if they wanted to just live here and raise families."

—*Now you see the shape of our plan. You were brought here to help* all *of Dunlath, not just wolves.*—

"That's twice you've said I was brought, like a cat in a sack. The wolves asked me to come help, but I came on my own two feet, and on Cloud's four."

—*Were you not surprised to get a request for help from Brokefang? Is it the nature of wolves to think to ask for help?*—

"Well, no . . . Maybe—"

—*They do not ask their kinfolk. Packmates already know what is needed. And those beings who are not Pack are unimportant unless they serve as food.*—

"But he changed, because he licked my wound—"

—*He didn't change that much, not in the beginning.*—

"Well, then, why *did* he think to ask for me to come?"

—*Old White suggested it. We thought that if you came for the wolves, you would ease into the true matter, the problem of* all *Dunlath. I had hoped you would see for yourself what is required by now.*—

Daine blushed, feeling absurdly guilty and stupid. "I'm not a seer or a diviner," she protested. "I need things spelled out. That isn't a crime."

The badger rumbled.—*Then here is the spelling. Fish, fowl, four-leggers, two-leggers, no-leggers, you are to set this whole valley to rights.*—

She listened with dismay. *"How?"* she wailed. "I'm fourteen! *Only* fourteen! How do *I* set everyone to rights? Get someone bigger! Get someone older!"

—*Someone older and bigger will not do.*—His voice was tightly patient.—*You are the* only *one for the task. If you weren't tired and wet and frightened, you would see it for yourself.*—

"No I wouldn't," she muttered rebelliously. "I still don't—"

—*Shape a bridge between kindreds.*—He pressed his blunt head to her palm.—*Find allies, my kit—not just among the People, but among humans and immortals.*—Idly he added,—*How do you deal with the Stormwings, may I ask?*—

She made a face. "We've had words. You know how they are. They're here in force, and it looks like they're serving the Carthaki emperor once again."

—*It may be they have no choice. If hurroks can be bound to the service of humans, so can Stormwings.*—

"Why is everyone I meet defending them? You sound like Maura." Remembering her friend's behavior with the immortals, Daine snorted. "Though I'll tell you, yesterday I almost felt sorry for Rikash and his crew. He wanted Maura to go home as bad as I do, but she said no, and he wouldn't make her. It was funny."

—*They sound almost like real people, not monsters.*—The badger's voice was so bland, so clean of any emotion, that Daine looked at him suspiciously.

"What's *that* supposed to mean?"

—*Nothing, young kit.*—Rising, he nudged her in the side, hard.— *Get some rest, then go to work. Unless you want to be here for the Big Cold?*—

"Goddess, no!" Smiling, she added, "Thanks, Badger."

—*Stop feeling sorry for yourself, mind. My patience has its limits.*— As if to prove his point, he glared at the wide-eyed Flicker, who had listened to the entire conversation.—*What are you staring at, nibbler?*—

He didn't wait for a reply. Silver fire bloomed around him and he was gone.

Badgers, Flicker remarked wearily. They always have to be wiser and grumpier than anyone else.

The next day dawned gray and wet, a mixed blessing. It meant they didn't need to worry much about Stormwings or hurroks: they had trouble staying aloft with damp wings. However, she and her friends were *also* wet, which did nothing for moods. They were all aware of the long trip to the northern fort.

"At least we can dry off and get some hot food here," Daine told the others as they reached the caves. "We can't stay long, though."

When they entered the big cave, Maura squeaked and ran to hug Daine. "I'm so glad you're back!" she whispered. "Are you done with your counting?"

Daine felt a guilty twinge. Her comments to the badger about a two-legger who got in her way felt as if they were branded on her forehead. "I have to do the northern fort yet," she said. "How is everything here?"

Maura pulled away. "Fine," she said, the tone of her voice falsely bright. "Tkaa's teaching me'n Kitten—"

"Kitten and *me*," Daine corrected automatically.

"About rocks. You know, how you can tell what's what. He teaches Kitten how to change them, too, but I can't make the noise."

—*Some of the wolves frighten her,*—said Tkaa, emerging from one of the rear caverns. Daine looked for the pack. The pups, napping beside the pile of human gear, thumped their tails and dozed off again.—*The gray-and-white female, Frostfur. The older male, Longwind. They do not harm her, but they watch her, and she knows it. The female growls if Maura comes too close.*—

"Oh, dear." Daine looked at the girl. "Tkaa says Frostfur and Longwind are upsetting you."

"Oh, no." Maura's eyes avoided Daine's. "I hardly notice them. Fleetfoot and Russet are nice, and the pups will play with me. Would you like corn cakes? I still have some batter. I made it from the food the pack brought."

Daine tended Cloud, feeding her the last barley and oats. Her pony cared for, she tried the cakes, and praised them. Flicker liked them too, particularly with honey. It will be a shame to go back to the trees, he confided to Daine. I like the variety of food you have.

You'll get fat as a marmot, Daine said, oiling rough spots on Kitten's hide.

"Daine?" Maura asked. "I was thinking, don't you need help with your counting? I could write numbers down for you. I wouldn't be in the way."

Dismay warred with pity. "We've only one horse," Daine said, "and I have to move fast. The only way you could go would be if we had a mount for both of us. I can't call your horse—he's in his own stable by now. And there's nothing else you can ride."

"A deer, maybe, or an elk? No. I guess that's a stupid idea. I'm sorry. I didn't mean to bother you. I know you'd rather I went home."

Daine winced. It was what she thought, but hearing it in that polite, well-bred voice made her feel like a bigger monster than a Stormwing.

"If travel is the only problem, I may be able to help," Tkaa remarked. "I will carry Lady Maura on my back."

Kitten whistled: the basilisk nodded. "You may ride in my pouch, Skysong."

Dumbfounded, Daine stared at the tall immortal. He looked no stronger than a birch sapling. "Impossible."

"You of all people should know better than to use that word," reproved Tkaa.

"Even if you could carry both, which I doubt, you couldn't keep up."

"I do not see how so young a mortal came to believe she knows all there is to be known of immortals. I would not offer if I felt I could not do it."

Daine was a well-mannered girl, but she liked being talked down to no better than any other teenager. "Very well," she said, standing. "If you can fit Kitten in your pouch, carry Maura piggy-back, *and* keep up with me and Cloud—"

"Cloud and *me*," Maura interrupted. She blushed and covered her mouth with her hands when Daine made a face at her.

"—then you're welcome to come," the older girl finished, feeling beset on all sides. "But if you fall behind, I won't linger for you."

Before they had been on the trail more than an hour, Tkaa caught up to Cloud, Daine, and Flicker and passed them. Maura drooped over his shoulder, sound asleep. Kitten sat up in his pouch, watching the trail.

They traveled all day, getting soaked as the damp turned to rain. At midafternoon they passed the cliff where Daine had first seen the mines. She sighed. That spot would have been good to work from if she only had to listen to the fort's animals, but she wanted to be closer before Flicker went there. She wasn't sure how far her new magic would stretch.

So they followed the mountains farther north, around the fields of heaped and barren dirt. Tkaa found a wooded ridge that overlooked the fort. It was ideal. Large trees nearby would shelter them from the hurroks Daine was sure lived in the northern fort. Also, a line of rock formed a clear path from the base of their ridge to within fifty yards of the palisade.

Flicker agreed. Easy as eating corn, he told her.

Using branches and a fallen log over a pocket in the earth, Daine and Maura built a rough shelter where Tkaa, Kitten, and the girl could sit out of the wet. Daine unsaddled Cloud. As she did so, Maura, Kitten, and Tkaa returned to the ridge, looking not at the fort, but at the mines. The weather might have been damp and miserable, but operations below were in full swing. Human and ogre workers labored in thick mud while overseers cursed those who fell.

When Daine joined them, Maura said quietly, "These poor ogres are *ugly*."

"I don't know," replied Daine. "At least they're of a piece, all one thing. They prob'ly think *we're* funny looking, all pink and hairless."

"You don't hate them? But I hear so many stories. Outside the valley they fight with humans all the time. It's said the King's Champion lives in the saddle these days because she's always battling them."

Daine shrugged. "It's not so bad. Lady Alanna doesn't *always* fight them. Ogres just don't understand they can't take things that belong to others." Since her talk with the badger, she had done a great deal of thinking. "I wonder—if humans didn't attack and tried to be nice, maybe ogres wouldn't be so nasty." She pointed at the mines. "And I know one thing for certain. This is just plain wrong. Look at their ribs— you could count them. When d'you suppose they had their last meal? And whatever it was, it can't have been much."

Maura stared at the scene below, small face unreadable.

Come *on*, Flicker said. We'll have to do some of this in the dark, and I *hate* the dark. Can we get moving, before we have to do it *all* in the dark?

"I have to go," Daine told the others. "Keep your heads down while you're here, and get under cover soon. No fire, mind, and talk *softly*."

Tkaa looked at her. "We will be fine. I will keep the little ones safe."

Daine smiled. "I know you will."

Seated in a corner of the shelter, Daine shut her eyes and entered Flicker's mind. The squirrel's hide itched with anxiety over the coming of night. He scratched, then clambered down the ridge to the line of rock.

The mine workers were trudging home as Flicker reached the fort. Daine was glad to find a chink where the log palisade met the ground: she had not liked the idea of climbing up when they could be seen by those being herded past. Once inside the wall, Flicker scaled one of the watchtowers, tucking himself in where two of the supports met the platform floor.

What is that building over there, the newish one? he wanted to know. It has a terrible smell.

She peered at the structure he meant. It was set apart from the other buildings in the enclosure. Built like a stable, its doors extended from ground to roof. When the wind blew from its direction, a scent of hay, dead meat, and rage, one she had first smelled as a bat, filled the air.

Hurrok stables, she told Flicker. They patrol this part of the valley. They're nasty. Lucky for us, I don't think they can fly in weather like this.

She examined the rest of the fort. It was larger than the one in the south, and older—no doubt it had been here before the mining began. There were painted shutters open on the buildings' windows. The men wore the uniform of Maura's house, green tunic over gray shirt and breeches, with a shoulder badge of the Dunlath coat of arms, a green two-headed griffin on a gray field.

Stands to reason that it's fancier, she told Flicker. Most local visitors must come from the north, from the City of the Gods or Fief Aili. Only traders come in from the south.

The sun is *going*, the squirrel replied.

I'm afraid we have to let it go, she said, as kindly as possible. That room with the light in it looks to be the commander's office like the one we visited in the south. We have to wait for him to leave, and that probably won't be till it's time to eat. Look at it this way—at least we're out of the rain.

We're going back to our friends in the *dark*? asked Flicker.

We must.

He sighed. I know you wouldn't ask it of me if it weren't important. I just *hate* the dark.

The meager daylight was gone and torches were lit when the mess call was sounded. The lamp in the commander's office continued to burn, but the commander emerged to join the flow of men to the mess. Daine and Flicker waited until everyone but the guards in the towers had left the yard, then raced to the headquarters. Swiftly they climbed in the window through an open shutter.

Like its counterpart, this fort had slates with the duty roster nicely laid out in white chalk. I love soldiers, Daine confided to Flicker. They always try to do things the same as every other soldier. She read what was on the board, counting forty soldiers, four corporals, four sergeants, one captain.

More soldiers because of the two-leggers entering this way? asked Flicker.

Has to be, she replied. Come on. Let's get out of here.

Their return took longer than the trip out. Flicker was almost as blind in the dark as a human, and more nervous than Daine had ever seen him. Each rustle and squeak was an owl, a bear, a bush dog, or something worse come to eat him. Daine nursed him along as patiently as she knew how. Flicker had done great things for her, things no squirrel would dream of, and that knowledge kept her gentle when he made one of his many stops to hide. She stayed with him up the face of the ridge and over its edge, rather than leaving him to do it alone.

He nearly expired when a huge shadow moved and snorted. Hello, squirrel, said Cloud. Bad night?

Flicker sat down against a tree bole, shuddering. It was *terrible*, he told the pony. How can you stand walking in the dark?

Daine knew Cloud would ease the squirrel's shattered nerves if the two were alone, so she thanked Flicker again and left him, to open her eyes in the shelter.

There was no light anywhere, only noises, the sounds of large bodies moving nearby. Nervous, she looked around, ears twitching. Now she could see a little, but what she saw was *not* reassuring. Two monstrous shapes moved just outside the shelter's door, one tall and thin, the other wide across the shoulders and slumped. Between them was a smaller but still big shape.

A whistle by one of her ears nearly deafened her, and a face thrust itself near hers. It was long and sharp-toothed on the end. Large, faintly glowing eyes with catlike pupils looked her over. She squeaked and tried to back away.

The smaller of the big shapes turned, showing a face like a pale blur in the darkness. Its owner crawled toward Daine on hands and knees.

It was very strange to find Maura so much bigger than she was.

"Oh, dear," the girl said. "Uh—Daine, you, um, you shrank."

Tell me something I don't know, Daine said: it came out as angry squirrel chatter. She looked at her hands and feet. They were still human, but a fine gray fuzz covered them, and the tips of her nails were now black claws.

She closed her eyes and tried to remember who Daine the human was. It was easier to remember her wolf self, or her bat self. Who was she?

An image appeared before her eyes, a pool of copper fire with a central core of white light. Between core and pool lay a wall of clear power, like glass, flickering with sparks of white and black fire. The white core was her inner self; the sparkling wall was the barrier Numair once put between her self and her magic, to stop her from forgetting her humanity.

Start there, she thought. She found memories of Ma, of Grandda, of the house where she grew up. Next were the Snowsdale humans who tried to kill her for running with wolves. She saw Onua, who gave her work in Galla and a home in Tortall. Here were others who filled important places in her life, a mixed bag of nobles, commoners, warriors, and animals. So *that's* who I am, she thought, pleased to have so much that was good in her human life.

She opened her eyes.

## ⇥ EIGHT ⤙

# FRIENDS

ॐ Maura sat with her back to Daine. "I can't look anymore," she was saying. "Tell me when she's done." The nearby, cat-eyed shape was Kitten, who made a questioning sound. Daine lifted the dragon into her lap, then looked at the bigger shapes at the opening of the shelter. One was unmistakably Tkaa. The other was a stranger.

"I'm done," she announced.

Maura turned and gasped. "You're you! I mean, you were always you, but you were starting to look kind of—squirrelish."

I'm sorry I missed that, commented Flicker from outside the shelter.

Tkaa said, "It is good you have returned. We have a guest. Iakoju, this is Daine, the human Maura spoke of."

The stranger nodded. She was an ogre, clad only in a short, ragged tunic in spite of the damp. "Are you cold?" Daine asked. "We have a horse blanket somewhere." She found one and offered it to the immortal.

"I *said* Daine would welcome her," Maura informed Tkaa. To Daine she added, "Iakoju's our friend. She wants to help us get rid of Yolane and Tristan."

Iakoju stared at the blanket, pointed ears twitching back and forth. At last she took it. "Thank you," she said quietly, and bowed from the waist.

Maura helped the ogre drape the blanket around her shoulders. "She's running away," the ten-year-old explained.

Placid eyes met Daine's without blinking. Despite skinniness and poor clothes Iakoju was clean, and smelled of soap, earth, and something vaguely spicy. Daine sniffed, trying to identify the spice odor. "Are you eating something?"

Iakoju smiled. "Maura give me candy."

Maura blushed. "Well, she looked so scared when I found her, and I remembered what you said, about people being mean to them and maybe if somebody was nice . . ."

There's one for your side, Badger, thought Daine.

"Did you succeed at your mission?" asked Tkaa.

Daine nodded and found her water canteen. Politely she offered it first to Iakoju, who shook her head and held up a gourd water bottle of her own. As Daine drank, Maura said, "Iakoju thinks some of the ogres will help us."

"Why?" Daine sat by Tkaa, where she could see their guest. Kitten and Flicker joined her, Flicker curling up on one shoulder, Kitten on her lap.

"Stormwings and Tristan lie," Iakoju said flatly. "They say, come through gate, we give you farms to keep, so we come. Only farms here are rock farms, under ground. We say, don't want mines, where are farms? Tristan say, you farm what we say farm." She scowled. "Ogres are angry. They send me from valley to find kin clans. Kin clans come help, bashing lying men on the head."

Flicker yawned and nearly tumbled off Daine's shoulder. She slid him into the crook of her arm and asked, "Didn't you have farms in the Divine Realms?"

Iakoju shook her head. "Too many ogres. No room. We come here for farms."

Maura frowned. "I don't understand. If you're peaceful—if you really only like to farm—how come you're called 'ogres'? Ogres are monsters, aren't they? And how come your people are always fighting with ours?"

"We are big," replied Iakoju quietly. "Ugly. Our color different from men color. No all ogres are same, either. Some take what they want. Some fight with men. My people, kin clans, we only like farming, not fighting. Some ogres only like fighting. Are all men the same?"

"No," Daine said thoughtfully. "Of course not."

Maura poked the dirt with a stick. "It's a shame the lake's east shore can't be plowed. It's too steep."

Daine sensed what her young friend had in mind. "The fief is Yolane's. I don't think she'll approve of ogre farms on the east shore."

"Under law she forfeits her lands for treason," argued the ten-year-old. "And the fief isn't all hers. Half is mine—Papa willed it to me, and maybe the king would let me keep it. The way it was supposed to be, Yolane would buy my half when it came time for me to marry, so it's my dowry. That's why I got the eastern half. It's mostly uphill, though," she said with a sigh.

Iakoju's eyes lit. "We make farms. Find ridge, dig out cup, pour in growing dirt. Make small valleys up and down, grow corn, beans, flowers. Peas, herbs—we *like* growing. If ogres help you, will you give us farms?"

"Maura cannot promise," Tkaa reminded her. "It may be she will lose the land. Her sister, whose holding this is, plots against the Crown."

"Tkaa's right," Maura told Iakoju, hanging her head. "I guess I can't promise, not if it might not come true."

The ogre looked at her, at the basilisk, then at Daine. Her mouth curved in a smile. "Maybe I don't leave Dunlath. I go with you instead. We will talk."

Daine was about to object, and changed her mind. The badger's words were still very fresh in her memory. In any event, it couldn't hurt. Before she slept, she wrote a report for Numair, using a glowstone from her belt-purse as her light. Once the report was done, she napped uneasily, dreaming of hurroks.

The company awoke at dawn. The clouds had gone, and the day promised to be lovely. Daine's enjoyment of its beauty was soured by the knowledge that winged patrols would be aloft today. Cloud told her, We had best take another route to the pass, one with lots of trees. Iakoju will stand out like a bear in a puddle.

A nearby stag told Daine of trails lower on the slopes, ones that skirted the mines and lumber camp and passed almost entirely under the trees. She led the way to them with a thank-you to the stag. The tip was a good one. The path was wide and much-used, taking advantage of every bit of cover the forest provided, perfect for much-hunted animals like deer.

As the morning ended, the path took them by the round meadow, past Flicker's tree and the Coldfang statue. Daine passed it with a shudder. Twice since meeting the creature she had awakened with a pounding heart, sweat-damp hair, and the feeling that something icy advanced on her, slowly and relentlessly. She would be glad if she *never* saw another live Coldfang, and it pleased her to leave the stone one behind. One other fear, that Flicker might choose to stay, faded when the squirrel made no mention of returning to his home.

An hour later she heard an animal's call and signaled for the others to halt. Where are you? she asked. What do you want?

A dog broke from the pines fifty yards ahead and raced up to her. It was the huntsman's head dog, one of the wolfhounds Daine had met at the castle.

Dismounting, she said, "I'm sorry—I didn't get your name, before."

I am Prettyfoot, the dog replied. Daine covered a smile with her hand. It is the name the man gave me, the wolfhound insisted. It is a good name.

"It's a lovely name," Daine replied soothingly. "How may I help you?"

Please come, the hound begged. The man is hurt. The wolves did it.

Daine looked at her friends. "Something's up. I have to go with this dog." To Prettyfoot she said, Is it complicated? Will it take me awhile to help?

I don't know if you can help at all, Prettyfoot said, dark eyes sad under wiry brows. Our pack could do nothing.

"Tkaa, will you take this to Numair?" Daine asked, pulling the letter she had written from her shirt. "I think the sooner he gets it, the better."

"Very wise," the basilisk said, lifting Kitten from his pouch. "When it is delivered, I will walk back this way to find you again." He took the letter and set off down the trail, long legs carrying him quickly out of sight.

"We go with dog now?" asked Iakoju.

Daine nodded. "His master's in trouble, he says."

"Tait?" Maura said, alarmed. "Then what're we waiting for?"

Prettyfoot led them onto a new trail, explaining that his pack had been calling for help for a day and a night. No matter what they or the man did, there was no way to take him from the hole. In a small, rough clearing crossed by the trail, they found the rest of Tait's dogs beside a pit. They came running to bark greetings to her and Maura.

Going to the rim of the hole, Daine peered in. Tait, coated in mud, leaves, and filth, sat at the bottom. Suddenly she knew what the wolves' plan for Tait had been. "Huntsman," she said. "You're in a fix."

"Laugh all ye like, girly," he said tiredly, "but get me out of here."

"I don't know," she drawled. "May I ask if this was a wolf pit, to start?"

"It was a lot smaller!" he bellowed. "And the trail marks I put here t' tell me where the damned thing was got moved! If that was your work—"

"I haven't been next or nigh this spot," she retorted, "so don't raise your voice to me!" She was tempted to leave him there. Maura had told her, during the morning's ride, that Tait had killed the last wolf pack to live in Dunlath.

Do not be angry, begged Prettyfoot. He is cold and wet and hungry. And he *smells*.

Daine turned to Iakoju. "I have a rope. Can you pull him out?"

The ogre went to the rim of the hole and leaned over. A sound like a yelp rose from the pit. "It's all right, Tait," called Maura, trotting over to stand next to the large, aqua-skinned immortal. "She's with me."

"Lady Maura?" the captive said. "What kind of company are ye keepin' now?"

The ten-year-old scowled. "Better company than is at home," she snapped.

"And what's that supposed to mean, miss?"

"Never mind. I'll tell you later."

Iakoju looked at Daine and nodded. "Man not too fat. I bring him up."

With a sigh, Daine got the rope and gave it to Iakoju. "I'm not doing this for you, Tait," Daine called. "I'm doing it for your dogs."

"I don't care who ye do it fer, long as ye do it afore I turn gray!"

Iakoju took several turns of rope around her waist and dropped the free end into the pit. Tait wrapped it around his waist in the same manner, and grabbed the rope between them with both hands. "Haul away!" he yelled.

Iakoju backed up. With some cursing on Tait's part, she dragged the hunter from his prison. The moment he was on solid ground, the wolfhounds surrounded him, yipping their pleasure as they nuzzled him.

Seeing him up close, Daine winced. The pit didn't seem to be the cleanest spot in the forest. Tait now smelled greatly of wolf urine and dung.

"Have ye water?" he asked, petting his dogs. "And food would be fair nice."

Maura gave him Daine's canteen. The first gulp went to rinse his mouth; the rest went into his belly. "Weiryn's Horn," he gasped, "I needed that."

Maura offered him sliced ham and cheese. He shoved the cheese into his mouth as the dogs watched, licking their chops. "Ye shouldn't be here," he said when his mouth was empty. He looked at Daine and Iakoju. "No offense meant."

"Berate her all you like," Daine replied. "If you can make her go home, it's more than I could do, *or* that Stormwing lord."

"Things are crazy here now," the man grumbled. "The lords don't care for land or people, bringin' monsters t' keep their servants in fear . . ." Shaking his head, he tore the ham up and gave it to his dogs. Seeing that Daine watched him, he looked down. "Don't care for more'n cheese just now," he growled. "M' throat's that sore from bellowin'."

Why, you softy, thought the girl. She got more cheese and two apples, and gave them to him. For the dogs she cut up the rest of the ham.

"Kind of ye," muttered the huntsman.

"They're good dogs," she replied shyly. "They really love you, you know."

"I know. They could've left me, but they didn't. They run off a bear last night, when it wanted t' come a-callin'." He looked at Iakoju. "Give a man a hand up?" he asked. "M' legs went t' sleep, bein' cramped down there."

The ogre held Tait by the elbows and lifted until he got his feet under him. He winced. "I need t' get this stink off me." He looked from Maura to Daine. "Will ye wait so I can wash? I've clothes and such hid by a stream nearby. I came out here with no plans to go back. Don't like what's happenin' in that castle these days."

Daine smiled. With luck, she had another recruit. "Go ahead. We'll wait for you."

With Iakoju to lean on and the dogs frisking around him, Tait hopped off to his bath. As they passed out of sight, Daine heard him tell the ogre, "No peekin' once I'm out of my clothes, mind."

"I want to check something," Daine told Maura. "Don't stray." She leaned against a tree and closed her eyes. Finding an eagle, she got permission to enter his mind. From the spot where he glided in the warm air that rose from the trees she could see glimpses of Tkaa. The basilisk was on all fours and galloping, his long, delicate limbs taking him faster than she would have believed possible. He was close to the western pass already.

Knowing her letter would soon reach Numair, she let the eagle take her where he wished. He flew low to avoid the barrier overhead, but he was still high enough to have a good view of the valley's heart. Not far from Tait's pit Daine glimpsed the lumber camp. The wolves, it seemed, had achieved their aim. All work was at a halt. The camp was nearly empty; the few humans there lay idly about or walked lazily around the area.

The eagle then flew south. Below lay the village and the castle, like toys. Smoke of an ugly green-brown color billowed out of a tower window in the castle. Every flying creature gave the weirdly colored plume a wide berth.

Why? Daine asked the eagle.

I do not need to fly through death to know what it looks like, replied her host. I do not have to bathe in danger when I know what it smells like. There is always something bad going on in that tower.

We're going to stop it soon, Daine assured him. It's almost over.

Good, replied the eagle. Tell me if you need help, and I will give it.

When the bird wheeled north, Daine saw trouble. Three creatures flew in criss-crossing patterns along the slopes where she had been the night before. The eagle squinted, and shapes came into focus: the bodies and heads of horses, batlike wings as big as sails. The hurroks worked their way south, skimming above the treetops. They were hunting for something, and she had an unhappy idea of what it might be.

I have to go, she told the eagle hastily. Thank you!

She opened human eyes. Something huge and brown filled her vision and surprised her into a yelp that came out a keening screech. I wish this would happen when I need it, not when I'm rushed! she thought peevishly, and blinked. The brown thing moved to show a patch of hairy skin.

Trying to rush the change was not going to work. With a sigh she began to remember Daine the human. She thought of nights in the Rider barracks hearing stories, of sword practice with the King's Champion, and of stargazing at Numair's tower. Under her memories now she felt talons become feet, and wings become arms. When she opened her eyes this time, Tait sat beside her, a golden brown feather in his hand. It was his rough tunic and skin that had seemed so close.

"Sorry. Didn't mean t' scare ye, lass." He offered her the feather. "Ye lost one. Actually, ye lost a few. Maura's got one."

Daine looked around and saw only Kitten and Prettyfoot. "Where is she?"

"Iakoju took her fishin'."

Raising her voice a bit, she said, "Kitten, get Maura and Iakoju. Hurroks are searching the valley—they're coming this way." To the man she said, "Is there cover around here?"

"The laurel bushes can hide Maura and the dragon." Tait stood. "There's a willow by the stream for Iakoju and the pony. The dogs can go where they like—I don't think the hunters will care about them."

The ogre and Maura came at a run. All of them listened as Daine explained where to hide. They hid their belongings, too. Daine kept her crossbow and quiver. Tait had a bow of his own, a fine weapon polished and supple with much use. He strung it quickly.

"They hunt me." Iakoju's eyes, the dark green of oak leaves, were sad. "They count us in morning, before work. My brother supposed to say I am sick."

"I guess they didna believe him, lass," Tait said, patting the ogre's arm. "Not yer fault. Get under cover. We'll sing out when all's clear." Iakoju tramped off toward the stream with Cloud and Tait's dogs behind her.

Daine pointed to a spot where a fallen tree leaned against an oak.

Where they met, the dirt underneath had worn away, leaving a hollow. From that spot they would be able to see the clump of laurel and the stream. Tait nodded and followed her to it. Flicker was already there, sunning himself on the log.

Sitting next to the huntsman, Daine put an arrow in the crossbow's notch and secured it, then placed it at her side, ready to fire—just in case. At the limits of her awareness came the first tingling sense that hurroks were near.

Tait had tucked the eagle feather behind his ear. Now he ran it through his fingers thoughtfully. "Can ye change entire?"

"No," the girl replied, fingering the badger's claw around her neck. "I can't even control what changes. I just learned how to turn myself all human again the night before last."

"Aye. Maura said at first ye thought ye were mad." Tait's brown eyes met hers. "She told me why she left home. Do you believe me when I say I'd no idea treason was afoot? I knew things was strange— that's why I left. But treason . . . That's worse than I thought."

Daine studied him. His was a square, stubborn face. He looked as if he would be as bad a liar as she was herself. "Yes," she replied, and smiled.

He smiled back. "Truthfully, I'm as glad she's here and not home. I don't think Tristan has the grip on what's goin' on that he thinks he does."

"What do you mean?"

The man teased Flicker with his feather as the squirrel tried playfully to grab it. "Two days ago I was in the courtyard when the female mage, Gissa, came out screamin'. She was holdin' her wrist like her hand turned into a serpent, yellin' fer someone t' 'take it off.' I saw a wee drop of red on th' hand. Th' skin was *bubblin'*, like, and red streaks was growin' on the back toward the wrist, like they do when a wound's gone bad. Tristan and Master Gardiner was on the steps, and they just stared at her." Sweat appeared on Tait's forehead. "So she run t' th' woodpile, grabbed th' ax, and chopped her hand off."

Daine stared at him. "She cut off her own *hand?*"

"Weiryn leave me hungry if I lie." He wiped his face on his sleeve. "Praise the Goddess the lass wasn't there. She'd've had nightmares for months, what with the blood and Tristan not carin' about Gissa, but yellin' if she let 'it' boil over they were all dead. He run inside—didn't even try t' help Gardiner make the wrist stop bleedin'. He—"

Daine put a finger to her lips, then pointed up. A large, winged shape passed overhead, its shadow falling on the spot where Flicker had lain. Nearby she felt the other hurroks, their presence tainted, as always, with rage. They remained directly above for some time before moving higher on the mountainsides.

"I think if we're quiet, they won't hear us," she whispered. "They've gone off a ways, but they might come back."

"Ye can tell where they are?"

"When they're in range."

"More witchcraft, then?"

"Yes," she replied, and he shook his head. She knew this attitude too well. Some people were uncomfortable with magic; the more things they heard she could do, the more uncomfortable they became. Rather than argue, she changed the subject. "Who's this 'Weiryn'?" she whispered. "You mention him all the time, and I don't think I ever heard of him."

"A mountain god of the hunt. He's rooted in the forest and rock, kin to all that walks or swims or flies. On Beltane ye can see him pass in the woods, with his hounds. Got antlers like a deer, he does. All us huntsmen swear by 'im."

Something about that description was familiar, but she couldn't place it. "I never had much to do with huntsmen at home. Well, *they* didn't have much to do with *me*. Have you heard of my village, in Galla? Snowsdale?"

The look he gave her was thoughtful, and very sharp. "So ye're *that* one."

Daine felt herself turning red. "I don't know what you've heard, but it's prob'ly blown way out of proportion."

"Not after what I've seen today," the man said, and grinned.

They waited for a long time. As they waited, Daine filled Tait in on all she knew, from the wolves' summons to the orders she'd seen from Carthak. Just as she thought the hurroks were going, she sensed fresh arrivals: Stormwings. Keeping low, she checked on the others and warned them the danger was not over. As she rejoined Tait, screams and snarls exploded overhead. It seemed hurroks and Stormwings did not get along.

"We could get old here," she whispered to Tait. "What are they looking for?"

"The dragon, perhaps?"

She winced. "Kitten. It figures." She made herself relax, and took a nap. When she woke, the Stormwings and hurroks were gone, and Tkaa had returned. They all left their hiding places, hungry and stiff. While Maura introduced Tkaa to the huntsman, Daine did some thinking. She did not like the story of Gissa's hand, not after seeing that oddly colored smoke over the castle. What were the mages brewing there—more trouble, like the barrier?

A touch on her arm was the basilisk.—*I am to tell you soldiers are at the southern gate to the valley. Also, the King's Champion and the Knight Commander of the King's Own are there. Master Numair says that should cheer you up.*—

Hope surged in her mind, and she asked silently, Can he break the barrier with Lady Alanna's help? She's a fair powerful mage.

—*He said you would ask. He and the Lioness cannot break this working. It continues to absorb what power they strike it with, not reflect it. No mages can be spared from the City of the Gods. Some are riding here from the south, and will be here in four days.*—

The girl shook her head. With Tristan up to something, she wasn't sure they had four days. She had to know more, and that meant entering the castle.

It took time to convince the others to push on without her. At last they agreed to move on toward the western pass until dark, then camp, while she and Cloud rode to a spot near the village. No one liked that decision, but Daine's growing fear that something bad was brewing made her overrule them. If Tkaa, Iakoju, and Tait could not keep Maura and Kitten safe, no one could, and only she could wander the castle with no one the wiser.

Cloud worked hard to reach a place near the village before sunset. Twilight had fallen when they halted inside the trees on the town's fringe. Murmuring compliments, Daine rubbed her friend down. Stop that, Cloud said when she was dry and clean. Go do what you must.

Daine opened her bedroll and lay down under the trees. I don't know how long this will take, she warned her friend. Cloud was nibbling the grass that grew close by and did not answer.

Daine's magic flowed out readily, reaching the castle before she had taken more than two deep breaths. Inside its walls she found horses, goats, chickens, geese, and pigs, all nice animals in their way (although she detested chickens), but ill-suited to a search in a human dwelling. She was nearly resigned to asking the mice for help, and praying they would not be seen. Then, in the kitchen garden, she found two cats.

She approached the elder, a fat, dignified tom who busily washed the inky black fur of a cat not far out of kittenhood. Since the younger cat objected to the tom's vigorous methods, he kept her in place with a powerful forepaw as he cleaned her white bib. When Daine interrupted, he stopped washing, but kept his grip on the younger cat as Daine politely explained her errand.

The tom—named by men Blueness—listened with interest. When

she finished, he inspected his claws. I am not sure that I am the cat you need, he told her. There are nooks and crannies where a creature of my noble bulk may not go. He looked at the other cat. You take the Scrap, here. Even for a kitten she is most inquisitive, and she can get into anything.

Say yes, pleaded Scrap. Please!

Daine had to smile. Thank you, Blueness.

Do not get dirty, Blueness warned Scrap, or I will wash you again.

I can wash myself, the young cat retorted.

Not as well as I can, the tom replied. Now sit quietly while Daine does whatever she must to ride with you.

Daine turned her attention to Scrap, hearing the cat's eyes blink, and the soft pound of her heart.

Are you here yet? asked Scrap, breaking Daine's concentration.

No, Daine said. Almost. Hold still, and hush.

She listened. That was the sigh of Scrap's lungs, and her heartbeat. Her stomach growled softly, digesting milk a cook had left unattended.

Scrap yawned. Well? she demanded. Are you ready?

Now you know what I put up with, muttered Blueness.

Daine focused hard, and Scrap gave a squeak. Now the two of them scratched an itch, and looked at Blueness with Scrap's eyes. He was the most handsome tom she knew, his glossy fur a mix of pure white and sable black. She *loved* Blueness. She would follow him anywhere, particularly if she could attack his tail. She pounced. Blueness, with the ease of practice, whipped the tail clear and gave her a solid cuff with his forepaw.

Come on, Daine said, and showed Scrap images of Tristan, Yolane, Belden, and the other mages. I'm looking for them.

I can find them, but the female will screech and throw things if she sees me, Scrap replied.

Then don't let her see you, Blueness ordered. Daine, keep her safe.

I will, and thank you, Daine called as they galloped through the kitchen. Why is he named Blueness? she asked as they trotted up a long flight of stairs.

My mama said when he was my age, he fell into a bowl of color the cook uses on food, and he came out all blue. I can't believe he would be that undignified, but that's what my mama said, and she knows everything. Here we are. The man with the yellow magic lets the others visit him here.

"I can't fit the hand if you won't hold still," a man was saying as Scrap entered. She went under a table and peered out. The room was big, with shelves of books along the walls and silk carpets to cushion feet from the stone floor. Scrap, heedless of the expense or quality of the carpet that extended under the table, kneaded it luxuriously, sharpening her claws.

Daine examined the humans. The mage Redfern sat with Gissa of Rachne on a sofa. He worked on a metal skeleton hand fixed to the stump of the mage's wrist, making tiny adjustments to it with instruments from the table before them. Gardiner leaned against the sofa's back, watching with interest.

"If Gardiner and Master Staghorn had kept their wits about them, this wouldn't be necessary!" snapped the woman. Pain had aged her face ten years.

"Recriminations are due on *your* side of the ledger, Gissa." That smooth, oily tone could only be Tristan, Daine thought, and she was right. He sat in a chair beside the table where she had taken refuge. "You are no greenling, fresh from the country. Letting bloodrain splash as you stirred it was—"

"Tristan!" cried a feminine voice. The door opened and humans entered. Scrap looked out cautiously, and Daine saw Yolane, Belden, and Alamid. "Tristan, Alamid showed us the warriors at the southern pass in his crystal. That's the King's *Champion* out there, and the Knight Commander of the King's Own!"

"Alamid shouldn't worry you with minutiae." There was more than a hint of poison, and meaning, in Tristan's voice.

*"Minutiae?"* cried Yolane. "The Lioness and Raoul of Goldenlake are *minutiae?"*

Tristan sighed. "My dear Yolane, calm down." He went to a wine table and filled the goblets there, bringing one to her and keeping one. "If I faced Lady Alanna and the Knight Commander with weapons they have mastered, I might feel some concern. I am not such a fool. Believe me, we were prepared for this. In three days they will cease to be even a mild irritation."

Belden went to the wine table, drank the contents of one of the goblets Tristan had filled, and poured himself a second drink. "Why?"

"My colleagues and I have prepared a little something to welcome the king's representatives. It's called 'bloodrain.' You might say Gissa already tested the brew for us, and that was before it reached its full potential."

"She cut off her *own* hand," Yolane said.

"It was my hand or my life," snapped the female mage. "If the poison had gotten into my blood, I would have rotted from the inside out."

"But how will you poison them?" Yolane asked. She finally sat down in the room's biggest chair. "Surely they'll have magical protections on their camp."

Tristan sat on the chair's arm, sipping his wine. "I don't plan to go near them. At sunset the day after tomorrow, I will take the bloodrain to the southern pass, where the river runs through the barrier, and dump it in." Gardiner shivered. "By sunrise of the next day, there won't be a living soul in that camp."

"Or anywhere else for ten miles," Gardiner said.

Yolane looked at him. "What is that supposed to mean?"

"Bloodrain will kill anything that uses moisture from the river." The cold, metallic voice was Alamid's. "Animals, plants—it doesn't matter. The zone of destruction will extend nearly five miles on each side of the river, and ten miles downstream." All the hair on the cat's—Daine's—back stood up.

"For how long?" Belden finished his second cup of wine and poured a third.

"The effects begin to fade after seven years or so," Gissa replied softly.

"It's necessary," Tristan said firmly. "Our departure for the capital is scheduled for a week from today. Nothing can be permitted to interfere."

"What if they're warned?" demanded Yolane. "They might withdraw."

"If they do, they should meet the two companies of mercenaries we have been keeping across the Gallan border," replied Tristan. "I took the liberty of calling them up in your name, and they will be at the southern gate in three days. Gardiner, tell Rikash to warn Captain Blackthorn to bring his own food and water supplies."

"And Numair Salmalín?" Belden's drinking hadn't affected his hands or voice as he poured another refill. "He's still in the western pass, isn't he?"

"I have a net I will use to bottle him up. The emperor wants him alive. It is *always* a good idea to give His Imperial Highness what he wants."

"I don't like it." Yolane's face was white under her makeup. "I swore an oath to keep Dunlath safe, when my father gave me his signet. This bloodrain—"

"My dear, you are overscrupulous." Belden's tone was scornful. "It isn't going to kill anything in Dunlath proper, is it? And what will you care, once you sit on Jonathan's throne? Dunlath is a long way from Corus. Besides, you heard Master Staghorn. It will all grow back in less than a decade."

Tristan picked up one of Yolane's hands and kissed it. "Yolane, leave command decisions to your generals. As queen, you must get used to sacrificing the lives of a few for the good of all. Think of this as a masterly stroke, which it is. In one move you deprive the king of his champion and the commander of his most personal guard. Those are tactics you need. You have to convince not only your enemies, but your allies, that you deal promptly with opposition."

"Believe me," Gissa added, accented voice quite dry, "once they see what is left of those who interfered with you here, they will hurt themselves for the chance to be the first to swear to you."

Yolane looked at all the mages, frowning. "Why does it have to wait two whole days? Why can't you kill them now?"

"Bloodrain takes time," Redfern told her. "Once combined, the ingredients must brew for three full days and three full nights."

Tristan smiled at Yolane in a way Daine thought Belden should object to. "You see, Majesty? Everything is under control. You chose your generals well."

Yolane looked as if she were about to object again, but Tristan put his finger to her lips. She sighed and looked around the room. Her eyes rested on Daine, and her mouth went tight. Picking up her goblet, she hurled it at Scrap, who ducked out the door, soaked in wine. "If I see that cat again, I'll kill it!" Daine heard her snarl as Scrap raced down the stair.

Now Blueness will wash me again, the youngster told Daine with a sigh. Did you hear what you wanted to?

I heard too much, replied Daine. I think I have to go. Thank you. A lot of people will owe their lives to you for this.

She fled to her body, scrambling to rethink herself human. She succeeded only partly—there were claws on her hands and she appeared to have a tail—but at least she was almost normal size as she entered her skin. Rolling up her bed, she jammed it under some bushes, thinking fast. Could she build wings for herself and fly up to Numair?

You will tire and fall, Cloud informed her. Use common sense. If you are in a hurry to get to Numair, take the way you know best. But don't ride me—I'm not up to a mad dash to the western pass, not after today. Steal one of the big horses from the village. I will follow you as quickly as I can.

Daine nibbled a fingernail and winced as the claw dug into her lip. I hate to steal, she admitted. But I think I must. She sent out an urgent call.

A large, bony horse grazing nearby came racing over. You want the fastest horse in this valley, he told her. I am the one.

Daine heard the other village horses agree: Rebel was the best at running.

You don't look like much to me, Cloud said, looking the stallion over.

Rebel snorted. That is what everyone thinks. That is why my man wins money when he races me against strangers, and that is why I am fed oats every day.

I am not impressed by your oat ration, Cloud retorted. Seeing that Daine was about to mount, she said, Don't forget your pack, or the crossbow.

Daine slung the pack over one shoulder and the bow over the other, after popping a bolt into the crossbow's notch and clipping it in place. Satisfied? she asked the pony.

And don't take any sauce from this jackanapes. I will follow soon.

Daine had ridden fast horses in the king's service and with the Riders, but none matched Rebel. The ride through the village, past the crossroads, and onto the road to the western pass left her breathless. Once the last farmhouse was behind them, Daine began to call for Tkaa, Tait's dogs, and the pack as she hung on for her life. When she felt their reply, she told them what she had learned. They agreed to meet her at the barrier.

No fighting, she ordered dogs and pack. We don't have time, and the stakes are too high. She felt some wolves ignore her, and some dogs. I mean it! she cried. I'll *make* you obey if I have to!

We will not fight, she heard Brokefang say, iron strength in his thoughts.

We will not fight, Prettyfoot said reluctantly. Any dog who wishes to fight may fight *me*, right now.

Daine relaxed. Let the dogs and the wolves concentrate on the *real* enemy: those who planned to dump bloodrain in the Dunlath River in two days' time.

In the pass, Daine halted Rebel under some trees and dismounted. Briskly she rubbed him down. "You need to rest. You'll find grazing over there. And don't mind all the weird folk who are coming here. Nobody will hurt you." He lipped her shirt and wandered off to graze, as Daine walked to the barrier.

Shapes that looked like rocks on the slope under the three-quarter moon rose to their feet and came down to her: the Long Lake Pack. Daine knelt so her eyes would be on a level with theirs. Adults and pups alike, they surrounded her in the greeting ceremony, licking her face and wagging their tails. Brokefang let the girl hug him fiercely about the neck and nuzzled her in reply.

You will stop it? he asked.

*We* will stop it, she told him. By ourselves if we must, but I don't think it will come to that. We have friends now.

Two-leggers? That was Longwind, the conservative. They never cared before.

They were not friends before, Daine replied firmly. They are friends now—*strong* friends. They can go places and do things we can't, hunt brother.

The dogs are *almost* wolves, offered Fleetfoot. If we sing, they listen. They have their own songs.

Two-leggers? Wolf killers? Longwind sneezed. I am too old for such changes.

Brokefang turned on his uncle, teeth bared. You are *not* too old for changes until I say you are, he snarled, advancing. You will change for now because the pack *needs* you to change. When it is done, we will return to the old ways.

If we can. The comment, unusually quiet and thoughtful, came from Frostfur.

I *like* changes! The thin, high voice in Daine's mind was Runt.

Me, too, added Silly. We see new things and do new things.

"I hear them," whispered Daine. "I can hear the pups. It's because of Scrap, maybe. She was a young cat at the castle," she explained. "I was with her when I heard of the bloodrain."

Would we like her? asked Berry. What is a cat?

Thinking of the castle reminded Daine that she had a letter to write. She left the explanation of cats to Fleetfoot and Russet, who had met them in their journey to fetch her. Taking her pack, she entered the stone lean-to where she had hidden to write once before.

With the help of her glowstone and cat eyes that had not changed during her ride, she put down all she had heard. Once the facts were laid out, she added:

*We must do something. I won't let them put bloodrain in the river. I hope you know a smart way to fight them. If you don't, I will think of a stupid way to do it. I was wrong to call Stormwings monsters. The creature that could brew and use this bloodrain is the real monster.*

Gently she blew on the wet writing to dry it, then put her tools away.

## ⇥ NINE ⇤

# WAR IS DECLARED

In the distance she felt the approach of Tkaa, Flicker, Kitten, and Iakoju, which meant that Tait, Maura, and the dogs had come as well. Tkaa immediately took the letter through the barrier, and Iakoju went with him. Flicker muttered a greeting and crawled into Daine's pack to finish his night's sleep.

"It's true, what the basilisk said?" Tait asked, sitting next to Daine. "They've cooked up some infernal broth?"

"Gissa had a drop of it on her hand when she cut it off," Daine replied grimly, tickling Kitten's belly. The dragon, sensing her agitation, voiced a soft run of clicks and chirrups that had always comforted Daine in the past. The girl smiled at her young charge. "I'll be all right, Kit," she whispered.

Tait watched Maura as the girl, yawning, bedded down in the shelter of the rocks. "How can ye speak with Tkaa and not Iakoju? She told us she couldna hear ye, and that's fair strange."

Daine shook her head. "No, it's not. I can't mind-speak with immortals that have some two-legger in them. Only the ones who're made entirely like animals."

The dogs came to lie down with Tait even as the pups, Russet, and Fleetfoot arranged themselves around Maura. For a moment both groups, separated by only a few feet of ground, stared at one another. Then Prettyfoot yawned, and Silly yawned in reply. Daine felt something relax in both clusters of shaggy bodies, and gave an inner sigh of relief.

"I'd like t' ask a favor," Tait said, his voice soft. "If aught's to happen in the castle, let me warn my brother, so he can get the servants out. He'll make sure none of the nobles or their guests are the wiser."

"You don't think someone might warn Tristan or Yolane?" she asked, examining the silver claw at her throat.

The hunter shook his head. "Nay. We accepted milady—she's Dunlath blood, and Mithros knows ye can't pick your lords—but none will back her in treason. And the outlanders she foisted on us treat us like slaves."

Daine heard a soft whistle from the barrier: it was Tkaa, half in and half out. Getting up, she ran to him, with Tait close behind.

"You may breathe easier," Tkaa informed them quietly. "The Stormwings and hurroks are at the soldiers' camp, harrying those who would sleep. The Lioness says they spend as much time battling one another as they do the mortals."

"How can ye know what goes on more'n a day's ride from here?" asked Tait.

"A speaking spell?" Daine asked. Tkaa nodded. To the man she explained, "It helps mages to speak to other mages, no matter how far off they are. They know about the bloodrain and the mercenaries coming?"

"Yes," the basilisk replied. "Once all may speak without interruption, Master Numair wishes you to cross the barrier. Perhaps the marmot who helped you there before will serve?"

Daine checked the eastern horizon. "She won't be up until dawn."

"It may take that long for the harriers to break off their attack. I will return when all is secure." Tkaa went back to Numair.

They trudged up to the stone cluster, Daine yawning until her jaw ached. "Sleep," Tait ordered. "I'll wake ye when Tkaa says they're ready t' talk."

"We need a plan," Daine mumbled. "And we don't have much time."

"Sleep," Tait repeated. "No one will make a plan without ye."

Cloud had arrived when Tkaa summoned Daine at sunrise. The girl watched her pony join Rebel, then sat back to listen for Quickmunch. The marmot was glad to hear from her, and eager to serve Daine again in communicating with her friends.

As they made their way from Quickmunch's burrow to Numair's camp, Daine felt a crackling tension in the pass. Numair was the source. She never had seen a look on his face like the one that was there now. He radiated fury. Iakoju watched his every movement, dark green eyes wary. Tkaa, as impossible to read as ever, munched quietly on a small pile of rocks.

When he saw Daine, Numair spoke a word. The air near him developed a sparkling blotch the size of a floor-length mirror, then opened to frame two figures Daine knew well. The smaller was a redheaded warrior in chain mail, breeches, and boots—Alanna the Lioness, the King's Champion. She was cleaning a sword. The other was a mammoth a few inches shorter than Numair and much wider. Raoul of Goldenlake, Knight Commander of the King's Own, wore plate armor over a sweat-soaked, quilted tunic. Sipping from a mug, he saw the image of Numair and his cohorts before his companion. "Alanna," he said, and pointed.

The woman looked up, her famous violet eyes grim. "I hope you have a plan—I don't. We could retreat, but that leaves Dunlath secure and you in a bad position. Numair, you told the king Daine's news?"

"Yes, but you know the problem as well as I. It will be days before more help can reach us."

"And maybe Tristan still put bloodrain in river," Iakoju pointed out.

Sir Raoul made a face. "It goes with what we know of the man."

Alanna's eyes narrowed. "Daine, is that really you inside this animal?"

Quickmunch nodded, but she said to Daine, I'm a *marmot*, not an animal.

Two-leggers, Daine replied with a mental shrug. She made a note to tell her friend Alanna that marmots were touchy, prideful creatures.

Numair sighed. "I'm afraid we must implement the plan we discussed earlier." The other two humans nodded.

"I do not like it," remarked Tkaa. "Is there no other way?"

Alanna shook her head.

Daine chattered with annoyance. Was somebody going to tell her *anything?*

An unhappy look in Numair's eyes silenced her. "Daine, there is one other way to break the barrier."

"It means a lot of risk." Alanna put her sword down. "And it won't work unless your friends can draw the mages out of the castle."

Daine looked at Numair, thinking, So what do *I* do? He was in a brown study, pressing his nose and staring into the distance. She was about to ask Quickmunch to get his attention when she thought, Can Tkaa hear me? He hears mortal animals. It's worth a try, anyway. Reaching with her magic, she called, Tkaa!

The basilisk peered at her. "You can speak to me through this creature?"

The "creature" barked. Daine said, She's a marmot. Her name is Quickmunch.

Tkaa bowed. "Forgive me, Quickmunch. I spoke from ignorance, not contempt."

Numair, Alanna, and Raoul were looking from the marmot to Tkaa. "Daine can speak to you even when she isn't doing it from her own body?" asked Numair.

Tkaa listened to Daine and said, "She has learned she has that ability only now. She asks me to say if you do *not* tell her what she can do once the mages have left the castle, she will ask Quickmunch to bite you."

Raoul snorted; the Lioness covered a smile. Numair sighed. "Patience is a virtue you should cultivate. Daine, not you—Quickmunch, is it?"

The marmot squeaked her reply.

"Of course," Numair said. "Daine, remember what I told you of image magic?"

Yes, Daine told the basilisk, who translated for her. If you do something magical to an image of a person, it's the same as doing it to the person.

"That is true not only of people," Numair said. "As it is impossible for Tristan and the others to walk around the valley to create the barrier, they must have enclosed a model of the valley itself. You must find that image in the castle. Once you have broken the circle of magic around it, the barrier will evaporate, and we can enter the valley."

"Opals," the champion put in.

Numair cracked his knuckles. "Alanna and I have assaulted the barrier. It continues to absorb, not reflect, our Gifts. This shows power stones are being used to take magic and feed it into the working. Those stones will be embedded in the model of Dunlath Valley. You'll have to break them to break the circle."

Daine said to Tkaa, I understand. Now what about the diversion? Tkaa repeated the question.

The Knight Commander leaned forward. "We think Tristan will send the other mages to deal with a disturbance at the forts, especially if the trouble is odd in any way. If it's serious, he'll probably go himself. Numair says Tristan never thinks underlings can handle real trouble without him. If both forts are attacked, there's a good chance the castle will be left unguarded."

"That ties up the Stormwings, maybe even the hurroks," Alanna said. "They're the quickest transport for the mages. Iakoju thinks she can raise her people—"

Iakoju nodded. "If I say so, my kin will fight human masters. We make plenty of ruckus in north."

"I can cause trouble in the south," added Tkaa. "But I will need help" He cocked his head to one side. "I am too big a target even for humans to miss."

Quickmunch scratched a flea, and Daine said, Tkaa, will you and Iakoju cross back to talk to everyone with me? Let's see what we can come up with. And tell them that Tait thinks he can get all the local people out of the castle.

"One thing," Numair said after Tkaa was done translating. "Time is vital. To be at the southern barrier by sunset tomorrow, Tristan must leave the castle no later than noon, and there is a chance he will leave earlier. Whatever you do, it must be ready to go by tomorrow morning."

Wait a moment! Daine cried, alarmed. What about the mercenaries who are supposed to come—that Captain Blackthorn and his men?

When Tkaa passed this on, Sir Raoul grinned. "We have two Rider groups here—sixteen irregulars *and* their ponies—plus a company of the Own, a hundred warriors. Yes, Blackthorn has a hundred more men than I do, but if we're in Dunlath when he comes, the game is *ours*— not his. Blackthorn also hates to fight mages even more than he hates to work with them. If he even *hears* that Alanna and Numair are waiting, I think he'll run like a rabbit."

"If that's all the questions, would you get moving?" Numair hinted with awful patience. "It's going to be a long day."

Tristan's crew aren't the only ones who need to fly, Daine thought, resuming her human shape. I will, too. The animals in the forts should be warned, so they can escape somehow. And I can ask local animals to do some damage, like the pack's raids on the lumber camp. I hate to endanger them, but this is too important *not* to involve them.

When Daine, Tkaa, and Iakoju explained the attack plan, their friends in the valley had plenty of ideas. The wolves chose to visit the northern fort, to support the ogres and to attack the hated mines. Maura offered to set the southern fort afire if she got close to it, and promised to leave the gate alone so the horses could run. Tait wanted to go with her, and the dogs followed him. Rebel, who itched to help, agreed to carry the man and girl south.

Kitten whistled a query. Daine smiled. "You're with me, Kit. I need you for locked doors." The dragon chuckled and sharpened her claws on a rock.

Flicker said that he would go with Maura and Tait to the southern fort. He also advised Daine to recruit the valley's squirrels. They could free the fort horses. They also could chew ropes, bowstrings, and the like, once the sun was up. "You think squirrels will want to get involved that much?" the girl asked.

Yes, replied Flicker. The walls in the forts are made of logs, aren't they? Plenty of my kindred lost homes and lives when those places were built. And the southerners have family by the river where they want to put bloodrain.

"Then I'll talk to them. What about the castle servants?" Daine asked Tait.

"I'll give ye a note t' my brother Parlan," the huntsman replied. "He's the innkeeper. He'll see it's done, and done quiet."

"If we fight at dawn, I must go," Iakoju commented. "I have to talk to ogres, give them hope for freedom. Talk might run all night."

"Let's take a bit more time," advised Tait. "Gie the squirrels a while with the sun to work in. If the mage hits the barricade hard, we'll all hear it. The ninth hour, say? Then Maura can start burnin', and the ogres can rise."

Iakoju frowned. "Big noise? Like being inside a bell?"

"It is very hard to ignore," Tkaa remarked dryly.

"Ogres hear. Ogres hear good, four-five days ago. That's *good* signal."

The basilisk went to tell the plan to Numair. While he was gone, Tait wrote his brother. When he was through, Daine summoned a crow and asked if she would carry the note to the inn. The crow, intrigued, accepted it and took flight.

Tkaa returned. "The ninth hour, three hours past dawn," he told them.

"Does everybody know what to do?" asked Maura, hands on hips.

The dogs and wolves yapped; Flicker squeaked. The humans, Kitten, the ogre, and the basilisk nodded. Rebel and Cloud stamped.

"I'm off to the northern squirrels, then," Daine said. "And everybody?" They all looked at her. "Be careful," she cautioned, eyes stinging a little. "Goddess bless us all."

"Goddess bless," whispered Maura and Tait. Silently the animals called on their gods, and perhaps the immortals did the same.

When the others had gone, Daine turned to Cloud. "If I tie myself to you and make sure Kitten's secure in her pack, can you carry us to the place we were last night? I don't want to linger here while I talk with the creatures in the north and south if I can help it." She studied her friend: Cloud *looked* fresh. "If you can't, say so. I'll call another horse from the village, if I must."

And risk thief catchers coming after you? retorted the pony. I think not. I can do this. You forget, I took my time walking here, and I've had plenty of rest and water and grazing. How will you be traveling?

"I thought to try that eagle again."

So much the better. You won't weigh as much as you do now. I noticed the first thing that seems to change is your bones. If you have bird bones, you'll hardly weigh anything, just like *her*. Cloud nodded to Kitten, who was tucking herself into Daine's pack. And make sure you bring that bow.

"Cloud, it'll be too much, me and Kit and a crossbow—"

Don't be a fool, retorted the mare. You need a weapon.

The girl sighed and got the rope. "This is going to be fun."

With the help of some birds and a marmot colony from inside the barrier, Daine tied herself, her crossbow, and Kitten to Cloud's back, with the knots in easy reach. When everything was secure, the pony set off at a walk.

As Kitten chirped soothingly, Daine relaxed and listened for Hunt-song, the golden eagle who had taken her so far the day before. She found him nearly a mile away, about to leave his treetop nest. When she explained what she needed, he agreed to help. Quickly she slid into his mind, and they were off.

Word of Flicker's adventures had gone from tree to tree in the days since the making of the Coldfang statue. The eagle too had been gos-siping with other birds, and the Song Hollow bats had added their in-formation. Daine was startled to find that the woods and rocky slopes all along the western side of the Long Lake buzzed, not only with her name, but with the names of her companions—humans, immortals, *and* animals. When she called from Huntsong's mind to the squirrels near the north fort, they asked what they could do to help end the destruction. Wood rats, overhearing what she told the squirrels, wanted jobs of their own. Three flocks of starlings reminded her that they had come at her call before, to drive off Stormwings. Did she have more fun for them?

With the wild beasts clamoring for Daine's attention, the domestic animals who lived in the fort were eager to listen to her. The dogs and cats left right away, not waiting for the next sunrise. The horses agreed to flee to the docks, once Daine promised that the wolves and other hunters would leave them alone.

As Huntsong wheeled south, Daine saw the pack running single file down the trails, the steady pace eating up the miles between them and the fort. Iakoju, heavy legs pumping in an equally constant tempo, brought up the rear. When the eagle dropped down to eye level, the ogre realized who it must be and waved, grinning cheerfully.

On their way to the southern fort, they found a trio of Stormwings going from there to the castle. With a shiver, Daine saw Rikash was one of them.

Have they ever bothered you? she asked Huntsong.

The great bird glared at the approaching immortals. Not in a general way, he replied, talons clenching. We had a few misunderstandings when they first came here, until they learned the error of their ways. His wrath faded, and he added, All the same, I shall give them a wide berth. They cut my mate to ribbons when she defended our nest.

He drifted to one side. Two Stormwings flapped past, making rude noises. Only Rikash changed course, to fly around Huntsong in a wide circle. The other two, a blond female and the K'miri male, came back and joined him.

"They soar, don't they?" Rikash asked them. "Wheeling, wheeling, always in the same place?"

"Like toy kites, and twice as wood-skulled," joked the K'mir.

"But now here is this one, flying in a straight line, going somewhere. You don't see prey when you go too fast, am I right?"

Get ready to drop, Daine warned Huntsong.

Rikash spat, not looking to see if anyone was below. "This valley has a disease, one where cute little animals don't *act* like animals. Did I tell you about the squirrel?"

"Only a million times," said the K'miri Stormwing with a groan.

Daine saw muscles bunch in Rikash's neck. Drop! she cried. Huntsong threw up his wings and dropped, hurtling earthward at terrifying speed.

"Go, go, *go!*" screamed Rikash.

The female whooped, and steel-winged bodies followed Huntsong down. Grimly Daine hung on, urging him into the trees that covered the road south. The eagle shot into the clear space between road and branches, scudding down the corridor they made. There was a scream and a crash: a Stormwing had come to grief. Huntsong risked a glance back. The female, scratched and bleeding, was trying to free herself from a chestnut. Seconds later the K'mir came in view, fighting to pull out of his stoop before he slammed into the dirt. He failed.

Relieved, Huntsong looked forward. Rikash awaited them ahead, where the trees fell briefly away from the road. Land, Daine urged.

I look stupid when I walk, complained the eagle as he obeyed. Hopping like a sparrow is not eagle's work.

If you think *you* look stupid, imagine how *he* will look, Daine consoled him.

Rikash cursed and darted forward, flying low, trying to keep his great metal wings from clipping the earth or trees. Called from their nests, the squirrels leaped on him, biting with very sharp teeth. Rikash screeched, tried to cover his eyes with his wings, and slammed into an elm. Now *run*, Daine told the squirrels; they obeyed. Huntsong liked that advice, too. He took off, flapping lazily past the spot where Rikash fought the elm's entangling branches. The air filled with the Storm-wing's curses as Huntsong broke free of the trees.

With battle already joined, Daine had no trouble persuading the southern animals to do what they could to help Tkaa, Maura, Tait, and Flicker. The fort's animals, told what was going on, were as eager to stop the use of the bloodrain as Daine was.

I think we're done, the girl told Huntsong, feeling more tired than ever. Let's go home. I'd return by myself, but I'm prob'ly outside the range of my magic, and I don't know if I would make it.

Would you mind terribly if I left you inside your range, and went back to that fort? the eagle inquired. I could help there. It would be a pleasure.

Daine smiled and replied, Of course.

Flying low over the treetops, keeping away from the road, they passed Tait, Maura, Tkaa, and the others. Daine pointed out the basilisk. Talk to him, she told Huntsong as they continued to head north. He can translate for the two-leggers, and they should know of something you can do.

The moment she felt the tug of attraction that was her true body, she wished the eagle good luck and separated from him. Instantly he turned south again as she slid into her human self. With regret she changed his farsighted eyes to her own, limited orbs, and his hollow, light bones into a human's heavier ones. Talons became feet; wings became arms. When she opened her eyes, all that remained was a layer of down between her clothes and skin.

"I'm back," she muttered. "Huzzah."

Cloud halted. That crow came by, the mare said. She wanted to tell you she dropped the note into the man's lap. He read it, and the last she saw of him, he was on his way to the castle.

Daine took a deep breath. "I hope he's as trustworthy as Tait says." The girl extracted herself and Kitten from the ropes that kept them on the pony's back. Then, with Daine afoot and Kitten walking or riding, they took the remainder of the day to approach the village, staying clear of outlying farms. They stopped as the shadows lengthened, so Daine could catch and cook some fish and Cloud would have a chance to graze; it was near dark when they moved on.

Everywhere the People were talking. Dunlath's nonhuman residents had much to say about recent events. They spoke to kinfolk, distant relatives, even enemies (at a safe distance). Their opinions and questions were so loud that Daine wondered if the two-leggers didn't guess something was up.

If they did, she saw no sign of it at the village. Hidden in the trees at the spot where she had left her bedroll and saddle, she watched the local people go about their end-of-day chores, then vanish into their homes. Lamps flared briefly in most houses, then went out; farmers rose and went to bed with the sun. Only the inn and the castle windows stayed lit for any time after dark.

Over the night the Song Hollow bats checked in, waking her with news of her friends. Iakoju had made it safely to the ogre dwellings around nightfall, starting a great deal of movement between buildings and a constant hum of ogre voices. The Long Lake Pack busied itself among the mine wagons, working pins that held wheels to axles out of their settings with their teeth, and chewing the reins until only scraps held them together. In the south, wood rats laid dry twigs and grasses at the base of the wall and around all structures but the gate and the stables. Dogs howled incessantly outside, as little fires erupted in the commander's office, the mess, and the barracks, keeping the men up all night.

At last, with only a few hours left until dawn, the activity ended. The People, and Daine, used the time in unbroken sleep.

She awoke at dawn, aching from tense muscles. In contrast to the racket of the day before, the animals were quiet. Even the birds who greeted the sun were silent, awaiting events. From the trees Daine watched as castle servants crossed the bridge in pairs, small groups, or alone, to enter the village. Parlan waited on the other side of the causeway, steering them to the inn. There were no soldiers to worry about; Yolane relied on Tristan and the forts for protection.

Daine called to the castle mice as the sky brightened. Soon they reported back to her: only the nobles and Tristan remained there.

The sun rose. In the north and in the south, squirrels were working hard to free the fort horses and do as much damage as possible. The soldiers were finding that their morning bread, tea, porridge, and cheese were inedible. The ogres were collecting weapons and moving their children to safety.

Daine combed her hair and tied it back, then removed her clothes and shook them out before putting them back on. She ate cheese and stolen apples, groomed Cloud, and fed Kitten what remained of their previous night's fish. Last of all, she saddled the mare and tucked Kitten into her carry-sack.

Give them time, Tait had said, but she hadn't known the hours needed by her allies would strain her nerves so cruelly. Her tension was made worse by the fact that she heard little movement in the village. The cows had been milked before sunrise, livestock had been fed, but apart from that, the local two-leggers kept out of sight. It made her feel as if she had a ghost town at her back.

At last, she heard a sound like a huge bell hit from the inside, as loud here as it had been in the caves. It was followed by another sound from the south, a hollow *thwap*! Billows of smoke appeared on the lake's southern shore. She would have to ask Maura what on *earth* her friend had managed to blow up.

Silver caught her eye from that direction: Stormwings, flying hard and homing in on the castle. She noticed they were as soot-blackened as chimney sweeps as they vanished inside the curtain wall.

She felt the hurrok trio come from the north. One bore a scroll in its left forepaw, and the gems in all their collars burned a bright yellow. They were in pain, clawing at the bands around their necks. Screaming in rage, the hurroks darted into the circle of the castle's wall. Checking the northern sky, she saw faint columns of smoke. Something was afire, but she couldn't tell what it was.

She waited briefly, and the fliers reappeared. This time the hurroks had riders who controlled them with reins and bit. They fought these as they had the collars, with no success. Two flew north. Daine shut her eyes and thought of Huntsong, then opened them to an eagle's vision. The mages on the hurrok pair were Redfern and Gissa. One hurrok tried to turn back, but Gissa was having none of it. Her mouth moved. A cloud of orange fire appeared on the immortal's rump. From the way he leaped forward, the fire must have hurt.

She turned to check the others. The Stormwings bore two humans in rope slings. Tristan rode the hurrok: he too used fire to sting his mount forward.

Daine made her eyes human again, then mounted Cloud. "Now," she told her companions. The pony raced for the causeway. All down its length, past the dock where the nobles kept a few boats and through the gate, Daine cringed, feeling exposed. Only when they were in the courtyard did she dare to sit up. There were no watchers on the castle walls, and the courtyard was empty.

Don't bother unsaddling me, Cloud told her when she dismounted. Find what you came here for. I'll hide in the stables.

"And rob every feed bag you see, right?" Daine whispered as she freed Kitten from her pack and put her down on the flagstones. Hanging the crossbow on her belt and the quiver over her shoulder, she trotted into the castle, the young dragon close behind.

Blueness and Scrap met her in the great hall. They looked smaller this way, though Daine could see that Blueness *was* a creature of noble bulk, for a cat. Scrap was a dainty thing, and fascinated by Kitten.

Have you seen anything like this? Daine asked the cats, picturing what she thought the model would look like.

No, said Blueness. Scrap! he said imperiously when the youngster, sniffing Kitten's muzzle, didn't reply. Answer the question!

The young cat sneezed. No, she replied. But I have not seen all there is to see. We are not allowed in the mages' workrooms.

Show me where those workrooms are, Daine said. Quickly, please.

The cats led the way up a broad flight of stairs to a gallery on the second floor, and down a hallway. Kitten made as little noise as they did: her talons, which Daine thought might click like a dog's, only made tiny scratching sounds.

The new humans sleep here, Blueness said, stopping at the end of a long corridor. In those two sets of rooms, and those two.

Daine tried one door: it was locked. "Kit, remember how you popped the lock at the inn?" The dragon nodded. "Give this a whirl, will you?"

The dragon sat up on her hindquarters and eyed the lock with interest. She gave a soft trill, as she had at the inn. The lock shone gold for a moment, then went dull. Kitten made a clucking sound and trilled again, breaking the sound into a high note and a low one. The door swung open.

Can she teach me to do that? asked Scrap as they entered the suite.

You do not need to know it, replied Blueness, disappearing into the bedroom. You are too much of a pawful already.

The model was not there, nor in the other three suites. Daine frowned as they finished their search. They had seen magical workrooms, but none had contained models. Also, she had seen nothing that looked like the room where she and Scrap had heard of bloodrain.

"Where are Tristan's rooms?" she asked. "The man with yellow magic?"

They are near the ones of the human female who hates cats, replied Blueness. This way.

They returned to the gallery and circled its rim, then went down a short hall. Scrap's tail twitched angrily when they reached Tristan's door: it was shut. Daine grabbed the knob. It stung her hand, making her yelp. "Kit? This one's magicked. Can you do anything?"

Kitten stood on her hind feet and peered into the lock, then whistled two cheerful notes. Nothing happened. She scowled and whistled again, less cheerfully, more as a demand. Nothing happened.

Daine was trying to decide what to do now when the dragon moved back and croaked. The lock popped from the wood to land at Daine's feet, smoking, and the door swung open. Kitten muttered darkly and kicked the lock mechanism aside as she went in. Daine followed, trying not to laugh.

I wish I could do that, remarked Scrap wistfully as she and Blueness brought up the rear.

Tristan's suite was bigger than those granted to his fellow mages, the furnishings more expensive. The central room was where Scrap had brought her last time. A study and a bedroom opened onto it; a dressing room and privy opened onto the bedroom. Unlike the other mages, Tristan did not have his own workroom. There was no sign of a model of the valley in his study. Indeed, except for a few scrying crystals and assorted books, they found none of the tools commonly used to work magic.

"What are you doing here?" a shrill, furious voice demanded. Daine, Kitten, and the cats faced the unlocked door. Yolane, in a thin nightdress covered by a lace robe, stood there. "Where is Tristan?" With a sneer she added, "I should have guessed you'd be a thief."

Daine put a hand on her bow. It was loaded, but she didn't want to kill Maura's sister. "I wouldn't call names, if I was you," she retorted.

Yolane backed up. "Tirell! Oram! Jemis! To me! Oram, on the double!"

Daine shook her head. "Yell all you like, they won't come. They're gone."

"What do you mean, 'gone'?"

"I mean it's at an end—the king knows what you're up to. The rebellion's uncovered. You'll never be queen."

"Tristan!" called Yolane. "Gissa! Alamid?"

"They have more important things to do right now," Daine told her. "The southern fort is burning. The ogres in the north are fighting the overseers. The mages went to deal with all that."

"You—" Yolane's face wasn't so attractive, twisted as it was in rage and hate. She turned and ran.

Kitten whistled an inquiry. "We can't," Daine replied. "The model's the important thing right now." Mice! she called silently, and added a picture of the model. Have you seen this? Will you look for it?

All over the castle the mice stopped to think and answer. Soon she knew none of them had seen it. "I don't understand," she muttered. "It's got to be somewhere. They haven't seen anything like this bloodrain, either, and I know that has to be cooked in something."

Did they mention the tower? asked Blueness. That is where all the mages gather to do their work.

When he said "tower," she remembered a column of greenish brown smoke, and Huntsong's remark that he did not need to fly through death to know what it looked like. "That's a good question, Blueness. Mice, what about the tower?"

Silence that reached through every nook and cranny of the huge building in which they stood was her answer.

"Mice?" Her eye fell on Scrap. The young cat was backed into a corner, fur puffed out. She was trembling. "Scrap, what is it?"

I know what they mean, she whispered. There is a lizard in the tower, a cold one. Colder than *anything*.

When Scrap said "lizard," the hair went up on the back of Daine's neck. It was the most sensible course, if the mages kept precious secrets in the tower. Tkaa had said a Coldfang would guard a thing until the end of time.

Outside in the gallery she heard Yolane cry, "Belden, wake up!"

There was no time to waste. "Scrap, how can I get into the tower?"

The cats ran out of Tristan's rooms. Daine followed, taking her bow off her belt and checking the bolt already loaded. It was blunt, more to stun than to slay, though it might have killed Yolane at close range. She switched it for a razor-pointed bolt, the tip hardened to punch through almost anything. She hoped it could put a hole in a Coldfang; if it couldn't she was in *real* trouble.

Scrap led them to another gallery, then a spiral stair. They climbed it high above Tristan's suite, passing broad landings that led to other floors. At last there was a window. Looking out, Daine could see over the curtain wall.

Here she felt the first touch of cold. Blueness, Scrap, go back, she told them silently. There's no sense in risking your lives.

But I *want* to, protested Scrap. She was so terrified that all her fur was puffed out and her ears lay flat.

Blueness, take her away, Daine ordered. There's nothing you can do.

Come, Scrap, the older cat said. The fear that had puffed his tail up to bottle-brush size didn't show in his voice. We could only get in the way.

Daine knelt beside Kitten. "You don't have to come," she whispered. Kitten glared and tried to climb past her. Daine shook her head and went first.

Thinking of Wisewing, she changed her ears to a bat's as they climbed, and listened to each scrap of sound. The cold thickened. Frost gleamed on the walls; curls of icy mist drifted around the small windows. Daine shivered in her thin shirt, and her nose ran. The stair narrowed; the curves tightened. How was she going to get off a shot around a corner?

The sound that made both ears twitch forward was a body, thirty-one feet ahead. Beaded hide brushed stone in a space much wider than the stair.

Fear made Daine's chest tight. When she could bear no more, she yelled, "Coldfang!" The echo hurt her ears: she made them human. "You'd best move—you're standing between me and where I want to go!"

Kitten whistled insults.

She heard a soft thud, then the buzz of a Coldfang rattle. Biting her lip so hard she drew blood, Daine raised the crossbow. "Don't let it catch your eye, Kit. That's how the other one almost got us."

It came tailfirst, on all fours and low, not headfirst or standing as she expected. The sight of the rattle and tail confused her for a second too long. The immortal half lunged, half slid, its weight slamming into her. Daine loosed, but the bolt went high to shatter on the wall. With a yelp the girl fell backward, the bow flying from her hand.

Kitten squeezed to one side. The girl kept rolling down the steep risers, losing arrows from her quiver as she fell. She was lucky the turns in the stair were so close: she couldn't build up any speed. All the same, her rattling progress, bumping into walls and stairs, knocked her silly. Protecting her head and neck with her arms, she kept her body tucked into a round ball and prayed. Kitten, trying to keep away from the advancing Coldfang, scrambled to avoid getting caught under her friend.

At the first landing they reached, Daine came to a halt. She grabbed the knob of a door leading from the stair and shoved. It opened on a hall furnished with suits of armor, old hangings, and wall decorations. Lunging to her feet, she ran in, the sound of talons on stone and that buzzing rattle loud in her ears.

## ⤛ TEN ⤜

# THE FALL OF TRISTAN AND YOLANE

ʕ•ᴥ•ʔ Kitten darted under a table against the wall, her scales turning the same gray-black as the stone. Daine looked frantically for a weapon of some kind as the Coldfang entered. Watching it, she knew coming here had been a mistake: the narrow stair had hampered the immortal as much as it did her. Now the Coldfang had room to move.

Like the one slain by Tkaa, this Coldfang was beaded in bright shades of green. Frost flowers sprouted ahead of its advance. It was quicker than the other, and pursued her down the hall. She raced away from it, checking the weapons on the wall. Broadswords were the main choice, but these were the two-handed kind favored by mountain lords—she never could lift one. She saw two maces, but they were higher on the wall than the swords. Trying to get one would slow her down too much.

Looking back at her pursuer, she crashed into a suit of armor. Quickly she rolled out of the way as it went over. From a metal glove dropped a long-handled, double-bladed war ax. She seized it, as heavy as it was, and got up.

The Coldfang stared, long tongue slipping out and in, tasting the air, then sidled to her left. She backed, keeping the blade between them, trying not to meet the thing's eyes. Her arms shook in an effort to hold her weapon up. It was *not* meant for a teenage girl's use.

Suddenly the immortal lunged, far more quickly than she would have dreamed, jaws popping open and fangs dropping down. She squeaked and darted back. The ax proved her undoing, as the long handle tripped her. She threw it to the side and rolled, then scrabbled to her feet. When she looked for the Coldfang, it caught her eyes, and held them. Although she fought, she was frozen in place.

Kitten, now rage-scarlet, jumped from the rear to fasten her jaws in the Coldfang's spine. Blueness and Scrap, behind her, leaped for its eyes. The immortal keened, half rising to its hind feet as it tried to rid itself of the cats with one paw and the dragon with the other. Scrap went flying, to strike the wall.

Free of the Coldfang's grip, Daine seized the ax and moved in close. *"Let go!"* She put all her power into the order. Blueness and Kitten jumped clear.

She swung with all her strength to bury the ax in the Coldfang's skull. It wrenched away, yanking the weapon from her grip, but the ax was firmly seated. The immortal thrashed on the stone floor, weakening with each convulsion. At last it was still.

The girl looked at the mess she had made, at the ax, the shattered immortal, and the gouts of dark blood all around, and vomited.

When she was done, she wiped her mouth and went to Scrap. Blueness crouched beside her, trembling and trying to wash the younger cat's still face.

"No, Blueness," whispered Daine. "Let me." She picked up the small body. It was limp in her hands, without any trace of life.

She is just a kitten, Blueness remarked, sounding lost. She is forever telling me she is a grown cat, but she is only a kitten.

Daine's eyes were streaming as she took the badger's claw from her neck and put it on Scrap's body. "Badger, you owe me. You and Old White and the other animal gods owe me. She would be alive right now if you hadn't *brought* me here. Now *do* something!"

No reply came, as precious seconds crawled by. She had failed. Hugging that soft body to her chest, Daine rocked back and forth.

—*It is for you, Queenclaw.*—Whoever the speaker was, he wasn't the badger. There was a hint of pack song in his voice, of cold nights filled with wolves singing.—*She is one of yours.*—

—*I am glad you see that, Pack Father,*—purred a new voice, silky and cruel. Blueness jumped to his feet, looking frantically for the speaker.—*As it happens, it pleases me to grant this prayer. A kitten deserves another life. Do not make a habit of asking, though, Daine. The gods are not at your beck and call. And finish what you came here to do!*—

Life roared under Daine's hands like a fire. Scrap opened her eyes. Where is Blueness? I dreamed I was in the fog, and he wasn't with me.

Daine put her down, tucking the silver claw into a pocket. The tom instantly began to wash his Scrap, purring so loudly he roused echoes. The younger cat screwed up her face and let him do it.

The girl rose, feeling weak in the knees. "You stay here and rest," she said. "I have something to do." Picking Kitten up, she wiped the dragon's muzzle clean of Coldfang blood, and carried her to the stair. As they climbed, she reclaimed those arrows that were unbroken and her crossbow.

The tower door was locked. "Why did they bother?" she asked bitterly, putting the dragon down. "They had their monster to guard it, didn't they?"

Kitten peered into the keyhole, tail twitching. Standing back from it, she croaked. The metal of the lock glowed dull orange. The wood around it began to smoke. Then the color faded, the lock still firmly in place.

Kitten stretched out her neck and croaked again, holding the note twice as long. She stepped aside just as the lock blew off the door. It fell down the stairs and continued to fall, its rattling audible long after it had gone out of sight. Without a word Daine opened the door.

Inside was a table on which lay the model of the valley, complete with its barrier. Behind that, on a tripod over a low brazier, a small pot of reddish brown liquid bubbled gently. That alone was interesting, because the fire was out. Daine stared at it. Could such a tiny amount of liquid, barely two cups full at best, really cause so much damage?

"Don't go near that," she ordered. Kitten shook her head emphatically, and Daine turned to the model.

What looked like a solid wall of fire in the western pass was a thin line of light that curved over the miniature valley as if a clear bowl were placed on top of it. The "bowl" sparkled with multiple colors, the yellow of Tristan's magic being the most common one. Embedded in the "rivers" into the northern and southern passes were two round, polished black opals.

Drawing her belt-knife, the girl reversed it, gripping it tightly where hilt met blade. She slammed the pommel into the north opal hard, and a crack snaked over the face of the stone. The barrier darkened, then brightened. She struck the opal again, and it cracked in half. Dark lines pursued each other over the curve of the magical light, but she could still see that curve.

"Stands to reason," she told Kitten, walking around the model to the far end. "If you've got two stones holding the thing in place, you have to break 'em both. After all, nothing *else* has been easy since I came to Dunlath, so why should this be?"

She slammed the knife hilt into the second opal, knocking loose a tiny chip. A thin whine filled the air; she glanced at Kitten, who also looked for its source. The whine built in volume, higher than anything the dragon or Daine could produce. It raised the hair on the back of the girl's neck. Gritting her teeth, she adjusted her grip on the abused hilt of her belt-knife.

"For the wolves," she whispered, and slammed the stone again. Whether the previous blow had weakened it more than it had appeared, or whether Old White lent Daine his strength, this did the trick. It shattered explosively. Daine covered her eyes with her free hand, and the room blew up.

Her return to awareness was heralded by a dreadful stench in her nostrils. She gagged and struggled against the iron band that clamped her arms to her sides, then sneezed repeatedly.

"Relax," a familiar voice said. "It's just wake-flower."

She blinked. The dark shape in her blurry eyes sharpened into a long nose, a full mouth, and black-fringed eyes. A bruise puffed up his left cheekbone, and his shirt was ripped. "No flower ever smelled like that," she said.

Numair helped her to sit up and eased his grip on her arms and back. "But it does," he replied innocently. "It grows in swamps, and its scent attracts flies to carry its seed rather than bees, but botanists judge it to be a true flower all the same." He let her go and placed the stopper in the tiny vial he had put under Daine's nose. The vial itself went into his belt-purse. "Are you well enough to sit unaided? I should deal with the bloodrain."

"Go ahead. Be my guest." Daine eased back until the wall supported her. Kitten, who had been poking in the remains of the table, came to examine her, making sure the girl was in one piece. Numair went to the small, bubbling cauldron. "How long have I been out?" the girl asked.

"If your unconsciousness commenced with the barrier's destruction—"

"It did."

"I believe it's some two and a half hours, then, judging by the length of time it took me to reach you. Once the barrier vanished I assumed bird shape and flew here, but I ran into delays. Also, my flight skills are rusty."

"What kind of delays?"

"I believe two of the hurroks managed to shed the magical binding that kept them here. They crossed my path and took exception to me for some reason. It took me an hour to get rid of them."

"What about Spots and Mangle? Did you leave them up there alone?"

"And risk your wrath? I told them to find you, and made sure to lead the hurroks away from them. Now give me a moment here."

His lips moved, though she heard nothing. A feeling of tension built up in the room, centering on the pot of liquid. Kitten rocked to and fro, intent on Numair, whistling under her breath. His hands moved, to write a letter or rune of some kind on the air in black fire. Just when Daine thought she might scream from the pressure, there was a pop! and the cauldron vanished.

"Where did you send it?" she asked when she could breathe again.

"Somewhere else," he replied. "Not a place as you would think of one. I am sorry I did not think to warn you of the possibility of a backlash from the barrier's destruction. It was Tristan's little joke—a surprise for whomever he asked to undo the spell. He often pulled such pranks when we were in school together."

Stiffly Daine got to her feet. "Some prank," she muttered.

Without warning she was caught up in an extremely tight hug. "You have no idea how glad I am to see you, magelet," Numair said, and put her down.

Daine wiped suddenly leaky eyes on a sleeve. "Maybe a little," she replied, and grinned at him. "It's mutual, you know." She collected her bow, checking to see if the knocking-about it had received broke any important parts.

Numair picked up Kitten. "Now to find Tristan, if he survived the excitement. I hope he did." A cold glint in his eyes made the girl shiver. "I have some things to say to him, and none of them are 'Goddess bless.' "

They went down into the castle, then to the courtyard. Outside, Daine felt an immortal's approach. "Numair, look," she said, and pointed.

Overhead soared a hurrok, Tristan on its back. Sweat darkened the weary creature's sides, and blood flowed from around the bit in its teeth. Crows, led by the one who had carried Tait's note for Daine, mobbed hurrok and rider, stabbing with beaks and claws. Tristan hurled darts of yellow fire at them, which the crows scrambled to avoid.

*Move*, Daine ordered the birds. They jeered, balked of their prey, and drew off. The girl swung her bow up, took aim, and let a razor-sharp arrow fly. She was fitting another in the notch as the first struck the hurrok in the throat. Tristan threw himself free: yellow fire cushioned and slowed his fall to earth.

Daine's second bolt, as the hurrok dropped, struck home just under his left wing. The creature screamed hatred, wings beating. She grabbed a third bolt and loaded it, just in case. The scream, however, had been a last defiance: the hurrok's wings collapsed, and it plummeted into the lake.

Tristan drifted, like a dandelion seed, to land on his feet near the gate. Numair advanced to meet his foe as black, sparkling fire gathered around his hands. "Tristan, I am *very* disappointed in you," he said amiably.

Tristan pointed. Yellow lightning crackled through the air between them, splintering on a shield of black fire that appeared around Numair.

"C'mon, Kit," Daine said, backing toward the wall. "I don't think he wants help." She swore as she sensed the approach of more immortals—Stormwings, this time. Rikash and his flock were coming in fast.

Ignoring stiff and bruised muscles, the girl raced for the stair that led onto the wall, ignoring an explosion in the courtyard. Kitten, who had climbed enough for one day, stayed to watch the mages with fascination.

A fresh explosion from below made Daine stumble and nearly fall on the open stair. She caught herself and forced her aching legs on. When she reached the parapet, the Stormwings were almost directly overhead, twenty yards up.

From below came a howling screech, and Tristan's furious "You can't beat me, Arram! You never had the belly for combat magic!"

Daine glanced at her friend. Numair stood on a rock spire; except for that, the earth around him was a giant crater. A line of blood ran from his mouth, and he was coated in dust, but he seemed well. Tristan battled the tendrils of a clump of roses that twined around him. Between the crows and those thorns, the mage's elegant clothes and skin were in tatters. His look of amused good nature was gone, replaced by a fury that twisted his handsome face into a mask.

The Stormwings could throw the contest Tristan's way, if she allowed them to interfere. Daine swung her crossbow up and sighted on their chieftain. "Lord Rikash!" she cried in her best parade ground voice.

He hovered, waiting. The others also hovered, watching him. Several had arrows in their living flesh. Others bore wounds from swords, claws, and teeth. All were streaked with smoke and soot.

"I should have seen it would come to this," Rikash said. "What do you want?"

She blinked. What did she want? Once she had wanted to kill every Stormwing she found, but was that still true? It seemed as if, ever since she had come here, someone was telling her that because she didn't like a creature's looks, it didn't mean that creature was bad. She *still* didn't like Stormwing looks, but Rikash seemed almost—decent. And how could she tell Maura that she had killed her friend?

"I'd like to end this bloodshed, I think," she replied. Her voice squeaked a little with embarrassment and nerves. She cleared her throat.

"You'n me have no quarrel here—not really. We don't like each other, but you can't go killing everyone you don't like. Isn't that so?"

"Your rustic philosophy amuses me," drawled Rikash. "Go on."

"Kill the ground-pounding bitch!" gasped the brunette female who once had told Maura that Daine was a Stormwing killer.

"Silence!" Rikash snarled at her.

Daine waited for them to be quiet. "Maybe you've heard of my aim. I don't miss often. I put out Queen Zhaneh Bitterclaws's eye, in case you hadn't heard. That was before she pushed me into killing her."

"But that shot was made with a longbow," the Stormwing lord pointed out.

"I'm as good with a crossbow. At this range it's like shooting fish in a barrel. I'm willing to negotiate, though. Since you're a friend of Maura's."

"You boast!" barked a male Stormwing. "Crossbows have no range, fifty feet at best. Don't they?" he asked Rikash.

The Stormwing lord looked at Daine and shrugged. "He's new from the Divine Realms. He thinks humans run screaming at the sight of us."

Daine sighted, loosed, and swung the bow down to redraw the string and load, all before the newcomer had registered the fact that the crossbow bolt had tapped his wing. A single feather dropped away and plummeted into the lake. By the time it struck the water, the bow was back on her shoulder and she was ready to fire again. "I've a two-hundred-yard range on this," she called. "Care to try me?"

Rikash watched her for a long time, metal wings fanning the air. Daine waited him out. When he spoke at last, his voice was quiet. "I am not as old as Zhaneh Bitterclaws was—not as crafty or as powerful. But I believe I may be wiser." To his flock he said, "Let's go, my friends. We must tell the emperor to expect no more Dunlath opals." He looked at Daine and shook his head. "I suppose we're both losing our minds. Please tell Maura I said good-bye and good luck." Gliding to the lake's surface, he banked and turned south.

"No!" yelled the noisy female. She stooped, talons ready to strike. Behind her, in the same fast attack mode, came the male who had lost a feather to her arrow.

The angle they had picked was opposite the sun. Its rays hit their feathers, blinding Daine. She didn't panic, but listened for the nearest moving body, and aimed. Eyes filled with sunspots, she fired: the female shrieked. Down with the crossbow, foot in the stirrup, both hands on the string, *pull* it up over the release.

Something big clacked nearby. She ducked as the male hurtled over her head. He would return with a fresh attack. Bolt from the quiver into the notch; clip in place; bow to her shoulder. Her vision began to clear: he was coming down, almost directly on top of her. She aimed, shot. The arrow slammed into his chin and up through his skull. The impact knocked him askew. He plummeted into the wall with a crash of metal and slid to its base. The female was already in the lake, sinking as her blood spilled into the water.

The rest of the flock had watched from above. When she looked up to see if they might avenge their friends, they wheeled as one and resumed their flight south. Automatically she redrew the bow and placed another bolt in the notch.

She had locked her attention so hard on the Stormwings that the mages' fight had slipped her mind briefly. Now she looked down. Numair was clothed in a clear, jellylike substance that burned white-hot. His mouth moved inside the burning sheath. It melted away like thawing ice, flame shrinking as it sank into the ground. Tristan was tearing away the strands of a giant silk cocoon.

"You are not taking me to that weak-willed idiot in Corus!" he cried. The cocoon flamed and vanished, leaving him covered in powdery ash. He looked the worse for wear, swaying as he stood, his breath coming in gasps. Lifting his hands, he threw a storm of yellow arrows at Numair, who shielded himself.

"Tristan, enough," the taller mage snapped. "If you rush me, I'll do something we'll regret. Your death would be a criminal waste of your talents."

Tristan glared at him. Sweat made tracks in the ash on his face. "You puling, gutless bookworm." On the gravel at his feet—it had once been stone blocks—a spin of brambles, old cocoon, and leaves caught flame. "You think you'll come away golden, don't you?" The fiery dust-devil roared high to become a tornado of flame. "You and your 'honor code,' your sermons on what we owe the unGifted—you made me sick in Carthak and you still do. Well, you will *not* walk away unscorched!" He pointed at Daine, and the funnel leaped for her.

She fired; Numair said a word that made the air scream. The tornado vanished. Her bolt plunged into the tree that was now Tristan Staghorn.

Daine gaped, leaning for support on the bow as her knees wobbled. "So," she remarked, when she had the breath. "Um—thank you. Was that a word of power?"

"Yes. What is he, can you tell?"

"I think it's fair rude to make him a tree and not know what kind he is."

"*Daine*—"

"Apple. Knowing him, prob'ly a *sour* apple tree. Will this hurt some other part of the world?"

Numair sighed. "As I recall, this word's use means somewhere there is a tree that is now a—a two-legger." He looked around. His stone pedestal was still intact, but the crater around him was at least four feet deep and six feet wide. "How do I get out of this thing?"

Daine remembered one more vital task. "Use a word of power, or something," she called, and ran for the stairs. "I need to find Belden and Yolane!"

Belden was easy to find. He lay on his bed, dressed plainly in black, his face white. The cause of his final sleep had spilled from a tipped-over cup on the bedside table. It was a thick, pale liquid Daine recognized from Numair's poison collection. Beside it was a note written in a sharp, decisive hand.

She knew it was rude to read others' letters, but she wanted to see why he had picked what she felt was a coward's way out of the mess he'd helped to make. The note read:

*She has learned the king knows of our plan. Nowhere in Tortall is safe when the king is a mage who knows who to look for, she says—the very trees will reach out to capture us. She said we must get away, that there will be a welcome for us in Carthak. I refused. We gambled, and lost. I will not bring more disgrace to my name. I do not blame her for luring me from the loyal path. I did not have to be tempted. My wrongdoing is my own, and I accept the responsibility.*

Daine left the room and closed the door behind her, feeling sick and angry. She could not think about Belden now. The important thing was that Maura's sister was going to escape. Mice! she called. Is Yolane here? Their denial came back instantly: Yolane was long gone.

She left, said Cloud in the stable. It was about the same time as the explosion in the tower. I tried to stop her, but she got away, on horseback.

Daine ran outside to Numair. He had reached the steps, where he sat with his head on his knees. "Yolane's gone. We have to go after her."

"Daine, I can't. I'm used up for the moment." He was gray under his swarthiness. "What about Belden?"

"He killed himself. He's in there." She indicated the castle with a jerk of her head. "If she's to get away clean, she must be headed west.

She could see from here the north and south passes are pretty hot right about now."

"Daine?" a voice called. "You here?" Iakoju, armed with a longbow that looked like a child's toy, walked in the gate. With her was the Long Lake Pack. They raced to greet Daine in wolf fashion. Numair was included in the ceremony, and had his face eagerly washed by Short Snout, Fleetfoot, and Russet.

Daine looked at the ogre. Her aqua skin bore collections of bruises, grazes, and soot, and a rip in her tunic revealed a shallow cut on her belly. "What's wrong? Were you driven back? How did you get here so fast?"

"No," replied Iakoju. "We win. My brothers lock up men that still live. Two mages dead—one fall from hurrok when I shoot with this." She held up the bow. "One killed by many little speckled birds."

"Starlings," Daine said.

"Speckled birds," Iakoju agreed. "I take boat to find you. Pack come, too."

There is no more for us to do there, explained Brokefang. Once the ogres chose to fight, nothing could stop them. The humans were scared already, after the work the People did on them. Perhaps they could have fought better with their weapons and horses, but the horses were gone and the weapons were ruined.

"You look bad," Iakoju was telling Numair.

He smiled up at her. "So do you."

Daine had an idea. "If you have Yolane's scent, could you track her? Even if she's on horseback?"

She is one of the two-leggers that brought this on us? Frostfur's eyes glittered angrily.

"All of it was done in her name," the girl replied.

Then we will find her, Brokefang said. Where is her scent?

Blueness and Scrap guided Daine to Yolane's rooms. The girl returned to the pack with a handful of the noblewoman's clothes. Everyone carefully sniffed the delicate gardenia scent that rose from the garments as Daine removed her belt, purse, dagger, and boots. She left the crossbow as well.

"What are you doing?" Numair demanded.

"The pack's going to find her, and I'm going with them, sort of. I have to sit in the lake, though, to help with the magic. I'm awfully tired, and I am *not* going to risk her getting away! Head out, Brokefang. I'll follow."

Numair did not protest as she ran to the docks where the fief's boats were kept. She had learned from him the trick to add to her power when she was tired by getting cold or cold and soaked. She only wished the Long Lake were salt water, since that worked best of all. You can't have everything, she told herself as she tied a rope to the ladder that led to the water. When the knot tested firm, she jumped in.

She gasped: the lake was icy, a product of mountain streams. Tying the rope to her waist, she clung to the last step and reached out, listening for the pack. They were near the end of the causeway.

Her mind blurred when she joined with Brokefang. When it cleared, she knew she couldn't stay in the water, not for as long as pursuit might take. She fought to heave herself onto the ladder, scrabbling at the wooden stair with her paws. The effort to drag her soaked body from the lake was painful. Her muscles screamed; then she was out and leaping up the steps to the dock. At the top something tugged at her middle—a rope tied much too loosely. She didn't need that anymore. Wriggling out of it, she paused and shook out her fur, ridding herself of what felt like pounds of water, then looked for the wolves.

They waited for her where bridge and land met. She raced to join them. Let's go, she said when they would have greeted her all over again.

Brokefang stood in front of her, ears and tail erect, upper lip barely skinned back over his teeth. Are *you* going to lead the hunt? he demanded.

She looked at him as if he were crazy. You know more about hunting this way than me, she retorted. I'll follow you.

Very good. The upper lip went down. He turned and cast around in the dirt for a moment. She watched, impressed. How can he sort through these incredible smells? she wondered. There were dozens here, a baffling patchwork of scents.

Come, Brokefang ordered, and trotted away. Daine let Frostfur go next, standing well back in case the chief female decided to bite. She followed them and the other wolves strung out behind her. Outside the village, she picked up the first clean scent of gardenia and horse. It was the newest odor on a road littered with yesterday's droppings. For the first time she was glad that the humans had chosen to remain out of sight today: it made Yolane's trail stand out all the more.

At the crossing with the north road they met Spots and Mangle. The horses went to the side of the road farthest from the wolves and waited for them to pass, ears flat, eyes rolling. It was only because they knew these wolves that the horses stayed on the road at all.

She halted. Spots, Mangle, she called, It's me. Don't be scared.

*Daine?* Mangle took a hesitant step closer. It really *is* you!

Daine? Spots also took half a step closer, badly confused.

Numair's at the castle with Cloud, she told them. Go on—I'll see you soon.

Come *on*, ordered Brokefang. You hold up the hunt!

With a sigh Daine followed.

Time passed, how much she could not say, as they followed the scent and the road to the western pass. Brokefang kept them to a strict schedule of short gallops broken up with longer periods of easy trotting, much as the palace training masters directed those periods of torture known as "cross-country runs." Daine gloried in the power of this strange/familiar body. In her own skin she had been tired; now she was not. She could run all day if the weather stayed like this, with a touch of crispness in the air.

The pack had reached the tree-covered shoulders of the mountains when she began to feel an ache build in her paws.

They are tender because you are new. That was Sharp Nose. You must build up your pads and your wind to stay with a pack. You will have to practice.

We had to do that, Runt called from the rear of their column. You can, too.

Daine licked a paw, then had an idea. Wading into the stream by the road, she let the water bathe, then numb, her sore feet. I never thought of that, Short Snout commented.

So two-leggers are good for something, retorted Daine. He nipped playfully at her, and she at him.

Stop, Brokefang ordered. And behave. He had checked each horse pat in the road: this time he called for them to join him. They gathered around the dung, tails wagging, to confer. The spoor was only an hour old. The horse was young, healthy, female, and beginning to overheat.

The pack speeded up. Daine panted as she ran, the day catching up even with her wolf shape. When they next stopped to inspect the mare's leavings, tails wagged harder than ever. This pile was soft and wet, barely five minutes old. Nearby a splash of heady horse sweat marked the ground. The mare's rider was pushing hard. She hadn't rested her mount on the climb to the pass; perhaps she even had tried to make the horse go faster. She had thrown away the advantage of her long head start on the wolves.

They moved out. Now their noses caught the mare's odor on the wind, mixed with saddle leather, oil, and gardenias.

The road topped a crest. When the pack reached it, they saw the horse and rider below. Dark with sweat, the mare was drinking too fast from the stream. Ironically, they had stopped where the trail to the caverns crossed the road.

Spreading out to form a horizontal line, the wolves began to run. With the quarry's scent in her nostrils, Daine forgot her aching feet and ran with them. They knew the mare had to catch their odor soon, but this was a good spot to circle her. She could only run west, and Daine already was calling the marmots to block the road. On either side the horse was walled in by rock and loose earth. Footing that would cripple her was not a problem for the wolves.

The mare smelled them and spun, white showing all the way around her eyes. Yolane, riding sidesaddle, was nearly thrown. She kept her seat and tried to whip her mount into flight. The wolves streamed over the rocks to either side of horse and rider, and surrounded them.

Daine's blood was up. A run meant a hunt to her wolf self; a hunt meant a kill. She wanted to leap for the mare's throat, to bring her down and feast, but caution held her, though she fought it. The mare was shod in hard metal. To lunge in would be to court broken ribs or a broken head. If Yolane had not been riding her, the pack never would have gone after such dangerous prey.

The wolves drew away from those hooves and waited. The mare held still. Yolane screamed and kicked, flailing at her mount with her riding crop. The horse staggered and came within jumping distance of Daine.

Forgetting the danger, the girl-wolf lunged. Battle slammed against her side and knocked her down. Stupid! the pack told her as one. You will get your brains bashed in, and we will lose a hunter!

Sheepishly, Daine flattened her ears and whined, backing to her place in the circle. Once there, she turned to lick her ribs, and thought, What am I doing?

Straightening, she called, Hoof-sister!

The mare faced her, quivering. You are not hoof kin, she said, breath coming hard. You are a hunter. I will not have you in my herd!

I'm not a hunter, not a *true* hunter. The girl freed some magic to connect her to the horse. Briefly her form shifted, trying to develop hooves, but she gripped her wolf shape and held it. Hoof-sister, she said, Dump the human. Run to your stable. You will be safe. It is not you that we want. It is her.

The mare hesitated. Enraged, Yolane struck her mount's tender ears.

The horse had borne enough. She bucked the human off and raced for home. Those wolves between her and the village moved aside and let her pass.

Yolane lay white and still on the ground. Daine trotted over and put her nose close to the woman's face. Her keen ears heard the soft drag of breath: Dunlath's lady was alive.

The pack made themselves comfortable, keeping their circle around Yolane, and Daine walked over to the stream. Sitting down, she began to recover her true shape. It was harder than she had expected. Her body *liked* the wolf shape. Bruises and hot feet notwithstanding, the wolf shape felt good, even natural. The girl had to fight a sense that she was meant to stay a wolf. Every little distraction—birdsong, the pups romping, the call of a distant horn—meant she had to stop and begin again. At last she found her two-legger self and slid into it. Opening her eyes she made an unhappy discovery.

Her clothes were gone. All she wore was the silver badger's claw on its leather thong. "And why am I still wearing you and nothing else?" she demanded.

Where is your flat fur? Are you taking a bath now? asked Runt curiously.

Luckily she had left most of her packs in the nearby caverns. "I'll be right back," she told the wolves. "Don't let her go anywhere."

When Daine returned, wearing clothes she had wanted to wash before she put them on again, Yolane was conscious. She greeted Daine with a flood of bad language.

Daine listened until the woman began to repeat herself, then said, "Shut up." As it went against the grain to be so rude even to Yolane she added, "Please."

To her surprise, Yolane gulped, then fell silent.

*Much* better, Brokefang said. The wolves had not moved from their circle around the captive. Will you take her alone, or shall we drive her? I think you will need our help.

"On your feet, milady," Daine ordered. "We're all going to walk back to the village. If you behave yourself, you'll be fine. Just don't try to run, or my friends will bring you down."

Yolane got to her feet. "If they're going to eat me, get it over with."

Daine sighed. "They don't eat humans."

We could try eating one *once*, Short Snout offered. Just to see what she tastes like. It seems this one isn't doing the human pack much good as she is. He walked closer to the woman, grinned up into her face, and licked his chops. Yolane backed away so quickly she tripped on her skirts and fell.

Don't help, Daine chided her friend. "Let's go," she ordered as the noblewoman got to her feet once more. "You walk in front of me."

Yolane dusted her rump and passed the girl, nose in the air. Daine followed. The wolves ranged around the humans as they turned east. It was plain they did not mean for the walk to be pleasant for the captive. They often darted in at her to snap heavy jaws close to her hands, then dashed away. Short Snout liked to draw close to sniff and nibble on Yolane's skirt.

Daine chose not to call them to order: they had worked hard, and they needed a bit of fun. As far as she was concerned, the woman who had helped to bring so much destruction on Dunlath needed harrying.

Halfway to the village, riders came to meet them. In the lead were Numair, the King's Champion, and Sir Raoul. The knights wore armor marked by the day's hard fighting. The warriors behind them, a mixed company of the King's Own and Riders, also looked the worse for wear.

Alanna grinned at Daine when the two groups met. "I hear you can shape-shift these days."

"Any ill effects?" asked Numair.

"I didn't have my clothes when I changed back. Luckily we were by the caves. How are Tkaa and Maura and Tait and Flicker?"

"Waiting at the castle," said Numair. "The squirrel needs some of your help."

Sir Raoul dismounted and ruffled Daine's hair with one gauntleted hand. "Good work," he said with a grin. "We'll make a king's officer of you yet. Speaking of which—" He went to Yolane and put a hand on her shoulder. Voice formal now, he said, "Yolane of Dunlath, I hereby arrest you in the name of King Jonathan and Queen Thayet of Tortall, for the crime of high treason."

The pack lifted their voices in a triumphant howl. Yolane shuddered. "I am guilty as charged. Now will you get me away from these monsters?"

"They have a different idea of who's the monster here," retorted Daine. "And I think *they* have the right of it. Will someone give me a ride? My pads—my feet—are killing me."

# ⤛ EPILOGUE ⤜

ᏣᎦ Daine was in the castle orchard petting Blueness and Scrap one last time when Maura found her. The girl's eyes were red and puffy. "I wish you weren't leaving," she commented, and sniffed.

Daine smiled. "You'll hardly know I'm gone. You've been that busy, what with Belden's funeral, and working things out so the ogres have farms and all."

"But once the king sends me a guardian, I won't be busy."

"Of course you will. Tkaa and the animals already said they'll deal with no one but you. You're the only noble in Tortall with a basilisk, ogres, bats, wolves, and squirrels as advisers on running a fief. Not to mention a golden eagle." Shading her eyes, she looked at the tower. Branches protruded from the window to Tristan's workroom. It had been specially widened so Huntsong could use it as a nest.

"Don't forget Blueness and Scrap." Maura petted the cats gently.

"Cats aren't *special* advisers. They advise us all the time, whether we want them to or not." Daine gently tugged at her friends' hair. "I'll visit, I promise. *After* the Big Cold, though. Twelve years I lived through mountain winters because I had no choice. That's enough."

"But winter here is *beautiful*," protested Maura. "The lake's all hard for skating, and the trees look like they have sugar frosting—"

Daine shivered. "Enough! You're too good at describing!"

"Will you write? Tell me what you're doing, and Kitten and Numair?"

"I'm not very good at writing letters," Daine said. The wistful look in the other girl's huge brown eyes made her sigh. "I'll try. Honest."

හි

Most of their friends—Iakoju, Maura, Tait, the dogs, Blueness, and Scrap—accompanied Daine, Numair, Kitten, and their mounts to the edge of the village, and stopped there. Daine gave Maura and Iakoju a hug and petted each of the dogs. The cats said their farewells to Kitten as Daine took Tait aside. "No more wolf hunting?" she asked him.

"No need to, since Brokefang promised they'd leave th' farm animals alone." The huntsman tweaked her nose. "Weiryn guide your aim, lassie."

"Take care of those dogs, and Maura."

Tkaa, who carried Kitten, and Flicker, who rode with Daine, stayed with them as the small company of horses and humans took the road south. Each time Daine or Numair looked back, the others were still there, watching until the road along the lakeshore took them from sight.

Kitten whistled unhappily. She and the cats had become good friends in the three weeks since the capture of Yolane. Tkaa murmured to her in dragon.

Silently appearing from the trees, the Long Lake Pack fell in step with the travelers. Once the champion and the soldiers had taken their captives south for trial, the wolves had left the populated areas. They had returned to their former habits, now that they had an understanding with the valley's humans.

Dismounting from Cloud, Daine walked among her friends, sharing their thoughts one last time, though she fought to keep her shape her own. Changing to wolf form had taken its toll: she had lain in bed for several days, drinking nasty herbal teas Numair gave her to ease the pain in all her bones. It would be a long time before she tried a full shape-shift again. When she did, she hoped her skeleton would be more accustomed to such changes. For now she walked in a universe of keen smells and sounds shared with her by her pack.

They stopped to eat lunch near the spot where the southern fort had once stood. It was a ruin; no buildings were left inside the blackened remains of the wall. Daine eyed the destruction, awed. "Kegs of *flour* did this?"

"Flour heated under pressure explodes," replied Numair. "They had gotten supplies for the entire valley the day before the barrier came down. Maura couldn't have done better if she'd burned kegs of blasting powder."

Shaking her head, Daine looked at the empty stockade where Blackthorn and his mercenaries had stayed until being taken south with Yolane. With advance warning of their arrival, the King's Own and the Riders had captured Tristan's allies with no bloodshed and only a little magical assistance from Numair and the Lioness. Now all that remained to show that mercenaries had come to Dunlath was this rough and empty fenced yard.

Flicker shared Daine's lunch, handling food gingerly with his left forepaw. It had been nearly severed in the fight at this fort, when the squirrel stopped a Stormwing from killing Tait. Daine had saved the paw, but nothing she could do would ease the tenderness in the bone. Now she let him go through her pockets one last time. His raiding done, Flicker pressed a cold, wet nose to hers. His whiskers tickled.

It was fun, he said. We had excitement before the Big Cold. We fought evil. My kits will know it, and their kits, and every other squirrel in Dunlath through all of time.

"I know. I don't s'pose you'd want to come with us, then?"

No, he replied. Somebody has to tell Maura how us "rodents" feel, and the mice won't do it. They are too afraid of Blueness and Scrap.

"Take care of yourself," she said, wiping her eyes on her sleeve. "You're getting as many lives as a cat, you know."

He gave her a last squirrel kiss, then allowed Tkaa to pick him up and put him in his pouch.

"Take care of my young cousin," the basilisk said in his whispery human voice. "Do not let her eat so many potatoes and cookies. She is getting fat."

Daine smiled at him, lips quivering a little. "Watch over our friends. Don't let the humans bully the People the way they did before we came."

"I doubt the People will allow them to do so," Tkaa assured her. He touched her cheek gently, and bowed to Numair. "I shall visit when things are settled here," he promised.

Numair smiled at the basilisk. "I'll collect rocks for your welcome feast."

Tkaa nodded—he had expected no less—and set off along the road to the village. Before they were gone from view, Daine saw the squirrel climb onto the top of the basilisk's head, where he could see better. Kitten chirped softly as Daine's eyes spilled over once more.

"Good-byes are sad things," Numair remarked, voice soft.

That is why wolves don't say them, commented Fleetfoot as Daine translated.

"I always knew your kind was smarter than mine," the man replied, smiling.

We knew that, too, agreed Short Snout, making Daine giggle.

"Enough moping," she said, getting up. "Let's move on."

They had reached the wide cleft where river and road left Dunlath—the spot where Tristan had planned to dump bloodrain—when a flash of white on a nearby ledge caught Daine's eye. A giant white wolf stood there, calmly watching them.

"Brokefang," she asked, "didn't you say there are no other wolves here?"

That is Old White, Brokefang replied. The patch behind him, which looks like a shadow, is his mate, Night Black.

Calling on a deeper level of her magic, she looked again. When she found Old White and Night Black, they were blazes of silver fire—the same kind of fire that shone from her mentor, the badger. She touched the silver claw at her throat. "I hope you're happy with all this," she called. "Just don't blame me if the People here aren't as obedient to you gods as they were before you brought me in to teach them things."

"Whom are you talking to?" Numair's question made her look at him.

"Old White," she said. "He's up there, him and his mate." She pointed to the ledge, but the wolf gods had vanished. "They *were* there." Checking for the Long Lake Pack, she found that they too had disappeared in a more normal way, fading into the trees that grew on the mountainside.

"Good hunting," she called to them. From the shadows under the trees, she heard her friends wish her the same.

Numair tousled her hair. "Let's go home, magelet."

# EMPEROR MAGE

To those who took a struggling young writer,
cushioned her in her early months in the Big Apple,
and agreed that no idea was too crazy:

Ellen Harris-Brooker

P. J. Snyder

Craig Tenney

and

Robert Wehe

How could I forget?
I couldn't have done it
without you!

# Acknowledgments

Once again I would like to express my thanks to those people without whose expert help I would have been hard pressed to get things right:

Mr. Ford Fernandez of Bird Jungle, on Bleecker Street in Manhattan, for advice on how tropical birds get sick;

Mr. James Breheny, the head camel mahout of the Bronx Center for Wildlife Conservation, for his aid in tracking down the ills to which camels are prey (and for the knowledge that there are very few diseases to which camels are prey), even though I had to cut the camel diseases in the final draft (!);

Usborne Publishing Limited of London, England, whose many reference books on classical and medieval times gave me invaluable help in visualizing Carthaki life and society;

Craig Tenney, who introduced me to metal and hard rock;

MTV and the Headbanger's Ball; and

Richard McCaffery Robinson, whose timely advice regarding galleys kept me from venturing into rough waters, and who owes me a freebie or two when his own work gets into the stores.

# CONTENTS

# ⤛ ONE ⤜

# GUESTS IN CARTHAK

🜂 His Royal Highness Kaddar, prince of Siraj, duke of Yamut, count of Amar, first lord of the Imperium, heir apparent to His Most Serene Majesty Emperor Ozorne of Carthak, fanned himself and wished the Tortallans would dock. He had been waiting aboard the imperial galley since noon, wearing the panoply of his office as the day, hot for autumn, grew hotter. He shot a glare at the nobles and academics on hand to welcome the visitors: they could relax under the awnings. Imperial dignity kept him in this unshaded chair, where a gold surface collected the sun to throw it back into his eyes.

Looking about, the prince saw the captain, leaning on the rail, scowl and make the Sign against evil on his chest. A stinging fly chose that moment to land on Kaddar's arm. He yelped, swatted the fly, got to his feet, and removed the crown. "Enough of this. Bring me something to drink," he ordered the slaves. "Something *cold*."

He went to the captain, trying not to wince as too-long-inactive legs tingled. "What on earth are you staring at?"

"Tired of broiling, Your Highness?" The man spoke without looking away from the commercial harbor outside the breakwater enclosing the imperial docks. He could speak to Kaddar with less formality than most, since he had taught the prince all that young man knew of boats and sailing.

"Very funny. What has you making the Sign?"

The captain handed the prince his spyglass. "See for yourself, Highness."

Kaddar looked through the glass. All around the waterfront, birds made use of every visible perch. On masts, ledges, gutters, and ropes they sat, watching the harbor. He found pelicans, birds of prey—on the highest, loneliest perches—songbirds, the gray-and-brown sparrows that lived in the city. Even ship rails sported a variety of feathered creatures. Eerily, that vast collection was silent. They stared at the harbor without uttering a sound.

"It ain't just birds, Prince," the captain remarked. "Lookit the docks."

Kaddar spied dogs and cats, under apparent truce, on every inch of space available. Not all were scruffy alley mongrels or mangy harbor cats. He saw the flash of bright ribbons, even gold and gem-encrusted collars. Cur or alley cat, noble pet or working rat catcher, they sat without a sound, eyes on the harbor. Looking down, Kaddar found something else: the pilings under the docks swarmed with rats. Everywhere—warehouse, wharf, ship—human movement had stopped. No one cared to disturb that silent, attentive gathering of beasts. Hands shaking, the prince returned the glass and made the Sign against evil on his own chest.

"You know what it is?" asked the captain.

"I've never seen—wait. Could it be—?" Kaddar frowned. "There's a girl, coming with the Tortallans. It's said she has a magic bond with animals, that she can even take on animal shape."

"That's nothin' new," remarked the captain. "There's mages that do it all the time."

"Not like this one, apparently. And she heals animals. They heard my uncle's birds are ill—"

"The *world* knows them birds are ill," muttered the captain. "He can lose a battalion of soldiers in the Yamani Isles and never twitch, but the gods help us if one of his precious birds is off its feed."

Kaddar grimaced. "True. Anyway, as a goodwill gesture, King Jonathan has sent this girl to heal Uncle's birds, if she can. And the university folk want to meet her dragon."

"Dragon! How old *is* this lass anyway?"

"Fifteen. That's why *I'm* out here broiling, instead of my uncle's ministers. He wants me to squire her about when she isn't healing birds or talking to scholars. She'll probably want to visit all the tourist places and gawp at the sights. And Mithros only knows what her table matters are like. She's some commoner from the far north, it's said. I'll be lucky if she knows which fork to use."

"Oh, that won't be a problem," said the captain, straight-faced. "I understand these northerners eat with their hands."

"So nice to have friends aboard," replied the prince tartly.

The captain surveyed the docks through his glass. "A power over animals, *and* a dragon . . . If I was you, Highness, I'd dust off my map of the tourist places and let her eat any way she wants."

At that moment the girl they discussed inched over as far on the bunk as she could, to give the man beside her a bit more room. The dragon in her lap squeaked in protest, but wound her small body into a tighter ball.

The man they were making room for, the mage known as Numair Salmalín, saw their efforts and smiled. "Thank you, Daine. And you, Kitten."

"It's only for a bit," the girl, Daine, said encouragingly.

"If we don't wrap this up soon, *I* will be only a 'bit,' " complained the redheaded woman on Numair's other side. Alanna the Lioness, the King's Champion, was used to larger meeting places.

At last every member of the Tortallan delegation was crammed into the small shipboard cabin. Magical fire, a sign of shields meant to keep anything said in that room from being overheard, filled the corners and framed the door and portholes.

"No one can listen to us, magically or physically?" asked Duke Gareth of Naxen, head of the delegation. A tall, thin, older man, he sat on the room's only chair, hands crossed over his cane.

The mages there nodded. "It's as safe as our power can make it, Your Grace," replied Numair.

Duke Gareth smiled. "Then we are safe indeed." Looking in turn at everyone, from his son, Gareth the Younger, to Lord Martin of Meron, and from Daine to the clerks, he said, "Let me remind all of you one last time: *be very careful* regarding your actions while we are here. Do *nothing* to jeopardize our mission. The emperor is willing to make peace, but that peace is in no manner secure. If negotiations fall through due to an error on our parts, the other Eastern Lands will not support us. We will be on our own, and Carthak will be on *us*.

"We *need* this peace. We cannot match the imperial armies and navy, any more than we can match imperial wealth. In a fight on Tortallan soil, we *might* prevail, but war of any kind would be long and costly, in terms of lives and in terms of our resources."

Alanna frowned. "Do we have to bow and scrape and tug our forelocks then, sir? We don't want to seem weak to these southerners, do we?"

The duke shook his head. "No, but neither should we take risks—particularly not you."

The Champion, whose temper was famous, blushed crimson and held her tongue.

To the others Duke Gareth said, "Go nowhere we are forbidden to go. Do not speak of freedom to the slaves. However we may dislike the practice, it would be unwise to show that dislike publicly. Accept no gifts, boxes, or paper from *anyone* unless they come with the knowledge of the emperor. *Offer* no gifts or pieces of paper to anyone. I understand it is the custom of the palace mages to scatter listening spells through the buildings and grounds. Watch what you say. If a problem arises, let my son, or Lord Martin, or Master Numair know *at once.*"

"Kitten will be able to detect listening spells," remarked Numair. "I'm not saying she can't be magicked, but most of the common sorceries won't fool her."

Kitten straightened herself on Daine's lap and chirped. She always knew what was being said around her. A slim creature, she was two feet long from nose to hip, with a twelve-inch tail she used for balance and as an extra limb. Her large eyes were amber, set in a long and slender muzzle. Immature wings that would someday carry her in flight lay flat on her back. Silver claws marked her as an immortal, one of many creatures from the realms of the gods.

Looking at the dragon, the duke smiled. When his eyes moved on to Daine, the smile was replaced with concern. "Daine, be careful. You'll be on your own more than the rest of us, though it's my hope that if you can help his birds, the emperor will let you be. Those birds are his only weakness, I think."

"You understand the rules?" That was Lord Martin. He leaned around the duke to get a better look at Daine. "No childish pranks. Mind your manners, and do as you're told."

Kitten squawked, blue-gold scales bristling at the man's tone.

"Daine understands these things quite well." Numair rested a gentle hand on Kitten's muzzle and slid his thumb under her chin, so she was unable to voice whistles of outrage. "I trust her judgment, and have done so on far more dangerous missions than this."

"We would not have brought her if we believed otherwise," said Duke Gareth. "Remember, Master Numair, you, too, must be careful. The emperor was extraordinarily gracious to grant a pardon to you, and to allow you to meet with scholars at the palace. Don't forget the conditions of that pardon. If he catches you in wrongdoing, he will be able to arrest, try, even execute you, and we will be helpless to stop him."

Numair smiled crookedly, long lashes veiling his brown eyes. "Believe me, Your Grace, I don't plan to give Ozorne any excuse to rescind my pardon. I was in his dungeons once and see no reason to repeat the experience."

The duke nodded. "Now, my friends—it is time we prepared to

dock. I hope that Mithros will bless our company with the light of wisdom, and that the Goddess will grant us patience."

"So mote it be," murmured the others.

Daine waited for those closest to the door to file out, fiddling with the heavy silver claw that hung on a chain at her neck. Once the way outside was clear, she ran to the tiny room below decks that had been granted to her. Kitten stayed topside, fascinated by the docking preparations.

In her cabin, Daine shed her ordinary clothes, changing to garments suitable for meeting the emperor's welcoming party. They wouldn't see the emperor himself until that night—the palace lay three hours' sail upriver—but it was still important to make a good impression on those sent to welcome them.

First came the gray silk shirt with bloused sleeves. Carefully she tucked her claw underneath, then slid into blue linen breeches. She checked the mirror to fasten silver buttons that closed the embroidered neck band high on her throat. Over all this splendor (as she privately thought of it) went a blue linen dress tunic. It was hard to believe that back home the leaves were turning color. Here it was warm still, warm enough that the palace seamstresses had kept to summer cloth while making her clothes for the journey.

A few rapid brush strokes put her curls in order, and a pale blue ribbon kept them out of her face. Carefully she put sapphire drops, Numair's Midwinter gift, in her earlobes and sat on the bunk to pull on her highly polished boots.

From a hole in the corner emerged the ship's boss rat. He balanced on his hindquarters there, his nose twitching. So you're off? he asked. Good. Now my boat will get back to normal.

"Don't celebrate yet," she advised. "I'll come back soon."

What a disappointment, he retorted. When do I get to see the last of you for good?

Silver light filled the cabin; a heavy, musky smell drifted in the air. When the light, if not the smell, faded, a badger sat on the bunk where Kitten slept.—*Begone, pest*—he ordered.

The rat was brave in the way of his kind, but the smell of *this* friend of Daine's sent the rodent into his hole. He had not known Daine was on visiting terms with the badger god.

Daine smiled at the first owner of her silver claw. "You look well. How long's it been?"

The badger was not in the least interested in polite conversation.—*Why are you here?*—he demanded harshly.—*What possessed you to leave your home sett? You are a creature of pine and chestnut forests, and cold lakes. This hot, swampy land is no country for you! Why are you here?—*

Daine made a face. "I'll tell you, if you'll stop growling at me." She sat on the bunk opposite him, and explained what the Tortallans in general, and she in particular, were doing this far south.

The badger listened, growling softly to himself.

*—Peace? I thought you humans were convinced Emperor Ozorne was the one who tore holes in the barriers between the human realms and the realms of the gods, to loose a plague of immortals on you.—*

Daine shrugged. "*He* says it wasn't him or his mages who did that. Renegades at the imperial university stole the unlocking spells. They were caught and tried last spring, and executed."

The badger snorted.

"Well, no one can prove if it's the truth or not. And the king says we need peace with Carthak more than we need to get revenge."

*—No one needs to talk peace or any other thing here. This is the worst possible place you can be now. You have no idea . . . Turn around and go home. Convince your friends to leave.—*

"I can't, and *we* can't!" she protested. "Weren't you listening? The emperor knows I'm coming to look at his birds. If I go home now, when he expects me—think of the insult to him! And it's not the birds' fault they live here, is it?"

With no room for him to pace, he was forced to settle for shifting his bulk from one side to the other as he muttered to himself.—*I must talk them out of it, that's all. When they know, even they will have to understand the situation. It's not like a mortal girl has the freedom they do, after all.—*

"Who will understand?" Daine asked, intensely curious. In all the time she had known him, she had never seen him so uncertain, or so jittery. Like all badgers, he had rages, and would knock her top over teakettle if she vexed him; but that was very different from the way he acted now. "And what's going on here? Can't you tell me?"

*—It's the Great Gods, the ones two-leggers worship*—the badger replied.—*They have lost patience with the emperor, perhaps with this entire realm. Things could get very—chancy—here soon. You are sure you cannot make your friends turn back?—*

Daine shook her head.

*—No, of course not. You said it was impossible, and you never mislead me.—*Suddenly he cocked his head upward, as if listening to something, or someone. He growled, hackles rising, and snapped at the air. Then—slowly—he relaxed, and nodded.—*As you wish.—*

"As who wishes?" asked Daine.

He looked at her, an odd light in his eyes.—*Come here, Daine.*—

"What?" she asked, even as she obeyed.

—*I have a gift for you. Something to help you if all goes ill.*—

His words made her edgy. "Badger, I can't misbehave while I'm here. There's too much at stake. You ought to talk to Duke Gareth of Naxen. You know every time you teach me a lesson or give me a gift or anything, there's always an uncommon lot of ruction, and I've been told not to cause *any!*"

—*Enough! Kneel!*—

She had thought to refuse, but her knees bent, and she was face to face with him. Opening his jaws, the great animal breathed on her. His breath came out visible, a swirling fog that glowed bright silver. It wrapped around Daine's head, filling her nose, mouth, and eyes, trickling under her shirt, flowing down her arms. She gasped, and the mist ran deep into her throat and lungs. She could feel it throughout her body, expanding to fill her skin.

When her eyes cleared, he was gone.

Stunned and trembling, Daine got to her feet. What was all *that* about?

The door opened and Kitten entered. "You just missed the badger," Daine informed her.

Kitten, who had met the animal god before, whistled her disappointment.

"I'm sorry. He was being *very* strange, and he left in a hurry." Worried both about what he had said, and about what he didn't say, she picked up Kitten and steadied her on one hip, then walked out on deck. When they reached the ship's rail, the animals awaiting her on the docks burst into an ear-piercing welcome. Dogs howled; birds cried out in their many languages. Only the cats welcomed her quietly, purring as hard as they could. The girl listened with a smile. She was so lucky to have friends wherever she went!

Thank you for meeting me, she called silently, her magic carrying the words to her listeners. It is very kind, and I liked it so much! I hope I'll have a chance to get to know some of you while I'm here. For now, though, please stop calling, and go home. We're making the two-leggers nervous!

They knew she was right. Birds took flight by groups, careful not to bump into one another; dogs and cats left the docks. Only the rats stayed, their attitude of decided *un*welcome a steady itch in her mind.

Piffle to you, she told them, and went to join Numair at the rail. He was dressed simply, but well, for their arrival. His soft, wavy black hair was tied in a short horsetail, accenting a long nose and full, sensitive mouth. A black silk robe that buttoned high on the throat billowed around his powerful frame. Long, wide sleeves covered his arms to the wrists; the hem stopped short of the toes of his boots. That robe was donned by only a handful of mages, the most powerful in the world. Not even the famed Emperor Mage was allowed to wear it. Numair always played it down. He said the learning needed to win the black robe was not worth much in the real world, but Daine knew better. Once, when Numair was pressed by an enemy sorcerer, she saw him turn the other man into a tree.

"Are you all right?" she asked, squinting up at him. The effort strained her neck: he was a foot taller than her five feet five inches. His dark eyes were emotionless as he watched the dock. Only his big hands, white-knuckled as they gripped the rail, showed tension. She had wanted to talk about the badger's visit, but she could see that this was not a good time. "Is something wrong?"

"No, magelet," he said, using his private name for her. "And I am as well as may be expected. I can't say which prospect makes me more apprehensive—that of meeting old enemies, or old friends." His voice was unusually somber.

"Old enemies, surely?" She understood his concern. Carthak's great university had been his home for eleven years. Shortly before his twenty-first birthday he had fled, accused of treason against his best friend—the emperor. Now, almost thirty, he was, in a way, coming home.

"I don't know," was his quiet reply. "I was very different then. And you know what the wise men say—'Only birds can return to old nests.' " He shook his head, and smiled down at her, white teeth flashing against his swarthy face. "Mithros bless. *You* look very pretty."

Kitten chortled while Daine blushed. "You think so really?" she asked, feeling shy. "I know I don't hold a candle to Alanna, or the queen—"

He held up a hand. "That isn't strictly accurate. The Lioness is one of my dearest friends, but she is *not* an exemplar of female beauty. Years and experience have given her charm, and her eyes are extraordinary, but she is not beautiful. Queen Thayet is astoundingly attractive, it's true, but you have your own—something." He scrutinized her as she giggled. "You should wear blue more often. It brings out matching shades in your eyes."

"I heard that about *my* looks," Lady Alanna said, joining them. "I'll get you later." Like Daine, she wore a tunic and breeches. Hers were violet silk trimmed with gold braid, over a white silk shirt. At her waist hung her sword. She grinned at Daine. "You do look good."

"Thanks," Daine said, blushing once more. "So do you."

The others, clad in daytime finery, joined them now that the ship was about to dock. Under their conversation, Daine tugged Numair's sleeve. "I need to talk to you as soon as you can manage," she whispered as the sailors made the ship fast. "It's really, really important."

He nodded, but his eyes were on the ships around them. She couldn't be sure he'd even heard.

Across the harbor a gong crashed three times. The Carthakis on the docks knelt and touched their heads to the ground as slow, regular drum-beats sounded. A path had opened from their ship across the busy harbor to what appeared to be a canal lock. Down that path came a high-prowed boat rowed by shaved-headed slaves. Its gilded surfaces threw off pain-ful flashes as it swept along.

Daine peered at the man seated on a thronelike chair on the deck. He wore a crown like a cap, one covered with diamonds, that glittered fiercely. "Who is *that*?"

Gareth the Younger said, "Probably a lesser prince, one of the im-perial court."

"This prince isn't a lesser one." Numair's stage whisper carried to those behind him. "See the lapis lazuli rod in his left hand? That is an attribute of the heir—what's his name?"

"His nephew Kaddar," one of the others said. "Age sixteen. Studies at the university."

The Tortallans got into the ship's boat and were rowed to the galley, where a heavy ladder was dropped to them. Daine waited for the senior members of her party to board, then followed. Kitten lost patience with her slow progress up the ladder and scrambled up past her, beating her onto the deck. Their order, as they gathered before the prince, was roughly that of importance, with Duke Gareth, Lord Martin, and Lady Alanna in front, Numair and the other officials behind them. Gareth the Younger, Daine, Kitten and the Tortallan clerks kept to the back.

Someone called orders. A drummer sounded a beat. Sunburned and tanned backs on Daine's left stretched forward. The left bank of oars dipped; the boat began to turn.

Standing by the prince was a herald. He wore a gold robe cut like those Daine had already seen on other Carthakis, a knee-length tunic with short sleeves. Thumping his staff of office on the deck, he cried, "His Imperial Highness, Kaddar Gazanoi Iliniat, Head of House Khazoi, Prince of Siraj—"

Daine lost track of the rest. She was interested in the boat: once it had turned, both sets of oars rose and fell on drumbeats, and the vessel raced across the harbor. On either side of the deck the rowers sat at their benches. Each time they stretched forward or pulled back, she heard a clatter under the drum's thud and the men's grunts of effort. It took her a moment to realize that it was the noise of the chain that linked their ankle cuffs.

Her skin prickled. She made herself look away and listen to the herald. "—His Most Serene and Imperial Majesty, Ozorne Muhassin Tasikhe, Emperor of Carthak—"

Kitten went to the end of a bench, chirping and peering at the man seated there. The girl went after her. "I'm sorry," she told the man, who watched the dragon from the corner of his eye. "She doesn't know not to interrupt when folk are working—" The slave looked up at her, startled.

"Eyes to your oar!" snarled a voice nearby. A lash snaked out to flick the man on the cheek. The slave hardly blinked, though the whip had come dangerously close to his eye. Daine bit the inside of her cheek and went back to her place, hoisting Kitten onto her hip.

Someone passed a handkerchief to her as the herald began to name their company to the prince. She quickly wiped her eyes. By the time she was under control, Gareth the Younger and the dean of mages at the Tortallan royal university were bowing to the prince, who greeted them both with distant courtesy. They bowed again, and stepped to the side so that Daine and Kitten were revealed.

Awed, the girl saw that the odd shape of the prince's eyes came from dark lines drawn on both lids and extended to his temples. He was a light-skinned black, with thin lips and long, thick eyelashes, dressed in a calf-length tunic of crimson silk. His jewels shimmered in the sun. He boasted three gold rings in his left ear, a gold bangle shaped like a many-flamed sun, and a ruby drop in the right. Another ruby served him as a nose button. He wore a collar-like necklace of gold inlaid with mother-of-pearl strips. Rings decorated fingers and thumbs; bracelets hung on both wrists. A flash drew her eyes to his feet, where she found rings on toes bared by his sandals. It occurred to her that she might not possess as much jewelry in her entire lifetime as the prince wore right now.

"Veralidaine Sarrasri," the herald proclaimed. "The dragon Skysong."

"I greet you in the name of my august kinsman, the Emperor Mage of Carthak," the prince said formally. Then he leaned forward, eyes sparkling with interest. "It's a true dragon?" His voice was light and fast. "Not a basilisk, which we've seen, but maybe a young basilisk—"

Kitten walked to the raised chair and rose, balancing on her hindquarters as she gazed at the young man. "She's a true dragon, Your Highness," replied Daine. She saw intelligence in his eyes, paint or no. "Basilisks have pebbled skin, almost like beading. Kit—her name's Skysong, but mostly folk call her Kitten—she has scales. Her ma was the same."

The prince frowned. "A mother? We were told there is only one dragon in the mortal realms."

"There is. Her ma was killed by—" She almost said "Carthaki raiders," but stopped herself. As she had been told over and over, no one could *prove* they were Carthaki. "Pirates," she went on. "She gave birth to Kitten a week before she died, and I've been raising Kit ever since."

"Is it hard? What does she eat? Does she hunt live prey, or—"

The herald coughed. "Your Highness, the ambassadors have yet to greet the delegation."

The prince looked like any of Daine's Rider friends caught in a misstep. He made a noise that sounded like a sigh and eased back in his chair, holding the blue stone rod and gold fan crossed on his chest once more. "It is my hope that, should you have idle hours during your stay with us, you will permit me to show you some of Carthak's wonders."

Duke Gareth had told her such an offer would be made by a Carthaki noble, so Daine had an answer ready. She bowed. "I'd be honored, Your Highness," she said, while thinking, He sounds *so* thrilled.

"May I present you of Tortall to your colleagues and fellow ambassadors," intoned the herald, more as a command than a request. He led their group to the spot where men, some dressed like the prince, some in robes cut in the same fashion as Numair's, waited under a canopy. Most of their names escaped Daine, at the rear of the Tortallan delegation. She would have to deal with almost none of these dignitaries, and saw no reason to memorize alien names and titles.

Once, a mage, did make an impression. He was a different fish among so many black-, brown-, and olive-skinned southerners—a tall northerner, tan and weathered from sun and wind, with earnest blue eyes and silver streaks in his flyaway blond hair. He stood with lesser mages and nobles, wearing a scarlet robe with earth-brown cuffs and hem. He wore his robe unfastened, over a northern-style shirt and breeches made of undyed cotton. When the herald gave his name— Lindhall Reed—he and Numair embraced. Daine smiled. Ever since she had met Numair two years ago, she had heard much of his old teaching master.

"Arram," Lindhall said, using Numair's birth name, "welcome, if that is the proper word."

Numair's eyes were overbright. "I'm surprised you remembered our arrival," he replied, voice scratchy. "I thought I'd have to root you out of your workroom."

"No, no." Reed's voice was quiet, cultured, and fast, as if he fought to breathe. "I have a good assistant, better than you were. She keeps track of everything. Unfortunately, she's about to go live with the mer-folk and study their culture. I hear they're moving in all along the Tortallan coast. I'd thought they'd live in rookeries, like sea lions, but their nature appears to be more tribal. And you are Arram's student," he said without a break, looking at Daine. She jumped at the change of topic. "He wrote me so much about you. He says you *know* how bats avoid objects and catch prey. When I was a student I incurred censure when I hypothesized that they do it with manipulation of sound, and Arram said you proved that to be true."

Daine smiled up at this man, who was nearly as tall as Numair. "Well, yes. They squeak at things. Their ears move separately, to gather in what they hear, and each sound has a meaning—"

"I don't like to interrupt," Numair said apologetically, "but, Lindhall, I have questions that require answers. Forgive me, both of you."

Lindhall looked wistfully at Daine. After friendship with Numair, she recognized someone who would rather talk about learning than anything else. "Duty calls," the older mage commented. "And I know we shall have other chances to confer, since you are here for the emperor's birds, and I help him to care for them. Very well, Arram, I am yours, for the time being. Unless—" His face brightened. "I know you've always had encounters with whales. It is true, their songs are communication, not merely noise? Or communication in the sense of birdcalls, proclaiming territory, and so forth? I—"

"*Lindhall,*" Numair said firmly, and dragged his old friend away.

I didn't even get to ask him what's wrong with the emperor's birds, Daine thought, and sighed.

"Daine," called Alanna, "can you spare Kitten? Duke Etiakret and Master Chioké would like a closer look at her, if she doesn't mind."

Kitten whistled an inquiry to Daine, who smiled. "Go on. They want to admire you." Kitten, always open to admiration, galloped off.

Trying not to look at the slave rowers, Daine went to the prow of the boat, where she could see the riverbank. During the introductions, they had left the port city of Thak's Gate behind, following canals that led finally into the River Zekoi. As the oars tugged the barge south, the city on Daine's side of the boat gave up its claims to the riverbank.

An army replaced it. From here she saw barracks in long rows, taking up hundreds of acres. Companies of soldiers stood side by side on the riverbank, each soldier with a bright, rectangular shield on one arm, a spear in the opposite hand. Looking at them, she swallowed hard. She was no stranger to military camps. Since her arrival in Tortall she had visited home bases for the army and the Queen's Riders alike, but none of them were as big as this.

As the imperial vessel passed the first company of soldiers, Daine heard a shouted order. As one man, the soldiers banged their spears three times on their shields, then thrust the spears into the air with a roar. The second company followed suit, then the third, then the fourth. It seemed to go on forever, drowning out all conversation and making Daine's ears ring. Duke Gareth is right, she thought, feeling ill. Even if we could *beat* so many, what would be left afterward?

The gods are up to something, she remembered abruptly. Something that might put a crimp in the style of this army. If only I could find out what's going to happen!

"That is just the Army of the North." The prince joined her at the rail as they sailed past the last soldiers. "My uncle has three other armies of identical size, all in combat readiness."

It was hard to read his face, but he sounded as if he wasn't proud of the imperial forces. "What's over here?" she asked, turning. They now had a good view of the far bank also. This side of the Zekoi was untamed. Reeds grew head-high; a web of streams emptied into the river. The loglike shapes on the far bank were not dead wood, she realized, but animals.

"Crocodiles." The prince had seen what she looked at. "Do you have them in the north?"

"No," she replied, calling with her magic. They stirred, drunk with the sun. "They're giant lizards, aren't they? I have a book that tells of them." She called again, and felt a soft reply.

"*Giant*, water-swimming, *vicious* lizards," replied the prince.

Daine counted to three, then said politely, "There's few animals that're 'vicious' by nature, if you'll forgive my saying so. Usually there's a good reason for them acting nasty—like you're stepping in their nests, or you're stealing their food."

Food, agreed a low voice in her mind. Hungry, commented another. A third voice added, Waiting for food.

"Like all females, you are sentimental about animals," the prince replied, his tone superior. "If you had a croc after you in the water, you wouldn't be so quick to stand up for them."

"They came after *you* personally?" She couldn't see this painted fellow doing anything that might wrinkle his clothes.

"Well, no, but everyone says they do."

Someday I must read this scholar Everyone, she thought as she bit her tongue to keep from giving a rude answer. He seems to have written so much—all of it wrong.

She called to the crocodiles again. I'm Daine, she told the great creatures. I come from the north.

You are odd, replied the one who had spoken last. You smell of frozen water and too many trees. Do not scold that two-legger. If he enters our water, we will eat him gladly.

A private boat, brightly painted, floated by. A man in a low-backed chair read under a canopy; a slave chased a boy who ran with something that struggled in his arms. Cornering the child at the rail, the slave tried to make him release his prize. The child leaned away. Suddenly he screeched. His arms flew open, and his captive tumbled into the water.

"If you can't hold on to pets, you don't deserve to have any," scolded the slave. The child screamed as she dragged him away without another look at the animal in the river. The crocodiles did not share her disinterest. They slid into the water from their riverbank.

"No, don't!" Daine cried to them aloud, forgetting her companion. "Let it be!"

Hungry, said a voice. Food is food.

It will die anyway, replied the one who spoke most. Look at it.

The crocodile was right. The tiny creature, whatever it was, couldn't swim. It fought to stay up, but the current dragged on its fur and limbs.

Stripping off her boots, Daine jumped over the rail and into the river. Swimming against the current, she struck out for the drowning animal. Please stop, she told the crocodiles silently. It isn't more than a mouthful! One last pump of her arms, and she had reached the sufferer.

I hope you do not interfere in too many meals, remarked the talkative crocodile as the reptiles swam off. We do not have enough food as it is.

I'll try not to, Daine promised. Treading water, she pumped liquid from the pet's lungs. He gasped. "Shh," she said. "It's all right. I've got you." He was a monkey, tiny enough to sit on her palm, with huge gray-green eyes. Around his neck was a jeweled collar. "No wonder you couldn't swim." She unbuckled the thing and let it fall. "That was probably too heavy dry, let alone wet."

Black, sparkling fire yanked them from the river and pulled them through the air. Daine soothed the frantic monkey until Numair's magic deposited them on the deck of the imperial barge.

The Carthakis, from prince to slaves, gaped at her and her new friend. Kitten began to scold as Daine blushed. Muddy water formed a pool on the polished deck; her hair dripped. Her linen and silk were ruined. Someone—a female—giggled. A man snorted. Daine glanced at Duke Gareth and saw that he had covered his face with one hand as his son's broad shoulders quivered with suppressed laughter. More than anything at the moment, she wished she had the power simply to vanish.

They went from their quarters to the women guests' baths soon after their arrival, to Daine's relief. Not only was she able to wash, but maids brought a basin and extra mild soap so that she could bathe her new friend. They even gave her towels for him. She dried him quickly there, then returned with him and Kitten to her room to do a more thorough job.

She used the work to get acquainted with this odd creature. Lindhall had called him a pygmy marmoset. Imported from the Copper Isles, he'd been the pet of the child he called the Monsterboy, the one who had let him fall into the river. His fur was strange—a mix of yellow, brown, gray, and olive green, which looked as if it might turn its wearer invisible in a proper forest. The marmoset gave his name, but it was in whistles and clucks, impossible for her to pronounce. She asked if he would mind if she called him Zekoi, or Zek, after the river she had taken him from. He seemed quite taken with that, even trying to pronounce it on his own.

Finished with Zek's grooming, Daine got to her feet. "I need to change," she told the marmoset when he clung to her. "Hold on to Kitten." Zek eyed the dragon with misgiving. Kitten chirped, and offered her forepaw. He clutched it and watched Daine's every movement.

Drawing on a shift, the girl surveyed her room. It was simple, elegant, and costly. Walls, floor, and ceiling were polished marble. Carved cedar window screens gave off their famous scent. The bed was delicately carved, the sheets fine cotton. Over it lay a silk comforter in autumn colors. The clean, sweet-scented privy lay off a small dressing room. That chamber, a few feet from the bed, was furnished with a table and matching chair, a long mirror, and a number of tiny jars which held various cosmetics, salves, and perfumes.

There was but one feature she disliked—a tiger-skin rug. Its jaws were open in a snarl; yellow glass eyes glared at the world. "I have to ask them to move this," she told her audience. "I can't sleep with it here." Kneeling, Daine touched it sadly. She had seen tigers in the king's menagerie. They were magnificent cats, and she preferred the ones whose skin was still attached.

Her palms felt hot, itchy. Suddenly they pulsed. White fire spilled from her hands onto the tiger. Slowly the eyelids fell, and rose again. The jaw relaxed; the great mouth closed.

She thrust herself away so quickly that she fell over. "Did you *see* that?" she demanded of Kitten and Zek. "What *was* it?" Both stared at her, plainly as bewildered as she was.

Although she waited, the skin did not move again. Using a long-handled brush, she shoved it under her bed, poking it repeatedly to keep any part from sticking out. At last it was securely tucked away, and she could dress.

# ⇥ TWO ⇤

# IMPERIAL WELCOME

∞ Some hours later, Daine looked round the antechamber to the throne room with awe. Kitten did the same. The marmoset Zek, who had refused to stay behind, observed everything from his hiding place under her hair, at the back of her neck.

There was much to stare at. The room was filled with nobles and mages dressed in their finest. Shave-headed slaves were everywhere, offering food, drinks, flower garlands, and feathered or jeweled fans. Huge screens had been pushed back to reveal a broad terrace and gardens. Light came from large globes hung by chains from the ceiling. As the sky darkened, the globes shone brighter.

"How do the lamps keep burning?" Daine asked.

"Magic." The speaker was Harailt of Aili, dean of magical studies at the royal university in Tortall. He was a stocky, round-faced man with an endless supply of jokes. Stuck in his outer room, waiting to bow to the emperor, Daine had been grateful for each and every jest. "Numair, why didn't you tell us about this light spell?" Harailt asked. "To have strong, steady illumination—"

Numair looked up. "They didn't have it when I was here," he said absently. "They did something with glass balls, but they faded after a short time. These aren't glass."

"The globes are filled with crystals," Lindhall Reed explained. "Remind me and I'll have one of the craft mages explain it for you." Seeing the door to the emperor's audience chamber open, he added, "You'll be all right, Arra—I'm sorry—Numair?"

The younger mage smiled. "I have to be, don't I?" As a page beckoned their group forward, he took a deep breath. "Here we go, into the presence of the one and only Emperor Mage. Huzza."

The Tortallans entered the imperial audience chamber, Daine, Zek, and Kitten at the back of the company with the clerks. The admiring looks of that group of young men told Daine that not only had she been wise to wear this twilight-blue silk gown, but that she had done well to accept the royal gift of a wardrobe for this trip. "You go as a representative of the Crown, just like the ambassadors," Queen Thayet had said, hazel eyes smiling. "My lord and I insist. Trust me: there is nothing like a good appearance to give a woman confidence." The queen had been right. It was hard to feel insignificant in a gown that whispered as she moved and winked with silver embroidery.

Introduced by a herald, Duke Gareth gave his speech to the emperor, announcing their desire to meet Carthak halfway and their hopes for a lasting peace. He then presented gifts from the king and queen to the emperor. As he spoke, Daine studied the ruler of Carthak, who sat on a tall throne before them, flanked by his ministers and nobles.

She had never heard of him until two-and-a-half years ago, when she had come from Galla to Tortall after her mother's death. Now she knew him all too well. Most Tortallans believed it was this emperor who had managed to break the walls between mortal and divine realms on frequent occasions, turning loose the creatures known as immortals to prey upon Carthak's enemies. Daine herself, working with Numair a year ago, had found evidence that Ozorne was helping to plan a rebellion against the rulers of Tortall. When the monarchs of the other Eastern Lands, those countries north of the Inland Sea, had learned of Emperor Ozorne's plot against one of them, they had united. The threat of the entire northern continent going to war against the southern one had caused Emperor Ozorne to back down, and to open peace talks with Tortall.

Her first sight of the infamous Emperor Mage filled her with awe. She had thought the prince was fine, but he was a barnyard rooster to his uncle's peacock. Gold frosted Ozorne's hair; gold beads hung from a wealth of thin braids. Gold paint shimmered on lips, brows, even his eyelashes. Gold rings marched up the curve of each ear; a diamond hung from his left earlobe. His neck was ringed with six rows of deep-blue stones that sparked with many-colored fires: black opals, expensive stones prized because they could hold magical power. Beneath them he wore the calf-length, short-sleeved robe of his people in heavy gold brocade. Looped at his right hip and passing over his left shoulder was a crimson drape. The long end of the cloth was linked to the emperor's left wrist by a gold bracelet. Each finger sported a ring. His sandals were gilded. Like the prince, he wore toe rings, and added to them ankle bracelets.

She'd heard of Carthak's wealth and power, but it was one matter to hear such things, another to see one man decked out like an idol in gold and gems.

Duke Gareth had finished. Now the line of Tortallans started forward as Duke Gareth gave their names, each bowing to the emperor as they were presented. Watching them, Daine felt a rush of pride. Carthak might be proud and great, but Tortall had sent wise and famous people to work out a peace settlement. Alanna the Lioness was a legend in the Eastern *and* Southern Lands, one the Carthakis couldn't match; and as far as Daine was concerned, Numair was the fish their hosts had allowed to get away.

At last her name and Kitten's were called. Taking a deep breath, Daine walked up to the first step of the dais on which the throne stood, and curtsied, spreading her blue skirts at her sides. The queen had worked on the movement with her for hours, and she was glad to do her teacher proud. Kitten walked up the steps, halting only when she reached the emperor's feet.

"Greetings, dragon child. This *is* a pleasure." He reached down. Kitten sniffed his fingers, and sneezed. Grasping his hand with her forepaws, she examined the gems on his rings with interest. "And you are her keeper?" inquired the emperor. "The one who is also a healer of animals?"

She didn't like that word, *keeper*, but she nodded. Lord Martin cleared his throat, and she realized she was supposed to answer the ruler of Carthak. "I take care of her, Your Imperial Majesty. And I have wild magic with animals of all kinds."

"How was she taken, your dragon? A trap, or a pit? A net?"

Daine swallowed. Traps or snares for Kitten? "I don't think you understand our relationship, Your Imperial Majesty. I'm not a keeper; I didn't take her. Kit's—Kitten's—ma died to protect my friends and me. She left Kitten to my care."

"Indeed?" He looked at her with curious amber eyes. "It is true, then. You are able to commune with the immortals."

"The ones like animals, sire. The griffins, and winged horses. Dragons. The ones that are part human, no." She made a face. "They can communicate without my help."

Kitten, bored with the conversation, voiced a whistle-croak. The gems on the emperor's fingers blazed with light.

"Amazing!" he cried, delighted. "Has she always been able to do that?"

"No, sir. She learned a year ago, from a basilisk. She learns things fast."

"Then she is blessed, as we are blessed to look upon her." He nodded a dismissal, and Daine stepped back to join the others.

Introductions over, the emperor said, "To you, representatives of our royal cousins Jonathan and Thayet, we say, welcome to Carthak. We pray that peace will reign between our lands and know that with such a distinguished company to smooth the way, peace is all but assured. And now, there is food outside, and drink, music, and good company. In your time among us, we have arranged for entertainment that we hope will arouse wonder and interest in our empire. Enjoy all these things, please. If you desire anything, only voice it to our servants. Within reason it shall be granted you."

Dismissed from the imperial presence, the Tortallans bowed as they backed up, until they were outside again. Once they had left the area closest to the door of the audience chamber, a gong sounded and a grinding noise filled the air. Everyone, guests and servants, froze in place. Slowly the walls that cut the audience chamber off from the antechamber sank into the floor. Now the emperor's dais commanded a view of the combined rooms. Everyone bowed or curtsied deeply to the golden man on the golden throne. He waved a hand; talk and movement picked up where they'd left off. A slave knelt beside the throne, offering a bowl of fruit. The emperor selected a fig, and nibbled it.

Daine felt like a puppet whose strings had been cut. Luckily niches in the walls held couches, with brightly colored pillows to cushion those who wished to sit. She nearly fell into the closest one. Zek squeaked and left his place of concealment to climb into her lap. Duke Gareth and Numair sat beside her, and the remaining Tortallans gathered around.

"Are you all right?" Numair asked softly, cupping her cheek with one large hand. "I had forgotten how intimidating he can be when he has all his imperialness on."

The girl looked at the gilded figure on the dais. "I noticed. Are *you* all right? Did he say anything to you?"

He smiled. "No. If I'm lucky, he'll ignore me for the rest of our stay. That's how he always managed such things when we were boys, anyway. If someone bested him at anything, he just pretended that person didn't exist. He got to be very good at it."

Duke Gareth remarked, "It went quite well. You did us credit, Daine."

The girl blushed and smiled at him. "Thank you, Your Grace."

Gareth the Younger and Harailt, who had quietly left them, returned with servants bearing trays of cups. "Fruit juices," the mage said as his companions helped themselves.

"So far, so good." Lindhall had come with the servants. "Numair, did he speak to you?"

"He didn't even look at me. He spoke the most with Daine."

"But what about his birds?" the girl asked, confused. "I came all this way to see them, and he didn't mention them at all."

"Rulers don't act as other men," Duke Gareth told her. "All requirements of protocol must be met before personal considerations may intrude. You must be patient until he sends for you."

"But more of them might get sick then," she muttered. Numair looked at her and put a finger to his lips. Daine sighed, but obeyed the command to be quiet.

"*Arram,*" said a female voice. Everyone looked around. A blue-eyed blonde in an open mage's robe of cream-colored silk approached, hands out. Her pretty face was artfully colored with the contents of pots like those that were on Daine's dressing-room table. Under the robe was a northern-style dress of rose-petal pink, cut to accent a narrow waist and a richly curved figure. Daine, thinking of her own modest curves, sighed with envy.

Numair rose, a stunned look on his face. Alanna slid into the place he'd just left.

"Varice?"

"The same old Varice Kingsford," the newcomer replied, smiling. "I'm surprised you remember me."

Numair kissed first one of her offered hands, then the other, and continued to hold both. "How could I forget you, my dear? You're lovelier than I remember. You must tell me *everything* I've missed. What changes are in the palace, and at the university? Are you married; may I kill your husband—" Laughing, Varice drew Numair through the crowd, leading him to a niche across the room, where they sat down.

"Is that who I think it is?" Alanna directed the question to Lindhall, who had come to lean against the wall beside the Lioness and Daine.

"She was his lover before he fled the country," the older mage replied. "Apparently there were no hard feelings."

Daine frowned. "Why didn't she go with him?"

"He didn't ask, and evidently she didn't offer," said Lindhall. "But she never married, either, and she's had a few serious proposals."

One by one, Ozorne's ministers came to speak with various Tortallans and to introduce them to Carthakis. Mages came for Harailt. Lord Martin and both Gareths were led away by the minister who'd stood closest to the emperor in the audience chamber. Even Alanna, who was uncomfortable in social situations, was deep in talk with a general in the crimson kilt and gold-washed armor of the Imperial Guard, better known as the Red Legion.

Lindhall beckoned to a slave with a tray of fruit. "Your small friend will like grapes," he told Daine, pointing to Zek. "You may also." He put a bowl of grapes and plums beside her. Zek devoured the grapes, while Kitten selected a plum.

"What does *she* do here? Lady Varice?" Daine asked.

"She is Ozorne's official hostess," Lindhall replied, his voice neutral. "Her magic allows her to specialize in things such as entertainment and cookery." He frowned. "I hope Arram—Numair—realizes that Varice is now completely devoted to imperial interests."

Daine looked up at him and realized that here was someone who genuinely cared about her lanky friend. "You've missed him, haven't you, sir?"

Lindhall smiled. "I never had another student whose interests so closely matched my own, and when he was no longer my student, we became friends. It's good to see him now, though I am apprehensive. The emperor never forgives. I doubt that he would imperil the peace talks to settle his score with Numair, but I cannot feel easy in my mind about his reasons for issuing that pardon."

Daine looked down, fighting the urge to tell this man of her own worries and the badger's ominous warning. She knew it was a bad idea, however nice Lindhall seemed, but she needed to tell someone. If only she could get Numair or Alanna someplace where they couldn't be overheard! She *didn't* want to tell Duke Gareth or any of the others. They didn't know her like Alanna and Numair did, nor did they know about the badger.

"Master Lindhall, could we have a word?" someone called.

Lindhall sighed. "You'll be all right here?" he asked Daine.

"Yes, thank you," she replied, smiling. "I'm not going to budge."

Lindhall looked at the crowds before them. "Probably that's just as well. I promise, when we get the chance, I would like to have a good, long chat about wildlife."

"Master Lindhall, the emperor's birds—"

The mage smiled, pale eyes sympathetic. "The emperor will explain, in his own time. That is how things are done here."

She watched him thread his way through the crowd, and shuddered at the thought of meeting so many strangers. Zek gravely offered her a grape; she accepted, with thanks. Looking around, she wished her pony, Cloud, were here. It had made sense to leave her at home, but now Daine longed for Cloud's horse sense and tart opinions. She felt lost among so many adults and such magnificent surroundings. The rulers of Tortall didn't have the kind of wealth, or surplus of mages, to create rooms like this for their palace.

Suddenly Kitten began to trill, producing sounds that rose and fell like music. At intervals she uttered a *chk!* sound. Each time she did so, the girl could see a man-sized distortion in the air to her left where Kitten stared intently.

"She sees you," the girl told the distorted spot. "It's the first thing student mages at the royal university try—the invisibility trick. It doesn't work with her. You do it well, the best I've ever seen, but if you don't show yourself now, she'll bite. She *really* dislikes invisibility spells."

The air rippled: there stood the Emperor Mage. "I trust she won't bite me," he said in a mild voice. "I would hate to bleed on this robe."

Daine's jaw dropped; she turned to look at the throne. He sat there, too, a figure identical to the one beside her. "Simulacrum," he explained. "A living puppet. I'm uncomfortable at state occasions. They really don't want *me* in attendance, just something to awe the empire's guests. I mastered the art of magical copies so that I might be able to move around. May I sit down?"

"It's your couch," she replied. For a moment she had spoken to him as she might have to King Jonathan or Queen Thayet, monarchs who insisted on informality. Belatedly remembering her instructions on proper behavior with the emperor, she said, "I'm sorry, Your Imperial Majesty. I should bow, or stand, but I'd upset Zek and the fruit and all."

"Then let us not upset Zek," said Ozorne, looking at the marmoset in Daine's lap. "He is the creature you dived so impetuously into the river to save?" The girl blushed and nodded. A smile tugged the emperor's lips. "It was a kind deed. We need more of them."

Embarrassed, Daine changed the subject. "About the copies of you—can't the mages tell it's only sorcery?"

Ozorne snapped his fingers, and a shimmering curtain of light enveloped the dais, hiding the other emperor from sight. "No. I *am* very good at them. Practice, you see—plenty of state occasions that require the emperor's image, not the man. I tried to teach your master, the former Arram Draper, how to make them, but he was never as adept as I am."

She ignored the jibe about Numair. "Can it do magic or look like it has magic? The sim—"

"Simulacrum." He put his chin on his hand, amber eyes thoughtful. "No. The fabric of the copy won't hold the chain of spells that would give it the seeming of my magical Gift."

Numair can do it, she thought. If the emperor hasn't heard it, though, *I'm* not going to tell him. "Why did you pardon Numair and let him come back, if you're still angry with him?"

He smiled. "My dear girl—no, you don't care for that, do you?" he asked, correctly interpreting the look on her face. "Then I shall call you Veralidaine."

"Daine, please, Your Imperial Majesty."

"Daine? What is the point of so beautiful a name if it's not used? Veralidaine. At the risk of destroying your illusions, I must tell you I have little control over what is done in this kingdom." He offered his hand to Kitten. The dragon shook her head, and crouched to examine his toe rings.

"I don't mean to be rude, but of course you do. It's your kingdom, isn't it?"

"Indeed, but—does my royal cousin Jonathan have complete freedom to order what he likes? I assume he has councils and nobles and law to answer to, does he not? I believe Sir Gareth the Younger is the head of his private council, to which Master Numair and Lady Alanna also belong. Duke Gareth leads the Council of Lords, which numbers also Lord Martin of Meron, and Harailt of Aili is head of his Council of Mages. Such men are the real power in any realm, Veralidaine."

"But they're just advisors. The king can do as he wants, surely."

The emperor shook his head. "Alienating one's nobles is a sure way to put a nation into chaos. There are always those who think they can do a ruler's job better. They need little encouragement."

Daine thought of Yolane of Dunlath, who had planned a rebellion in Tortall with *this* ruler's encouragement, and bit her tongue. Her orders from the king and queen had been specific. She was not to mention the emperor's attempts to weaken Tortall, no matter how much she might want to.

Zek, unconcerned by the emperor's nearness or his scent, a mix of amber and cinnamon, picked his way through the bowl of fruit. When his stomach bulged with his discoveries there, he offered Daine the next grape he found.

"No, thank you," she said. "Perhaps His Imperial Majesty would like it." Zek held the grape up for Ozorne.

He accepted it gravely. "Thank you, Master Zek."

Watching him eat the grape, Daine said hesitantly, "I—heard your birds are sick. It's why I came, but—are they better? Do you not need me to look at them?"

Ozorne's face brightened. "No, but I thought—after your journey, and all this—when do you wish to see them? I can arrange it for the morning tomorrow, if you don't mind."

"Um—if they're sick, I'd *like* to see them now. If you can have a servant show me the way—"

"Servants don't go near my birds, except to prepare their food. Are you certain? It seems too much to ask, to have you look at them the night you arrive."

She grinned. "Keeping me here when you have sick animals is asking too much."

He got to his feet, and she followed. "Do you mind if I veil us?" he asked. "Otherwise we will be followed; my ministers will want me to stay.."

Daine looked around. "I really should tell the others." The problem was that she could spot no one else from her company. While she had been in conversation with the emperor, the crowd had moved away from them to watch dancers in the garden. All she could see were richly dressed backs.

Ozorne raised a hand, and a slave appeared at his elbow. "Inform Duke Gareth of the Tortallan guests that Mistress Veralidaine has gone to look at our birds. And send the mage Lindhall Reed to us in the aviary."

The slave bowed deeply, and the emperor offered Daine his arm. She didn't see how she could refuse without being rude, and surely the slave would obey the order to tell Duke Gareth where she was. Carefully she rested her palm on Ozorne's forearm, as she had seen court ladies do at home. The emperor gestured, and a copy of him split away from them to walk back to his throne. The shining barrier that hid the raised seat vanished when the copy reached the dais, and the illusion blended with the copy on the throne. Daine watched it, fascinated, as Ozorne led her through a small door at the back of the antechamber and into a narrow hall. Kitten followed, while Zek settled himself comfortably on Daine's shoulder.

Globes like those in the room they had just left were placed at intervals along the hall. Passing the first, Ozorne gestured. It lifted free of the clawed iron foot that held it up and followed them, lighting their way through a maze of corridors and empty public rooms.

"I've tried everything," he explained. Since the humans they passed bowed to them, Daine realized he must have dropped the invisibility spell once they'd left the reception. "The new quarters were finished this spring, and after we moved them in they seemed fine. Then some of my birds took sick. I noticed a palsy in their heads. They became listless; their appetites fell off. Within two weeks of the first signs, the victims die. I know a great deal of bird medicine, and Lindhall Reed has made a study of it, which is why I asked him to join us. Indeed, there he is now."

Lindhall awaited them in front of a pair of broad white doors on which green flowering vines had been painted. He bowed low to the emperor and smiled at Daine, then turned and opened both doors, thrusting them wide. He clapped twice. Light-globes in the hall that lay before them came to life, to reveal a wonder. On the walls, birds had been inlaid with gold strips. Tiny gems served them as eyes, while craftsmen had used pieces of bright, colorful stone for their plumage. Kitten trilled her appreciation.

"Oh, *glory*," breathed Daine. "Your Imperial Majesty, this is—*wondrous*."

"It is well enough," the emperor said coolly, surveying the inlays. "We thought it pretty when we designed it, but no image can take the place of a living bird."

She couldn't disagree, but the walls still had to be the finest thing to come from human hands.

At the end of the hall stood another pair of doors, these made of long glass panels. They were frosted and set in a network of metal pieces enameled a bright, emerald green and shaped like vines.

"I am a *fool*." Ozorne was upset. "They will be asleep. We can have light-globes—they are used to that; I often read here at night, but to disturb their rest, even to care for sick ones . . ."

"You must leave that to me," Daine told him. "I won't frighten them, and I won't let the ones who are well interrupt their rest. It's more important to start work now."

"Master Lindhall, will you remain and get whatever Veralidaine needs?" inquired the emperor. When Daine looked at him curiously, he tried to smile. "To see them ill, and to be helpless—do you think less of me? I cannot watch."

She smiled. "I don't think less of you, sire. I know what it's like to be helpless when a creature you love is ill and you can't do anything."

Lindhall sketched a rune in the air with a glowing finger. When the design was complete, the glass doors opened. He bowed deeply to the emperor, holding the posture, until Daine realized that both of them were waiting for her to do the same. Again she'd forgotten that she was not dealing with King Jonathan! She curtsied, wobbling a bit, as Zek squeaked and hung on to her curls. Kitten sat up on her hindquarters and bowed, too.

Emperor Ozorne nodded and left, vanishing in plain view as he passed the white doors.

Lindhall went into the aviary first, using fingersnaps to wake two small light-globes near the entrance. They illuminated the area around the door, revealing a marble bench and walks that led between banks of large, thick-leafed plants. Daine looked up and saw the shadows of trees overhead. In the darkness she could hear the murmur of fountains and brooks, and the brush of damp greenery. In her mind, she could hear the whispers of sleeping and waking birds, both well and ill.

Lindhall closed the doors behind them.

"You don't have to stay," she said quietly. The number of birds in this chamber was surprising, and the thread of ill health weaving through her senses made her feel slightly ill herself. She was starting to regret the last grape she'd eaten. "It'll be fair boring."

"I believe I will stay in any event," he said, breathy voice kind. "Partly because I should like to see you at work, but also partly because I know Numair will feel better if I am with you."

Daine nodded. "Would you mind holding Zek, then?" she asked. To the marmoset she explained, "I'm going to need that shoulder."

Resigned, the tiny animal climbed down her outstretched arm and onto Lindhall's immense palm. Zek was beginning to realize that his new friend had her own ways of doing things. Lindhall sat on the bench, stroking Zek's many-colored fur with one finger, while Kitten leaped up beside him and settled down to wait. "Daine, may I give you a word of warning?"

Looking around, the girl saw the immense bole of a tree nearby. "About what, sir?" She settled into a fold between two large roots, resting her back against the tree.

"The emperor." Lindhall's pale eyes were troubled. "He shows his best side in regard to his birds, and to animals in general. He possesses—other sides."

She smiled at him. "I'll keep it in mind." She didn't think she had needed the extra warning—not after two years of finding imperial claws hooked into all parts of Tortall. Closing her eyes, she called her patients to her.

The ones in the best condition came first, heads bobbing on weakened necks. Some barely had the strength to fly, a result both of the disease and of the appetite loss that went with it. Daine looked deep inside herself until she found the pool of her magic. She drew it up not in threads, but in ropes, sending fibers of it into each of the birds resting on her shoulders and legs.

If they had a disease, it was like none she had ever seen. To her inner eyes, it shadowed the dab of copper fire that was each bird's wild magic, leaving a film that grew until it blotted out the animal's fire, and its life. She burned the shadows away in every bird that could reach her, then rose to find those that couldn't. She ached all over, particularly in her joints. She ignored it and felt her way into the shrubbery that concealed the rest of her patients from her. Many were on the ground, too weak to move. Three had died since the last time the place was cleaned. She stubbornly went after each flickering life light she could sense.

Some had made it to aboveground nests. The thought of climbing the large trees of this indoor enclosure was daunting, but she found a stair that followed the walls in an upward spiral. Using it, she searched out the rest of her patients. At last she had seen to all of them. Lindhall must have heard her coming down the stair: he, Kitten, and Zek met her at the bottom.

"How did it go?" the man asked.

"They're healed—for now, at least. Oh, dear." Now that she was in somewhat better light, she could properly see that her hands, arms, and dress were coated with heavy, white droppings. Before coming down, she'd scraped the worst off with leaves and twigs, but her splendid gown was ruined. Even one of Kitten's magical sounds wouldn't save the cloth.

"Perhaps I should continue to hold Zek," Lindhall said tactfully. "Would you like me to show you to your room?" She brightened, looking up at him, and he laughed. "My dear, I've lost more garments to animal droppings than I can count. Clothing is not worth a candle when placed against what you have done here. Come. We'll go through the gardens, where no one will see you."

Kitten, following them down the hall with the bird inlays on the walls, whistle-croaked. The stone birds lit up. Lindhall grinned with pleasure as lapis, jade, and citrine shimmered in their natural colors. Once that had faded, they went out into the gardens.

"What was wrong with the birds?" he asked, navigating the tangled paths.

"It's not a disease. Could they have eaten moldy seed or anything like that? I think they were poisoned somehow."

"It's possible, though the slaves are vigilant with the food that goes to those birds. They have to be. Do you think the poisoning was deliberate?" They passed a large, many-tiered fountain lit from within by glowing stones.

"I don't know. If they get sick again, I can check their food and things like that. Should I mention poisoning to the emperor?"

"Please don't. He would kill the slaves. It wouldn't matter to him if the poisoning were deliberate or not—only that it happened. He might torture them first, to see if it *was* deliberate, but it wouldn't do much good. All his personal slaves are mutes."

Daine shivered as they entered another wing of the palace. Now she knew their surroundings: the guest quarters, near the wing set aside for the Tortallan delegation. A slave dozing in the central area onto which the rooms opened jumped to his feet and held the door to Daine's room, trying not to stare at her.

"She will be going out to bathe in a few moments," Lindhall said. The slave nodded without looking up. "Daine, will you be all right? Shall I have Lady Alanna look in on you?"

She smiled up at him. "I'm just tired, and I need to wash, that's all. Thank you, Master Lindhall. Numair said you are *very* kind, and he was right."

To her amusement, the lanky mage blushed. "Well, good night, then."

About to enter her room, she said, "Oh, wait—if it's possible, can the birds be left alone all day tomorrow? They can be fed as long as food's left *quietly*." She had seen food trays and water bowls somewhere in the aviary. "If there's a way to keep it dark in the aviary for half of the day, I'd use it."

He looked interested. "Of course—I can manage it, actually. Glass walls conduct magic well, and it's no great matter to make them dark. You want the birds to sleep? Even the healthy ones?"

"It won't harm them, and the rest will get the sick ones over their reaction to the healing. Birds are funny." She yawned. "When they're up and alert, their bodies use energy faster than any other animals. The magic sticks better if they can sleep for a while after I'm done."

"I shall take care of it. Try not to fall asleep in your bath. Good night, Veralidaine—and welcome to Carthak." He closed the door for her.

"I like him," the girl told Zek and Kitten drowsily.

So do I, replied the marmoset as Kitten also nodded agreement.

Slowly, half asleep already, Daine began to gather her bathing things.

She woke early, with no ill effects from the previous night's work. By the time she dressed and left her room, a large breakfast had been laid out in the area common to the bedchambers occupied by the Tortallans. The others were emerging from their rooms to eat there.

"It went quite well last night," Duke Gareth said once they were settled. "Some of the imperial ministers are more forthcoming than others, but that is to be expected. I am *particularly* happy with the reports I've had of *you*, Daine."

Startled, the girl looked up, her teeth halfway into a bite of melon. Blushing crimson, she put the forkful onto her plate again. "*Me*, Your Grace?"

"Emperor Ozorne heard from Master Lindhall that you cured his birds in one session," explained Harailt of Aili. "The emperor is *very* pleased—says he has to think of a proper way to express his thanks."

"It's like that with some men in high places," commented Gareth the Younger, buttering a roll. "Things that would impress *us* have no effect on them, but a kindness done to creatures they love, they never forget." He looked at Daine, brown eyes uncomfortably keen. "I hope you'll continue to stay on his good side. The ministers' definition of concessions they will and won't make changed to our benefit after the emperor thanked us for bringing you."

Daine frowned as she passed a roll to Kitten. That didn't sound much like the way Ozorne had described himself—as a ruler whose lords told *him* what to do.

"Which reminds me," Numair said, feeding Zek as the marmoset sat on his lap. "We're scheduled to have a tour of the imperial menagerie after breakfast."

Daine gulped. "A menagerie?" King Jonathan had possessed rare, caged animals when she first came to Tortall. Even going near it had been a torment until the king began to change it, making it into enclosures that resembled the captives' original homes.

"Ozorne would never ill-treat his animals," said Numair, seeing the discomfort in her eyes.

"Don't slight him by staying behind," added Gareth the Younger.

Alanna hugged Daine around the shoulders. "She wouldn't think of it, Gary. Leave her be."

Daine smiled at her friend, and slipped the rest of her melon to Kitten. Somehow she wasn't hungry anymore.

They had just gotten up from the table when their guides arrived, Prince Kaddar and Varice Kingsford. Daine scowled as the lady, dressed in clinging green silk with a transparent white veil over her hair, kissed Numair's cheek, smiling flirtatiously at him. "I shall walk with His Grace," the lady told Numair, "but stay close, please. You know so much more about animals than I do."

Duke Gareth bowed over Varice's hand. "Numair's loss is my gain, Lady Varice."

Prince Kaddar bowed to Alanna. "May I offer you my escort, Lioness?"

Alanna grinned, resting her hands on her sword belt. "On such a beautiful day you shouldn't be stuck with an old lady like me," she said wickedly. "I don't believe Daine has an escort."

Kaddar smiled and turned to Daine. "Then I am free to offer my arm to you, lady."

My friend, Daine thought, glaring at the Lioness. To Kaddar she gave a lukewarm smile. "I'm no lady, Your Highness—just Daine."

The amenities over, the group was led by Varice and the prince down a maze of paths that led past a formal garden and partway around the shore of an ornamental lake. Daine closed off the links her magic formed to the animal world around her. She could no more hear Zek's thoughts and feelings than she would hear the zoo captives, but the marmoset understood when she explained why she was closing herself off. I don't like cages either, he said balefully, chittering in anger. They put my mate and our little ones and me in a cage, and then we were sold.

At last they walked through wrought-iron gates topped by the imperial seal: a crossed sword and wand, topped by a crown, wrapped in a jagged circle.

## ⇥ THREE ⇤

# HALL OF BONES

∞ "My uncle loves animals," the prince said dryly as the girl stared at the scene before her. "He tries to give them room, and the foods they prefer, and companionship. The ones that don't thrive in captivity he sends back to their homes."

She should have realized that the man who showed such devotion to his birds might pay similar attention to other creatures. While the animals here were contained, they had far more space in which to move than she had seen in the royal menagerie when she had first arrived in Tortall.

Lions basked in the sun, living at the bottom of a well too deep for escape. A lively brook flowed through the enclosure, and desert trees grew on one side, offering shade from the midday sun. Chimpanzees raced around an immense cage equipped with a large, many-branched and leafless "tree" for their enjoyment. On an island in the middle of a deep pond, strange, reddish-faced monkeys Kaddar identified as macaques climbed over and around heaped rocks.

Giraffes gazed at her solemnly over a tall iron fence. Daine couldn't help herself: she went to them, hands out, letting the wards on her power fall slightly. Startled, the giraffes dropped their heads low on their impossibly long necks to lip her fingers and say hello while Zek warned them to behave themselves.

"It's all right," the girl told him, smiling as a young giraffe snuffled her tunic. "They're grazers. They won't hurt you."

We don't have *anything* like that where *I* come from, the marmoset replied with offended dignity. We have *proper* animals there.

Kaddar, who'd been taken aside by a keeper, rejoined her. "Has your king anything this good?"

Daine bristled at the smugness in his voice. The hot reply on her lips was cut off by Harailt. "Actually, we're trying something a bit uncommon." He gave Daine a half wink. "We *royal* university mages are working with builders on a new kind of menagerie, a bit like this one, but much broader in scope. We duplicate the lands each animal comes from—plants, weather, and all; you see where the mages come in. When it's done, within the confines of the royal menagerie, a guest will visit small pieces of Carthak, and the Copper Isles, and Scanra."

Kaddar's eyes lit with enthusiasm. As he pelted Harailt with questions, Daine wandered down the curving path with Zek and Kitten, out of sight of the others. Here she discovered a pit in which giant, long-nosed pigs drowsed in a deep pond. Their noses, shorter than an elephant's but nearly as flexible, pointed toward Daine as she passed. Opposite them, a colony of mongooses watched her from behind wire mesh that enclosed a high and far-reaching mound of burrows. Beyond them the path took an abrupt left turn.

This last enclosure lay below ground level, inside a glassy wall four yards down from the girl's feet. The area was less well kept than the others. A small pond lay near the wall, but much of the water in it had evaporated. The grass was brown-edged and lay in patches on bare, dusty-looking ground. The remains of shattered bones lay everywhere. In back, lying out of the sun in a shallow cave, were three shaggy, spotted brown bodies.

She opened a wider crack in her magic's defenses, reaching for these strangers. "Please come out," she called aloud. A twitch of movement: three rounded pairs of ears came to bear on her.

You smell of cold places, one voice, commanding and female, said. You smell of frozen rain and pine trees. You smell of far away. Me and my boys never had a whiff of someone like you.

Blinking huge eyes in the sunlight, the speaker came to the foot of the wall. She was followed by two smaller males.

Daine wished she could meet the god who had molded these creatures. There was a god with *imagination*. The source of the shattered bones had to be those powerful jaws, equipped with strong teeth. The least of these creatures weighed more than she did. On their fours they were tallest and heaviest at the shoulder, their spotted fur covering slab-like muscle. Their hindquarters were low and short, but strong. Small tails sported jaunty tufts at the end.

"They're *beautiful*," she breathed.

"Spotted hyenas," Numair said at her elbow. "From the grass plains of Ekallatum, far to the south. Night hunters, for the most part—see the eyes? They have the strongest bite of any mortal predator—it crushes even the bones of water buffalo. Hyena packs are matriarchal—"

"Matri-what?" she asked. Kitten voiced an inquiring whistle of her own.

Numair smiled. "Their society is ruled by females. Each pack is led by sisters."

"Sensible of them," Daine said, grinning up at him.

"Excuse me." It was Varice. She bore down on them with a brittle-looking smile. "I'm sorry. These animals aren't to be shown to visitors. I don't know why the emperor keeps them, when he doesn't even like them . . . Numair, Daine, please come back. There's another part of the menagerie you haven't seen." Linking her arm through Numair's, she led him away from the hyenas.

Come back sometime, offered the female hyena. Me and my boys are always around.

"I'll do my best," Daine promised. "C'mon, Kit."

When she caught up to the rest of the group, the prince led them through a second barred gate. "This is my uncle's other collection," he announced. "Each and every one was captured and brought here for causing trouble for humans."

Kitten screeched. Daine hushed her, but felt like screeching herself. The cages in this wide courtyard, none of them as pleasant as those for the mortal animals, held immortals. Brass plates on each cage identified killer unicorns, griffins, the flesh-eating winged horses called hurroks, and giant, lizardlike hunters known as Coldfangs. Here, too, she saw unlikely combinations of human and animal: giant, human-headed spiders called spidrens and centaurs of both the peaceful and blood-hungry kinds, the former with hooves and hands, the latter with talons.

To her surprise, one cage held a man and a woman with steel-feathered wings and claws instead of arms and legs—Stormwings. The male had a pale, intense face, aquiline nose, and fixed, hungry eyes. The female's nose was hawklike, her dark eyes imperious. She had been beautiful in her youth, it was plain, and now, older, she was haughty and commanding.

Daine looked at Kaddar. "I thought your uncle was allied with the Stormwings!"

"He is," replied Ozorne's nephew. "The price of the pact with the Stormwing King Jokhun was that Queen Barzha and her mate Hebakh be kept here. Believe me, she would have caused as much havoc in Carthak as Stormwings have in the north, if my uncle had not made the alliance."

Daine was trembling. "What do you feed them?" she asked, shaking off someone's restraining hand. "Do you bring folk in and scare them, so they can live on that? And these cages are too small. The griffin can barely open its wings." Kitten muttered unpleasant things in dragon.

"They don't need food, and they don't require more room," said Varice impatiently. "You know these monsters don't fall ill and die. Unless you kill one, they live forever. Would you rather let them raid villages and destroy crops?"

"We mean no criticism of the way the emperor chooses to run his domain," said Duke Gareth. His eyes locked on Daine with a message she couldn't ignore. She looked at her shoes, biting her lip before more rash words spilled out. "Daine speaks only because her bond with all creatures gives her a dislike of cages. Your Highness, my lady, I regret to say I am not as young as I was. Might we find someplace shaded, and sit for a moment? Your sun is fierce, even this early."

Their group streamed out through the gates. Daine alone hesitated, staring at these captives. She had no reason to like spidrens, Stormwings, hurroks, Coldfangs, and their kind. Too much of her time in Tortall had gone to fighting immortals like these. Stormwings in particular had caused her, personally, a great many problems. She ought to be glad these were locked away from doing more harm—oughtn't she?

At midmorning she returned to her rooms, to find an old servant woman there, straightening things. "Don't mind me," she said, her grin revealing a handful of teeth. "You sit down. I won't be but another minute." She flicked a duster over one of the carved screens.

Awkward and unsure of what to say, Daine sat on a chair. She guessed this was a slave, though she was much older than the other palace slaves that she had seen. The woman's dress was undyed cotton, looped over one bony shoulder and hanging just to skinny knees. She wore straw sandals. Her only ornament, if it could be called that, was a tattooed bracelet of snaky lines that twined around each other.

Putting aside her duster, the old woman took the pillow from the bed and plumped it. "You're from up north, aren't you?" she asked. "Up Tortall way?"

Kitten trotted over and tugged the woman's dress, chattering loudly.

"Not now, dearie," the slave told her, apparently comfortable with a dragon in the room. "I have things to do."

"Over here, Kit," summoned Daine.

The slave laid her hand on Kitten's muzzle. "Enough," she said, black eyes dancing wickedly in a seamed face. The dragon was instantly silent. Turning back to the bed, the woman grappled with the slippery comforter.

Daine barely noticed Kitten's abrupt silence. Her upbringing got the better of her, and she stood, placing Zek on her seat. Ma had not raised her to sit idle, not when housework was to be done. She also had not been raised to let an elder work without aid. "Here, grandmother—let me help. Kit, move." The dragon ducked under the chair. Together the girl and the old woman bared the sheets on the bed and began to neaten them.

"Yes, I'm from Tortall," Daine said. "From Galla, before that."

"Your first trip to Carthak? What do you make of us Southerners, eh? D'you like it here?"

It occurred to Daine that the woman might be a spy, there to get information from her. "It's all right," she said hesitantly. "It's very different from home, of course."

"It's in trouble, you know—the Empire." The gnarled old hands were busy, tugging and straightening. "Famine in the south, five years running—did they tell you? Locusts—folk out of work—wells drying up. It's as if the gods have turned their faces from the emperor."

"It—it's not my place to say," Daine stammered.

"You ought to look around a bit. *Really* look. Long as you're here. The priests don't like the omens, you know. They whisper that a cold wind's blowing from the Divine Realms. Might be next time you visit Carthak, it won't be here. Hard to argue with gods, when they're done being nice to mortals." Briskly she patted the coverlet into place.

Daine blinked at the woman. Her words sounded too much like what the badger had said. And weren't slaves supposed to be quiet and timid? None of the others had talked to her like this one did: all they'd said was "Yes, Nobility," "No, Nobility," and "Right away, Nobility."

"Do *you* think the gods are vexed with Carthak?" she asked, digging her hands into her pockets.

The slave ran her duster over the writing desk. "Ask them to show you the temples," she advised, apparently not hearing Daine's question. "The shrines. They used to be the glory of the Empire. Now they think mages and armies are imperial glory. They think—the emperor thinks—he doesn't *need* the gods." Wickedly, she reached with the duster and flicked the end of Kitten's nose as the dragon peered out from under the chair.

Kitten sneezed, then squealed with outrage as her scales turned angry red. Her voice rose as she hooted and chattered with fury. Daine begged her to be quiet, but there was no silencing the dragon this time. The girl knelt and clamped her hands on her muzzle. "Stop that this instant!" she ordered. "Look at Zek—you're hurting his poor ears, and you're hurting mine!"

Kitten glanced at Zek. The marmoset sat gravely on the back of the chair, paws over his ears. Slowly turning a sullen gray, the dragon whistled what sounded like an apology.

"She wants discipline," remarked the old lady, sounding breathless. "Her own folk would never allow her to speak out of turn."

Concentrating on Kitten and Zek, Daine had taken her eyes off her visitor. When she turned to ask the servant what she had meant, she discovered that the old woman had dragged the tiger-skin rug from under the bed and was attempting to stand with it bundled into her arms.

Daine's reaction was automatic. "Here, grandmother—I'll take that," she said, holding out her hands. "Just tell me where it goes—"

The woman dumped the bundle into Daine's grip, and white light flared. Kitten shrieked as the skin began to writhe. The girl dropped it, horrified. Her head swam, and she toppled over, landing on her hands and knees next to the fur.

As she gasped for air, the skin rippled. The great forepaw, by her toes, flexed. Long, razor claws shot out, then resheathed themselves. By her nose a hind paw stretched, then braced itself on the floor. The rump, no longer flat on the stone, wriggled. Slowly, as if a body filled the empty hide, the cat got to its feet, hindquarters first, then forepaws. The tail lashed.

Daine scooted away from it. "Grandmother, you'd best get out of here!" she cried.

The door opened. A slave peered in, seeing first Zek and Kitten by the chair, then Daine. The door hid the rug from her view. The slave knelt and bowed her head, putting her right fist on her left shoulder. "You called this unworthy one, Nobility?"

"No," said Daine. "I mean, yes, I mean—"

The slave touched the floor with her forehead. Daine lunged to her feet. "Please don't do that," she pleaded, not sure if she spoke to the slave or the tiger. "I don't—I can't—I'm not a Nobility, all right?"

"Forgive this one's faults, Nobility. What do you need? This unworthy one is here to serve."

She took a breath and got herself in hand. "Please get up. And—where's the old woman?"

"Old woman, Nobility?" asked the slave. "There is no old woman here."

Baffled, Daine looked around. The old servant was gone, feather duster and all. "She was just here a moment ago—you must have passed her." She grabbed the door, holding it so that the kneeling slave would have no glimpse of the tiger behind it. "She was cleaning in here."

The slave looked up. "The care of your room is this unworthy one's task, Nobility," she said, clearly frightened. "It was done some time ago, shortly after the Nobilities from the north went with the prince and Lady Varice."

Daine thought fast. The old slave must have fled in that moment when the light blazed. No doubt she'd been frightened out of her wits; Daine knew her own knees were decidedly weak. She had to calm down, because now she was scaring this poor girl as well. "It's all right," she said, attempting a smile. "I—I must have been napping, and had a—a dream or something. I—"

She looked behind the door. The tiger skin lay on the marble tiles, all four paws tucked underneath, tail curled around its chest. The head rested on the floor, eyes closed. If she hadn't known better, she would have sworn the thing looked smug—except, of course, that dead animal skins couldn't manage that kind of expression.

"Would you do me a favor?" She closed the door so that the slave could see the tiger skin. "This—rug. It's very—upsetting, to have it here. Will you take it away? *Far* away?"

From the look on her face as she rose, the slave was used to odd requests. "Yes, Nobility." The rug offered her no more resistance than a blanket might have done. With a last bow, she left.

Trembling, Daine said, "Thank you," and started to close the door.

"Daine?" Alanna was in the central room outside, dressed for the opening of the peace negotiations. "You'd best hurry or we'll be late for the banquet."

Daine winced and shut the door. Between talking to the old slave, having the rug come to life on her, and handling the young slave, she had forgotten she had to clean up and change again. "I don't know how much more excitement I can take," she told Zek and Kitten as she stripped off her tunic and shirt. "To think the king thought I might get bored while I was here!"

The opening banquet started at noon, a feast of the light, cool foods preferred in warmer lands for daytime. From the talk around Daine, such meals were Varice Kingsford's special pride. It was the kind of thing that had foreigners from all over the Eastern and Southern lands singing the praises of the emperor's table. The girl surveyed the bewildering variety of choices and let Zek help her choose. The marmoset was an expert on plant foods, at least.

Varice was everywhere, seeing to the comfort of the Tortallan delegation and the foreign ambassadors to Carthak who had been invited to observe the talks on behalf of their rulers. With so many lords to attend to, she didn't appear to notice that Numair barely touched his food.

Daine noticed, and felt sorry for her tall friend. Varice had filled his plate herself, heaping it with delicacies like eel pastry, elephant-ear soup, and snake medallions in a black bean and wine sauce. It was the worst thing she could have done. Numair's body did not always travel well, particularly not after a sea or river voyage. Usually he spent several days in a new place eating mild, simple foods—the only things he could keep down. He nodded and gave polite thanks when she stopped to ask how he did, but Daine could see a tinge of green around his lips.

Luckily the dogs and cats who served as palace mouse and rat catchers were everywhere, even here in the banquet hall. Daine silently asked two dogs for help. When a paw on the mage's knee caused Numair to look down, he saw them at his feet, willing to be fed. The look he gave Daine was filled with gratitude. She didn't see the costly food leave his plate, but she didn't expect to: Numair's hobby was sleight of hand. The dogs she heard clearly. They were delighted with their feast.

At last the emperor led them to the room where the talks would be held. Tables and chairs had been placed in a loose square, and unshuttered windows allowed breezes and garden scents to pass through. The Tortallans, the foreign ambassadors, and the Carthaki ministers were given seats, their places marked with nameplates of gold inlaid with silver. Jugs of water, juice, and herbal teas were at all the tables. Carthaki scribes sat cross-legged against one wall, ready to take notes, while the Tortallan scribes had their own table, directly behind Duke Gareth's seat. Those who would not take part, such as Lindhall Reed and lesser nobles and officials, sat in chairs behind the delegations. Daine sat at the end of her table, uncomfortable even there. Kitten had a stool to perch on, beside the girl; Zek hid in his usual place under Daine's hair.

Ozorne rose to speak, dressed in a blindingly white robe and green shoulder wrap. His hair, ungilded today, proved to be reddish brown, though it was still in many fine braids, each tipped with a gold filigree bead. Black paint lined his amber eyes back to his temples. He glittered with gems.

"We bid you welcome, representatives of our eminent cousin, King Jonathan of Tortall, and of his queen, Thayet the Peerless, and of our fellow monarchs and neighbors." His voice filled the room. "This day has been too long in coming. At last we are met in a spirit of mutual aid and support for our lands, so long at odds. Villains conspired to bring us to the brink of war, but wisdom and vigilance have kept us from stepping over. All our hearts desire only peace.

"Without our knowledge and consent, evil men contrived four years ago to steal arcane learning secretly held for centuries. With this ill-gained knowledge, they reversed what the writers of those spells had dedicated their lives to achieve, the banning from our human, mortal existence those creatures loosely called immortals, the semidivine beings who may live forever unless accident or force brings their life spans to a halt.

"To our sorrow, our person and our university were blamed for this dreadful misuse of power. Our cousins of Tortall, sore beset by immortals and by those who prey on a land open to attack, felt we were to blame, and who could contest it? Loving freedom and commerce, we kept too little watch on our library, on our shipwrights, on those who hired men and paid them in Carthaki gold. To our shame and sorrow, our lack of awareness caused our Tortallan cousins to think we condoned the behavior of pirates, bandits, and rogues. Let us now set the matter straight. Let us strive together for peace between our peoples, and put aside all past misunderstandings.

"May the gods bless our endeavors, and may they foster the peace for which we all long." Clasping his hands together, he touched them to his forehead in a kind of salute, and sat down.

Duke Gareth rose to make his reply, reading from a letter written to Ozorne and his ministers by King Jonathan. Daine hid a yawn under one hand. She might have found the letter more interesting if she had not heard discussions about its contents on the voyage to Carthak. Instead her mind kept skipping away from Duke Gareth's voice, returning to the tiger-skin rug, or to the badger's visit, over and over. She had mentioned the need to talk to Numair and Alanna on their way to the noon banquet, but she knew it might be some time before they could get the chance to safely hear what she had to say. As the emperor's guests, most of their time away from the talks would be taken up with entertainments and activities. Both had promised to do what they could, and Daine had to be content with that.

If only I *knew* what the gods had in mind, or *when* it was going to happen, she thought as the foreign ambassadors read messages from their own rulers. I don't know what Numair or Alanna can do with "Something bad is going to happen." I don't even know what *I* would do with it!

Once the ambassadors were done, each of Ozorne's delegates had a speech to make, followed by a speech from each Tortallan official. Daine's yawns began to come thick and fast.

Suddenly a clerk tapped her on the shoulder and passed her a note from Duke Gareth.

*There is no reason for you to remain for all this—your presence*
*in Carthak has nothing to do with being bored to death. Why*
*don't you go? No one will mind. Just remember to be changed*
*and ready for the supper banquet this evening, and go nowhere*
*that is not permitted.*

When she stuffed the note into her pocket, Zek woke from his after-lunch nap. We're done now? he asked, hopeful.

That was enough to decide her. Maybe *they* aren't done, but I am, she told the marmoset. Leaning around Alanna, she caught the duke's eyes and nodded. He smiled at her, and Alanna gave her shoulder a pat.

"Kit," the girl whispered, "I'm leaving. Come on."

The dragon shook her head. She appeared fascinated by the speakers. Daine tugged her paw; Kitten shook her head again. With a shrug, the girl left her, and quietly made her way out of the room. Looking back as she let the door close, she saw her dragon climb into the vacated chair.

Outside, she found herself in a long breezeway that opened on both sides to gardens. She sat on a marble bench with a sigh of relief, and lifted Zek down into her lap. "Amazing how much two-leggers can talk, isn't it?" she asked him.

"Given that the alternative to speech this time is war, I imagine talk is a little better." Lindhall had followed her. He sat on the end of the bench and offered a hand to Zek. Curious, the marmoset went to inspect his fingers. "I would like to show you something of interest—something you would not see at home. Unless you had planned to return to the deliberations of the mighty?"

"Goddess, no!" she exclaimed with a shudder, and picked up Zek.

As they set off through the palace, Lindhall said, "I wanted to ask—is it true marmosets form monogamous groups in the wild? No one's ever been able to actually observe them in their native wilderness. There are other tales, of course, such as the one that claims they vanish in plain sight and reappear in another part of the forest, which is clearly false—isn't it?"

Daine, politely waiting for him to finish, realized that he had. "Zek says they don't vanish. They freeze. The way their fur is colored, they seem part of the tree. Or they zip around to the far side of the trunk and keep it between them and whoever is watching. And yes, they have just one marriage. Zek used to live with his wife and their three children before they were trapped."

Lindhall shook his head. "Wild things should remain in the wild. Down this corridor."

They now entered the heart of the palace, where throne rooms, reception halls, and waiting rooms were located. Lindhall stopped before a large double door that bore a brass nameplate: The Hall of Bones. The handles on each flap were very large bones of some kind. Daine and Zek touched one with curious fingers.

"What do you know of fossils?" the mage asked.

"They're creatures and plants that lived so long ago no mortals remember them. There are some in the royal museum—shells, batlike creatures, fishes and such. Numair says there are others, skeletons of huge beasts called dinosaurs, but no one has found any in the Eastern Lands yet."

"Quite true," replied Lindhall. He spoke a word in a language she didn't know, and both door flaps swung inward. Daine squeaked; Zek darted under her hair. Peering at them from the shadows was a *very* large skull. Three horns sprang from the bony face: a short one, near the end of its nose, and two longer ones that pointed forward over the eyes.

"Oh, you beautiful thing," the girl whispered, and went up to it, hardly believing what she saw. She only came as high as one of the large eye sockets. "What is it?" With trembling fingers she touched the beaklike plate of bone that seemed to be the creature's upper lip.

Lindhall clapped. Overhead, throughout that immense hall, light-globes began to glow. "One of the horn-faced lizards. We call them lizards because they resemble lizards more than other creatures, but they didn't *act* like our modern reptiles do." Daine blinked up at Lindhall, who smiled. "This one is a great three-horn. All the horn-faced lizards had some type of facial protrusions. The three-horns and one-horns also had a simple or ornate bone frill behind the skull. This fellow was the largest of his family—the others varied from eighteen to twenty feet in length."

She saw a massive, curved fan of bone behind the long horns. "Neck armor?" she asked. The hand with which she touched the skull itched.

"Apparently."

"And they weren't lizards?"

"No. The appearance was reptilian, but most were quite agile, and less vulnerable to changes in temperature than modern lizards are. They seem to have behaved more like birds than lizards. We know so much thanks to those seers who are able to look back in time. The real world has little use for them, but in a university they are in great demand."

"Nobility—" A slave had appeared in the doorway. Lindhall went to speak to him.

Slowly enough that at first Daine thought she imagined it, the skull turned to train a single eye socket on her. The girl stared at it, appalled. She had missed that flare of white light in the flicker of the overhead globes. "Hold still," she hissed, flapping her hands at it. "Quit moving!"

The head cocked slightly to one side, as if to ask why she made such an odd request. Carefully the dinosaur raised a bony foot and wriggled its three toes.

"Daine, are you all right here?" asked Lindhall. "There's something I must tend to."

"I'll be fine," she replied, not taking her eyes from the skeleton. She watched it for some time after the mage left, but the bones' period of movement was over.

That was fun, Zek remarked. Why were you angry with it? Touch some more of them.

Dead should *stay* dead, she replied silently and firmly. I will not touch *any* of them. To emphasize her point, she thrust her hands into her pockets, where they could start no more trouble, and looked around.

To the right of the three-horn, where the large hall connected with a smaller one, she discovered a far different dinosaur. Ten inches tall, it stood beside a nest of eggs, some whole, some broken.

"A mountain-runner lizard. We don't know what killed him, but at least we kept him with his nest." Lindhall had returned. "There's an adult of his kind standing guard." Daine looked where he pointed, and found a somewhat larger skeleton, eight feet long, peering at her. They were clearly the same animal, and there did seem to be a protective air about the big one. It stood in front of a doorway that led to a chamber full of smaller dinosaurs.

"They almost look as if they could move, don't they?" the mage asked.

Daine winced. "How did you fit the bones together?" she asked. "Did you find them like this?"

"The process is fascinating," replied Lindhall. "It was developed by the School of Bardic Arts and the School of Magecraft. If you understand magical theory, you know that things once bound to one another retain the occult tie, even when separated. Knowing that, the bards and mages create special musical pipes. Played correctly, they call the bones together to form the original owner."

Daine nodded; she had seen Numair do the same thing with skeletons at home. Together she and Lindhall roamed the collection. Behind the three-horn she had briefly awakened, she discovered another, smaller three-horn, whose neck frill was larger and flatter and whose brow horns curved up, rather than pointed straight ahead. A brass plaque set into the base of his stand identified him as a bull three-horn, listing his

height, weight, and the place he was found. Following this line of skeleton stands, which ran down the center of this branch of the hall, she
discovered other horn-faced lizards, whose neck frills grew more and
more ornate: a spiked three-horn whose frill was topped by large, curved
spines; the thick-nosed horn-face with extra bone plates instead of a
nose horn; and the so-called well-horned three-horn, who boasted down-
turned spikes on his frill. None of them were less than eighteen feet in
length, from nose to tail tip.

"Don't you wish you could have seen them when they were alive?"
the girl asked Zek.

The marmoset, as fascinated as she was, shuddered. Daine translated
his answer aloud for Lindhall: "Only if they were grass eaters. Even so,
I should prefer to see them from the top of a very tall tree." The mage
laughed at that.

They saw bony-headed skeletons like giant, long-legged crocodiles,
covered with back and head spikes and wearing solid bone clubs on
their tail tips. All were more than ten feet long and belonged to a family
called armored lizards. They gave way to cousins, plated lizards, each
with leaf-shaped plates and spikes running along their backs. These, too,
were giants, ranging from thirteen to thirty feet in length. Each one's
tail was laden with a collection of spikes that looked like a mace.

"There's so much learning here," she remarked softly. "The king's
trying to build a university to equal yours, but it'll take years. And when
it comes to things like this . . ."

"Once Carthak was famous largely for its treasures." Lindhall's
voice was equally soft. "It was a citadel of learning, arts, and culture.
It still has those things in abundance, but now the army and the navy
garner the attention of the world and of the emperor."

When she glanced to her left, her jaw dropped. The skeleton before
her, labeled Great Snake-neck, was ninety feet long. Its tiny head, at
the end of an extremely long neck, stared down at her from nearly
twenty-five feet in the air. With small teeth only at the front of a light
jaw, and eyes that faced to the sides like the three-horns, she knew it
was a plant eater—"A very *large* plant eater," she told Zek quietly. The
marmoset, who had climbed on top of her head for a better look, agreed.
Behind this one, she saw other snake-necks, though none so large.

Near the snake-neck was another, frightening skeleton, for all he
was only two-thirds as long as his neighbor. His eye sockets faced
forward, and his heavy jaws bore a collection of sharp and jagged teeth,
marks of a meat eater. He had cousins, too, Daine saw.

They found a cluster of duck-billed skeletons and, behind them,
dinosaurs who sported odd, bony crests on their skulls. One reminded

her of a basilisk, only the skeleton had a long, freestanding head knob, like a large bone feather on its owner's head.

"Now *there's* a hat," she remarked. Zek sniffed with disdain.

She had viewed nearly ten crested skeletons when she found a second hall in the rear of the collection. Curious, she ventured inside, Lindhall behind her. Here stood a double row of elephants. The four closest ones were strange-looking, with hides covered in shaggy fur and tusks curved up in an incomplete circle. The next four elephants had four tusks; two sharp ones on top, two smaller ones on the bottom.

"Mammoths," Lindhall told her. "The world used to be much colder, as I'm sure Numair has taught you. In those days, elephants needed fur."

"I don't understand. Were these alive once? How are they here, in their skins? Are they in a magical sleep?"

"They were brought from ice fields in the distant south," explained the mage. "They froze to death, and the ice preserved them until we could work the spells to keep them as they are. I use *we* in a general sense, since they were found a century to two centuries ago."

Daine stared at the great animals. "You have such wonders here. I almost wish I could stay longer and see them all."

"I noticed you said *almost*. I can't say that I blame you, though I wish that were not the case. I have a feeling we could learn as much from you as you might learn from us."

Daine laughed at that. "I doubt it, Master Lindhall. I'm just a girl with wild magic, when all's said and done. When I leave in six days, Carthak won't even remember I was here."

Lindhall smiled. "But *I* will remember, and so will the emperor's birds."

"I couldn't ask for more," she said with a grin.

Nightfall saw her in a lilac muslin dress and the long, sleeveless surcoat that had just come into fashion in the north. Hers was gold silk, as frail as a butterfly's wing, with a beaded hem to make it hang properly. The outfit made her nervous. She was sure that at any moment she would step on the hem and rip it out.

She and the adults were in a reception room with floors tiled in squares of night-blue lapis lazuli and white marble. The talks were over for the day. While the guests sipped fruit juices and nibbled delicacies, Daine waited for Numair to finish a conversation with the ambassador from Galla. At last that gentleman bowed to him, and wandered off.

Turning, Numair smiled. "You're becoming a young lady." He

brushed a curl from her cheek. "If I'm not careful, you'll be grown and married to a deserving fellow before I realize it."

She ignored this as being too silly for comment. "When can we talk?" she demanded. "You've got to find a way, somehow. It may be fair important."

" 'It *may be*'?"

"I don't know. I'm not sure." She thought for a moment and decided she had to take a chance and give him some clue as to what she wanted. "I spoke to the badger yesterday."

*That* startled him. "Where?"

"Aboard ship. In my cabin. He was"—she groped for a phrase—"not himself."

Long brows drew together. "*Not*—" The doors swung open. "Very well—I'll try to develop some opportunity," he said quickly. "They've scheduled these meetings so tightly we barely have time to scratch, let alone talk."

The group of people surged forward, taking them with it. In the banquet hall the emperor waited beside a long, low railing made of gold. Behind it large, open windows gave a view of the sky and a small lake. Ozorne was as splendid as on the night before, although his theme now was silver, from the beads on his hair to the paint on his eyelids. His long underrobe was silver cloth. Over it he wore a black velvet drape like a cloak that covered his back to the knees and left one shoulder bare. Strings of flashing opals linked the free end of the drape to his wrist. He blazed with gems at fingers and toes. Silver armlets like giant snakes wound about his wrists.

Now, through the windows, two Stormwings dropped in to perch on the gold bar. One was an older male with a pinkish-gray face, tight lips, and small brown eyes. He wore a black iron crown on thinning dark hair. The younger male was green-eyed and lean-faced. He wore bones braided into his long blond hair. While Ozorne and the crowned male spoke privately, the younger one shifted from foot to foot, clearly not pleased to be there.

Numair frowned. "Daine, isn't that—from Dunlath?"

"None other," she said. The last time she had seen the green-eyed Stormwing, he had been in her bow sight. "How nice for us all. We can have a reunion."

# ✦ FOUR ✦

# STRANGE CONVERSATIONS

Ozorne beckoned everyone forward. "Honored guests, we present King Jokhun Foulreek, our ally from the Stone Tree nation of Stormwings, and his vassal, Lord Rikash Moonsword. They will join us." He didn't seem to care whether or not his guests wished to meet Stormwings. Coolly he presented each of them to the immortals by name. Duke Gareth, bowing to them in greeting, caught a faceful of Stormwing odor and coughed.

Daine watched the immortals as the introductions unfolded. Jokhun stared at those being presented, not bothering to speak to them. The only time he showed emotion was when he saw Kitten: he frowned, and murmured to his companion. Rikash glanced over. Seeing Kitten, he found Daine and scowled.

"His face will freeze like that if he isn't careful," muttered Daine, shifting Zek from the crook of her arm to her shoulder. In Dunlath a year ago, Rikash had acted for Ozorne in the plot to overthrow King Jonathan, and had lost to Daine and Numair.

They were the last of the group to be presented to the immortals. Jokhun paid them no more attention than he might a fly on the wall, but Rikash bated her. "We've met," he said coldly.

*"Moonsword?"* She had never known his last name. "That's very pretty."

The Stormwing grimaced. "My ancestors were a sentimental lot. I know you, too, mage," he told Numair. "I remember the onion bomb you threw at me."

Ozorne smiled. "Lord Rikash, did you not say the wild animals of Dunlath behaved oddly?"

"I certainly did," the Stormwing replied.

"You have Daine to thank," said the emperor. "She is bonded to animals through wild magic."

The look on Rikash's face was one of mixed rage, chagrin, and laughter. King Jokhun turned watery eyes on Daine. "Some day we must meet less formally—when you are not protected by your host." There was an annoying hint of a whine in the king's nasal voice. "We will discuss a number of Stormwing deaths that are laid to your account."

"Anytime," Daine told him, smiling as sweetly as she could.

Numair bowed and nudged her to do the same. Once they were away from the emperor and the immortals, he murmured, "This visit gets better all the time, doesn't it?"

Daine nodded. She wasn't sure how she felt about seeing Rikash again. He was a Stormwing, a race of immortals she hated, but personally he hadn't seemed to be such a bad sort.

"*There* you are." Varice, in a red satin gown that fitted like her skin, took charge of them. Numair she guided to the very end of the head table, far to Ozorne's right. The only seat next to his was the one she would occupy herself. Daine, feeling cross, realized immediately that the woman had arranged things so that she would have Numair to herself.

With Numair seated, Varice led Daine to the opposite end of the main board, where Prince Kaddar waited. Daine curtsied slightly, pleased by the elegant sigh of her skirts, and once more silently thanked the queen for her wardrobe. She never could have faced these elegant people in the clothes she normally dressed up in—a blue wool gown for winter, and a pink cotton for summer. Even in *these* garments, she couldn't hope to match the prince. He was as finely dressed as he had been on the ship, in a calf-length robe of fine wool tinted a delicate aquamarine, and a shoulder drape of white silk shot through with gold threads. He glittered with jewels; against his dark face, his eyes could easily have been black gems, for all the emotion they showed as he bowed her to her seat.

"You'll be fine with His Highness," Varice told Daine, and left them there.

Kitten, unnoticed by Varice, sat up on her hindquarters and chirped, drawing a smile from the prince. "I don't know if your food will be very good for her," he admitted.

"She eats anything," Daine replied. "Trust me."

Kaddar lifted a hand, and a male slave appeared by his elbow. An exchange of whispers resulted in a stool being produced for Kitten. Discovering that she could see over the table if she sat on it, she cheeped and whistled softly.

"She's thanking you," explained the girl. "And so do I. It was a nice thing for you to do."

A smile tugged at Kaddar's mouth. "I read that dragons are curious about everything."

Daine nodded. "They understand as much as two-leggers. More, because they know the speech of animals as well as human tongues. I can't speak dragon, but if she wants me to understand her, she makes her meaning clear."

Ozorne clapped his hands. Slaves began to move in streams, bringing dishes to the diners so that they could select what they wanted. Female slaves, wearing loincloths, and nothing else, went from guest to guest, filling wine goblets.

For Daine and Kaddar, the dragon was clearly a safe topic of conversation. Her wariness of him began to fade when she found he asked intelligent questions, and listened to her answers. The moment he felt his friend relax, Zek popped out of the sleeve where he'd been hiding and climbed onto Daine's shoulder. For a moment the prince struggled with well-bred dismay, then suddenly grinned, for the first time looking like a young man not much older than she was.

"Anyone else?" he asked. "A sparrow in your pocket? A snake as your belt?"

Daine blushed and looked down. "No one else. Zek just doesn't like to be parted from me. I think he's so relieved to be in my care that he doesn't want to let me out of his sight."

"Understandably," replied Kaddar, stretching a hand out to the marmoset. Zek observed his fingers with the same grave air as he did everything, then climbed on. With that, the ice was broken between prince and guest. They talked about a number of subjects, comparing stories of their lives. The only awkward moment came when a slave arrived with the meat course: antelope steaks.

Daine swallowed hard. She had managed skewers of roast duck and peppers, smoked salmon and herring, and tarts filled with cheese and ham. She had even tried snails in garlic butter. At the risk of giving offense, she could *not* eat this. Worse, she knew Kaddar was bound by social custom to eat only the things she did. "I'm sorry," she whispered. "I can't."

Kaddar frowned. "Please? They're my favorite."

Her cheeks were hot. "Look—don't mind me. You go ahead."

"It would be churlish of me to eat something that causes *you* distress." Kaddar sighed and shook his head at the slave, who removed the offending dish. "At least tell me why."

Daine rubbed her face tiredly. "What do you know about me? About what I can do?"

"Well, you heal animals, and talk to them inside your head, and they do your bidding."

"You won't like that," Daine told Zek, who was investigating a small dish of hot peppers. To Kaddar she said, "I *ask* them to do things, most of the time. I don't like to order them around. Would *your* friends like it if you always told them what to do?"

Thin lips twitched. "Point taken. So you ask them to do things and you talk to them and heal."

"I can also *be* them. I learned how to shape-shift a year ago. My first mistake was when I thought I'd try deer shape, one day last winter. See, I didn't know the royal huntsmen would be out, looking for some game—"

"I think I can see where this is going." He watched her with interest, leaning his cheek on one hand. "So you can't eat deer—"

"Last spring we were rounding up killer unicorns, and bandits cornered me. I'd gotten separated from Numair and panicked. I changed into a wild goose." Remembering, she sighed.

"Big mistake?" There was sympathy in his voice.

"They got me with a barbed arrow. I escaped, but almost lost the arm. Anyway, ever since I could take on a creature's mind or shape, I can't eat game of any kind. I eat fish, and domestic meat like beef and chicken, but then, I never wanted to be a fish, and I close out the thoughts of barnyard animals. I'm sorry. I used to hunt and eat game with the best of them, but not anymore."

The prince looked thoughtful. "So there are drawbacks to your power."

"There's drawbacks to *any* power, Your Highness."

Musicians had entered the room as they talked. Now, in the cleared space before the main board, acrobats started a whirling, athletic dance. Kaddar was feeding bits of smoked eel to Kitten, leaving the girl free to admire the performance. When it was over, she remarked that she'd never thought two-leggers had that much bend in them, which made her companion laugh.

The acrobats were replaced by a number of unusually small black men and women and their animal companions. One old man held the leashes for a pair of tall, rangy, spotted cats. Twin girls carried an assortment of monkeys, while dogs of varying sizes and colors followed the entire company. The minute they saw Daine, all of the animals broke from their handlers to go to her. Quickly the girl stood and walked around to the front of the table, knowing that they would knock the table over to say hello if she didn't. Zek squeaked in fear and burrowed under Kaddar's drape as one of the cats rose on his hind legs to plant his forepaws on the girl's shoulders.

Daine petted her new friend. "Hello—you're a beauty, aren't you?" Silently she asked, How do they treat you, these trainers of yours? Do they hurt you to teach you things? In Tortall she'd found that many animal trainers used pain to make lessons stick.

The animals gathered around were quick to reassure her. Our two-leggers are wise, the cheetah male who had laid his paws on her shoulders said. They speak almost as clearly as other beast-People do. They never hurt us.

Daine saw why as the trainers, none of them taller than her earlobe, came to her behind their animals. Flashes of copper fire—wild magic—sparked in their eyes and around their hands as they chattered in word-like sounds. One woman coaxed the cheetah back from Daine, but the monkeys and dogs crowded into his place.

"They are Banjiku tribesmen, from Zallara in the south." Emperor Ozorne had left his dais and come over to the group. "They are saying that they think you are a god."

Someone laughed. Daine turned red. "Please excuse me, but I'm no such thing."

"You are god," said the oldest man in heavily accented Common. "I am Tano, the cat-man. The cats come to me, also to my wife. We have cat-children." Daine realized his face was tattooed with feline whiskers and ears. "Cholombi is dog-man." The man thus named raised his hands to show dog-pad tattoos on his palms. "Twins are monkey-girls." The young women with monkeylike tattoos bowed and grinned at Daine. "See? We all one-kind beast. If you are not god, then you god-child. Yes? Which god?"

Her blush worsened, and Daine knelt to bury her face in the female cheetah's fur. The cat chirped.

"I don't know who my da is." She wouldn't have minded telling these nice humans in private but doing so in front of the emperor hurt. "My ma died before she could tell me."

The Banjiku chattered briefly.

"They think it's too bad you don't know your father." Numair had also come over. "They wish they knew his name. They would sacrifice to him and ask him to visit their daughters as he did your mother."

Daine was about to protest that she was *not* the child of a god when she remembered visions she'd had since her mother's death, of her ma doing everyday tasks in a forest cottage. All included a horned man with hints of green in his darkly tanned skin. Could it be . . . ?

Ozorne watched Daine and Numair, face unreadable as he waved a jeweled fan idly. "The Banjiku skill with animals is legendary," he remarked. "It was through their legends that your teacher came to believe in the existence of wild magic. It seems he was right—in this case, at least. And now, if they would be so kind as to do the work for which they have been summoned?"

The Banjiku bowed to Daine, and moved into place for their performance. She returned to her seat and watched the entire thing without seeing it. Surely it wasn't possible that her da, unknown for all these years, was a god! And yet—Ma had always told her that she'd been conceived in the forest on Beltane, and that her father was a stranger.

Applause brought her back to her surroundings. The Banjiku and their animals had performed beautifully and were leaving the room. Daine nodded when the cat man winked at her. They would see each other again.

The banquet over, the emperor's guests returned to the reception area. Musicians played in a corner while slaves offered pastries and drinks to everyone. Daine was talking about the habits of griffins with Numair and Lindhall when a slave approached, pushing a wheeled cart. Perched on its surface was Rikash. Jokhun had left during the banquet, but evidently his vassal had other plans.

"Go away," he ordered the slave, then nodded to Numair and Daine.

Zek, on Daine's shoulder, craned forward to stare at the immortal, holding a tiny paw over his nose.

Rikash grimaced at him. "Still consorting with tree rats, I see."

Daine smiled. Rikash's last encounter with her had involved a squirrel named Flicker. "Now you know what disease the Dunlath animals had."

"Was that you, shape-changed?" he asked.

The girl shook her head. "Not then. I had just learned how to put myself within an animal's mind. Flicker and that eagle were helping me."

"Shape-shifting goes with that skill," the Stormwing lord pointed out. "I would have thought you would know that by now."

Numair grinned. "She does."

"How delightful for us all," the immortal said, voice extremely dry. "I must remember to give Tortall a wide berth."

Idly he scratched the brass that sheathed the top of the cart under his feet, drawing squeals from it with his steel claws. Daine gritted her teeth; Numair winced.

Lindhall bowed. "If you will excuse me?" He patted the humans on the shoulders and left.

"We were having a nice talk before you came," Daine informed Rikash.

"I am devastated to have ruined your fun." Looking down, he asked in a very different voice, "Do you hear from Maura of Dunlath?"

"She writes Daine often," said Numair.

"She misses you," Daine told the Stormwing. "She says her guardian is nice, but he doesn't have your sense of humor. You *could* visit her, you know. She'd like that."

Rikash pried up a bit of the metal he stood on. "I must remain here with King Jokhun, for now," he replied. "I believe my stay will not endure for much longer, and then I may be free to pursue my own life. If that is the case, I would like to see Maura again."

"Oh?" Numair asked. "It sounds as if you anticipate a momentous event. What is it?"

Rikash looked at him sharply, then grinned. "Finish your business here quickly, mage. Carthak's unhealthy. It will get worse before it gets better." To Daine he said, "Frankly, I'm surprised to find either of you at this court. It is wise to make a peace with the man who tried to overthrow your king?"

"It's very wise, if the greatest army and navy are on your enemy's side," Numair said dryly.

Daine toyed with the silver claw at her throat. "It's no different from what you did, is it?"

Rikash stamped the pulled-up brass into place. "What is that supposed to mean?"

"Don't play innocent." It was such a relief to be able to speak her mind to *someone*. Rikash, at least, would never complain of her lack of diplomacy.

"We've *seen* the menagerie, *Lord* Rikash. They have one of your queens and her consort here."

Kitten whistled confirmation, and silenced when the Stormwing glared at her.

"You are wrong," he said flatly. "There are no queens missing from the other flocks, and I have no queen in mine. The old one was slain in combat by King Jokhun, after our custom."

"Then maybe the prince was mistaken," said Numair with a shrug. "He seemed convinced that Barzha was a queen."

Rikash's steel feathers ruffled, then settled into place with a series of muted clicks. "*What* did you say her name was?"

"Barzha," Daine replied as she scratched Kitten behind an ear. "Her consort was named Hebakh. The prince said their being in a cage here was the price of the alliance with King Jokhun."

Rikash's frown deepened. Suddenly he leaped from the cart, wings pumping. Guests scattered as he flew through the window into the night. In his wake, nobles and slaves alike struggled to repair their dignities.

"I wonder where he was going," murmured Numair. "Is it possible he did not know of Ozorne's special menagerie? And what was that about the health of Carthak?"

Daine chewed her lower lip. She had a feeling Rikash meant the same thing the badger had.

I don't like all this, Zek told her. Back home, we know the feeling of a coming storm, and we hide. This feels like a really bad storm in the air, but it doesn't smell like water.

What does it smell like? Daine asked silently as Numair went to find Lindhall.

Zek thought for a moment or two, tiny nostrils flaring as he took deep breaths of the air. *Fire*, he said at last. A storm of fire.

Soon after that, Daine found the emperor at her elbow. "Veralidaine, good evening. The birds have been left all day, as you ordered," he said, offering Kitten one of his rings to play with. "Can they be visited to-morrow?"

Daine nodded. Off and on during the day she had called to the aviary with her magic, touching the minds of the occupants to see how they did. "They'll be up with the sun if they can see it. I should warn you, they'll be fair hungry. Figure they'll need at least double, prob'ly triple rations."

The emperor smiled. Daine realized that his watchful air vanished only when he talked about his birds. "They shall have them," he promised. "You may ask any price of me, any reward."

"I got the only reward I want—knowing they're better. I'm not always lucky enough to save animals when they're sick. Sometimes they die, no matter what I do for them. It happens often enough that I never get tired of making them well again."

Kitten offered the ring back to Ozorne with an inquiring whistle. Smiling, he replaced it on his finger, then vanished. Kitten squawked her irritation.

Daine sighed, feeling as if she'd been clamped in a vise for hours. She yawned and stretched. "Let's get some air, Kit."

With a cheerful whistle, the dragon led the way onto the terrace. Prince Kaddar found them there, watching the moon rise.

"This is beautiful," Daine said, waving at the formal garden lying off the terrace. It was laid out in patterns, with hedges and flowers forming precise, graceful curves and spirals. "We don't have anything that's this fine."

"Your king spends his money on very different things," replied the prince, watching the silver-gilded pattern. Before she could ask what he meant, he said, "I have to go, but I wanted to ask, would you like a guided tour in the morning? I could meet you when your friends leave for the talks. Your Duke Gareth said it was all right, when my uncle asked him."

Daine inspected his face. "Are you sure you don't mind? I would be at loose ends, it's true, but I can always amuse myself."

He grinned, teeth flashing wickedly. "I would like something to do, frankly. We're between quarters at the imperial university, and there's little going on for me until classes start."

"Then I accept with pleasure," she replied, seeing no resentment in him.

"I'll come for you tomorrow, when the talks open," he promised, bowing over her hand. He left her there, and once more the girl, marmoset, and dragon had the terrace to themselves.

Taking advantage of her solitude, Daine went down and around the side of the steps, where the raised wall of the terrace met the ground. Out of sight in this niche, she slid off her surcoat, folding it neatly and giving it to Kitten to hold. Zek she placed in an opening of the marble banister, where he would be safe. Unencumbered, she let the garden bats come to say hello, as they had clamored to do since she had walked into the open. They arrived a dozen at a time, to cling to her hair, dress, hands, and shoulders, talking in their high, clear voices. She loved bats, but had learned years ago that few humans agreed. It was always better to sit and gossip with them in private.

She didn't keep them long. There were still pounds of insects for them to catch, and she ought to return to the silk-and-perfume air inside. She sighed as, one by one, the bats left her, and wished them good hunting. More than anything, she would have liked to shape-change and go with them, but she had the feeling that Alanna and Numair would frown if she did. That was funny in itself, because Alanna liked elegant parties far less than Daine did.

"And I'm getting fair tired of them myself," she murmured to Zek. "Kit, would you do the neaten-up trick?"

The dragon drew herself up. Suddenly her eyes glowed silver; she made a soft, cooing sound. Curl by curl, Daine's hair, mussed by the small mammals that had clung to it, straightened to lie neatly under its lilac velvet ribbon. Small threads in her gown, pulled free by claws, plunged back into their proper weave once more. Little spots, the kinds left by creatures who never had to worry about clothes, vanished. Creases flattened; pockets of musty odor evaporated. It never would have worked on a dress saturated with bird droppings, but it was perfect for little messes. Daine had discovered this bit of dragon magic months ago, when Kitten fixed her appearance after she'd been called from riding to hear a noble's complaint about winged horses.

"Thanks!" The girl accepted the surcoat from the dragon and donned it. "Why did you do it so quiet? You—"

The dragon held a claw to her muzzle, signaling Daine to hush, and pointed to the terrace behind them. Confused, Daine peered through the openings in the rail. In the shadows where terrace met building, hidden from the view of those inside, was the old slave woman. Perched on the rail in front of her, talking softly and fiercely, was Rikash.

Daine frowned. She wasn't sure which was odder: the conversation itself, or the parties to it. Why would Rikash talk to a slave, *any* slave? He was hopping in fury, waving his wings as he tried to make a point; the slave shook her head. A slave, refusing an order from *anyone*?

Something else troubled Daine. She was sure this was the slave she had seen that morning, but now the woman's shaved head was covered by stubbly hair. Her rough gown hung from both shoulders, not just one, and her sandals were leather, not straw. They laced all the way up to those bony knees.

Suddenly the old woman produced a gleaming silver cup. Showing it to Rikash, she rattled it, producing the unmistakable sound of dice.

Daine collected Zek and marched up the short flight of steps, Kitten beside her. Rikash would get the poor old thing into trouble, and the gods alone knew what might happen to her if one of her masters saw this.

"Seven," the slave remarked. She and Rikash stared at the flat surface of the rail beside the upended dice cup. "You win. For now." She turned, and winked at the approaching Daine. "Push this bad boy off the rail, there's a dear," she said. "He's going to beat a poor old lady out of her life's savings."

Grabbing the dice cup, she placed a hand on the rail and nimbly vaulted over. When Daine ran to stare down at her probable landing site, sure the woman had broken an ankle at least, she was nowhere to be seen.

"Who was that?" demanded the girl of Rikash. "What were you doing with her?"

The immortal's eyes danced. "You saw her? Who was she?"

"The poor old slave they made clean my rooms this morning!"

The Stormwing guffawed. "Oh, indeed?" he said when he had calmed down. "Well, if you want to believe that, go right ahead. You'll learn."

"There's something you're not telling me."

"No, it's *her*. Ask *her* what she's not telling you. And be careful. She's tricky."

Something glittered on the rail where the dice cup had been. It was a metal feather. "Are you molting?" asked Daine. "*Do* you molt? You don't *look* like you lost a feather."

"Never mind that," he snapped. The girl shrugged and turned to go. "No—wait. Please."

She moved to stand upwind of him. "Well?" she asked, when he didn't seem inclined to speak again. "Anything?" He remained silent, frowning in thought. "You left in a hurry before."

"I would apologize for my rudeness, if I had manners. Happily, I don't. You ought to try *our* shape sometime. People expect you to be crude. I'm told it's liberating for most humans."

She snorted. "You won't catch *me* that way. Numair warned me what happens when humans take on the shapes of immortals—we can't change back."

"Wanted to try dragon's shape, did you?"

She stuck her tongue out at him, and he smiled.

"I wasn't lying—about the Stormwings in the menagerie." She fiddled with the feather on the rail, careful not to touch the edges. If it was one of his, it would cut better than a knife.

"I know. I saw them—Barzha and Hebakh. They told me how they came to be there."

"I'm sorry."

"I am angry, not sorry. Jokhun lied when he took over our flock. He said he killed Barzha and Hebakh in combat, and their bodies dropped into one of your oceans." Rikash had begun to rock from foot to foot; his green eyes sparkled angrily as his feathers bristled. "We believed him because we were tired of battles . . . Stormwings—tired of battles! We betrayed her, just as he did. And to find *this* smiling, lying mortal in league with him—"

Humans came onto the terrace. Globes sailed overhead to light the darkness. Ozorne was in the forefront, with Alanna on his arm and Duke Gareth on his other side. Seeing them, he came over.

"Follow my lead," Rikash muttered softly. "Please."

She looked at him, puzzled, but nodded. She didn't think he would get her into trouble, enemy or no. She did have to admit their talks here weren't hostile—more like the exchanges between friends who enjoyed a good argument. That was enough to make her head spin.

"Veralidaine and Lord Rikash," said the emperor, smiling mischievously. "Now here is an odd pairing. We had heard this young lady hates Stormwings."

The immortal shrugged. "We value a good enemy, Imperial Majesty. If I may be permitted to say so, opponents come in many guises. It is well to get to know them all."

The emperor nodded. Alanna frowned, looking from him to Rikash to Daine. The girl shrugged to let her friend know that she hadn't the least idea of what the Stormwing meant.

"Forgive me for my departure earlier, but I had thought of a gift to make to you, as a personal token of my appreciation for our association. It would be my very great pleasure if you would accept it." Rikash nodded toward the feather. "Give it to him, if you please."

Daine carefully picked up the feather and offered it to Ozorne, who smiled and took it, holding it with care. "Is some *particular* virtue attached to this gift?" he asked.

"Indeed," replied the Stormwing. "Any such token from an immortal has—qualities." Daine touched her throat, brushing the chain for the badger's claw.

"Heed me," Rikash went on. "If ever you are in peril of life and throne—and it must be peril that drives you, not curiosity—take this feather and thrust it into your flesh. When it mixes with your blood, you will fly from your enemies as if winged with steel, and escape beyond the Black God's reach for all time."

Ozorne replied evenly. "Neither our life nor our throne is in peril, Lord Rikash, nor do we believe they will ever be. Our hold on our empire is firm indeed."

"But the wheel turns," Rikash answered. "What is up may come down; what is brought low may rise. The gods are not fickle—but they have been known to change their minds. One day you will know the value of Stormwing esteem." He bowed to the emperor, then looked at Daine. "I never know what to make of you," he said dryly. "I suppose I never will."

He took off, and vanished into the dark. Daine watched for the last sweep of his wings. You aren't alone, she thought.

The sun was not even above the horizon when she woke the next morning. It would be an hour or more before Numair and the others began to stir, and Kitten and Zek were still deep in slumber. With no mind to go back to sleep and no books to read, she decided to visit the emperor's birds. Leaving the dragon and marmoset, she asked the mousers and rat catchers for a path to the aviary. The one they gave her took her through gardens to a door in a glass wall. It was open, with no magical lock to undo. She slipped inside and closed the door softly behind her.

The first to come meet her were small, green birds with red faces and tails, called parrot finches. They eyed her from a branch several yards away before dropping to her shoulders. The next arrivals were unlike any bird she'd ever seen, finches who looked as if they had rolled on an artist's paint board, sporting red, yellow-orange, or black faces, aqua collars and tails, emerald wings, yellow bellies, and purple breasts. Twittering, they hopped on nearby twigs and on her fingers, eyes bright in their vivid faces. What had she done to herself, to be dressed as a dirtwalker? they asked.

I was born this way, she told them silently, hearing quiet male voices from the direction of the door into the palace. I'm a two-legger *and* People.

The finches were not sure they approved.

Red-crested cardinals arrived. With them came tanagers whose plumage shimmered green and gold or green and blue. None of the birds could remember much of their first encounter with Daine; they had been too sick. Now they inspected her eagerly.

Greetings over, a tanager pair invited Daine to come see their nest. Finding the stair nearby, she accepted the invitation, ascending as quietly as she could.

Most of the birds stayed with her, though some left to get food. Chattering, being rude to their companions, they explained that the Man fed and talked to them. He came at all hours, but he didn't wake them if it was dark, and he always brought their favorite treats in his pockets.

Daine shook her head. The more she saw or heard of the emperor, the more confused she felt.

At the topmost level of the aviary, she found a very small colony of leafbirds, some with blue-violet stripes breaking their bodies into halves, the top green and the bottom orange-gold, some with orange heads and red edges to their wings. Here, too, were royal bluebirds, who appeared drab until they turned in the light to reveal wings and tails of a blue so intense it seemed to glow.

She was beginning to see why humans from the western islands to the eastern kingdoms of the Roof of the World came to see the emperor's aviary. These birds were like feathered jewels. She also noted the care they received, which impressed her more than all the emperor's wealth.

Checking the sun's position, she saw there was plenty of time before she needed to return for breakfast. I'm going to change, she told her new friends. Don't worry—I won't hurt anyone.

Removing her boots, she crouched on the platform and closed her eyes, remaking herself as a starling. Her body shrank swiftly, clothes falling away. She sprouted bronze-and-black speckled feathers, and grew a yellow beak. Her legs became stilts, her feet three long toes. Done, she ruffled her feathers and cackled, then took to the air.

The leafbirds joined her. The parrot finches came behind, twittering in their eagerness to show her the nooks and crannies they had discovered. The birds had nests tucked everywhere in this huge room. Not only had they made use of the trees and bushes that were natural choices, but they had built in the joints of the enameled green metal strips that supported the panes of glass forming the ceiling and most of the walls. Only one wall was stone. This the birds followed down, headed for the Man and his treats. While the food and water dishes throughout the aviary were kept full, the Man always had something extra good.

She was so wrapped in the flock that she nearly followed them to beg a treat from Ozorne. Only when she saw him and a newly arrived companion did she back up hurriedly, almost colliding with the finches. The emperor would know that a starling did not belong with his exotic treasures. She perched, concealing herself in a clump of leaves. Ozorne's companion was Numair.

Once out of view, she changed the shape of her head and ears, becoming more like an owl than a starling. Now she could hear the men clearly.

"—checked the baths, and the gardens, and she is nowhere to be found. If she is here and you are concealing her from me—"

"Be assured, Draper, she is *not* here. We had hoped she would be, to see how our birds have improved."

"If they have, then you have no further need of her. We *all* prefer that you leave her in peace."

"*We* are inclined to give her grace and favor." Ozorne's tone was haughty. "She has served us well, and we wish to reward her."

"She requires no rewards for your providing, *Your Imperial Majesty*." Never before had the girl heard Numair sound this harsh. "She is well enough as she is."

"Such heat over a girl child, and one without family or connection to recommend her. Why concern yourself in her affairs? You will forget she exists the moment some rare tome of magic comes into your hands, or some arcane toy. That has always been your way. You take up with someone, make them feel you are their sworn friend, then turn on them the moment you have what you wanted from them."

"How like you to see it in those terms," retorted Numair. "She is my *student*. You will never understand that. You never could sustain so profound a tie. Once you gained your throne, you decided you no longer required mere *human* bonds."

Stop it, Numair! Daine thought, watching the emperor's eyes flicker with some odd emotion. Can't you see he *wants* to upset you?

"Human bonds," Ozorne said quietly, studying gilded nails. "I am certain you and your lovely *student* have a most profound bond. Must you share a bed with her animals as well as with her?"

Numair's hand lashed, and slammed against the suddenly visible sheet of emerald fire that appeared around the emperor. Lights flared where he struck; he yanked the hand back, rubbing it. "If you interfere with her, if you harm her in any way, it will be a breach of the peace accords." His breath came hard under the words. "All of the Eastern Lands will unite to destroy you." He stalked out of the aviary, dark cheeks burning crimson.

Daine was breathless. What had *possessed* him to hit Ozorne? The suggestion that Numair was interested in her for sexual reasons had been made before; he'd laughed it off. If *anyone* took offense over such things, it was Daine herself, and only because the speaker did not understand Numair was too honorable ever to take advantage of her.

The emperor remained oddly still for several long moments after Numair's exit. Wondering if he were in a trance, she changed once more, until she looked at him with an eagle's eyes. Now she saw fine-pearled sweat on Ozorne's face. The pupils of his eyes had opened all the way up, in defiance of the light that streamed through the glass walls. His breathing came deep and soft; his mouth trembled slightly.

Slowly he lifted his right hand and held it palm up. Emerald light in four different streamers spiraled from the air before him, forming a small and fiery cyclone in his open palm. Bit by bit it solidified into a human shape. It was Numair dressed in rags, hair tumbling around his face.

When the image was complete, Ozorne, left hand palm-down, began to crush it. The image shrieked, its tiny voice a perfect copy of Numair's own. It screamed and screamed as Ozorne bore down. The emperor was smiling.

Daine fled to her clothes. She heard the image's cries as she became human, dressed, and left the aviary as silently as she could. Racing back to the guest wing, even with her hands over her ears, she thought the screams followed her.

Numair said nothing when she came late to breakfast, picking at his food as she told the others she'd paid a predawn visit to the aviary and gotten lost coming back. If anyone noticed that she barely ate, or that she trembled so hard that she spilled her juice, they made no comment. Afterward, as they were preparing to go, Numair said, "Daine, you asked to speak to me alone. Let's go to my room."

Alanna heard. "Then I go, too."

"It isn't needful—it's just a magic thing," explained the girl. She'd prefer to confront him about what she'd seen with no witnesses.

"If you visit a man's room, you need a chaperon." The lady knight shook her head. "Really, Numair, you know Carthakis. They think an unveiled woman is no better than she ought to be. Until we leave here, you can't talk with her unless she is chaperoned or you can manage it in public."

"A fine thing, when I can't talk to my student alone," said Numair, red-faced. "Let's go, then."

Inside his room, Daine smelled perfume in the air, a mixed-flower scent she recognized. "Did *Varice* have a chaperon?" she muttered to Alanna.

The woman kicked her lightly. "Perhaps she didn't *want* one for what she was here to do."

Daine scowled. A midwife's daughter, she knew very well that men enjoyed going to bed with women they weren't necessarily married to. Lately, the knowledge that Numair had such affairs had begun to irk her. She didn't want to mention that to him; she was afraid he'd laugh.

Once inside, the door closed, Numair spoke a word. Black fire bloomed in every corner, covering the windows and door. "It's safe now." He sat on the bed next to Alanna. "Talk."

Daine told them what the badger had said, and reminded Numair of Rikash's words. "It's hardly new," the mage said once she was done. "Seers throughout the Eastern and Southern Lands have been giving warnings of some disaster that looms over Carthak. Without better information, we have no reason to break off the talks and return home. Have you such information?"

Daine shook her head.

"Next time, tell the badger he must be more specific, if the warning is to be of any use."

"What about that breath thing the badger did?" Alanna inquired. "Do you know what it is?"

"Oh, I know," said Daine grimly. "And I don't like it—not one bit."

A dead animal was on display in this room as well as in hers: not a tiger, but a stuffed king vulture, fully two-and-a-half feet long. It was posed on a tall pedestal in the corner, the purples, reds, oranges, and yellows of its head were as bright as if the huge bird were still alive. Daine went over and removed the handkerchief someone had put over its skull. Looking at it, she saw that the fine cambric bore a delicately embroidered initial, V.

Scowling, she thrust it into her pocket and looked at the adults. "*Here's* what the badger did." She rubbed her palms on her breeches, then grasped the vulture with both hands. Light blazed around her fingers, blinding her. She blinked rapidly, trying to clear her vision, but the first hint that she had succeeded came when a wing brushed her ear. When the spots were gone, she found the vulture leaning forward, his many-colored face inches from hers.

Daine smiled. "Hello," she told him. "I need to sit." Her knees quivered; she went to the bed. Once sitting, she put her head between her knees to hold off a faint.

## ⇥ FIVE ⇤

# PALACE TOUR

૭૭ "Daine?" Alanna came over to check her pulse.

"I'm fine. Just dizzy." She closed her eyes and took a few deep breaths, then sat up. From some pocket Numair had produced his vial of wakeflower, a scent guaranteed to revive the dead. Just the threat of having to smell it cleared her mind.

The vulture flapped awkwardly across the room, clutching the wooden screen over the window. He pecked at the openings in the wood. Six feet in wingspan, he made the room *much* smaller.

"Is your weakness part of this new working?" asked Numair.

"I don't know. The times it happened before—the tiger rug in my room, and a three-horn skeleton in the Hall of Bones—it was just a flash. They didn't move about for long."

"I need to sit," Alanna said, and did. "The—what did you say?—tiger, and the three-horn. Did you bring them to life on purpose?"

"No. It was an accident." The vulture hopped onto the bed and leaned against Daine.

"That may explain why you're weak. This time you *tried* to do it." The Champion looked at Numair. "Do you agree?"

The mage tugged his long nose. Daine braced herself. That tug always came before a flood of learning. "To reason without information is fruitless. To acquire more information, Daine must conduct further experiments." Numair rubbed his temples. "What precisely did the badger say?"

She repeated it as closely as she could remember.

"The tiger and three-horn—what happened?" He paced as she explained, the vulture watching him with interest. "You are sure neither the slave in your room nor Lindhall saw anything?"

"No. I don't think they could have covered up if they saw."

Alanna laughed shakily. "Nor could I!"

Daine tickled the bird's foot, and he nibbled her hair. "I can't talk with him. It's like he's got no mind. But he must, mustn't he? He *looks* like he can think."

"The timing is inconvenient," Numair said, toying with his black-opal pendant. "We can't investigate properly while we are here. I will say this much—what you have done sounds like no wild magic I have ever heard. Only the gods can bring the dead back even to a seeming of life."

"I'm no god," protested Daine. "What if the badger passed some of his godness on to me?"

The mage shook his head. "There is nothing in the writings about animal gods to indicate they are able to do such a transfer. Not only that, but normally their power affects only those of their own species. The badger's magic should apply to badgers alone, as the wolf god applies only to wolves, and so on. Only the great gods have power that translates across species: Mithros, the Goddess, the Black God, the Graveyard Hag, the Master of Dream Gainel—"

"Don't name them all," Alanna said, too patiently.

Numair smiled. "No—of course not. In the meantime, Daine, I think it would be best if you said nothing of this and, in particular, *did* nothing with it until we got home."

"I'll *try*. It keeps getting away from me, though."

"What about him?" asked the Champion, pointing to the vulture. "We can't just let him run around in here. He's losing feathers, for one thing."

It was true: the bird's movements had shaken a number of small feathers from their moorings.

Daine asked, "What do *you* want to do, wing-brother?"

The vulture hopped from the bed, landing on the deep windowsill. Keeping his balance with the help of his wings, he pecked at the cedar screen.

"You want out?"

"Taking him out now is tough," Alanna remarked. "People will ask questions. I assume you want this kept quiet."

"As quiet as possible," Numair said. "You don't know Ozorne. If he found out she could do this . . . You don't ever want him to find out."

Daine said nothing. After what she had seen that morning, she planned to give Ozorne as wide a berth as possible. Something about the way he'd made the image scream without letup had chilled her to the bone. To the vulture she said, "If I take you to my rooms, will you stay there and pretend to be stuffed if the servants come in? When it's dark, we'll go outside."

The vulture nodded.

Numair reached into his belt pouch and produced a round stone. "This cat's-eye agate will make you two invisible once the spell is activated. When you re in your room, put it in your pocket. Out of the light, the charm will end. Don't bump into anyone, or they will see you, spell or no."

"Come on," Daine told the vulture. "You'd best walk. You're too big to carry."

The bird hopped to the floor, wings half opened for balance. Numair made a sign over the cat's-eye, then gave it to Daine. Without looking at her tall friend, she said quietly, "Numair—you shouldn't have tried to hit him. I don't think he liked it."

Quickly, before he could answer, she left, the vulture hopping beside her.

Kitten dropped a pawful of ribbons and screeched when Daine walked into her room. Zek, absorbed in the paint pots on the dressing table, didn't see Daine and her companion until the girl put the invisibility stone away. The vulture looked at him, and Zek chattered unhappily.

"He's all right," Daine assured the marmoset. "He's dead. He won't hurt you."

Did you do the thing to him you did with the tiger and the big skeleton? Zek asked.

"Yes. Seemingly, if I do it a-purpose, it lasts longer." The vulture hopped onto her desk and folded his wings. "Tonight I'll take you out and put you where you won't be found," she told him. "And you two leave all this alone," she scolded Zek and Kitten, seeing the mess on the dressing table. "Pick those things up, Kit." Replacing tops on the jars, she noticed her hair in the mirror.

"Goddess!" Sitting, she grabbed the brush and attacked her curls. "It looks like birds nested in it." Someone tapped on her door. "Come in."

Alanna entered, smiling when she saw Daine in front of the mirror. Then, looking at each corner of the suite of rooms, she flicked her fingers, sending balls of purple fire into them. Once they reached their destinations, they stretched, lengthened, and turned into sheets of purple light that covered the door and windows. Coming to Daine, she took a ribbon from Kitten and began to thread it through the girl's hair.

Daine looked at her in the mirror. "Why'd you ward the room? Are we talking secrets now?"

"Who did Numair try to hit?"

Daine related what she had seen. When she was done, Alanna cursed under her breath. "You're right to be upset. I can't believe he was so foolish!"

"He gets fair protective of me, sometimes."

"He also as much as *told* the emperor you're his weak spot." Daine nodded.

"I don't *think* Ozorne would endanger these talks, but—there is life after them to be considered. When we go home, it will be hard to stop Ozorne's spies from trying to hurt either of you. Men! Why they can't just keep *quiet* about things—" Outside a gong sounded the call to the talks. Alanna sighed. "I have to go. Be *careful* in what you say to the prince. Remember he *is* the emperor's heir."

"I'm hardly likely to forget, as much jewelry as he wears," Daine said dryly.

Alanna grinned. "Be polite. And if you see Numair about to do anything else stupid, try to stop him."

Kitten chattered agreement. Daine nodded. "Believe me, I will."

Alanna clapped her on the shoulder and left.

The girl looked at the vulture. "Are you still awake?" Its great wings spread, and folded again. "All right. Remember what I said."

The bird's feathers ruffled, then went smooth, as another hand rapped on the door. "Excuse me—Lady Daine? It's Prince Kaddar."

"And here we go," she told Kitten and Zek, lifting the marmoset onto her shoulder. Kitten raced ahead and opened the door.

Kaddar blinked when he saw her companions. "Won't they be happier inside?"

"No, they would not, thank you. Kitten's a smart creature. If you don't give her new things to do and see, she finds them."

"Like a puppy and my new slippers?" he inquired.

"Like a bear cub in your wardrobe, only bear cubs don't have magic. *She* does. She can whistle locks off doors—among other things."

"Very well. You would know best, of course. Since we're touring the palace, is there any area in particular that you would like to see?"

She took a breath. "Actually, I'd like to look at chapels and temples and such. Have you any here?" Until that moment she had forgotten the old slave woman had suggested it. I'd like to have a nice long talk with her, next time I see her, she thought grimly.

Kaddar frowned. "Well—yes, but—they're nothing special. You probably have finer ones at home. Except for the temple of Mithros in Carthak City—it's very beautiful."

"If it's all the same, I'd like to see your temples here, please." His reluctance hardened her resolve. She smiled up at him. "I'm making a study of them, you see."

It was the right argument to employ with a young man who attended the imperial university. "Very well, though I still think you'll be disappointed. It's also a bit of a walk."

When he offered his arm, Daine put Zek there instead of hanging on to it as he seemed to expect. He laughed, and let Zek climb to his shoulder, then set off through the gardens.

Daine walked beside him, looking at him sidelong. He looked different from the times she'd seen him before. He still wore his ruby drop and ruby nose button, but had switched his other earrings to small hoops. He wore only a single, heavy silver bracelet and no rings; boots; a white shirt; and loose, maroon breeches. An open collar revealed a muscular chest, and his dark hands were large and strong-looking.

"Are you related to the emperor on your mother's side, or your father's?" she asked, curious.

Kaddar, grinning as Zek inspected the gold rings in his left ear, asked, "What?" She repeated the question. "My mother, Princess Fazia, is my uncle's sister. My father was a prince of the Chelogu province in Zallara, far to the south. As you can see"—his teeth flashed in a broad grin—"my father was *much* darker than my mother."

"Forgive me for asking, but you said he *was?*"

"Five years ago he was killed, putting down a rebellion in Siraj— What in Mithros's name is going on here?"

They had turned onto a broad walk lined with trees. Coming toward them was a squad of five soldiers, marching in order, armed with spears and small, round shields. Instead of armor they wore gilded breastplates over knee-length scarlet tunics. The emblem on shields and breastplates alike was part of the imperial seal of Carthak, a crown wrapped in a jagged circle.

"What's the matter?" she asked.

"They're members of the Red Legion—soldiers—and they're here. The army isn't allowed on palace grounds—*ever*. Will you excuse me for a moment? I must speak with these men."

Daine took Zek back from him. "Go ahead."

He left briskly, seeming to grow an inch or two in authority as he advanced on the soldiers. They bowed deeply in unison, right hands placed on their hearts. When he spoke to them, Daine could see he addressed them as a prince, not as a teenager, and their leader spoke to him with respect. She wondered if she ought to improve her hearing to eavesdrop, and decided against it. Instead she looked around, wondering where she was.

To her left, on the far side of a bed of late roses, she saw an arch that led to an enclosed garden. At its center was a fountain, a tower of ornamental sculpture rising from a wide, deep bowl. On its rim sat the old slave woman. At least, Daine was fairly sure of the sitter's identity, but her appearance had changed again. The black stubble on her head was now at least an inch long. Parts of it were even longer, and gray. Her gown reached to her calves; the leather sandals of last night had been changed for worn slippers with holes through which the lady's bunions protruded. A knobby walking stick leaned against the rim beside her.

More startling than the change in her appearance was her company, a mass of black and brown rats. She was feeding them—at her feet, in her lap, and from her hands. Frowning, Daine headed for the fountain. Whatever was going on here, she wanted to know what it was—no more hints!

Kitten squawked a demand, and the old woman looked up. One of her wicked black eyes was gone; a mass of old scar tissue filled the socket. The other eye danced at the sight of Daine as its owner grinned and waved. The rats turned to stare at girl, dragon, and marmoset.

Daine stepped up her pace, only to find that no matter how fast she walked, the woman and courtyard moved away, keeping the same distance from her as they had been when she first saw them. Kitten stretched her long neck out and trilled, the sound harsh in Daine's ears. Undoubtedly it was a spell of some kind, but it had no effect on the gap between Daine and her quarry.

When the girl halted to catch her breath, the receding courtyard picked up speed, getting smaller and smaller as it moved away. At last it vanished.

That was interesting, commented Zek. Can *you* do that?

"No." Vexed, Daine put her hands on her hips. "Something *funny* is going on here."

Kitten nodded agreement, her eyes half silver, her scales pink with irritation.

"Daine, what in the name of Bright Mithros are you *doing*?" Kaddar, panting, ran up to them. "Didn't you hear me call? You were supposed to stay where I left you!"

Her legs and feet suddenly felt odd, the muscles loose and trembling, as if she'd run, or walked hard, for a long time. She slumped onto a nearby bench and rubbed her aching calves. "But I just turned aside to look in the courtyard—"

"*What* courtyard?"

"It was right off that walk where you left me." She looked around, and gaped. The trees, the walk, the five soldiers—all had vanished. Instead they were at the top of a long, dusty street, with no courtyards or fountains in sight. Buildings, each with a statue over the door, lined the avenue. At its far end loomed a big temple-like structure with a golden dome. "Where are we?"

"The Sacred District." Kaddar yanked out a handkerchief and wiped his sweaty face, patting carefully to avoid smearing the paint that lined his eyes. "And you couldn't have seen it from where we were, because it's a quarter mile away from there. You've been here before, haven't you?"

She stared up at him. "Are you crazy? I've never been to Carthak in my life." The additional thought—that she was starting to wish she hadn't come now—she kept to herself.

"Nonsense. You walked as if you were born here. And you didn't stop for me! Don't you *realize* you can't run around here without an escort?"

Daine blotted her own face on her sleeve. The direct sun was brutal without trees to shield them. "I *didn't* walk here. I saw the old slave woman by the fountain, and I was *trying* to reach her. Do *you* know who she is? An old woman, about my height? I thought she was a slave. Yesterday she straightened my room—"

Kaddar's eyebrows snapped together. "Why would I care about *any* slave, young or old?"

Daine felt as if she'd been punched. She fiddled with the cuffs on her shirt and collected herself. At last she said quietly, "Because I thought you were a decent human being."

Kaddar scowled and walked away for a few paces, rubbing the back of his neck.

All right, Daine told herself, it's plain the old woman isn't a slave. A slave wouldn't feed rats, or dice with Rikash. And I'm sorry he's in a pet, but I *did* think maybe he cared more about other people than some of them that live here.

None of the furred ones care about no-furs—what you call slaves, said Zek. That is, they care when they hit the slaves, and that's all. The slaves work and try not to make the furred ones notice them. When furred ones—

Owners, Daine told him silently, to keep the prince from hearing. Two-leggers with fur—with hair—who order slaves to do work are the owners of the slaves.

Like the Monsterboy owned me? asked the marmoset.

The girl petted him gently. It's much the same.

Kaddar had mastered himself. "I'm sorry if I was rude," he said as he returned, his voice cold and clipped. "You must understand, I'm responsible for you. If any harm came to you, my uncle would be— displeased. And your old woman cannot be a slave. When palace slaves reach a certain age, they are given tasks better suited to them, in the weaving rooms or warehouses or nurseries. The slaves in the guest quarters, and the imperial and nobles' quarters, are young. Now, if you please, you asked to see our chapels."

Kitten made an extremely rude noise. For a moment Daine thought the prince would lose his temper again. He fought the urge, and smiled at last. "She knows what that sound means?"

"She knows the meaning of every sound she makes." Daine tried on a smile of her own as she got to her feet. After hearing that the old weren't allowed to work where they would be seen by anyone important, she knew it wasn't a good smile, but Kaddar accepted it.

He guided her into the first of a series of small chapels. This was dedicated to a god of the inner desert, far to the south, and a statue made of red sandstone was placed over the altar.

While statues and altars changed from building to building, certain things were the same everywhere. Dust lay in corners and under what few benches or offering tables remained. Daine saw none of the things she expected to see: incense, flowers, candles, lamps. The air in these houses of worship was stale and unmoving. The dust in the shrine dedicated to the Threefold Goddess was so thick that Daine couldn't make out the details of the wall mosaics.

There were exceptions to the lack of offerings. The Trickster, god of thieves and players, presided over an altar where lay scattered playing cards and a few wilted bouquets of weeds. Several someones had left shells or bits of coral for the Wave Walker, but the gilt on the sea goddess's statue was peeling. Hidden behind the altar of Shakith, goddess of seers, were a score of candle stubs and a battered lamp. For Gainel, the Master of Dream, Kitten found two lavender-stuffed packets, too small to be called pillows, concealed under a bench.

"Are these less-known temples?" Daine asked. "Are there others— more popular ones?"

Kaddar's smile was crooked. "These are the only palace temples. The ones in the city are not in such bad shape as these."

Only Mithros's temple, the one with the golden dome, had serving priests—a three-man staff, explained Kaddar, with two boys as acolytes. All of them came running to greet their guests by dropping to their knees and touching their heads to the ground, a gesture that made Daine uncomfortable. Priests of any god should only bow to other humans, not genuflect as the Carthakis expected their slaves to do.

This temple was in better condition. Brightly polished sun disks caught outdoor light and reflected it into the sanctuary, but streaks of soot above wall brackets told her that light after sunset came not from lamps or candles, but inexpensive torches. She smelled incense burning, and freshly cut flowers lay on the large altar, but the priests were underfed.

Once they'd looked around, Kaddar led her toward the back of the temple, past the altar. "Where are we going?" she asked. "Aren't we returning the way we came?"

"There's one more," explained the prince. "Mithros is the best known, and the king of the gods, but our empire had its own, personal goddess. Uncle built her a temple behind Mithros's house, so he could make offerings to her once he was finished with his duties as the Sun Lord's high priest."

Passing through a small door, they entered a long, open gallery. At its end was a door inlaid with a patter of black-and-scarlet dice. Statues of hyenas sat on either side of the portal. A group of three rats sat over it.

Daine looked at those carvings for so long that Kaddar had to reach back and pull her through the entrance. Inside, the air held a faint odor of perfumes, but the silver candlesticks and chalices on the altar were tarnished, and the floor was unswept.

Behind the altar was the image of the temple's goddess, the most unusual statue Daine had ever seen. For one thing, hyenas and rats crouched at her feet like pets. One hyena held a dice box in its jaws, while two rats offered a die each to their mistress.

Except for the Threefold Goddess in her third aspect of the Hag, or Crone, goddesses tended to be young or mature women. This one did not show wisdom or grace as statues of the aged Goddess did. This Hag was bent, leaning on a gnarled stick, grinning so widely that the onlooker could see that she had only a few teeth left. Her eyebrows were bushy; one of them was cut in two by the strip of an eye patch.

Daine and Kitten stared at it, gape-mouthed, while Zek chittered his shock.

"What is it?" asked Kaddar, bewildered. "Daine? What's the matter?"

"It's—I think it is. I can't say for sure, with her hood up, and being stone, not colored like a—"

"What *are* you talking about?" Kaddar demanded.

"Her. It's—" She was about to say "the slave" when her throat closed off, and she half swallowed her tongue. She choked, then coughed until her eyes ran.

"Are you all right?" The prince thumped her between the shoulder blades. "Would you like water, or something else to drink?"

Daine shook her head. "I'm fine," she gasped. "I was just going to say, that statue—"

Coughs erupted, tearing at her throat. Both her nose and eyes ran this time. Whenever she thought she was better, each time she tried to explain about the resemblance between the slave and the Graveyard Hag, she began to hack as if she had lung disease. The explosions didn't let up until Kaddar took her outside, into a garden. She sat on a bench and took deep breaths through her nose, while the prince went to find water for her.

I know what this is, Daine thought furiously, clenching her teeth to stop the explosions. She thinks she can silence me this way. What I'm going to say to her the next time we meet . . .

Who are you talking to? asked Zek, confused.

Her. That—*Hag* these southerners worship. I'm coughing because she doesn't want me telling Kaddar she's been about!

Then don't say anything, if she doesn't like it, Zek said. Our gods, Chrrik and Preet, don't like us talking about them to outsiders.

Daine blew her nose. Chrrik and Preet?

Chrrik is the first male of the pygmy marmosets, explained Zek. Preet is his mate. They are very private gods.

Daine ran a finger down the marmoset's vari-colored fur. That I can believe, she told him. But from all Numair has said this is *not* a private goddess, and she cannot play with me! I don't know why she's here and showing herself to me, but she can either let me speak out or leave me alone!

She doesn't only show herself to you, Zek pointed out. She was talking to the Big Stinker—Rikash—and to the rats.

Kitten, following the conversation, nodded vigorously. The girl scowled. They were right. Moreover, Rikash had acted like the old lady was someone important.

"And he didn't tell me who she was," she remarked aloud, her voice a croak. "Maybe he couldn't. But why stop me from talking about her?"

"What did you say?" Kaddar had returned. With him came a young slave bearing a tray, a pitcher, and two cups. "I thought grape juice might help." At his nod, the boy put the tray on a nearby bench and poured juice for both of them. Once he presented the cups to Daine and Kaddar, the prince ordered, "Leave us, but don't forget to return and clean this up."

"Thank you," Daine told the boy with a smile. He bowed deeply and retreated, still bowing.

"Perhaps your body reacted to the incense or flowers in the temples," Kaddar remarked when Daine emptied her cup. "My life is a misery with sneezes and coughing at haying time, and my mother cannot be near roses without her eyes watering."

Daine knew her problem had a very different cause, but she appreciated his concern. "I feel better now, thank you," she told him, thinking that seemingly she'd go *on* feeling better if she didn't tell anyone their Hag was out and about!

"No doubt you're wondering about the temples." He didn't meet her eyes, but fiddled instead with his ruby-drop earring.

"Perhaps folk here keep shrines in their homes?"

Kaddar shook his head. "I wish I could explain. There *is* no good— never mind."

"What's the matter?" Daine asked. "Is something bothering you?"

Kaddar shook his head and put a finger to his lips. The girl frowned, not understanding. With a sigh, he reached up and tugged his ears. Pale green magical fire sparkled around his fingers.

Magic? Ears? Daine thought, then remembered Duke Gareth's warnings. "There's no listening spells on *us*, Your Highness. Kitten wouldn't allow it."

Kaddar frowned. "What is that supposed to mean?"

"Kit?"

The dragon voiced an ear-splitting whistle. Light flared, from the rubies at Kaddar's nose and ear, from the etched and heavy silver ring on his left wrist.

"So the only magic is on the things that glowed—is that so, Kit?" asked Daine. The dragon nodded. "Your jewels are magicked," the girl told Kaddar.

He covered his bracelet and the ruby drops with his hands. "Not by Uncle or his mages."

"What are they for?"

He looked at her, tugging the drop. "Kitten really knows if there's magic near?"

Daine nodded. "If she feels it, she uses a sound to make it appear. Unless it's invisibility or illusions—those she sees normally. She caught your uncle, our first night here, sneaking around the reception while he was invisible."

Kaddar took his hand from the bracelet. "Do you want to stay here?" he asked Kitten. "You'd have whatever you desire. Do you know how valuable she is, Daine? A creature that can tell when a spell is in place? Our nobles would give you her weight in diamonds."

"She's not for sale," replied Daine. "She's her own self, and goes where *she* wants."

Kaddar sighed. "Oh, well. Did you know rubies are protective stones?" Daine nodded. "Mine ward me from the sendings of lesser mages, though they may not work against a powerful one. The bracelet works on drugs and poison in my food. Even if I eat them, the magic turns them harmless. That one was so costly my mother won't tell what she paid the Shusini mage who made it. I think she sold family heirlooms to pay for it, but I don't like to ask, because it's saved me five times."

Daine shuddered. "What of the temples?" she asked, putting the subject of Kaddar's close calls out of her mind for now. "You were going to say why they're so neglected."

"My uncle decreed that, since the gods are eternal and his is not, the people should not spend their money on offerings, but on taxes. Anyone caught making an offering to a god is fined the cost of the item. The priests, all but one or two, and those the oldest, have been put to work for the empire as clerks and overseers. City temples fare somewhat better than the ones here, but even they don't look their best anymore. On the other hand, the treasury is full. That's all my uncle cares about—more gold for weapons, and the armies, and mages." He seemed relieved to be able to criticize his uncle without fear of being overheard.

They stood and followed a walk that led away from the Hag's temple. "But people need to worship, don't they? If they haven't got someone to call on, someone bigger who helps them with their troubles, what can they hope for? All creatures need hope—two-leggers or beast-People."

"My uncle says if they need to worship someone, they can worship him." Kaddar's shoulders drooped. "He says that he can change or ruin their lives more quickly than gods bother to."

The hair on the back of her neck stood up. "But that's fair *crazy*."

"You noticed."

For a long time they walked in silence, Daine mulling over what she'd learned. They reached the gardens that supplied the kitchens with common herbs, part of the working areas behind the palace.

"We have a choice from here," Kaddar said. "We can turn south and visit things like the wood shops, forges, stables, kennels, and so on. If we turn north, we'll come to the training yards used by the nobles and bodyguards. The warhorses are stabled out that way. My friends should still be there, practicing their battle and hunting skills."

She had made him take her to the chapels, knowing he didn't really want to go. "Why don't we see the training yards?" Shielding her eyes to look up at him, she was rewarded by his grin.

As he led her down the small roads that marked this area into neat squares, she asked, "Why were you so upset by those soldiers before?" The worry and concern that had marked him behind the Hag's temple returned to his face, and she almost wished she'd kept quiet.

"It's a breach in custom," he explained, nodding to the group of hostlers who bowed to him as they led horses past. "Traditionally, the army is forbidden to come closer than a mile to the palace. The men said the orders came from my uncle, who commanded regular small patrols through the palace and gardens, starting last night." He shook his head.

"Is that such a bad thing?" she wanted to know. "At home we have the King's Own, the Guard, and the Queen's Riders all quartered at the palace."

"Tortall's armies have never had a habit of rebelling against its rulers—ours do. Evidently my uncle—" He looked at Kitten. "No one's listening?" The dragon shook her head. "Thank you. My uncle doesn't think he needs to be wary of the army. He looks more at certain nobles who have protested the state of things in the empire, and who live here. He should worry about the army. Too many officers come from conquered lands and have no reason to love any of us."

At the archery butts they found a handful of males their own age, practicing with short, double-curved bows. They were laughing, well-groomed young men, their skin ranging from tan to brown to black. All were dressed simply in brown, knee-length tunics and leather sandals. Their rank and wealth showed only in their jewelry—earrings, nose rings or nose buttons—and in the high quality of their weapons.

When Daine stayed with the Queen's Riders, she took a daily turn shooting with them, or with the guardsmen, pages, and squires. Now her hands fairly itched to try that short, well-made bow, but she was too shy to ask. Instead she watched, leaning on the fence that separated yard from street, as the youths joked and pummeled Kaddar. They didn't appear to be in awe of the heir, but treated him as an equal. For a moment she saw Kaddar relax, becoming as carefree as any of them. The sight of his wide grin and dancing eyes told Daine how much on guard the Prince acted with her.

As she waited, Zek climbed onto the fence to observe. Kitten wriggled under the bottom rail and sat up to watch. It was the flash of the dragon's blue-gold scales that drew the attention of the young men. Kaddar, recalled to his duties, introduced Daine to everyone. The foreign names and titles flew in and out of her ears. She hoped no one expected her to remember all of this information, but nodded and smiled cautiously. She did *not* like the way they looked her over, bold eyes lingering on her face, her chest, and everything from the waist down.

Of course, she thought, red-cheeked from embarrassment and irritation. They don't usually see women with no veils, and in breeches.

"Daine is from *Tortall*," Kaddar said warningly, noticing the same thing that Daine had. "She came with the peace delegation to care for my uncles' birds."

"I have birds, sweetling," teased one youth. "Would you care for them, if I asked you nicely?" He barely flinched when Kaddar jammed an elbow into his ribs.

"Tortall—that's where they have a *female* as King's Champion," remarked another.

"Maybe Tortallan men are easily beaten," said one. "No *Carthaki* men are bested by a woman."

Daine inspected her fingernails. Anger was a warm, comforting fizz under her cheekbones and along her spine, driving off the gloom she had felt since her visit to the chapels. "And are you willing to bet on that?" she asked gently.

"Bet that we could beat your Lioness?" asked someone.

"Oh, no—she's busy. I can't bother her to teach a lesson to *boys*. *I'll* beat you. At archery."

They laughed, even Kaddar, and her blush spread. Kitten was muttering to herself, not at all happy with the way this talk was going.

"Sorry, Daine," said Kaddar, "but we have only men's bows. You couldn't draw one."

Her blue-gray eyes glittered up at him. "Oh?" She let herself into the yard. "You'd be surprised what I can do," she told the grinning young men. "Have you longbows?"

The young nobles laughed, or groaned. One of them teased, "Oh, I'm scared."

"Careful, Kaddar, she might be one of those Queen's Riders, the ones that let *females* join!"

"Or so they say. *I've* never seen one of these Rider maidens, have you?"

Daine's smile was sweeter than ever. "I work for the Rider Horsemistress. Trust me—there are females in the Riders, and they *work* for a living." To Kaddar she said, patiently, "A bow?"

The prince took her into a shed at the side of the yard. "They will be too strong for you," he remarked as she checked the unstrung longbows placed in wooden racks on the wall. Much as she wanted to try the recurved bow they used, she felt she ought to stick to the weapon she knew best.

"I'll judge what's too strong for me, thank you." Running her fingers down two bow staves, she shook her head. The next felt better, but when she lifted it down she could tell that the balance was off.

"We assumed those tales of women fighting among the Riders were only tales. No woman has ever asked to enter *our* armies."

"With you so open and welcoming of the idea, I'm not surprised." She found one that might suit her and examined it carefully, warming the stave in her hands as she checked grain and texture. "This will do. Have you strings?"

He stalked to a cabinet, reminding her of an offended cat, and opened a drawer to reveal coils of bowstring, each in oiled paper. She picked one out.

"Women aren't up to the discipline of military life."

Looking over quivers full of arrows, she chose a handful. "You must tell Lady Alanna that sometime. I'd do it from a distance."

"I hope you lose," he muttered as she went outside.

In the yard she backed up to the fence, since her bow had greater range than theirs. The targets were eighteen inches across, with two rings and a bull's-eye—a difficult shot even for a good archer. The Carthakis watched as she stuck her arrows point-first into the ground, keeping two. These Kitten held as Daine looped the string around the foot of the bow and stood that end between her feet.

"She'll never bend that," she heard someone mutter.

If only she had her *own* bow, the one that even the Lioness had trouble bending! Holding the stave in one hand, the free end of her string in the other, she easily slid the loop over the top end of the bow. When she had taken her stance, left side toward the target, Kitten handed over the first arrow. Daine put it to the string, careful to keep the arrow pointed at the ground.

"Stand back, or I'll hurt you," she warned her observers, then added, "Tortall and the Queen's Riders!" She swung the bow up, and loosed. Bow down, second arrow from Kitten, to the string, up and loose. The target was in her mind, not her eyes; she didn't have to take the time to aim that these males did. Now, pulling the arrows one by one from the ground, she fired until they were gone. Done, sweat gleaming on her forehead, she told the Carthakis, "You may check my aim."

At first nobody moved. Finally one of them went to look. Their judge carefully examined the arrows, by eye and by touch, where they were clustered in the center target. At last he called, "We must cut them loose from the bull's-eye. They are too deeply embedded to be removed by hand."

The young nobles crowded around her. She was incredible, they told her; could all the Tortallan women shoot like that? When she mentioned she'd like to try the recurved bow, six of them were offered at once.

## →» SIX «←

# CARTHAKI MAGECRAFT

∞ Finally Daine and Kaddar returned to the palace, the prince carrying the dragon, Daine cradling Zek. They entered by the marble water stairs that led from the river to the guest quarters.

On her arrival that first day, the girl had been too busy keeping Zek warm to notice the statues on either side of the stairs. She stopped now to look them over. The crowned images were both Ozorne: one simply dressed, with birds on his shoulders and a pile of scrolls and books at his feet; the other draped in robes, a jeweled scepter in one hand, a crystal orb that sparked with gold-and-green fire in the other.

"In case you'd forgotten whose house this is." Kaddar's dry remark was made quietly, for her ears alone—the ambassador from Tusaine and his staff had come out to take the air. "You could say my uncle has two faces." He smiled politely as the others approached.

The ambassador shook his head. "It did not go as well today," he remarked with a sigh. "Problems arose over fishing rights. One could have wished for a more flexible attitude from all parties. If only the strait between your lands were not so narrow—"

The sky was bare of even the tiniest cloud. None of them expected a loud crack of thunder to interrupt the ambassador as it ripped through the air, drawing shrieks from Kitten and Zek. Lightning flashed down from above. Splitting in two above the stairs, it struck each of the imperial statues with a roar. When Daine's vision cleared of spots, all that remained of Ozorne and his two faces were globules of molten gold and charred, shattered marble.

No one moved for a long moment. Then, without speaking, they all rushed inside.

Returning to her room to calm down, bathe, and change for supper, she discovered something was missing. Where was the king vulture? The desk where he'd settled was empty, but its top shimmered. Rising on tiptoe to look at its surface, Kitten squawked in outrage.

Daine looked. There was a message scratched into the varnished wood, in writing that glowed.

*Dearie, I came to fix your room, but some mortal took care of it first. Very nice work on the vulture. I'm taking him with me, so don't worry about him. We'll talk soon, never you worry.*

Burned into the wood in silver was the print of a rat's paw.

"She is getting on my nerves," Daine told Zek and Kitten. "The things I am going to tell her—"

The writing vanished. Only the paw print remained. Furious, the girl shed her clothes, muttering about gods who hung around where they weren't invited or wanted.

That night's banquet was held aboard a large boat kept for the emperor's use. Once his guests took places at tables in the stern, the emperor— seated in lonely state on a deck raised above them—nodded to a nearby slave. The man lifted a silver pipe-whistle to his lips and blew a wavering string of notes. In the bow and in the stern, three men and a veiled woman, in the scarlet master-of-sorcery robe from the imperial university, clapped their hands and bowed their heads. The vessel shuddered, and began to move north on the river, slowly at first, then gaining speed. Soon they were moving faster than oars or sails could drive them, while other craft drew closer to the banks to get out of their way.

*What a waste of magic,* Daine thought to Zek. *We could have stayed at the palace.*

"Would you like to visit the university tomorrow?" asked Kaddar, offering her a bowl of olives. "Master Lindhall will be here, and he's said he wants you to see his workroom."

"I'd like that. Kaddar, what did your uncle say when you told him about the lightning that—"

She stopped, puzzled. The prince was shaking his head vigorously. "Don't talk about it," he ordered, lips barely moving.

"Why? It happened, didn't it? And he can't have a listening spell on us, or Kit would've said something." The dragon, sampling pumpkin slices stewed in cumin, and sea urchins in bay sauce, shook her head. "So why can't we talk about it?" Daine asked reasonably.

The prince took a deep breath, as if he were about to yell, then let it out slowly. Still hardly moving his lips, he said, "Among the servants, he has spies who read lips."

She digested that for a moment, and accepted the olive that Zek offered. "Are there *many* things you aren't allowed to talk about?"

Kaddar propped his chin on his hands. "You have no idea."

They had just finished their main course, stuffed goose, when Numair came over to their table. "May I join you?" he asked, and sat down. He leaned forward, smiling at the prince. "We haven't really had a chance to chat. I understand you're studying with my friend Lindhall Reed."

The prince nodded. Daine peeled an orange for Zek while Kitten munched on a goose bone.

"What course of studies, may I ask?"

"The relation of men, animals, and plants to one another, with a matching course in law. Next spring, if things permit, I hope to go south with Master Lindhall and a group from the university to look into the causes of the drought. We're hoping—well, the masters are; I'll just be there to carry things—we hope to find some way to end it. Five years is a long time."

"I see. Commendable. With regard to your position as his heir, has your uncle arranged a marriage for you?"

Daine looked sharply at her teacher. What was he doing, asking such a personal question?

Kaddar passed his goose bones to Kitten. "He is negotiating with the king of Galla for the hand of one of his daughters. There is also a princess in the Copper Isles who my uncle feels is a possibility."

"I see. But you are involved with girls, are you not? Students at the university, young noblewomen. Are they aware you are not permitted to marry to please yourself?"

Daine, cheeks flaming, kicked Numair under the table.

Kaddar stiffened. "No gentleman deceives a woman in that manner, sir."

"Indeed not. Stop kicking me, Daine. You understand, she is very important to a number of powerful nobles and mages in Tortall." Numair's voice was quiet, almost friendly; his eyes were hard. "Their majesties. Lady Alanna and her husband, the baron of Pirate's Swoop. Me. All of us would take it amiss if we thought for one moment she was being trifled with, particularly by a young man who wasn't free to do the right thing by her."

"Numair," Daine growled. "Can I speak to you *privately* for a moment?"

"No. Stepping on my foot won't work, either. Do I make myself clear, Prince Kaddar?"

The younger man sat up straight, eyes glinting. "I understand you well, Master Salmalín."

"Good." Numair stood. It seemed to take him forever to rise. When he was up, he looked taller than ever, and faintly shadowy around the edges. "Lindhall tells me you also have an excellent memory. I hope so."

Daine covered her face with her hands as he returned to his own table and Varice. "I'm going to *kill* him," she whispered, shamed almost to tears.

Kaddar drained his cup of pomegranate juice. "Nonsense. He was just looking out for you."

"I can look after myself," Daine retorted.

Kaddar smiled. "You are lucky to have someone who cares so much about you. He knows we're spending—"

Drums began to hammer, on their boat and in the distance. Ozorne rose and walked to the bow, his guests following him. Moving under the power supplied by the master wizards, they had reached the imperial harbor in Thak's Gate in little more than an hour, a voyage that normally took three hours. A lighthouse on the far side of the lock admitting vessels to the commercial harbor shone its beacon overhead. Even with its beam it was hard to tell what lay past the lock, but Daine could just make out a forest of masts.

A horn call sounded from the harbormaster's tower on the breakwater. Sparks of magical Gifts flared from a hundred sources just beyond the lock. Fiery ivy sprang from those sources to climb masts and twine around yardarms. More and more such "vines" sprouted, until Daine realized that each belonged to a single ship, docked or anchored in the commercial harbor.

Another horn call: a shout went up from the assembled ships. The vines grew brighter, larger, until they burned like trees around the shadowy masts. Now the entire harbor was visible, as colored lights bounced off shield rims, armor, and spear points. They were looking not at civilian shipping vessels, but at war galleys with two or three banks of oars, fully manned.

The whistle on the emperor's barge trilled again. From among the guests, Master Chioké and three other mages, who'd been pointed out to Daine as the most powerful at the imperial university, stepped up to join the red-robed mages. Chioké and those wizards who had been with the guests lifted their arms to point upward. Magical fire stabbed into the cloudless night sky. The mages who had brought them downriver leaned over the rails, allowing their power to fall into the water.

Timbers creaked; wooden joints popped. Fire ran from one red-robe's hands to the next, until the hull lay in a disk of light. Chioké and the three mages in civilian dress cried a single word; the streams of light from their hands broadened. Slowly, its timbers groaning, the boat rose into the air.

Kitten shrieked. "No, Kit, stop," Daine whispered. "Be quiet, understand?" The thought of what might happen if any mage lost his or her concentration made her queasy.

The dragon shifted from paw to paw, chattering angrily as she buried her face in Daine's skirts.

Kaddar knelt beside them, petting Kitten's slender neck. "I can't say that I blame her," he growled softly. "I hate it when he does things like this. Why can't he put such power to use against the drought, instead of staging idle dis—"

"Hush," Daine said gently. "It isn't safe to talk, remember?"

The boat continued to rise. Sweat gleamed on the faces of the mages who controlled its motion.

At last the whistle shrieked again. The rising boat stopped, nearly eighty feet above the imperial harbor. The lighthouse beacon went out. From the harbormaster's tower came another, different horn call, one that was picked up by horns in the ships below. Kitten, Daine, and Kaddar returned to the rail. Zek, seeing where they were, squeaked and tore Daine's hair from its knot so that he could hide, trembling, in her curls. She didn't have the heart to scold.

More horns bellowed. New fires sparked past the white finger that was the lighthouse tower. Like those in the harbor, these new flames became vines growing up and along some dark trellis. They flared, magic piercing the night, to reveal hundreds of vessels lying at anchor past the harbor.

There was a roar or shout of some kind. Torches were set to globes that burst into flame. They were balls of liquid fire, lit as they rested in the slings of catapults aboard the infamous Carthaki war barges. At one catapult per barge, Daine calculated, there were twenty outside the harbor, forming solid ranks between the breakwater and the naval vessels farther out.

"Is he *mad*?" Kaddar whispered, appalled. "This isn't just the northern fleet—he's brought the western one up as well! Did he do it to—to *brag*—"

A hand gripped his arm. "Shut up," Varice said fiercely. "What's the matter with you? Do you want to disappear like his *last* heir?"

"But—"

Daine elbowed him—hard. "She's right—shut up!" Kitten closed her jaws lightly on the prince's leg. "If I tell her, she'll bite," Daine said coldly. "And you haven't been bit till a dragon does it."

Kaddar's hands clenched, but he shut his mouth and gritted his teeth; they could see his jaw muscles twitch. The emperor's boat hung in the air for a few more moments, then descended slowly. Except for sailors passing on orders, no one aboard said a word. Only when they were safely in the River Zekoi again did Kitten release the prince's leg.

The red-robed mages who had brought them downriver were replaced by four new, fresh masters. They clapped in unison and were bowing their heads when a ringing sound, like a gong being struck, shattered the air. It was followed by another, and another, and another. It sounded, Daine realized, like a horse's walk.

The air around the harbormaster's tower was glowing. From the emperor's frown, this was not part of his planned entertainment.

The clanging drew nearer. Around the tower's side and down the shortest breakwater, enclosed in a loose ball of light, appeared a golden rider on a golden horse. The clanging sound came from the animal's hooves as they struck the boulders. Together rider and mount were twice, nearly three times larger than normal. Both slumped, as if stricken with weariness or grief, the horse's muzzle barely a foot off the ground. The sword and shield that the man held drooped from his hands.

"Goddess bless," whispered Kaddar. All around them hands made the Sign against evil.

Do two-leggers grow so big? asked Zek, awed.

"No," Daine whispered. "That's not a two-legger. Zek was asking," she explained when Kaddar and Varice looked at them.

"It's a statue," Varice replied softly. "Of—of Zernou, the first emperor. It stands in Market Square, in Carthak City, before the Temple of Mithros."

"I don't think it's standing there anymore," Alanna commented from the shadows nearby.

Horse and rider reached the lock between the imperial boat and the harbor, and stopped. The horse reared, pawing the air with his forelegs. The rider cried out a word in a voice like a giant gong. Again he cried out. The third time, he shouted words in a strange, guttural language. He pointed to their vessel with his sword. Instantly magical defenses went up, forming walls of light between those onboard and the statue, but no attack came.

The horse gathered itself and leaped, clearing the lock, to land on the seawall on the far side with a ringing crash. Horse and rider galloped down the wall, striking sparks from the granite boulders. Just before they reached the lighthouse, the glowing figures leaped off onto the ocean's surface, and raced across it, dodging the naval vessels and heading north. Daine watched in silence as the glow that surrounded them faded, and was gone.

"What did he say?" Varice asked Kaddar, voice hushed. "It was Old Thak, wasn't it? The first language of the empire?"

"He said 'Woe.' " The prince's voice was quiet and even. "And 'Woe.' Then he said, 'Woe to the empire—we are forsaken. The gods are angry!' "

In her dream, she glided down a green river in a flat-bottomed barge, a silly, overdecorated affair painted yellow and white. A dainty yellow awning kept off the sun overhead. A rat offered her a white straw tray filled with a choice of small tarts. Two more rats slowly waved huge fans made of black feathers. Looking around, the girl saw vultures perched on the forward rail.

"Don't worry, child. I may not even need you." The Graveyard Hag reclined in the straw-and-white striped cushions next to Daine, choosing tidbits from the tray held for her by yet another rat. These appeared to be made of worms, beetles, fungi, and moss.

Daine shuddered. The food being offered to *her* seemed normal enough, but she decided not to take a chance. "No, thank you," she told the rat serving her. "I'm not at all hungry." He waddled away, awkward on his hind legs.

"It's quite possible Ozorne will heed the three warnings." The Hag chewed noisily, her mouth open. "Still, here you are, the perfect vessel, should I need one. I wanted to give you the power, just in case. Give you a little time to practice, to get used to it."

"Won't someone else do? I'm supposed to behave myself here. And don't you already know if he'll listen to your warnings? You're a god, after all."

The Hag crackled, spraying food on the cushions. "You *are* a funny thing! No, a vessel for a god's power can't be just anyone."

"Is it because my da really is a god, like the Banjiku said?"

"No, or we'd have even fewer vessels than we do now. Most mortal women die giving birth to a god's child, for your information. No, for a vessel we need a mortal with imagination, a strong will, and determination. And anger—plenty of it."

"I'm not angry."

"Nonsense, dear. Think of your mother's death. Think of how you were treated in that awful village you came from."

Daine looked down at her hand. The goddess's words had awakened memories of those times, as fresh as when she'd lived through them. For a moment she actually knelt beside Ma's body, feeling how cold she was. Memory flickered: she was shivering, naked, running, the village hunters close behind, calling her name.

As if she'd spoken, the Hag said, "Well, there you are." Briskly she wiped her fingers on the cushions. "And no, I can't tell if he'll attend to the warnings or not. We can see ahead a bit, but not far, and not when the events concerned will create so much change. Ozorne's choice will determine the path that history takes thereafter, which means it's like trying to see through mud. You mortals have to make your own choices. We poor gods only get to come in and straighten up *after* you choose."

Daine raised skeptical brows. The goddess's self-pity was laid on a bit too thick. "I'd no idea what a struggle it is for you."

"Oh, you don't appreciate me. Just because you're a good vessel doesn't mean I'll stand for your sauce! Back to bed with you!" The Hag flapped a hand.

Daine sat bolt upright in bed. She was in her room in the imperial palace. Kitten and Zek were grumbling at her. "Just a dream," she whispered, and sank back onto her pillows.

Entering the common room for breakfast, she saw only Alanna. "I got rid of the servants," the Lioness said tiredly as she put food on a plate. "I hope you don't mind. I can't deal with slaves, not today."

"Where's Numair?" Daine asked, sitting down. "And Master Harailt?"

"In their rooms, reading." Alanna handed the plate to Daine. "The Carthakis have allowed us to see the spells that open gates into the Divine Realms, but we aren't allowed to copy them, and *we* can't take them with us. Harailt and Numair are memorizing as much of them as they can."

Daine buttered a roll. "Where's the rest? Duke Gareth, and his son, and Lord Martin?"

"Talks won't start today until noon," explained the Champion with a yawn. "If they have any sense, they'll sleep in. Same with the clerks."

"You're not sleeping in," Daine pointed out.

"More 'rest' like I got last night and you'll find me atop some tower, baying at the moon."

"Bad dreams?"

Alanna flicked her fingers at the room's corners. Purple fire raced to encircle them, shutting out eavesdroppers. "Bad thinking," the Lioness said grimly, peeling an orange with callused fingers. "Bad sights."

"What's the matter?"

"Prince Kaddar is right. Carthak's northern fleet is small—about thirty vessels. They don't have many troop ships or war barges—they aren't necessary. This shore of the Inland Sea is all theirs: none of the lands on our side have a navy worth sweating over. They have the war barges and transports for men and horse on the western coast, against Scanran raids, or trouble with the Copper Isles, or to keep their southern holdings in line. They *need* those ships there, unless—"

"Unless he's got something for all of them to do," Daine said. "But—he's going to sign a treaty with us! *No*body brings in the navy during peace talks, do they?"

"If we were actually having peace talks, no; but we bogged down yesterday."

She remembered the Tusaine ambassador's remarks. "Fishing rights?"

"That, and something else. We were told Ozorne wants Kaddar to marry Kalasin in the spring and bring her here to live. No marriage agreement means no treaty, in spite of the fact that he never mentioned a wedding when he and the king arranged these talks."

Daine's jaw dropped. "But she's only *ten*. Queen Thayet won't hear of a marriage being set up till she's thirteen or fourteen!"

"I think the emperor knows that, Daine." The woman looked tired, and older than she had when they landed. "Look. Perhaps I'm being an alarmist, but—he showed us that fleet for a reason, and he's pressing this marriage for a reason. Be *extra* careful, understand? Watch your step. We may have to leave in a hurry. Our permits to be here are good only so long as he says they are."

She explained everything to Zek and Kitten as she fed them and got ready to go. On their way to meet Kaddar in the guest courtyard, she peered into Numair's room, hoping for a word with him. Although the door was open, black fire sparkled in the entrance. She could just see him through it, stretched out on the bed with a book in front of his nose. Zek touched the fire and squeaked, yanking his paw back.

Did that hurt? Daine asked.

No. It was only strange. I don't think he wants to talk to anyone, though.

No, probably not, she agreed.

They walked on, emerging into the morning sun in a yard where the guests who rode came and went. Awaiting them was Kaddar, holding the reins of a pair of horses.

They raced to the ferry landing, then crossed the broad river to Carthak City. Zek burrowed into Daine's shirt once they boarded the ferry so that he wouldn't have to look at the river that had nearly killed him. Kitten, sitting up in Daine's saddlebag, observed with interest every sight that met her eyes.

At the top of the far bank the capital stretched before them, avenues beckoning. To their left stood a walled enclosure: the famed imperial university. Humans, afoot or mounted, passed through the gates in a stream.

Once inside, they followed a paved avenue lined by handsome buildings set on groomed lawns. Around her Daine saw every human color in the world, from the blue-black of southern tribespeople to the pale skins of the far north. Most wore over-robes of the same loose cut as those worn by the mages, in a variety of colors. White robes, explained Kaddar, plain or with colored trim, meant a novice in any program of study. Wide bands of color at cuffs and hem meant the wearer was a journeyman in his course of study. Solid-colored robes indicated mastery; trim on a solid-colored robe meant advanced mastery. Daine simply enjoyed the human scenery as they rode down the avenue.

"That's it," Kaddar said, pointing to the large five-tiered building that straddled the avenue. Tall, graceful columns painted a deep blue were arranged across the front of the ground floor, their bases and capitals gilded and bright in the sun. "Lindhall's study and workrooms are there."

Hostlers took Kaddar's mare, Westwind, and Daine's gelding. Something about them was strange, Daine realized, and about the gardeners who trimmed the grass and bushes along the avenue. Stretching her legs, she puzzled out what it was: all of them had hair. "Kaddar, aren't there any slaves here?"

"None inside the university complex. The academics won't allow it. Too many northerners teach here, and they aren't comfortable with slaves."

"I can't imagine why," Daine muttered.

"What is that supposed to mean? Are *you* uncomfortable with slavery?"

"Yes."

"It's the first time you've mentioned it."

The girl shrugged. "Ma always taught me that when you're visiting someone else's house, you shouldn't be carping about the way they clean. Besides, we're supposed to be on our best behavior here. The peace between us is more important—that's what Duke Gareth said." Thinking of those warships the night before, Daine shivered. To a girl whose family had been murdered by raiders, those ships were a bloody promise. She would do anything to prevent its unfolding.

Kaddar picked up Kitten and led the way to doors behind the blue pillars. "And what *do* you think of slavery? Don't worry—I won't repeat it." To Kitten he said, "And no one's listening, right?" The dragon nodded vigorously.

"It makes me think of cages," replied Daine. "And cages make me feel like I can't breathe."

Me, too, said Zek, peering up at her. They put us in a cage. Then they took my family away.

"I know," she whispered, stroking his fur. "He reminded me that he was a captive," she explained to the prince.

He looked at them. "I thought it must be wonderful, to be linked to animals the way you are, but it isn't always, is it? I have a bad enough time just knowing human sadness, let alone the sorrows of every other living creature." He shifted Kitten's weight to his hip, so that he could carry her one-armed. "You aren't anything like what I expected."

He led her into a huge, high-ceilinged room where plants grew and fountains played. Daine stopped, awed by the great mosaics that lined the walls. Kaddar followed her, still carrying the dragon, as she went to inspect each one. Mosaics were a Carthaki specialty, but these were splendid even by their standards. Each panel, ten feet by ten feet, depicted a craft or branch of learning. One showed Carthak's famous dyes: a woman dipped cloth into a vat to turn it a rainbow of colors. One panel was dedicated to mages: a red-robed man was halfway transformed from human to horse, a yellow-robed woman had plants growing from outstretched palms, and behind them a black-robed figure, back to the viewer, opened a fiery portal in a nighttime sky. Other panels were dedicated to astronomy and engineering, as well as to glassmaking, weaving, and metalworking. The picture Daine liked the least was of a soldier in the scarlet tunic and gold armor of the Red Legion, standing with one foot on the back of a fallen black man who reached vainly for a spear. To his left, a brown woman in green brocade lifted her hands, pleading; to his right, a pale woman in the tall headdress and tiered gown of Ekallatum pushed forward two naked children, a boy and a girl, in chains.

"Our glorious heritage." Kaddar's voice was very soft; his lips barely moved. "The splendid empire. We loot our conquests until they can no longer feed themselves. Then we take the money from what food and goods they buy to pay for wars to acquire more conquests."

She stared up at him, astonished.

He noticed, and smiled crookedly. "It's true. What's the matter?"

"You're not exactly what *I* expected, either," she said frankly.

"And what did you expect?"

She brushed Zek's mane with her fingers as she considered her reply. "Someone who enjoyed being imperial more. What did you expect of me?"

He grinned and tweaked her nose. "Someone who ate with her fingers."

"There you are!" Lindhall approached, hands out in welcome, open robe flapping behind him. "I am late—forgive me. I just found a reference to ichneumenons, and I was trying to locate its source. Come! I think perhaps the *Analects of Utuhegal the Blasphemer*, or perhaps it was Thorald Moonaxe . . ."

Kaddar rolled his eyes at Daine as they followed their host down a long corridor.

"I do *not* eat with my fingers," she whispered, trying not to smile.

"The improvement in the emperor's birds is astonishing," Lindhall told Daine over one shoulder. "It's impossible to tell if they were ever ill. He is very pleased with your work. Don't be surprised if he invites you to remain, and even offers you a bribe to do so."

"There's nothing he has that I want," Daine said. "I was just glad to help the birds."

"Which is as it should be," the mage said with approval. "Is she heavy?" he asked, looking at the prince and Kitten. "Could I hold her?"

"Kit?" Daine asked, and the dragon nodded. Kaddar gave her to Lindhall, who looked startled. "She hasn't the weight I would expect of a creature of her mass."

"Dragons are hollow-boned, like birds," the girl explained. "Numair found a scroll that told all about dragons from when they lived in the mortal realms."

"*The Draconian Codex*," Lindhall and Kaddar said together, and smiled at each other.

Making several turns down long corridors, they finally reached their destination, a door with a brass nameplate bearing the words: *Master Lindhall Reed—Plants, Animal Behavior and Habits*.

"Let me in, dolt," Lindhall said, and the door opened.

"That's how he talks to the key spell," explained Kaddar.

"I almost feel as if there is a sprite at work, not a spell." Lindhall placed Kitten on the floor and dumped his robe next to her. "A small, not very clever, *spiteful* one." The robe glided through the air to drape itself over a hook on the wall. That spell Daine had seen before, in Numair's tower.

"What about your assistant?" she inquired, greeting a very large turtle who seemed to have full run of the room. He was pleasant enough to Daine, but tried his best to take a bite of Kitten, who screeched at him. Zek, mistrustful of anything that tried to bite, climbed to the top of Daine's head and clung there.

"Out on fieldwork for the day." Lindhall glared at the still-open door. "Close up," he said crossly. "I don't want any visitors until further notice." Meekly the door obeyed. To the turtle he added, "And that will be enough out of you, Master Sunstone." Picking up the great reptile, who was pursuing Kitten's tail, he carried him across the room to a door beside a cluttered desk. He opened it and put the big reptile inside. Daine, watching, noticed something in there that looked uncomfortably like a human form on a bier, covered with a dark cloth.

Lindhall shut the door before she could get a better look. "What do you think?" he asked, waving a hand to include their surroundings.

Daine put the odd shape out of her mind and looked around. Along the walls were small kingdoms in huge glass tanks. Some were landscapes with plants, streams, and enough room for small animals to live comfortably. One tank was set up like a pond, with underwater greenery and rocks to feed and shelter the fish and frogs who lived there.

"I inherited the pond from my master. The rest I made, with help. That is the advantage of a university: someone is always there to help create things, just to see if it can be done. Mages helped glassmakers with the tanks, or we never could have made them so large and so clear. I try to keep the environments as much like the animals' true homes as possible." Lindhall watched as she examined a tank that housed a trio of large green lizards, whose comblike crests ran the length of their spines. "They are iguanas, from the Copper Isles. Are they happy? Do they need anything? I think I would know if they were pining, but I can't ask them, and I don't wish to be cruel."

Daine held up a hand, laughing. "Master Lindhall, if you'll wait a moment, I'll ask!" Well, sun-brothers? she inquired silently. Are you happy in there?

They rushed to the glass. Lindhall reached in and lifted them out, to Zek's dismay.

"They like you," Daine said, listening to the iguanas. "Their only complaint is that it gets close in the tank, but since you let them out all the time, they don't really mind. No, the turtle isn't here right now," she told the lizards, who had asked. As Kitten and the iguanas sniffed each other, Daine walked around, talking to the inhabitants of the other tanks. They had only good to say of Lindhall. Most didn't even know they were confined.

Kitten's voice called her away from these small kingdoms. The dragon stood before an empty corner expressing indignation as only she could, with a series of bone-piercing whistles. Before Daine could warn whoever was using the invisibility spell, the air shimmered, and Numair appeared.

# SEVEN

# WAKING DREAMS

ᴑᴑ "You *had* to inform everyone," the mage scolded the dragon, scowling. Kitten nibbled on his breeches. He sighed and scratched the top of her head.

"But—I saw you, in your room," Daine protested, feeling decidedly odd.

"It was a simulacrum. I'm expressly forbidden to leave the palace."

"What if one of their mages came around, looking for you? What if the emperor spies on you?"

"I embodied it with sufficient amounts of my Gift to deceive anybody. Should someone try to disturb the copy, it will enclose the room completely, so no one will enter until I am back inside."

"And if you're caught?" she demanded. "He'd love to catch you breaking the rules!"

"Daine, we had to talk." The voice, surprisingly, was Kaddar's. "There's no other way we can do it without being spied on."

Daine faced him and Lindhall. They watched her, not her teacher. "You knew he'd be here this morning. That's why you brought me."

"I also wanted you to see *my* friends." The kindness in Lindhall's voice broke through her anger. She knew him well enough by now to realize that he was telling the truth. "You are more than welcome here in your own right, my dear."

She smiled at him reluctantly, and nodded. To Numair she said, "You *could* have trusted me."

He took her hands in his. "I *do* trust you, magelet. I simply didn't wish to discuss it under Ozorne's roof. You aren't particularly adept at concealing your state of mind. You would have been visibly apprehensive if I had left with you and His Highness, whether I was invisible or not."

Since there was no answer she could make to that, she scowled. "How *did* you get here?"

"Hawk shape. And now, we've little time and much to discuss. Would you mind looking at the aviary for a while? Or would you rather be privy to our discussions?"

"I'll go look at birds," she said hastily. "I'm that tired of secrets. Kit? Stay or go?"

Kitten, who loved secrets, shook her head and sat. The iguanas promptly began to climb on her.

Lindhall opened another door, different from the room with the turtle. Daine entered a large, sunny area with a ceiling that was half glass panes, and closed the door behind her. Under the glass and behind a silken barrier net was an aviary. It was different from Ozorne's: the plants were northern, not tropical. On the trees the leaves had turned color and were falling. Something in the room produced a faint chill, like the kind she'd feel at home at this time of year. The air was drier, and the birds who inhabited the aviary were northerners: lapwings, turtledoves, crested larks, nightingales, song thrushes, and green and gold finches.

"Here's a man who wants to go home," she said to herself, looking at the birds. "Of all the pretty southern birds he could have, he picks you. I like his taste."

The birds flocked to the netting to peer at her and talk. She chatted with them for some time, listening to them gossip about their neighbors and Lindhall. Like the inhabitants of the glass kingdoms next door, these birds had nothing but good to say of the mage.

Once each bird had been greeted, she looked at the counter on the far side of the room. Writing materials were scattered over its length, and a number of animal skeletons stood on it, posed as they would have been in life. She also found a large slab of limestone. Embedded in it was an incomplete skeleton, that of a small animal with only three extremely long, birdlike toes to a leg, and a lizard's bony tail. Its skull was odd compared to those of the birds she knew, but its end formed a beak. Most interesting, in the chipped-away stone around it, she saw outlines of what looked like feathered wings. Missing were the lower ribs on the right, part of the spine, the right femur, and the end of the tail. A label on the front of the shallow box that contained the limestone read, Lizard-bird, found in the Jalban Quarry, Zallara.

"Have you ever seen a bird like this, Zek?" she asked.

No, replied the marmoset. Never.

After the Hall of Bones, she wasn't about to touch the complete skeletons. On the other hand, surely there was nothing wrong with touching a collection of bones embedded in rock, particularly if parts of the entire skeleton were missing. Gingerly, she touched a thin claw with her finger.

The flash burned into her eyes. Blinking to clear her vision, Daine heard the last thing she wanted to hear in the world: the sound of crumbling rock. First to come free was the skull, followed by the heronlike neck. Next came the overlong arm bones, spine, and bits of ribcage. Pieces moved as if connected, even when they weren't. Outlying chunks of bone jumped from the rock and gathered around the main skeleton as the hipbones separated from their tomb.

Look! said Zek, squeaking in excitement. If there's any missing, the bones leave room for it!

"Wonderful," she whispered. She didn't share his enthusiasm: it made *her* queasy to look at those absent—or invisible—chunks.

The legs yanked themselves free. The skeleton tried to stand and was brought up short, its tail still embedded in limestone. It looked back over its rump to see what the holdup was. The beak opened in a soundless cry that revealed small teeth. It switched its hips, freeing its tail. At liberty, the lizard-bird extended its arms, then its legs, having a good stretch after a long nap.

Daine sat on a nearby stool, hard. Zek, who couldn't understand why she was not pleased, jumped from her shoulder to the countertop, skidding until he turned and brought himself around. The skeleton was about the size of a crow. It turned to peer at Zek, crouching to get a better look.

"With eyes that aren't there," Daine said, and giggled helplessly. Both the skeleton and Zek looked at her reproachfully. "Sorry."

"Mithros bless, I didn't know you had the magical assemblage spell!" cried Lindhall. Numair and Kaddar, behind him, only stared.

As if I weren't having enough fun yet, thought Daine.

"It doesn't seem to matter if pieces are missing." Lindhall walked to the counter for a closer look at the creature. "But that's why I didn't use the assemblage spell on my own. It doesn't work if the skeleton is incomplete."

If it knew it was incomplete, the lizard-bird didn't act it. Looking around, it stretched, wagged its arms clumsily, then leaped off the counter. All four humans lunged to catch it, but the skeleton had other ideas. It flew up, bony arms flapping awkwardly, as if it still wore the feathers that had left their imprints in its rock tomb.

"But there aren't any birds with claws in their arms!" Daine protested as the skeleton swooped and turned around the light-globe over-head. "And its bones are solid, not hollow like a bird's. Bats have sort-of fingers, but those are genuine clawed toes, not like a bat's wing."

"It was no bat. It is a link, between the dinosaurs in the Hall of Bones and animals—birds—alive now," Lindhall explained without tak-ing his eyes from the flier. "The seers who look back in time have seen lizard-birds in the same era as the largest snake-necked dinosaurs and the lesser tyrant lizards. They have followed the lizard-birds develop-ment, and it is true—it comes from the land walkers."

"Instead of scales, feathers," said Numair, as interested as Lindhall. "Also a bird's wishbone and a bird's gripping foot. But it has abdominal ribs, as reptiles do, and a flexible tail."

The skeleton, tired of exercising invisible wings, settled on Lin-dhall's shoulder. Kaddar leaned in to inspect the empty spaces in the bones, and nearly got pecked. "Stop that," Lindhall ordered, stroking the creature's beak. "He was only looking."

"This isn't the assemblage spell," the prince said, looking at Daine. "I've never seen anything like this in my life. What did you do to it?"

Kitten, who had followed the men, squeaked a reproach at Kaddar's tone. The iguanas came in from the other room, prepared to defend Daine.

"I can't—I'm not—" Daine stammered.

She looked at Numair, who was rubbing one temple. "I think you must explain," he told her.

"These rooms are warded," Kaddar said. "That's how I could talk with Master Numair safely."

"What's in place here is unlike normal warding spells," added Lin-dhall, leaning against the counter. The lizard-bird on his shoulder ran his beak through the mage's fine, gray-gold hair, grooming him. "The emperor must never suspect these rooms *are* warded, or he would come to discover what I have that's worth concealment. If he or his servant mages try to eavesdrop in these rooms, they will hear only dull, innocent conversations and noises made by my animals."

Daine whistled. After two years with Numair, she had an idea how complex a spell-weave like that would be. "It's a new thing that's hap-pened," she told Lindhall and Kaddar. "I'm not sure of the details . . . Numair, what should I say?"

"All that you told me yesterday," was the quiet reply.

She obeyed. When she finished, no one said anything. Waiting for *one* of them to speak, Daine went to talk to the aviary birds. They wanted reassurance that the bone thing was not going to get into their home. Daine soothed them until they returned to their normal pursuits.

The first to speak was Lindhall. "You mean it isn't permanent?" The skeleton, bony tail hooked around the mage's neck, was gnawing his shirt buttons. "He'll stop being alive?"

Daine nodded. "I'm sorry, but it does seem to run out, after a time." She wanted to add that she wasn't sure if the vulture *had* run down, since the old woman had taken him, but thought the better of it at the last minute. She didn't want to start coughing again.

"You should try this in the Hall of Bones," the older man remarked, turning the skeleton's head from a necklace he wore under his shirt. "Stop that. If you bite it, you'll hurt yourself. Although I suppose it would be a bit inconvenient if any of the dinosaurs were to walk away."

Kaddar made a face at Daine, who giggled. "*Inconvenient* puts it mildly," the prince drawled. "But Daine's right to keep this secret. I hate to think what my uncle would do with someone who has such power. Can you imagine? An army of dead creatures that can't be hurt by normal means?"

Daine thought of the great fused lizards, with their plates and spikes of bone, and shivered. One of them would do serious harm in a small village.

"It would be precisely to his taste," agreed Numair. "He might decide such power is worth a war in Tortall, perhaps even all the Eastern Lands."

"Well, while he's with us, I am going to call this one Bonedancer," Lindhall declared, stroking the lizard-bird's skull. "There's one thing I find troublesome about all this, however. Numair is right—wild magic does not function this way, as far as we can determine. What *is* the provenance of this power? Even the Black God is unable to give a semblance of life to the dead."

"Mynoss—?" suggested Kaddar. "No. He judges only."

"In *The Ekallatum Book of Tombs* it's said the Queen of Chaos once raised an army of the dead," murmured Numair.

"But the *Scrolls of Qawe Icemage* refute it," Lindhall replied. "According to him, the Queen of Chaos assembled dead wood and stones to be her army. No, the only god, I believe, who can resurrect that which was once flesh and is now dead is the Graveyard Hag."

"That's right," Kaddar said. "Remember? There are legends of bonedancers—the resurrected dead—from the fall of the Ikhiyan dynasty, and the end of the Omanat priest-kings—" He stopped, realizing what he was telling them, and the men looked at each other.

Daine's throat locked as if a bony hand gripped it.—*Don't even think of it, dearie*—a voice advised insider her head.—*It doesn't suit me that these handsome friends of yours should know I'm about. My,*

*they're a tall set, aren't they? Not a one of them under six feet. I like
these big fellows. Make a girl feel sheltered and fragile, that's what I
always say.—*

You're as fragile as *granite*, thought the furious Daine.

*—Of course,—*was the amused reply.—*I'm a goddess after all. But
it's nice to feel as if I might be fragile, old and rickety as I am. Now,
remember, I'm keeping an ear on you, so don't try to warn them. If you
force me to silence you fast, I might hurt you.—*

The hand on her throat squeezed, and Daine gasped, fighting for
air. When her knees buckled, Numair caught her and held her to a seat.
"Are you all right?" he asked, dark eyes worried. "Bringing things to
life tires you, doesn't it?"

She nodded. Kaddar went into the other room and returned with a
pitcher and a cup, which he filled and handed to her. Daine sipped. It
was water, freshened with a leaf of mint.

"We have to be careful talking about the Graveyard Hag," he said,
gently teasing. "Yesterday she had a coughing fit in the Hag's temple.
It didn't let up until we were outside."

Lindhall frowned, troubled. "Should you have visited her temple?"

"We visited them *all*," said Kaddar.

"It's my fault," Daine said, voice hoarse. "I wanted to look at them."

"Uncle can't fault me for doing it when he told me to take her
wherever she wanted."

"No, of course not." Lindhall still looked uneasy. Clearly shaking
it off, he said, "Numair, I think you must be getting back—it's almost
noon. And what will you young people do? I could have lunch brought
to us and then show you around a bit."

Daine smiled at the fair-haired man. "I'd like that, if it's all right
with Kaddar. I can get to know *your* friends better."

Lindhall smiled as the lizard-bird preened feathers that were long
gone. Numair took a deep breath and began to shape-change. Only when
he was completely a hawk, oversized and black, did Lindhall open a
door so that he could fly into a garden, and away.

That night, Varice shifted the banquet to a series of broad, shallow
terraces overlooking an ornamental lake. Daine and the prince were
dinner partners once more, seated at the end of the main group. Harailt
was on Daine's other side. When the opening course was served, he
amused himself by slipping tidbits to Kitten as he filled the two younger
people in on the uneasy progress of the talks.

The emperor hadn't even made an appearance at the talks that day.
Duke Etiakret, head of the Carthaki negotiators, walked out after Duke

Gareth said King Jonathan and Queen Thayet would not agree to buy silk, dyes, and glass from no one but Carthak. Etiakret returned, only to say that Carthak refused to surrender one of its lords, a pirate who often raided Tortall, to northern justice.

When Harailt turned to the woman seated on his other side, Daine told Kaddar, "It doesn't look at all good, does it?"

"Do you see *any* happy faces around here?" he asked, indicating to the servers that they would have the catfish.

Daine shook her head. "Nary a one." She leaned back and reshaped her ears, knowing the growing shadows would hide the change from most. Scraps of talk came to her and faded as she twitched them to and fro.

"—am *not* going to let those things ruin his party, Numair. His Imperial Highness was simply in a mood. Etiakret will come to your people tomorrow, all smiles and conciliation—just you watch. Try the dormice, won't you? They're rolled in honey and poppy seeds—"

Daine winced—in her view dormice were food for owls, cats, and snakes—and listened elsewhere.

"—the result of a misunderstanding on my part, my dear Lord Martin. The emperor has taken me sternly to task and, I assure you, the progress of the talks in the morning will be far different—"

"—to honor her for her service to our treasured pets, Duke Gareth. Surely your rules will not ask a penniless child to turn down a title and property of her own."

Daine made a face. She wanted no lands or title from the Emperor Mage! With a sigh she returned her ears to their normal shape and concentrated on the meal and her companions. As the sky darkened, they nibbled fried pockets of noodles and pork in a sweet sauce and talked about Kaddar's mother and sisters. Kitten, thinking herself unobserved, gobbled boar's tail with hot sauce, then had to leap for the water pitcher.

"Does she ever get sick from eating human food?" Kaddar watched as the dragon managed to dump half the water down her throat and half all over herself.

Daine smiled. "She never gets sick from *anything*. Once she ate a box of myrrh. She was only three months old. I thought every little accident she had would harm her for life."

"She didn't get sick?"

"She burped smoke for a week, that's all."

"I should have a stomach like hers. Especially these days." Kaddar's eyes flicked to where Ozorne sat, fanning himself idly.

"Come back with us," she said impulsively. "Make a *real* life, one with no cages in it."

His smile was both sad and bitter. "I cannot. He's got my family, my friends, even my horse. Do you think he would stop at hurting them to bring me home?" He patted her hand. "No. Once he claims something, he never, *ever* lets go. It's a miracle your Master Salmalín has managed to remain free and unharmed all this time."

Daine, knowing that Numair had worked as a street magician and nearly starved during his first years in Tortall, shook her head. Not daring to use his Gift out of fear that Ozorne would learn of it and hunt him down, changing his appearance and name, moving often before he made friends who brought him to the king's attention—to her that said he'd paid a high price for his miracle of survival.

Dishes came and went until the meal was over at last. By then the light-globes were burning, and musicians tuned their instruments at the far end of the terrace. Slaves arrived pushing a large metal cart slowly down the line of tables. It bore an immense cake, the pinnacle of a pastry cook's art, shaped like the imperial palace down to each bay, ell, and tower. Looking at it, Daine now saw that the palace was built like a rising sun, a large half circle with wings like short and long rays.

"The cooks made each piece and all the spun sugar, cream decorations, and so on," explained Kaddar, "but it's Varice who designs the cake and puts it together and supervises the decorating. Without her magic they couldn't do anything so fancy."

The guests applauded; Daine, reluctantly, clapped as well. Varice looked proud of herself as she offered the pastry knife to the emperor. Ozorne smiled and indicated that she should do the cutting.

As the blonde turned to the cake, Daine realized that something was wrong with Kitten. The little dragon was clawing at her muzzle and rocking back and forth. Bending close, Daine could hear her squeak, as if she were trying to talk with her jaws glued shut.

"Kit, what's the matter?" She bent down to grab the dragon's forepaws. "You're—"

Varice's shriek raised echoes on the lake. A slave filling Gareth the Younger's glass dropped his pitcher; it shattered on the flagstones. Daine jerked upright.

Rats—mostly browns, with a smattering of black ones—poured out of a hole in the front of the cake in a stream, their numbers far greater than even this cake would hold. They tried to climb Varice's skirts as the blonde continued to scream. Alanna was on her feet, groping for a sword she didn't wear; the mages were helpless, unable to throw fire at the animals without hurting Varice.

"Stop!" Daine cried, running out from behind her table. The rats turned to stare at her. "I said, *stop!*" Opening herself up, she let her power flood out until it swamped them. In their minds she read the knowledge that they were passing through a magical gate from their riverbank homes into the center of the confection. She also saw clearly the image of the Graveyard Hag in their thoughts, pointing them to the gate with her gnarled walking stick.

"Imperial Majesty!" someone cried, shaking Daine's concentration. The moment she faltered, the rats broke free. Six of them launched at her face; she slammed them with her power, killing three instantly. Two fled; one fastened his teeth in her sleeve. Coldly Daine shook him off.

The man who'd broken her concentration was still yelling. "Majesty, even you can't continue to ignore the portents! You must—"

Ozorne pointed; emerald fire lashed to wrap around the speaker, a Carthaki nobleman. Emerald flames leaped from his skin. He had time for one agonized shriek before the fire ate him up.

Daine took a breath and renewed her magical grip on the rats, yanking them back from tables and guests. They fought hard. She dug her nails into her palms, hunting for something to make her furious. She found it when she saw the ruin that had come to the cake Varice had worked so hard to create. Gathering up the anger she felt on the part of Varice, she turned it on the rats.

We don't have to obey you, snarled a brown. We don't owe you anything!

We serve a powerful mistress, added someone else. Next to *her*, you are only a shadow!

She bore down, producing shrieks of rage and pain from them. "Back into that cake, buckos," she ordered, eyes glittering. "Back where you came from. Do it *now*, before you *really* vex me."

They struggled wildly, but she had them. When she began to tighten the pressure, she felt their surrender like the buckling of a wall. She called silently, Tell your mistress, if she has a bone to pick with Ozorne, pick it with *him*, not with them that have to obey him!

The rats leaped onto the cart and into the cake, vanishing through the gate. When the last of them had gone, the pastry collapsed.

She looked around. Slaves propped up a fainting Varice. Numair climbed over his table. Giving his wakeflower vial to Harailt and pointing to Varice, he came over to Daine. "Are you all right?" He cupped her cheek in one large hand, eyes worried. "One of them bit you—"

She held up her arm to show him the rip in her sleeve and smiled. "Didn't even nick the skin. It was only *rats*, Numair."

He looked at the chaos around them. Slaves who had fled the rodents stayed in the shadows, afraid to come out. Duke Gareth and Duke Etiakret were debating hotly in whispers, as Gareth the Younger looked on. Harailt was pulling the wakeflower from under Varice's nose as she coughed and gasped. Alanna talked softly into Kaddar's ear; she had to stand on tiptoe to do it, and Kaddar had to stoop a little.

"We need to get out of here before the sky starts raining blood or something equally pleasant," Numair remarked "Where's Ozorne?"

The emperor had left.

The banquet was over. Varice, hysterical after she roused from her faint, was only able to cling to Numair and cry. All the guests, Carthaki and foreign alike, talked of the ominous signs they had seen and heard of in tense, lowered voices. No one seemed to care if the emperor spied on them or not.

Daine and Kaddar watched, quickly getting bored. "It's not as if we can *do* anything about all this," complained the girl, cradling a dozing Zek. "I get the feeling the only ones who can do something are your uncle and his ministers."

"Would you like to go for a walk, then?" Kaddar asked. "Is there anything you'd like to do?"

Daine looked around. On the far side of the lake, behind the willows on its shore, she could sense the menagerie. "Can we go look at the animals again?"

"Let me ask." The prince went to talk briefly with Alanna, who came back with him.

"I don't blame you for wanting to go someplace else," the Lioness said with a glare at Varice. "Just don't be gone too late. Tomorrow is another day—provided it comes, of course."

Daine stared at the Champion. "Do you know something we don't?"

Alanna shook her head. "Only that I didn't reach my station by ignoring the gods. If his imperial majesty doesn't consult them—soon—he will wish he had. Now scat, before *I* start crying."

They scatted, passing a squad of guardsmen on their way around the lake. Kaddar slowed and stared at them after they passed, his mouth tight. Then he shook his head, and they walked on. On reaching the menagerie, he left her at the closed, locked gate. When he returned, he bore a huge key ring. Sorting through the keys, he read their tags by the mage-light he cast over their heads.

"What kind of Gift do you have?" Daine asked. "Nobody ever said what you can do."

"Very little." He chose a key and fitted it in the lock. "Call light, move things a short way, call fire." The gate swung open. "What I do best is grow things. Trees, flowers, vegetables. I like to garden. The plants Lindhall has for his creatures—I grew those." He closed the gate behind them.

"That's wonderful," Daine replied, opening herself to the captive animals. "A shame you're stuck being a prince when you can do something important. Do those keys open the cages and enclosures? I want to go inside."

Startled, he yelped, "You want to—" Remembering where they were, he finished in a rough whisper, "—what? Go *in*? Out of the question. Absolutely out—"

"Don't be missish, Kaddar," she replied flatly. "If you don't let me in proper, I'll ask Kitten to do it, and maybe she'll melt the locks off."

Kaddar looked at the first enclosure, the lions'. "You swear you won't be harmed?"

"Goddess strike me if I lie," she said, holding up her right hand.

Shaking his head, Kaddar went to a door set into the wall next to the lions' pit, looking for the right key.

Zek watched, fascinated. These keys things—do they always open cages and doors?

"One of them is just called a key," replied Daine. Kaddar glanced at her. "Zek's asking," she explained. To the marmoset she added, "They open what doors and cages they're made to open. Two-leggers make locks to keep doors shut unless you have the right key. It keeps folk from stealing what's ours. It also helps us keep prisoners."

Then a key is magic, Zek said, gray-green eyes locked on Daine's face. If I'd had *keys,* I could have freed my little ones and my mate. *Next* time, I will have a key.

Daine cuddled him, "No one's ever going to cage you again, Zek; I promise."

Kaddar unlocked the door. Open, it led to a small, dark stairwell that wound downward.

"Lights?" asked the girl.

"Just snap your fingers."

She made a face at him. "I can't snap my fingers, Your Highness."

"You *can't*? Really? But it's easy. You just—"

"I know what you just. I've been trying to for years."

He grinned, teeth flashing against his dark skin. "You don't know how much better that makes me feel. You can outshoot me and talk with animals, but you can't do this." Raising a hand, he snapped his fingers, and small light-globes embedded in the wall flickered on.

"No need to rub it in," grumbled Daine. "Kit, are you coming?"

The dragon went in, but Kaddar hesitated. "Maybe Zek would rather stay with me."

I would, Zek told Daine, nostrils flaring as the scent of big cat rolled up the narrow stair.

Daine handed him to the prince. "Will I need keys down there?" she asked.

"No. The inner doors are held with bolts. They aren't locked."

May I see his keys? asked Zek. When Daine translated, the prince smiled and held the ring up for the marmoset to examine.

Daine followed Kitten down the stairs and opened the door that took them into the lions' pit. The cats were awake. Moving to look at Daine, they caught a whiff of Kitten's alien scent and snarled. "It's all right," Daine assured them, bathing the big animals in reassurance. "She's a friend. I'd think, downwind of those immortals, that you'd be more open-minded."

There was a laugh from above. She looked up and saw Kaddar leaning on the rail. "Is that what upset them?"

She smiled crookedly. "You'd think they never smelled a dragon before," she joked, holding her hands out for the lions to smell.

Entering their minds, she could feel they missed open ranges, even the ones who were bred in captivity, who learned of their true, wild life from the others. That had bothered her from the first, the sadness of their days even in confinement as pleasant as this. She could not turn them loose. Even if she could, they would be hunted down. Now, at least, she could do something for them. Lindhall had given her the idea when he showed her the small worlds he'd fashioned for his friends.

She asked the cats' permission first; they gave it. Starting with those born wild, she used their memories to build a waking dream. From different parts of their minds she drew scents, images, sounds, until she felt as if she'd been transported to a hot, distant land. She gave the dreams shape with the chill of winter rains, air perfumed with dry grass, zebra dung, fresh blood, the grunts and lowing of herds of fat prey. Carefully she sowed the dream in each lion, rooting it firmly in their minds. Now, when they chose, all they had to do was shut their eyes and remember. The dream would awaken; they would be home and free.

With Kitten she climbed back up the stair and went to the chimpanzee enclosure. Kaddar moved away from her as she passed, and looked at her with awe as he unlocked the chimps' prison. One by one, she visited all the menagerie captives. Dream planting wasn't physically hard, but it was time-consuming. Kitten grew bored and joined Kaddar and Zek. The prince, to his credit, never complained about how long this took.

At last she reached the hyena enclosure. All three inhabitants sat at the bottom of the glasslike wall, dark eyes up and watching, rounded ears pricked forward.

"Perhaps you should pass by these," Kaddar suggested.

She stared at him. "Goddess bless—why?"

"They're not like other animals, Daine, They're cowards. If an animal fights them, they run away. They steal kills from lions, cheetahs. They even devour their young."

She scratched her head. For some reason, what he said irritated her. "Steal kills, is it? Doesn't Carthak do the same? Carthak has eaten all her young—Siraj, Ekallatum, Amar, Apal, Zallara, Shusin—even Yamut, all the way to the foot of the Roof of the World." He stiffened up, offended. "Forgive me for speaking so plain, but you *do* make them sound like this country of yours. I'm sorry to be rude when you've been kind to me, but animals, at least, do *every*thing for a good reason—to eat. To survive."

His smile would have gone unnoticed if she hadn't given herself cat eyes to see into the shadows around them. It was sour, but it was a smile. "You just reminded me that hyenas are sacred to our patron goddess. You know—the Graveyard Hag."

"How delightful for them," she replied, also sour. "Will you let me in there or not?"

He shrugged and opened the door that would admit her to the stair down. Once she emerged into their pit, the hyenas surrounded her, sniffing eagerly.

So you came back after all, remarked their leader, the female. I am Teeu. Meet my boys—Aranh is the one with the nicked ear. Iry has more spots than he can use.

Daine smiled, running her hands over powerful shoulders, exploring the muscles under the hyenas' rough and wiry fur. "I'm honored to meet you, all of you."

Too bad you weren't here before, Teeu said, touching Daine's closed eyes with her cold nose. This close, the reek of mush and dead meat made it hard for the girl to breathe. The hungry one was here.

This time he wasn't just hungry; he was scared. It's the best we ever smelled him.

"What hungry one?" she asked, curious.

*The* hungry one, said Teeu, sniffing Daine from top to toe. The one who wants to eat the world. He hates us, but he can't stay away. And tonight he was *sooo* afraid.

"How do you know?"

We smell it, Iry's voice murmured. We can smell him quite well when he stands up there.

May I? Daine asked Teeu. The female let her into her mind, to experience the world as they did. Kaddar was partly right when he spoke of hyena nature. Teeu had killed her twin not long after they were born; it was hyena custom. In some ways they thought like a wolf pack, but their noses were ten times better than even a wolf's. They mapped their landscape with scent as a bat would map it with sound. She breathed with Teeu, and learned. The wind brought a bouquet of odor to the nose, one the hyena sorted through for her. She smelled Kaddar: lavender from his clothes, his own unique personal smell, each food he'd consumed that night. Kitten's scent was completely alien, even to one who lived on the other side of the wall from the immortal's menagerie. Teeu savored it, making sure it would never be forgotten, before she turned to Zek. His odor was musky, touched with hints of the fruit he loved, and mixed with the fear he felt as the hyenas' smell reached *him*.

What about the hungry one? she asked Teeu.

The hyena's memory for scent was as vivid as Daine's for sights. Their "hungry one" smelled of expensive cloth, soaps and hair oils, amber and cinnamon, spicy food and wine. The girl was startled to recognize it, though her memory of that particular odor was far less strong than Teeu's.

Leaving the hyena's mind, she comforted Zek briefly. When he was calm she called up to the prince, "Kaddar? Why is your uncle afraid of the hyenas?"

The prince leaned over the wall to look down at her. "Who told you that?"

Daine rested a hand on Aranh's sloping shoulder. "*They* did. They smell it on him. Kaddar, I swear these creatures can smell *anything*."

Kaddar fingered his eardrop. "Kitten, is there a listening spell on us?" The dragon whistled. The sound produced flares from Kaddar's gems—nothing else. "Thank you. Whenever you wish, you may live with me." Lowering his voice, he told Daine, "When Uncle took the throne a prophecy was made that hyenas would lead his doom to him. If Chioké hadn't reminded him that hyenas are sacred to the Graveyard Hag, he would have killed every one in the empire. Instead, he keeps these. We have a saying about things like that: 'buying off the grave diggers.' " He lifted his head. "What was that?"

She gave her ears bat shape and listened. "There are humans in the immortals' menagerie."

"No one can go there without my uncle's permission." Kaddar examined the keys. "I should check."

"Can't we leave it be?"

"No. Do you know the magic that can be done with griffin's blood or spidren wool? If you want to wait, fine."

She looked at her new friends. "Do you want the waking dream, the one I gave the others?"

Teeu yipped her amusement. We would rather have what is here, she replied. The smells in this place are much more interesting than the ones at home.

She left them, racing up the stairs to the main walk. Kaddar was quietly trying to fit keys into the special menagerie's lock. When she joined him, he was scowling.

"Splendid," he muttered. "The guards have a way in, at the back of the immortals' enclosure, but I don't want to go past them. I'd hoped I'd find a normal lock, one for the cleaning slaves, but there isn't one. This lock is magical and my Gift won't open it. I don't know if the underground tunnels come out this far, either."

She heard voices on the far side of the gate. "Are you sure this is needful?"

"A drop of saliva from a flesh-eating unicorn in a man's food will kill him after three days of intense pain. It's undetectable as a poison unless you know *exactly* what to look for."

Daine sighed. "I suppose that means yes. Kitten? Don't melt it; just open it."

The dragon sniffed the keyhole. Backing up a few steps, she gave a demanding whistle, and the gate swung open. Kaddar strode past Daine. Zek, on his shoulder, leaped into the girl's arms, and she and Kitten followed.

## ⇢ EIGHT ⇠

# THE BADGER RETURNS

Humans were in the courtyard between the cages. Some were the Banjiku she'd met, as well as other tiny black men and women who could only be their kin. The remaining humans were slaves. They were placing offerings—fruit, flowers, incense—before the immortals' cages. Apparently they'd heard nothing outside the gate: they froze in shock when Kaddar reached them.

No one spoke. At last the Stormwing queen unfurled great steel wings, the metal flashing in the light of torches set around the courtyard. "So, girl who slew Zhaneh Bitterclaws." Her voice was dry and stern. "Do you come to taunt my consort and me?" The humans went to their knees, bowing to Kaddar until their foreheads touched stone flags.

"Does *every* one of you know what I look like?" Daine asked the Stormwing.

"Your face is in our minds," was the icy reply. "It is rare that we are bested by one so small, and unGifted." The queen turned dark eyes on the prince. "Have you come to see what you will inherit, mortal? Do you think to master *us*? You mean nothing. These others at least know they are slaves and give me fear because they know nothing else."

Her mate shifted on his perch, sidling to and fro, never taking his eyes from Daine and Kaddar. The female was Barzha Razorwing, Daine remembered, and he was named Hebakh.

"I'm not that different from these slaves," Kaddar said politely. "Perhaps all I know is fear. It seems that way, often enough."

"A pretty reply." The queen spat on the floor of her cage. "That is what I think of it."

"Stormwings," Daine muttered. "Anything they do, they have to be disgusting first."

"How else may we act, mortal?" demanded Hebakh, burning eyes fixed on Daine. "Our nature is what it is, don't you see? Our very immortality makes us immune to change."

"Mortal? No, no!" The protest came from Tano, the Banjiku who had done most of the talking when Daine first met him and his people. "She is a god, or the daughter of a god whose name she does not know. She is no mortal."

"Nonsense," scoffed Barzha.

"Forgive, forgive," said Tano, "but how can Banjiku be wrong about god things? Our tribe was birthed by Lushagui, sister to Kidunka, the world snake, the all-wise. To us it is given to bind men to beast-People, to know gods, and to be slaves."

They must thank their gods every day for that last, Daine thought to Zek, who nodded.

"Nonsense," Barzha repeated. "Look at her. She is a scrawny, underfed, unattractive spawn of mortal get, a killer of Stormwings."

Hebakh bated, then settled down. "There's evidence of the Banjiku gifts, my dear. I recall hearing about it from Lushagui. Girl. You know Rikash Moonsword?" He sidled across the cage to a perch near the bars, where he had a better view of her. "You told him we are here."

"Yes, sir," Daine replied.

"Why? Why tell Rikash anything?" demanded Hebakh. "You hate Stormwings."

Suddenly the griffin gave a shuddering, screaming roar, unfurling her wings as far as the confines of her cage would permit. She took a breath, then roared again, and again.

"We must go," said a slave urgently. "The guards will come any moment to silence her."

"Follow us," Tano instructed Daine and Kaddar, pointing to an open trapdoor. "There are tunnels for slaves to work here. We will guide you away, and no one will be the wiser."

"So the tunnels *do* come out this far," Kaddar muttered.

Daine hesitated, wanting to help the griffin. Reaching with her magic to ask the great creature to be quiet, she felt what was in her mind. The griffin was half crazy from imprisonment. Soothing her would take precious time. She could already hear raised voices behind the door at the rear of the courtyard, the guards' entrance that Kaddar had mentioned.

"Daine, come on!" hissed Kaddar.

Daine, Kitten, and the prince raced to the opening and down the ladder that led from it. Last came Tano, who drew the door shut and threw the bolt. A gnarled finger to his lips, he grabbed a lantern on the floor. Already the others were gone.

They followed their guide down a long, winding corridor for nearly sixty feet, where it branched in three different directions. Each one was marked with pictures in softly glowing paint: a bucket on one, a trio of brooms on another, and a horse's head on the third. That was the one chosen by their guide.

"What were you doing?" Kaddar demanded softly. "You know you aren't supposed to be in that area unless you work there, and even then only during the day."

The old Banjiku replied, "We worship captive gods."

"*Worship*—" sputtered the prince.

Tano stopped and looked up at the tall young man. "Worship," he said firmly. "Someday they will no longer be caged, young master. When they are free, will not their anger be terrible? Better to make offerings now, so the great ones will remember not all men are jailers."

Daine shivered. His words had sounded much like a prophecy.

"They aren't gods," argued Kaddar. Now they passed other stairs out of the tunnel, each marked with a picture. "They can be killed. That means they're not gods."

"No more is your master a god, Nobility," Tano said cheerfully, "but he wants offerings from all. When Black God claims us, who will be punished for giving worship and power to a false god? The prince? Or Banjiku? Now." He stopped by a ladder marked by an image of a flower and a fountain. "Go up here and you will be in garden of guests, where lady stays." He bowed to Daine.

"I'm not a lady," she said, offering her hand. "Just Daine. Thank you, Tano."

He took her hand in his callused ones. "We are friends of the People together."

Kaddar had gone ahead and was holding the trapdoor open. "There's no one about. Come on."

Impulsively, she leaned down and kissed the little man on the cheek, then followed the prince.

They emerged between two hedges. The guest quarters shimmered whitely nearby. Once Kaddar shut the trapdoor behind them, it looked like part of the gravel walk. There was a small birdbath next to it; Daine suspected it was there so the gardeners might find the door again. "Are there tunnels just under the gardens?" she asked. "There are tunnels everywhere under the palace," he replied. "Mostly used by slaves, but others find them handy, too." They fell silent, enjoying the cool evening.

Kaddar moved first, stretching his arms. "We're in trouble, Daine. All Carthak is. See that?" He pointed at the sky.

Daine looked up. Stars spilled everywhere overhead. The moon was a sliver; another night, or two, and it would be full dark. The dark moon, for the working of dark magics, she thought, and shivered. "See what? Stars?"

"You *shouldn't* see them. This time of year, the skies *should* be thick with cloud. Maybe an opening or two, but not clear skies, night after night. We've had very little rain. In the south, people starve while my uncle readies for another war, so he can waste taxes, food, slaves, men . . ." He looked at her and smiled bitterly. "You are too gods-blest easy to talk to, Veralidaine. You watch me with those big eyes, just listening, and the words drop off my wagging tongue." He shook his head and offered an arm. "I'd better escort you to your room. It's getting late."

She rested a palm on his arm and looked away as he led her inside. She wished he hadn't found her easy to talk to. There was nothing she could do to help a Carthaki human friend. He wasn't a mongoose or giraffe. She couldn't give the emperor's heir any waking dreams.

In her dreams, she stood with Kitten and the Graveyard Hag at a cross-roads in the middle of a barren land, and argued. An audience of rats and hyenas looked on. The Graveyard Hag wanted her to go left, into a fenced-in graveyard, where the tombstones leaned at strange angles and human bones poked through the earth. Daine wanted to go right, where she could see dinosaur skeletons embedded in the ground. Kitten, chattering furiously, wanted Daine to go back the way she had come. She slashed at the old woman's legs with a forepaw.

"Enough, dragon," the Graveyard Hag said. "I can't stop your coming here, but I don't need to put up with your impertinence, either. You aren't *near* old enough to do battle with me." She smacked Kitten on the muzzle with her gnarled stick, and the dragon's jaws snapped shut. She pawed at her mouth, but it remained closed.

"You stop doing that to her, and stop pushing me around," Daine told the goddess flatly. "I'm not one of yours, and I'm getting tired of your playing with me and my friends."

The Graveyard Hag grinned, showing all five teeth. "You're a sassy one, dearie," she said with approval. "Well, I always did like a girl who could stand up for herself. But you're being naughty all the same. Come into my little garden here and play."

Hands on hips, Daine shook her head. "By the time you bury two-leggers, they're glad to rest," she retorted. "I don't *want* to play with them. They've earned the right to be let alone. Look at the way you've left them, all higgledy-piggledy like that. I should think you'd have the decency to straighten up around here." Part of her mind knew all this was a dream, but what on earth were they talking about, anyway? It made no sense.

A gnarled hand that had been empty suddenly boasted a silver dice cup. The Hag rattled it, her one good eye twinkling cheerfully at Daine. "Toss you for it."

"No. You cheat. C'mon, Kit." They marched toward the dinosaur bones. At first the going was hard. It took all Daine's might to lift her legs, and she could tell that Kitten was having equal trouble. The girl clutched the heavy silver claw around her throat. It dug into her palm, drawing blood, and suddenly she was moving forward along the barren dirt road.

Then she slowed, frowning. Things were changing, as they did in dreams. The dirt under her bare toes felt like cold marble, polished smooth. The blackened hills and barren trees of the orange-lit world around her were fading, becoming shadows that hinted at great shapes within.

Daine opened her eyes.

She was not in her guest bedroom, with its luxuriant bedclothes and sweet-smelling wood. Though she still wore her nightgown, cold stone under her bare feet was much too real to be a dream, and the draft that flowed against her back made her shiver. Kitten was dragging on the hem of her nightgown, chattering softly with anger and fear.

"Kit?" Daine asked, kneeling to cuddle the dragon. "I'm sorry— did I sleepwalk?" She'd never done so before, but things had been too strange during this journey for her to be much surprised. She changed her eyes to those of a cat, thinking she'd wandered out into the common room, or even the hall.

They were in the Hall of Bones.

"What in the name of the Great Goddess—" she breathed. "How did we get in, without the spell to open the lock? Kit—did you open it?" The dragon shook her head.

Crazy as it seemed, Daine had a very good idea of how they'd gotten here. "When I get hold of her, I will snatch what hair she's got left," she growled. "That's it for toying with *me!*"

Turning to leave the hall, she stumbled and went down. Throwing her hands to catch herself, she struck the thing that had tripped her, the stand for the mountain-runner nest. One hand plunged in among the eggs.

There was a blinding flash, one that etched in lightning both the baby dinosaur standing by the nest and the eggs. She heard a distressed shriek from Kitten, but lacked the strength to tell her dragon that she was fine, just a little tired. She fainted before her body crumpled.

She and Kitten walked a trail that led up a densely forested hill. Suddenly the girl felt better than she had for days. Surrounding her was a northern woods, the air scented with pine, leaves turning color. The day was fading, but even so, everything she looked at seemed extra clear. An owl called; in the distance a wolf sang the first song of the night. All around she heard small woodland creatures prepare to go to bed, or to start their night's foraging.

The peace around them seemed to cow the dragon. Staring at everything, she walked so close that Daine nearly tripped over her several times.

Ahead was a thatched cottage, its white plaster walls gleaming as the night drew down. Light poured from the open door and windows. On the threshold, a man with antlers rooted in his curly hair argued with a badger. She heard them clearly, though she was only halfway up the hill.

"—ask you to keep an eye on her, keep her safe, and you allow my child to be used in *that*!"

"Flatten your fur, Weiryn," replied the badger. "What makes you think I had any choice?"

"The Great Ones can find another instrument! Why didn't you tell them so?"

"I did tell them, you horn-headed idiot. They didn't listen. *She* didn't listen. If you have a complaint, *you* take it up with the Graveyard Hag."

A woman appeared in the doorway behind the horned man, drying her hands on a cloth. She was graceful and solidly built, firelight from indoors gleaming on her pinned-up golden hair. "Weiryn, does the badger want to sup with us? We—" Looking past the man's shoulder, she caught her breath; one hand went to her cheek. Man and badger turned to see what had gotten her attention.

Weiryn pointed at Daine, but it was the badger who spoke. "There! *You* said she would be fine, and here she is. You know what that means! You *never* should have left her there—"

"If you were so interested in fathering, you shouldn't have put her in my care. She's old enough to get into her own tangles, whether you like it or not." The badger sighed. "I'll take them back. Talk to the Great Ones if you want, but I think it's too late. Can't you feel things moving forward?" He trundled down the path toward Daine and Kitten. "This place isn't for you. Turn around—"

"Badger, that's my ma," she protested. "And—my da?"

"Yes, yes; you should listen when the Banjiku tell you things. Turn around."

She obeyed, and fell into a mass of rolling gray clouds.

When she opened her eyes, she was flat on her back.

The badger stood on her chest, claws digging into her shoulders.

—*Idiot kit!*—he snarled.—*You drained your life force for this. You're supposed to use a spark, just a spark, to wake them up!*—

She blinked dazedly at him. "How was I to know that, pray? You didn't tell me anything. You just breathed on me and left."

—*Nonsense. Of course I told you.*—Daine shook her head.—*No?*— The badger climbed off her.—*Then I lost my temper, at being used to place this on you. I should have taken time to explain. It was a grievous mistake, and a disservice to you.*—

Kitten, much vexed, chattered at the badger, punctuating what she had to say with earsplitting whistles.

Daine groaned and covered her ears, while the animal god turned on the immortal.

—*When I wish for your opinions, dragonling, I will ask for them. Silence!*—

Kitten subsided, muttering under her breath.

Daine sat up. "Kitten was there with me," she said, frowning.

—*Of course,*—the badger said—*Dragons go where they will, even the young ones.*—He snorted rudely.—*Pesky, interfering creatures.*— Kitten made an equally rude noise in reply.

Daine heard a rapid clicking, as if something bony ran on the marble tiles. Instantly she checked the mountain-runner nest. Not only was the standing skeleton gone, but the eggs had hatched.

—*That is why it killed you,*—said the badger, peering at the nest.— *You woke them all. What were you thinking of? The energy to spark this waking magic has to come from wild magic. Waking the whole nest drained you. You'd better find a way to draw the spark from other sources. I can't bring you back from the Divine Realms whenever you make a mistake and die.*—

"Die? But—I thought—humans go to the Black God's realms when they die."

—*Humans do. You will have a choice, the Black God's kingdom or the home of your father, when the time comes. You must be careful not—What do you lot want?*—

His question confused Daine, until she noticed the mountain-runner skeletons to her left, the ones from the nest. Seven of them were only a foot tall. The last was the eighteen-inch skeleton. All watched the badger, the tilt of their small skulls giving them an odd look of attentiveness.

"Oh, no," she whispered, and covered her face with her hands. "However do I explain *this*? Badger, I can't be going about waking up dead creatures. I'm no god!"

—*No, but the Graveyard Hag granted you this power to further her own ends,*—he retorted.—*I am sorry, my kit. I was not given a choice.*—

"She can push you around?"

—*In Carthak, which is her own, she can do whatever she pleases. Here she is one of the great gods. In Tortall you would be safe,*—he snarled.—*We would be safe from her: She is only a minor goddess anywhere but the empire. Here, Bright Mithros, the Threefold Goddess, all but the Black God must bow to her; and she is the Black God's daughter. In Carthaki matters be listens to her.*—

"Lovely," Daine grumbled. "The boss god of all Carthak wants to get me in hot water. Next time I get the notion to travel, I'll remember this and stay at home." She sighed and looked at the mountain-runner skeletons. One, braver or more foolish than the rest, had crept forward, and reached out to touch the badger's coat.

—*Don't you dare*—snarlea the badger. The mountain-runner leaped back and tripped on its bony tail. Kitten rushed over to place herself between the downed lizard and the badger, scolding loudly, the color in her scales turning pink.

"Kit, hush! He didn't mean to frighten the little one. Someone will hear; *please* be quiet."

The badger sighed.—*It is time for me to go, and for you to return to your room.*—To Kitten, he said,—*If you do not behave, I will tell your family that Daine is spoiling you, and that they had better take you from her care if they do not wish you to be ruined for life.*—

Kitten shut up with a last cheep.

Daine hid a smile. Looking at the mountain-runners, she said, "But what about them? I cant hide these. And I've no idea of when they'll go back to sleep. The lizard-bird I woke at Master Lindhall's was still up and about when we left."

The badger scratched an ear.—*Most of those you wake will sleep when the Graveyard Hag's need, whatever it is, ends. Only a few will care to stay, when their kind and their world are gone. As for these*—He eyed them. They had crept around Kitten and were stroking his fur with gentle forepaws.—*They will go with me. It is the least I can do. I made a mistake, not helping you to understand what you can now cause.*—

"Badger—do *all* gods make mistakes?"

He glared at her.—*Rarely. I have not made one in ten centuries, so perhaps I was due. Even the greatest gods err now and again. When they do, the results are catastrophic.*—He looked at the dinosaur skeletons looming in the shadows.—*Their world ended through a god's mistake.*—

"Horse Lords," whispered the girl, eyes wide.

The badger looked at the mountain-runners.—*Climb on. And no pulling my fur.*—

The mountain-runners lost no time in obeying. Clustered on the god's broad back, they reminded Daine of nothing so much as children on a boating holiday. "Badger? Does it hurt them to die again? Or if a mage blasted them, say?"

—*How could it hurt flesh that is not there? This awakening you give them is not true life. When they sleep again, they will return to the otherworld that serves the spirits of the People. Now, go back to bed,*—he advised.—*And tell the Banjiku that Lushagui never meant for them to be slaves.*—

Silvery light bloomed. It winked out, and Daine and Kitten were alone.

As they sneaked back to Daine's room, the girl began to yawn. Her body ached as though she had been pummeled. Gently moving Zek from the center of the bed to the side, she got in next to him. Kitten gave a small croak, and the lamps went out. Daine's last thought was of moving her feet to make room for the dragon, and then she slept.

The odd night she'd had didn't cause her to sleep late, but as she cleaned her face and teeth, dressed, and brushed her hair, she felt as if a griffin had landed on her. Kitten roused as she buttoned her shirt and uttered a forlorn cheep.

"No, don't," the girl said, voice gravelly. "One of us ought to rest."

Kitten nodded agreement and went back to sleep. Zek, curled up on Daine's pillow, sat up. You vanished, he said. Kitten got angry and vanished, too. Why didn't you take me?

Daine smiled. "I didn't know I was going anywhere, Zek, or I would have taken you. Remember, I promised you'd be safe from now on. I won't leave you behind. Now, go back to sleep." Ever agreeable, the marmoset obeyed.

Closing her eyes, Daine reached with her magic for the emperor's birds: she wanted to check their progress. The moment she found them, she knew something was wrong. Each appeared in her magical vision as a tiny ball of light. On a handful, shadows dimmed their fire. Some of the birds were falling sick in the same way as they had before.

Leaving a note in the common room, she trotted along the shortcut to the aviary, frowning. In conversation with Lindhall the previous day she had learned he would never change the birds' feed without an excellent reason. He'd also said that the emperor was too good with birds to meddle with their diet when they'd been sick, and she believed him. Then why were they ill again, and how long would it be until the disease spread to the entire flock?

When she reached the door in the glass wall, she saw emerald fire around its edges. Gingerly she touched the knob. If the magic was to foil intruders, it failed: she felt nothing. She went in and closed the door quietly. When she turned away from it, an oval patch of emerald fire hung in the air before her. It rippled; the face of the Emperor Mage appeared. He was bare of all makeup save for the black paint around his eyes, with only a few gilded braids in his casual hairstyle.

"Veralidaine, good morning," he said. "I thought it might be you. Will you come to my table? I'm by the door into the palace."

She scuffled a shoe against the ground, not wanting to say why she was there until she had a better idea of what was wrong. "Could I look at the birds first, please, Your Imperial Majesty? They need me to check them over a bit, now they've had a couple days free of the sickness." To excuse herself the half-lie, she crossed her fingers behind her back, where he couldn't see.

"Far be it for me to come between you and your charges." His smile was sweet, if a bit melancholy. "You will come to see me, though? Once you have spoken with them?"

She didn't want to, but there was no graceful way to refuse. "Yessir."

"Very good." The image faded; the fiery oval collapsed on itself and vanished.

Parrot finches came to lead her up the curved stairs to a pair of stricken birds, red-crested cardinals. They clung side by side to a branch well away from the sun, blinking. She saw no signs of trembling, and their eyes were bright, but she could feel the illness starting to work in their bodies. She gathered the male into her hands.

What have you been into? she asked silently so that the emperor wouldn't hear. What have you been eating or drinking to make you sick again?

The bird looked at her dully. He couldn't remember. He was fine the day before, visiting all his favorite places. And he wasn't sick, precisely. Just a bit off his feed.

She opened her mind to his. The illness showed as black threads running along the bird's nerves, growing toward his spine and brain. Once they reached those, he would know he was sick. She bore down with healing fire, burning out every thready trace.

When he was well, she opened her eyes to find he'd marked her arms and feet with thick white droppings. She frowned. The night she'd first come to the aviary, her mind was too full of the thing she had seen and the work she was doing for the birds' dung to register as anything more than the reason for the loss of a pretty outfit. Now she scooped up a bit and rubbed it in her fingers. It was heavy, almost pastelike. What it should have been was compact, wet, dark, with perhaps a few undigested seed hulls mixed in.

The female red-crested cardinal had the same kind of droppings.

Daine spread her power through the aviary, calling the other three whose new illness she had detected: a green-and-gold tanager, an orange-bellied leafbird, and one of the royal bluebirds, with its impossibly blue wings and tail feathers. All three nested close to the glass wall. All three of them emptied themselves of heavy white droppings as she healed them. She held them away to spare her clothes more damage.

With them taken care of, she summoned the red-crested cardinals back to her. All five of her patients clustered on branches around her at the top-most level of the stair, looking at her curiously. Where do you nest? she asked the cardinals.

The male flew to the tree where he lived, and back. Like the others, he nested by the glass.

Some kind of magic gone awry in the windows? she wondered. Getting her handkerchief, she scrubbed her hands with it as she thought. Glass splinters falling into the nest or the food? she wondered, but that wasn't right. If splinters had caused the damage, the birds' dung would be bloody and black, not white. White paste—why did she think there was something important about white paste?

A picture came to life in her memory, of Numair making paints, using—

Lead compounds, she thought, eyes lighting up. They're getting *lead*! That's what's coming out of their bodies when I heal them! Tell me what you eat here, she ordered.

Red-faced parrot finches had come to watch everything she'd done, fascinated. Now they chorused, Seeds.

What *kind* of seeds? she asked. What do they look like? Show me. All the birds came, to shower her with images of seeds.

Enough! she ordered when they began to repeat themselves. Only seeds, or is there other food?

Fruit, said the tanagers. Figs, grapes, fluffy leaves with plenty of wet in them.

Daine smiled, recognizing the image of lettuce in their minds. What else?

Sometimes green food, said a parrot finch, perching on Daine's shoulder. It's good. It's different. His red face twisted up to hers. *They* had green food, he said, meaning Daine's patients.

So what is it? she asked. What kind of plant?

Not a plant, exactly, the helpful parrot finch said. He gave up trying to see her face from her shoulder and perched on her hand.

Not a plant. Green *seed*? she asked.

No, said the parrot finch. It is green food. Over here.

He fluttered up into the air, and darted at the glass. She was about to warn him not to hit it when he stopped, clinging to a vinelike tendril. It was a decoration on one of the metal strips that held the glass panes there. He pecked at the green enamel surface.

"Goddess bless," she whispered. She reshaped her eyes and face to give herself a hawk's vision, and focused on the metal strips near the parrot finch. With so much extra visual power, she noticed a glossy surface on the enamel that was clear, a layer that had to be lacquer of some kind. Cracks ran through it like fractures in ice, and tiny bits had flaked off, revealing the less-shiny green enamel underneath. Everywhere she looked, the clear surface was pitted. In a number of locations, the damage to the clear lacquer was even greater, and there were pocks in the green material itself. She would know the distinctive marks of beaks and claws anywhere.

Is that what you've been eating? she asked her patients, remembering to do it silently.

It's good, replied the green-and-gold tanager, cocking his head at her. It tastes different. I'm always thirsty after the green food, but I still like it. The others chorused agreement.

Daine put her hands on her hips. Salt in the enamel, she thought with disgust. Only they're eating lead along with it.

She called the birds to her, even those begging tidbits from Ozorne. Now listen to me, she told them when they were quiet. The green food is *killing* you. It's poison. You have to promise me you'll never, *ever* touch it again. As she spoke, she pressed down, reinforcing her words with magic so that they would avoid the stuff forever.

I still have to tell the emperor to have the coatings changed, she thought as she trotted gleefully down the stairs. Or new strips put in, or something.

"I found out what made them sick!" she said when she found him. He was seated in the area with the marble bench, a seed-filled bowl at his side. A table and two chairs had been placed there, and breakfast was already laid out. "The enamel on the metal things that hold up that glass? They're eating it for the salt and taking in lead. If you change the paint, or cover it with something that won't crack or break, they won't get sick again. I've talked to your birds"—they were coming back to him now, perching on his shoulders and on nearby branches as he offered them food from the bowl—"and *they* won't go near it anymore, I made fair sure of that! But you'll have to fix it before any chicks hatch, because doubtless I won't be here to make them leave it be."

He smiled up at her, holding seed-filled palms steady as birds perched and ate. "You have done me a tremendous service, Veralidaine. Will you do me another and take breakfast with me?"

She looked at the table, set with filled crystal goblets, delicate porcelain and silver, then looked down at herself and blushed. "Your Imperial Majesty, I'm a mess. It would hardly be fitting—"

With a gentle movement he dislodged the birds and moved the bowl away so that they could sit on the rim and stuff themselves. He closed a hand and opened it, to reveal a ball of green fire. "We require a washbasin and those things necessary for the cleansing of hands. Also a robe—blue, or lilac, blue-gray—suitable for a young lady who stands as high as our chin." He closed his hand, and the fire was gone. Looking up at Daine, he smiled wistfully. "Please accept. I dislike meals taken alone, and it seems—of late—I am not the most sought-out of companions."

What could she say to that? "Thank you, Your Imperial Majesty."

Three slaves came through an arch partly shielded by greenery. One carried a gold basin that steamed faintly; another soap, a washcloth, and a neatly folded towel on a tray; and a third something lilac and very fine draped over his arm.

"Our rooms open into this aviary," explained Ozorne. She noticed that he'd switched instantly to the imperial *we* on the arrival of the others. "Our birds will not come there—it is too bright and noisy for them—but we enjoy the sound of the aviary fountains at night."

The slave with the basin knelt on one knee before Daine, holding it above his head like an offering. She stepped back, confused.

"Go on," the emperor said. "Wash."

She was supposed to clean her grimy hands this way? With a human washstand?

The slave with the tray set it on one of the chairs. She and her companion proceeded to delicately unbutton Daine's cuffs and roll her sleeves above the elbow. The girl gritted her teeth and did as she was expected to, wetting her hands and scrubbing them. With the best intentions in the world, she couldn't avoid splashing the boy underneath the basin. When she was finished, the slaves dried her hands and helped her into the lilac robe. She winced as it closed around her dung-streaked clothing. The garment, a finely made thing with silver braid and tiny pearls worked around hem, collar, and cuffs, would never be the same.

Once she was covered, the slaves served the food as Daine and the emperor each took a chair. When they were done, Ozorne dismissed them. "I find mutes make the best slaves," he remarked, curling one hand around a crystal goblet. Daine had one just like it before her, filled with something that was the bright red of fresh blood. "They do not chatter. Shall we have a toast, then?"

Daine stared at him, hands tucked into her lap. "A toast, Your Imperial Majesty?"

He raised his goblet. "To birds," he said gravely.

Relief filled her: she had feared he'd want to toast Carthak, or the ruin of Tortall. Don't be silly, she scolded herself as she raised her goblet. He wouldn't try to make me do something bad like that, not when I just helped him.

She sipped the red liquid. It was pomegranate juice, a bit thick and oversweet. She would have preferred to water it down, but the emperor drank all of his straight down. Good manners dictated that she do the same. When the goblet was empty, she drank from another filled with cold water, to rinse the heaviness out of her mouth.

"What do you think of the progress being made in the peace talks?" he asked, delicately cutting a bite of ham. "Have you been kept abreast of what transpires here?"

She fiddled with the napkin she'd put on her lap. "I know it's not going very well."

"No. It was too much to hope for, really, with so much else taking place—all these dark omens. Do you know why the gods are angry?"

The girl shook her head. It was much too hot in here. Sweat was trickling down her temples, and it was a little hard to follow what he was saying. It also didn't seem like the time to mention that she had some idea of the source of the gods' displeasure.

"I let a threat to Carthak exist. A powerful criminal, sheltered by my enemy, Jonathan of Tortall. The gods do not love a ruler who permits a threat to survive. It was made clear to me, the night of the naval review. Zernou himself pointed out my error, and suddenly I understood."

She took a deep breath. It was an effort to draw air in. "He pointed to you," she whispered.

Ozorne's smile was amused and pitying. "Not to me, Veralidaine. To the criminal. To Arram Draper—your teacher, Numair Salmalín. I knew that I was moved to allow his return for a good reason. My hand was guided by the gods themselves." Rising, he came to her side of the table and lifted one of her arms, placing his fingertips over her pulse. She tried to yank away, but all she could think of was Numair.

"You cannot fight dreamrose," Ozorne remarked. "It's a cousin of wakeflower, and very strong. A spear dipped in it will drop a charging elephant. Frankly, I am amazed you are still awake."

"You—can't hurt us." She fought hard to say it. "Ambassadors. Sacred—"

"I will hurt no one, my dear." He placed her arm in her lap again and brought his chair close, sitting where he could watch her face. "You will run away and vanish into the kingdom. I will be furious. For all I know, you are among criminals in the underground, urging them to rebel against me. Your friends will be forced to leave immediately, under guard. Even Tortall's allies will be able to see that these talks failed due to *you*, not to me. I will have my Tortallan war, and no one will stop me.

"Better, I know that he loves you—the traitor Salmalín. That I could see when he came here seeking you, and the night Zernou pointed him out to me—the night the traitor warned my heir not to trifle with you. Since we will go to war in any case, Salmalín will return for you, and I will have him." There was nothing in his voice, or eyes, but kind interest. "This will turn out for the best. I *like* you, Veralidaine. The way you have with my darlings—" He shook his head admiringly. "You will have a title—countess, perhaps? Even duchess. You will have your own estates, your own slaves, whatever you wish. You will even have the dragon, too. It will be necessary to keep her under the sleep until you are well settled here, but once you are, she will be content as long as *you* are content. I will not risk waking her until I am certain she will not turn on me.

Sleep was wrapping around her like a cloud-filled blanket. "Numair . . ."

Ozorne stood. "He dies, my dear. The gods demand a blood sacrifice, and so do I."

# DAINE LOSES HER TEMPER

**ၑၓ** She had the oddest dream. She was Zek, and the world was *huge*. Kitten, who to Daine was the size of a medium-tall dog, looked like a three-horn to the marmoset. He watched the dragon sleepily from the bed as she walked to and fro on the floor, talking to herself. He could tell she was worried, but not about what.

Then a section of the wall that was farthest from him swung open with a sound. Zek/Daine leaped from the bed, and hid underneath. Kitten whirled, turning orange with fright, as the Emperor Mage came in, a solid black crystal in his hand. He lobbed it gently at the dragon. It shattered on the floor without a sound, filling the air with smoke. When Zek could see Kitten once more, she was frozen in place, unmoving.

Ozorne knelt in front of her and drew a hank of thin, black cord from the pouch at his belt. Swiftly he unrolled it and bound Kitten's muzzle and paws, tying the two ends together when he was done. When he let go of the cord, it shone green, then vanished completely. Kitten's eyes closed, and she collapsed into the emperor's arms.

Ozorne pointed to the door; green fire left his finger, spreading to cover the opening. He then waved to someone in the hole in the wall. Slaves came, gathering up Daine's things. "Be certain you take *all* of her belongings," he instructed quietly. "Not a single hairpin must remain."

Zek, wits made sharp by exposure to Daine, looked around. There was no place under the bed to hide if they looked there, and there was magic on the main door. He didn't know what lay beyond the opening in the wall, but in any event the emperor was between him and it. He peered at the corner near the windows. A cloth hanging was on the wall. Above it, near the ceiling, he saw a rectangular opening: an air vent.

The emperor's face appeared under the foot of the bed. "There you are." Fire collected at his hand, and lashed forward.

The time to think was past. The marmoset raced from under the bed, scrambled up the hanging. Emerald fire lashed the cloth below. It burst into flame. Zek jumped into the vent and found himself in a long, dark tunnel not much bigger than he was. Turning, he saw that the tunnel ended nearby in an opening with a fine screen over it: no escape that way.

"Where are you, little rat?" he heard Ozorne say. Zek fled down the long end of the tunnel, into the palace depths.

Daine continued to dream after that, funny images that had little in common with the dreams she was used to. She wondered if she ought to complain to whoever was in charge of these things, but Gainel, the Master of Dream, was not one of the easily found gods. With no one to protest to, she paid attention once more to the dreams.

Guards formed a square around the Tortallans, marching them to a waiting ferry. Alanna walked grim-faced behind the covey of clerks, eyes watching everywhere. Duke Gareth, Lord Martin, and Gareth the Younger kept their heads together, whispering urgently. Harailt gripped one of Numair's arms, talking fast as he half trotted beside the much taller man. Daine wondered at the look on Numair's face. His nostrils and lips were white-rimmed; his eyes blazed. His unfastened robe spread behind him like black wings.

The scene changed. She was in the immortals' menagerie, watching as Ozorne himself gently placed the sleeping Kitten on a giant cushion inside a cage. Next to it, flesh-eating unicorns looked on with eyes that blazed hate.

The next dream was an entire play set in a cramped shipboard cabin. It glowed in the corners with sparkling fire, shielding against eavesdroppers. Harailt, Gareth the Younger, and the clerks were absent. Lord Martin and Duke Gareth were side by side on one of the bunks, watching Numair on the other. Lindhall was also present, Bonedancer the lizard-bird on his shoulder; he looked deeply worried. In her dream, Daine was mildly surprised to see that Bone was still awake. She noticed, fascinated, that his empty eye sockets followed each speaker.

"Impossible," Lord Martin said curtly. "Our duty is to return home and warn the king."

"She's one of *ours*," retorted Alanna. The Champion leaned against the wall, fisted hands thrust deep into her breeches pockets. "That letter's a forgery—it must be. He's keeping her somewhere, and using it as a pretext to end the talks and declare war."

Duke Gareth looked at her, eyes sad. "We cannot prove that, my child. Neither can we help Daine; we *must* warn the country. As it is, Tortall will stand alone against him. By announcing it before the foreign ambassadors, he made certain they believed his proof that Daine conspires against him. As far as our allies are concerned, *we* caused the talks to fail."

"You can warn Tortall, then, and the king," Numair said quietly. "I won't leave without her."

"We never should have brought that child," snapped Lord Martin. "I knew it would be trouble!" Standing, he approached the door. "Let me pass," he ordered. A hole appeared in the magic; he opened the door and left. Once he was gone, the fire sealed the room tightly again.

"Arram, there is more at stake than any girl, even this one." Lindhall's absentminded air was gone. "The information passed to you—contacts, new routes for the slave underground, conspirators' names—it *must* go north, *now*, before the borders are closed by war. We may have to get the prince out in a hurry if the emperor begins to suspect him, and the only way to do it safely is to have all prepared on your end."

Numair shook his head. "I don't care. Someone else can take the information to the king."

The Champion whirled and slammed both fists into the wall. "I *hate* not doing something!" she cried. "I *hate* it! I want to go back there and-"

The lizard-bird leaped from his perch on Lindhall, flapping clumsily across the room to land on Alanna's shoulder. He ran his beak through her hair, trying to comfort her. "Go away, you old Bone," she whispered, but her heart wasn't in it.

"You cannot, my dear," Duke Gareth said, his voice filled with pity. "We are going to war. Your place is at home with the king and his armies."

Alanna's eyes brimmed with tears; she turned away from the men.

"Numair, if you choose to remain, I cannot stop you—you are too great a mage," the duke said. "Please think, then. The emperor is mad, but not stupid. He *knows* you wouldn't leave Daine here. My concern is that he has planned for just that eventuality."

Numair and Lindhall exchanged looks. "I'm aware of the danger, Your Grace," Numair said quietly. "I have taken precautions. They may be enough. Ozorne has trouble believing in his heart that anyone else has more of the Gift than he does, even when his mind knows there are more powerful mages. I can use that to fool him. As for the knowledge of the prince's conspiracy—"

"Give it to me," Alanna said curtly. "It's the least I can do." She handed Bonedancer to Lindhall.

Numair looked at the duke, who sighed and nodded. Getting up, the tall mage went over to Alanna and placed his fingers on her temples. Black fire sparkled where they touched.

Daine would have liked to view more, but the dream was pulling her away, and her head ached.

The dream headache turned into a real one as she awoke. Putting up a hand to shield her eyes from a light-globe overhead, Daine found that she was stiff in places she hadn't known could get stiff. Arms and legs alike were slow to respond as she sat up and put her feet on the floor.

Here was a strange thing—she sat on the floor. The bed on which she lay was only a thick pad covered with a blanket. A stack of clean, fresh clothing lay next to the pad.

As her eyes got used to the light, she realized that she was some-place totally unfamiliar. The room was a box; its white plaster walls, floor, and ceiling were bare of any ornament. Three skins of liquid and a napkin bundle rested beside the pile of clothes. The skins contained water, the napkin stale rolls and grapes. A wooden bucket sat in the corner, she assumed for use as a privy.

Fear chilled her. The door had no handle or knob. Running her fingers along the frame as high as she could reach, then down to the floor, she sought a lock or latch without success. She stripped off the clothes soiled in the aviary and put on the clean garments. It didn't escape her attention that they were her own things. She ate the rolls and fruit greedily and could have eaten more. How long had she been asleep? How long would it be until someone let her out?

Did anyone mean *ever* to let her out?

She searched the room, seeking locks, vents, or anything else. Only plaster met her fingers. A year earlier Numair, telling her of his captivity before he'd escaped to Tortall, had said there were rooms under the palace that canceled magic, used from within them or from without. If she was in such a room, Numair, Alanna, and Harailt might seek her with their Gift and never find her. And what about her dreams? Had they been true? Were her friends still in Carthak?

By then she was trembling. She was caged.

"I want out," she whispered. The room was stuffy. She tried to fill her lungs, without success. With no vents, she might run out of air. The walls drew closer. In a moment she would stretch out both arms and be able to touch them—"No!" she screamed, slamming into the door. "No! No!"

The pain cleared the last traces of drug from her mind, and she could hear her friends outside. Her prison might cancel the Gift, but not wild magic. The People screamed with her, throughout the palace and in the city, over the river. Daine roared her fury. Animals turned on the two-leggers. Dogs set on master, cats the nearest passerby. Birds drove nearby farmers out of their fields. Daine was in all of them, shrieking defiance of cage builders.

In the palace, dogs and cats leaped for the mage Chioké. He threw up his hands: orange fire lashed, crisping their bodies. Daine shrieked as their agony shot through her.

"Stop!" she cried to the others. "No, don't! Stop! They'll hurt you, they'll kill you!"

A hunter shot his horse with a crossbow; a soldier speared his camel; Ozorne flamed a charging pet monkey. The rest of the People calmed down and hid from sight. Daine collapsed to the mattress and wept. She had gotten her friends killed, and she was still trapped.

She heard a thump somewhere near, and a click. Taking a deep breath, she shaped herself. Bones shifted. Skin and senses changed swiftly; claws sprouted from paws the size of plates. Daine the bear plodded over to a corner behind the door. Rearing up on her hindquarters, she waited.

The door opened. A cheetah entered the chamber, with Zek on his back. The marmoset clutched silvery metal in his paws. He looked at the bear, and showed her his prize.

*Keys*, Zek said proudly.

Zek and his new friend, Chirp, the Banjiku performers' male cheetah, led Daine through the web of branching tunnels under the palace, avoiding humans. At last they came to a round chamber deep underground, where odd-looking signs and runes had been painted on the walls. Tano, Chirp's trainer, waited there with fruit and water for Daine.

"It is safe to speak here and to be here," he told the girl as she ate. He pointed to the signs on the walls. "This is protected place. Slave magic protects here from owner-mages. Tell me what you need, and we will find."

She swallowed a mouthful of grapes. "My friends—are they here?"

He shook his head. "Two days ago emperor say you run off to get slaves to rebel. His warriors take your friends to boat and guard it until they leave. The armies prepare for war. Their great drums pound all night." He shook his head. "Sleep very bad."

She thought over what all of that meant. The armies wouldn't march; her animal friends would see to that. "I need to talk to Prince

Kaddar. Will you trust him if you bring him down here? Or you could blindfold him, if you aren't sure. But I trust him, if that means anything."

Tano nodded. "You will leave this place, go home?"

"I have to do one or two things, but then I'm going." Now that she was awake, her dreams felt *solid*, more like visions than dreams. If that was so, then Numair was here, somewhere. "Tano—I have a message for you, from the first badger. The male badger god. He said to tell the Banjiku that Lushagui *never* meant for you to be slaves."

The black man frowned. "Never?" Daine shook her head. Tano thought this over, pulling thoughtfully on his lower lip. "We must talk about this, the Banjiku. Talk comes later. I go for prince now—you wait."

As he trotted away, Chirp curled up next to Daine, while the girl petted Zek. "How did you find the keys?" she asked. "Where were they? How did you know they'd be the right ones?"

I found the emperor when he went to feed his birds, Zek replied, nibbling a fig. Then he went to his room. In his wall, there was a way down to the cage where he put you. He went down twice to look at you. Afterward he put the keys near his bed. I took them and asked Chirp to bring me to you a different way than through his room. All the People knew how to find you once you woke up. Smugly he added, But I am the only one of the People who knows about *keys.*

"You are the wisest, cleverest creature I've ever met," she whispered, cuddling him. "You saved my life *and* my wits. Did you see where he took Kitten? I dreamed he enchanted her."

Zek shook his head. He did not visit her, the marmoset explained.

Daine leaned back against the wall. "He wouldn't hurt her. I'm not at all sure he can. So he's put her somewhere—perhaps in the menagerie with the other immortals. I dreamed that's what he did, anyway. We'll look and see."

Still cuddling Zek, she dozed off until Chirp nudged her awake. Kaddar and Tano were coming. When the prince saw her, he stopped, dark face turning ashen. "Daine? Tano didn't say—"

She glared up at him. "You know what your uncle did to me?"

"We have to get her out of here," Kaddar informed Tano. "Once he finds her gone, he'll tear the palace apart."

"I'll go happily, once I get Kitten back," she said. "Tell me something, if you please. Do you know anything about a drug called dream-rose?"

"It produces sleep," he replied promptly. "And true dreams."

She nodded. "All right, then. I think—I'm fair certain—Numair's still in Carthak. Once I find Kit, will you smuggle me to the university? I can't leave this place without him. He—" The look on the prince's face brought her up short. "Something's wrong."

"Daine—"

She rose. "*What?*"

Kaddar put a clumsy hand on her shoulder. "Please, try to remain calm."

"*Your uncle* tricked me, drugged me, put me in a locked room with no air and stale food, and then he made my friends leave without me. He also kidnapped my dragon, and I want her. And he's using this as an excuse to start a war with Tortall. I won't be calm for *weeks*, so you'd best tell me!"

"They caught him. Master Numair. He gave them the slip in Thak's Gate, but they found his hiding place at the university. And my uncle wouldn't risk his escape. Not a second time. He was executed, a day ago."

For a moment she listened but heard only an ominous thudding in her ears. Then she said flatly, "You're lying."

He squeezed her shoulder. "Not about something like this."

"Then Ozorne lied to you."

"*I saw it.* He made me watch, along with everyone else at the university. Daine, I'm sorry. Numair Salmalín is dead, and we *have* to get you out of Carthak."

Coolness trickled into her mind until her skull was filled with it. Her world seemed extra sharp and extra real. Part of her, someplace deep inside, wailed; *that* seemed unreal, as if she watched a crying baby from a great distance.

Kaddar was shaking her. "Daine! Can you hear me?"

She gently pushed his hands away. "Stop that. I'm thinking."

His eyes and Tano's held the same worried, frightened look. "You weren't answering. You looked frozen—"

She put a finger to her lips, and he shut up. A thought was coming in the distance. She waited, patiently, skin rippling in brief shivers, until it reached her: Ozorne had to pay.

The gods had taken too long to say whatever it was they'd planned to say here. With all those omens and portents they had sent, the sole effect had been her kidnapping and her friend's execution. Plainly she would have to take care of this herself. If any gods tried to stop her, they would regret it.

"What time of the day is it?" Her voice sounded distant, but reasonable. Something about her, though, must not be right. She saw that

Chirp backed away to press against Tano's legs, fur on end. Both men began to sweat.

"Mid-afternoon," replied the Banjiku, eyes bright with concern.

"Where is Emperor Ozorne, Your Highness?"

"Across the river, reviewing the Army of the North. They march in two days to the staging point in Thak's Gate."

She had no interest in armies at this moment. "Will he return today?"

"Yes. He has to meet with some officials—"

"When?"

Kaddar wiped his forehead on his arm. "After sunset."

"Tano, could you pass word to all the slaves by dusk, if you had to?" The black man nodded. Daine looked at Kaddar. "Does anyone that you care about live in the palace?"

He wet his lips with his tongue. "Yes. But—"

"Tell the slaves and your friends to be ready by nightfall. When things break loose, they must leave the palace. I don't care where they go, so long as they do." She sat down again and let Zek climb into her lap.

"You can't just—"

Something in her face made him stop back. "Please don't say what I must and mustn't do, Highness." It was amazing, how cold she felt. "Hurry, now. Dark comes early here, I've found. Tano—the emperor's birds."

The little man bowed deeply, hands crossed over his breast. "One of the tunnels opens inside the glass birdhouse, Great One."

"If I tell them to go with you and your folk and not be frightened, will you carry them to a safe place? They won't try to escape you."

Tano nodded. "We will take them away, gladly."

Daine nodded. "Thank you. Before dark, please!"

Tano bowed again, and drew the prince away. Chirp followed them into the tunnels.

Dry-eyed, the girl stared at the ceiling. "You don't have to stay, Zek. It may be scary."

I will stay, replied the marmoset. Scary with you is better than scary without you.

Daine tickled his stomach gently, then closed her eyes. "I didn't get to say good-bye or anything." She swallowed hard. Her friend, her teacher—he had shown her the use of her wild magic, looked after her when her first trial with it backfired, taught her the science that enabled her to learn more about the People than she had ever dreamed of knowing.

Gathering up her power, she spoke first to Ozorne's birds. It was quick work to persuade them to go with the black men and women who had already begun to emerge from an opening in the aviary floor. Once all of them had gone back into the tunnels with the Banjiku, she cast her wild magic to the far side of the River Zekoi, and summoned every small creature that crawled, walked, or flew to the camp of the Army of the North. Let Ozorne see how far his soldiers could march with gnawed rope and leather, bad food, foul water, and useless weapons. Anyone who tried to use ballista or catapult would be in for an unpleasant surprise, as would the wagon drivers. Mule skinners and horsemasters wouldn't go very far without their charges.

She had done it before, calling on her friends to harass the enemy in a siege or to keep soldiers too busy to go to anyone's aid. Never before had she done it on this scale, but it wasn't that hard to summon thousands instead of hundreds or tens. It was almost a relief.

If Ozorne's gods weren't prepared to instruct him on polite behavior, she would have to do so.

The mingled voices of her friends above the ground told her at last that dark had come. Guided by a helpful cat, using cat's eyes to see in the dark, she found her way through the underground tunnels, until they had reached a trapdoor that opened into the Hall of Bones. "Thank you," she told the cat as she tucked Zek into her shirt. "And now, you'd best get out. It's going to be very busy here for a while."

The cat rubbed affectionately against her shins and raced off into the darkness.

"Ready?" Daine asked Zek. She could see his wide eyes and feel him tremble slightly.

No, he told her. Go ahead anyway.

She climbed the ladder to raise the trapdoor half an inch. The room above was dark and empty. Climbing out, she looked around.

She was in a niche between the mountain-runner nest and the hall where the smaller skeletons were kept. These wouldn't do. Turning, she entered the hall of the larger dinosaurs, and went to the threehorn that faced the main door. It seemed right to begin with him. Rubbing her hands, she touched the skeleton's long nose horn. White fire blazed. The dinosaur tossed its head, as if to shake off sleep.

"Now, that's the wrong way to go about it," said a cracked voice. "You'll kill yourself again, and you won't rouse nearly enough of them."

Daine faced the Graveyard Hag. "You," she hissed coldly. "Am I angry enough now? Isn't this what you wanted?"

"No," was the frank reply. "I *wanted* you to wake the human dead. Give 'em a start to see corpses dancing in their streets. It'd be just like the old days. Well before *your* time, of course."

Daine rested a hand on the three-horn's neck frill. It had moved up beside her and stood firmly braced, as if telling the goddess that she would have to go through it to get to Daine. "And when the dead lie back down, the mortals will forget. A couple weeks, a month, and it'll seem like a bad dream. I want to give them a lesson that will keep them busy awhile."

"What might that be, dearie?"

"Palaces are important," replied the girl. "Rulers keep their gold and gems and art in palaces. The tax rolls and imperial records are here somewhere. If I rip this palace apart, it'll take them *years* to clean up. They'll have something besides going to war with their neighbors to do. And if I kill *him*, a new emperor might not be so bad. Guaranteed, they'd go back to proper worship of the gods—I imagine that would make all of you happy."

The goddess frowned. "It's not what I would do."

"What *you* would've done you should've done *years* ago!" Daine cried, voice breaking. "If you hadn't let it go, and let it go, things might not have come to this state! But you didn't, and you left it to me, so now we'll do it like *I* want to! Add your own flourishes if you wish, but either help me or get out of my way!"

The Hag sighed. "You don't understand."

"I don't *want* to understand!"

"We can't just *do* whatever we feel like," the goddess said. "There are rules, even for us. We can only work on something like this through a mortal vessel, for one thing. Do you know how *few* mortals can be used as a god's vessel without dying on us? And I was reluctant to act, I confess. That nice boy Ozorne wooed me like a maiden—flowers on my altar every day, precious oils, public feasts in my honor—oh, it was grand! So, maybe I wasn't strict with him, and now he's too big for his breeches. It hurt when he stopped leaving flowers, you know. I was the last god still defending him in Mithros's court." She sighed and shook her head. "These men say they care for me, and I fall for it every time. Too good-hearted—that's me."

"My heart bleeds buttermilk," Daine snapped.

The Graveyard Hag shook her stick at the girl. "If I didn't need you—"

"But you do. You said it yourself—vessels are hard to come by. So, can we get on with it, please? I need strength enough to wake up *all* these big ones."

"Strength." The Hag rubbed her chin. "There's always the rats. You'll have to offer them something, though. Even *I* can't make them help for nothing. There's—"

"Rules, yes, you told me."

The Hag tapped her on the head with her stick. "Don't be impudent, Weiryn's daughter! And think up something nice to offer my rats!"

The tap made her ears ring and her eyes burn. She rubbed both; when she looked around again, the Graveyard Hag was gone.

Zek poked his head out of her shirt. Are you all right? he asked. Your bones are humming.

"I'm not surprised," she murmured, patting the three-horn's neck frill when he nudged her. "Zek, what can I offer rats?"

Food, he replied immediately. Rats are *always* hungry. I could do with a bite myself.

She dug in her pocket for raisins left from the meal Tano had given her in the tunnels. As the marmoset nibbled them, she thought hard and fast. On the edges of her awareness, she could feel rats approaching, hundreds of them. Where could she get enough food to bribe them all?

She was in a palace. Most of the provisions for Varice's fancy dinners were already here. Of course, the food stores were guarded by an army of rat catchers.

Smiling grimly, she called to the hundreds of cats and dogs who worked the palace and grounds.

As she conferred with them, rats streamed into the Hall of Bones through every hole, vent, and crack. Once the dogs and cats agreed to her request, she looked around. The great dinosaur skeletons now bore passengers: rats, black ones and brown, large and small; well-fed, glossy ones and scrawny river rats decorated with scars.

A brown female with one missing eye stood at Daine's feet. Herself told us you want to make a deal, she said. Something to trade for our wild magic, so you can wake these old bone piles.

The three-horn apparently heard this. It looked down and nudged the rat with its nose horn.

The rat bared yellow incisors. You don't scare me, dead beast! she snarled. There's enough of us here to do for you!

Daine patted the skeleton's neck frill. "It's all right. They're on our side—I think."

We don't side with anybody that ain't a rat, the female snapped. From the darkness all around them came chittering agreement from the others. Pipe down! ordered the rat chieftain. So what's the deal, then, two-legger?

"I plan to leave this palace a wreck; plenty of supplies buried under stone and in rooms the men can't reach," replied Daine. "So, *if* you give me what I need, the dogs and cats agree not to hunt anywhere in the palace or on the grounds for a year and a day. I can't get rid of the human mages, but the dogs and cats will go—if you help me. That's the deal."

The rats conferred, their whispers loud in the echoing hall. Finally the one-eyed female—who looked like the Graveyard Hag herself— squealed, We have a bargain!

The rats moved into the second hall, where the smaller dinosaurs were kept. Once they were settled, Daine got to work, drawing on the power they gave her as, one by one, she woke the great skeletons. Down the row of horn-faced reptiles she went, rousing each of their kindred: the bull, spiked, close-horned, one-horned, thick-nosed, and well-horned dinosaurs. None were shorter than a man's height at the shoulder, and some were half again as tall. Each came to life at a white-fired touch, and stretched lazily. They seemed to know she had business with them, for while they flexed limbs, tails, and bodies, they stayed in place, wait-ing.

Next she went to the armored lizards, with their back and head spikes and their bone-tail clubs. Mixed in among them were their cous-ins, armored lizards, who had traded the tail club for heavy side spikes. Most of the armored lizards were as tall as the horn-faces. They, too, woke readily at her call, working kinks out of muscle and cartilage that were no longer there.

After them she went to the plated lizards, remembering their ma-celike tails. Next she woke the snake-necks. While they weren't armored as the others were, their bulk and long tails would make fast work of obstacles.

At last she reached the tyrant lizard and his kin, the meat eaters. Originally she'd thought they would be little help, since their arms were so weak-looking, but she had reconsidered. Something about those great skulls, with their forward-pointed eyes and saw-edged teeth, told her they would make excellent hunters. Their cousins the wounding lizards had stronger arms, with large claws.

Once they and the eight mammoths were awake, she went to the front of the hall. Now she heard booming sounds at the doors; evidently someone had raised an alarm, and humans were trying to come in. Even if they had a mage to speak the opening spell, it would still take them awhile to enter. The bull three-horn leaned against the inward-opening doors, holding them shut.

"Friends," the girl said, voice echoing, "the master of this palace killed my friend, stole a dragon, and tried to cage me. He is a thief and a murderer. He needs a lesson. You can't be hurt as my mortal friends can. *You* are ancient and powerful. Will you help me get revenge? I would like to rip this palace apart, stone by stone. I want to topple the columns, break the walls, crush the fountains. Will you do it?"

From tyrant lizards to horn-faceds, the skulls of her allies pointed to the ceiling as one. She couldn't hear their roar of agreement, but she felt it in the quiver of the ground under her feet.

A four-toothed elephant wrapped his trunk around her waist, and placed her gently on the back of a shaggy mammoth, out of harm's way. "Thank you," she told him. To the others she said, "I'd druther not kill any two-leggers, but I know if you're attacked, you'll fight back. Just, please, look where you step, and don't hurt anyone who's smart enough to run."

The bull three-horn backed away from the doors. Both leaves slammed open, to reveal a very young mage and a squad of men from the Red Legion. The Hall of Bones was still unlit: the mage clapped to waken the light-globes. When they blazed into life, they revealed nearly seventy long-dead creatures who had left their pedestals and were walking toward the intruders.

The mage screamed and ran. The guardsmen followed, dropping their spears.

Outside the Hall of Bones, Daine's army split into three groups. One, led by the great three-horn she had awakened first, turned in the direction of the wing in which the palace records were kept. The second group, led by the chief tyrant lizard, began in the great hall where they now stood, smashing pottery, windows, and benches; ramming the walls; and toppling fountains. A plated lizard discovered the anchor chain of an immense light-globe chandelier and began to tug it from its mooring.

The third group, which included Daine, her mammoth, the bull three-horn who had blocked the door into the Hall of Bones, and others, was ready to go. "Zek," she asked the marmoset, "could you find the way back to the emperor's chambers?"

He clambered down the front of her shirt and along the mammoth's back until he perched in solitary grandeur on the creature's head. That way, he said, pointing left.

Daine tapped the mammoth with her left foot, and he obediently moved forward. The tiny animal on his skull lurched and almost fell, then grabbed tufts of the mammoth's fur to use as reins.

Two snake-necks, each over eighty feet long, wound their tails through the door handles to the Hall of Bones, and began to walk away. They didn't stop, even when their tails were stretched as far as possible.

In the end, it was the doors that gave way, snapping out of the frame and leaving it in splinters. The snake-necks then followed Daine, freeing their tails from the wreckage.

Behind them a ringing crash signaled the end of the plated lizard's attention to the chandelier.

Zek's next turn brought them into a long gallery lined with niches. In each stood a gold statue of a Carthaki emperor, decorated with gems and designed to show the monarch with those things that symbolized his reign. The dinosaurs got to work, pulling statues down and trampling them flat. One plated lizard made the windows his sole task, smashing each and every one with his spiky tail. A four-toothed elephant ripped doors off hinges with his trunk. People spilled from the rooms that opened into the statuary hall, stared at the dinosaurs, and fled.

Near the end of the gallery, a side door leading to the nobles' wing crashed open. Five people rushed in. Two of the women were veiled; a female slave carried a baby. When the women saw Daine's friends, they began to scream. The old man and the boy put themselves between their womenfolk and the threat, though their hands trembled as they gripped their weapons.

"Stop that noise," Daine ordered. "No one's hurting you." The only one to listen was the slave, who tried to calm the shrieking infant. "Get out of here," the girl went on. "My friends won't hurt you if you don't attack them and don't get under their feet. Now move!" The humans ran.

Daine looked at Zek. "Do we go the way they did?"

Zek shook his head. Straight, he said, pointing to the doors at the end of the hall.

In the distance they heard the crash of falling stone. Behind them the thick-nosed horn-faced dinosaur leaned on the marble wall. When an armored lizard joined him, the blocks of stone began to give way.

Zek led them through a tree garden, which they left as it was. The next turn brought them into one of the palace's many bathhouses, this one set aside for nobles. It seemed that those inside had not heard the distant sounds of mayhem. They were taken completely by surprise and fled without recovering their clothes. Tyrant lizards ripped up sections of the tile floor, laying bare a forest of gleaming pipes. A mammoth and a four-toothed elephant seized these, yanking them from their moorings and showering everything with hot and cold water. Armored lizards walked through rooms where clothing, robes, and towels were kept, catching them on their side spikes and dragging them along. Mud baths were overset, rubbing tables torn apart, steam rooms dismantled.

Their next turn led them through storerooms. Snake-necks destroyed countless jars of raisins, olives, dates, fresh fruits, and vegetables, wielding their tails like whips. Tyrant lizards tore their sharp teeth through pounds of dried and salted meat. Daine noticed coolly that the food vanished once it had entered their mouths. The others preferred the grain stored in great burlap sacks.

The last storeroom held drinkables in bottles, jars, and barrels. They had gone to work when the other mammoth in their group lifted a screaming female from a hiding place behind the casks. Pale blue fires danced around her body as she fought the trunk around her waist, without success. The mammoth brought her to Daine and set her gently on the floor.

Daine stared down at Varice Kingsford, fingers knotting in her mammoth's long fur. "Tell me why I shouldn't have you ripped to pieces?" she demanded. "Were you at his killing? Were you serving pretty food and fancy wine?"

Varice got herself under control, and shook her head.

"Did you betray him to the emperor?"

"I don't expect you to believe me, but no. Maybe I would have, if he'd come to me. You don't know what it's like, to be in the service of a man like Ozorne. But I didn't betray Arram."

Zek looked at Daine from his seat on the mammoth's head. Why are you angry? he asked. She has been sad. She isn't wearing the smelly stuff she likes, or the pretty colors on her face and hands.

He was right. The woman was pale, her eyes red with long weeping. She wore no makeup at all. Her blonde hair, uncurled and unarranged, hung lank and straight down her back. Even her dress was plain, a loose-fitting gown of dove-gray cotton. Her mage's robe was nowhere to be seen.

Varice met Daine's eyes. "You must think I'm useless and silly. Maybe I am. I just like things pretty. Is that so bad, to want people to enjoy themselves? Only, when you have the Gift, you can't just go to parties and keep house. They expect you to study, and to *do* something in life. Arram—he always wanted me to learn more spells and be famous. I don't want to be famous! What I do is useful. And I *like* using my Gift for cooking and baking. Great power hasn't brought the mages I know happiness or peace of mind."

Daine stared down at the blonde. Varice sounded like Ma, whose greatest pleasure had lain in dancing and working in the garden or kitchen. Quietly she said, "You needn't explain yourself to me."

Varice blotted her eyes on her sleeve. "I begged," she said, voice hoarse. "Sometimes it works. I said, what's the point of killing Arram? Other monarchs would fear Carthak more, if he showed mercy to his betrayer. But it didn't help. He made me watch when they killed—I'll never forget that as long as I live."

"Varice," Daine said. The cold inside her prevented tears, but she felt bad for the older woman. "We have no quarrel with you. The gods are unhappy with Ozorne, and I'm helping them, but you don't have to be involved. Get out of here. Shelter at the university, if you can get across the river, or the estates outside the palace grounds. You won't be safe here."

Varice nodded and gathered up her skirts. Daine's army parted to let her pass, then set about destroying the room. The horn-faced lizards, testing the walls, found they were wood, not stone. They began to smash them, wall after wall, working back through the storage rooms. When Daine moved on, some armored lizards and a mammoth stayed, as did the bull three-horn, to handle the stone walls. The echo of crashing stone followed Daine out.

## →→ TEN ←←

# STEEL FEATHER

**ᔕᓂᔕ** They came to a long passage where the ceiling was supported by columns studded with semi-precious stones. At the end waited a squad of determined-looking soldiers. Half bore small, double-curved bows; the rest long-bladed pikes.

She held up a hand; her army stopped. "I wish you no harm," she called. "But I want the emperor. Give him to me or get out of my way, but choose."

"We will defend our emperor to the death!" cried one.

"That's fair foolish. My friends are a bit hard to kill. They've been dead already."

One of them fired. His hands shook so much that the arrow flew wide.

"Witch!" a man screamed. "Sorceress!"

Did they think names *mattered* anymore? "For the last time, *get out of my way*."

They did not move. She waved: the spiked three-horn came up and lowered his head, the spines on his neck frill like rays of the sun. Five armored lizards stumped into place behind him. A wedge formed, the skeletons headed for the guards. Arrows flew. Those that struck their targets shattered; the rest could as well have been rain. The pikemen lunged, to find their weapons gripped in bony jaws and wrenched from their grasp.

Those still on their feet ran. Three lay on the floor after being knocked down. The armored lizards nudged them out of the way.

Impatient, the spiked three-horn rammed the door. It shattered. Orange fire billowed out of the room; the skeletal creature exploded into a million fragments.

The armored lizards opened their jaws in what Daine knew was a silent roar, and charged. Orange fire ripped the side off a double-armored lizard and broke the right-side spines on its neighbor. The remaining skeletons kept going. Daine covered her eyes against a bright flare of magic beyond the door, then urged her mammoth forward. Inside the doorway, Chioké lay crushed. He was pinned there by a thirty-three-foot-long armored forest lizard whose skull and front half were melting. Daine slid down and went to the dinosaur, trying not to cry as it fought to look at her.

"Go back to sleep," she said, patting the undamaged spine. "You've done a wondrous thing here, and I thank you. Go back to sleep."

The dinosaur relaxed, letting what remained of his head drift to the floor. For a moment copper fire shone brightly in the girl's eyes, running along her friend's bones. In it she saw the forest lizard as he must have looked in life, skin a gleaming chestnut brown, all his spines and plates whole. He was trotting away from her, bound for a lush forest that shone in the distance. When her vision cleared, even his skeleton was gone.

Checking the pair who had been half destroyed outside the door, she saw that they, too, had vanished.

A snake-neck grabbed her by the waistband and lifted her onto the mammoth's back. Please be careful about getting down! scolded Zek. Even if we fight the ones with magic, you are safer up here!

The mammoth waited for the last of the skeletons to enter Ozorne's rooms, then followed. Two snake-necks, finding that they would never get their large bones through the door, began to lean against the walls, trying to force them.

"Emperor Ozorne!" shouted Daine. No one answered. The girl looked at her warriors. "I think you'd best go to work."

They ripped the elaborate suite of rooms to shreds. They tore open chests and closets, broke whatever could be broken: furnishings, tiles, glass, pottery. The secret exit through which Zek had seen Ozorne go to visit a captive girl was laid bare. Daine urged her mammoth through the different chambers until they passed through. Ozorne's bedroom and entered the aviary.

Here were the benches, and the table where he'd fed her dreamrose. A book lay open on it, and a decanter of wine had shattered on the floor. Someone had been here recently, and had left in a hurry. Looking around she saw that the panes of the rear wall were shattered, as though a giant fist had punched through the glass and its green metal fittings. Soot streaked the panes on the outside; the odor of scorched bone hung in the air. More than ever, she was glad she had arranged for the birds to be taken away before any of this began.

Her mammoth followed the tyrant lizard through the broken wall and into the gardens. Here lay some of the warriors from another part of her army: a four-toothed elephant, two plated lizards, and a snakeneck. Their remains were blackened and twisted by magical fire.

"Thank you," she whispered to all of them.

Copper fire bloomed; scorched bones rose and became whole bodies. The dinosaurs headed toward a distant forest, to vanish as the copper light faded.

"Curse it," she muttered, looking at the burned area where they had lain. "Curse it, curse it—" She pounded the mammoth's back in fury. Where had Ozorne gone, if indeed he was the one who had done this? He could be anywhere, up to any kind of mischief!

A small, winged shape with long, leathery ears dropped to flutter before her nose, squeaking a welcome. This was a large, mouse-eared bat, on his night's hunt for insects. He was glad to see her, he said. All kinds of strange things were going on tonight. Was there anything he and his colony of the People could do?

Zek eyed him suspiciously. Can they be of any use? he asked.

"One way to find out," she replied with a grim smile.

Cradling the bat against her shirt, she called the others, both mouse-eared bats and common pipistrelles. The ones close by came to Daine herself, gripping her clothes or lighting on the mammoth's wide back. Those bats within the range of her magic but not close enough to reach her in person found roosts and waited to hear what she had to say.

As Zek peered curiously at these new guests, Daine built for them an image of Ozorne as he would "look" to bats, his face and form drawn with sound, not light. She gave them everything, from the tinny echo of beads in his hair to the clear whispers that would return from his gems. "Can you hear him?" she asked. "Is he anywhere near you?"

Wait, they told her in a single voice, and took to the air.

As the rest of her third of the skeleton army caught up, Ozorne's chambers now so much rubble, she wondered what to do if the bats were unsuccessful. They could find him outdoors, even if he were invisible: no cloaking spell was invulnerable to sound. If he were indoors, or wore another shape, that was a different matter. They would recognize the form, not the wearer.

If he couldn't defeat the dinosaurs, would he run? It was hard to imagine the Emperor Mage running from a girl and her army of dead animals. Still, blasts like the one that had finished the dinosaurs outside the aviary had to be costly in terms of his magical strength.

Reports began to come back from her spies. Bats were fast in the air, and they built sound pictures quickly. Within minutes Daine knew that not only was the emperor nowhere in the gardens, towers, or outlying buildings, but that parts of the complex were in flames.

"Pull back, then, all of you," she said, wanting to cry. "It's no good you getting cooked."

Maybe we can help, a voice said from behind her.

Daine turned, and gasped. The hyenas were out.

"How—what—?" she stammered.

Teeu, the boss female, came forward to sniff Daine's mammoth. The Mistress let us out, she said. Old One-Eye. She is a goddess of two-leggers, but she helps us, too, now and then.

Light reflected from metal in the air. Rikash landed on a balcony nearby. "I believe she felt you would require assistance," drawled the green-eyed Stormwing. "You might want to know, a company of dinosaur skeletons opened the menagerie cages and dumped trees into the pits so the animals could climb out."

"Kitten?" she asked Rikash. "My dragon? I dreamed she was in the immortals' menagerie."

"You dreamed truly. She is there under a sleep spell," he replied. "Your friends tried to break into that collection, but failed. The spells on the gate and cages are keyed to Ozorne. They won't give way until he dies."

We are going to find this Ozorne, Teeu said cheerfully. The Mistress reminded us: we have a score to settle. She said you might want to come, too.

Daine thought fast. A hyena's sense of smell was keener than any other living creature she'd ever met. She was willing to bet Ozorne wouldn't think to change the unique scent given off by his body, no matter *what* shape he took. Better still, Teeu and her "boys," Iry and Aranh, were creatures Ozorne had reason to fear. What better hunters could a girl bent on vengeance ask for?

"Lift me down, please?" she asked the mammoth, who complied. On the ground once more, she looked at Teeu. "I want to shape-shift and become one of you. Then we can hunt the emperor together, if you're willing."

Teeu gave a strange-sounding yip—a hyena laugh. Get on with it, the hyena urged. The night is young, and Ozorne has a head start.

Daine looked up at Rikash. "It just occurred to me—what in the name of all the Horse Lords are you doing here?"

The Stormwing ruffled his feathers. "I was paying my respects to my *true* sovereign, Queen Barzha, and her consort."

"Rikash—" she said warningly, not believing him.

"Well, as it happens, I'd heard that tonight would be an interesting night for Carthak."

"You mean the Graveyard Hag told you."

"Perhaps." The Stormwing's eyes glittered as he smiled. "There's a chance the emperor might feel the need to use the gift that I gave him. I wanted to be here to see the fun."

"If he has any sense, he's run off."

"Ah, but a man with sense never would have ignored so many warnings. I doubt he has fled."

"He killed Numair," Daine said hoarsely.

"I know." The immortal rocked to and fro, cleared his throat, and said, "I am sorry."

"Me, too," she whispered. She rubbed her sleeve over her eyes and turned to her skeleton army. "Will you go on tearing things up? I don't know if you can follow where I'm about to go, and I really want to leave this place a ruin."

All of them nodded. Zek clambered down from the mammoth's back. She patted each skeleton and elephant as they passed her, wishing them a good hunt and giving them her thanks. When they had gone, she asked Rikash, "Would you look after Zek and see he comes to no harm?"

He frowned, but nodded. "If he does not object, I will place him in the dragon's cage." He jumped to the ground, using outspread wings to slow his fall.

It will be good to see Kitten, Zek said. Even if she's asleep.

"I'd hate for anything to happen to Zek," Daine said quietly, meeting Rikash's eyes with hers. "Mithros knows why, but I trust you." She kissed the top of the marmoset's head, then held him out to the Stormwing. Zek climbed over Rikash's shoulder, where steel grew out of flesh, and hid under the Stormwing's long hair, grasping handfuls of it.

He smells *terrible*, the marmoset confided to Daine.

"Good hunting," Rikash said, and took flight. Before he and Zek had gone from sight, Daine began the painstaking business of entering hyena form. She drew her memories of Teeu's mind around her, letting her body shift. Her jaw spread and lengthened to become a muzzle. Her teeth broadened, widened, sharpened. At last she sat on the stone of the courtyard, a spotted hyena.

We can pick up the scent inside, she told her companions. His rooms are through that hole in the glass.

Teeu grinned, showing bone-crushing teeth. By all means, let us get a whiff of his lair. Daine and the males grinned back.

The dinosaurs still at work inside paid no attention to the four hy-

enas sniffing the emperor's bedclothes and garments. The reek of
Ozorne's many perfumes made Daine feel queasy; smells that had been
almost too much for her as a human were far more powerful to a hyena's
nose.

I don't see why he soaks himself in all this, Iry complained. It's
disgusting.

Don't whine, ordered Teeu. You should be grateful he left such a
clear trail for us.

As they followed the scent through shattered glass to the outside
once more, Daine found changes in it. Bitter tones, more powerful even
than the perfumes, lingered around his steps. Outdoors, where smells of
burned ground and scorched bone filled her nose, she could still find
those bitter traces. The hyenas snuffled the earth, their nostrils taking
information from the odors there. Daine growled, her rage surfacing at
last as a hunter's eagerness to find her prey.

Got it? Aranh asked.

She realized she would know Ozorne's scent for the rest of her life,
perhaps even in human form. Got it, she replied.

Then let's go, Teeu said.

The hyenas picked up the trail along the outside wall of this wing
of the palace. Teeu led the way, Daine at her side. The males spread
out behind them, chattering in yips and whines.

What are those bad smells in his spoor? Daine asked the female.
The ones that came into his odor as he left his rooms?

Teeu bared her teeth in a laugh. Fear, she replied gleefully. Your
friends chased him from his lair and into the dark, on foot. Those are
fear scents in your nose. If he were a wildebeest with that smell, you'd
know it was beaten and you were about to make a nice kill.

They stopped at a fresh battlefield. A dead human in armor lay
against the wall. He'd dragged himself away from the mammoth that
had crushed his lower body. The mammoth itself was a pile of embers
that burned copper and vanished when Daine pawed at it, whining. Two
more skeletons nearby had been crisped by magical fire. They vanished
like the mammoth's remains when she touched them with her paw. A
red-robed mage lay moaning in the bushes where he'd been thrown.

Come on, Iry called to Daine. The trail will get cold!

They found two more sites where the Emperor Mage had been
forced to defend himself. There were so many bodies at the second—
seven in all—that Daine thought of the sacrifices demanded at the fu-
nerals of ancient kings, whose households were put to death so that the
king might have attendants in the afterlife. Carefully she thanked each
of the fallen dinosaurs and elephants that had died a second time for

her, and watched as their remains vanished from sight before moving on.

Next the trail brought them around a corner and into the light. At the end of a short mall ahead, the palace was ablaze. Between the hyenas and the fire stood a squad of armed guards. One of them yelped, seeing the beasts, and brought up a loaded crossbow.

Aranh leaped, strong legs propelling him across the distance between them, and tore the weapon from the guard's hand. Bats swarmed out of the dark, blinding the other men with their wings before they could shoot the attacking hyena. Snarling, Aranh crushed the bow stave, making the weapon unusable. The rest of the guards dropped their weapons and fled.

The hyenas moved on.

The night air carried a thousand messages. Daine ignored the unimportant ones and concentrated on the odor of her prey. The emperor's scent changed as they followed, as if it were a living thing that grew under her eyes. In his rooms it had been one of a very well tended man, tinged with almond rubbing oil, aloe lotion, orris-scented shampoo, perfumed makeup, the acrid smell of gilding powder and gold, lavender from his clothes, and the personal scent of a man who ate and drank richly. In the aviary, anger and then fear had been added to the mix. Outside he'd acquired a touch of charred hair and bone. Now the smell of burned things was much thicker. So was the fear.

Thunder rolled overhead. Flagstones gave way to gravel as the hyenas followed a path between tall hedges. The smell of recent burning drifted into their faces. Three dinosaur skeletons must have come at Ozorne from the far end of the path: their blackened remains lay in a heap there. The emperor had fled through an opening in the hedge. Stopping to thank those fallen allies, Daine trembled. He'd escaped her army again. A growl rumbled in her throat, and her mane stood up.

He's weakening, remarked Teeu as the heaped skeletons shimmered and vanished. All the bones of the others were black through and through. These had white in them, and they still held together instead of breaking apart.

Good, snarled Daine. The less magic he has, the better!

The hyenas yipped agreement and picked up the emperor's trail, laced now with blood and sweat. His thin shoes had given out on the gravel, leaving footprints etched in blood. Their path twisted around a fountain, followed the curve of the artificial lake, and headed straight down a path shaded by willows. Here the great three-horn, the first dinosaur she had awakened, and a huge snake-neck must have been waiting for him.

The snake-neck was the first they'd seen who bore few marks of burning. Instead tiny cracks had riddled its bones. Some had disintegrated completely, leaving small powdery heaps. When Daine nudged its skull, the skeleton shaped itself, becoming a living dinosaur. The snake-neck waited patiently while the girl turned to the three-horn. Ozorne had tried to burn him without success, then melted him, the way Chioké had melted the bull three-horn. The great skeleton had gone down fighting: blood painted the tip of a long, sharp brow horn. Daine sniffed it: the blood was Ozorne's.

He's running out of fire, Iry told the others with savage glee. Look at this one—barely charred!

Sadly, Daine licked the three-horn's beak. It gave under her tongue as flesh might.

Why are you unhappy? Teeu wanted to know. Does it hurt them to die?

No, Daine replied softly as copper fire raced over the half-melted skeleton, calling the owner back to the true shape of its living days. The badger said it didn't, anyway. It just hurts me.

The great three-horn stood, his beaded hide a deep, golden bronze, his face, with its horns, restored. Through him Daine could see the trees dimly. Good-bye, she said, though she knew he couldn't hear. I'll miss you.

The three-horn bowed his head, touching her gently with his nose horn, then followed the snake-neck down a road to a distant jungle. The vision faded as they left the hyenas, until only the garden trees were left.

Rage and sorrow built in Daine's heart until she thought it might burst. I want Ozorne! she snarled at her companions. I want to rip him up like he's ripped me up!

Then *hunt*, cried the hyenas, eerie voice echoing in the dark. Smell, and find!

Daine set off, nose to the ground, the others behind her. Ozorne's scent was nearly fresh and thick with the sourness of exhaustion. Drops of sweat had fallen with his blood, the red liquid dripping heavily now that the three-horn had marked him.

The trail turned beside a wall and passed through the shattered gates of the menagerie. Inside the moral animals' enclosure, no animals were left. The cages were open, the fences pulled down, and trees reached from the pits to the ground level. The gate of the immortals' menagerie stood open and whole: someone who knew the spells had unlocked it.

He's here! she cried, and leaped.

Kaddar stood before the griffin's cage, hand upraised. At the hyenas' snarl, he whirled, and the shape he wore evaporated. It was Ozorne.

The moment he spotted her and the others, the reek of fear almost wiped out his other smells. He was disheveled, sweat-soaked, bleeding, soot-streaked. He wore only a light green robe and costly, shredded slippers. The fabric over his chest was torn: beneath lay a long, open wound that still bled sluggishly.

He's trying to escape on the griffin, I bet, Daine told her companions. He can think again!

She sprang and hit the emperor's magical shield headfirst, making it flare briefly. She howled, barely noticing the pain of a bruised head and neck as she dropped. Far more important than pain was the fact that the magical shield had weakened a hair when she struck it.

Teeu and Aranh leaped and hit the barrier, sparking twin flares in it. They fell, snarling in fury. Daine, watching, saw that the flares weren't as bright as when she'd hit. Iry attacked from Ozorne's left. This time the emperor's shield only flickered from the impact. It still held firm, but he was losing strength.

The caged immortals watched silently.

Emerald fire gathered, slowly, around Ozorne's hands; he swayed as it grew. There was a white-hot edge to its glow, the kind that left a streaky imprint on eyes that watched it too long. The hyenas circled to the man's left and right, yipping with excitement. Daine stayed in front of him, teeth bared, mane erect.

One more blow should do it! she told the others. One more and he's *ours*.

"No!" cried a human voice behind her. Sparkling fire leaped through the air to form a bubble around the emperor.

Daine snarled without looking away from her quarry. How *dare* two-leggers cheat her of what she had won? She threw herself against the new fire barrier, and received a nasty shock on her delicate nose.

"You'll have to choose, Uncle." This voice was different from the one that had cried "No." "Abdication and imprisonment—or the hyenas. You must give in. Your Gift is almost used up. We can see you're taking it from your own life force now."

Ozorne's fire had evaporated. He swayed, his skin gone cheesy white under streaked facial paint. "Abdi—? Never!" His voice was hoarse with effort.

"Then it must be the hyenas, Uncle, just as the Graveyard Hag promised."

"Give him to the animals!" cried the female Stormwing, Barzha.

"They have worked hard for his flesh—let them have it! Let them feast, so *we* can sup on his fear!"

The emperor stared at the female immortal in open terror. Daine, Teeu, Aranh, and Iry cried their triumph in a series of hollow yips that made Ozorne shudder. Daine stalked up to the sparkling barrier, intent on the man inside. You're *mine*, she thought, and bared white, bone-crushing teeth. For Numair, you're *mine*.

Ozorne's eyes brightened feverishly. "Promises, is it? Well, I have a promise in reserve!" he grabbed the hair on the back of his head, fumbling among its strands.

A rattle of steel made Daine glance to the side. Barzha and Hebakh were at the bars of their cage, staring at the Emperor Mage with grim concentration. Above them, on the roof of their prison, Rikash had also come to watch.

"See!" Ozorne cried. Daine's head whipped around. The emperor held a metal feather—the one Rikash had given him, pulled from a braided strand of hair. "I have *this* promise!"

She snarled in fury and threw herself at the barrier as Ozorne drove the feather through his arm.

Something exploded in a burst of light. Daine, falling through a vanishing barrier, slammed into metal that cut. She rolled away and struggled to her feet. A Stormwing with Ozorne's face and hair stood where he had just been. Steel feathers and talons gleamed as if newly minted. The gash on his chest was now a clean, broad scar.

Chimes filled the air. One after another the cages disappeared, releasing the inhabitants. The griffins and hurroks wasted no time: they fled into the night sky, filling Daine's ears with the sound of flapping wings. Magic of a deep-gray shade, almost like fog, washed and wrapped itself around the killer unicorns, spidrens, and killer centaurs, holding them where they were, as the more peaceful centaurs fled. Kitten, in a cage at the far end of the courtyard, sat up with an inquiring cheep; Zek clambered up her back to perch on her shoulder. The Coldfangs looked around, tongues sliding out to taste the breeze.

Barzha and Hebakh stretched their wings in a slow, ominous movement, exercising each feather. "Humans, stay out of this," commanded the queen. "Now he is in *our* form; he must answer to Stormwing justice!"

Ozorne gaped in horror. "No! I am the Emperor Mage, lord of Carthak."

"No immortal may hold a mortal throne," Hebakh said, rocking to and fro. "Wake up, *Emperor Mage!* Do you understand *now* the trap that was laid for you?"

"No immortal may rule over humans or use human magic." Rikash had drifted gently to earth, wings outstretched, when the Stormwing cage vanished under him. Now he stood behind his queen and her consort, razor-sharp teeth bared in a nasty grin. "Go ahead—try it."

Ozorne croaked a word. Something boomed, and he went flying end over end, as if blown by a powerful wind. He smashed into the menagerie's rear wall and lay stunned.

"You forgot our earliest lessons, Ozorne," said a voice behind Daine. It struck a chord in her memory, but if her life had depended on it she couldn't have looked away from the drama taking place before her nose. "Once you take immortal shape, you can never change back."

"We are free!" cried Barzha in triumph. "First I take payment from that motherless worm Jokhun and then I will tend to *you*, Ozorne!" She took to the air, Hebakh behind her.

Ozorne screamed and struggled to stand up on his awkward new claws. "I have magic! I—I have Stormwing magic!"

"Of course you do, sweetheart," Rikash said pleasantly. "Do you know how to use it?"

A scarlet bolt edged with gold struck from overhead to blow a hole in front of Ozorne. For a moment he stood there, panting, mouth working as he tried to speak. Sweat rolled off him.

"You'll get the hang of it in a few days or so," Rikash told him with false sympathy. "If you live that long, of course. There is a reason the former King Jokhun didn't want to fight Barzha Razorwing on her terms."

A second bolt struck the flagstones behind the new Stormwing, spraying him with sharp fragments. Ozorne cursed blackly, then leaped, pumping his wings clumsily. For a moment he dropped. At last he began to rise, bit by slow bit. Everyone watched as he climbed into the darkness overhead.

Rikash sighed. "I must go after him. I wouldn't like him to lose interest, not after it took so much work to get him into the proper claws. Barzha will want him eventually, after all." He looked at the hyenas. "Is one of you Daine?"

The girl trotted to the edge of the dais that had once been a Stormwing cage.

Rikash waddled over to look down at her. "If it counts for anything—though I'm not sure that it does—you have my gratitude. And things aren't as bad as you think. You might look around." He took flight and sped away, calling, "Ozorne, my precious, where are you?"

The hyenas gathered around Daine. What did that mean? asked Teeu. Look around for what?

I don't know, the girl replied, turning to find the human mages behind her. Kaddar was standing by the griffin's empty cage. Lindhall, Bonedancer on his shoulder, was keeping the killer centaurs, spidrens, and killer unicorns penned with his fog-colored magic.

In the gateway stood Numair Salmalín.

Daine gasped and lost her grip on the hyena shape. She turned human instantly—human and unclothed—and sat down hard. "No," she whispered, breathless. "Gods, this is too horrible. Don't do this to me."

The hyenas shifted to form a circle of furry bodies, concealing her, as the man came forward.

"I'm real, sweetling. It truly is me."

"Kaddar and Varice saw them kill you. You're a—a ghost, or a—puppet. A simu-thing."

He lifted a hand: black, sparkling fire grew around it. "Ozorne couldn't attach magic to a simulacrum, remember?" He let the fire die as the hyenas watched, heads cocked in interest.

She swallowed. "Very well, then—you're one of *Numair's* simal—"

"Simulacra. Magelet, remember how we met? I was a shape-shifted hawk. You nursed me until Alanna helped me regain my true form. Last year, in the courtyard of Dunlath castle, I changed Tristan Staghorn into an apple tree with a word of power." He removed his cloak and tossed it toward her. Borne by his magic, it settled onto Daine.

Rising, she wrapped the cloth around her with numb fingers. She didn't *think* a fake would know so much. Gingerly she stepped away from the hyenas and reached for him, then yanked back, terrified that if she touched him, she would know he was dead.

"Kitten?" she cried. "Is it really him?"

The dragon chortled happily and nodded.

Numair waited, one hand extended to her. Steeling herself, she reached again and placed her hand in his. Roughly he pulled her into an enveloping hug, arms encircling and lifting her off her feet. Nose buried in his shirt, she breathed his unique smell, one of spices, soap, and clean clothes. No one would think to copy that, she realized, and began to cry.

He murmured softly to her, arms wonderfully tight. When at last she stopped, he let her go and produced a handkerchief.

Obediently she wiped her eyes and blew her nose. "Where have you been?"

"At the university. Once the emperor's men arrested my simulacrum, I had to play least-in-sight for a day or two."

"But—they knew—Varice and Kaddar were *sure* it was you."

"It was a very good simulacrum, my dear. I worked on it for weeks in secret and had it shipped to Lindhall from Tyra. I didn't quite trust Ozorne's good intentions, I'm afraid."

Memory flared: in Lindhall's office, Lindhall had placed the turtle in another room, and she had seen a shape like a body covered with cloth.

"Why didn't you tell me?"

Numair sighed and smiled ruefully down at her. "I have no idea. I think I forgot."

"Oh." That made more sense than it didn't. "How'd you find out? About—all *this*, then?"

"Kaddar made it across the river. We have enjoyed a most informative evening. Are you aware that the entire west wing and Astronomer's Tower are burning?"

She scuffed a foot on the ground. "I thought they'd killed you. I lost my temper."

Numair's eyes danced. "Magelet, that is the greatest understatement I have heard in my life."

"She had help," said a cracked female voice. "She couldn't have done it without me." The Graveyard Hag had appeared at the back of the immortals' enclosure, cane, eye patch, and all. The badger waddled at her side.

"That's true enough," Daine snapped. She hadn't forgotten her anger with the goddess. "But if you'd done what you're supposed to, none of this would've been necessary."

"And *I* told *you*, we have rules." As she passed the Coldfangs, they slid their tongues out, tasting her cape. "Oh, go away, you," the goddess ordered. Silver light gathered around the Coldfangs, and they were gone. "You, too," she said, pointing at the spidrens, then at the killer centaurs and unicorns with her cane. "I'll talk to you when I get back." Silver fire gathered, and they vanished.

"Interesting company you keep these days," Numair told the badger as Daine stifled a yawn.

—*If I'd had a choice, I would have given up the experience,*—was the grumbled reply.—*You did very well, kit,*—he told Daine.

She smiled at him. "Thank you, Badger. Coming from you, it means a lot."

The Graveyard Hag came over to Daine. "Well, dearie, it's been fun, but you have something of mine, and I want it back."

Numair put a protective arm around Daine's shoulders. "She doesn't have anything of yours, Goddess—does she?"

"Bringing the dead animals back," Daine said, yawning. "That part's hers. You can have it," she said, extending a hand to the goddess. "It makes me nervous."

The Hag wrapped a gnarled hand around Daine's. White light blazed, and vanished. Suddenly the girl's knees felt rubbery. She swayed, and Numair caught her. Kitten, who had managed to leap down from the platform of her former cage with Zek on her back, trotted over, whistling angrily at the goddess while her scales turned pink.

"Oh, stop it," chided the Graveyard Hag. "She's just a bit tired. It's only to be expected."

"Goddess—will you listen to me for a moment?" They had forgotten that Kaddar was also there. When they turned to look at him, he went down on one knee. "Please?"

The Hag grinned cheerfully and leaned on her gnarled stick. "What have you got for me, handsome?"

"Gracious lady, my uncle's palace is a shambles, its treasure burning or scattered or buried. His chief mage is dead, as are many of those mages who supported him. There are people of good will in this realm, people who feared to cross my uncle while he ruled. I know the gods are angry, but—please, will you stay your hand from more destruction? Intercede for us before Mithros's court? Give us a chance to prove our worth. I represent a secret fellowship of nobles, academics, and merchants who genuinely wish things to change here. Carthak is not beyond hope."

Lindhall bowed deeply to Kaddar. "Your Imperial Majesty," he said.

"So he is," remarked Numair, and bowed.

Daine, after a moment's hesitation, copied them, yawning. When she straightened, the Hag fixed the girl with her one good eye. "What do you recommend? Seems to me, since you did the hard work, you ought to have a say."

"Give him the chance," Daine said, fighting yet another yawn. "Prince—*Emperor* Kaddar, I s'pose—he cares about the land and the people. If you gods were only interested in destroying the empire, not saving it, you wouldn't have waited to use me. You'd've gotten on with it."

The Graveyard Hag grinned and looked at the badger. "You were right about her," she said. "Sharp as a Shang blade, she is." Looking up, she said, "Well, my brothers and sisters? What do you think? I say let's give 'em the benefit of a doubt."

For a moment nothing happened. Then a rich wind filled with the scent of growing things filled the air. Overhead, thunder boomed again, a long, rolling crash that seemed to peal forever. When it ended, rain poured down in sheets, drenching everyone.

"Very good," the Graveyard Hag said with approval. Gripping her cane, she stumped over to the new emperor. "Get up," she commanded. "Silly for a ruler to kneel in a cloudburst."

Kaddar obeyed, looking dazed.

"I hope your memory is better than Ozorne's, sonny," she informed him. "I won't be ignored! Not in my own empire! Now, give me your arm. We need to talk."

The young man swallowed and offered his arm to the goddess with a courteous bow. She took it, cackling.

"*That's* more like it," she said, leading him toward the gate. "Now, don't worry about the army and the Guard. They were told to stay put or they'd risk the gods' wrath if they came to help your uncle tonight. By dawn they'll be ready to go to work. Oh, wait."

She looked back over her shoulder. "Arram, or Numair—whatever you call yourself—put that girl to bed. She'll sleep for three days, give or take." To Kaddar she said, "Where was I? Now, I like fresh flowers in my temples, and no more cheap pine incense." Her voice faded as they walked off into the gardens.

"Three days?" Numair asked, looking at Daine with concern.

—*It was divine power moving through her,*—said the badger.

Daine found that talk was too much work just now, as was standing. She sat and smiled up at Numair.

—*Sleep is all she needs.*—

She smiled agreement, then hugged Kitten and a deeply unhappy, wet Zek.

—*Don't worry about the escaped menagerie animals.*—

The badger's voice was the last thing she would remember as she closed her eyes.

—*We animal gods will see to it that they reach their proper homes unhurt. It is the least we can do.*—

# →→ EPILOGUE ←←

ʚɞ When she opened her eyes, it was raining softly outside her window. A breeze carrying the scent of wet earth came in, to mingle with the scent of sun-dried cotton sheets. She inhaled, smiling, and a joyful, earsplitting trill sounded from around her feet. When she sat up, Kitten leaped forward to strike her chest, almost knocking her back down. "Easy, Kit, easy," she protested, laughing. "Calm down!" Zek jumped onto the bed and came to curl up on the girl's shoulder.

"So you're awake." Alanna came over to the bed. "How do you feel?"

"Rested." Cuddling dragon and marmoset. Daine frowned. "Weren't you shipped back home?"

"We were called back. You were busy to some purpose here, youngling!"

Daine had the grace to blush and look down. "I lost my temper—"

"And the gods did the rest. At least you're alive and well, after such an experience!"

"Is Carthak still going to war against us?"

Alanna shook her head. "Kaddar's—the emperor's—ministers are signing the treaty with Duke Gareth today. Not that the Army of the North could march in any case. They seem to have run out of supplies that are fit to use." She lifted an eyebrow at Daine, who blushed again.

Alanna filled her in as the girl cleaned her teeth and dressed. She had slept for four days, and they were in guest quarters at the university. At first they had gone to Kaddar's mother's house. That had lasted until the princess learned the full story of the events at the palace. Once the word got out, nothing the new emperor could say would convince her or her servants that Daine, asleep in the women's quarters, would not pull the villa down around her ears.

"That's what they'll think back home, too, isn't it?" asked Daine.

Alanna handed the girl some breeches. "Not necessarily. See, youngster, it's a good thing that all this happened in Carthak. By the time those in Tortall hear the tale, they'll think it's just a tale."

"Really?" Daine asked, clinging to her friend's hand. "They won't shun me, like the servants and the princess and all?"

"Trust me. There will always be *some* who dislike you, but that's life. Over this business?" The Champion grinned. "People like to *hear* tales of things in distant realms, but they never believe them. There might be strangeness at first, but you'll be surprised how quickly they forget."

Daine rested her head on the woman's shoulder. "Good," she whispered. "I don't like the person I've been here."

Alanna held her. "No one can refuse a god." Her voice was kind. "It's over, and you're the same person you've always been. Once you're home, it will seem like a tale even to you."

The next day, in a break between rains, she and Numair were sitting in a garden, watching Bonedancer, Kitten, and Zek play with brightly colored stones, when Alanna brought Kaddar to them. He smiled hesitantly as the girl and Numair got to their feet.

"May I talk with you briefly?" he asked Daine. "I won't take much of your time."

"Take all you want, Your Imperiousness," she replied with a grin, patting the chair next to hers.

"Here, laddybuck," Alanna told Numair. "You come with me."

The tall mage sighed, but didn't argue. The Champion led him back into the house.

"Sit, please, Daine. I know you haven't been up very long." Kaddar joined her. The new emperor was dressed simply, as he'd been on his tours with her. The only changes she saw were a gold sunburst ring on his left index finger, and an air of purpose. For a moment they watched the animals play.

"What about Lindhall's Bone?" he asked. "The other dinosaurs you awoke have vanished, but he's still here."

"I don't know," Daine admitted. "It seems to be up to Bone."

Bonedancer looked up at them and nodded, a trick he'd learned from Kitten.

"This is the first time I've seen him away from Lindhall. He must like you." Kaddar looked at his hands. "They'll be going north, too, it seems."

"Numair mentioned it. I'm sorry," she told him. "I know you'll miss Lindhall."

"I offered all I could to get him to stay. Gold, books, a menagerie like your king is building. Head of the university, or just of the School of Magecraft. He says he's borne it here as long as he can. He wants to go north, where he won't see another slave." He laughed shortly. "It seems his only reason for staying this long was to help runaways out of the country!"

"Are you surprised?" Daine asked.

"No, not really—I had my suspicions all along. I just wish he could stay. I trust him. I don't know about some of these other people, particularly the ministers who served my uncle."

"Can't you get rid of them?"

Kaddar shook his head. "The country's already in turmoil. I need to keep a few of the same faces around, at least until I get their measure."

"It doesn't sound like much fun. I wish you luck with it."

"I'll need luck," Kaddar took her hand. "Daine, I found my uncle's papers. He was going to have me arrested and charged with conspiring against him—which means he planned to have me killed. I owe you my life. I know this will sound trite, but I mean it: whatever you want that I can give, even to half of my kingdom, all you need do is ask."

Daine gave him a skeptical look. "Your ministers wouldn't like the half-kingdom part."

He grinned. "Actually, they want to arrest you for crimes against the state."

"*Me?*"

"It will take a year just to figure out how much we lost. We have to do a census now, and draw up new records and tax rolls for every part of the empire." Daine whistled, impressed. He went on, "What amazes me is that creatures dead long before man ever walked the earth fixed on the treasury and the imperial records, where they could do the most damage. We'll never replace it all, and what we do replace will cost a fortune."

She fingered the badger's claw around her neck. "I had help," she reminded him.

"Yes, but haven't you seen how often people look for someone to blame? Not to find a way to keep some bad thing from repeating itself—just to blame."

"Send them to the Graveyard Hag," Daine suggested impishly. "*She'll* set them straight."

Kaddar shuddered. "My blood runs cold at the very thought." He squeezed her hand. "I mean what I say. I want to reward you, so think fast. Your ship sails at dawn. I know you've no family or home of your own, so shall it be gold or jewels? My own wealth was invested here in the city, and there are imperial treasures all over the empire. We may not have a palace, but neither are we poor. Name your desire."

She stared at the dragon, marmoset, and skeleton. Bone had discovered a puddle to splash in. "I want some humans—slaves—to be freed, with enough in their purses to start a new life. A *good* life, with work they enjoy, the chance to buy apprenticeships for their children, and proper clothes and food and such. If they want to return to Tortall with us, they can."

"All these things for others? Nothing for yourself?"

"No, Kaddar. The Graveyard Hag did most of this, not me. Use whatever you might have given me to help them that suffered in your famine."

He looked her in the eyes for a moment and saw that she meant it. "Name these people, then."

"The Banjiku—all of them, please, and their animals. And the emperor's mutes."

"The *mutes*?" She nodded. "But—they're useful, and since they're mute already—" Daine stared at him. The emperor sighed. "Very well. I have to bustle, if they're to leave tomorrow."

As he tried to get up, Daine held him back. "Kaddar, it's not my place to criticize the way you live, but if I were you, I'd think about your slaves. Animals endure cages if they must, but not two-leggers. If your slaves ever think to break out, it'll make what I did look like mud pies."

He sat down again. "It would beggar the empire if we freed them. No one could pay wages to so many when they pay only for room and board now. My nobles would rise against me. Even my soldiers would rebel, thinking that freed slaves would attack and their homes and families would be in danger."

"I know it'd be hard, but please, think about it. If you whip an animal long enough, it turns on you. If all the world were slave, I don't know if it would be so dangerous, but all they need do is look across the Inland Sea to know life doesn't have to be like this."

To her surprise, he lifted her hand to his lips and kissed it. "I will think about it; I promise."

At dawn, she stood on one of the ships that would convey the now much larger Tortallan party north to Corus, the Tortallan capital. Their small convoy would raise anchor once the Banjiku and their animals boarded Daine's ship. The mutes—those who had chosen to come— were already aboard another vessel. To Daine's surprise, half of them had chosen to stay behind. Talking in sign language to Numair, they had explained that they preferred to stay with the life they knew. Emperor Kaddar would be far kinder than his uncle, they were sure, and Carthak was their home.

"When's the coronation?" she asked Kaddar, who had come to see them off. Numair, standing nearby, picked up Kitten, trying to pretend he wasn't listening.

"Full moon," the young man said. "I wish you could be there."

"I don't," grumbled Numair. Daine kicked him gently.

"You'll write?" asked Kaddar, turning to go. The Banjiku had finished boarding. "You promise?"

"I'll write," she replied. The early fog had burned off at last, giving her a clear view of the palace. While some parts remained as they had been, she saw plenty of cracked and broken walls. The upper reaches were scarred by flame and soot. Of its five towers, only three remained standing.

She also saw one more thing. "Your Imperial Majesty? Kaddar!" On the dock, he looked up at her. "Yes?"

"About the palace? I wouldn't rebuild over there, if I were you. You're going to have a dreadful problem with pests, and no dogs or cats will stay in it." The captain shouted the order to cast off. She waved cheerfully.

"Pests?" Kaddar glanced across the river. The entire slope between palace and water was covered with rats.

It's ours, now, they thought to Daine.

It's only fitting, she told them, and waved goodbye. Thunder rolled softly overhead as, once more, it began to rain.

# The Realms of the Gods

To Claire Smith and Margaret Turner
who teach me that heroism includes
facing sorrows each and every day with courage,
humor, and practicality.

## Acknowledgments

When I complete a series, I like to thank all those who assisted me in some fashion. With *The Immortals,* I had a great deal of help from general reference and wildlife sources. While I have thanked some persons or groups in the book for which I most needed their help, I would like to thank them again, so they know the debt I owe them, but also so that anyone who also has an interest in these areas can find them. My heartfelt thanks to:

Subscribers to *two* computer networks, including but not limited to CompuServe's Pacific Forum, members of the Australia Section, particularly Douglas Dow, who gave me invaluable tips on duckmole (platypus) lore; Barbara Delaplace, CompuServe's Science Fiction Literature forum, who has given me sound advice on professional matters.

America Online: the KMart Shoppers, particularly MaxEntropy for her extra assistance with duckmole information; Steven and Lisa Dawson for the loan of their imperious orange-marmalade cat; Virginia Caputo, who helped me to find a different name for platypi and named Broad Foot; also, KO Gen and the KO staff, Guides and kids of America Online's Kids Only, where I have found such friendship, warmth, community, advice, enthusiasm, and input as I never would have expected to come from a computer {{{{{Gen & Co.}}}}}

Richard McCaffery Robinson, for his valued critical comments, his eleventh-hour naval and plot pointers, and his way of cheering up woebegone persons under deadline: Our friendship alone is worth every penny I pay to CompuServe!

Ellen Harris, who would be very happy to do a Daine doll.

Cat Yampell, for her enthusiasm, moral support, and her own wonderfully wacky writing—I hope she gets the recognition that she deserves.

Ms. Vivian Ellner and the kids of U.N.I.S., who have invited me to read for their book fair three years in a row.

Tas Schlabach, who helped set Daine's feet on the path of the horsehearted.

My foreign editors, agents, and publishers, who have kept me afloat: in the United Kingdom, Jacqueline Korn and the staff of David Higham Associates, and Julia Moffatt and David Fickling at Scholastic Children's Books (and David Wyatt, who does most cool covers!); in Europe, Ruth Weibel and Liepman AG, which has been tireless on my behalf, and Barbara Küper, my editor at Arena Verlag, her staff, and Arena's dedicated translators.

Robert E. J. Cripps, Celtic Wolf Medieval and Renaissance Style Crossbows, for making me look at crossbows in an entirely new light.

The wildlife researchers and experts whose work I relied on for insights, ideas, and research, and whose efforts to preserve wildlife deserve aid and applause across the world: L. David Mech, researcher and writer on wolves; Farley Mowat, the author of *Never Cry Wolf*; Marty Stouffer and his *Wild America* television series; The Nature Conservancy; the National Wildlife Federation; NYZS The Wildlife Conservation Society; Sir David Attenborough, whose many programs and books on nature changed the way I looked at it; and the International Wolf Center of Ely, Minnesota, which tries to make it possible for future generations to hear pack-song.

Friends whose contributions are intangible but vital all the same, including Amelia and Molly Bonnett, whom I got to meet at last; Nikki Johnson, who went from fan to friend; Kelly Riggio, whom I think of far more than my rare letters would lead her to believe; Iris Mori, because *Benkyo ni narimashita* (It's been educational, literally!); Heather Mars, who's earned a much-deserved degree after wading through quanta, vectors, and m-m-m-math; Stacy Norris, who is never afraid to speak her mind; and my inspirational helper, Andy Foley, who has made me laugh (on purpose) at times when I could use a laugh.

Peter, James, Rich, Tim, and all the other wonderful people at Books of Wonder, still my favorite bookstore.

Jean Karl of Atheneum, who has borne with me during crazy times, and Howard Kaplan of Atheneum, for the work he's put in.

And, as always, my own personal family constellation: my husband Tim, who nurses me through my deadlines as I nurse him through his; Raquel, who at last sighting had submerged in nineteenth-century New York for *her* current book; Thomas, whose approach to artistic growth and experience always gives me guidance on staying young from the neck up; my sister Kim, who rescues people and keeps them alive for a living; Pa and Ma, who teach me to age with Attitude; Melanie, Fred, and C.J., who share my love of animals; and the agents, accounting department, assistants, and receptionist of Harold Ober Associates, who do so much for this grateful ex-employee and client.

# Contents

# ->> PROLOGUE <<-

A magical barrier had separated the realms of the gods from the mortal realms for over four hundred years. While it stood, mortals were safe from the legendary creatures known as immortals, so named because, unless they were slain, they lived forever. Giants, Stormwings, griffins, basilisks, tauroses, Coldfangs, ogres, centaurs, winged horses, unicorns: In time all became the stuff of children's tales, or the concern of scholars who explored the records of times long gone.

In the eighth year of the reign of Jonathan and Thayet of Tortall, mages in Carthak found the long-lost spells that were the keys to gates into the Divine Realms. Ozorne, the Carthaki emperor, turned those spells to his own use. His agents opened gates into other kingdoms, freeing immortals to weaken Carthak's enemies for later conquest. Even those immortals who were peaceful, or indifferent to human affairs, created panic and confusion wherever they went. Gate after gate was opened. No thought was spared concerning the long-term effects on the barrier.

In the autumn of the thirteenth year of Their Majesties' rule, Ozorne's great plan came to a halt. In the middle of peace talks with Tortall—whose agents had revealed his involvement in the current troubles of his neighbors—Emperor Ozorne made a final attempt to regain his advantage. He ignored omens that proclaimed the gods were most displeased with his stewardship of his kingdom. For his pains, he was turned into a Stormwing and barred from human rule. His nephew took the throne; the gate spells were destroyed. By that time, however, the barrier had been stretched in a thousand places to cover the holes made by the magical gates. Its power flickered like a guttering candle.

ΩΩ

At the dawn of the Winter Solstice, the shortest day of the year, all those with any magic—Gift, immortal, and wild—woke suddenly, laboring to hear something that was not a sound. In Tortall, Numair Salmalín, one of the world's great mages, sat up in bed, pouring sweat. Though he could not see them, he *knew* what all the other mages in the palace and city were doing. The king, awake and at work in his study, knocked his chair over when he jumped to his feet. Harailt of Aili, dean of the royal university, flailed in bed and fell out with a thud. Gareth the Elder of Naxen pressed a hand to his laboring heart; Kuri Taylor swayed on her feet, half fainting. Even those with wild magic registered on Numair's senses. Onua of the Queen's Riders jumped out of her dawn bath, shrieking a K'miri war cry. Stefan Groomsman dropped out of his loft, landing safely on bales of hay while the horses who loved him whickered in concern.

And Daine, Numair's teenage friend and ally of the last three years, sat up in her bed-nest of cats, dragon, marmosets, martens, and dogs, eyes wide in the gloom, soft lips parted. The young dragon Skysong trilled without stopping, her voice spreading in a series of rippling pools, soon to reach and fill the palace itself.

"Kit, hush," Numair heard Daine say, though the girl didn't try to enforce the order. "Numair, what is it?"

He didn't question her knowing that he could hear what she'd said, in spite of hundreds of yards and a number of buildings between them, any more than she questioned it. In that moment, as the sun climbed over the horizon, any wall seemed vague and ghostly. "It's the barrier," he replied softly, but she heard every word. "The barrier between the realms. It's—gone. Evaporated."

He could feel her blink, as if those long, dark lashes of hers touched his cheek. Suddenly he learned something that he'd never considered before. For a brief moment, that fresh knowledge erased even his sense of magical cataclysm.

"The immortals—they'll be on us like a ton of bricks," she said, her voice matter-of-fact. "I'd best get up."

# ✦ ONE ✦

# SKINNERS

The Stormwing sat on a low wooden perch like a king on his throne. All around him torches flickered; men spoke quietly as they prepared the evening meal. He was a creature of bad dreams, a giant bird with the head and chest of a man. As he moved, his steel feathers and claws clicked softly. For one of his kind, he was unusually clean. His reddish brown hair had once been dressed in thin braids, but many had unraveled. His face, with its firm mouth and large amber eyes, had once been attractive, but hate deepened the lines at mouth and eyes. Dangling around his neck was a twisted, glassy lump of rock that shimmered in the torchlight.

Now he stared intently at a puddle of darkness on the ground before him. An image grew in the inky depths. In it, a tall, swarthy man turned the reins of his black-and-white spotted gelding over to a young hostler. Beside him, a girl—a young woman, really—lifted saddlebags from the back of a sturdy gray pony. When the hostler reached for *her* reins, the mare's ears went flat; lips curled away from teeth.

"Cloud, leave be," ordered the girl. She spoke Common, the main language of the eastern and southern lands, with only a faint accent, the last trace of her origins in the mountains of Galla. "It's too late for you to be at your tricks."

The mare sighed audibly, as if she agreed. The hostler took her reins carefully, and led mare and gelding away. Grinning, the girl slung the bags over her shoulder.

She is lovely, thought the Stormwing who had once been Emperor Ozorne of Carthak. The boys must swarm around her now, seeing the promise of that soft mouth, and ignoring the stubborn chin. Or at least, he amended his own thought, the ones with the courage to approach a girl so different from others. Boys who don't mind that she converses with passing animals, not caring that only half the conversation can be heard by two-leggers. Such a brave boy—or man—would try to drown himself in those blue-gray eyes, with their extravagant eyelashes.

Ozorne the Stormwing smiled. It was a pity that, unlike most girls of sixteen, she would not make a charm this Midsummer's Day to attract her true love. On the holiday, two days hence, she—and her lanky companion—would be dead. There would be no lovers, no future husband, for Veralidaine Sarrasri, just as there would be no more arcane discoveries for Numair Salmalín, Ozorne's one-time friend.

"I want the box," he said, never looking away from the dark pool.

Two new arrivals entered the image in the pool. One was an immortal, a basilisk. Over seven feet tall, thin and fragile-looking, he resembled a giant lizard who had decided to walk on his hind legs. His eyes were calm and gray, set in a beaded skin the color of a thundercloud. In one paw he bore his long tail as a lady might carry the train to her gown.

The other newcomer rode in a pouch made of a fold of skin on the basilisk's stomach. Alert, she surveyed everything around her, fascination in her large eyes with their slit pupils. A young dragon, she was small—only two feet long, with an extra twelve inches of tail—and bore little resemblance to the adults of her kind. They reached twenty feet in length by mid-adolescence, after their tenth century of life.

"Numair! Daine! Tkaa and Kitten—welcome!" A tall, black-haired man with a close-cropped beard, wearing blue linen and white silk, approached the new arrivals, holding out a hand. The swarthy man gripped it in his own with a smile. As the young dragon chirped a greeting, the basilisk and the girl bowed. Jonathan of Conté, king of Tortall, put an arm around mage and girl and led them away, saying, "Can you help us with these wyverns?" Basilisk and dragon brought up the rear.

Something tapped the Stormwing's side. A ball of shadow was there, invisible in the half-light except where it had wrapped smoky tendrils around a small iron box. The Stormwing brushed the latch with a steel claw; the top flipped back. Inside lay five small, lumpy, flesh-colored balls. They wriggled slightly as he watched.

"Patience," he said. "It is nearly time. You must try to make your mistress proud."

Mortals approached from the camp. They stopped on the far edge of the Stormwing's dark pool; the image in it vanished. Two were Copper Islanders. They were dressed in the soft boots, flowing breeches, and long overtunics worn by their navy, the elder with a copper breastplate showing a jaguar leaping free of a wave, the younger with a plain breastplate. The third man, a Scanran shaman-mage, was as much their opposite as anyone could be. His shaggy blond mane and beard were a rough contrast to the greased, complex loops of the Islanders' black hair. Hot though it was, he wore a bearskin cape over his stained tunic and leggings, but never sweated. Few people ever looked at his dress: All eyes were drawn to the large ruby set in the empty socket of one eye. The other eye glittered with cold amusement at his companions.

"Still watching Salmalín and the girl?" asked the senior Islander. "My king did not send us for your private revenge. We are here to loot. The central cities of Tortall are far richer prizes than this one."

"You will have your richer prizes," Ozorne said coldly, "*after* Legann falls."

"It will take all summer to break Legann," argued the Islander. "I want to reunite my fleet and strike Port Caynn now! Unless your spies have lied—"

"My agents can no more lie than they can unmake themselves," replied the Stormwing coldly.

"Then an attack from my fleet at full strength will take port and capital! I want to do it now, before help comes from the Yamani Islands!"

Ozorne's amber eyes glittered coldly. "Your king told you to heed my instructions."

"My king is not here. He cannot see that you forced us into a fruitless siege only to lure a common-born man and maid into a trap! I—"

The Stormwing reached out a wing to point at the angry Islander. The black pool on the ground hurled itself into the air. Settling over the man's head and shoulders, it plugged his eyes, ears, nose, and mouth. He thrashed, ripping at the pool. It reshaped itself away from his clawing hands, flowing until it pinned his arms against his sides. The onlookers could hear his muffled screams.

When the man's thrashing ended, Ozorne looked at the remaining Islander. "Have *you* questions for me?"

The younger man shook his head. Droplets of sweat flew from him.

"Consider yourself promoted. Bury that," the Stormwing ordered, meaning the dead man. He looked at the Scanran shaman-mage. "What do you say, Inar Hadensra?"

The man grinned. Crimson sparks flashed in his ruby eye. "My masters sent me to see that Tortall is stretched thin," he said in a cracked voice. "Where our forces go is no matter, so long as this bountiful realm is weak as a kitten in the spring."

"Wise," Ozorne remarked with a shrug of contempt.

Fire blazed out of the ruby, searing Ozorne's eyes. He covered his face with his wings, sweat pouring from his living flesh, but the agony went on, and on. A harsh voice whispered, "Remember that *you* are no longer emperor of Carthak. Take care how you address me." The pain twisted and went icy, chilling Ozorne from top to toe. Each place where his flesh mixed with steel burned white-hot with cold. "The power for which I plucked one eye out of my own head is enough to defeat the magic of a Stormwing, even one so tricky as you."

When Ozorne's vision cleared, he was alone with the dark pool on the ground, and the shadow next to him. "I'll gut you for that, Inar," he whispered, looking at the box, "But not before I settle my score with Veralidaine and the one-time Arram Draper." Grabbing his iron box in one claw, he took off, flapping clumsily into the night sky.

Two days later, the girl and the man who had drawn Ozorne's attention hovered over a cot in a guard tower at Port Legann. Their eyes were locked on the small blue-white form curled up in a tight ball at the cot's center. The dragon's immature wings were clenched tight on either side of her backbone. The tall gray basilisk Tkaa was there as well, gazing through a window at the courtyard below.

"I don't like her color," Daine said. "She's never been that shade before. Pale blue, yes, but—going white along with the blue? It's as if she's turning into a ghost."

"She is weary," replied the basilisk, turning away from his view. "For a dragon as young as Skysong, the effort of will required to send a wyvern about his business is tiring. She will be fine when she awakes."

"What if the wyverns return before then?" Numair Salmalín showed the effects of the spring's fighting more than Daine or Tkaa. Too many nights with little or no sleep had etched creases around his full, sensitive mouth and at the corners of his dark eyes. For all that he was only thirty, there were one or two white hairs in his crisp black mane of hair. "The king was—unpleased—when *I* attempted to fight them last time."

Daine smiled. *Unpleased* described King Jonathan's reaction to Numair's use of his magical Gift on wyverns as well as *breeze* described a hurricane. "You were ordered to keep your strength in reserve," she reminded him. "Archers can do for wyverns as well as you, and there might come something archers *can't* fight. *Then* he'll need you."

"The wyverns should not return for at least a day," the basilisk added. "They too used up their strength, to defy a dragon's command for as long as they did."

"I can't believe they ran." Daine pushed her tumble of smoky brown

curls away from her face. "She's not even three years old." She and
Kitten had risen at sunrise to handle the attacking wyverns; there had
been no time to pin up her hair, or even to comb it well. With a sigh,
she picked up her brush and began to drag it through her curls.

Numair watched her from his position next to the sleeping dragon.
He could see weariness in Daine's blue-gray eyes. The two of them had
been in motion since the spring thaws, when Tortall's foreign enemies—
an alliance of Copper Islanders, Carthaki rebels, Scanran raiders, and
untold immortals—had struck the northern border, western coast, and a
hundred points within the realm. With the wild magic that enabled Daine
to ask the animals and birds of Tortall to fight the invaders, Kitten's
dragon power, Tkaa's ability to turn any who vexed him to stone, and
Numair's own great magical Gift, they had managed time after time in
the last twelve weeks to stave off disaster.

Port Legann was their most recent stop; the four had ridden all night
to reach the king. Remembering that ride, just two days ago, Numair
wondered how much more of this pace they would be able to stand.

The rest of the country was in little better shape. "Our true allies
are pressed to the wall," King Jonathan had told them over supper on
the night of their arrival. "Maren, Galla, Tyra—immortals hit them at
the same time they hit us. Emperor Kaddar does his best to guard our
southern coast, but he's got a rebellion on his hands. The emperor of
the Yamani Islands has promised to send a fleet, but even when it
comes, it will be needed to relieve the siege on Port Caynn and on
Corus."

Kitten stirred in her sleep, interrupting Numair's thoughts. "Shh,"
he murmured, stroking her. The dragon twisted so that her belly was
half exposed, and quieted again.

A boy stuck his head in the open door. " 'Scuze me, m'lord Numair,
Lady, um—um—sir." His confusion over the proper title for a basilisk
was brief. "His Majesty needs you now, up on the coast wall, the northwest drum tower. If you'll follow me?"

Now what? was in the looks Daine and Numair exchanged, before
the girl remembered the dragon.

"Kitten—"

"I will remain with Skysong," Tkaa assured her.

Daine stood on tiptoe to pat the immortal's cheek. "You're fair
wonderful, Tkaa." She and Numair followed the runner at a brisk walk.

A man, a commoner by his sweat-soaked clothes, knelt at the king's
feet, drinking greedily from a tankard. Beside him was a tray with a
pitcher and a plate of sliced bread, meat, and cheese. The king, in tunic
and breeches of his favorite blue and a plain white shirt, leaned against

the tower wall, reading a grim sheet of parchment. In direct sunlight, Daine could see that Jonathan had also acquired some white threads in his black hair since the arrival of spring.

"This is Ulmer of Greenhall, a village southeast of here," the king said when he saw them. "He has ridden hard to reach us, and his news is—unsettling."

Watching the man eat, Daine realized he didn't kneel just from reverence to his monarch—gray with exhaustion, he was too weak to stand. It seemed that all he could manage was to chew his food.

" 'Unsettling'? I don't like the sound of that," Numair remarked.

"The village headman writes that five *things* came out of the Coastal Hills near Greenhall the day before yesterday. They kill what they touch—"

"Skin 'em, with magic," Ulmer interrupted. "Can't shoot 'em." He refilled his tankard with trembling hands. "I mean, y' *can*, but it does them no hurt. Swords, axes—" He shook his head. Realizing that he'd interrupted the king, he ducked his head. "Beggin' your pardon, sire."

"It's all right, Ulmer." To Numair and Daine, Jonathan added, "Sir Hallec of Fief Nenan went to fight them at sunset yesterday. They killed him." He grimly rolled up the parchment. "Fortunately, the Skinners don't move after dark, and are slow to start in the morning—they seem to need to warm up. The people of Greenhall have fled, but . . . there are rich fields in this part of the realm, as you know. We will need those crops this winter." He looked at Numair, then at Daine. "I'm sorry. I know you're exhausted, but—"

"You need your other mages to deal with the enemy fleet, and the siege," Numair said. "This *is* why you've kept me in reserve, Your Majesty."

"The wyverns—" the runner who had brought them said. He blushed when the others looked at him.

Daine understood his worry. The giant, winged, legless dragons breathed a yellow fog that gave humans a dry, long-lasting cough and made the eyes burn and blur. The crew of one of the great catapults, breathless and half blind, had dumped a boulder among their own soldiers. Legann's only insurance against another wyvern attack was Kitten. Wyverns might resist, but they *had* to obey an order from one of their dragon cousins.

"Kit stays," the girl said firmly, looking at the king. "Tkaa knows more about helping her than I do, anyway."

"She won't protest?" Jonathan asked. He knew the young dragon well.

Daine shook her head. "She doesn't like us being apart for long, but she's gotten used to it since the war began. Sometimes we're more useful when we're apart."

"I'll guide you to—home." Ulmer tried to get up, and failed.

"There's no need," said Numair gently. "If you do not object, I'll take the knowledge of the route to your village from your mind. You're in no condition to ride."

"I'll pack for us both, and give the word to Tkaa," Daine said. "Meet you at the stables soonest." She turned to go. A hand grabbed her sleeve. Puzzled, she looked at the king. "Be careful," he said, giving her the parchment letter. "These Skinners sound like nothing that anyone has encountered before."

Daine smiled at this man whom she had served with love and respect for the last three years. "Numair will set them to rights, Majesty," she said. "Just make sure you're still here when we come back."

"I think we can manage that much," the king replied, and released Daine's sleeve. "Unless they get reinforcements, we can hold them all summer if we must." He and Daine tapped their own skulls with closed fists, their version of knocking on wood. "Look at the bright side. It's Midsummer's Day—maybe the gods will throw some luck at us!"

"Midsummer—do you know, I'd fair forgotten?" Daine smiled wryly. "Maybe I'll look in a pond along the way and find out who my true love will be."

Jonathan laughed. Daine grinned, bowed, and trotted off, waiting until she knew he could no longer see her before she let her smile fade. With Numair's magical Gift to hide their presence, there would be no problem in leaving the city—it was how they'd entered it in the first place. Her concern was for the king—and for the queen, commanding at the embattled capital; for Alanna the Lioness, the King's Champion, in the far north since the spring; for the many friends she had made all over Tortall.

We need Midsummer luck for fair, she thought, returning to their rooms. All along, the enemy's known what we're about before we do it. We need luck to counter him, and luck to find his spies. I don't know where it's to come from, but we need it *soon*.

They left Port Legann separately. Numair rode his patient gelding, Spots, carrying his pack and Daine's. While two of the three roads that led into the city were still open, they were unsafe; he cloaked himself and Spots magically, as he'd done on the way into Legann. Daine herself flew out in the shape of a golden eagle to see if she could find the Skinners and get an idea of what she and Numair were up against.

She soared on columns of warm air that rose from the land. From the upper reaches, the walled city and its surroundings looked much like a wonderfully detailed map. The enemy's main camp lay a few miles off the north road. On the road itself, a mixed band of enemy soldiers and immortals was camped. On the eastern and southern roads, soldiers in Tortallan colors had dug in to keep the way open for help and supplies. From aloft, she also saw the motley fleet that waited outside Legann, thwarted from entering the harbor by the great chains stretched across its mouth.

In her years in Tortall she had lived among warriors and mages, and could read a battle situation like a book. What she read now gave Daine hope. The enemy army was about equal to Legann's; if they had any magical surprises, they would have used them before. With armies that were matched, and neither side having the advantage in magic or weapons, the battle on land and at sea was a stalemate. The king was right: Legann might hold all summer, particularly if they could keep at least one road open.

She wheeled, turning her eyes east. Twenty miles from the city, a wide swath of pale brown, black, and gray, naked of greenery, straddled the east road. Trees stripped of leaf and bark thrust into the air like toothpicks. As she approached, she saw, and smelled, corpses—most of them animals—bloated and stinking in the heat. They came in all sizes, from the smallest mice to cows and sheep. The closer Daine came to that dead zone, the fewer animal voices she heard. Most of the Beast-People who could do so had fled.

Gliding over the last bank of living trees, she found the Skinners. There were five in all: wet, flesh-colored, two-legger things. They had no eyes, ears, noses, or mouths, but they didn't seem to require such niceties. They forged ahead blindly, touching anything that lived. When they did, plants became dull instead of glossy. Tree bark vanished. Within seconds, vegetation went dark, brittle, dead. As the creatures touched things, parts of their own flesh changed color—brown, green, reddish, like bark or leaves in texture. Those patches would grow, shrink, and vanish rapidly.

She had come upon the Skinners as they worked their way through a village. They ignored small obstacles, like tossed-aside buckets or sacks of food that had been left in the street. If the object was big—a well, or an abandoned wagon—they split up, walked around, and rejoined to walk abreast once more.

High overhead, Daine reached into the copper fire of her wild magic. Gripping it, she cast it out like a net, letting her power fall gently onto the Skinners. She didn't expect it to stop them. Wild magic only helped her shape-shift and talk to the People. Still, if wild magic was something she had in common with these things, perhaps they could talk. Perhaps she could get them to break off their mindless, deadly ramble.

Her net touched something—and suddenly a hole yawned in the center of her magic. She felt the closeness of things she couldn't name; they shifted and rolled just at the corner of her mind's eye. Creatures that should not exist wailed in voices that made her ears bleed; dreadful scents reached her nose and tore at the delicate tissues inside. She lost control over her eagle body and dropped.

In losing her form, she broke the magic's grip. Frantically Daine shifted into the first shape that came to mind. Just before she hit the ground, crow wings grabbed the air and dragged her aloft. When she was safe in the new form and out of reach, she looked down.

The Skinners had formed a circle. Their eyeless heads were turned up, as if they could see her. She scolded with the excitement of fear, cursing them in a crow's beautifully nasty vocabulary.

Her foes were not impressed. Spreading out in a line, they began to march forward. Daine shuddered. What had she sensed? What were those things made of? She would have to ask Numair. For now, she slowly made herself an eagle again. A bird of prey was a better glider than a crow, and she needed the eagle's sharp eyes.

Below, the monsters lumbered on. The leftmost Skinner was about to step over a small hutch when it stopped. Bending down, it grabbed at the small door, yanking it off its hinges. A rabbit streaked by on its way to freedom. Before Daine could even guess what was happening, the Skinner seized its prey and held its prize up by the ears.

The hare convulsed. Its fur and hide vanished, ripped off in an eyeblink. Patches of fur appeared all over the Skinner, dull against the gleaming stickiness that was its own flesh. The hare now dangled, motionless. The thing dropped it, and touched a patch of fur that had appeared on its belly. The patch grew, then shrank, and was gone.

Horrified, Daine called up her magic again while the Skinners walked on. She searched the village for more abandoned animals. There was a chicken coop on the edge of town. Its occupants could sense nearby monsters; they shrieked their alarm. She didn't stop to remember that she despised chickens for their stupidity and their smell. Once more she dropped, taking on her true shape as soon as she touched the ground.

Fumbling at the rope latch on the coop, she glanced around. More than anything, she wanted to see the Skinners before they saw her. The rope gave. Chickens erupted from the coop, showering Daine with feathers, scratching her and squawking in her ears. "Stop it, you idiotic birds!" she whispered. "Shut up, clear out, and get away from here!"

She used her magic to give them brief wisdom. The chickens raced into the forest, away from the approaching monsters. Daine took eagle shape for the third time, watching the Skinners from high above as she waited for Numair to arrive.

He threw off his cloaking spell when he and Spots reached the dead zone, and Daine glided down to meet him. Taking her pack, she dressed behind a tree as she reported what she had seen. When he dismounted, she unsaddled Spots and sent the gelding into the still-living woods, out of the Skinners' path.

Numair passed her crossbow and quiver to her. "Can we beat them?" he asked.

Daine's blue-gray eyes met his dark ones. "I don't know," she said truthfully. "I've never seen the like of these things." Putting a foot in the crossbow's stirrup, she drew the bowstring until it hooked over the release.

The man sighed and dropped his cloak over their packs. Black fire that sparkled with bits of white appeared around his body. "Give me that quarrel," he said, holding out a hand. She obeyed, passing over the bolt that she'd been about to load. He closed long fingers around it, lips moving, then handed it over.

Daine placed the quarrel in the clip, then led him to their quarry. The Skinners had finished with the village of Greenhall and had entered a nearby peach orchard. Half of the trees were stripped of their bark. Even the green fruit had lost its skin.

Numair looked ill. "Is it all like this?" he asked.

"Worse. There's acres of it, clean back to the hills." She raised the bow to her shoulder, taking deliberate aim. The Skinners, in the middle of the orchard, turned to stare at them—if they could stare.

Daine shot. The quarrel flew straight, and buried itself in one Skinner's head. Numair gestured; an explosion tore the air. The Skinner blew apart, showering its companions with pieces of itself. The others looked around in apparent confusion.

Daine started to grin, but stopped. Swiftly each of the Skinner chunks doubled, redoubled, and spread. Each sprouted a pair of stumps to stand on, and stretched. Now there were ten Skinners, five large and five smaller ones. Their attention fixed on her and Numair, they came at a run. Daine slipped another bolt into the clip of the bow.

The mage raised a hand. Black fire jumped away from him and swept over the monsters, pulling them into the air. The Skinners thrashed and broke through his control, hurtling to the ground. Slowly, they got up.

"I hope the owner of this orchard forgives me," muttered Numair.

Stretching out his hands, he shouted a phrase that Daine couldn't understand. The ground before the advancing Skinners ripped open. They dropped into the crevasse.

Numair trotted toward it, Daine right behind him. "If I can seal them into the earth, that may be the end of it. I certainly hope so." Halting at the edge of the crack, they peered in. "I *hate* simply blasting them with raw power like this. There is always a spell to uncreate anything, though the consequences may be—oh, dear."

The Skinners were climbing the sides. Numair jerked Daine back, shouting a word that made her ears pound. The earth rumbled, knocking them down; the crack sealed.

"Please Goddess, please Mithros, let that stop them," whispered Numair. Sweat dripped from his face as Daine helped him to stand. "Grant a boon on Midsummer's Day—"

Daine heard something behind them and whirled. Ten feet away, crude hands erupted through dirt. "Numair!" she cried, and shot the emerging Skinner. Unmagicked, her bolt had no effect. The creature rose from the ground as if it climbed a stair.

Numair cried out in Old Thak. The creature that Daine had shot turned to water. The man whirled to do the same to another Skinner. Half out of the earth, it dissolved.

Five spots near them exploded as Skinners leaped free of the ground. Daine screamed. Numair reached to pull her closer, and discovered that someone else had the same idea. Two pairs of hands clutched the girl by the arms, dragging her into a patch of air that burned silvery white.

"No!" shouted the mage, wrapping both arms around Daine. The phantom hands continued to pull.

Sinking into white pain, Daine heard a man shriek, "Curse you, follow them! Follow, *follow, FOLLOW!*"

Unseen by her or Numair, an inky shadow leaped free of the grass to wrap itself around her feet. Girl, man, and shadow vanished into bright air. Every inch of her throbbed. Hands gripped her; she fought. "The Skinners! They'll kill Numair, they'll kill the People, they'll kill the crops! Let me *go!*"

A female voice, one that she knew, said, "If she doesn't rest, she won't heal. He's just as bad. Both keep fretting about those monsters."

"I'd best take care of it, then." The second, gravelly voice was even more familiar.

"Why?" The speaker was an unknown male. "Leave mortal affairs to mortals."

"Nonsense," barked the gravel voice. Whiskers tickled her face; a musky scent that she knew well filled her nose. "Listen, Daine. Numair is here, with you. He's safe. I'll fix those Skinners. I can handle them. Now rest, and stop fussing!"

She sneezed. "All right, Badger." If her old friend the badger god said that things would be taken care of, she could believe him, even if all this was only a dream.

The woman's voice was fading. "I'll tell Numair."

The next time Daine woke, the pain gnawing at her had turned to a dull, steady ache. Cloth rustled nearby; the faint odor of sweet pea and woods lily filled her nose. Like the female voice she'd heard, she knew that scent well. She opened her eyes.

A blurred face hung over her. Daine squinted, trying to see. The face became clearer: blue eyes, a dimple at the corner of that smiling mouth, creamy skin, straight nose, high cheekbones. The whole was topped with a braided crown of heavy golden hair.

In a second the girl forgot the last four years. She was twelve again, and in her bed in Galla. "Ma?" she croaked. "I dreamed you was dead." With a frown, she corrected herself—she knew how to speak like cultured folk nowadays! "I dreamed you *were* dead."

Sarra Beneksri—Daine's mother—laughed. "Sweetling, it was no dream, I *am* dead."

Some of Daine's confusion faded. "Well, that's all right, then." She tried to sit up. "Where am I?"

Sarra moved pillows to help her. "You're in the realms of the gods."

Moving dizzied the girl. "How'd I get *here*? And why do I hurt so?"

"We brought you. Sadly, passage between realms was fair hard for you. Here's something to drink against the pain."

"Talk about familiar," Daine grumbled, taking the offered cup. With each swallow, she felt an improvement; by the time she'd swallowed all of the liquid, her pain was nearly gone. "Your messes have gotten better," she remarked with a grin.

"It's the herbs here." Sarra pinched Daine's nose gently. "They're stronger. Open your eyes wide." She used her fingers to pull back Daine's eyelids. "Where were you born?"

"Snowsdale, in Galla. Why are you asking?"

"To see if your mind's unhurt—though it being you, I wonder if I'll be able to tell."

"Ma!" squeaked Daine with a laughing outrage.

"How old are you?"

"Sixteen." Memory returned in a rush. "Where's Numair? The Skinners—"

Her mother stopped her from getting up. "Easy. Master Numair is here, and safe. The badger took care of those skinning monsters. He turned them to ice, and they melted. They won't trouble anyone now."

"So I didn't dream that." Daine sank back against her pillows gratefully, fingering the heavy silver badger's claw that hung on a chain around her neck. "Where did they come from, do you suppose?"

"You know as much as me" was the reply. "I've never seen the like of them."

"Sarra?" The voice coming from the next room was deep, male, and unfamiliar.

The woman's face lit up. "In here, my love. She's awake."

The door opened, and a man dressed in a loincloth entered. Although the doorway was unusually large, the crown of antlers firmly rooted in his brown, curly hair forced him to duck to pass through. He was tan and heavily muscled, with emerald eyes. Daine was unsettled to notice that there also were olive streaks in his reddish brown skin.

"So." He touched his antlers uneasily as she stared at them. "We meet at last."

"This is your father," Sarra told Daine. "This is the god Weiryn."

## ✦✦ TWO ✦✦

# MEETINGS WITH GODS

**∞** He looked so—odd. No one else's father had antlers, or went half naked. What was she supposed to say? "Hullo, Da." She hid trembling hands under her blankets.

"Daine!" Sarra cried. "Is that the best you can do? He's your da!"

The girl couldn't begin to describe her feelings. Only months ago, she had learned that the horned man she saw in visions was her father, and that he was a god. She had tried not to think about it ever since. "It's not like you ever told me who he was, or what he was," she reminded her mother. "Not even a *hint*."

"I thought we'd have time later," replied Sarra. "I never meant to be killed by bandits!"

"Daine?" Numair came to the door, looking pale and tired. "You know that the badger destroyed the Skinners, yes?"

"Ma told me. You don't look so good."

He smiled. "I'll survive. Are *you* all right?"

"I hurt a little." She couldn't help but note, with some amusement, that except for the tips of his horns, Weiryn was shorter than her friend.

Numair smiled twistedly. "I am informed that passage between the realms has an adverse effect on mortals." He clung to the doorframe.

Silver fire glimmered on the floor, and a large badger appeared. Daine smiled as her mentor waddled over. He looked up at her with black eyes that were bright in his vividly marked face. "Hullo," she told him. "So we've you to thank for handling those Skinners?"

"You wouldn't rest until you knew they were dealt with." Balancing on his hindquarters, the god rose to plant his forepaws on her covers. Her nose filled with his musky, heavy scent.

Gently she scratched him behind the ears. Since she had left her

Gallan home, the badger had visited her, teaching her the use of her wild magic, and warning of danger to come. The claw she wore around her neck was his; he could always trace it to find her.

Sarra frowned at Numair. "You are supposed to sit, and stay sat." She made a tugging gesture at the wall beside the mage. That part of the room began to move; the floor buckled and rose. The wall stretched to meet it, then sagged to create a chair. "Down, Master Salmalín!" ordered Sarra. Meekly, he did as ordered.

Daine's jaw dropped. "But—Ma, you can't—You never—"

"Things are different here," the badger said. "In the Divine Realms, we gods can shape our surroundings to suit ourselves."

"Sometimes," added Weiryn.

"Wonderful," the girl said weakly. She was not sure that she liked to see unliving things move about under their own power. "Tell me— how did we come here? The last thing I remember is the Skinners."

Weiryn and Sarra traded glances. "You were in danger of your life, against a foe you could not fight," the god said. "We had meant to bring you only, but this—*man*"—he glared at the mage—"refused to let go of you. We were forced to bring him as well."

"I just thank the Goddess that you met the Skinners on one of the great holidays, when we *could* pull you through to us," added Daine's mother. "Otherwise you would have been killed. It fair troubles me that no one we've asked has ever heard of those creatures."

Light bloomed through the curtains on a window that filled one of the walls, growing steadily brighter, then fading. Just as it was nearly gone, another slow flash came. "Oh, dear," remarked Sarra as Weiryn opened the drapes. "They're still at it."

"What's going on?" Numair asked, lurching to his feet.

"Will you *sit?*" cried Daine's mother. "Men! You're so stubborn!" Numair quickly sat, this time on the bed. Sulkily, the chair that Sarra had made for him sank into the wall.

Daine stared at the view. The ground here dropped away to meet a busy stream. There were no trees between stream and house, although the forest grew thickly on the far side of the water. In the oval of open sky overhead, waves of rippling pea green, orange, yellow, and gray fire shimmered and coursed.

"What is it?" she whispered. Numair took her hand and squeezed it gently. "I feel that it means something bad, but it's so beautiful . . ."

"It means that Uusoae, the Queen of Chaos, is fighting the Great Gods," said the badger. "That light is her magic and her soldiers, as they attack the barriers between our realm and hers."

"She has been at it since Midwinter." Weiryn put an arm around

Sarra. "Normally the lights that burn in our sky reflect your mortal wars, but this is far more important."

"Thanks ever so," muttered Numair. Daine grinned at him.

Sarra looked at her daughter and said reproachfully, "Speaking of war, I never raised *you* to be always fighting and killing. That's not woman's work."

"It's needful, Ma. *You* taught me a woman has to know how to defend herself."

"I never!" gasped Sarra, indignant.

"You taught me when you were murdered in your own house," Daine said quietly.

Sarra turned back into Weiryn's hold, leaning on his chest, but not before the girl saw tears in her mother's eyes. A hand patted her ankle; a broad head thrust itself under her elbow. Against her mother's hurt, she set Numair's smile and the badger's approval.

"Sarra, our war in Tortall may seem unimportant to the gods, but not to us," Numair said. "Daine and I must return to it. They need every fighter, and every mage."

Daine nodded, and closed her eyes. She felt dizzy. Her bones were aching again.

Sarra glanced over and saw what was wrong. "We'll talk of that later," she said crisply. "You both need to drink a posset, then sleep again. It will be a few days before the effects of your passage are over." She went to the hearth and ladled something from a pot into a pair of cups. One she gave to Numair, the other to Daine. "Drink."

The liquid in the cup smelled vile, but Daine knew better than to argue. She gulped it down when Numair did, praying that her stomach wouldn't reject it.

"Back to bed, sir mage," ordered Sarra.

"Good night, Daine," Numair said. The badger echoed him.

"G'night," she murmured, eyes closing already. She sank back among pillows that smelled of sundried cotton. "Oh—I forgot. G'night—Da."

She heard a deep chuckle; a hand smoothed her curls. "I am glad that you are here and safe, little one."

Daine smiled, and slept.

Waking slowly, she heard familiar voices, and thought she dreamed them.

The speaker was a mage, Harailt of Aili. "—from Fiefs Seabeth and Seajen." He panted, as if he'd been running. "A Yamani fleet's been sighted to the west. The bad news is, somehow the Scanrans knew they were coming. They fled overnight."

"Father Storm's curses!" That voice was Queen Thayet's. "How does the enemy get his information? I'd swear on my children's lives that there's no way for a spy to report our plans—and yet the enemy continues to stay one step ahead!"

"I'll ask the mages to start using truthspells and the Sight, and see if we can identify an enemy agent." Harailt sounded worn out.

"Please do," replied the queen. "And when we find him—or her—I hope that person is good with his gods."

Daine opened her eyes. The little room was silent, and bathed in sunlight.

What a strange dream, she thought, and sat up.

There was an even stranger animal on her bed.

At first she thought that someone had played a very bad joke on a young beaver; her visitor had that same dense brown fur. No beaver, though, had ever sported a duck's bill. The tail was wrong, too. It was the proper shape, but it was covered with hair. As the creature, a little over two feet in length, toddled up the length of her bed, she saw that it had webbed feet. Reaching her belly, it cocked its head first one way, then the other, examining her with eyes deeply set into the skull, near that preposterous bill.

"G'day, Weiryn's daughter," the animal greeted her. "Glad to see you awake."

Daine had stopped breathing—she made herself inhale. "Are you a—a god?"

"We're all gods here, except for the immortals," replied her visitor.

She sat up carefully. "Excuse me for asking, but what *are* you, exactly?"

"I am Broad Foot, the male god of the duckmoles."

"Duckmoles? I never heard of them." His fleshy bill *was* the same shape as a duck's, but with comblike ridges inside the bottom half. "May I pick you up?"

He nodded. "Mind the spurs on my hind feet, though. I've poison in them."

She lifted him gently. The fur under her fingers was springy and thick. Examining broad, webbed feet armed with heavy claws, she handled the rear ones—and their venomous spurs—with care. "What on *earth* do you eat?" she asked, putting him down.

"My people eat shrimp, insects, snails—frogs and small fish if we can get any. I usually eat the same things as my people, though gods are more venturesome. Sarra cooks the best fish stew in the Divine Realms. I spend warm seasons here, just for that."

"You come here for Ma's *cooking*?"

His eyes twinkled. "That's right. She sent me to tell you that she has food ready for *you*, if you care to dress and come out."

Daine eased out from under the blankets, careful not to dislodge her guest, and saw that she wore a cotton nightgown. "How long have we been here?" she asked Broad Foot.

"Four days. See you in the garden." Silver fire bloomed; the duck-mole vanished.

Four days was too long. What were Kitten, Tkaa, and King Jonathan doing now? Did they know that Numair and Daine weren't dead? Frowning, she washed her face and cleaned her teeth; all that she needed to do those chores lay on a table.

Looking about, she saw a simple red cotton dress at the foot of the bed. Under it lay a pink shift, underclothes, and red slippers. She wished they were a shirt and breeches, but knew she might as well put them on. There was no sign of her old clothes, but even if she *could* find them, she doubted that they would be in very good condition.

Once dressed, she had to sit briefly to catch her breath. The weakness and ache weren't as bad as they had been, but she was still shaky. Tidying her bed required another rest before she could leave the room. She did not see the pocket of shadow that separated from the gloom under her bed and followed her.

The main room of the cottage was empty of people. Looking around, she saw the things that she would expect in her mother's house, as well as three heavy perches—as if very large birds often visited. She guessed that other bedrooms lay behind closed doors. Two doors, however, stood open. Outside one, a path led downhill into a forest. Going to the other, she looked into a walled kitchen garden. A small well, a table, benches, and an outdoor hearth were placed on the open grass. Her mother sat at the table, peeling apples. The duckmole sat on the table beside her, pushing a bit of peel with his bill.

Sarra beamed as Daine sat opposite her. "It's long past breakfast, but I thought you might still want porridge." She filled a bowl from a pot on the hearth. Pitchers of honey and cream were on the table; Daine used both. The porridge was rich, with a deep, nutty taste that shocked her. It was stuffed with bits of dried fruit, each tasting fresh-picked. The cream and honey also were intensely flavorful. She ate only half of the bowl, and put it aside. Her mother drew a mug of water from the well. That was easier to swallow, although it was as powerful as if it came from an icy mountain stream.

Sarra frowned. "You should be hungrier, after all that sleep and the pain from crossing over."

"You forget how things tasted when *you* first came here." A fluffy orange-and-white-marbled cat leaped onto the table to sit in front of Daine. She stared at the girl with large amber eyes, pink nose twitching. "In the Divine Realms, you eat the essence of things, not the shadow. I am Queenclaw, goddess of house cats."

Respectfully, the girl bowed. Queenclaw was an impressive creature. "It's a very great honor, meeting you."

"Of course it is." The cat began to wash.

"How'd you come to be here, Ma?" Daine asked. "I thought the mortal dead go to the Black God's realm."

Sarra cut her apples. "So I did," she replied. "Your father came for me there. He petitioned the Great Gods to allow me to live with him. They decided it was well enough." She eyed Daine warily. "You blame me for not telling you about him?"

Daine looked at the cat, who was still washing, and at the duckmole, who was grinding apple bits in his bill. She'd forgotten her ma's way of discussing private things before others. "It might've helped later, is all. Ma, we can't stay, you know. We're—"

Queenclaw hissed, and leaped off the table. Briefly Daine suspected her of creating a diversion, until she saw that a black shape, almost like a living ink blot, was tangled in the cat's teeth and claws. It wriggled and shifted like water, trying to escape. Only when the duckmole jumped down to stand on one of the thing's tendrils did it quiet.

"What is that?" the girl wanted to know.

"I've no notion," replied Sarra, frowning. "I've never seen anything like it. Unless it's one of Gainel's—the Dream King's. It *could* be one of his nightmares."

"No," Queenclaw said, looking up. "He's strict with his creatures. They lose their power over mortals if they're allowed to wander, so he keeps them close."

"We'll hold it for Weiryn to look at when he returns." Sarra reached down, white light spilling from her fingers. When it touched the shadowy thing, Queenclaw and Broad Foot moved away from it. Kneeling, Sarra picked the creature up, using the white fire as a kind of scoop. "What manner of beastie are you?" she asked, frowning.

The creature rolled itself into a small, tight ball.

"I command you, give me your name!" ordered Sarra. There was a crack, and a smell of blood. *"Darking?"* She looked at the animal gods. "Have you heard of it?"

"Never," Queenclaw said, washing a forepaw.

Broad Foot shook his head. Vanishing in a wave of silver fire, he reappeared on the table next to the girl. "Easier than climbing for a little fellow like me," he explained.

Daine's mother shrugged, dropping the creature into her apron pocket. "That will hold you for now." She drew a line of white fire across the pocket's opening. Seeing it, Daine was uneasy: Sarra's magical Gift had always shown as rose-pink fire, not white.

"Don't fuss," the woman told her pocket as the darking began to thrash inside. "You'll just—" She fell silent abruptly and cocked her head as if she listened to someone.

When Daine opened her mouth, the cat placed a paw over it, silencing her. "Hush," Queenclaw whispered. "Someone needs her." Fur tickled Daine's nose; she sneezed.

"You are known to the Green Lady, Isa," Sarra remarked, oddly formal. "You seek aid for a breech birth? Who is the mother?" She listened, then sighed. "Nonia. I see."

Daine frowned. They had known an Isa and a Nonia in Snowsdale. Her mother had always claimed that Isa would be a good midwife, if she could ever stop having children of her own. Nonia was barely a year older than Daine herself.

"Harken, Isa. You must turn the babe before it comes. No—listen to me, and I will help." Absently, Sarra walked into the cottage, looking at something very far away.

Daine was the only one who saw the darking—whatever it was— drop to the ground through a hole in its pocket prison. She thought, just like Ma to fix the opening with magic and forget there's a hole in the bottom. She said nothing as the darking vanished into the shadows by the cottage wall. If Queenclaw and Broad Foot hadn't seen its escape, she wasn't going to tell them. After all, the darking hadn't done any harm.

"She's not the same as she was back home," she whispered, more to herself than to the cat or the duckmole.

"Of course not." Queenclaw stretched. "Only gods or immortals may dwell here."

"You're telling me that Ma—*my* Ma—is a god."

"There was a need," Broad Foot explained. "The northern forests had no one to watch over village gardens and childbearing—the Great Mother Goddess can't be *everywhere*. It wouldn't have worked if your mother hadn't liked such things already. Since she does, she became the Green Lady."

"Is she my Ma, then?" demanded the girl. "Is she who she was, Sarra Beneksri?"

"Are you who *you* were?" asked the cat.

About to say that of course she was, Daine stopped herself. Daine of Snowsdale could no more heal animals—or turn into one—than the sun could rise in the west. She got up, ignoring a slight dizziness that overtook her. "Please excuse me. I need a walk."

"Be careful," both gods chorused.

"Do you wish a guide?" added Broad Foot, concern in his voice. "Some mortals find the Divine Realms overwhelming—"

"No company, thank you," Daine said, heading toward the gate.

Outside the wall lay a well-marked path. To her right it curved around the house. To her left it crossed a log bridge over a stream and led into the forest. Near the trees a rocky bluff rose in tumbles of earth and stone until it breached the leafy canopy. Anyone who climbed it should have a view that would stretch for miles.

Crossing the bridge, she found that her head had cleared; strength was returning to her legs and arms. She left the path at the foot of the bluff, taking a track that wound through piles of stone, leading her gently upward. When she stopped for a breath after steady climbing, a nearby chuckling sound drew her to a spring hidden in the rocks. A couple of sips of water were all that she needed: Her veins seemed to fill with a green and sparkling energy that carried her on upward.

There was plenty to think about as she climbed. Her Ma, a god? She loved her mother, but there was no denying that Sarra needed looking after. Without it, she would seek plants on a cloudy day without taking a hat. Gods were dignified, all-knowing, all-powerful creatures, weren't they?

She knew that lesser gods entered the mortal realms only on the equinoxes and solstices, and her mother had said it was good they met the Skinners on Midsummer Day. There were degrees of strength among gods, then. If this was so, then perhaps lesser gods weren't all-anything, and Sarra could now be a divine being.

"There would be *worse* goddesses than Ma, I guess," she remarked, then sighed.

She left her thin, pretty slippers under a bush when they began to pinch. Thickening the soles of her feet by changing them to elephant hide, she climbed on in comfort. The way was rocky and steep. By the time she reached the rocky summit, she was gasping.

Below was the forest roof, an expanse of countless shades of green, pierced by clearings, streams, and ponds. Turning, she found mountains that stabbed into the sky, their heads wrapped in cloud, their shoulders white with snow.

"Oh, glory," she whispered, and went to see what lay below on that side. Passing a dip in the rock, she halted. A pool of some eerie substance was cupped there. It shimmered with green, yellow, gray, and blue lights, much like the colors that she'd seen in the sky the night before. They moved over its surface in globes, waves, or strips. Watching the pool made her giddy. She swayed, and put out a hand.

"Don't touch it!" a voice behind her warned.

She fought to yank her eyes away in vain. There was something terrible in those moving colors, something that she rebelled against as it drew her in. Pain flared on her ankle; it broke the pool's grip. She stumbled back a few steps.

"Careful!" Clinging to her foot was a lizard, a striped skink. "I'm sorry I hurt you, but I thought you needed help." Green with white and black stripes and a yellow muzzle, she was large for her kind, a foot in length. Her black eyes glinted with intelligence.

Daine bent to pick up the lizard. "So I did." She crossed to the far side of the bluff, putting yards of stone between her and the shifting pool. There she sat, placing the skink beside her. An inspection of her ankle showed that it bled a little. "Thank you."

"You're welcome." The skink jumped on top of a nearby rock to put herself at eye level with the girl. "The next time you find a Chaos vent, don't look into it," the lizard advised. "It'll pull first your mind, and then the rest of you, into the realms of Chaos."

"Chaos vents?" She licked her finger and dabbed at the bite, cleaning it off.

"You'll find them all over the Divine Realms," replied the skink. "They serve as gods' windows into the home of Uusoae, the Queen of Chaos."

"You'd think they'd put warning markers on such things," grumbled Daine. "And why are the gods keeping these windows open if they're fighting this Uusoae?"

"The vents have always been in both the Divine and Chaos Realms, whether they're at war or not," explained the skink. "Father Universe and Mother Flame ordered things that way. Are you over your scare?"

"I think so." Daine leaned back, bracing herself with her arms as she looked at the view. "Why didn't I sense you?" she asked. "I should've known you were here the moment I got in range." In the distance, a hawk wheeled over an opening in the trees. Her finely tuned ears picked out the distant call of crows, jays, and starlings. "I never *felt* any of the People. I can't hear you in my mind."

"Nor will you," the skink replied calmly. "We are not mortal animals, Veralidaine Sarrasri—we are gods. If we are killed, we are instantly reborn in new bodies. We have our own magic, powerful magic. Mortals cannot hear us, or know us."

Daine rubbed her ears. "I feel deaf. I feel—separate from everything."

"It's all right," said her companion. "Bask awhile. The sun will do you good."

Daine smiled to think that sunning would help, but she obeyed. The rock warmed her and banished the fear caused by the Chaos vent. Below, woodpeckers tapped trees; squirrels called alarms. Nearby a pika chirped. From the mountains behind them, first one, then another, then more wolf voices rose in pack-song. She grinned, hearing the feeble, shaky notes of wolf pups joining their elders, perhaps for the first time.

The wind shifted, and brought with it a hint of wood smoke. Looking for the source, she found her parents' house and garden, cradled in the bend of the stream that ran past her window. A white plume of smoke trailed from the chimney.

"Look," said the skink. "To the west."

A large, dark bird of some kind flew up from the tree canopy in a twisting pattern. Daine couldn't see it clearly; one moment it was shadowy, the next almost transparent. It was larger than any bird of prey, though not as big as a griffin. She would guess that it was four or five feet long, with a seven-foot wingspan. Up it flew, its spiral tightening. When it seemed as though it spun like a top in midair, the bird opened its wings to their widest, spread its tail, and faced the sun.

Daine gasped as spears of orange, yellow, red, white, and even scraps of blue light flared from the creature's feathers, turning it into airborne flame. It flashed its blazing wings three times, then folded, shedding its fire, or covering it. Once more it was simply a nondescript bird, now flying downward in a spiral.

The skink sighed with pleasure. "Sunbirds," she said. "They do this from noon until sunset. I never get tired of watching it."

For a while they sat in quiet comfort, enjoying the vast scene before them. In the distance an eagle screamed. The breeze changed, to come out of the south, carrying with it the scent of water from still pools and busy streams.

The skink's head shifted. Daine looked and saw three bird forms rise from the trees in that distinctive corkscrew flight pattern. Eagerly she watched the sunbirds climb far above the leafy canopy. At last the three faced the sun, spreading wings and tails in an explosion of color. Daine gasped at the brilliance of the hues: There were more dabs of blue and green light among these birds, even a strong hint of purple under the flame.

There was also something like a picture. Startled, she closed her eyes; the image was clear on the insides of her lids. Queen Thayet and Onua, Horsemistress of the Queen's Riders, stood back to back on the wall before the royal palace in Tortall. Stormwings fell on them, filthy and open-clawed, mouths wide in silent shrieks. Grimly the two women, armed with small, recurved bows, shot arrow after arrow into the flock overhead, hitting Stormwings almost every time. A mage raced along the wall to join them, raising both hands. Something glittered like crystal in his palms.

The image faded. Opening her eyes, Daine got up. "I have to go," she told the reptile, who watched her curiously. "It was very nice meeting you."

"Come back when you can visit longer," the god replied.

Daine frowned at the skink. "Why are you being so nice?" she asked. "I'd have thought a god would be more, well, aloof."

The skink couldn't smile, but Daine heard amusement in her voice. "When you were a little girl, you once saved a nest of young skinks from two-leggers who wished to torture them. For my children, I thank you—and I hope to see you again."

Daine bowed to her, then began her descent. She had to stop more often to rest this time. A drink from the spring helped, but her legs were trembling by the time she reached the bottom.

Weiryn was there, waiting, strung bow in one hand, a dead hare in the other, quiver of arrows on his back. "Your mother is worried about you." His leaf-colored eyes were unreadable. "It's not always a good idea to wander here, these days."

Daine wiped her sweaty face on her sleeve. "I know what I'm doing," she said shortly. "And what is *that*?" She pointed to his kill. "Surely a god doesn't need to hunt."

"Don't vex that tender heart of yours," he replied. "As gods themselves, my prey are reborn into new bodies instantly, or there would be no game anywhere in these realms. And a hunt god *must* hunt." He turned and walked toward the cottage. Daine fell in beside him. "Didn't those mortals teach you anything? The tasks of gods bind us to our mortal followers."

"But you don't need to eat. You're gods."

"We don't need to, but it's fun. Which reminds me—I don't like how *you've* been eating lately. What kind of hunter's daughter won't touch game?"

Daine sighed. "One that's *been* hunted, in deer shape and in goose shape." She tried to smile. "I'm down to mutton, chicken, and fish, Da. I'm just too close to the rest of the People to be eating them."

Weiryn shook his antlered head. "To think that—" He whirled, dropping the hare. "I *thought* so."

"What?" she asked.

In a single, fluid movement, he put an arrow to his string and shot. His arrow struck, quivering, in a patch of shadow under a bush.

Daine frowned. *Something* keened there, in a tiny voice she heard as much in her mind as in her ears. Trotting over, she saw that the shaft pinned an ink blot. What had Ma called it? A darking? "What did you do that for?" she demanded, cross. Gripping the arrow, she yanked it out of the creature. It continued to flutter, crying, a hole in its center. "You don't even know what it is!" She tried to push the blot in on the hole in its middle.

"I don't have to," was the retort. "It came into *my* territory without leave, sneaking about, following us. Now, don't go coddling it—"

Sitting, she picked up the darking and carefully pinched the hole in its body, holding the edges together. "It's fair foolish to shoot something when you don't even know what it is." The darking ceased its cries; when she let go, the hole was sealed.

The god picked up the hare. "When you are my age, you may question what I do. Now, come along. Leave that thing." He set off down the trail.

Daine looked at the darking. "Do you want to come with me?" she asked, wondering if it could understand. "I won't let him hurt—"

The darking fell through her hands to the ground and raced under the bush. That's a clear enough answer, thought Daine. "Don't let him see you again," she called. "For all I know, he'll keep shooting you." She trotted to catch up to her sire.

"I never thought a daughter of mine would have these sentimental attachments," he remarked. "Pain and suffering trouble gods, but they don't burden us as they do mortals."

Daine thought of the two-legger goddess that she had met the previous fall, the Graveyard Hag. Certainly *she* hadn't been troubled by the ruction that she had caused. "Maybe that explains more than it doesn't," she replied grimly. "Though I believe gods would be kinder if things hurt them more."

Her father turned to look at her. "What makes you think our first duty is to be kind?" he wanted to know. "Too much tenderness is bad for mortals. They improve themselves only by struggling. Everyone knows that."

She blinked. He sounded like those humans who claimed that poverty made the poor into nobler souls. "Of course, Da. Whatever you say."

Sarra met them on the other side of the log bridge. She kissed her mate, then ordered, "Go skin and dress that hare, and not in the house." He left, and she looked at Daine. "You shouldn't wander off like that, sweet. You're not well yet—"

"Ma, if I'm well enough to climb that"—she pointed to the bluff that thrust out of the forest—"then I'm well enough to go home. Me 'n' Numair can't be lingering here."

Sarra blinked, her mouth trembling. "Are you so eager to get away from me? After not even a full day awake in my house?"

Daine's throat tightened. "I don't want to leave *you*. Don't think it!" She hugged her mother. "I missed you," she whispered. "Four years—I never stopped missing you."

Sarra's arms were tight around her. "I missed you too, sweetling."

Memory surged: The girl could almost smell burned wood, spilled blood, and the reek of death. The last time that she'd held her mother, Sarra had been stone cold, and Daine had been trying to yank out the arrows that had killed her. Tears rolled down her face.

Gentle hands stroked her hair and back. "There, there," Sarra whispered. "I am sorry. Never would I have left you willingly, not for *all* the gods in these realms." Softly she crooned until Daine's tears slowed, then stopped.

"Forgive me." The girl pulled away, wiping her eyes. "It was—remembering . . ."

"Me too." Sarra drew a handkerchief from a pocket. Tugging on it until two handkerchiefs appeared, she gave one to Daine, and used the other to dry her own eyes.

"Grandda?" asked the girl. She blew her nose.

"In the realms of the dead. He's happy there. Well, you know we never got on well. We like each other better now that I only visit now and—" Sarra cocked her head, that odd, listening expression on her face. "Someone needs me?" she asked, her smile wry. "Two in one day—I must be getting popular." Her voice changed, as it had in the garden before. "Yes, Lori Hillwalker. The Green Lady hears you." Turning, she walked away, crossing the stream on the log bridge.

Daine wasn't sure if she ought to follow. Looking around, she saw Queenclaw trotting toward her.

"Don't just stand there," ordered the cat goddess, "pet me. Did she get another call?"

Daine knelt to obey. "I don't see why they *would* call on her. They liked her well enough when they needed a healer. The rest of the time, they thought she was silly, and odd . . . and shameful." Queenclaw looked up, and Daine answered the unspoken question. "Well, there was me, and no husband, and there was—*were* always men around Ma."

"Cats have more sense," Queenclaw said. "We don't keep toms or kittens about any longer than we must. Mind, your people don't know it's her they pray to. They call on the Green Lady, who started to appear over the town well in Snowsdale. She told them to summon her for help in childbirth and sickness, or for matters of the heart."

"I'll be switched." Daine was impressed in spite of herself.

The cat's eyes followed something in the grass that only she could see. "You'd better go do something with the stew," she remarked, tail flicking as she crouched low to the ground. "It hasn't been stirred in a while." She pounced. A mouse squeaked and ran for its life, Queenclaw in hot pursuit.

Grinning, Daine went inside. The stew smelled wonderful. Stirring it, the girl realized that she was half listening for a courier to arrive, wanting her or her friends to arm themselves and come quickly. There were no horns calling for riders to mount and ride out. There was no thunder of message drums, pounding signals to those who had no mages to pass on the latest news. Her parents' house breathed rest and quiet.

I wish I could stay, she thought wistfully. I never realized how tired I've been, till now. And I can't stay—neither of us can.

## →→ THREE ←←

# DREAMS

**∽∾** As she moved the stew off the fire, she heard an assortment of sounds from one of the other rooms. She grinned: Numair had a habit of talking aloud as he fixed information of interest in his memory. Walking to an open door, she looked inside. Bent half double, the mage stood at the window as he tried to shave, using a mirror propped on the sill. *That's the trouble with being so tall,* she thought, not for the first time. *The things most folk can make use of, like windowsills, are that much farther away from him.*

When he took the razor from his skin, she asked, "Need help?"

His dark eyes lit in welcome. "It's good to see you on your feet."

"It's good to be on them." Getting the mirror, she held it for him. "Have you talked to Da or Ma about sending us home?"

He smiled crookedly, and wet his razor again. "Let us say rather that I have *attempted* to do so. They are amazingly elusive on the subject. The best I've gotten so far is that we may discuss it once you have recovered."

"I've recovered," she assured him. She knew that wasn't entirely true, but the images she had seen in the sunbird's display worried her.

"Daine," he said, then stopped. She waited. Something was troubling him; she could hear it in his voice. "Perhaps—perhaps you should stay here when I return. This is your home. You'd be safe here."

She put down the mirror, outraged. "How can you say that? *Tortall* is my home!"

"You'd be with Sarra—I know you've missed her. You'd get to know your father." He put the mirror back on the sill and scraped the remaining bristles from his chin. "Look at it from my perspective." He wouldn't meet her eyes, but his soft voice was pleading. "I was powerless against the Skinners. There are so many foes in this war, and too many are strange. I would like to know that *you*, at least, had a chance to survive."

"I'll make my own chances, if you please." Standing, she fought sudden dizziness. Carefully, she sat on the bed as Numair rinsed and dried his face.

"Will you at least consider it?" he asked, draping the towel over the window ledge.

"No."

"Daine . . ." Picking up the mirror, he examined his face. His dark brows twitched together; he shoved the mirror under her nose. "What do you see?"

Instead of her reflection, the glass showed battle. Sir Raoul of the King's Own, Buri of the Queen's Riders, and a mixed company of the Own and Riders fought in a temple square. Ranged against them were Carthaki warriors in crimson leather. Overhead, creatures swooped down to attack the Tortallans with long-handled axes. Daine gasped: These were some kind of bat-winged, flying apes, their long black fur streaked with gray.

The image vanished. Numair put the mirror down with fingers that shook. Quietly, the girl described what she had seen in the sunbirds' dazzling flight.

"In the Divine Realms, *we* observe mortal affairs," said Broad Foot, waddling into the room. "Liquid is the most reliable, but flame and mirrors work. Mortals who visit tell us that in their sleeping, just before they wake, they hear what is said as well."

"Is it possible to observe specific people and events?" inquired Numair.

"Yes," replied the duckmole. "It is how Sarra could observe you, Daine. With practice, you could master it in a week or so, and hear as well as see what goes on in the mortal realms."

Numair picked up the mirror and sat on the bed.

"We'll finish our chat *later*," Daine told him, standing. "I'm not done with you!" He was not listening. With a sigh, she left him, trying not to use the furniture for support.

The animal god followed her into her room. "Are you well?"

"Just tired is all." Sitting on the bed, she rubbed her face. "Maybe climbing that bluff wasn't the cleverest thing to do my first day out of bed."

The duckmole vanished from the floor, reappearing beside her on the coverlet. Careful not to bump him, Daine lay back. "Of all times for him to go protective on me. Maybe he ate something that was bad for him." She closed her eyes.

"Maybe he loves you," Broad Foot said.

She didn't hear. She was already asleep.

In her dream, a pale wolf approached. Instead of the plumed tail that her kind bore proudly, the wolf's was thin and whiplike. "Rattail!" Daine ran to meet the chief female of the pack that helped to avenge Sarra's murder. It didn't seem to matter that Rattail was dead, or that a nasty female named Frostfur had taken her place in the pack.

When she was close, the wolf turned and trotted away.

"Wait!" Daine shouted, and followed.

Rattail led her down a long, dark hall, stopping at a closed door. When the girl caught up, the wolf held her paw to her muzzle, as if to say "Hush!" Daine knelt and pressed her ear to the door.

"Gainel, Uusoae's power worries you too much." While Daine had never heard that booming voice before, she knew that the speaker was Mithros the Sun Lord, chief of the gods. "We have always contained her. She has not the power to break through the barrier between her and us."

"If she's got no power, how is she holding her own against you for the first time in a thousand years?" Daine stifled a gasp. That was Carthak's patron, the Graveyard Hag. "She's using tricks we've never seen before, and I don't like it. You're fighting her the way you always have. What if she's found a new way to overset us—a way that we've never encountered and don't know how to defeat?"

"She will not consume us," Mithros said flatly. "She cannot fight us all, and she has no allies in any realm but her own."

The dream faded as Daine opened her eyes. She was still tired; her legs and back felt limp. Her nose worked as well as ever, though. She breathed deeply, enjoying the flood of good smells in the air. One was stew, the other bread. She was *hungry*.

Her dress should have been wrinkled from her nap, but when she flapped her skirts, the creases vanished. Quickly she splashed water on her face and combed her hair, then went outside, hearing voices from the garden.

There was a bit of sunlight left, but globes of witchfire hung over the table, growing brighter as night fell. Three men stood when she arrived. Sarra, Broad Foot, Queenclaw, and the badger nodded to her. Weiryn gestured to the new male. "Daughter, this is Gainel, Master of Dream, and one of the Great Gods. Gainel, my daughter, Veralidaine."

The girl looked up into a pale face framed by an unruly mane of dark hair. The eyes were shadowy pits that stretched into infinity. Staring into them, she thought that she saw the movement of stars in the distance—or was it Rattail? Cold hands took hers, jolting her back to the present. The god brushed Daine's fingers with a polite kiss.

"He says it is a pleasure to meet you," Weiryn told her. "You must excuse him—as the Dream King, he's only permitted to speak to mortals in dreams. We gods hear him"—Weiryn tapped his skull—"but you won't."

Daine curtsied to the god. "I'm honored, Your Majesty."

Gainel smiled, and took a seat at Sarra's right. Numair was at Weiryn's left, a place had been left for Daine between the mage and the duckmole. She stumbled trying to climb over the bench. Numair caught her and braced her arm until she was seated.

As utensils clattered and plates were handed around, there was no way to avoid noticing that the company included a duck-beaver creature, a man crowned with antlers, and a lanky, pallid man who seemed to fade into the growing shadows even while his face shone under witch-lights. More than anything Daine had observed since she and Numair were yanked out of that orchard, that dinner table said that Sarra Beneksri was not the Ma she had lived with in Galla.

The animal gods, her parents, and Gainel spoke mind to mind—she could see it in the way they turned their heads, moved their hands, or leaned forward. Daine concentrated on her food. She was fascinated by the variety. She hadn't seen a cow, a wheat field, or a grape arbor, but there was wine, bread, and cheese as well as the hare. Even knowing that the hare god lived on in a fresh body, she couldn't bring herself to have its meat. When the wine pitcher came to her, she passed it to Numair without pouring any for herself. If the food and water of the Divine Realms made her senses reel, she didn't want to think what liquor might do.

Numair asked Weiryn a question, keeping his voice low.

"Petition the Great Gods, for all the good it will do." Weiryn's reply could be heard by all. "They are too busy fighting Uusoae to ferry mortals back home. They won't even reply to mind calls from us lesser gods."

Numair looked at Gainel. "Forgive me," he said, "but our friends are hard pressed. Might *you* send us home? You are one of the Great Gods, and you don't look as if you are locked in combat with the Queen of Chaos."

Gainel smiled, shadowed eyes flickering, and shook his head.

"He says you forget your myths," Sarra told them. "Of the Great

Gods, the Dream King alone cannot enter the mortal realms. He can only send his creatures to do his work there."

"Forgive me," Numair said politely. "I *had* forgotten."

On Daine's foot, caught in a beam of light that fell between her and Numair, something moved. Reshaping her eyes to those of a cat, she looked harder. An inky shadow had thrown a tentacle over her bare foot. Was it the darking that Weiryn had shot?

"Pass the cheese?" asked Broad Foot, nudging her with his head. She obliged, forking slices onto his plate. As the duckmole happily mashed cheese in his bill, she glanced at her companions. Queenclaw mildly batted a piece of bread to and fro. Her mother seemed to be conversing with Gainel, while Numair tried to learn from Weiryn if a human mage might have better luck in approaching the rulers of the Divine Realms.

"I don't see why you fuss about it so," Weiryn snapped. "Come the fall equinox, *you* at least will be dragged back to your wars, and I wish you joy of them!"

"They don't *give* me joy, and I didn't ask for them," Numair said, voice tight. "Would you prefer we let Ozorne and his allies roll over us?"

Daine palmed some cheese. Breaking off a piece, she let her hand drop to hang beside her leg, and offered the tidbit to the creature. Tentacles grabbed the cheese and pulled it into the shadow. Daine offered another morsel. The darking made that vanish, too.

"By the way," Sarra told Gainel, "I think one of your servants might have escaped somehow and wandered here. It called itself a darking."

Daine flinched. The shadow flinched, too, and slipped off her foot to hide in the darkness under the table.

The woman fumbled with her apron, then sighed, exasperated. "Look at this." She lifted her hand. Her fingers stuck out of the hole in the pocket. "It got away."

The pale god covered Sarra's pocket with one hand. White light shimmered, and an image of the darking appeared. Immediately the Dream King shook his head.

"He's never seen its like," Weiryn told the humans. Gainel's light faded; he withdrew his hand from Sarra's apron.

"I *told* them you are strict with your subjects," said Queenclaw, grooming her tail.

Rising to his feet, Gainel nodded to them all, and vanished.

"He's terrible at good-byes," remarked Broad Foot. "Worse than a cat that way."

"I prefer to think he's as good as a cat," retorted Queenclaw.

Sarra got to her feet. "Well, no amount of wondering and chatter will see that the dishes are done. Let's get started, Daine."

The girl looked up at her mother, surprised. It had been a long time since anyone had told her to assist with cleanup. She wanted to say that she was tired, but if she did, her mother would fuss, and no doubt feed her nasty-tasting potions. With a sigh, the girl rose. Accepting a stack of plates from Sarra, she bore them inside. A washtub sat on a table in the common room, steaming faintly.

Daine set her burden next to it and turned. Sarra blocked the garden door, a bottle in one hand, a cup in the other. The girl winced—so much for fooling her ma.

"You overdid today, and you know it." She poured dark liquid into the cup. "Drink this, and off to bed with you."

Daine took the cup, but didn't drink. "Ma, why am I so weak? Are you sure it's because I'm half mortal, or might it be something worse?"

Sarra shook her golden head. "You came here long before it was time," she said firmly. "The balance between your mortal and divine blood is delicate—a crossing like yours usually causes problems. They're only temporary, I promise you. Now, drink, miss."

It tasted as vile as she had feared. She kissed her mother's cheek, went into her room, and closed the door.

A dull hiss filled Daine's ears. Darkness covered her eyes.

Light dawned far ahead. It was impossible to tell if the scene that she now saw moved toward her, or if she flew to it. Within moments she was close enough to see two-leggers standing in a ring, arms overlapping, hands clasping their neighbors' shoulders. In the middle of their circle a lump of material shifted and pulsed in the same colors as the Chaos vent had done. Daine turned her face away.

"It's all right." Rattail appeared beside her. "You can look. You *must* look."

Daine obeyed.

At first the ring of men and women, and the thing at the hub, stood on black, empty space. One by one stars winked into being around them. With the added light, she could see the faces of those who formed the circle. Their names sprang into her mind as if she'd always known their true appearance: the Black God in his deep cowl and long robe, the Great Mother Goddess. Daine identified Kidunka, the world snake, lord of the Banjiku tribes, and even the K'miri gods of storms and fire. The large, powerful-looking black man in gold armor was Mithros himself. Looking from face to face, she saw that all of the Great Gods but one formed the ring.

The lump in their center began to rise, changing color swiftly. When it halted, a person stood there, bent nearly double. The hunched figure straightened. At first it was a gold-skinned woman with stormy gray hair and a simple gray dress. Within a breath, she changed. Her skin went yellow, her hair became twigs, her body sprouted a mass of tentacles. That, too, lasted briefly. She never kept one shape for long, but shifted constantly from patchwork to patchwork in combinations of things that lived and things that did not. Pincers grew on a cheetah's forequarters; a cow's head and a man's legs were attached. Just to look at the changing thing made Daine's stomach roll.

The creature lurched to the side, diving for the opening between the Wave Walker and the Black God; white fire appeared, to form a dome between gods and their captive. Half lion, half crone, she dropped and crawled for the gap between the Thief and the Smith, only to retreat howling after she touched the barrier.

"Why don't they kill her?" Daine asked. "They just wear themselves out holding her in their circle, and she doesn't seem to weaken at all."

"They are forbidden to, as she is forbidden to slay them," Rattail explained. "They can imprison and enslave each other, but Father Universe and Mother Flame, who made them all, will not let their children murder a sibling."

The scene rippled like pond water and dissolved before her. Daine was flying backward now, over a broad, perfectly flat plain. Looking around, wondering what had happened to the circle and the shifting monster, she discovered a lone figure, Gainel. A gale whipped his shirt and breeches. He reached one hand out to her. A balance hung from his white fingers.

A crack opened under the Dream King's feet. His left foot rested on that flat and barren floor. His right was planted to the ankle in gray-green muck that boiled and twisted.

Gainel vanished when Daine opened her eyes.

"I have such peculiar dreams here," she complained to the ceiling. "Seemingly the Dream King wants me to know something, but why? Given my druthers, I'd druther have a good sleep." She sighed and rolled out of bed, to hit the floor with a bang. The floor was comfortingly solid.

Her old strength was returning faster than it had the day before. She tried to puzzle out the rest of her dream as she made her bed, cleaned her face and teeth, and brushed a multitude of tangles out of her hair. At least she felt like her old self for the first time in days, even if she couldn't decide what Gainel meant.

The items in her room had been added to during the night. She found boots and a belt. On a chair lay neat stacks of folded breeches, shirts, loincloths, stockings, and breast bands, all in her favorite colors. Unlike her dream, Daine could read Sarra's message easily. Her mother had provided as if Daine would spend the rest of her life here. She would not be happy when Daine insisted upon leaving.

Daine needed to clear her head to prepare a campaign against her parents. Putting on yesterday's dress, she gathered clean garments, towels, and brush, and went into the main room. Broad Foot was there, nibbling a bunch of grapes on the counter.

"Is there a place I can swim?" she asked. "My head feels like mush."

The duckmole's eyes lit. "There's the pond where I stay when I am here," he replied eagerly. "It's clean and quiet, and not too far. Come on."

Daine followed. After a few minutes' walk along a forest trail, they reached a very broad pond, almost a small lake, set just below a ridge crowned with brambles. Her guide plunged in as soon as they reached the water. Finding a cluster of broad, flat-topped rocks on the pond's rim, Daine put her things on them and began to strip off her clothes.

The duckmole surfaced, a frog sticking out of his bill, and swallowed his meal. "Hurry up," he urged. Daine wondered if the meal that he'd just eaten was a god, too. Would it be reborn, as her father claimed the hare had been?

As if to answer her, a small frog, identical to the one that Broad Foot had just eaten, rocketed out of the water to land on the duckmole's head. It gave a rasping trill, then leaped on the path and out of sight as Daine giggled and the duckmole glared.

"Some gods always have to comment when they're being eaten," he grumbled, and dove once more.

Wearing only a loincloth and breast band, Daine slipped into the water. It was *cold*, drawn from mountain streams. She yelped with the first shock, then took a deep breath and submerged. Long experience had taught her to keep moving until she warmed up.

Opening her eyes, she could see most of the area around her—the water was crystal clear. Broad Foot swam up and ran his bill over her face; his eyes were closed. Spinning, he sank to the bottom and glided snakelike over it, passing his bill over everything in his path. Soon he was gone from sight, questing for prey.

The gods of bass, minnows, sticklebacks, and brook trout fled Daine's approach, then returned in small groups to nose her. She squirmed—they tickled—and dropped to the bottom. There she sat, looking around as the fish continued to examine her. A snapping turtle, bigger than those she knew in the mortal realms, eased out of the mud and glided over. Daine watched him uncertainly, not liking the idea of those formidable jaws closing on any part of her. Instead the turtle circled her twice, inspecting, then swam away.

Thrusting herself to the surface, she filled her lungs with fresh air, then submerged again. A black, inky blob rose to meet her as she swam farther out. She stopped, treading water. Before her, the blot spread until it was plate-sized. Gently she reached out and touched it. Was it a darking? She felt warmth and a slippery resistance.

Against the darking's blackness, a face she knew far too well appeared: Ozorne the Stormwing, once called the Emperor Mage. He was perched on a wooden fence above her, staring into the distance.

Suddenly he looked down; he seemed to be staring directly at her. His mouth stretched in a savage grin. Throwing his head back, he voiced a screeching call that she heard even underwater.

Gasping her shock, the girl choked as the pond filled her mouth and throat. With a kick, she drove herself to the surface, trying not to breathe more water before she got there. She broke into the air, liquid pouring from her nose and mouth.

Was that another darking, or the one from yesterday? she wondered, treading water and coughing. And how could a darking show her a vision of Ozorne? How—

A low, grating hum filled her magical hearing. It was faint to begin with, but swiftly turned into a roar. Frantic, she looked around for the source. Only an immortal would affect her magic like this. The sound was new, which meant that she'd never met this kind of immortal. She hated that; she hated surprises in general.

Her things lay on rocks on the beach of an inlet that opened onto the rest of the pond. On the far side of the inlet, air bent and rippled. From its warping center came a reddish brown arm, with a black-nailed hand, and a powerful, shaggy leg tipped with a splayed hoof. Daine caught her breath as the owner of the arm and leg finished his crossing between the mortal and divine realms. It was a tauros.

Her skin crept. She had seen drawings and heard tales, but they had never frightened her as much as looking at one did now. The immortal was seven feet tall with short, strong horns. He had a bull's broad, powerful neck and slablike shoulders, but the large eyes pointed forward, like a predator's. His nose was almost human, but squared off and flat. The jaws were large, the teeth nearly too wide for them. Most of the remainder was human, though built on a large, powerful scale to support his massive head. Since he wore nothing like clothes, she could see that he was quite definitely male. As he turned to one side, she glimpsed a bull's tail at the foot of his ridged spine.

She held very still, treading water lightly. The stories claimed their sight was poor. Smell was the thing to worry about with a tauros. Could it smell her?

The creature swayed, eyes shut, nose lifted. He snuffled wetly.

If he catches me, he'll rape me, she thought, scalp prickling. The stories were far too detailed about the fate of women who met these particular immortals. Quietly, without lifting her arms or feet from the water, she thrust herself to shore, mind fixed on her clothes. She always left her bow with them when she swam. Then she remembered, her strength evaporating. She had no weapon. Her bows were in the mortal realms.

She heard a bone-rattling bellow and looked back. The tauros had her scent; it was wading into the pond. The need for quiet was over. Making for the rocks, she swam in long, practiced strokes. She had a head start on the thing; she'd outrun it to her ma's.

Too busy watching the tauros to see where she was going, she plowed into the mud at the water's edge. Gasping, she lurched to her feet and ran the few steps to her clothes and towels, grabbing them. The immortal was a third of the way across the inlet. He was an ungainly swimmer, wallowing like a bull, but wise enough to use his arms to pull himself through the water.

She turned and ran three steps, then halted. If she escaped—

He would find her mother.

Nearly four years of protecting others from immortals fused with a lifetime of looking after Sarra. Weiryn was forgotten. Her frightened mind seized on one thing: If he didn't get her, the tauros would go after her ma.

The tauros bellowed. Daine spun. She had to do *something*—in a minute he would be on her. Hands shaking, she dropped what she held. If only she had a bow! Even the sling she'd used as a girl—

The towels lay across her fallen clothes in a pair of clean white stripes.

She grabbed both, slinging one over her shoulder, keeping the other in hand. The brambles grew to the pond's edge on her left. Even if she had seen ammunition there, it would be impossible to get. She'd have to go to her right, around the open edge of the water. Trotting around the cluster of rocks where she'd left her things, she scanned the ground. In a heap of stones and gravel, she saw five rocks the size of hen's eggs.

The tauros moaned, a sound that made her own throat go tight. He was two-thirds of the way across the neck of water between them.

Daine seized a rock. Fumbling slightly—it had been years since she'd used a sling—she folded the towel into a sling and placed the stone in the cradle. Cloth and rock felt awkward, even wrong, as she began to twirl her makeshift weapon. Her body protested the large, strong movements required for a sling.

When she felt the best moment, when the weight of the stone and the speed of her arm seemed right, she released one end of the sling. The rock shot past the immortal's head, skipped over the surface, then dropped from sight.

The tauros watched her missile sink. Horrified, Daine could see that he stood on the bottom. The water was up to his chest.

When I was little, I would've been *glad* to skip a rock four times! she thought, grabbing a new stone. She neatened the towel-sling, keeping an eye on the tauros. He decided that her first missile was not worth his interest. He plowed into the shallows, drooling as he stared at her.

"Goddess, help me," she whispered. Bringing the sling up higher, she twirled hard. The motion felt better. She let fly.

It struck the tauros on the shoulder, opening a large gash. He roared with pain and fury; silvery blood coursed over his chest. Frantically he scooped pond water to splash on the wound, flat nose running.

Daine seized two more stones—all she could hold—and backed up, putting the cluster of flat rocks between her and the immortal. It was hard to neaten the sling one-handed. Still retreating, she took the time to do it right; sloppy work now would kill her. When the tauros advanced, she loaded a rock and began to twirl. The circles of her wrist and elbow were broad now; her sense of when to release was exact. She let fly.

Her stone hit the tauros in the throat. His bellow was a strangled croak; he dropped to his knees with a splash, scrabbling at his neck. Dripping sweat, the girl flipped her sling into place and loaded her final rock.

The tauros lurched to his feet, wheezing. He stumbled forward, flat teeth bared.

"Don't," she called, lips quivering. She didn't want to kill a beast who could no more help his nature than she could. "Give up, please!"

He roared and came on, the ground quivering under his weight. When he was six yards from her, she loosed her final shot with all her strength. It slammed between his eyes and stayed, embedded in his skull. The tauros gasped, flailed blindly, and toppled into the mud. There he thrashed, and choked, and died.

"I'm sorry," she cried, eyes overflowing. "I'm sorry, I'm sorry. . . ."

Broad Foot surfaced nearby, plainly upset. "What happened? If I'd known that a tauros was about, I wouldn't have brought you here! Where did it come from?"

"It crossed between realms," she replied, still trembling. "I think it may've been sent. I had a vision of Ozorne, anyway, right before it came."

"But how did he know where you are?"

"I've no idea."

"And why do you weep? You've killed before."

"And I hate it!" she cried. "Especially when this poor, idiot thing couldn't do no different!" She tried to gather her things, and dumped them into the mud. "Look at him—what else is he made for but to prey on females? *Are* there any lady tauroses?"

"No. No, there aren't."

"Wonderful! No one cared enough to give them mates of their own kind. All they know to do is grab two-legger females. They either kill them or get killed themselves. It's wrong!" Pulling her belongings from the mud, she ran to her parents' house.

Broad Foot eyed the dead tauros. "She has a point," he told it. "Someone ought to bring the matter to the Great Gods' attention—once things quiet down a bit."

Halfway to her parents' home, the girl paused: A Stormwing awaited her there. She hesitated only for a moment, then re-formed her towel-sling and grabbed stones for ammunition. If that Stormwing was an enemy, he or she had a surprise coming!

Emerging from the cover of the trees, she saw that her father and Numair were seated on the slab of rock that served the cottage as a doorstep. The immortal she had detected stood on the ground before them. He turned as she approached, his movement setting the bones that were braided into his long blond hair to clicking.

Daine relaxed and tossed her rocks aside. She wouldn't need them for Rikash Moonsword.

"What happened to *you*?" asked the green-eyed Stormwing as Broad Foot appeared on the path between him and the men. Numair got to his feet, frowning.

"Broad Foot will explain," Daine said, weaving between the mage and her father. "I need to clean up."

She scrubbed, then pulled on clean garments with hands that still trembled. As she was combing out her hair, Sarra knocked on the door.

"We're having lunch in the garden," she called. "If you're decent, come take a perch out for your Stormwing friend to sit on."

Quickly the girl finished. Feeling calmer now, she did as she was told. Once she'd set up the perch by the outdoor table, Rikash glided down from the rooftop and took his place. For the moment they were alone. Numair and Weiryn were nowhere in sight.

"You let me down," the girl told the Stormwing. "We thought your Queen Barzha would finish Ozorne once he was a Stormwing. Instead, he shows up in the spring with our enemies, and hundreds of Stormwings at his back."

"Two hundred and forty-eight Stormwings to be exact," Rikash said bitterly. "Those who did not care that he held a queen and her mate captive. Those who ignore the fact that he took his Stormwing crown by killing Jokhun from behind. Those without regard for Stormwing law. *They* are the army that followed him to the mortal realms." He laughed. "Queen Barzha and her followers are fugitives, Daine. We stayed in the Divine Realms when the barriers fell. Here, at least, we are partly safe from Ozorne and his flock."

Ignoring his pronounced odor, Daine put a comforting hand on the Stormwing's shoulder. "I'm sorry to hear it. How *are* Queen Barzha and Lord Hebakh?"

"Tired," replied the immortal. "As am I. Ozorne sends groups back to harry us. It is not enough to have most of us as followers—those who will not follow, he wants dead."

"How many are on your side of it?"

Rikash shook his head, making the bones in his hair clatter. "Sixty-three, in all." He tried a smile; it was half bitter. "Don't take us to task for not killing him. We've tried our best."

Daine sighed. "We humans haven't done so well at it, ourselves."

Sarra, Weiryn, and Numair came out, carrying their lunch, as the three animal gods materialized at their places by the table. With Rikash positioned downwind so that his odor wouldn't spoil their meal, the plates and bowls were passed.

"Has anyone thought of a way that we can go home?" asked Numair.

"There is none," growled Weiryn. "The Great Gods are speaking to no one as long as Uusoae fights them."

Daine moved the food on her plate. "What about the animal gods? I came here last fall, while I was in Carthak. *You* took me back to the mortal realms then, Badger."

"Not possible," replied the great animal. "You were dead then. All I had to do was put you back into your mortal body. With both of you still alive, not all of the animal gods together could move you between the realms."

"You are far better off here with your mother," said Weiryn. "If you insist on leaving, then wait until the fall equinox, when the gates open for the likes of us and you. And there's one of those *things* again!" he cried as the darking oozed onto the table, having climbed up Daine's leg.

"Leave it be, Da," she told him. "It's not hurting anyone."

Stretching to make itself taller, the darking changed. Up came a serpentlike neck, supporting a wedge-shaped head. The body the darking made was long and slender, with powerful hindquarters and long forepaws that were as nimble as hands. Two great wings unfurled out of the blot's shoulders.

"Dragons," Rikash said. "This creature is right, whatever it is. They might very well take you back. You *have* been looking after their young one."

"You mean for my daughter to journey to the Dragonlands? Absolutely not," Weiryn snapped. "It's too risky."

"They might refuse to help," Queenclaw pointed out. "I never met a dragon that wasn't perverse—they're worse than we cats. Even the Great Gods can't force a dragon to do *anything* it doesn't wish to."

"I'm almost positive they will do it," said Rikash, bating. "Don't forget, we Stormwings know them best—our eyries border on the Dragonlands. They are proud. One or two of Skysong's kin will feel they *must* repay you for what you've done, and one is all you need to go home." He looked at Numair and grinned. "Well, it may take two. There's so much extra of one of you."

The girl smiled, then asked, "How do we find them?"

The Stormwing looked at Weiryn. "I'm sure a map can be drawn—unless you plan to cage them?"

"Da, Ma, please listen," pleaded Daine. "Humans and People *need* us. I've friends that would risk their lives for me and Numair. If you won't help us, then we'll muddle along on our own—but we can't just sit here, seeing them in visions, and laze about."

The god sighed and rubbed his antlers. "No—no, I won't cage them."

Sarra wiped her eyes. "Not even a day I've had to talk to you. But I know you can't sit idly by when them you care for are in trouble."

"Lord Rikash," the house cat said, "they will need help to cross the Sea of Sand."

The immortal sidled, digging into his perch with steel claws. "I will see what can be done. It will take persuasion." He looked from Daine to Numair, frowning. *"Be careful,"* he told them. "The Divine Realms are perilous. Maybe Queen Barzha is right, and I am getting sentimental, but I would hate to see anything happen to either of you." Jumping into the air, he took flight, blowing waves of stench over the table.

## ❧❧ FOUR ❦❦

# TRAVELERS

❧❧ "Forget sentimentality," the badger grumbled. "*I'd* like to see him lose that *smell*."

"And from a badger, that's saying a great deal," quipped Queen-claw.

"I will go with them," said Broad Foot. Everyone stared at him. "I can't transport them, but I can act as guide and protector. The three of us should manage."

"The *four* of us," the badger told him. "I will come as well. I haven't put so much time into looking after this young one to stop now."

"Lord Weiryn, will you and Sarra come with us?" Numair asked.

Daine's mother smiled wistfully. "As a new goddess, I'm bound to Weiryn's lands for a century."

"As am I, for requesting her admittance here," added Weiryn. "You will do well with the badger and Broad Foot."

"If we're to leave today, I'd best get a little extra hunting done," commented the duckmole, and vanished.

"I will join you tomorrow morning," the badger said. "There are a few things to deal with at my sett before I go." He, too, vanished.

"Ma, Da," the girl said thoughtfully, "are there horses we might trade for, or buy? We'd go faster than afoot."

"No, dear one," Sarra replied. "Every horse in the Divine Realms belongs to itself, or its herd. They do not serve anyone." She rose. "I'd best pack your things—No, Daine, I don't need help. You'd only be in my way."

"Besides," added Weiryn, also getting to his feet, "I need you both to come with me." He led Daine and Numair inside.

"What about making horses?" Numair asked. "Could you—"

"No," Weiryn said flatly. "Any being created in the Divine Realms belongs to itself and serves no one else. You would be lucky if such a horse only dumped you in the dirt. It *might* take you for a ride that would last a century of mortal time."

In the main room, he opened a door that the girl was positive hadn't been there the day before. It gave onto a small, dark chamber that was more like a shed than a room. Here, to her surprise and delight, she saw a woodcarver's tools, staffs, boxes of feathers, boxes of arrowheads, coiled strings, and completed bows.

Weiryn ran long brown fingers over the finished weapons, checking the feel, rejecting this one and that. "These are my gifts to those I favor." He selected an ebony-colored bow with startlingly pale horn nocks over both tips. "And if my own daughter isn't one I favor, who is?" He laid the stave across his palms, and offered it to Daine.

It was air-light in her grip at first, but it got heavier, until it reached the exact weight she looked for in a bow. Weiryn offered a string. Fitting the loop over the lower nock, she braced that end against her instep. She drew the upper nock down and slipped the other loop over it in a flash. "She's sweet, Da," she told him, smiling.

The god offered her a quiver full of arrows. "I should have given you a proper bow long before this," he told her, wrapping extra strings in a square of oiled cloth.

Handing that to Daine, he went to the staffs in the corner. "Here, mage." Weiryn selected one that was six feet of thick, knotted wood. About to hand it over, he frowned. "A moment." He looked at Numair, then cupped the top of the staff in one hand. White fire shone from his palm; when he drew it away, a fist-sized crystal knob sat on top of the staff, embedded in the wood. He gave the staff to Numair.

The mage took it and stood for a moment, one hand wrapped around the wood, the other around the crystal. Daine saw no magical fire but knew he examined the staff with his Gift, looking for its secrets. When he looked up again, his eyes were filled with respect. "Thank you. I've never had something that was so—attuned—to me."

Weiryn scowled and went to a wooden counter along one wall. "Come here, both of you." An ink pot and brush appeared on the surface next to him. The god wet the brush, and began to paint symbols directly onto the wood. "Here we are," he said, tapping the brush against a painted square. "Here's the stream, and the pond where Broad Foot stays. And this is the path you must follow."

Daine, following the brush, thought for a moment she saw trees and streams along the dotted line of ink. When she blinked, she saw only glossy black dots sinking into the stained wood.

"If you walk steadily, you will spend the night beside Temptation Lake," Weiryn informed them, drawing that body of water close to the trail. "Do *not* drink from it—unless you desire to be tempted, of course."

A vision of Numair reclining among three naked, lovely women who fed him grapes, or rubbed his feet, or finger-combed his hair, filled the air over the counter. From Numair's deep blush, Daine could tell that he saw it, too.

"Not funny, Da," she told her father, her voice very dry.

"Neither of us is in the mood for temptation, Lord Weiryn," the mage added quietly.

"Hmpf," snorted the god. "Well, just don't drink the water there. It's a good place to stop—no dweller of the Divine Realms may harm another within a league of Temptation Lake." He rewet his brush and continued to draw. "The trail will carry you to Long Drop Gorge, which you will cross on the First Bridge." Briefly Daine glimpsed a wood-and-rope bridge in the air over the counter, like the bridges that filled the mountains of Tortall and Galla.

Weiryn continued the line of the path for an inch or two, then stopped to create a blurred area around it. "This is Mauler's Swamp." The vision in the air over the map showed a pair of yellow, slit-pupiled eyes sticking out of murky water. They moved. A ripple of passing square ridges like those on a crocodile's back cut through the image of water, followed by the snakelike curving of a long tail. "Give no offense to Mauler, if you can avoid it.

"Here is the Stonemaze." The vision was one of rocky canyons and a distant, small river, as seen from high overhead. "Watch your footing, never leave the path in the maze, and harm no stones."

"Lord Weiryn," said Numair, "it would help if you were to explain what will happen if we make a mistake in these places."

Weiryn looked at him, leaf-colored eyes glinting. "Who can tell?" he asked. "The gods in most places never punish a trespass in the same manner twice. Mauler once ate the mortals who disturbed his afternoon nap, but that was a while ago. He may not choose to eat the next intruder. Of course, he may have young to share his swamp, and they always need a meal. Just use caution. Cut no green wood. Take no fruits without asking the bush or tree. If you don't, you might spend a century with wild pigs trying to dig you up by the roots. Blackberries in particular have a very nasty streak."

"Wonderful," Daine whispered.

"Where was I?" asked her father. He rewet his brush, and sketched another blurred area on the wood. "Oh, yes. At last you will come to the Sea of Sand." The vision revealed dunes; for a moment Daine's face was hot and painfully dry. "If the Stormwing can't find help, the winds will strip your body of moisture in the time it takes your mother's pan bread to bake. Don't you see what folly this is?" he demanded, eyes on Daine. "The Divine Realms are too dangerous for a pair of mortals!"

"We will have Broad Foot, and the badger," Numair said. "And we have protected ourselves, from time to time. Mortals have survived in the Divine Realms before."

Weiryn sighed. "That's what I thought you would say." His brush and ink pot disappeared. Palms down, he tapped the inked surface of the wood. "At least I can tell Sarra that I tried." Like bark that was barely attached to its parent tree, the surface with the map cracked away from the wood, thinned until it could have been heavy parchment, and rolled itself up. Weiryn gave it to Numair. "You need not fear that it will go to pieces, or that water will smear the marks," he said grumpily.

Daine leaned over and kissed the god's forehead. "Thanks, Da."

When the three returned to the main room of the cabin, Broad Foot, dripping, was on the table. "Are we ready?"

Sarra offered them cloaks—a blue one for Daine, a black one for Numair. Once the two mortals had donned them, she handed over their packs.

"How do you want to do this?" Numair asked Broad Foot. "You can't use your power to move us, and—forgive me, but—I doubt that you can walk at our pace."

Broad Foot looked at the mage; Numair jumped. Visible through the opening of his cloak, his cream-colored shirt twisted. When it stilled, a deep pouch had formed in the cloth over Numair's belly. The duck-mole vanished, then reappeared in shimmering fire, tucked into the pouch. He looked back and up at Numair. "The view from here should be very nice," he said as Daine and her mother giggled. "Mind you don't bump me."

Sarra hugged Daine. "You'll come to stay a bit when your war is settled?" she asked. "Please?"

"I will, Ma—I just don't know when that will be."

"We'll know. We'll come for you on the holiday that's closest." The woman scanned her face intently. "You'll visit for a season, or two?"

"I'll come, Ma."

"Promise?"

Daine hugged her mother hard, tears in her eyes. "I promise. We— we'll catch up on the time them bandits took from us."

Sarra gave her a last squeeze, then turned to Numair. Daine slung her pack and quiver over her shoulders, then looked at her father.

Weiryn leaned down and kissed her gravely, first on one cheek, then the other. "We shall see you again, so what's the point of good-byes?"

"None at all," she said, and brushed a hand along his horned crown.

Weiryn opened the door; they filed outside. "Straight down the path," instructed Broad Foot. "We've a couple of hours of light still."

Daine let Numair take the lead. She glanced back only once, to see her mother crying in the circle of Weiryn's arm. They both waved. She waved, too, and didn't look again as the path led her into the woods and out of sight.

They walked quietly, descending into a mountain forest on a much-used track. Listening for the voices of the People, as she did in walks at home, Daine once more had that odd sense of being deaf. Her physical ears picked up the rustle of small creatures moving on the forest floor and the many calls of local birds. Magically she heard nothing. She had no way to know what was said in the conversation between a squirrel and a jay—though she could guess from the rage in the squirrel's voice and the mockery in the bird's. Far in the distance, her sense for immortals registered a small herd of killer centaurs on the move. About to warn her companions, she realized that the centaurs were traveling in the opposite direction. Soon afterward, they faded from her awareness.

"Goddess bless," Numair said, coming to a halt. They were in a dark hollow where only slivers of light touched the ground. The cause of the early twilight grew beside the path: a white oak tree, or what Daine thought *might* be an oak, except that it was the largest that she had ever seen. If she and Numair stretched out their arms, together they still could not reach all the way around the bole.

"She is a First Tree," Broad Foot explained. "From her acorns, the first mortal white oaks were born."

*"Her?"* asked Numair, looking down at his passenger.

"She is a god," the duckmole said. "She is aware. All of the First Trees are."

Daine snatched her hand from the bark.

Stepping back, with Broad Foot held away from him, Numair bowed deeply, sweeping an arm before him as if the tree were a queen. Straightening, he frowned. "What's that noise?"

"What noise?" chorused Daine and Broad Foot.

Numair approached the girl, hand cupped around one ear, and bent. "Easy, there," the animal god cautioned. Giving Daine a half turn, Numair put his ear close to her pack. Now Daine heard a thin, high shrilling.

Numair opened one of the pack's side pockets and reached inside. When he drew it out again, he brought a small clay pot with a wax seal, and a darking.

"Now where did *you* come from?" he asked, holding the blot up to eye level.

"Is it the one that's been following me about Da's?" inquired Daine. Shaping a head for itself, the darking nodded.

"Were you in my pack by accident?"

The inky creature shook its head.

"You *wanted* to come?"

The darking nodded.

Daine shrugged and held open the breast pocket of her shirt. "Pop it in here, then." Numair hesitated, then dropped the creature into its new residence. "Now we've each got a passenger." She smiled into his face, so close to her own just then. Briefly, his eyes changed; a strange, burning excitement filled them, and made her catch her breath.

He straightened abruptly. "We shouldn't dawdle," he said, striding off down the path. "We've a lot of ground to cover."

Puzzled, confused—feeling as if she'd glimpsed something important, only to have it vanish—Daine trotted to catch up.

They walked long after dark, stopping only to eat a brief supper. As night drew down, Numair called light from the crystal on his staff to illumine the way. At last the path emerged from under the trees. They had come to the rim of a stretch of water—a large pond, or a lake.

"Temptation Lake?" asked Numair, looking out over the water.

"Yes, indeed," Broad Foot said. "And I could do with a swim."

Daine sighed her relief and let her bow, quiver, and pack slide to the ground. The thick, lush grass that grew almost to the water's edge looked better than the softest feather bed at that point.

Numair first lifted the duckmole from the pocket in his shirt, putting him on the ground, then removed his own pack. "Broad Foot, if I bespell our camp for protection, will it inconvenience you?"

Broad Foot clapped his bill in a laugh. "No, not in the least. Though you don't *need* to spell it—Temptation Lake is sacred. No one of the Divine Realms would harm anyone here. If anything *does* happen, mind," he added, looking at them soberly, "just call or think my name, and I'll come. And remember—don't drink the water!" He vanished in a cloud of silver light.

Numair gave his pack to Daine. She pulled out folded squares of cloth and spread them. There was more cloth in their folds than she had expected. Laid flat on the ground, they were big enough to wrap each of them completely.

Exhausted, Daine stripped off her boots, dagger, and belt, and freed the darking, who vanished into the shadows. "Don't let me step on you," she warned, and heard a squeak in reply. "I hope that means 'yes,' " she muttered. Rolling herself in her blanket, Daine watched as Numair gathered rocks, placing them in a circle around their things.

Once the stones were placed, he walked counterclockwise around the rim of his circle. She couldn't hear what he said, but when he finished the first circuit, all noise from outside the barrier stopped. He walked the circle again; this time, when he was done, the rocks began to glow faintly. To Daine's surprise, they warmed, throwing off a mild heat without scorching the grass. The third time that he walked his route, black fire glittering with white sparks flowed behind him. When he completed this circle, the magic blazed, then vanished. The only sign that he had done anything was the glow and warmth that came off the stones.

"We're shielded from sight and sound." He tugged off his boots.

"And the rocks?" she asked.

He smiled tiredly. "We only have one blanket and a cloak each. You know I don't like to get cold." Using his cloak as a pillow, he rolled himself into his blanket and turned on his side, his back toward her. "Good night, magelet."

Dreams brought Daine once more to that vast, empty space. There were the Great Gods, standing in a wheel of linked arms. Their focus was the changing thing that wore the colors of the Chaos vent. Daine got queasy as she watched its constant shifts—did others feel ill when *she* shape-changed?—but this time she kept her eyes on circle and captive. The creature leaped for a gap between Kidunka and the Thief, and was blocked by the white barrier that made a dome between gods and it. The creature shrank into the center of the ring and fell in upon itself until it was a heaving mass.

Lightning fast, that mass split into a star, shooting its many arms toward all of the openings between its captors. Each arm of the changing thing sprouted a wide mouth with outsized, jagged teeth. The Great Gods shifted, and the fiery barrier shone more brightly than ever. The mouths shrieked and retreated into the central mass, smoking where they had made contact with the white fire. In the meantime, unseen by the ring of Great Gods, small puddles of multicolored liquid appeared behind them. The puddles grew, spreading to the left and right, until they formed a ring at the backs of the Great Gods.

The scene dissolved. Daine was back on the plain, seeing the Master of Dream as he stood poised, one foot on each side of a great chasm. He still held a scale in one hand. The foot that rested on the flat side of the crack skidded. He fought to regain his balance on that polished surface without taking his other foot out of the wriggling muck. At last he was steady again. A bubble grew in the strange liquid. When it burst, thousands of exotically colored butterflies swirled around Gainel in a spiral dance.

Daine thought that she'd opened her eyes, but although she could see clouds drifting over a pink-and-gray sky, it felt as if her dreaming was not over. The sound of oddly muffled voices, coming from some-where close by, met her ears. In case the voices weren't part of a dream, she wrapped her fingers around her dagger and grew bat ears to hear every word.

"—you ordered what is left of the Razor Scream nation to attack those mortals in the harbor. Eleven Stormwings were killed out there— *eleven!*"

"That is the cost of battle, Qirev. Everyone takes casualties."

Daine stiffened. It had been six months since their last meeting, but there was no mistaking that cold, distant voice. It was Ozorne's.

"The cost of *mortal* battle! When the kings chose to ally themselves with you, it was your promise that while we might *harry* two-leggers, we would kill *only* to sow fear!"

"I lied." There was bleak disinterest in the former Emperor Mage's tone.

"We are no army for mustering. We *feed* on armies," said a cracked and aged voice. "You promised feasting to glut us—not to throw our kindred against archers and mages. Mortal wars are not Stormwing wars."

"Jachull?" inquired Ozorne. "Do *you* feel Stormwings have no part in mortal wars?"

A third, female voice replied, "What does it matter if we kill a few or many to sow the fear we dine on? Whether they shoot us for eating the dead, or for attacking the living, what difference does it make?"

"There, sires. Jachull of the Mortal Fear nation does not disagree," announced Ozorne, "and *her* subjects number more than your—sadly reduced—nations combined."

"Humans attack on the north road!" someone cried. "Warriors come!"

"Fellow Stormwings, I would love to chat all day, but as you can hear, business intrudes." Ozorne sounded friendly and false. "If you don't mind?" He paused briefly. Then, in a cold, direct voice, he continued, "Number fourteen, report your position. Where are you? I can see nothing!"

Daine's bat ears filled with a voice both closer and louder than her enemy's. It sang a bizarre tune that sounded like nothing on earth. She sat up.

Numair's things were packed. The rock circle around their camp had gone cold; two stones had been moved to open the last of the protective spells on the camp. There was no sign of Broad Foot, either. The sun was clear on the horizon, but not by much. It was time to get moving. If she could just find Numair . . .

She spotted him nearly a hundred yards away. He was striding into the lake, without even bothering to roll up the legs of his breeches.

"Numair!" she called. He gave no sign that he'd heard. *"Numair!"*

He never even looked her way. The water reached his belly; still he walked on.

Bespelled! she thought. Jumping up, she raced across the grass and waded in after him. Closing the distance fast, she lunged and grabbed air. He'd gone under.

She dove. He was speeding away. Worse, she could see he was not swimming: His arms were flat against his sides; his legs fluttered. Something was towing him.

Daine surfaced and gasped, filling her lungs with air as she filled her mind with sea lions. Her body shifted. She dove and arrowed after her friend. She was gaining on him when she realized that she was now a saltwater animal in a freshwater lake.

Too late to fret, she told herself. I just won't eat or drink here.

The thing that towed Numair picked up speed. Daine poured her strength into her rush through the water and drew even with the man. Now she saw his captor. A naked blue female with hair like silver tentacles, she dragged her prize on a gold rope as she sang the weird tune that had captivated Numair.

The song pressed on Daine's ears; she flattened them and did her best to ignore it. Lunging, she clamped a sea lion's sharp teeth on the gold rope. Acid pain seared her mouth, making her cry out. The leash dropped from her jaws.

Muddled and dizzy, she almost slammed into Broad Foot, missing the duckmole by inches. She's got Numair! Daine cried, speaking mind to mind.

The duckmole took up the chase, easily keeping pace with her.— *That's no she.*—

Of course it's a she, the scheming wench! A—a river god, or lake god!

Broad Foot fell back slightly, letting her slide by. Rising above Daine, he swept his bill over her eyes.

The thing that had stolen Numair bore right in a broad arc, trying to get by its pursuers. It clearly *was* a thing now, a blobby mass of burned orange and pale lilac that towed the mage not with a gold leash, but with a tentacle of its own flesh.

Daine shot across the arc, slamming into Numair. She knocked him aside, but not free—the tentacle was wrapped around his throat.

—*Again,*—urged Broad Foot.

Speeding at her friend, Daine prayed she wouldn't break his ribs, and crashed into him. Broad Foot opened his bill and shouted in a voice that filled each drop of water around them. The blob shrieked and dissolved. The peculiar song was cut off.

Numair came out of his trance, to find himself in deep water. He tried to yell, and inhaled liquid. Daine shook her head to clear it of Broad Foot's cry and dove under the man, pushing him up to open air. Taking on her own form, she looped an arm around the choking mage and struck out for the shore. As soon as the water was shallow enough that he could manage, she left him. Racing onto dry land and into a clump of tall reeds, she threw up, rejecting every trace of whatever she had bitten.

Wiping her face in wet grass, she saw Broad Foot go by, sweeping his bill over the ground as if he looked for breakfast. Nearby, she could hear Numair doing what she had just done, and decided to give him privacy. Hardly aware that she wore not a stitch, except for the badger's claw on its chain around her neck, she caught up with the duckmole. "Where are you going?"

"I want to look at something." Now that they were on land, he spoke as the other animal gods did. "Why didn't you call me?"

She stopped, horrified. Why *hadn't* she summoned him? Red-faced, she said, "I forgot. I'm used to it being just him and me, and I had to move so fast . . . I'm sorry!"

The tall reeds opened onto a broad, flat stretch of clay. In it, spilling into the lake, was a pool of shifting tan, pale gray, and blood-red light. Nothing stayed the same for more than a breath; she thought that she saw images, but they changed the moment she focused on them. She leaned closer, drawn by the play of colors.

"Wake up!" cried Broad Foot.

The girl straightened. She'd come to within a few steps of the pool—and pieces of it had risen in the air to meet her. When she moved back, the raised goo collapsed with plopping sounds, like boiling mud. Weakly she asked, "Is—is that a Chaos vent?"

"It is, and an active one, too. Activity I don't mind. That's Chaos for you. But this . . ." He waddled to the water's edge, where the fluid ran to mingle with the lake. "*This* worries me. It means the whole lake is tainted—and Chaos bile is dangerous to us."

"Numair's been poisoned?" she gasped, suddenly dizzy with panic.

"No, no. It affects only immortals and gods," said Broad Foot. "Mortals are half Chaos naturally. He is completely safe, and it sounds like you rid yourself of it before any entered your blood. But . . ."

He paused so long that Daine thought he might have forgotten her. "Broad Foot?"

"It doesn't poison gods or immortals as *you* would think of poisoning. It brings them closer to Uusoae. They go from enemies to—to potential allies. I wish we knew all those who've drunk here. This lake is very popular."

Even though he'd said Numair would take no harm from the water he'd inhaled, she wanted to check on him and make sure. Leaving the duckmole beside the Chaos vent, she picked her way through the reeds and returned to their camp.

There she found the mage, looking the worse for his experience. He sat with his back to her, talking to the badger, who must have arrived while she was off with the duckmole. "I think I hear—" Turning, he blushed scarlet and looked away.

She had forgotten she wore only the claw necklace that stayed with her each time that she shapechanged. "Oh, for—!" she cried. Getting her pack, she went behind a tree. Fumbling with her garments, the girl shouted the details of her talk with Broad Foot.

When she emerged, stockings in hand, Numair was close by, ready with her boots.

"Are you *sure* you didn't drink from the lake?" she asked quietly, fixing him with a stern eye. "That creature looked to me like a blue, naked female with a big chest, until Broad Foot changed my vision. She looked like *just* the kind of female you might want to be tempted by, Master Salmalín."

He blushed. "I give you my solemn word that I did not drink the lake water and request temptation," he said, combing his wet mane back with his fingers. "I tested it with my Gift, and sensed there was something very wrong with it. You know, magelet, the gods may be losing ground against Chaos."

Broad Foot had arrived and was talking softly to the badger. Hearing the mage, they broke off their conference and came over. "What makes you think so?" asked the badger, dark eyes sharp.

"I know my legends and myths," explained the man. "The creators of the universe ordained that the gods, who stand for order, and Chaos, who stands for—"

"Chaos," Daine interrupted with a smile.

Numair tweaked her nose. "They must stay in balance. The only problem is that it's the nature of each to fight the other. It's written that a day will come when the Queen of Chaos will break free of the prison made for her by her siblings, the Great Gods."

"When that day comes, the mortal and divine realms will melt into Chaos. The gods—all gods—will perish, as will mortal life." Broad Foot's voice was grim.

"You know your legends well, human," remarked the badger.

"I have to report this," the duckmole told them. "It's more than just the lake being poisoned. The creature that had you captive was no part of this place. It was a Chaos dweller, masked as a lake being. How one of *them* managed to escape into the Divine Realms . . . You start without me—I'll catch up." Without another word, he vanished.

Packing, Daine filled Numair in on what he'd missed while bespelled, as the badger went to examine the vent. Once she was ready, the girl realized that she hadn't seen the darking.

"We have to go," warned Numair. "We can't spend the day searching for it."

"I know," replied Daine, scanning the grass around them. "I think it does, too. I just hope it didn't fall into the lake."

When the badger rejoined them, the humans shouldered their packs and returned to the path. There, stark against sandy dirt, was an inky pool. "Is that you?" she asked it. "Did you come back?"

The ink split. Half flowed over to her and reached up with a pair of armlike tentacles. The other half thrust up a part of itself shaped as a head, cocking it to one side.

Daine stooped and picked up the one that clearly wanted her to do so. Cupped in her hand, the darking was light, but still had weight and a presence against her skin—like a bubble filled with water, she thought. "You brought a friend?" The darking on her palm grew its own head and nodded.

"More of those?" grumbled the badger. "Don't they have anything else to do?"

Both darkings shook their heads.

Daine smiled. Giving her bow to Numair to hold, she lifted the newcomer in her free hand. "I don't know where you two will sit, though."

The first darking trickled up her arm and curled around her neck, a bit of coolness on her skin. The other flowed over her wrist until it could drip into her belt pouch.

"I guess we're set," she told her companions. Numair returned her bow. They set off briskly, mage and badger in the lead, Daine bringing up the rear. It was something she and Numair did automatically: She could trust him to pay attention to what was ahead; he knew that she would guard their backs.

The duckmole rejoined them as they stopped for their noon meal. "Not good, not good," he said, pacing the clearing where they sat. "They have placed a ban on the lake, but they won't be looking into the matter of those who have been tainted. I think—" He came to a halt and sighed. "I think it is all they can do to hold the barriers against her."

"Then if we can do nothing here, let's be on our way," suggested Numair. "Daine and I would like to go home, where we *can* do something."

## ➤➤ FIVE ◄◄

# THE BRIDGE

**∞** They made good time that afternoon. Black mountain pines gave way to maples, chestnuts, and paper birches, and larger clearings. Flashes of bright color darted through the tree canopy as the sunbirds began their afternoon's homage to the sun.

Suddenly the travelers emerged onto a long, wide grass shelf. Ahead the land fell into a vast gorge. Approaching the edge, Daine looked down and whistled. Far, far below lay a thin silver curl: a river.

"Long Drop Gorge," the badger told them. Nodding at two splintery logs planted upright in the ground at the cliff's edge, he added, "And there's the First Bridge."

Daine gulped. What had looked like a sturdy enough wood-and-rope construction in the vision over Weiryn's map was in reality fraying, twisted hemp and ancient slats. Twin ropes, as old and unreliable-looking as the rope of the floor, were strung as rails at waist height and attached to the logs. The whole structure didn't look as if it would support even one of them, let alone their whole group.

"The first rope-and-*wood* bridge," corrected the duckmole. "The first rope bridge is farther up. We didn't think you'd like that."

"First Bridge or First Wood-and-Rope Bridge, it won't break," snapped the badger. "It was set here after the first humans were done with it, and it's been here ever since. No force in the Divine Realms may break it, until the realms themselves are broken."

"Is there an easier way to cross?" Numair asked. "Anywhere?"

Both gods shook their heads. "Long Drop Gorge extends several days' march in both directions," explained Broad Foot. "You *did* say you are in a hurry."

"Would you be able to carry our belongings if you and Broad Foot transported yourselves across?" the man wanted to know.

"No," said the duckmole. "Weiryn and Sarra both put some of their power into what you carry to help you. Those things are bound to you. If we tried to take them, they would not come."

Numair eyed the crystal in his staff and said dryly, "I didn't know Weiryn cared."

Daine looked at the canyon floor again and winced. It was just too far down. First Bridge or no, the thought of seeing that distant ribbon far under her toes made her sweat. I could take eagle shape, she thought. Heights never bother me when I fly.

That was no good. Numair carried his staff; she couldn't burden him with her belongings, not when he'd need a free hand to grasp one of the ropes that served as rails.

An arm slipped around her shoulders. "Are you all right?" Numair asked. "Heights don't bother you."

"It's the bridge as much as the height," she replied.

"I will carry our things, if you want to shift," he told her softly. "A shape change is out of the question for me. We must keep our food and weapons, for one. For another, I would hate to use my Gift to fly across, then need it to handle trouble on the other side."

"If we are going today, let us begin," urged the badger. "I would like to be across before anyone, or anything, else comes by."

The thought of being caught on that bridge by an enemy made Daine's stomach roll. "He's right." She tried to smile at Numair. "We'd best start walking."

Numair put down the duckmole and stood back. Silver fire bloomed, shrank: The gods vanished, to reappear on the far side of the canyon.

Daine insisted that Numair go first, and tried not to watch as he carefully moved away from the cliff. When he was well ahead, she bit her lip and stepped onto the first plank. It shuddered beneath her weight; the whole structure shook with her friend's movement. Trembling, she seized the rope handholds: firmly with her right hand, awkwardly with her left, the one in which she carried the bow.

Numair slipped, making the bridge rock. Like Daine, he'd managed the barest hold on the left-hand rope, hampered by his staff. "It takes getting used to," he called to her.

"It's stood for time out of mind!" The badger's voice came from the air near them.

"That's what I'm afraid of," they both chorused.

Numair glanced back at the girl, and grinned. She had to smile as well. Carefully, he walked on, eyes on the planks before him.

She'd meant to keep her eyes forward. Instantly she discovered that would be impossible. Gaps lay between the wide boards. To avoid putting a foot through an opening, she had to look where she stepped, and was treated to a view of the river as it wound between tall, jagged rocks far below. She forged ahead, a step at a time.

Away from the cliff, she walked into a brisk, playful breeze. "Of course," she growled. "What would a First Bridge *be* without its own plank-rocking first *wind!*"

Movement pulled her attention to her chest, rather than her footing. Shimmering with light, the darking that had been tucked into her belt purse now hung by a tentacle from her belt. The other darking had flowed off her neck to swarm over the belt darking, hitting it with tentacles shaped like hammers. She heard small plops as each blow landed.

"Here, you two, stop it! This isn't the time—"

"What's wrong?" The breeze was strong enough that Numair was forced to shout. He was more than forty yards distant, a third of the way across the bridge.

"I don't know!" she yelled. "It's the darkings! *Enough!*" she told her passengers. Clutching the left handhold with fingers still wrapped around her bow, she released the right-hand rope and grabbed the top darking. She pulled it away from the one on her belt and stuffed it down the back of her shirt. Seizing the belt darking, she held it up.

Examining the darking, she gasped and nearly dropped it. Its center was filled by Ozorne's face. He grinned and waved, then vanished. The darking was solid shadow once more. Daine stuffed it into her belt purse and tied the pouch shut with one hand. As she seized the right handhold again, her magical senses prickled. Wind made the bridge jump. Clinging to the rails, the girl looked for the disturbance. Far overhead, the sky rippled.

"Uh-oh," she whispered. Like the tauros, something, or someone, was crossing from one realm to the other.

Winged shapes came into view, as if they flew through a waterfall or beaded curtain. Please let them be friendly, Daine thought, shaping her own eyes to those of an eagle. Now she saw the new arrivals clearly: horse-shaped, with powerful, batlike wings and a predator's talons and fangs. They were not at all friendly.

"Hurroks!" she yelled to Numair, pointing. "Eleven of them!"

The immortals drew their wings in and dropped, coming for the bridge like plummeting falcons.

Numair planted his feet and raised his staff, holding the rail with his right hand.

The girl couldn't afford a handhold. Kneeling, spreading her legs to balance herself, she grabbed two arrows. One she put to the string; the other she held in her teeth. She refused to think about the rocking bridge, or the gaps on either side.

Five hurroks formed the first attacking wave. Carefully Daine selected a target. Black fire shot from the crystal on Numair's staff even as the girl loosed; the hurrok struck by the mage burst into flame and dropped. Another screamed in rage: Daine's arrow had grazed its chest and punctured a wing. With her second arrow Daine shot the next hurrok coming in. It shrieked and fell, her shaft through one eye.

She yanked two more arrows from her quiver, putting one between her teeth, one to the string. Sharp pain dragged across her scalp: A hurrok had come from behind to rake her with his claws. As momentum carried him far below, into the gorge, the impact of his strike knocked Daine forward. The arrow in her bow fell as something ink-colored hit the board in front of her. Daine flinched.

It was a darking. Keening, it clamped onto the board, locking itself down with a half-dozen tentacles. She couldn't believe it might attack— something in its shrill cries told her it was too busy keeping itself from dropping into the gorge to do her an injury.

Rolling, hampered by her pack and trying not to crush her quiver, she put her second arrow to the string. Carefully, she turned over, tracking the hurrok with her blood on his talons; correcting for wind, she loosed. The arrow soared across the air below to plunge into the hurrok's belly. Shrilling, he tried to claw the missile from his flesh as he dropped. Two more attackers plummeted, one set ablaze by Numair, another fighting silver fog wrapped around its muzzle. The animal gods had joined the fight.

Daine sat up, holding the bow at an angle to keep it from tangling in rope or boards, and groped for her quiver. Two arrows met her fingers. Glancing back, she saw that the darking she'd put into her shirt was spread over the quiver's top. It had saved her arrows from the chasm; now it handed them to her. "Thank you," she whispered, getting to her knees again. She touched the back of her skull: Wetness trickled through her curls. "Hope you don't mind getting bled on."

Other hurroks, including the one that she had first wounded, spiraled down to the attack. Daine shot and killed the injured hurrok. A sparkling black net enveloped a pair of the immortals and exploded, leaving nothing. Two more hurroks, one nearby, one higher up, dodged frantically, trying to evade the badger's deadly silver fireballs.

Coldly, Daine drew the bowstring back to her ear. Silver fire overtook the hurrok farthest from her. It turned black and charred, dissolving as it fell. The last hurrok, screaming its rage, plunged toward Daine, claws outstretched. The girl shot.

The arrow flew as neatly as if she were in the practice yards of the palace. It slammed into the hurrok's throat, cutting off its scream. The immortal beat its wings to stop, and flew right into sparkling fire. Instantly transformed into a charred skeleton, it broke up, raining into the canyon.

Carefully Daine put down her bow. "I want to go home," she whispered. "I've had enough excitement for a while."

A darking head peered over her shoulder.

"*You* have some explaining to do," she told it. "The one in my pouch was spying on us, wasn't it?"

The darking squeaked and hung its head.

Daine pointed to the darking that clutched the plank. "What about this one? Is it coming with us?"

The darking on her back squeaked at the new-comer. It trembled like jelly, and finally shrilled a reply. Her passenger nodded to Daine.

"Is it a spy, too?"

The small, inky head shook emphatically. The newcomer was no spy.

"Well, it's certainly a deserter from Ozorne's army, at the very least." Carefully the girl reached forward to peel the newcomer off the board. Quivering, it pooled in her hand. "Why did you come over to my side, hm?"

"Daine," called the mage, "may we move on?"

"Sorry," she yelled. "Just a moment." To the darkings, she said, "You'd better come up with some answers that make sense, and soon." She dropped the newest of the blots inside her shirt. The darking on her shoulder stuck its head under her collar. Their soft, peeping conversation was drowned out by the creaking of the bridge as Daine carefully got to her feet. Gripping the rope handholds, she caught up to Numair.

"You're hurt," he said, touching the back of her head, when she reached him. The girl winced. "I'll tend it later, though. Let's get off this thing!"

"I don't know," she remarked, following. "It seems like a nice little bridge." He looked back at her, eyebrows raised. "It never dumped us, now, did it? And it could've."

"Yours is a happy nature," the mage answered, wry. "I confess, this is too much like excitement for me."

"It could be worse," Daine said, and giggled. "It could be raining."

Numair shook his head, then returned his attention to crossing the bridge. "I wonder if that hurrok struck your head a little too hard."

"Nonsense," the girl retorted. "I couldn't have shot straight if it had."

When they stepped off the bridge, Numair swept her into a tight hug, and examined her scalp as he held her. Daine rested gratefully against him. He'd sounded calm on the bridge, but his heart pounded; his shirt was sweat-soaked.

"We should clean this," he remarked over her head. "Didn't Sarra give you ointment for injuries?"

"Mm-hm." Daine rubbed her nose in the patch of chest hair that peeked through the V of his shirt collar.

He drew back. "Stop it," he said sharply. "I can't think when you do that."

"You think too much," she retorted, but she stopped anyway.

"I smell water," said Broad Foot. "Fish, and frogs, too."

"Let's find it," the badger ordered. "Before something else happens."

They found their way down into a valley. It was cut in two by a lively stream that flowed out of a deep pool. Broad Foot plunged in. Seconds later, Daine saw him on the bottom, riffling through sand and rocks with his bill.

On Numair's orders, Daine washed out her cuts. The darking that had deserted the hurrok remained inside her shirt, clinging to her waist, enduring without complaint the cold water that dripped onto it. The darking that had protected her arrows helped the man to gather firewood. The third darking remained in Daine's belt purse. She ignored its bumping as she dipped water and poured it over her aching head. The badger hunted for his supper among the ground-squirrel, snake, and mice gods nearby.

By the time he returned, the fire was burning well, and a pot of tea water was heating. Daine submitted patiently as Numair examined her scalp wounds, made sure they were clean of grit, and rubbed ointment into them. Neither he nor the girl were much surprised when the cuts healed as the ointment was applied.

"She said the herbs she finds here are more powerful," Daine remarked when Numair patted her shoulder and moved to another seat, one not so close.

The badger settled across the fire from the two mortals. Broad Foot was there already, half tucked under a fallen log.

"Daine, what in the name of all the gods was going on at that bridge?" the badger demanded. "It looked as if you were dancing!"

The girl rubbed an aching temple and sipped her tea. She felt weak and watery, a bit like tea herself. "It's these darkings." She explained what had taken place, while the darking that had saved her arrows nodded vigorously. Somewhere it had acquired a faint streak of gold through its body, color that filled the tiny head that it fashioned for itself. "Seemingly they were fighting, or disagreeing," the girl finished. "And then I saw Ozorne." She bit her lip. "There was another time, when the tauros almost got me. A darking was in the water—was that you?" she asked. The gold-smeared blot nodded. "I saw Ozorne then, too, inside *him*." She pointed to the darking.

"You never mentioned this," Numair remarked, eyes glittering dangerously.

She stiffened. "I had other things to worry about! I *thought* maybe I saw Ozorne because the darkings are liquid, kind of, but they aren't, are they?" Her gold-streaked companion shook its head.

"We need answers," said Broad Foot. "Where is the spy—in your pouch still?"

The leather purse thumped at the girl's belt, the creature inside trying to free itself. "Oh—and I've another one."

"Another—?" asked Numair, his brows coming together in a frown.

"It dropped off the hurrok that cut my head. I think it deserted to our side."

Broad Foot waddled over to Daine and cut a circle in the earth with a claw. Before he closed it, he told the gold-touched darking, "Inside, you." The shadowy thing cowered away from him.

"It won't hurt," the badger said. "Getting answers in other ways takes too long."

"But Ma tried that," protested the girl. "She only got its name."

"Because that was what she asked for," Broad Foot replied. "We're doing something else. Stop dawdling!" Flattening itself like an anxious dog, the gold-streaked darking trickled across the ground unwillingly. It hesitated outside the mark in the earth, then flowed into the circle. The duckmole looked up at the girl. "Where's this new darking?"

Daine fished out the deserter. "Go with your friend." She put it on the ground, and the darking rolled into the circle.

"Now the third," said Broad Foot.

Quickly the girl upended her belt purse over the circle. Her captive fell out with a plop; Broad Foot closed the circle. The darking from the pouch surged against the line in the ground, and flattened as if it had met a wall of glass.

"Stand back," ordered the duckmole. Opening his bill, he uttered a strange noise, half croak, half bark. Silver fire bloomed over the darkings, who shrank away from it. The glittering light stretched; deep within, a picture began to form.

There was Ozorne, streaked with soot, cuts on his face and chest, a clump of braids singed. At his throat he wore a black, glassy stone on a frayed cord. His lips moved as if he talked to himself. The view spread: The former Emperor Mage stood alone in a cave, a pool of water at his feet. Outside the entrance, snow fell in a thick veil.

An image formed in the water. It showed Daine as she read a book. Ozorne reached for her. When his outstretched wing touched the water, she disappeared. Though the image was soundless, they could see him shriek, baring sharp silver teeth. Veins in his chest, neck, and face stood against his skin. He spun, and came to an abrupt halt, a look of sudden cleverness on his face.

His lips moved. A thick worm of gold-edged scarlet fire appeared before him.

"So he'd mastered Stormwing magic by winter," murmured Numair. "Possibly even before the barriers between the realms collapsed."

"This is months ago," said the badger. "I remember this blizzard. We don't have that many, even here in the colder climates—it was the first full moon after Midwinter, the Wolf Moon."

Neatly, Ozorne cut his cheek on a razor-edged feather. The fiery worm flew to the cut, battening on it as a leech might. Ozorne spoke again. The tube fell away, turning into a bowl as it moved back. It brimmed with dark blood.

Lurching to the pool, Ozorne drank. When he straightened, his eyes were bright; he grinned. Returning to the magical bowl, he breathed a red-gold mist on its surface. It sank into the depths of the blood and swirled, making wavy patterns. Quickly the Stormwing cut both lips, flicking the blood drops into the bowl.

"For speaking," guessed Numair, engrossed. "Blood also for life, and to bind the fruits of the working to him. He couldn't have done it as a mortal, but here—"

"Here magical laws are what you make them," Broad Foot said. "He seems to have learned that better than most who are *born* immortal."

Numair raised an eyebrow. "I doubt that he learned that at all," Ozorne's one-time friend replied. "He merely wanted to do the thing, and so he forced it to happen. Subtlety has never been his strong suit."

Again that delicate flick of a feather edge, this time across each ear. The blood went into the bowl. Closing both eyes, Ozorne raised the same wing feather. Even more carefully, he just nicked the skin of his eyelids, producing two scant drops to add to what he'd already gathered.

Slowly, he raised his wings, pointing at the cave's ceiling. As he did, the liquid surged upward. Ozorne lowered his wings; the bulge remained. Twice more he repeated the motion; each time the liquid in the bowl rose higher. After the third raising, it formed a red-black column nearly eighteen inches tall.

Ozorne was sweating. Now he shouted; the bowl vanished. Its contents dropped, breaking into a myriad of blobs. Each turned black. The Stormwing's face was mirrored in each newborn darking.

The vision dissolved. Only the trio of darkings remained.

"There you have it," said the duckmole. He broke the circle to release the captives. "Your enemy made them to serve as his voice, eyes, and ears."

Free, the darkings did not try to escape. Instead they created heads for themselves so that they could nod. Again Daine noticed that one still contained a streak of gold. Somehow, while in the circle, another had picked up a small leaf. This it wore on its head, like an absurd hat. She was nearly positive that the third—the plain, shivering one—was the darking that had dropped from the hurrok.

"So you *are* Ozorne's spies," she said.

The answer was a head shake, first on the gold one's part, then on that of the one that bore a leaf. The third blot shrank lower to the ground, trembling.

"You showed Ozorne that we were at the bridge," Numair reminded them.

Gold-streak pointed an accusatory tentacle at Leaf.

"You'll do it again when he summons you," growled the badger.

The answer was emphatic head shakes from the gold-tinged and leaf-wearing blots. The third shrank against the other two.

"But he *created* you," Numair said.

Gold-streak began to tremble.

"Don't be afraid," Daine said. "You needn't—"

"I don't think it's fear," interrupted Numair.

"It's trying something new," added the duckmole. "Wait."

The streaked darking's companions leaned against it to somehow give it strength. An image formed in Gold-streak's depths, growing to cover its surface. There was Stormwing Ozorne: He glared at a darking on the ground before him.

"*Obey,*" whispered Ozorne. Its victim began to shrill; the darkings with Daine and her friends shrilled, too, tiny voices rising and falling. When the image vanished, they stopped.

"He hurts you," Daine said. "Is that why?"

Gold-streak showed a fresh image: a red-clad female giant—a blot's-eye view of Daine—as she tugged an arrow shaft away from the onlooker's vision. That picture blurred, to form a fresh image.

"Your leg, isn't it?" asked Numair, grinning. "From the foot up?"

A large hand came into view, cheese in its fingers. It dropped the scrap and pulled away.

"You fed it." The badger sighed. "Sometimes I think you'll feed *anything*."

"You were trying to warn me, in the pond?" asked Daine. The visions disappeared. The tinted darking nodded. "And on the bridge? Your friend here—Leaf, and you're Gold-streak, and this little fellow—" She scratched her head, looking at the trembling creature. "You'll be Jelly."

The darking's shivers slowed, though they didn't stop. It rose a bit in the middle, no longer trying to merge with the ground.

"So on the bridge, Leaf was reporting to Ozorne. Gold-streak, you tried to put Leaf in the pouch to keep Ozorne from seeing where I was, but it was too late—Ozorne had already sent the hurroks. You hadn't told Leaf not to do as Ozorne bids you."

Both Gold-streak and Leaf nodded.

She looked at Jelly. "And you abandoned the hurrok when you saw I had Gold-streak?" A bump that might have been a head lifted in Jelly's mass. Stiffly it shook its new head.

"Or did Gold-streak call to you?" inquired the girl.

Jelly nodded.

The badger chuckled. "Ozorne mastered Stormwing magic," he remarked, "but he created the darkings *here*."

"Are you sure?" inquired Numair. "That cave may have been in the mortal realms."

"He did it here," Broad Foot said firmly. "We gods can always tell the difference."

"Here, life is forbidden to remain a slave of its creator," explained the badger. "It's why so many children and servants of gods act against the interests of those who gave them life. The darkings are forming their own ideas and ways to communicate, and they're getting names."

"They're his *blood*," argued Numair. "Blood will bind anything. How can they refuse when he commands?"

"I don't know, but they can." Daine looked at the gold-tinted blot. "This morning I heard Ozorne say, 'Number fourteen, report.' I thought I dreamed it, but I didn't. Gold-streak was still in my pack then, so Ozorne couldn't see where we were. Gold-streak refused to tell him!"

Gold-streak nodded vigorously.

"That's why Ozorne sent Leaf, because he couldn't make you tell, and Jelly chose to be with you, not Ozorne."

Both Leaf and Gold-streak nodded.

Daine picked up Jelly. "You were brave to jump off that hurrok," she told it gently. "Why don't you talk to Leaf and Gold-streak a bit, and hear what they have to say?" The darking nodded, then—abruptly— rubbed its head against her thumb before she put it down. The three came together in a shadowy pool. Dane realized that she was exhausted.

"We'd best turn in," Numair said, eyes on her. "We've had a long day."

"Doubtless tomorrow will be longer still." The girl dug in her pack for her blanket.

"We will stand guard," the badger said. "Broad Foot and I have things to discuss."

Daine's last awareness was of the badger and the duckmole rocking to and fro, their heads together as they conferred mind to mind.

Rattail, who Daine was now sure spoke with the Dream King's voice, awaited her when she fell asleep. Again she called the girl's attention to the changing creature that was Uusoae, the Queen of Chaos, sur- rounded by the Great Gods who kept her captive. The fiery barrier between her and them blazed. Daine couldn't see her under that bright light, but she could *feel* the creature's changes, and wished very much that she could not.

Behind the Great Gods, multicolored liquid ran, not as puddles that spread and merged, but as a stream that whirled in a circle, seeming to flow both right and left at the same time. Watching it made the girl feel giddy. Suddenly columns leaped from the stream, rising and curving over the gods. If the columns met at the peak of the circle, the gods would be under a bowl of Chaos light, just as Uusoae was under a bowl of light.

White fire winked into existence at the backs of the gods. Instantly the columns turned to spinning drills, trying to bore their way through. The second barrier flickered.

"I hope you don't expect me to get excited over all this," Daine remarked, finding that she could speak for the first time. "*Or* that you mean the gods want my help." Part of her quivered at speaking so lightly of the gods; she rudely stepped on that fright. "I can't help the gods against Chaos—I have troubles of my own, back home. It's not as if they came to *our* aid when the barrier between us and them gave way at Midwinter."

"Why in the name of Father Universe would they meddle in that?" demanded Rattail. "The barrier was made by human mages, who never asked permission to do it."

"I still don't understand why you're showing me all this," the girl told her stubbornly. "It's like I'm being asked for help. Forget it. I've none to give."

A paw cuffed her soundly on the ear, knocking her over. Suddenly she was pup-sized; Rattail towered over her as she had over her own wolf pups. "You cannot have been attending to the duckmole, then," the wolf told her sternly. "Look there!" Planting her nose on Daine's behind, she scooted the girl forward.

Before them was the image that Daine had just seen, with the columns of shifting light connecting over the heads of the gods. They spread to cover the outer barrier. Mouths, distorted with jagged, sharp, and weirdly angled teeth, opened throughout the cover of Chaos light, and sank within it.

Suddenly everything sagged inward; Daine felt the white-light barriers evaporate within her very bones. Shapes thrashed under the rippling, glimmering Chaos stuff as it fell inward. At the center was Uusoae, born from the muck that she commanded, her eyes—when she had them—shining with triumph. She opened a mouth with swords for teeth and sprouted a hundred arms. They lashed out, seizing animals and two-legger gods from seemingly empty air, carrying each to the Chaos queen's jaws. She ate, and ate, and ate. Blood of all colors streamed over her chin and body and was soaked up, to add its colors to the muck in which she stood. The last two struggling figures she raised to her lips were Sarra and the badger.

With a gasp, Daine sat up, eyes open. Her curls and skin were dripping sweat. Sometime in the night she had thrown off the cover. It lay beneath her, dragged into folds and ridges. Her back and head ached.

"Numbers eleven, twenty-seven, fourteen, report!" That voice was Ozorne's; the girl looked around for the darkings. "How *dare* you defy me!" The commands issued from Daine's pack, where the blots had spent the night. "If you will not show what I wish—"

Crimson light shone through openings in the pack. The darkings keened, tiny voices shrill. He was hurting them! She yanked the flap open, furious; black tentacles streaked with red veins reached out to pull it shut again. The darkings wanted her to stay out. Rather than listen, she went to the pool to clean up. It took her longer than usual; she was trembling with rage, and dropped things. The sky in the east was just turning pink.

"Did you hear me?" Numair stood on the rise near their camp, wearing only his breeches, hair tousled. "It's how our enemies seem to know every move!"

Daine rubbed her face with her hands. "I didn't hear."

"It's the darkings. *They're* the answer."

She felt a powerful urge to yank him into the pond, just for being awake and chatty, let alone for having poked up the fire and set tea water on to boil. Mastering the urge—barely—the girl returned to her pack.

The darkings came out. She cuddled them, asking if they were all right. All three nodded, but Jelly quivered more than ever, and even Gold-streak and Leaf were trembly.

The badger waddled over to her. "Did you dream?"

Daine glared at him. "I dreamed, all right," she said grimly. "Amazingly clear dreams, like all the ones I've been having here. Amazing and *long*, since I don't remember sleeping much!"

Numair scooped up the darkings. "It's these little fellows," he said. "Or ladies," he added, squinting at them. "It's impossible to tell if you have a sex."

There was a splash; Broad Foot climbed out of the pool, a small fish in his bill. The resurrected fish god that had supplied his breakfast leaped from the water, splashing him. "What about the darkings?" he asked.

"They don't just spy on *us*," Numair said. "I *thought* Ozorne had created a number far in excess of his needs, if they were solely to keep an eye on Daine or me. Your kinfolk are with our leaders, aren't they?" he asked the darkings. "The king, the queen—"

"In the north," Daine said, realizing what he meant. "I heard in a dream that the Scanrans got away clean. Somehow they knew the Yamani fleet was coming."

"As I woke, I heard that yesterday the Seventh Riders tried to use a secret exit from Legann," Numair added quietly. "The enemy was waiting. Three of the Riders are dead."

Daine clenched her teeth. She had friends in the Seventh Riders. Their commander, Evin Larse, had pulled a roll from her ear the first time she'd eaten in the Rider mess. She looked a question at Numair.

"I don't know who they were, magelet," he said gently, smoothing a wet curl off her forehead. "No one mentioned names."

She nodded, and made herself think about the immediate problem. "The darking spies tell Ozorne. And other darkings with his commanders pass it on," she whispered. "That—dung-fouled, mold-eating—" She faced the badger, eyes blazing. "You could put an end to it!"

"The Great Gods don't like the People's gods to intervene in human affairs," the badger replied. "We are to keep to doings of our own children."

"You've always said I mean as much as your own kits." She knelt beside him. "Badger, please! I can't help them at home whilst I'm here—but *you* can! *Please!*"

The badger fluffed out his fur, snorted, and stamped.

"What good is knowing that your friends have eavesdroppers?" asked Broad Foot. "The darkings are very good at hiding."

"There are general spells to make an area secure," Numair said hesitantly. "I would hope that the darkings aren't immune to their effects. Of course, chances are that our friends are using such spells now, to hamper the enemy's spy-mages."

Colors rippled over Gold-streak's skin. The other two blots flowed into it to form a single, quivering mass. They seemed to be conferring.

Movement in the pot where Numair was brewing their tea caught Daine's eye. On top of the curtain wall at Port Legann, Tkaa the basilisk stood by Kitten. Yellow fog was drifting through the air over their heads: The wyverns were on the attack once more.

A burning log snapped, throwing up sparks, and the image dissolved. Mute, Daine pulled off the silver claw that hung around her neck, the symbol of the tie between her and the badger. She held it out to him. "I'm asking you now, by this symbol of the bond that's between us: Please help my friends."

The badger whuffled, wet nose quivering.

"If it helps, I will take them as far as I can," the duckmole told his fellow god.

"What is it, Gold-streak?" Numair asked. The three darkings were surging up and down beside Daine, reminding her of children trying to get an elder's attention. Gold-streak had stretched until it stood taller than Leaf and Jelly.

To her surprise, a slit opened in the knob that served Gold-streak as a head. The opening moved; a squeak reached the girl's ears. Quickly she bent down so that her ear was close to the blots. "I go," repeated Gold-streak. Its voice was tiny.

## ➤➤ SIX ◄◄

# CHESS GAME

Numair touched her shoulder. "What's the matter?"

She looked up at him. "It's Gold-streak. It—it talked."

"But they *don't* talk, do they?" he asked. "My impression was that they only communicate what is said *to* them, or *near* them."

Gold-streak stretched a bit more and said, "Now talk." It was louder this time, enough so that everyone heard. "*I* go. Talk to darkings. Teach them—" It returned to its huddle with Leaf and Jelly. They vibrated together until Gold-streak's head rose out of the mass. "Freedom," it said clearly. "Choosing."

"Do you know where your brethren are—who they spy on?" asked the badger.

All three blots nodded.

"And I can transport a darking from place to place, here or in the mortal realms," the badger commented. He sighed, and pointed out, "It will take us a while, even going from spy to spy by magical means. Transporting all over the mortal realms, I will need to rest. Numair Salmalín, look after my kit. Put that back on your neck," he ordered Daine crossly, meaning his claw.

She obeyed. Gold-streak ended a last conference with Leaf and Jelly, and rolled up the badger's leg to his back. The god looked at it. "Ready?" he asked. Gold-streak nodded. Silver light exploded, and they were gone.

Numair straightened their camp. He filled their fire pit and the trench that had served as a privy, scattering leaves and stones to make the place seem untouched. Daine packed, rapidly stowing their belongings. Broad Foot, Leaf, and Jelly watched from a safe distance.

"It's as good as the courtship dances of cranes," the duckmole remarked. When they finished, he created a pouch in Numair's fresh shirt, and materialized in it. "You never bump into each other, and you never try to do the same tasks."

Daine smiled up at her tall friend. "We've been doing this for a while," she explained. "I've lost count of the camps that we've put up and broken down."

Numair reached, as if he wanted to stroke her cheek, then dropped his hand. "Where do the darkings ride?"

Leaf coiled around Daine's neck. Jelly, still aquiver, tucked itself into a pocket of the girl's breeches, letting only its makeshift head stick out.

Today Daine set the pace. She knew exactly how fast she and Numair could walk together, just as she knew how often they had to rest. The man and Broad Foot talked quietly; Numair had a great many questions about the home of the duckmole's mortal children. Daine and the darkings watched their surroundings. The small blots were fascinated. Wary, the girl carried her bow in her free hand. She wanted no surprises.

Their trail led downhill, through a less heavily forested land. It was almost noon when they came to the narrow arm of a swamp. "Mauler's Swamp?" asked Daine, seeing that Numair was looking at their map.

The mage nodded. "There should be a bridge ahead."

Daine pointed. The bridge was a low one, rising a handful of inches over the water's surface. Fashioned of sturdy-looking logs, it would hold them clear of the murky water until they were completely across.

Mosquitoes and biting flies came for them as soon as they stepped onto the bridge. Killing the insects did no good: They were gods, and restored themselves instantly; their dead bodies fell into the mouths of waiting frogs and fish. Their bites raised welts that itched crazily. At last Numair spun a fiery magical shield to keep the things at bay.

The insects buzzed outside, on a level with the humans' faces.

"The bears and the deer let us feed off them!" protested a horsefly.

"Muskrats," a tiny voice said; Daine couldn't see who spoke. "Don't forget them."

"They are gods," Numair replied calmly, undisturbed by a chat with insects. "No doubt they replace their blood instantly. *We* are not gods."

"Mortal blood tastes best," added the small voice. "It has life in it. The blood of gods doesn't."

"I can't begin to tell you how sorry I am to deny you such a treat," Numair said.

"You know very well we could break that shield, if we wanted to," cried a blackfly. "We are *gods*, after all."

"What good is blood that's given so grudgingly?" the horsefly grumbled.

"What good indeed?" inquired the mage, voice mild.

"Selfish," a mosquito snapped.

"I hope that Mauler eats you! It would serve you right!" the invisible bug told them. The insects left as abruptly as they had come.

Daine wiped her forehead on her sleeve; it was hot and close in this marsh.

"Broad Foot, what is this Mauler?" Numair asked. He kept his staff—its crystal charged with his Gift—raised before him in case something larger than insects came to feed. "He looked like a crocodile in the image that Weiryn showed us."

"Lord Mauler is an older god of the People," said the duckmole. "He is a link between crocodiles and the dinosaurs. May we move faster?"

"Why?" asked Numair. Daine paused briefly to string her bow. When she reached back to her quiver, an arrow met her fingers—Leaf had gotten it for her.

"Mauler isn't entirely friendly to trespassers," Broad Foot told him. "He puts up with them on his good days, of course."

"You're afraid today may not be one of his good ones?" suggested the mage.

"Exactly."

Daine watched their surroundings closely as they followed the low bridge around the bole of an immense cypress. Below, in murky water, she saw an oddly regular pattern that ran under their bridge to emerge on the other side.

The pattern moved; water heaved and rolled. A hollow tree boomed like a giant drum. The bridge shook, then settled. The thing underneath headed for open water, pulling skeins of vines in its wake. Daine's jaw dropped. At best guess, the creature was over thirty feet in length; any three of the crocodiles she'd seen in Carthak, lined up head to tail, could fit inside its skin comfortably. It curved back around, then stopped.

Twin yellow rounds popped through the surface.

A tiny voice just under the girl's ear—Leaf's—said, "Uh-oh."

Dark shutters slid down over the orbs, then lifted. They were eyes. Daine gulped, sweating. It was one thing to see a creature in a vision over her father's map; such a vision was very misleading as to size. One of those eyes alone was larger than Broad Foot. If she used her bow, would her arrows do more than tickle him?

"What the—?" Numair stared at those two immense yellow eyes.

"Lord Mauler," Broad Foot whispered. "Greetings to you, cousin!" he called.

"And good day," muttered Numair. He broke into a trot, Daine behind him. To their relief, solid land was a few yards ahead. Mauler thrashed as they stepped off the bridge. The surface of the swamp rolled, and crested, and splashed the travelers. The great creature dove, leaving only surging water to mark his passage.

Broad Foot shook a clump of plants off his bill. "I don't know which is worse—when he's cross, or when he's trying to be funny."

Numair wiped his face on his sleeve. "If it's all the same, I won't stay around to study his moods."

Now the way led slowly uphill. The trees thinned. Clearings expanded; streams flattened and slowed. The air warmed and dried. They kept going after sunset, using the lights overhead, fired by the war with Chaos, to see by. At last they made camp beside a lazy, wide stream.

After eating, Broad Foot volunteered to stand watch until dawn, since he didn't always need to sleep. The two humans curled up under their blankets. Daine had thought she would sleep instantly. Instead she watched the war lights bloom and fade.

I know my Da, she thought. I could change my name. No more looks from them that know I'm Sarrasri because Ma was my only family—that I'm a bastard. I s'pose Da acknowledges me now. It's my right to change my name. Weirynsra. Veralidaine Weirynsra.

It didn't sound right. When all was said and done, she was Veralidaine Sarrasri, really. She'd been that for sixteen years. Changing now would be—uncomfortable.

That settled, she closed her eyes. What did the Dream King want to say tonight?

She had the answer almost instantly. Rattail appeared next to her; they were seated on clear air that had turned solid, enough so that Daine could hear her friend's tail slapping the invisible floor in back of her.

"So now we get down to it," said the wolf. "There is one thing that Father Universe and Mother Flame have forbidden Uusoae to do—*meddle in the affairs of mortals*. All of Chaos gets half of its strength from mortal creatures, because *they* are half Chaos by nature. My lord Gainel thinks that someone is helping Uusoae to tap into the other half of mortal fire, the half that does not belong to her. He thinks that she is playing this game, which she is forbidden to do."

Below them appeared a great chessboard in red and gold. Uusoae was the red queen, her appearance for the most part that of a woman in an orange gown, with tangled black hair. Only her eyes and hands changed shape, constantly. Her king was an empty shadow that tried to draw all that was nearby into it. At last a pincer-handed Uusoae ringed it with multicolored fire to save her other pieces from being gulped by her consort. The leftmost rook was a yammering, three-headed ape: "Discord," said Rattail when the girl pointed it out and asked. Uusoae's other rook was a lean, blue-skinned youth with six arms, each one holding a weapon. Smiling at Daine, he pulled, a seventh arm from behind his back—it held Numair's dripping head.

A hand rested on her shoulder; she jumped. The newcomer was Numair, well and whole. "Violence," he said, pointing to the blue youth. "With Discord, the gatekeeper of Chaos." Daine glanced at the rook Discord, and saw that it juggled her own head.

"Charming," she murmured dryly.

"It's their nature," said Rattail, with an unwolflike shrug. "They can't help being what they are."

Numair took his hand from Daine's shoulder and looked at the wolf. "Daine, would you introduce us?"

"I dunno," said the girl, looking at Rattail. "Are you Rattail, or are you the Dream King?"

The wolf's shape puddled, curved, and straightened into a rail-thin man with inky, tousled hair and bottomless eyes.—*I thought perhaps you would be less unnerved by hearing of these things from a friend.*—

"Maybe," she replied, looking at gold's ranking pieces. These were the Great Gods: Mithros and the Goddess as king and queen, the Black God and a white-eyed female—"Shakith, goddess of seers," whispered Numair—as high priests, the desert god Jihuk and the Smith god as knights, Kidunka the world snake and the Wave Walker as rooks. "Where are you?" Daine asked Gainel.

The Dream King smiled.—*Like you mortals, I have one foot in the Divine Realms, the other in Chaos. Lately that's been a most uncomfortable position.*—

"Understandably," replied Numair. He pointed to Uusoae's pawns as they materialized on the board all at once. "*Now* we have some answers!"

The central pawn was the Stormwing Ozorne. His closest neighbor was a blond Scanran mage who used a ruby in place of a lost eye.

Numair whistled softly. "Inar Hadensra. *That* explains far more than it doesn't."

"He's very powerful?" asked Daine.

"Yes, indeed. And he serves only the Council of Ten in Scanra, not whomever they have as king that week. The Copper Islander to his right? That's Valmar, the third of King Oron's sons, carrying a general's baton. And next to him is Deniau, the high admiral of the Copper Isles, and Valmar's brother. Ozorne has powerful allies."

Daine wasn't sure how mere two-leggers might compete with the spidren—a giant, furred spider with a human head—hurrok, dull-eyed female Stormwing, and winged ape that filled out the number of red pawns, but she kept that to herself. Looking to the row of gold pawns, she saw a piece that looked like her at the far end of the board, and one like Numair at the end closest to them. Between their pieces stood a gold-skinned, almond-eyed Yamani who carried a spyglass, Tkaa, King Jonathan, Queen Thayet, the King's Champion, and Kitten.

"I don't like being so far apart from you," she told Numair.

Pieces vanished and reappeared. Now the Great Gods struggled with the Chaos beings, neither side appearing to have the advantage. Ozorne and his allies, holding swords, spears, and axes that rippled with the constantly changing colors that filled the sky and Chaos vents in the Divine Realms, attacked the gold pawns. Gold's pieces were armed, but the attack took them while they were staring at the Great Gods' fight; red's pieces swiftly cut them down. When Daine, Numair, and the other gold pawns were dead, Ozorne and his allies slumped to the board and dissolved, blending with their weapons. Their melted selves flowed around the outside of the ring of struggling gods, to become the Chaos stuff from Daine's earlier dreams, flooding over, then eating, the Great Gods.

"I don't like that game," said Numair, his grin a bit forced. "Can we play a new one?"

In the blink of an eye, the whole board twisted. When it straightened, all the pieces had been returned to their original places. This time, as the gods and the lords of Chaos struggled, gold's pawns led the attack. The Scanran mage threw fire at them; King Jonathan blocked it. Alanna the Champion locked blades with an armed spidren. Daine's pawn went straight for Ozorne, Numair's for the Copper Islander Deniau. All over the board, opponents were locked in desperate battles.

The spidren was the first killed; Alanna raised her sword with a triumphant cry. Uusoae appeared, shrieking as she charged the King's Champion. Gold's pawns were swept out of harm's way as the Great Gods appeared in a circle around the Queen of Chaos. Red's pawns vanished.

—*If she is behind this, she will come to avenge her servitor, the one who found a way for her to use mortal power without Father Universe and Mother Flame knowing. Once she reveals herself, they will enter the matter, and end the fight. Gods and mortals will be safe again, at least for another thousand years.*—Gainel, who had stayed beside the girl and Numair all along, looked at them. Daine could no more read the emotion in those shadow eyes now than she had been able to the last time she met their gaze.

He disappeared, and was replaced by tree limbs and leaves. It took Daine a moment to realize that she was now awake and that Gainel's soft voice was in her mind, not her ears.—*Her ally may not be a spidren. It may be another immortal, or a human. Whoever it is, for the sake of your parents, humankind, and the beast-People, you must kill him, or her. It is the only way to end the war.*—

"Why didn't someone just tell us what the problem was?" demanded Numair. Daine looked: He, too, was awake and sitting up.

—*Because the Great Gods believe that no problem exists. They say that no mortal would risk the destruction of his or her own realm by helping Uusoae to break the walls that keep her contained. I no longer argue with my brothers and sisters. They only laughed, so I gave it up. Farewell then, mortals. Good luck.*—

Though he was nowhere to be seen, Daine knew the Dream King had left as surely as if she'd seen him walk away.

Later in their travels that day, as they ate lunch by a stream, the ground shook. Two sounds tore through the air. The first, Daine and Numair agreed later, was that of an iron door being slammed. The other, hard on the heels of the first, was undeniably that of a drawbridge being slowly, ponderously lowered.

Daine and Numair covered their ears, to no effect. When the booming echoes faded, she checked Leaf and Jelly. Both were shrinking, shivering blobs.

"Oh, my goodness," Broad Foot remarked sadly. "So it's come to that."

"Come to what?" Daine asked, rubbing her abused ears.

"Follow me." Broad Foot waddled to the stream, Daine, Numair, and the darkings right behind him. Leaning over the water, he breathed on it. An image—or rather, three images—grew on the surface.

The first, before Numair, showed the walls and ramparts of Port Legann from high overhead. A colossal spotted hyena gnawed on a tower, then on a siege engine outside the walls. Under her, around her, even through her, humans surged in battle. Was the hyena a ghost? Raising a muzzle that dripped blood, she gave the stuttering, eerie cry that made her kind so feared. Pricking cat ears forward, Daine also heard a distant, dim roar: human voices shouting and the clang of swords, shields, and armor.

In the water before the duckmole, Daine saw wheat fields. Cattle and sheep grazed nearby, herded by children and dogs. Over everything, in a form as sheer as the hyena's, slunk a yellow, mangy cur dog. He was little more than a skin-covered skeleton, as unhealthy an animal as Daine had ever seen. He took bites from everything: grapes, wheat, apples, herd animals. As he bit, things began to shrivel.

Daine looked at the water image in front of her, and shivered. It showed Corus, the Tortallan capital, with its crowds, rich marketplaces, and temples. A giant, ghostly rat crept through the streets, thrusting his nose into windows and doorways. He licked a man who was making a speech in front of the stocks: The man began to cough. A woman brought him a dipper of water; he could barely drink it. Two men helped him to sit. The ghosts of tiny rats flowed from his mouth, landing on those who had gathered around him.

"Slaughter has been out since May," Broad Foot said. "Malady, though, and Starvation—what you heard were the gates to their dwellings being opened."

"The Three Sorrows," whispered Numair, making the Sign against evil on his chest.

Daine copied him in the Sign; her skin prickled. Leaf curled around her neck to see. Now it rubbed its tiny head, with its green hat, against her cheek. Jelly had vanished into Daine's pocket when the three images had appeared in the water.

"They are the siblings of the gods," the duckmole explained. "Their appearance causes great changes, many for the good—"

"I doubt the ones they kill think so," murmured Daine. She looked at the duckmole, thinking hard. It was one thing to ask the badger for help, another to ask the duckmole. Broad Foot had nothing to do with her, really, or with humankind—there were no two-leggers in the lands where his mortal children lived.

"You know," said the mage casually, "the more disorder that is created in the mortal realms, the more power that Uusoae will have to use. Or so it appears to me."

Daine took her cue from the man. "I bet that Chaos will feed on this. How can she not, when all three Sorrows are wandering loose?"

The duckmole sighed. "So that's it. You want me to halt the Sorrows." He scratched himself. "I can't stop them all," he warned them. "They are strong. They ought to be, with humans feeding them for centuries. I can only hold one, and I'll have to remain in the mortal realms to keep it from breaking loose. The Great Gods themselves could do no better. Some powers cannot be ruled, even by the mightiest."

Daine and Numair traded worried looks. *Choose* between Slaughter, Malady, and Starvation?

"Who are we to say which roams free?" whispered the girl. "If we ask to hold Slaughter, Malady, and Starvation will kill hordes of folk— but if we hold Starvation, which kills slow, the other two will wipe out large numbers . . ." Her throat closed.

"Armed humans can defend themselves," Numair said, thinking aloud. "Hopefully Starvation can be held at bay through food imports. But Malady . . ." He shuddered. "Malady doesn't care who it takes, or how many. Malady can wipe out armies and leave no one in the Yamani Islands or Carthak to farm the land."

"And it's just out," added the duckmole. "It's weak still."

Daine shivered and tried not to think of friends killed in battle, or dying slowly of hunger. "Malady," she whispered. "If it can be only one, let it be that."

Broad Foot rocked from side to side, muttering. At last he stopped. "Stay on the path," he ordered. "It is a fixed thing, even on the Sea of Sand. It will lead you to the Dragonlands. Getting in, of course, is *your* affair."

"Of course," murmured Numair.

Daine knelt to face him. "I'll owe you for this, Broad Foot."

"So will I," added the man.

"It *is* only fair. If you can force Uusoae to reveal herself, and save the divine and mortal realms, *we* ought to do some things for *you*. Be careful, then." Silver fire gathered around his small body, and he vanished.

"What will we do if the dragons refuse?" Daine asked Numair.

"Fret about them later," he said, gathering their things as she quickly finished her lunch. "I'm worried about crossing the Sea of Sand, if Rikash doesn't help us."

Daine stowed her pack and quiver on her back. "What's wrong with the Sea of Sand?"

"I keep forgetting that we haven't both made a study of myths and legends," remarked Numair, shrugging into his own pack. "The Sea of Sand is more than a desert. It's said the Great Gods take mortal heroes there—though Alanna the Champion never mentioned such an experience. If the hero survives, it is a sign that his—or her—mortal impurities have been seared away."

Daine winced. "Please, Goddess," she said, looking up. "Send Rikash with help." She led the way to the path. "I'm fair confused," she told Numair. "If I'm in the Divine Realms, why do I look up to pray to the gods? Shouldn't I be looking somewhere else?"

"Thinking about things like that will give us both headaches," he replied. "Although I believe that Shuiliya Chiman had visions of the dead praying by looking down. Now, in the lost books of Ekallatum . . ."

Daine smiled. As long as he could talk of learning, Numair would forget anything else, including future dangers. At her belt and on her shoulder, two heads craned toward the mage: The darkings were fascinated.

The path ahead climbed; they stopped often both to rest and to get out of the sun. To the east, the ground fell to a broad river with a sea of grass on its far bank. To the west, the thinning forest gave way bit by bit to scrub and short grasses. Finally, as the afternoon sun beat down without mercy, they stopped near a spring tucked in a rocky cleft. First they ate a meal of bread and fruit, then curled up to sleep until the sun went down.

"What do you mean, 'no reports'?" The voice was young, male, with the accent of the Copper Isles. "All through this campaign you have been able to say exactly where the enemy is! Now, suddenly, you have no information from your spies? There is a Yamani *fleet* north of us—what if it is coming here?"

"I have but two spies there, as you know! If there is some way that they have been detected—Put your own idle mages to the task!" Ozorne's voice was twisted by fury. "You want everything handed you as a gift. But for me, you would have neither courage nor allies to take on Tortall, for all your vows of death to King Jonathan's line! If you want news, scry for it!"

A hoarse voice added, "General Valmar—if you think perhaps to take your fleet and slip away tonight, or tomorrow, or ever, know this." From a childhood spent too close to that harsh land for comfort, Daine recognized a Scanran voice. "Every skin of liquid fire that you possess will burn, should I touch it with my Gift. If you throw them overboard, our allies among the merfolk will fasten those skins to your hulls, and I will burn them then. We will not have the Copper Islanders act as they have so often, and forget their vows of allegiance."

Footsteps—hurried ones—receded. Daine heard metal claws digging into wood.

"The centaurs, too, grow restless," the Scanran remarked.

"I have hairs from every tail among them, to bind them to me. They'll sing a very different tune, should I scorch even one." Ozorne's voice was sullen.

"Sometime you must tell me how you first had information so detailed that one might think you perched on the shoulders of the northern defenders, and now you have nothing. I look forward to hearing."

ॐ

Daine opened her eyes and smiled. The badger and Gold-streak had visited the darkings in northern Tortall, then, and talked them into breaking contact with their creator.

Wanting Numair to sleep a bit more, she wandered over to the spring. On its glittering surface, she looked for news of home. An image formed immediately. In it, Broad Foot clung to one of Malady's feet. The rat-Sorrow tried to shake him off; the duckmole jammed venomous spurs into Malady's transparent flesh. Malady stiffened; his reddened eyes went blank. He froze.

Daine blinked. Now she was over Port Legann, so high that men and the ships that blockaded the harbor looked like toys. In the distance to the southwest—the direction of the Copper Isles—she saw the bright flare of torches. The image moved closer and brightened, so that even though it was night, she saw the shapes of ten ships. With the strange, clear sight granted by the water image, she easily read the flags that crowned the masts.

Numair asked softly, "Daine?" He was sitting up, frowning.

She began to stuff things into her pack. "The Copper Isles is sending ten ships—they're flying battle flags—north. I think they're making for Legann."

The sun had set. Quickly they packed; before they set out, Jelly changed its seat from Daine's pocket to Numair's shoulder.

The land was changing, turning to desert in the west. The path headed that way, gleaming silver under war light and the light of the newly risen moon, sloping down through huge clusters of rock. In the distance a bird leaped from a pinnacle, flying as if it meant to reach the moon. When it pulled in its wings and tail, Daine grabbed Numair's arm and pointed.

The bird opened itself, spinning on its tail. Lances of silver, blue, and gold light shot from its feathers, an explosion of color over the desert. Within seconds, more dark forms took wing. Each opened itself to the light in a shimmering dance of colors Unlike the sunbirds, these did not drop back to earth. They spiraled around one another, winding like a river across the scrublands, more of their kind falling in behind them.

"Beau-ti-full," whispered Leaf beside Daine's ear.

She had been holding her breath. Releasing it, she sighed. "Beautiful," she agreed, stealing a look at Numair.

Petting Jelly with a finger, he watched the spectacle, eyes glowing with awe. "I wish I could stay, or come back," he whispered. "So many wonders."

The way grew steep. Lizards that glowed pale blue or yellow darted across the path, or crouched in stone hollows, tongues flicking out to taste the air as the two mortals went by. The path led among stone formations that looked like cracked and broken pillars tightly jammed together. Wind and grit had cut the soft rock into laddered, fantastic shapes. They made Daine nervous: She had an odd feeling that some hollows in the columns were eyes that tracked her.

She tried to meet one pillar's gaze. Half hypnotized by it, she searched for the flash of intelligence that she *knew* was there. Numair and Jelly, far up the trail before they realized she wasn't behind them, returned for her. "I feel it, too," the man said quietly, drawing her away from the stone. "I don't know if this place is dangerous, but I will be happy to get out of here all the same."

For the next two miles the path followed a narrow slot between deep rock cliffs. Numair's crystal blazed with light, creating shadows within shadows, turning long hollows into mouths that screamed. The sense of eyes on her was almost unbearable. The hairs at the nape of her neck stood on end.

"Can you—put the staff out?" she asked. "I—I think it makes things worse."

He nodded. The crystal went dark. She took the lead, making bat ears and cat eyes for herself. Numair saw well in the dark; he also had the moon and the rippling battle flares to light the path.

A fresh breeze hit their faces, air from an open place being funneled into a narrow one. Looking up, Daine could see the edges of rock formations. It was nearly dawn. Just ahead, a stone pedestal rose into the air. On top of it, a massive boulder had been cut by the elements into the shape of a question mark.

"Well, *that's* fitting," Numair remarked.

Daine grinned, her mood lightening. Behind the question rock lay open air and, she hoped, an end to those frozen screams.

To their right, at the edge of a cliff, lay a drop; to their left, stone heights reared. They were on the side of a mountain. Sage clung to the pale soil of the shelf; junipers thrust twisted limbs into the sky from rock clefts above their heads. Across the path, in a swath too wide for them to jump, a Chaos vent had overflowed, its shifting yellow, green, and gray liquid a yard from the cliff's edge. To get around it and back onto the path, they would have to walk that narrow strip of bare earth between rim and air, then pass a massive clump of odd gray stones.

"Now *that's* curious." Numair frowned. "The indigenous stone is lava rock of the brown variety. These are different. They could be granite." He walked closer, eyebrows knit, halting a few yards from the spill.

Daine strung her bow and put an arrow to the string, then trailed him. "Indi—what?"

"Indigenous," he replied quietly. "Local."

"Why you couldn't just *say* local . . . ?"

He chuckled as the black, sparkling fire of his Gift flowed out of his hand to wind around the gray rocks. "I'm sorry. I'd meant to do better than my university friends, and not upset people by talking in that abstruse fashion. Then my *father* complained. He asked how did he know that I even *went* to those expensive teachers when I spoke just as I always had?"

Daine grinned. "You never told me that. I s'pose once you get used to doing it at home, you forget the rest of the time."

His magical Gift returned to him. "Those rocks *seem* all right."

Impulsively, she cast her magic over the stones. A chasm tore through her magical self, just as it had done with the Skinners. At the edges of her perceptions, the world shifted and rolled; she was drowned in odors and sounds like nothing that could, or should, exist in the natural world. She tried to cry out, but dripping hands closed her mouth.

A sharp pain lanced through her ear. The magical assault ended. It was her *own* hands that had closed her mouth. Tears ran down her cheeks.

"What happened?" Numair had one arm around her as he fumbled for his handkerchief. She took it with gratitude. "You're white, you're—"

"They're touched with Chaos, those stones," she replied, wiping her eyes. "If I try to use my wild magic to look at something like that, it—it pulls me in."

"You shouldn't generalize from one experience—"

"But it *wasn't* just one. This made me remember the *last* time!" She finished wiping her face—particularly her mouth, where she'd felt oozing fingers—and told him what had taken place with the Skinners.

"Then how did you break free this time?" Numair demanded.

"Leaf, you bit me, didn't you?" she asked, raising a hand to her right ear. Tiny spots of blood came off on her fingers.

"Sorry," the leaf-wearing blot replied, hanging its head.

"Don't apologize," she told it. "Do that whenever you think it's needful. You just saved me from maybe walking off a cliff." The darking rubbed its head on her finger.

"For now, we shall delay the question of where it got teeth," Numair remarked. "Let's get away from here. Can you walk by those rocks, Daine?"

"Chaos mostly gets me through my magic. I just won't use it. And it's not like they're *alive,* after all." She looked at the way around the Chaos vent and rocks, and gulped. Three feet was a small margin between her and the long drop. "You go—I'll come after."

Resettling his pack, Numair took the lead as confidently as if he had ten yards, not one, in which to move. Once he cleared the vent's spill, before he passed out of sight behind the rocks, Daine followed. Watching her feet, she skirted the vent, backing away an inch or two as the shifting-colored substance threw a tentacle in her direction.

Numair cried out. She looked up: A gray stone arm was wrapped around him, lifting him off his feet. Rocky, grinding sounds filled the air as the other stones began to move. Fumbling to get her bow up, Daine stepped back to get a cleaner shot.

The rim of the canyon broke under her weight. With a shriek, she dropped, bow tumbling out of her grip.

# ⇥ SEVEN ⇤

# FALLING

∞ The first tree didn't even slow Daine down. Branches, gnarled by the fight to get their share of sun in the narrow canyon below, snapped easily when she hit them. She pulled Leaf from her shoulder and tucked it into her middle, curling into a ball around the darking. Panic swamped her; she could think of nothing but the rush of air and the sickening drop.

The second and third trees that she struck held her a bit longer as they raked her back and legs. The quiver caught on something, nearly dislocating her shoulder. She screamed, and hauled her arm out of the strap. The fourth tree was full of thorns. It kept her for almost a full breath, and ripped her skin.

She clutched at the branches of the fifth tree, thorns or no, missed her grip, and fell into deep, ice-cold water. Down she and Leaf plummeted, dragged by the pack. Yanked along by a heavy current, she dumped her belongings and shot to the surface, choking.

White water swept her along. Battered against the stony riverbed, she fought to reach the shore. At last she was swept into a calm pool, out of the undertow. Gasping and cursing, she dragged herself and Leaf into the shallows, and looked up.

The sky was a distant blue strip. Earth and rock soared on either side of the canyon. Nowhere in those forbidding walls did she see the trail of broken trees that would mark where she'd come down.

"Not a problem," she told Leaf, slogging for the rocky shore. "I'll just take hawk shape and find him—once I catch my breath. Are *you* all right?"

The darking's leaf hat was soaked; Leaf itself trembled as devoutly as Jelly had. "No," it told her flatly.

"Me neither. At least we're alive." Daine waded onto dry land.

Had she been herself, she would have seen the odd regular pattern under scattered dirt and stone. Instead, the trap closed on her the moment that she stepped into it.

Heavy, sticky ropes clamped around her. One strand fell over her eyes; when she opened her mouth to cry out, two more dropped over her lips and nose. Suffocating, she tried to claw at them, only to find that her hands and legs were bound. She tossed her head, fighting to breathe.

Whatever covered her nose peeled back. She sucked in air, ordering her lungs to be happy with what came through her nostrils alone. Her instinct was to feel the gag in her mouth and panic. Sweating, she forced herself to calm down, and breathe slowly.

There was a new movement on her forehead. Slowly, a hair at a time, her blindfold slipped up. At last it was over her brows. Her left eye filled with a small, inky head. The bonds that wrapped *her* so well apparently had no effect on a darking.

"Thank you," she tried to tell Leaf. Whatever sealed her mouth kept the sound in.

"Badbad," Leaf replied.

Yes indeed, she thought. Badbad. I must've stepped into a snare laid for anything big and edible that came down here to drink.

Turning her head, she examined her bonds, and began to shake. Not rope, but dust-gray web, gripped her. She knew what it was, having seen enough such webs in both sunlight and in the dark, when they glowed. They were the creation of spidrens.

She trembled. Of all the immortals that she had battled over the last three years, those were the worst. They had furry spider bodies, at least five feet tall; the females were mottled, males black. Their heads were human, with sharp, predatory teeth. They leaped amazing distances, and preferred human blood to any other food. She had lost count of the times that she had found humans caught in their webs.

Immediately she listened, listened *hard*, for the web spinners. There was no telling which could be worse—that they had laid the trap and then left the area, or that they might be close by. At last, on the outer fringes of her magical range, she felt something immortal. If it was a spidren, perhaps she still had time to escape.

Taking a breath, the girl became a great jungle snake. Her clothes drooped around her scaled form. Gathering herself to crawl away, she ran face first into a shrinking web. As she fought to get her skull free, it closed so tightly that it pinched her coils together.

She changed: swan shape. The web fitted her new body perfectly, binding her. That sense of immortals on the fringes of her awareness was stronger, and familiar: spidrens for sure, three of them.

She wanted to scream, but stopped herself. They were very close now, moving fast; they must know they had a prize.

Perhaps small's not the best way, she thought. Focusing on the great bears of the north, Daine shed her swan shape. The web, instead of bursting, stretched. She was as captive as before.

If she had to face them, she needed clothes. No one could feel brave when naked, and all she wore now was the silver claw. Somehow she didn't think she would feel dressed, meeting spidrens with only the badger's token to wear. Eyes closed, she reformed her true self, easing human limbs into breeches and sleeves, re-covering her back and hips, until she was properly dressed. That done, she sank back. What now?

Her dagger. She twisted, looking for it. Her forearms were plastered against her sides, but if she could reach it . . . The hilt at her waist was covered by web. She couldn't even touch the weapon.

"Look, dears, we have a guest!" taunted a voice from above.

Daine looked up. Three spidrens—two males and a larger female—descended a nearby rock face on threads of web. Her stomach rolled as they jumped away from the cliff to land near her.

"Only think," said a male. "All the realms know that King Ozorne of the Stormwing Alliance will heap rewards on whoever brings a certain female mortal treat—"

"Or a long-shanked mortal mage," interrupted the other male.

"Quite right," said the first. "So everyone else searches—and the treat falls right into our nets. The gods must love jokes like these; they tell them so many times."

The female minced over. "Greetings, Veralidaine Sarrasri. How are we today? We look *terrible*." She bared silvery teeth in a grin.

"Eat my loincloth," retorted the girl, sweating. "It's bad enough *looking* at you, without hearing your blather."

"Oh, tut." The female patted Daine's cheek lightly with a clawed leg. The girl winced—even a light spidren tap hurt. "That empty-headed mother of yours should have taught you manners."

"Keep your mouth off my ma!"

The spidren crouched to bring her face closer. "You're in no position to dictate the rules of conversation."

"Where's the long man?" the male who'd spoken first wanted to know. "He's always close to this little morsel."

"Can we kill her even a little bit?" asked the second male. "Can we eat her?"

The female spun. Pink web flew out of the spinneret under her belly, plastering itself over the hungry male's face. He screamed and fell back, clawing at it.

"Remember Ozorne's reward!" she cried when he'd gotten most of the pink strands off. Unlike the gray webbing, the pink left thick, raised welts. "He'll give us human slaves for centuries! He—"

One of the two male spidrens exploded. The female spidren shrieked and kicked Daine to the ground behind her. The girl squinted. What had happened? One spidren was gone, blown to pieces. In the splatter of black blood that was his remains stood Numair. Livid with rage, he raised his staff as the female spidren reared.

Jelly raced over the ground to plaster itself over the spinneret on the female's belly, and bulged as the spidren tried to force liquid web through it. Leaf jumped from the top of a nearby boulder to cover the female spidren's face. Her shriek was muffled; she could neither see nor breathe. Numair pursued the remaining male, beating him with his staff.

Slowly the female spidren collapsed. When she stopped moving, Jelly dropped away from her spinneret. The liquid web that the darking had bottled up spilled to pool uselessly on the ground. The female's head fell back; Leaf peeled itself from her face. Daine saw lumps on the hatted darking, pieces of it that had been sucked into the spidren's nose and mouth. Leaf had suffocated her.

Numair's opponent was the last to die. When the immortal sank to the ground, head crushed, the webs on Daine turned liquid and flowed away. She was free.

"Numair?"

He stood motionless, his back to her, leaning on his staff. He appeared to be staring at the dead spidren.

Frightened, the girl dragged herself to her knees, then to her feet. Upright, she swayed. "Please . . . are you all right?"

He turned. "You—you're alive. I thought . . ."

She staggered over to him. "I hurt too much to be dead."

Dropping the staff, Numair swept her up in his arms; hers went around his neck. He stroked her back; Daine buried her fingers in his hair. Pulling away, she tried to get a proper look at him. Their eyes met for a breathless moment as heat surged through her body. Then his mouth was on hers, his breath warmly mingling with her own.

She had been kissed before, over the last two years. Perin the cle the most persistent of her swains, had done it a number of times si Midwinter, before the war broke out. A moment ago, she would h said that she liked kissing well enough.

This was different. *Liking* did not begin to describe the thund her body and heart. Hot sweetness raced from his lips through her body, making her tingle, making the breath come short in her tired lungs, making her knees watery. Powerful awareness of all the places their bodies touched—from his palms on her back to her breasts, belly, and thighs crushed against his—made the blood pound in her veins.

Numair took his mouth away. "No," she whispered, and pulled him back. He was gentler this time, easing his lips carefully over hers, pulling away briefly, then returning.

A good thing he's holding me up, she thought giddily. Elsewise I'd fall down.

He pulled away with a strangled laugh and scooped her up in his arms, carrying her over to a large rock. There he sat, cradling Daine in his lap. "Goddess bless," he whispered, smoothing her curls away from her face. "Magelet, I thought I'd lost you."

On top of her recent experiences, it was too much. She buried her face in his shirt so he wouldn't see the tears that trickled from her eyes. He seemed content to simply wrap his arms around her, lips against her hair. The darkings on the ground observed the humans, small eyeless heads cocked to one side. Noticing them, Daine smiled.

"We need to rest and eat," Numair remarked after a while. "It'll soon be too hot to travel, and there is the path to relocate as well. If I remember correctly, this river is on the map. It parallels our route and emerges from this canyon near the path. Once you feel better, perhaps you could fly up and locate it. What do you think?"

She didn't answer.

"Sweet?" Craning to see her face, he realized that she was asleep. ith a sigh, he got to his feet, cradling his student, friend, and love. ne's only reaction was to snuggle closer. To the darkings Numair "Let's find some shelter."

—if I have this straight—no disrespect, Lord Badger, but I confess ⁀ confusion."

ʜe smiled in her dream: Queen Thayet of Tortall was never

ᴛ           ɪnd this—"
ɪs         treak," a tiny voice said.
           that these two creatures—"
k,         " Gold-streak corrected.
ɪce        ⁀ings are made of Ozorne's blood, and they were created
ᴀᵛᵉ        ɪow they think for themselves, and they claim they will
           ɪs that correct?"

ᵉʳ ɪn      was the badger's mind voice, the one he used in the mortal realms.—*Now these darkings who spied on you will tell you where your enemy is.*—

"The possibilities are dazzling," murmured the queen.

Daine turned over, and realized that she was awake and thinking already: Reinforcements from the Copper Isles were approaching Port Legann.

Numair had brought them to a hollow under a rock shelf in the canyon wall. The river thundered nearby. Outside their shelter, heat rose from the flat, unshaded stone on either side of the river. It would be mad to start walking for several hours, unless they wanted to lose more time still to heat exhaustion. She also ached and stung from top to toe, as if she'd been pounded with a hammer and dragged through thorns. Which I have, she admitted to herself.

The mage leaned against the wall, dozing. Leaf and Jelly, seated on rocks by the fire, watched a small pot of soup. When she sat up, Jelly reached out a tentacle to grip the long-handled spoon and stirred. Creating a head, the darking squeaked, "Food done."

Numair woke up. "Very good," he told the blots. Glancing at Daine, he blushed and looked away.

"How in the name of Shakith did you find me?" the girl demanded.

The man fidgeted. "It was merely a simple magic, Daine—"

"Mouse manure," she replied. "D'you think I've lived all this time with mages without *knowing* what it takes to find somebody *and* go to them?"

"I had a focus," he mumbled.

"A focus? Something of mine to connect us?"

"Yes—and I'm glad I had it."

"Yes—but—may I see it?" She wouldn't like to find that anyone but Numair had a focus, something that had been hers for a long time, in his or her possession. There were all kinds of magics that could be done with focuses, including control of her body and mind.

For a moment he looked grave; she thought that he might refuse. Then he reached across the distance between them. A bracelet appeared on his left wrist: a gold chain with an oval locket. This was the first time that she had seen it.

The locket fell into her palm opened. Inside one half was a miniature painting of her face, perfect in every detail, from blue-gray eyes to stubborn chin. Tucked behind a gold clip in the other half was a smoky brown curl. It seemed more like a lover's token, not a magical device to find an errant student. She returned it to him.

"I thought you might laugh if I asked you to sit for a portrait." He attached locket to chain—both vanished. "The painting was done by Volney Rain." He was a court artist they knew. "The hair I got when you were delirious with unicorn fever six months ago."

Going to the fire, he took charge of the soup, filling three bowls. One he gave to Daine; one he kept for himself. The third he placed on the ground. The darkings flowed over their bowl.

Daine blew on a spoonful to cool it. "What happened to you? What about those rock things?"

"They carried me off. I used my Gift to shield myself, but it took them some time to learn that *I* was the source of their pain. Once they did, they fled. When I returned to the Chaos vent, and realized that you had gone over the cliff—" He swallowed hard.

"You can thank a number of trees and a deep part of the river that I'm reasonably alive." She sat next to him, inching over until he was forced to raise his arm. Flinching at the bite of her cuts and scratches—she'd have to tend them soon—she tucked herself into the curve of his arm, then rested her head on his chest.

"You're trembling," she murmured.

"I'm only tired." He was lying, she knew. "I used my entire Gift to reach you."

"You shouldn't have," she told him. "You need it to defend your-self—and we still have to reach the Sea of Sand."

Numair's arm tightened. She looked down so that he couldn't see her wince. "If I'd lost you and kept my power, I would hate myself. Eventually magic returns, even after a draining. I had no way to know if *you* would."

She looked into his face, and smiled. "It would take more than falling off a cliff to keep me from you."

Numair kissed her again, his mouth lingering. The flooding heat of desire nearly swamped Daine before he broke the kiss. "I'd hoped you felt that way," he whispered. He kissed her eyelids, and the tip of her nose, then found her lips again. When he stopped, Daine was limp within the circle of his arm; now she too was trembling.

He sighed regretfully. "I should look at your cuts."

Daine sat up as he drew the pack over. Gingerly—even her bones ached—she lifted her shirt hem.

*"Daine!"*

"What?"

He had turned crimson under his tan. "You—We aren't—You should be clothed!"

"I've a breast band on, dolt. Besides, this shirt's in shreds. Like the rest of me."

He shifted slightly. "It just doesn't seem *right*. I feel that I'm . . . taking advantage of your innocence. A man of my—years, and reputation—"

" 'Taking advantage of'?" she repeated. "And *what* reputation?"

"You of *all* people should know that I've been involved with ladies of the court."

"What has *that* to do with the price of peas in Persopolis?"

"It's easy for an experienced man to delude a young woman into believing herself in love with him. It is the basest kind of trickery, even when the man does not intend it."

"Do you love me or not?" she demanded.

"That is *not* the topic under discussion." He fumbled, getting Sarra's ointment from his pack. Jelly and Leaf trickled over, carrying a bottle of water between them. "Thank you," Numair told them as he took charge of it.

Defiantly the girl stripped off her shirt, turning her back to him. Her breast band was in little better condition than her outer clothes, but she didn't care. *He* was making the fuss, not her! "We're not talking about love?" she demanded, wincing as he began to clean the cuts on her shoulders and back. "What are we talking of, then? Canoodling?"

"Daine! Is that what you think I want?" he demanded, outraged. *"Sex?"* Despite his dismay and fury, the hand that smoothed ointment on her was gentle.

"It isn't?" Rising to her knees, she stripped off what remained of her breeches. She heard Numair move away.

Swinging to face him, she searched his eyes; when they met hers, she knew that she'd hurt him. But how? she thought, baffled. Why? Perin only wanted to bed her, as a few Snowsdale men had bedded her mother. Then she knew. Grabbing the hand with the bracelet, she held the locket. A lover's token, she'd thought before. She had been right. "You're in love with me?"

He looked away.

"Love's fair wondrous. Where's the harm?"

"I was 'canoodling,' as you so charmingly put it, when *you* were four. You're so young, Daine. I knew that if I spoke, you might think yourself in love with me; you might ma—" He stopped.

*"Marry?"* she squeaked. *"Marry* you?"

He wouldn't look at her. "One day you'd turn to me and see an old man. You'd want a young one." He got up and walked out of their shelter. She watched him go to the river and crouch there, a big shadow against sun-bleached rock.

She rubbed her face. Love was well enough, but *marriage?* There was so much to consider. All her life she'd heard that no respectable man would marry Sarra's bastard—though she wondered if the Snowsdale gossips would think Numair respectable.

All those things he'd said of her waking up someday could be turned to fit him. She had managed to get a look at all of the women whose names were linked with his. They were typically in their thirties or late twenties, buxom, well-groomed, beautiful, mature.

What if *he* woke up, later on, to see a baby where he wanted to see a woman?

If they married, they would be trapped. Daine had seen enough bad marriages to know a life sentence when she saw one. Some of those marriages had involved men whose marriage proposals her mother had turned down.

Unrolling one of Numair's shirts, she wrapped it around herself—the scrapes on her back were healing fast, thanks to her mother's ointment—and walked down to him.

"Can't we just go on as we have?" she asked. "This is a fair weight to solve when things are so—mad."

He looked up and smiled, just barely. "That is certainly true."

"I know I love you. Maybe I always have—"

"Which is what I was afraid of."

She ignored his frivolity. "Once we're home—once the war's done—we can work it out. We'll talk then."

Standing, he cupped her face in his hands, and kissed her gently. "Indeed we will."

Her mother's ointment made small work of her injuries. As Numair cut his spare clothes down to fit her, she took advantage of the powerful thermals in the canyon, letting them carry her in hawk shape above the rim. There she flew upstream until she found the path of destruction that she'd left in her tumble down the cliff.

Here was the trail they had been on, minus the cluster of gray rocks. She followed it through winding stone alleys, keeping high enough to see the river as well. Numair was right. If they kept to the water's course, they could find the path where the river met open scrubland. Beyond that lay the desert—the Sea of Sand.

She returned to him, and donned the clothes he'd cut down for her. Once the worst heat had passed, they set out again, pacing themselves to avoid heatstroke. After dark, nearing the spot where they could pick up the path again, Daine sensed Stormwings. Rikash was there for certain; she also thought she knew at least two of his companions.

Spying on the waiting immortals through a crevice between two rocks, Daine sighed with relief. She *did* know two of the others. One crowned female had the appearance of a mortal in her fifties. Her nose was prominent and forbidding over a mouth carved by a master sculptor, her dark eyes commanding under perfect black eyebrows. The girl thought that Queen Barzha of the Stone Tree nation of Stormwings must have been a beauty in her youth; age had added majesty. Her younger consort, Hebakh, had a pale, intense face lit by slightly mad gray eyes set over an aquiline nose.

Daine walked into the open. "Hello."

Some of the immortals idling near the path jumped, caught by surprise. The air was filled with metallic clicks as steel feathers ruffled and fell into place.

"Don't you make *noise*?" one of them demanded crossly as Numair came forward.

"You dine on fear, but you don't care to feel it yourself?" the man asked innocently.

When the immortal opened his mouth to reply, Daine said, "Enough, both of you." She bowed to the crowned female and her mate. "Queen Barzha and Lord Hebakh. May I present Numair Salmalín?" He had seen the Stormwings in Carthak last fall, but she didn't think they had been properly introduced. "This is Leaf." The darking nodded its hatted, knobby head. "And that's Jelly." The darking under Numair's shirt thrust out a tentacle, waved, then disappeared into its refuge.

"It hasn't met royalty before, that we know of," Numair explained. He bowed elegantly to Rikash's queen and her consort. "May I say that it is good to see you again?"

"As long as you don't get downwind of us, right, *mortal*?" taunted a male voice from the rear of the flock.

"Do you challenge my decision, Vekkat?" Barzha asked without looking away from the humans. "Have you questions left unanswered?"

There was no loud reply, though Daine could hear voices whispering, "Shut up!" and "Aren't you in enough trouble?"

Rikash came up beside his queen, green eyes glittering. "I confess, the most amusing part of our association is that I am not sure who is more puzzled by it—you or me," he said wryly. "I'm shocked Sarra let you go out dressed that way."

Daine looked at her clothes. "My things got lost. I fell off a cliff."

"You take such a fall well, Veralidaine," Barzha said, her voice wry. "Rikash tells me I should apologize for not killing Ozorne while I had the chance."

Daine smiled. She hadn't thought the formidable Stormwing queen *had* a sense of humor. "He's good at survival," she remarked. "I know you gave it your best."

Hebakh bated. He was a nervous creature, always shifting his weight from one clawed foot to another. "We have not put the matter aside yet. There will be other chances to explain to Ozorne how things are done *properly* among our kind."

"In the meantime," Rikash said, "Queen Barzha has agreed that we shall carry you over the Sea of Sand, to the portal of the Dragonlands."

"We are in your debt," added Barzha. "You freed us from Emperor Ozorne. We shall feel better if we may repay you."

Hebakh whistled. Two Stormwings flapped over, bearing some dark substance coiled in their talons.

"Your mother helped us to make these slings," explained Rikash. "It won't be an easy ride, but it's the quickest way to cross the desert."

Numair and Daine nodded. The pair with the slings, assisted by Rikash and one of the other immortals, spread their materials on the ground.

"I heard something that might be of interest to you, if you didn't hear it yourselves," Daine told the Stormwing queen. Briefly she related the conversation she'd heard by Temptation Lake, before she had known the darkings were Ozorne's spies.

The queen dug into rock with her claws, eyes glittering with malice. "So Qirev—"

"The other must be Yechakk," interrupted her mate. "He's the only old one left."

"They are finding mortal warfare a bit rich for their stomachs," said Barzha. "Perhaps Mogrul of Razor Scream also feels the pinch, after losing eleven. Perhaps—"

"You'll never turn Queen Jachull," Hebakh said, bating. "She is empty. There isn't a Stormwing inside of her, only a void. But the others—they might yet listen to reason."

Their conveyance was ready. After the humans secured their things and sat in the rope webs, Barzha croaked a word; shimmering with gold and crimson fire, the slings rose. On Hebakh's command, five Stormwings took flight, the ropes that cradled the humans in their talons. Three carried Numair; two bore Daine. Belatedly, she said, "You know, I could shape-shift and fly my own self."

"Save your strength for the dragons," replied Hebakh.

The Stormwings began to climb. The magic that had lifted the slings to a level where their porters could grab them released. Daine and Numair dropped an inch, then rose, borne by Stormwings.

The scrubland came to an end and was replaced by sand dunes.

Like all deserts, this one was cold after sunset. Daine shivered, but was resigned; at least the cold laid the Stormwings' odor.

Barzha flew close to Numair. Mage and queen spoke, but Daine couldn't hear; the wind bore their words away. Jelly was nowhere to be seen. Leaf, to the contrary, was looped around Daine's neck, its small, eyeless head stretched forward to take the full brunt of rushing air. It was talking softly. She had to bring an ear close to the darking to hear, and when she did, she laughed. Leaf was saying, "Funfunfunfunfun."

For a while, she was content to sit, shivering, as she watched the immortals. There were sixty-three Stormwings present, all of the queen's allies. These were the ones that Rikash had spoken of, those who took honor and tradition seriously.

*There's* a thing to boggle the mind, she thought, rubbing her shoulders to warm them. Stormwings with honor!

Rikash had been flying in the van, watching the sky. Now he fell back, gliding into position near Daine. A female Stormwing behind them called, "Mortal lover!"

The green-eyed male looked at her. "Repeat that on the dueling grounds at the next full moon, Zusha." The female shut up, and Rikash turned his attention to Daine. "A feather for your thoughts."

"Hm?" she asked, startled.

"Mooning over Long Lankin?" he inquired, jerking his head toward Numair.

Daine blushed, and glared at him. Long Lankin was the villain in a ballad, a tall bandit who lived for slaughter. "He's no more Lankin than you are a songbird," she retorted. "Besides, he's not what I'm thinking of"—which wasn't entirely a lie.

Rikash laughed. "What *were* you thinking of, then?"

"I heard somewhere that immortals are born in dreams. Or our dreams give them shape—something like that. Now, I can see folk dreaming winged horses and unicorns. Even dreaming that a winged horse or unicorn would go bad makes sense. Haven't we all thought something's a joy, only to find that it's evil inside? But—forgive my saying it; no offense intended—how could *anyone* dream a Stormwing?"

His smile was cruel. "Ages ago, a traveler in the mortal realms went from place to place and found only the leavings of war—the starving, the abandoned, the dead. It was the work of armies, fighting over ground they soon lost again. That traveler sickened of waste—of death. She wished for a creature that was so repulsive, living on war's aftermath, that even *humans* would think twice before battle. That creature would defile what mortal killers left, so that humans couldn't lie about how glorious a soldier's death is. *She* dreamed the first Stormwing."

Daine shivered. "But it doesn't seem to make a difference, most of the time." Leaf, who had trickled down to pool in her lap, nodded.

"That's humans for you," said the immortal cheerfully. "Nothing slows them down for long. *But*—if one person asks himself—or herself"—he nodded politely to her—"if the matter to be fought over is worth his corpse being ripped to pieces and smeared with our dung, and decides it isn't, that's all we need to justify ourselves. You'd be surprised how many people changed their minds, knowing that we'd come to live on their pain and play with their bodies. The barrier changed that. Humans forgot us. We've had to start all over. It will take a century before we'll make a difference again."

Daine shook her head as she stroked Leaf. "Am I a bad person, then, for wanting to fight to protect what I believe in?"

"I'm only a Stormwing, not a philosopher. For that, you must talk to Salmalín—if you don't mind the headache he'll give you."

She smiled. "Have people tried making offerings and sacrifices to you, to keep Stormwings from coming down on them?"

"Very good. You know human nature almost as well as we do." The Stormwings who carried Daine had been listening. They cackled their amusement, making the girl's hair stand on the back of her neck. "Of course humans have tried to buy us off." Rikash grinned, his sharp, silver teeth glinting. "We go after them first."

Hebakh called. "My master's voice," Rikash commented with a sigh. He winked. "Sweet dreams." He rolled in the air in front of her, and caught up with Hebakh effortlessly.

Daine thought long and hard about his words, curling up into a ball within the ropes of her sling. She was afraid to sleep, but she must have done so anyway. The next thing she heard was a voice in her ear. "Wake up!" it said. "We're setting down!"

She opened her eyes to dawn. They were indeed descending, bound for a flat expanse of sand. Before it roared a curtain of white and red fires, like a flaming waterfall.

The slings touched the ground; their porters dropped the ropes. Daine landed with a gentle thump, untangled herself, then lurched to her feet. She was stiff all over. Numair, too, winced as he straightened.

Barzha, Hebakh, and Rikash landed in front of them, while the other Stormwings remained aloft. "Our debt to you is paid," the queen informed them. "We are going now. If the dragons are unhappy with your presence, we prefer not to be nearby."

"Thank you," Daine said. "If you see Ozorne before we do, give him our regards."

Barzha and Hebakh nodded and took flight, the rest of the flock behind them. Rikash gently tapped Daine's arm, then Numair's, with his wing. "Be polite to the dragons, and watch your step." He leaped into the air, and soon caught up with his brethren.

Girl and mage surveyed the fiery curtain, standing well back from a heat that made them sweat. "Now what?" Daine asked her companion.

A voice chimed in the air around them. "Go away, mortals. You will not be admitted to the Dragonlands. We wish to know none of your kind."

"On the contrary," Numair said, voice mild. "One dragon knows a great deal of us. My companion is the guardian of the dragonet Skysong."

"The true guardian of a dragon is brave. You are shrinking, cautious beings."

"Oh, really." Daine stalked toward the curtain, feeling its heat grow to unbearable levels. Just when she thought she might scream with pain, she was through a hair's breadth of fire. On the other side of the portal lay rolling, sunny hills.

Numair burst through the gate behind her, glistening with sweat and gasping. Before Daine realized what he was doing, he'd dropped his staff and grabbed her by the shoulders. "Don't you ever—*ever*—frighten me that way again!" He shook her for punctuation, then wrapped his arms around her so tightly that she thought she might just pop. "*Ever,*" he added, and kissed her thoroughly before releasing her.

"I don't know," she said impishly, smiling up at him. "I like this particular kind of tantrum. Besides—at least now they know we're brave enough."

"Speak for yourself," the mage said weakly, fumbling for his handkerchief. He wiped his face with hands that still trembled.

"The darkings?" asked Daine, suddenly worried. "What if they—?"

The darkings popped their heads out of their hiding places. Jelly had dropped inside Numair's shirt. Leaf had trickled into Daine's belt purse.

"Warm," Leaf told them. "Fun."

Nervously Jelly crept up to Numair's shoulder. "I know it wasn't fun for you," the mage said comfortingly, stroking the darking with a finger.

The darking stretched until it could look Numair in the face, if it had possessed eyes. "Fine now," it assured him. "Get stick." Grinning, Numair picked up his staff.

"Wait," the portal's voice instructed. "Guides will come for you."

## ➤➤ EIGHT ◄◄

# DRAGONLANDS

Some time later, Leaf tugged one of Daine's curls, pointing at two creatures who trotted toward them. Like Kitten, they had long, reptilian snouts, slender paws like hands, and colorful scales. They were also like Daine's friend in that they were young dragons—the wings on their backs were tiny, incapable of bearing them in flight.

The smaller one reached them first. Snow white in color, it had black shoe-button eyes. It was four feet long from head to rump, with an extra two feet of tail. Its companion was as tall as Daine, with steel-gray and black scales intermixed. Unlike the white dragon, this one was more sedate, and walked with slow, deliberate steps.

*—We're to take you to our grandsire,—* the white dragon told them, speaking to their minds, not their ears.*—You're the first mortals we've ever seen. It's very exciting! I'm Icefall, only the elders call me Scamp. My cousin—well, she's really a third cousin twice removed—her name is Steelsings, only I call her Grizzle because she's so old.—*

*—Welcome to the Dragonlands,—*said Grizzle, mind voice grave.*— Ignore Scamp. She has only two centuries. She doesn't know very much.—*

*—You've only one more century than me!—*accused Scamp.*—You don't have your wings yet either!—*

Numair hid a smile behind one hand. Daine sighed. Perhaps it was just as well that Kitten still could not speak mind to mind, if all young dragons chattered.

*—Children should be seen, not heard.—*Grizzle cuffed Scamp, then looked at Daine and Numair.*—Follow us, please.—*

She led the way with composure. Scamp frolicked around them, asking questions nonstop, in spite of Grizzle's frequent orders to leave their guests alone. Scamp was convinced that humans spent their time fighting, and—sadly, Daine thought—she knew enough of the present state of things that it was hard to persuade her otherwise. Finally, Leaf stuck its head out of Daine's shirt and chattered angrily at her. The shock was so great that Scamp actually held her tongue for a moment before pelting them with questions about darkings.

"Is your grandfather the, um, king?" the mage asked as they turned downhill to walk beside a deep stream.

—*King?*—asked Scamp, distracted from her pursuit of a butterfly.— *What's a king?*—

—*They rule mortals,*—Grizzle replied smugly.—*The male ones, that is. The female rulers are queens.*—

—*Oh,*—was Scamp's comment.—*But you'd always have to change them, wouldn't you? Since they're always dying?*—

Daine bit her lip to keep from grinning. "It's true," she said gravely when she'd gotten herself under control. "Mortals must forever change leaders because they die. That's why we're called mortals."

—*I wouldn't like to be mortal,*—Scamp remarked wisely.—*Uncle Moonwind has been teaching me about mortality. It sounds uncomfortable.*—

—*He's not really our uncle,*—said Grizzle.—*Just like Grandsire isn't our grandfather, exactly. He's our great-great-great- . . . I don't remember how many greats. There are a lot of them. Grandfather. He's the oldest—*

—*No,*—interrupted Scamp.—*Moonwind, Rainbow, and Cometfern are older.*—

—*He's the biggest . . . Now what are you looking at?*—demanded the older dragon: Scamp was staring at the sky. When she did not answer, Grizzle looked up.—*Uh-oh.*—

An enormous blue-green shape crested the winds over a hill. Regally it glided toward them on huge, batlike wings boned in silver.

"Is there a problem?" asked Numair. Daine saw that both dragons' scales bristled.

—*It's Jewelclaw,*—replied Grizzle.—*He's not very nice.*—

—*He can't do anything,*—Scamp told them, but she trembled. Waves of pink, the color that Kitten turned at those rare times when she was afraid, washed over her body. Grizzle, too, had acquired a rosy tinge, harder to see against her darker scales.—*They're here to see Grandsire, not him.*—

The mature dragon lit on the ground and advanced, wings half extended. Until now, the only adult dragon that Daine and Numair had seen was Kitten's mother, a young female who had measured twenty feet from nose to hindquarters. This dragon was nearly forty feet long, with a tail that was half again as long as he was. His scales were a deep, almost glowing shade of blue-green on his back, then emerald green on his belly. Like other dragons, this one had silver talons and teeth, in addition to the silver bones that gleamed inside the delicate hide of his wings. His eyes, emerald around slit pupils like a cat's, were cold indeed. Sparks and threads of fire similar to lightning jumped over his scales; his head crest was raised.

—*Who let* mortals *into the Dragonlands?*—His voice was a roar in Daine's mind.—*You two will find this to be far more serious than your usual pranks!*—He bridled, scales ruffling. The grass under his talons began to scorch.

Grizzle jumped between Jewelclaw and the humans.—*You can't touch them!*—she cried. She was now an eye-smarting shade of pink, with no trace of gray, but she stood her ground. Scamp, also entirely pink, scrambled to stand next to her. Tiny sparks flared on both youngsters.—*They are under Grandsire's protection.*—

—*Then Diamondflame will answer to the Dragonmeet! Out of my way!*—Jewelclaw ordered, wings fanning.—*They will be my captives!*—

—*No!*—Scamp's voice was shrill, but firm.—*She's the one who's raising Skysong!*—

—*Raising? Or imprisoning?*—demanded the adult.

Numair crossed his arms. "If you know anything about the young members of your race, you know that captivity is not an issue," he said mildly. "I do not believe there is a cage that could hold Kit—Skysong— if she wished to get out."

Leaf, still on Daine's shoulder, extended its head to chitter angrily at Jewelclaw. After a moment's pause, Jelly thrust its head through Numair's collar and chimed in.

—*Must we tell Grandsire you took them from us?*—Grizzle asked.

—*The old newt has gone senile!*—snarled Jewelclaw.—*And I'm not the only one to object! I'm not finished with this!*—He took to the air, the back draft of his wings making both humans and dragonets stagger.

—*He is not senile!*—Scamp shouted. If Jewelclaw heard, he gave no sign, flying off with hard, rapid wing beats. In a small voice she added,—*I bet his mother was a wyvern.*—

—*Scamp!*—cried Grizzle, shocked.

—*I don't care. He's rotten. He's* always *rotten. Come on,*—she told Daine and Numair.—*Before anyone else comes after us.*—

When they reached a bridge that looked as if it had been spun from glass, the two young dragons raced ahead as if it were rough and sturdy wood. Daine and Numair, certain that mere humans might just slide off, were testing the bridge with their feet when crackling filled the air. Grizzle and Scamp halted in midspan, raising themselves up on their hindquarters as Kitten so often did. Jelly retreated inside Numair's shirt, while Leaf raised its head, looking for the cause of the disturbance.

—*There has been a change.*—The voice boomed in their minds all around them.

—*Grandsire, Jewelclaw came and yelled,*—cried Scamp.

—*I know it. He and the other Separatists have been dinning my ears since our guests came through the portal. They have called the Dragonmeet.*—

Scamp shrank inside her skin.

—*Uh-oh,*—Grizzle whispered softly.

—*Take them to the amphitheater,*—ordered the voice.—*Do not enter the floor with them, mind. Sit among our people.*—Voice and presence faded from their surroundings.

—*Turn back,*—Grizzle told them, dropping to her fours.—*At least it isn't far to go.*—

Daine and Numair exchanged glances. They needed to talk. "May we get a drink?" asked the girl as they stepped off the bridge. "And *I* need to relieve myself." The dragons nodded. Daine stepped into a cluster of bushes to empty her bladder, first making sure her urine wouldn't run into the water. Finished, she joined Numair. They crouched beside the stream to drink and wash their faces.

"What do you think?" asked the mage softly.

"We have to go. We can't force dragons, only persuade," she reminded him.

Scamp and Grizzle looked down at them from the top of the stream bank.—*Are you finished?*—Grizzle inquired.—*It's a bad idea to keep a Dragonmeet waiting.*—

Grizzle led them uphill from the bridge, following a broad track through knee-high grasses. When they crested the hill, they stood on the uppermost edge of a deep, tiered bowl in the earth. It was too regular to be natural, though grass flourished on the tiers. The floor of the amphitheater and the long ramps that cut it into eighths were bare earth, beaten and gouged by centuries of pressure from dragon paws and talons. At the far end of the giant oval was the only other exception to the grass carpet, a heap of glistening blue stones that was piled about the arena's rim.

Each tier was dragon-sized, big enough to contain even the largest of them when they crouched on all fours. A number of dragons were already present. Jewelclaw, for one, was installed near the western ramp. Miniature lightnings still played over his blue-green scales. He glared at them and returned to whatever he was saying to a sixty-foot dragon whose scales had the white glimmer of pearl. As Jewelclaw spoke, bursts of fire—Daine thought of heat lightning—came and went along the bigger dragon's hide.

Grizzle saw what the girl was looking at.—*The pearly one—that's Moonwind,*—the dragonet explained.—*She's one of the oldest. Her grandson Summerwing was the last dragon to willingly visit the mortal realms. That was before the Dragonmeet put a ban on visits. Um . . .* —

—*Stay away from Moonwind,*—Scamp said bluntly.—*She isn't even nice to people she likes.*—

"Just how old is this dragon?" asked Numair.

Scamp cocked her head, blinking.—*Fifty-five centuries, I think.*—

—*Fifty-nine,*—Grizzle corrected her.—*Come on. This way.*—She started down the ramp, headed toward the arena floor.

"Your grandsire said you weren't to come with us," Daine said quietly, watching the adult dragons. They were huge creatures whose scales blazed with color, some of them twenty or thirty feet longer than Moonwind. The girl didn't know if their kind formed lynch mobs, but there was enough mob feeling here that she didn't want to take any chances.

Busy watching the larger dragons, she didn't see the seven young ones until they swarmed around the humans, curiosity in their eyes. One was nearly as small as Kitten, still unable to use mind speech. Others were as big as, or bigger than, Scamp and Grizzle. Behind them, walking majestically, as befitted their age, came a handful of dragons fifteen and twenty feet long, the length that Kitten's mother had been—adolescents.

—*We'll* all *escort you,*—Grizzle announced proudly. The humans were swept along by young dragons, unable to protest, across the beaten earth of the arena floor.

The price of their escort was a hail of questions about the mortal realms. Daine left Numair to answer. She was counting the adults present—thirty-three thus far—when the air exploded to her right. Where there had been nothing but empty space a moment ago, a sixty-foot black dragon crouched.

—*Aunt Nightbreath!*—cried Grizzle.—*You're not supposed to materialize so close to everyone else!*—

—*Oh, tut,*—the dragon replied, coolly amused.—*I haven't fouled anyone in a materialization since* I *was your* age.—There was more than a hint of wicked glee in her eyes as she added,—*I was in a hurry. This may be my only chance to see humans before these two are made into fertilizer for Moonwind's rosebushes.*—

The young dragons protested her cynicism. Daine reached out instinctively, and Numair took her hand. He kept it as they reached the center of the Dragonmeet floor. Their escort remained with them when they stopped at last.

Three dragons appeared on the highest part of the arena. The blast of air caused by their arrival made the humans stagger. Daine gulped, and clutched Numair's hand tighter. All of the newcomers were over a hundred feet long. The biggest, whose scales were a pale, delicate green, was fully a hundred and twenty feet in length.

—*That's Wingjade,*—Scamp whispered, seeing where Daine looked.—*My father.*—

"Biiiig," commented Leaf.

"Too big," squeaked Jelly, its head protruding from the V of Numair's shirt.

—*We start,*—boomed a golden dragon directly across the amphitheater from the mortals.—*Diamondflame is charged with ignoring the will of the Dragonmeet, and with permitting humans to enter the Dragonlands. Humans, the question is asked: Why have you come here?*—

"You should do the talking," Numair told Daine softly. "You are Kitten's guardian."

Daine was about to reply when a mind voice yelled,—*No one cares what they want! Kill them!*—Looking around, the girl saw a mottled black-and-white dragon who sat up, balanced on his back legs.—*Kill them, and bring Skysong home!*—Slowly he fell back to his fours.

Nearby, a second dragon reared onto its haunches.—*Our law bids us to first bear what they have to say.*—

Moonwind sat up.—*They and their defenders lost their right to claim justice under our law when my grandson was murdered by their kind. Look at them. Already they cause trouble here. Already they try to seduce our young away from us.*—

—*We aren't seduced!*—cried a younger dragon hotly.—*They're new; they're different. We could learn from them—except you and your crowd have closed minds!*—

—*Silence!*—roared Moonwind. Daine and Numair cringed away from the force of her rage, while the young dragon who had spoken clawed at his muzzle.

—*Now you've done it,*—whispered Grizzle to the gagged youngster.—*You'd better hope that she takes the Silence off you before you get too hungry.*—

—*If you felt that humans were not to be treated with under our law, Sister Moonwind, you should have amended the law in the four centuries since your loss,*—snapped a new adult.—*You know as well as*

*I that all changes in law must be reviewed, debated, and considered. You cannot demand that it be changed here and now.*—

"Excuse me," said Daine, wanting to answer the initial question. The dragons continued to argue about legal issues. Red tinted the scales of most present; lightning, in sheets or threads, danced over more than a few. "Excuse me!"

"Try again," murmured Numair. Black fire glimmered around the hand he placed on the nape of her neck.

She took a deep breath. *"EXCUSE ME!"* she cried. Her voice, amplified by the mage's spell, thundered in the bowl of the arena. Daine winced, and used a quieter tone. "All we want is to go home—that's it. We don't like being here any more than you want us. So, if you could take us back to the mortal realms, we're quits."

—*No one asked you.*—Jewelclaw did more than sit up. He stepped onto the ramp and began to walk down toward them. Balls and rails of lightning raced around his hide as it turned a deep crimson, the color of dragon rage.—*You* humans. *How could we have allowed you to continue to exist, with your murderous hearts, your waste, and your noise? It's time to scour the mortal realms clean. We can start with you.*—

"You *dare*." Numair took his hand from Daine's back. Suddenly it was hard for the girl to breathe. She stepped away from him and the sudden bloom of his power.

—*Do you think we fear you, mortal?*—the black-and-white dragon asked as he stepped onto the ramp behind Jewelclaw.—*No human can face down a dragon!*—

A burst of wind threw Daine back. Moonwind had vanished from her station, to reappear on the beaten earth of the floor.

Numair handed Jelly to Scamp, ignoring the darking's unhappy cries, and advanced on Moonwind. With each deliberate step that he took, fresh power shivered the air around him, as if he gathered magic like a cloak.

Daine gave Leaf to Grizzle and unlaced her overlarge shirt, looking at the pair of smaller dragons on the ramp. Her skin was clammy and tingling with fear, her knees weak. She wished passionately that she knew more about dragons. Swiftly she reviewed forms she could take: A big one might slow her down, make her an easy target. A falcon's claws and beak could make an impression, and she would be fast.

—*There are mortals who may battle us on an equal footing.*—The speaker was a lean, knobby dragon who sat in the lowest tier. He did not bother to rise on his haunches. His green, red, blue, and yellow scales were pale, as if coated in dust. The two on the ramp halted; even Moonwind looked at him.—*Not many, but some. Your coterie has cho-*

*sen to ignore that which does not add to your overweening selfishness in regard to which species have importance, and which ones do not . . . Or are you merely stupid? I never could decide which it was, though perhaps I should have.—*

—*You do not understand the matter, Ancestor Rainbow!*—snapped the black-and-white dragon.

Pale eyes swept over Daine as the elderly dragon looked in the direction of Jewelclaw and his companion. Seeing no pupils, she realized that Rainbow was blind.

—*Do I not?*—he asked, voice mild.—*Well, you are entitled to your opinions, Riverwind, however foolish they may be. I too am entitled to my opinion, which is that I grow weary of your bad manners. Leave the Dragonmeet.*—

The black-and-white dragon reared. He clawed at the air with his forepaws, screeching so high and so loudly that Daine felt a pressure like thumbs in her ears. His screech dwindled rapidly, as did he, until he vanished from sight.

For a long, still moment, there was no sound in the arena.

Daine was taking a deep breath when all of the dragons spoke at once, mind voices blending into a wordless roar in her mind.

She heard one voice clearly: Jewelclaw's.—*The humans are mine!*— He trotted down the ramp. Moonwind raised a forepaw and unfurled her immense wings. Numair faced her, the air rippling and bending visibly where it touched him.

Daine jumped, taking goshawk shape as her feet left the ground. Her clothes dropped, empty. With a screech, she sped toward Jewelclaw.

—*Enough,*—said the crackling mind voice that had spoken to Daine and Numair near the bridge. Jewelclaw froze in his tracks.

—*When did my* personal *invitation to guests of my clan become a matter for every wing and claw in the Dragonlands to discuss, and interfere with?*—What Daine had thought was a huge pile of blue stones uncoiled, and walked leisurely to the amphitheater floor. Diamond-flame—Grandsire—was a dragon over eighty feet in length from nostrils to rump. While she could see larger dragons, none had a presence that made the air hum as he approached Moonwind and Numair.

Daine kept a wary eye on Jewelclaw as she drifted overhead. Diamondflame's scales were a shiny blue so dark as to be nearly black, picked out with flecks of gold and violet. A golden crest rose from his broad forehead and swept down to his shoulders, lending him a stern, crowned aspect. His large indigo eyes glittered with intelligence.

—*I understand your grief for your grandson, Moonwind, but only to a point. With no law passed by the Dragonmeet, I am entirely within my rights to welcome my grandchild's guardians to my home. It should not matter if they are human, dragons, or dragonflies. They are my guests, and no business of the Dragonmeet!*—

—*Ancestor Rainbow, I demand a ruling,*—hissed the pearl-scaled dragon.—*Humans in the Dragonlands are no matter of personal choice, as Diamondflame has said, but of the will of the Dragonmeet. I vote to dump them into the Sea of Sand and let them cook.*—

—*Will the Dragonmeet now tell each dragon what guest to have, what to read, when to have children?*—Diamondflame wanted to know.—*I am within my rights, the ones granted to me and to every dragon by the Golden Dragonmeet, to accept the visit of the guardians of my grandchild, without certain* meddlers *getting involved.*—

—*Now he calls "meddlers" those who wish only to see dragonkind return to power in all the realms!*—cried Jewelclaw.—*Have you old and conservative ones turned to wyverns and salamanders?*—

—*Humans or no human, I must say that I have not heard such insolence from the young in the last thousand years as I have heard today,*—said the one called Rainbow. Slowly he lowered himself from his grassy seat and walked over to Diamondflame.—*I will judge now.*—He sat on his haunches and rose up, many-colored scales tightening over his knobby, fragile-looking skeleton. Slowly, as gracefully as a dancer, he stretched out enormous, nearly transparent, bat wings. The sun glinted off the silvery bones within them, and painted glowing light over the old dragon.

—*I ordain as Rainbow Windheart, governor of the Dragonmeet, oldest of the Firefolk, with a hundred centuries under my wings. By the Compact of the Godwars and the vote of the Golden Dragonmeet, I speak for all of us, until the day comes that I am taken back to Mother Flame.*—

Settling a bit, he turned those blind eyes on the blue-green dragon.—*Out of my sight, Jewelclaw. If I see you before a century has passed, I shall not be so kind again as I am right now.*—Heat passed under Daine's tail feathers on its way from Rainbow to the younger dragon. Jewelclaw dodged the bolt with a snarl and jumped into flight, lunging at the girl-goshawk.

Something—not Jewelclaw—clutched her tightly. She felt *squeezed,* as if she had turned to icing in a pastry cook's tube. A strangled cry burst from her lips; she could feel herself dropping as her eyes went dark.

When she opened them again, she lay on the ground, fully dressed, staring at the sky.

—*The only way dragons can live together is to vow to keep their muzzles out of one another's private lives.*—The mind voice was Rainbow's; he sounded close by.—*When we wrote our laws at the Golden Dragonmeet, we made sure of that. When I spoke in my office as governor, they could not argue, under the laws of that same meet.*—

Two ink-blot heads stretched into her vision, one over her left eye, one over her right. Leaf squeaked, "Awake now!"

The next faces Daine saw were those of Grizzle and Scamp. Over their head, within a heartbeat's time, she saw Numair, his dark eyes worried. Behind him, the great blue dragon peered down at her.

"What happened?" she asked, blinking.

Scamp moved out of the way. Into the space she had filled in Daine's vision came the muzzle and blind eyes of Rainbow. His mind voice sounding like wind-tossed leaves, he said,—*Forgive my lack of precision in grabbing you out of harm's way, Godborn. I allowed Jewelclaw to upset me. What you felt was dragon magic, nothing more.*—

"I'm glad it *was* nothing more." Daine felt oddly peaceful. "Think how upsetting it might be to get squeezed from a shape—like milk from a teat—by something big."

"Is she all right?" Numair asked the blue dragon, worried. "Not— damaged?"

—*She seems well enough now,*—was Diamondflame's reply.

"You don't know her as I do. She's *never* this philosophical about surprises."

Reaching out, the blind dragon pulled Daine into a sitting position, his grip gentle. "My bones are all wobbly," she confided to him in a whisper. Looking around, she saw that many of the adult dragons had left. "Where'd everybody go?"

—*Where they would have been if Moonwind and her Separatists had not chosen to meddle in business that was not theirs,*—said Diamondflame.—*They have gone home. Ancestor Rainbow ruled that your visit, concerned as it was with returning to my grandchild, was a matter for my clan alone.*—

The blue dragon reared, towering over the girl. Numair and Rainbow steadied her as she got to her knees, then her feet.

—*Who will help me convey these mortals out of the Dragonlands?*—asked Diamondflame.

The young dragons, who had remained, clamored to go. When he looked down his muzzle at them, they silenced instantly.—*Those of you who can fly are too small. The rest of you cannot fly at all—and fly we must. You will remain here, and mind Ancestor Rainbow.*—

Daine's mouth twitched as Scamp grumbled,—*We never do anything interesting.*—

*—I will come with you.*—One of the few adults remaining, a gray-and-gold dragon fifty-six feet in length, came over to them. She was an elegant creature, slender without looking at all fragile.—*I am Wingstar. Your Skysong is my grandchild. The least I can do is bring her humans back to her.—*

*—Climb onto us,*—ordered Diamondflame.—*I believe the Dragon-meet is done.—*

He was right. One by one, the dragons were vanishing from the arena tiers. Only the youngsters and Rainbow stayed.

Leaf went to Daine, Jelly to Numair. Once the humans had settled the darkings into their favored riding spots—around Daine's neck and inside Numair's shirt—Wingstar sank low to the ground.—*I will take you, Weiryn's daughter. You do not appear to have so many bony angles to you.—*

Daine grinned at Numair and climbed onto the female dragon, settling in front of her wings. Numair had to ascend Diamondflame's foreleg to perch on the blue dragon's back.

*—Hold on to my crest,*—ordered Wingstar.—*It won't hurt me if you tug.—*

Under her legs Daine felt powerful muscles flex. "Wait!" she cried, remembering something. The dragons, Numair, and the darkings stared at her. "When we came through last time, we—more me, but both of us for a while—got fair sick. We need to tell you—"

*—Nothing,*—interrupted Diamondflame.—*You were brought here by lesser gods, not by dragons. You will not become ill in the least.—*

Disliking the slur on her parents, Daine muttered, "Pardon *me.*" Leaf giggled under her ear as the flap of immense wings blew her hair into her eyes. She closed them tightly as the dragons leaped up and forward, soaring into the air.

Wind buffeted her. Opening her eyes, she saw that Diamondflame was in the lead, taking them into a cloud bank. Daine shivered; it was cool and clammy, and she couldn't see. Feeling a tickle on her cheek that had to be Leaf's hat, she asked, "Still funfun?"

"More fun," the darking replied.

"You have a happy nature, little one," she grumbled.

Up the dragons climbed, flying a corkscrew pattern through the clouds. Daine sensed Stormwings only a few moments before they came upon them, but as before, she recognized at least one, and very likely three, presences among them.

When the dragons emerged in clear, very cold air, Barzha, Hebakh, Rikash, and their followers awaited them. All of the immortals were armed.

—*You have interesting friends,*—remarked Wingstar.

"If you don't mind, we will go with you to the mortal realms." Barzha's voice sounded odd in the thin air. "We have business to settle."

—*I will not wait if you fall behind,*—Diamondflame warned them.

The Stormwings grinned, steely teeth glinting, as they took up positions to the rear and sides of the dragons. Rikash was the only one to glide between them.

"Is this wise?" Daine asked. "Ozorne's folk outnumber you almost four to one."

"Since when are Stormwings wise?" he called, and laughed.

Diamondflame and Wingstar began their descent, gliding in a broad spiral that carried them into the clouds once more. Clammy, damp fingers brushed the girl's face and wound in her hair. Gray fog blinded her again. "More fun, more fun," commented Leaf.

They broke through the clouds.

She expected to see Dragonlands or desert. What lay below was a tangled web of barns and gardens, and a sprawling complex of gray stone buildings tucked behind high walls in front and low ones behind. From the high walls, the land sloped down a green, uncluttered expanse before reaching tree groves around low-lying temples. On the far side of the groves lay a vast city flung on both sides of a broad river.

They were over the capital, and royal palace, of Tortall.

Daine frowned. The voices of the People filled her mind, but they were not tense or wary, as they had been when Port Caynn and the surrounding areas were under attack. Shaping her eyes to those of a raptor, she examined palace and city. Soldiers were everywhere, afoot, on horseback, or patrolling the river, but she saw no fighting, and a great deal of rebuilding. People were hard at work all over the palace grounds, too, piling debris for wagons to carry away. There were patrols on the walls and within the palace grounds, but nowhere did she find evidence of the enemy, except for two large prison stockades that lay east of the palace.

The dragons circled high above the palace; their Stormwing escort did the same. "Why come *here*?" Numair shouted to Diamondflame. "Skysong is at Port Legann!"

—*Why are we here?*—asked Wingstar, mind voice dry.—*You guided us, Diamondflame, and I too thought you would take us to our grandchild. I don't even see an army in this place.*—

—*The god of the duckmoles is here,*—said Diamondflame.—*I want to know why.*—

Wingstar stared at the blue dragon.—*Broad Foot? In this city?*—

—*On the other side of the world from his mortal children,*—Dia-

mondflame replied grimly as Numair and Daine exchanged looks.—
*Involving himself in mortal affairs.*—

"How do you know all this?" the mage asked loudly.

*—I am a dragon,*—was the haughty reply.—*My power tells me a
great many things that you are blind and deaf to.*—

Silver glittered in front of them, condensing very slowly as Broad
Foot appeared. Daine reached for him before she remembered where
they were. The duckmole was thin, his eyes sunken. "What's happened
to you?" she cried. "You look terrible!"

He clapped his bill gently in a duckmole laugh.—*I overestimated
my ability to contain Malady. It will not break free of me, but . . . it
fights.*—His mind voice—the only way the animal gods could speak in
the mortal realms—sounded weak.

*—This is incredible!*—boomed Diamondflame.

*—What possible interest have you in the affairs of humans?*—

The duckmole snorted.—*Have you dragons shut yourselves off so
completely from affairs in the mortal and divine realms? Can you not
feel the battle that is raging? Read the Chaos currents around you!*—

*—Humans and their wars,*—snapped Wingstar, but Daine heard
doubt in her voice.

*—If she overturns the mortal and divine realms, how long do you
think it will be until she turns on the Dragonlands?*—Broad Foot wanted
to know.—*You have made them separate from the Divine Realms, but
you share a common border with them, and Uusoae is nothing but
appetite. Even when fed to gorging, she hungers still.*—

"Would you dragons mind setting down for a moment?" asked Numair. "I would like to learn what the situation is here."

*—And I would like to talk to you, duckmole,*—said Diamondflame,
gliding down to light on a broad expanse before the palace wall. Daine
saw the soldiers' bows follow them down. The catapults on the walls
were being turned in order to dump rocks and liquid fire on the dragons,
if necessary. She crossed her fingers and prayed that none of the defenders would lose control—she had the feeling that Diamondflame and
Wingstar would have little mercy for human error. Looking over, she
saw Numair talking into a small, fiery globe on his palm. He'd opened
a speech spell to one of the mages below, and was explaining matters,
talking with a speed only he could manage.

When the dragons settled on the bare earth, a gate in the wall
opened, and two people came riding out. One, mounted on a horse and
wearing chain mail, was unmistakably a knight, albeit older than most
of the knights on active duty. His long-haired companion wore the
brown tunic and trousers of the Queen's Riders and rode a mountain

pony. Daine waved. She knew Duke Gareth the Elder and Buri, a commander of the Riders, almost as well as Numair did.

"They're friends," she told Wingstar as the female extended her forelegs, raising her chest, and the girl, higher in the air. "It's all right."

*—They may well be friends, but do they know that we are?—*The female sank down again. Once she was close enough to the ground, Daine slid off her back and went to their welcoming committee. Numair caught up with her, as Diamondflame, Wingstar, and Broad Foot turned their backs to everyone else and spoke mind to mind.

Tugging an earlobe, Duke Gareth eyed the dragons. "I had thought that I was past being shocked by your companions," the king's uncle said. "Clearly I was mistaken."

"You should have seen where we got them," Numair informed him, shaking hands with Buri. "Where's the queen? For that matter, where's the enemy?"

"Gone, except for our prisoners." Dismounting from her pony, Buri came to give Daine a hug. "They scrambled out of here half a day before a relieving force from the Yamani Islands came in—just pulled up stakes and vanished."

"We still maintain our forces on alert, however," the duke told them. "Just in case the enemy attempts something crafty. The army is camped throughout the Royal Forest, and between here and Port Caynn."

"Thayet took a picked force and some mages and went south on some of the Yamani ships," Buri told them. "They're going to try to break the siege at Port Legann."

Daine gasped. "There's a relief fleet going there from the Copper Isles! They'll be caught betwixt and between!"

"I'd ask how you know, except anybody can tell you've been strange places," the little K'mir remarked, looking at the dragons.

"We'll have to catch up with Her Majesty, then," Numair said. "You're certain everything is well here?"

Duke Gareth smiled. "Enough that you can go to them. We are well situated. You know that Her Majesty would not have left us vulnerable—"

"No more than she'd go if she thought there was still work to do here," added Buri.

Daine looked at the dragons and the duckmole. "Will you take us to the queen?" she asked. "They're at sea, on their way to Port Legann."

*—The badger and Gold-streak are with them,—*added Broad Foot. He had ended his secret conference with the dragons.

*—We will do more than convey you to her,—*said Wingstar.—

*Broad Foot has told us enough that my mate and I have decided to help you, and our grandchild, fight.—*

"Do you think your fellow dragons might be concerned enough about the danger from Uusoae to fight on our side as well?" Numair asked hopefully.

*—If you are prepared to wait a few decades for them to reach the decision,—*said Diamondflame, mind voice dry.*—That is one reason why few of us will argue with a personal choice. Long-lived as we are, we still would die of old age before our peers would agree on anything.—*

Numair winced. "Please, forget I asked."

Barzha glided down to join them, her elegant brows knit in a frown. "Why do you gab here like pigeons?" she demanded. "Ozorne is not here. Our people are not here."

*—I needed to speak to the duckmole,—*Diamondflame said.

"You have spoken, have you not? Then let's find our battle," snapped Barzha. "We didn't come to admire scenery."

Daine and Numair gave Duke Gareth and Buri a hasty farewell and climbed onto the dragons' backs once more. As they flew up, leaving the palace and the capital far below, Wingstar remarked,*—I see no reason for us to tire ourselves by flying all that way to their queen's ships—not if we can use the spiral spell to transport all of us.—*

*—Come, Stormwings,—*said the blue dragon.*—Let us keep our strength for our enemy.—*Up they flew until they disappeared into the clouds again.

# NINE

# THE BATTLE OF LEGANN

ᖬᖴ  Under the cover of dragon spells and the night, Daine watched as Queen Thayet of Tortall landed her army on a beach a day's march north of Port Legann. All around the girl, men, Riders, knights, mounts, and immortals waded onto the sand as carefully and quietly as they could. The two dragons, as well as centaurs and ogres, towed the ships' longboats. These were packed to the rim with arms and supplies, first to be emptied on the land, then to be sent back for more. In the morning, the relief force would try to cut through a dense forest that lay between this beach and the enemy's main camp. Their task would be easier than it had been for enemies of Tortall: It seemed that Wingstar knew spells that would hide and silence their passage. Ozorne and his commanders thought they were safe from attack on their rear, knowing the forest was nearly impassable, and having mages experienced at the detection of other mages' spells. The dragons had been quick to assure the queen that no mortal or immortal could sense *their* power. Remembering old tales of dragons who walked through cities unnoticed while shrouded in their magic, Thayet had accepted their offer of help.

Daine sighed. She would not be with the army: She was to act as courier between Thayet's force and Port Legann, with Diamondflame himself to take her back and forth. In a pack she carried things that the king and Lord Imrah of Legann should find helpful: bespelled mirrors for use in communicating with the queen and her generals, maps of the plan of attack both for the queen's land army and for the Yamani ships, and descriptions of the extremely varied collection of folk who would be fighting on Tortall's side.

Someone tapped her shoulder; turning, Daine found Queen Thayet. Co-ruler of Tortall, she was dressed in the simple Rider uniform and wore her crow's-wing black hair tightly braided. Only the helmet tucked under her arm bore any royal insignia, a small gold crown set over the visor. She also carried a soft leather bag, which she offered to Daine. Taking it, the girl realized that it held something heavy that was the size of her palm.

"If you'd give this to my lord, I would appreciate it," Queen Thayet told Daine. "And tell him that I said the *next* time he goes on a long tour of our embattled cities, he had better take the Dominion Jewel with him. *I* don't know how to wield the dratted thing."

"You know he hates to use it." Harailt of Aili, chief of the mages in Tortall's royal university, came over, rubbing his hands against the chill. "He thinks it's a crutch. He doesn't want to be too dependent on it."

"With a relief force coming here from the Copper Isles, we need all the help we can get," Thayet said flatly. She kissed the girl's cheek. "Good luck," she whispered, and went to the longboat that awaited her, Harailt close behind. Leaning over the rail, Daine waved to the badger and Goldstreak, who had been in the boat when they lowered it from the ship. Her reunion with them had lasted only half a day: They would stay with the queen and her generals, sending messages to the commanders through the darkings who had spied on them until recently.

Daine turned Thayet's leather pouch over in her hands. She'd heard tales that with his jewel King Jonathan could ask the very plants and stones to rise up in defense of the realm. "I'll believe it when I see it," she muttered. Tying the long drawstrings around her neck, she stuffed the pouch inside her shirt, to hang next to the badger's claw. Leaning on the rail, she squinted at the shore. She wanted to get *moving*.

"Fretting about your stork-man?" Rikash inquired, lighting on the rail beside her. He dug steel talons into the wood. "He'll be fine. Mages always are."

"I'd feel better about that if I could be here to look after him."

"Then stay."

"I can't," Daine replied, shaking her head. "I don't want Kitten there without me when the big noise starts. In the Dragonlands, I saw—she's just a baby still. She ought to be in a safe place. Since she isn't, I need to be with her, as much as I can."

"You're breaking my heart," drawled the immortal.

"Got a bit of sand in your crop?" she demanded irritably. "A swallow or two of oil should wash it right out the end that does your thinking for you."

To her surprise he laughed. Around them, she saw gold-skinned Yamanis and Tortallans make the Sign against evil. "I deserved that.

Don't mind me." He fell silent again, flexing his talons, digging chips of brightly colored enamel from the rail. All the Yamani ship rails looked tattered after two days of Stormwing company. "Barzha and Hebakh said to wish you happy hunting," he said abruptly. "And if they get Ozorne first, they'll save you a piece." He grinned, showing all of his pointed steel teeth. "Perhaps it's treasonous of me, but I really think *I* would like to reach Ozorne ahead of them. If I do, they may take all the leftovers from me. How about if I just tell him you said good-bye, before I rip him apart?"

"That's very thoughtful of you," Daine told him solemnly, her eyes dancing with laughter. "I appreciate that."

Rikash looked up at her, green eyes black in the lamplight. "I *think,* if I'm careful, I can at least keep one of his braids for you. I'll try, anyway." He tossed his long blond hair, making the bones that were braided into it click. "Souvenirs are always important." His tone changed to one of mockery. "Gods help us, it's the stork-man, come to make sure I'm not corrupting you. Has your grand conference ended, Longshanks?"

Numair joined them. "It has. There go Barzha and Hebakh now." He pointed to the silvery shapes flapping their way to shore. The rest of the Stone Tree nation was there already, perched on the limbs of trees that edged the forest.

"And I must follow, like a good servant," Rikash commented. "I'll see you both when the dust settles in two days." He took off, gliding over the water. At the last second, he swerved to avoid a collision with the back of Wingstar's neck. The dragon whirled and lunged, jaws snapping. The Stormwing rolled, inches from her muzzle, flipped up his tail, and sped on.

Numair put an arm around Daine's shoulders. "It's time," he said quietly.

"Come with me," she whispered, turning to grab a fistful of his shirt. Jelly squeaked at her. "Well, if you wouldn't hide in his clothes all the time," she snapped.

"Magelet, I can't." Numair caressed her face, eyes intent on hers. "No one else can take on Inar Hadensra, not without risking lives needlessly. He could have been a black robe mage like me, but—he thought the university was too confining. He's in the main camp for certain—I can sense him even at this distance. I *must* be there when Thayet attacks."

"You get into so much trouble without me to look after you," she whispered.

He kissed her forehead. "You belong in Legann. Make sure that

Jonathan understands what Gainel told us. It's not the kind of thing we can trust to a letter or speech spell. He's *got* to see that it's vital to capture or kill Uusoae's pawn, Valmar of the Copper Isles. Diamond-flame says he'll get Deniau of the Copper Isles when his fleet reaches Legann." He sighed, staring into the dark with troubled eyes. "And we'll just have to hope she is drawing on those two or Inar Hadensra, or Ozorne, not one of the other immortals that were in our dream, because we have no way to identify them."

Daine threw her arms around the man's neck. They kissed with hunger and desperation, holding each other tight. Jelly shrilled in protest; they ignored the darking.

Slowly, at last, she opened her arms, and Numair let her slide to the deck. "I love you," he whispered. "If you get yourself killed, I will *never* forgive you."

That got a laugh from her, albeit a wet one. Numair offered his handkerchief. "You'll need it," she said, and wiped her eyes on her sleeve.

"Something else." Reaching into his shirt, he pulled Jelly out. "We talked about this," he told the darking firmly. "You'll be much better off with Daine and Leaf."

The darking stretched its neck long until it could rub its head against his cheek, then retracted until it was a small blob once more. Daine turned. The mage tucked the darking into the compartment of the pack where Leaf already waited.

—*If these touching farewells are done with?*—Diamondflame hovered effortlessly beside the ship. They hadn't even heard his approach.—*We too must be on our way.*—

Daine and Numair exchanged a last, swift kiss, before the girl climbed onto the rail. Numair steadied her until Diamondflame's magic hands picked her up and deposited her on his back. They began to rise. Daine looked at Numair and blew him a kiss, trying to ignore an inner voice that said she would probably never see him again.

Light sparkled at the corner of her eye: a speaking spell. Phantom lips touched her cheek, and his voice whispered in her ear, "Goddess bless, my darling."

Two days later, in the hour before sunrise, the girl stood on Legann's Northgate watchtower. She knew what lay in the shadows below. Yesterday, as the queen's army advanced, she had mapped battlefields and camps, riding on Diamondflame's back, with his magic to keep them invisible. Copies of her maps went both to the city's defenders and to Thayet, borne by Wingstar. Now the Tortallan rulers knew their opponents' every position. The queen and her forces waited at the forest's edge. It was nearly time to ford the river between them and their enemies, time to begin the day's grim work.

The image of the land before her was etched into her brain. A swath of torn-up ground hundreds of yards wide lay before Legann's outer wall, littered with bodies that had begun to swell, blacken, and stink in the summer heat. With them lay abandoned weapons; shattered spears, arrows, and pikes; stones from Legann's catapults; and wide, scorched gouges where the war mages had battled.

Farther back, out of catapult range, Ozorne's allies had set their defenses. The first of these was a row of logs roped together in X's, their outer ends sharpened to gut any horse that tried to leap over them. Next came lines of trenches, designed to break the legs of horses and men that managed to get through the log fence, and to shelter the enemy's soldiers when arrows were flying. The third barrier was a low, rounded earthen wall. Behind that lay the main enemy camp itself, in a low valley with a river cutting through.

She'd mapped the positions of everything out there. As the light improved, she saw the shadowy forms of sentries on top of the low earth wall, just as she could see the tall, wooden towers that the enemy used as lookout posts. If the defenders ever let those towers get close enough, they would also give Ozorne's allies a way to reach the top of Legann's curtain wall.

Shivering, the girl drew the blanket that—with the badger's claw— was her only covering even closer. Beside her, Dominion Jewel in one hand, a speech-and-vision-spelled mirror in the other, was King Jonathan. With the mirror, he was in contact with his queen. His generals had such mirrors, too, to pass news to him more quickly than runners could.

"Are you sure you ought to be here?" Onua, Daine's first Tortallan friend, asked the king. She had come to Legann while Numair and Daine were in the Divine Realms, and had reserved the right to stick to the king's side. "It's foolish to risk yourself out in the open. If one lucky Stormwing slashes you, I'm left to tell Thayet why I let you do this."

"I distrust any advice that contains the words *ought* or *should*," he replied coolly. "And I can't wield the Dominion Jewel from inside, Onua. I have to see where I use it."

Daine leaned forward and mouthed "I told you so" to Onua. The K'mir smiled, wry. She hadn't really expected Jonathan to take her advice.

Kitten chirped to Daine. The girl awkwardly stooped, clutching her blanket, and used one arm to lift the dragonet into a rectangular notch in the wall. The sky over the hills in the east had gone pink.

In the wide, flat space inside the wall behind the king, light bent as Diamondflame moved. The tower guards couldn't see him, but they *felt* him, and walked, when they had to, pressed against the wall. The dragon's invisibility was less of a problem for his allies than visibility. Not only did it keep him from the notice of the enemy's spies, but at the few times that he *had* appeared, there had been panic in the city.

Hearing the clank of armor, Daine looked around. Lord Imrah, ruler of the fief of Legann, had reached the tower roof. He was no more able to see the dragon than his men, but he knew Diamondflame was there, and at least he did not press against the wall and sidle along. He walked as if he would normally follow the edge of the circular deck, rather than cut straight across it. Daine, with her hands on Kitten, could see that Diamondflame moved his tail out of the nobleman's way.

The girl made room so that Imrah could stand next to the king; the lord nodded his thanks. At first she had not liked this bald, large-bellied man. With his pale eyes and pockmarked face, he looked cruel. The night before, at supper with Jonathan and his leaders, though, she had caught Legann's master feeding Leaf, Jelly, and the Legann darkings under the table. "Well, they look like shadows of their former selves," he'd said then, and winked.

Now he smoothed his salt-and-pepper mustache. "Almost time, isn't it?"

"We'll get the queen's signal at any moment," Jonathan murmured, watching the view to the north. Shadows and light began to mark the landscape, outlining structures and the dead.

"I hope these Yamanis can handle those ships blockading my harbor," Imrah said to no one in particular. "They seem pretty confident they can handle them and that fleet from the Copper Isles."

—*It will not be Yamanis alone*,—Diamondflame said, mind voice crisp.—*Do you but handle your side of this mess. Leave ship warriors to those who can best handle them.*—

"I think your daughter Flamewing believed she could handle ship things, too," Daine said, shivering. "And they handled *her* instead." She smiled briefly at Tkaa, who had come to join them.

—*She was barely more than a kit*,—the invisible dragon said kindly.—*You will see. It is rare for adult dragons to be caught.*—

The sun's rim crested the eastern hill. To the north, beyond the enemy's defenses, light sparked.

Kitten chirped. "Wingstar is in flight," Tkaa said. Like Daine, he rested a paw on Kitten, or neither of them could have seen a thing.

Dragons, apparently, could not hide from one another, and those close enough to a dragon to touch it would see what the dragon saw.

Imrah scratched his bald crown. Jonathan drew a deep breath. Daine watched that spark as it rose and grew bigger.

Before Wingstar reached the agreed-upon position, the girl silently called out to her friends among the People. The enemy had gotten careless in the time that she was away. Ozorne must have told his allies that she had gone: They had resumed tethering their mounts with rope and leather, and leaving them unwatched. Now that Ozorne had no darkings to supply him with information—they had all gone over to the badger and Gold-streak—he didn't know that Daine was back.

Steadying the enemy's horses and mules, Daine warned them again of the fright to come. The mounts shifted at her request, stretching their tethers to the limit.

High above the enemy's main camp, placed so that she could also be seen from Legann's walls, the dragon shed the spells that kept her invisible. Stretching out her long neck, she gave a feral shriek that brought sweat to the face of everyone who heard it. Pearl-gray scales blazed silver. Gold scales flared with a brilliance that was the essence of light. Wingstar was a living beacon over the enemy tents.

Even with Daine's warning, the mounts were terrified. They reared and lunged—and each rope and strap, carefully gnawed in the dark by sharp-toothed rodents, snapped. In a thunder of hooves, mules, ponies, and horses fled as soldiers jumped out of the way.

On the wall, Kitten replied to Wingstar with a trill that made Daine's ears hurt. The crenelated granite walls of Legann had been capped with pale gray stones. These now shimmered and glowed, throwing off light, but no heart.

—*She is so much more advanced than our young at home,*—remarked Diamondflame as he rose onto his hindquarters.—*Perhaps more of them should spend time here.*—He launched himself, giant wings pulling him aloft. Daine, Kitten, and Tkaa followed his flight; the other two-leggers were staggering in his back draft, fighting to recover their balance.

"I wish we had a sign that this flaming dragon was part of an *attack* or something," Imrah grumbled. "Those dung heaps might think it's just one of their *own* monsters enjoying the sunrise."

Diamondflame reached the sky over Legann harbor before he shed his cloaking spells. Before him lay the ships of the invading fleet, balked by the harbor's defenders and the chain across its mouth. Daine couldn't begin to imagine how the enemy—or even Legann's friends—felt at the sight of eighty feet of dragon overhead. Diamondflame snarled: Sails burst into flame. Wingstar too snarled. The sharpened logs in front of the trenches and the wooden towers behind the enemy's earth wall began to burn.

"Is that enough sign of an attack for you, my lord?" the king asked.

Imrah of Legann was a deliberate man. He walked over to get a better view of the harbor and its blockaders. The sailors were scrambling to douse their flaming ships as first Diamondflame, then Wingstar, descended on them, howling with fury. Legann's master returned to Jonathan's side. "It'll do," he said, reseating his helmet on his armored hip. With a half bow to the king, he began the climb from the watchtower to the ground.

Onua checked the fit of her arm guards and archer's gloves, and strung her bow.

Daine shifted nervously; she hated waiting for an enemy to come at her. "You stay right there, and don't move," she warned the pale blue dragonet. "If you tumble out, your grandda will cook me—once he and your grandma finish with the enemy's ships, anyway." Kitten chuckled and rubbed her muzzle against the girl's face. Leaf, who was coiled around Daine's neck, squeaked a protest.

Her mind filled with a metallic roar, a shrill hum, and a rattling buzz. Damping her magical hearing as far as she dared, she told her companions, "They're coming."

The K'mir leaned out of the notch in front of her and waved her bow. From the wall below the tower, a familiar voice boomed, "That's the signal, lambkins—string your bows! Wake *up*, Master Wooley! Stormwings don't wait till you've finished your beauty sleep!" The hectoring voice faded as Sarge, the ex-slave who helped to train the Queen's Riders—and who fought with them—urged Legann's archers to prepare for the assault.

Daine, stretching the cramped muscles of her neck, smiled at the familiar roar that had woken her on so many days in the Rider barracks. She sent a prayer to the Goddess to shield him and his charges: Half of the archers on Legann's walls were as young or younger than she was, teenagers chosen for their precise eye and ability to hit what they shot at.

They needed prayer. Winged legions rose from the second enemy camp to the northeast. Sunlight blazed from Stormwing feathers, and glinted on the silver bones of hurrok wings and claws. With them flew winged apes armed with lances or axes.

At least there were no wyverns. Diamondflame had already told the king that they had sensed the arrival of mature dragons and fled. Though they had been willing to fight on with only a single, very young dragon to oppose them, they dared not try to challenge her grandparents.

"An ugly-looking crew, aren't they?" Marielle, Imrah's lady, joined them, recurved bow in hand, as the immortals came on. A tiny woman, she had lively brown eyes and kept her dark hair cropped short and close. She wore a leather jerkin studded with metal rings over a kilted-up dress; there were archer's gloves on her hands. Unhooking a spyglass from her belt, she surveyed the winged attackers. "You know, these look like they're *running* from something."

"They are," King Jonathan replied. "While Her Majesty's main force attacked in the northwest, her second force hit the camp in the northeast."

"What kind of force?" Marielle wanted to know.

"The badger god," replied Onua.

"Stormwing friends," piped Leaf. Jelly nodded.

Marielle raised her eyebrows. "If you say so, little ones," she said wryly. "Strange friends that we get in wartime."

Another darking stretched to put its eyeless head over Jonathan's shoulder—it was tucked into the king's belt purse. "Centaurs," it squeaked to Marielle. "Forty-four."

"Very true, Inkblot," Jonathan told Ozorne's one-time spy, now his companion and connection to other darkings. "Don't forget Sir Raoul, the Knight Commander of the King's Own. He mustered a hundred-odd ogres, as well as the centaurs. Those who chose to live with our laws are fighting for them."

The noblewoman laughed. "Do you know, sire, I think that if we live to tell our grandchildren about this war, they will accuse us of making it up."

Daine traded places with Tkaa, putting him at the king's side and herself in front of a stone notch in the wall. Far below, she heard the grind of chains and wood: The portcullises on the north, east, and south gates were being raised, the drawbridges lowered. Imrah led mounted knights and men-at-arms from the north gate, to confront the soldiers who fled the queen's forces. Another company of mixed horsemen, foot soldiers, and archers was leaving by the east gate, Daine knew, and two Rider Groups were trotting their ponies out of the southern gate. If it worked, Ozorne's allies on land would be caught between the queen's relief force and Legann's defenders, just as his seagoing allies, the blockaders, would be pinched between the arriving ships and the harbor's defenders.

Where is Slaughter? Daine wondered. She'll have plenty of work today.

The noise level rose, fueled by the howls of winged immortals and the roar of enemy soldiers as they topped the rise between their camp and its outer defenses. Seeing the wooden towers that Wingstar had flamed blazing in front of them, some tried to turn back. Roots—belonging to trees long cut down to clear the battlefield—shot out of bare ground and twined around the ankles of the enemy. More runaways dodged the roots, only to meet Imrah and his knights. From the valley where the enemy had camped, magic fires erupted and died as Tortallan mages attacked those serving the invaders.

The king was pale and gleaming with perspiration. Marielle and Onua also began to sweat as fear—Stormwing war terror—billowed ahead of the oncoming immortals. No one moved. It affected Daine as it did the others, but all of them had fought under the pressure of that fear before: The choice was fight or die.

"How many Stormwings did you say followed Ozorne?" Jonathan asked, his normally even voice strained.

"Two hundred and forty-eight, Your Majesty—if this is all of them coming at us now." The archers on wall and tower swung their bows up, choosing targets from among the oncoming immortals. Daine's was a winged ape that flew with others of his kind, ahead of the Stormwings. He carried double-headed axes in feet that were as nimble as hands.

Taking a deep breath, the girl closed her eyes and thought of merlins, fast birds of prey, able to maneuver well in the air. The blanket dropped to the stone deck. Tkaa pulled its folds back, allowing her to take flight.

The air below filled with the snap of bowstrings and the whistle of arrows and bolts. Daine shot straight at the ax-bearing ape, striking him as the hurrok had struck her on the First Bridge, dragging her claws across his brow and scalp. He shrieked and grabbed for her as blood streamed into his eyes. Turning fast, she tore at his wings, ripping holes in them with talons and beak. He fell, dropping both axes as he tried to spin around in midair. When she saw a peaked tower roof loom up underneath, she released her prey. He struck the tower back first, and rolled limply into the city street below.

Swerving fast, she returned to the watchtower roof and the king. A hurrok was her next target; once more she went for eyes first, then wings. Blinded and crippled, the immortal careened into a Stormwing, dragging it down and into the curtain wall as the Stormwing's feathers cut it to pieces. Daine glided back to a place next to the king, watching for a new target.

The archers on the walls shot as rapidly as they could, choosing ape, hurrok, and Stormwing targets with deadly accuracy as they fought

Stormwing terror. The king, examining battles on the land and in the air before him, continued to talk calmly into his spelled mirror, relaying what he saw to the queen. In his left hand, the Dominion Jewel glowed, violet light streaming from its many facets.

Jonathan quietly said, "Excuse me," into his mirror, and put it on the stone. Raising the Jewel, he aimed it not at the oncoming Stormwings, but at three hurroks bearing riders to the lower wall and the archers there. The riders were human mages; they lashed the fighters on the curtain wall, burning two of them alive. White threads of fire drifted from the Jewel, falling gracefully onto the hurroks and their burdens.

Kitten cried an alarm: A quartet of Stormwings—two males, two females—had come in low, where no one had seen them, skimming the ground until they reached the base of the curtain wall. Now they sped up its length, ducking the web of fire that was tangling the mages and their mounts, zipping past the archers on the lower levels. Clutching round clay pots in their talons, they were intent on the watchtower and its occupants. Daine recognized the bombs: A spell word from a Stormwing and the pots would explode, showering everyone with liquid fire.

Inkblot jumped from the king's belt purse onto the notch of the wall in front of Jonathan, who did not see his danger. The mages were fighting him and the Jewel with all they had. Jelly, clinging to Kitten's back, leaped to join the king's darking.

Marielle and Tkaa ignored the blots as they leaned through the crenelated wall. The lady aimed; when her chosen target was only fifty feet away, she loosed. Her arrow took one in the eye; the immortal slammed into the stone with a dying shriek. Jelly and Inkblot dropped to cover the face of the leading Stormwing, blinding him. He thrashed, dropping his bombs in his frantic attempt to scrape the darkings off. They abandoned their victim only when three of the archers on the lower wall had riddled him with arrows.

The two remaining Stormwings came on, deadly rage in their eyes. Tkaa opened his jaws. His throat gave out an ear-piercing song that was part shriek, with a counterpoint tune in it that sounded like an avalanche. The male Stormwing was half caught by the basilisk's song. His left side turned to stone; his right wing and claw thrashed. He dropped as archers scattered from the wall below. Moments later the occupants of the tower heard rock shatter on rock. His companion, the female, had come in to his rear and side; she escaped Tkaa's song. Before the half-stone male began to fall, Daine was arrowing down the side of the watchtower. Abruptly she changed shape to that of a larger, heavier golden eagle, and slammed into the female Stormwing's face. Steel teeth snapped; the girl-eagle got her claws out of the way just in time. Twisting, she slashed the immortal's throat, then jumped away. Cursing, the Stormwing hit the lower wall, silvery blood spraying everywhere, and from there tumbled end over end to the ground.

Daine circled, hunting for the darkings. She was relieved to find them rolling up the watchtower's side, clinging to it as easily as the sunlight did. For the moment the air around the watchtower was clear. Gliding in, Daine carefully picked the two inky creatures up in her claws and carried them back up to the king.

"Good work," Leaf said from its position on Tkaa's shoulder. Jelly went to Kitten; Inkblot flowed out of Daine's talons, pouring itself into Jonathan's belt purse once more. The king grinned, and stroked the purse. Looking for the hurroks and their riders who had run afoul of Jonathan, Daine saw only a heap of white bones on the curtain wall below, and shuddered.

A boom from the north shivered the tower stones. Mushrooming billows of arcane light climbed from behind enemy lines. One cloud was sparkling black, the other a deep ruby shade. Numair had found Inar Hadensra. Daine shifted from foot to foot, ruffling her feathers and praying as she watched tendrils of black fire wind through the red, and red through the black. Numair had tricked the Scanran into protecting their contest from the rest of the battle. Let Inar Hadensra think it was to keep someone from putting a spear through their backs; Daine knew it was to keep the magical battle from hurting anyone else.

Jonathan continued to speak to his queen and generals, passing on the numbers of the enemy and the directions of their movements. His companions defended him from every attack, physical and magical— Kitten and Tkaa easily handled the latter. Now that Numair had engaged the enemy's chief mage, and Thayet's wizards fought most of the rest, few human mages had the attention or strength to strike at those Tortallans who had no Gift, and thus no defense.

Fresh immortals raced onto the battle-torn ground between their camp in the northeast and Legann. Many bore torn nooses of vines and brambles: They had been forced to rip themselves free of clinging plants roused by the Dominion Jewel. On their heels came centaurs, ogres, and knights, all in Tortallan colors, fighting under Tortallan battle flags. When the enemy immortals turned south, to freedom, the ones who escaped the roots that snatched at them from the ground ran into companies of Tortallan soldiers, two Rider Groups, and a small detachment of centaurs who had settled east of Legann.

Behind the Tortallans rose a wall of brambles ten feet high. Anyone who tried to escape the battlefields and camps around the city would run into it. The Dominion Jewel, it seemed, could deliver what King Jonathan had promised.

Metallic shrieks drew the girl's attention. High above the Stormwings, hurroks, and winged apes, Barzha was locked in deadly battle with another Stormwing—a queen. "Jachull," Tkaa remarked, eyes fixed on the crowned immortals. "Queen of the Mortal Fear nation." Daine nodded; so this was the dead-voiced female she'd heard in her dream, the one who had said it wasn't important if some of her own kind died.

Crimson fires edged with gold tangled around the pair like an ill-made knot. For the most part they clawed at each other. The strange queen was adept at quick swipes of her wing feathers; soon Barzha was laddered with shallow cuts and covered in blood. Her enemy bore wounds as well—belly cuts that bled heavily.

Below the queens, Hebakh and Rikash fended off any Stormwings who tried to interfere. Seeing they were outnumbered, Daine called for the People. Sparrows darted into the fray, dashing around Stormwings, pecking and speeding away. Fighting them, or trying to, the immortals smashed into one another, slicing their own allies to pieces. They retreated from Barzha's guards, while the rest of her allies came to help the two males.

A net of scarlet fires wrapped itself around Jachull, its ends lodged under Barzha's skin; Jachull would have to kill the Stone Tree queen to escape. With a snarl, Jachull turned and sped at Barzha, talons forward, set to impale. At the last second Rikash's queen detached the webs of her magic and shot upward, Jachull passing under her by inches.

Barzha fell as Jachull fought to halt and turn; when Jachull stabilized, Barzha was behind her, chopping down with the edges of her right wing. Jachull spun hard to meet an attack she expected from her rear or from above. Instead she jammed her throat and chest into the razor of Barzha's wing. Barzha seized Jachull's face in one talon, dug in her claws, then let her enemy fall. Jachull's allies, who had watched the duel at a distance from Barzha's defenders, wailed.

"Daine?" Jonathan asked quietly. "Would you see how the Yamanis are faring?"

She nodded and took off, changing her shape to that of a gull to fly more easily over the ocean. She kept a wary eye out for winged immortals who might try to kill her. As far as she could tell, they were busy enough, caught between city forces and Thayet's army. Everywhere Daine saw the flash of magic: Stormwing crimson edged with gold; brown and gold from centaurs who were also mages; and varicolored fires that served human wizards. The winged apes laid down a blanket of thick clinging fog, the only magic they possessed, but it did little to hide them. Too many winged creatures and too many other mages took part in the fight; the fog would billow, then shred and blow away.

Soaring over the harbor, she saw that the enemy's ships were in poor condition. Many of the largest vessels had burned to the waterline, seared by dragonfire; nearly all of those left bore scorch marks. Five Yamani ships, half of the fleet that had brought Thayet to Legann, kept all but the smallest vessels from making a getaway. Like dogs herding sheep, they were driving those ships still able to maneuver toward the harbor, where they could surrender to Legann's defenders or be crushed against the breakwater.

Two miles past the blockade Daine found Diamondflame, Wingstar, and the other five Yamani warships. The ten-ship relief force from the Copper Isles, the one she had seen in a Divine Realms vision, was trapped in a circle formed by dragons and Yamanis. Two enemy ships were burning fast. Three more were disabled, their masts broken off. Skins of liquid fire flew through the air, hurled by catapults from vessels on both sides. Any that came too near the dragons swerved, burst, and showered their contents on the enemy's ships. Daine was no admiral, but the outcome of this contest was easy to read.

Circling, she returned to take on her own shape and report to the king. After hearing her description of the sea battle with satisfaction, Jonathan ordered her to rest. A runner gave her meat and cheese between slices of bread, and a cup of heavily sweetened herbal tea. Eating quickly, the girl felt her strength return with every bite and sip.

The sun was almost directly overhead when thick, multicolored smoke rose in an unnaturally straight column from the enemy camp in the northeast. Daine viewed it uneasily: It looked far too much like the Chaos vents in the Divine Realms.

"Sir Raoul, what is that?" Jonathan asked the mirror.

"Booby trap," Daine heard the knight reply. "A squad of men found a box in a tent. One was fool enough to open it before we had a mage check it. The gods-curst thing exploded. It killed everyone in the squad—and I don't think it's done making mischief."

The column bent and stretched, colors rippling, until it touched one end to the ground where the eastern road and the road that circled Legann met. Anchored there, it condensed until it was nearly thirty feet in height, and solidified until it formed a monstrous, three-headed serpent. Its scales changed constantly, from pale green to pink to yellow, never holding to one color or pattern. Only the eyes in the three heads remained the same, all blood red, with no pupils that Daine could see.

The smoke-snake turned on the line of Tortallan allies and struck in three directions, each head stretching its long neck for prey, baring overlong, onyx fangs. When the creature straightened again, one head gripped a shrieking man-at-arms in its jaws, the second a green-skinned ogre, the third a female centaur who fought to stab her captor with a javelin that she carried. The serpent devoured them, and searched for its next victims.

The Tortallan centaurs and ogres fled. One knight turned his warhorse to face the serpent. He was a huge man in brightly polished plate armor; his mount was armored as well, her size well-suited to her master's weight. A tight band around Daine's heart squeezed. Raoul of Goldenlake, the Knight Commander of the King's Own, was not a close friend, but she knew and liked him. She was used to thinking of him as a giant, but the serpent rose at least ten feet over his head before the body split into three necks.

Steel wings and claws flashed in the sun. Rikash—his blond hair with its bone decoration streaming behind him—plummeted, talons first, to slam into the monster's central head. The snake roared, its voice tearing at the ears.

Silvery fire bloomed on the snake's left head: The badger materialized there, burying claws and fangs into the thing's skull as a small, moving shadow dove into one of the creature's nostrils. Daine gasped. That was Gold-streak!

Starlings burst from the trees in a sizable, jeering crowd. Like a swarm of bees they swirled around the serpent's right head, blinding it, digging sharp beaks into its flesh.

Sir Raoul galloped in, massive, double-bladed ax in one hand, hacking at the serpent's body as if he were felling a tree. He struck a vital organ; blood of no particular color gushed forth to splatter his armor, smoking where it struck. His mount screamed when the drops lashed her rump. Hurriedly the knight guided the mare back from the stream of blood. The snake convulsed.

The starlings were not fools. They didn't need a command from Daine to get clear. Pulling back, they left the eye sockets of the head that they had assaulted packed with dead birds. The head that the badger had torn into lolled uselessly on its neck; he had chewed through bone to its brain, without taking harm from the thing's acid blood. Gold-streak looped itself around the badger's forepaw as the god vanished.

The middle head shrilled in rage and pain. It whipped frantically, tossing Rikash into the air. The blond Stormwing slammed into a boulder, and slid to the base of the stone.

The plate and cup slipped from Daine's numb fingers to shatter on the deck.

*"Rikash—no!"* someone cried in a voice that cracked as it rose. *"No! No! NOOOOO!"* It was her voice. If she screamed loud enough, long enough, he would live. She hadn't realized that he meant something to her. She hadn't known he was her friend.

It was the three-headed thing's last defiance. It drooped, then dissolved into a liquid soup with colors that shifted over its surface as it soaked into the ground.

Queen Barzha settled onto the rock that had broken Rikash, shrilling her grief. Hebakh landed beside her, keening, eyes ablaze. They had lost the follower who had brought them hope when Ozorne held them captive. They had lost the only Stormwing who had tried to set them free.

Their voices fell into an odd silence, one of those which came in battles when most fighters stopped briefly to catch a breath. Their eerie wailing sent shivers through everyone who could hear.

The battle resumed, but the tide had turned. Everywhere that Daine looked, she saw the enemy fighting to defend themselves, not to attack. Some humans began to lay down their arms. In the north, black fire flared around crimson still, but the lesser mage fires were dying.

In the northeast, so far away that only an eagle—or a girl who had turned her own eyes into those of a raptor—might see, a lone Stormwing took to the air and flapped away. He was trying to escape, leaving the others of his kind who fought on.

Daine had an idea who it was. "No you don't," she muttered, blackly furious. "Not this time, and never again! Sire, I request permission to go after that Stormwing!"

"This is not a good idea," Tkaa said, placing a gentle paw on her shoulder. "You risk capture or death from others of the enemy. He will be pursued, and caught."

She faced the basilisk, eyes ablaze. "That's what I said last time, and *look*!" She swept an arm to include the battlefield before them.

A hand rested on her other shoulder. "Then go," the king said, blue eyes direct. "Go, and the gods look after you."

"If they are not busy themselves," Tkaa pointed out. "Chaos must have plenty of strength to draw upon, with all this."

Daine shed the blanket that she had worn around her human form. Jumping into a wide notch in the stone wall, she leaped out, changing as she did, trading hair for feathers, arms for wings, and legs for talons. As a sparrow hawk, a small, fast bird of prey, she streaked after Ozorne.

## ➤➤ TEN ◄◄

# JUDGMENTS

ഇൽ  Her flight carried her over the ruins of the wooden towers and the enemy's dirt bulwarks. Fighting continued there, but even a quick glance told her that the enemy was losing heart. A growing number of men and immortals sat in clusters everywhere, guarded by wary knights and soldiers in Tortallan uniform.

On she flew. Beneath her lay the enemy's northern camp. The ground was littered with bodies, weapons, and the things men needed to live in hostile country; some wagons and tents were ablaze. Here mages battled, the fires of their Gifts waxing and waning. Some mages had surrendered; others lay dying, the loss of their power turning their bodies into skin-covered skeletons before they were dead.

Beside the river, the fiery black-and-ruby ball that was the interlocked Gifts of Numair and Inar Hadensta pulsed with unchecked fury. Daine glanced at it, then fixed her eyes on her quarry. She couldn't think about Numair, couldn't stop to watch—she was gaining on Ozorne.

Speeding over the river, she saw the queen enter the enemy camp. If she'd had a mouth, she would have grinned. She had been there when Thayet's commanders told the queen that she would not be permitted to ride to battle herself, not when the king was trapped and vulnerable in Legann. They had made Thayet agree that Tortall could not afford to lose both monarchs, but not before she had expressed her feelings in words that Daine usually heard only in the Corus slums.

Rising air bore her above the forest where the relief force had hidden. Her quarry was clearly in view—and much closer. Stormwings could fly, but not gracefully or speedily. Daine shrieked her elation. Ozorne looked back and saw her. He sped faster; Daine matched him.

He searched the land below, trying to spot a place where he might escape her.

It was harder to shape a human mouth and voice box in a bird than it was to give her two-legger self raptor's eyes, or bat's ears. She had no idea why that was true; it just was. After a few moments' struggle she had something that she could talk with.

"Ozorne Muhassin Tasikhe!" she called. "I am fair vexated with you!"

He turned, hanging in midair, smiling contemptuously. There were marks of soot, blood, and sweat on him; the scars of Stormwing battles decorated his chest. The black, glassy stone she had seen in visions of him still hung on a cord around his neck.

"I quiver," he said as she approached. "You have no notion of how terrified I am." For a moment he sounded as he had when she first met him, cool, aloof, and grand, seated on an emperor's throne. In those days he had been someone who placed himself far beyond the kind of life that she knew.

His eyes flickered as he looked over her shoulder. Daine turned. Two Stormwings, and three winged apes, crested the trees between her and Legann. He must have ordered them to wait for just this, so that he could set the trap, and she could fly into it.

The girl-eagle sighed. "Here I was thinking that, just once, it would be nice if you fought a battle *yourself,* without getting others to do your dirty work." She was thinking hard. She would have to be fast now, faster than she'd ever been in her life.

"*I* am not the one who gets my little animal *friends* killed by the hundreds for defending me," he taunted her.

Any anger that had clouded her mind vanished. "I made my peace with that—and with them—three years ago. Fight, damn you!"

"I won't soil my claws." He sneered. "I was the Emperor Mage of Carthak—"

"Oh, *please,*" she retorted, glancing back. The other immortals were coming on fast. "That's finished, and by your own acts did you finish it!"

"How *dare* you judge me?" he snarled. "You're a common-born bastard, a camp follower's brat who spreads her legs for any passing man—just like her mother."

To her own surprise—and quite clearly, to his—Daine laughed. "And you're as ignorant as you are evil," she retorted. "I'm done listening to you!"

Wheeling to face the immortals behind her, she changed, as quickly as thought. A giant strangling-snake, she dropped across two apes who flew close together, wrapping her tail around one throat, and her first three feet of length around the other. To her surprise, two small, blobby forms dropped past. Spreading themselves like kites, they steered until they fell onto the faces of both Stormwings. Leaf and Jelly had stolen a ride on Daine's back.

The Stormwings tried to scream; instead they only pulled darking bodies into their throats. Daine couldn't wait or watch. In one burst of strength, she squeezed, and heard dull snaps as both of her victims' necks broke.

Agony burned her side: The third winged ape wielded a sword. Daine fell away, forcing herself into raven form as she dropped. The cut was long, but shallow; with a grimace she made herself ignore the pain. If she didn't bleed too much, she would be fine. She would *have* to be fine.

Plummeting, she remembered the feel of wind under feathers and the loud calls of raven flockmates. The wind caught her outspread wings and carried her aloft.

There was a crash: The smothered Stormwings dropped into the woods. Leaf and Jelly fell away from their victims, gliding flat until they latched onto the naked limbs of a tall, long-dead tree. Daine swooped to get them as Ozorne screamed a word.

The two darkings flared crimson, and exploded.

Pulling her wings in, stretching her body, she banked, murder in her heart. The last winged ape was forgotten. There was no one bird that she drew on, but many, as Daine shaped angled wings to give her speed, a ripping beak and talons to match for combat, a starling's talent for quick, midair dodges. She stayed as large as she dared: She would need size to fight this battle. Hurtling through the winds, she came at Ozorne.

He lashed her with Stormwing fire. She barrel-rolled, spinning away from his bolts without losing a feather's worth of speed. Behind her, something grunted: The sword-wielding ape fought to catch up. She would have to deal with him: He was quicker than he had a right to be. Twisting herself until the air flowed over and under her just right, she emptied her large bird's bowels squarely into his face.

The ape's furious howl was choked and wet. Daine chanced a look back. He clawed at his throat, his sword falling to the earth. The silly clunch inhaled, she thought coldly, before she fixed her attention on Ozorne once more.

He burned her twice with crimson bolts, or tried to. She bent away from both and picked up her speed. He was sweating; she could smell it, a bitter combination of man oils and metal tang that spread through the air.

On the ground, the forest came to an end; they had reached the coast, far beyond the point where Yamani ships had landed the Tortallan force. Below, the sea battered the feet of high, rocky cliffs. The cliff thermals would help her along; she was beginning to tire, a little.

But if Daine was tiring, so was Ozorne. It cost him to fly. She could see it in his laboring wings and loss of speed. Twice he spun to throw flame at her. Ducking it easily, she gained altitude and circled to his left. He knew she was not directly behind him, an easy target. Forced to keep turning in order to see her, Ozorne lost momentum. Daine closed the gap. Once she was close enough, she changed again, and dropped onto his back, her wildcat's forepaws hooked over his shoulders.

Razor-edged feathers cut into her fur; she clamped her jaws on the back of his neck and bit, hard. Ozorne howled and writhed, falling. Daine bit harder. There was naked flesh on his back, too, where she put her rear claws to use. Red fire raced all over his skin, burning her paws and mouth. She hung on as long as she could, but in the end, she lost control over her shape and dropped off, while Ozorne spun and fell, bleeding heavily.

She strained, trying to regain her wings, but her mind was as exhausted as her body. She couldn't remember how winged creatures felt to her. I can't die! she thought frantically. Not whilst he's alive!

Her back struck a soft, feathered platform that slowed her fall. Gulls had come to her rescue, crowding together so that their outstretched wings overlapped, forming a platform of feather, skin, and bone. They sank to the ground, and drew away from her. She dropped an inch or two, striking thick, springy grass.

"Thank you," she whispered, rolling to her knees. "If I survive this, I will owe you and your kinfolk until the end of time."

She looked up. Ozorne's fall, like her long tumble in the Divine Realms, had been slowed and broken by a tree. He neared the ground, using his magic to cushion his own drop. When he landed, he was scant yards away. For a moment he stood, gasping, sweat-drenched hair in his eyes, bleeding from deep gouges and scrapes.

Daine forced herself to change, dredging up one last droplet of magic to arm herself. Her skin rippled, grew fur, developed patterns, changed again to human skin. "Like a Chaos thing myself," she mumbled, getting to her knees, and shuddered.

Ozorne shook his hair out of his eyes and grinned, lips peeling mirthlessly from his steel teeth. "What is Chaos to you?" he sneered, panting as he walked toward her.

"If you're for it, then I'm against it," she retorted, keeping her own face down.

"Then you're in trouble," he informed her. "With my help, Uusoae has the strength to defeat the gods at last. She has promised that I will be king of the world."

"And how long will that last? She'll only eat the world, too, when she's done with the gods." Daine thought she had something—her fingers and toenails were cooperating, at least. Driving up from the ground—she had to strike *before* he got those wing blades of his up— she launched herself at him with a scream of raw fury, finger-claws raking at his eyes, knees drawn up to her chest so that the claws on her feet could dig into his gut.

She knocked him back. Intertwined, they rolled down a slope, the girl ripping all the meat from him that her talons could reach, keeping her head down so that he couldn't fasten his metal teeth in her throat. He clawed at her with his own feet, tried to cut her with his wings, but it was hard for him to bend his metal flesh, harder still to grip a head cushioned by thick, long curls in his jaws. He screamed something.

A force lifted her up and knocked her yards away. She landed on her back, the wind knocked from her lungs. Trying to fill them again, Daine felt her claws turn back into toes and fingernails. As surely as she knew her name, she was certain that there were no more shape changes left in her. Perhaps if she had not lost so much blood, or flown so hard and so fast, or had kept her shapes to those of whole animals instead of using parts from many . . .

The sound of metal scraping rock woke her from a weary half-trance. She gasped, and coughed, found the air to roll over, and got on her hands and knees. He was coming for her, panting and exhausted himself, bleeding and triumphant.

"So here you are, without your precious *friends*," he mocked. "There is no one to save you: no human, no animal—no magic. Don't try to deny it," he said when she looked up at him. "Stormwing magic isn't good for much, but we *can* tell when someone is ready to die— when all her weapons are stripped from her."

Daine hung her head. At the edge of her vision the badger's heavy silver claw—the one thing that managed to stay with her through every shape change that she had ever worked—swung on its chain. The end of the claw was sharp; she knew that very well.

She let her curls fall forward, masking her actions. He was still a few yards away. With her right hand, she felt the chain until she found the catch. With her left, she groped for a rock. He would see that; let him.

A flick of a fingernail opened the catch. The chain ran off her neck and through the wire binding of the claw, pooling on the ground like water. Daine straightened, claw tucked into her right hand, a rock visible in her left. She hurled the stone at Ozorne. The weakness in her arm was terrifying; still, her aim at least was good. He threw up a magical shield, but it was barely visible. When the rock struck, the shield's pale red fires rippled and broke; the stone thumped his chest.

"I'm not the only one that's out of magic," she cried hoarsely. Manipulating the claw, she positioned it so that it thrust between the fingers of her fist, pointing out and down. "You couldn't light a candle, could you?"

He smiled, lifting a razor-edged wing as he approached. "I don't need magic to handle you now, Veralidaine. All I need is this. Why don't you just bare your throat, and make it easy on yourself?"

Come on, she thought, watching through her curtain of hair. And I have to make sure he *never* gets up from this. Just one . . . more . . . step . . .

He took it, bringing him within wing reach—or arm's reach. She threw herself forward, with no grace or coordination of muscle. Grabbing the upper edge of his open wing with one hand, feeling its bite in her palm, Daine slashed forward with the claw.

Ozorne screamed a doomed beast's scream as the badger's talon bit into his neck, and tore. Daine yanked the claw sideways, across his windpipe, through the veins on the opposite side. His blood sprayed, drenching them both; he thrashed like a mad thing. She dug the claw into his belly and dragged it down.

At last he was still.

For a long moment she lay there, too weary to get up—but the mess of blood and flesh made her stomach lurch. She rolled off him, barely feeling the small cuts from his outspread wings, too worn out even to vomit over the mess. When she was able to sit up, she found that the stone he'd taken to wearing was stuck to her bloody chest, with the remains of the cord on which it had hung. Claw must've cut the string, she thought vaguely. Groping, she seized cord and stone and hurled them away from her.

They struck a tree; the stone shattered. Beneath her, the ground lurched, rolled, then sank. Before her appeared an arch and pool of oozing, dripping muck, their shifting colors making her dizzy. In the spot where pond and arch met, a hunched figure straightened. The face changed without letup, no part of it ever still, from unmatched eyes to the overall shape.

Horrible as she looked in Daine's dreams, the physical reality of

Uusoae was much, much worse, The girl's hands and feet scrabbled in the dirt as she tried to get away from the Queen of Chaos, but her muscles were as soft as butter. Trembling, Daine covered her eyes. It didn't help. The Chaos queen was in her mind. Her constant shifts of body and face pulled at Daine's belly and ears and heart.

"You *dared* to interfere," the creature muttered, her breath scented richly with flowers and long-dead meat. "For my creature, and my plan—" Hard, sharp, gluey, oozing, pulpy, twining hands seized Daine's wrists.

The girl shrieked at the horror of that touch. Her scream went on, and on—

And ended, as if cut off by shears. They were nowhere, in a flat, dead space where there was no sound, no light, and no up or down. Mercifully, Daine could no longer feel Uusoae's touch. She only wished that she could no longer see the goddess, but her vision was crystal clear, even without light.

"It is as we said, Father Universe, Mother Flame," boomed a deep voice. Mithros, the Sun Lord, stood nearby. A huge black man with short-cropped hair, he wore gold armor over a kilted white tunic. In one hand he bore a gold spear with a blade that shone white-hot. "In defiance of the ban you laid upon her, she entered the mortal realms and made an alliance with one who influenced mortal lives. She did it to gain the upper hand against us, her brothers and sisters. Are your bans to be set aside lightly by her, or by any of us?"

Uusoae released Daine, and stepped away. The girl huddled in the space where she sat, teeth chattering, her many wounds bleeding and stinging.

Below, light blazed, all the colors of fire, stars, and the moon. "Uusoae, I am disappointed." The voice was somehow female and somehow the essence of light and heat. Daine heard it in her bones. "So soon after the last time, as well."

Overhead, the blackness moved. "It is her nature to strive, to overset, to imagine all as being different." This voice was male, a distillation of darkness and emptiness. "Still, to follow one's nature is no excuse to openly defy one's parents. Return to the confines of your own realm, Uusoae. There you will be confined in a cage of dead matter and starfire until your mother and I feel better about you."

"How long will that be?" demanded the ruler of Chaos.

A weight settled over Daine's shoulders; folds of black cloth wrapped around her. She looked up into Gainel's shadowy eyes. He smiled and gave her shoulder a gentle pat.

"Until the next star is born, my daughter," Mother Flame told

Uusoae firmly. "Rule your subjects from your cage, and think on the consequences of your behavior."

As one, the great powers—parents of gods and Chaos—spoke: *"It is done."*

Uusoae vanished. So, too, did that infinite blackness, and the ultimate light. Daine knelt on pale marble in the center of a vast courtyard rimmed with graceful columns and dotted with fountains. Half of the sky overhead was dark and blazed with stars; the other half showed daylight, with a sun just past noon.

Mithros sank into a backless golden chair with a sigh, and gave his spear to a young, brown-skinned boy in a blue tunic. Beside the Sun Lord a black cat slumbered in a silver chair. The Great Goddess tried to shoo it away, but the cat refused to take the hint. At last the Goddess moved the animal. Set on the marble court, the cat sniffed audibly and trotted over to Daine.

She held out a hand for it to smell. It did so, examined her with bright purple eyes, then sat in front of her and began to wash. All around them, gods settled into chairs, or onto fountain rims and benches.

Silver bloomed on either side of the cat: The badger and Broad Foot appeared. The duckmole still looked thin and worn, but there was amusement in his small eyes as he nodded to her.

"I think you'll be glad to know the Sorrows have returned to their kennels, all three of them," he informed her. "The mortal realms are rid of them, for now."

Gold-streak unwrapped itself from around the badger's neck and rolled over to Daine. "Miss you," it said, and trickled up her thighs to nestle in her lap.

Her eyes stung. Tears trickled down her cheeks. "Leaf and Jelly are dead," she told her first darking, the spy that Ozorne had set on her. "They were so brave."

"I know," Gold-streak replied. "They had freedom. They had choosing. They chose you. All darkings know. We never forget."

Sniffing, she wiped her eyes with a finger, and the Dream King's coat began to slide. Gainel, still behind Daine, resettled the garment around her shoulders. There was much less pain from that change than she had felt when he originally put the garment on her. Peeking under the coat's lapel, the girl saw that her injuries were mending themselves.

*—You will have scars,—*Gainel said,*—but those are signs of battles fought bravely.—*

"I don't hardly feel brave," she whispered. "I feel sad, and I feel *tired.*"

"Brother, there are things to deal with." Looking at the speaker,

Daine gulped and thrust herself backward, colliding with Gainel's legs. It was a serpent far larger than the one that had killed Rikash: Kidunka, the world snake, the first child born of Universe and Flame. "*Her*, for one." The serpent pointed its large, blunt nose at Daine.

Eyes—gods' eyes—turned to her. Daine wished very, very strongly that she could just sink into the marble floor.

"Leave be!" Sarra came from somewhere in the crowd to kneel and wrap her arms around her daughter. "You're frightening her!"

"What is there to deal with?" Weiryn demanded, joining his mate and child.

"She must choose," said the Great Mother Goddess, fixing emerald eyes on Daine.

"Choose what?" asked the girl. "I don't understand."

Mithros met her eyes with his. Daine quivered, but refused to look away. He was a god, the greatest of those who ruled two-leggers, but he was no Chaos queen. Her supply of awed terror was used up for today.

At last Mithros shook his head. "You are god-born, Veralidaine Sarrasri. Wherever the Godborn go, whatever they do, trouble—disorder—"

—*Change*,—interrupted Gainel.

Mithros glared at his brother, and went on. "All those things follow. We cannot have that, particularly not on the scale on which *you* seem to create it. We must then limit the area of your influence.

"Either you now return to the mortal realms to live out your life, or you stay here, a lesser goddess. Once you decide, you will never be able to change your mind. You will never again cross between the realms."

*Choose?* she thought, numb. Choose between Ma, who never should have died, and Numair? Her father, whom she barely knew, or Queen Thayet, King Jonathan, Onua?

But I could be a *goddess*. I could do magic like Ma does. I could visit Broad Foot's home. And Kit—seeing her won't be a trouble, since she can go where she likes.

What of Cloud, and Zek the marmoset, and Spots and Onua's Tahoi? Was she going to leave the Long Lake wolf pack behind? Confused, Daine buried her head in Sarra's shoulder. What of Alanna the Lioness, and Maura of Dunlath? Could she spend their lives watching them from the Divine Realms, without ever being with them?

Numair. From their very first meeting, he'd given her joy, delight, new things to learn. He was her teacher, her traveling companion, her comrade in arms. He was her love. When he kissed her . . . She could never give him up, not willingly.

She lifted her head as her heart turned to ice. She had promised Ma that she would return. She had given her *word*.

"The immortals, brother." A soft voice, filled with kindness, issued from the hood that shadowed the Black God's face. "For their part in Uusoae's plan, the Stormwings should be made to return here, and be forbidden the mortal realms for all of time. Perhaps *all* immortals should return. Humans have forgotten how to live with them."

"Too bad," growled the badger. "Once immortals had a place in things. Human mages threw them out—and *you* allowed it. You have a chance to fix a wrong here, not repeat it."

The Graveyard Hag thumped her walking stick on the ground to get attention. "The badger's right," Carthak's patron goddess said. "And it's good for humans to have a *few* things to be afraid of. Besides us, of course."

—*For nearly four centuries, I have labored with human dreams.*—Gainel's mind voice was firm.—*The immortals evoke rich dreams without my striving. Mortal spirits were poorer with the immortals gone, human imagination less fertile. I have enjoyed a few years' relief from a thankless task. Will you cripple me twice, brother?*—

Gold-streak put its small head beside Daine's ear and whispered, "Stormwings."

That tiny, high voice broke through her concentration on her choice that was no choice. "What?" she asked dully.

"Stormwings," repeated Gold-streak. "To be prisoned here."

"Good," she mumbled. "They're *evil*, they're—"

Memory silenced her. Cold air touched her cheek as a voice remarked, "That creature would defile what mortal killers left, so that humans couldn't lie about how glorious a soldier's death is." In her mind's eye, a tan-and-silver figure plummeted, claws extended, blond hair and bones streaming. Dark, imperious eyes, and pale, hypnotic ones, accused her.

She did not like raids on nests for eggs and nestlings, but her squirrel, crow, and snake friends did just that. Wolves chose scapegoats to bully, hurt, even reject completely from the pack. The sight of living prey fighting a hyena's devouring jaws or of a killer whale beating a seal pup to death might reduce her to tears, but those predators could not help their natures any more than Uusoae, or the Great Gods, could.

While she thought, the gods spoke, until Mithros cut off discussion with a wave of his hand. "Very well. Those immortals who dwelled in the mortal realms at the spring equinox may remain, if they choose. All others return here. As for the Stormwings—"

Gold-streak stretched itself wire-thin, raising its head until Mithros could see it. "What of Queen Barzha?" it asked.

Daine rose, gripping the edges of Gainel's coat to keep herself covered. "Gold-streak's right. Barzha's flock for certain—them that followed her into the mortal realms. Even—maybe even some that sided with Uusoae. Stormwings aren't humans. They aren't gods. They are what they were made to be. If you punish them for that, you may as well punish yourselves for what you are." She straightened, looking around at that magnificent assembly. If they wanted to admit her to their number, then they would have to get used to her speaking her mind. "You'll forgive me for saying so, but you don't look like you'd care to punish yourselves."

"Daine!" gasped Sarra, eyes wide with horror.

A weight pressed against her leg. She looked down: It was the badger.—*That's my kit.*—His mind voice spoke to her alone.

"Isn't *order* what makes you happy?" continued the girl. "Well, Stormwings are the nightmare of battle, pure and simple. What's that but a nightmare of disorder? How can you begrudge a mortal home to anyone that might scare two-leggers off war?"

Mithros glared. "The Stormwings may remain," the Sun Lord barked at last, his voice thunder in her ears.

The marble courtyard shimmered, then stretched, creating an immense bare space at the center. The moment that it ceased to move, Diamondflame, Wingstar, and Kitten popped onto it. Kitten whistled and chirruped, her scales red with anger. Seeing Daine, she trotted over and began to scold.

"I wasn't hardly given a choice," Daine told her, guessing what her charge was upset about. "They just grabbed me when that Uusoae appeared."

—*We* have *come to take Veralidaine home,*—said Diamondflame.— *The humans want to know what happened.*—

"She may not be able to return," said Broad Foot. "She has to choose either the mortal or the divine realms—she may not cross from one to the other."

—*And whose idea was* that?—Wingstar demanded. The duckmole began to explain.

"I ought to stay," Daine told Kitten, tears rolling down her cheeks unnoticed.

The young dragon replied in a stream of chatter and croaks. Tiny lightnings crackled over her scales.

*—She wants to know why,—*Gainel remarked in his soft voice.— *She wants to know why you will not go to your friends in the mortal realms.—*

Kitten reared onto her hindquarters and dug silver talons into the front of the Dream King's jacket. "Kit!" protested Daine, trying to work her friend's claws out of the fabric. "See, I promised Ma I would visit. I gave my word."

"Dear one, no." Sarra had moved away when the dragons arrived. Now she came forward, clothing over one arm. "You don't belong here. You would be so unhappy." She held out the garments. "I believe Gainel would like his coat back eventually."

Numbly Daine reached for the clothes, still trying to understand her mother's words. "But—I gave you my promise. I don't break my promises."

"You're not breaking it. I'm releasing you. There's a good man and true friends waiting for you at home. That man is a fair *strange* man, certainly, but he's a good one." Sarra motioned, and Daine was encircled by a glittering curtain. The girl couldn't see out; no one else could see in. "Hand me Gainel's coat, dear." A hand pierced the wall, and slender fingers beckoned. Daine gave the coat to her mother, who pulled it out of the enclosure.

Where the underthings, lavender dress, bodice, and slippers had come from, Daine could never guess. She put all of them on. "Ma, I'm decent."

The enclosure vanished. Weiryn had one arm around her mother; he clasped a bow and quiver in his free hand. Looking for Kitten, Daine was horrified to find that the young dragon was scolding Mithros quite emphatically.

"Your going back won't be so bad," Sarra told Daine, eyes filling. "We'll come to you on the equinoxes and solstices."

"But I *promised—*"

"We can't restore the years together that were taken from us," Sarra interrupted. "It was misery, but we can't change it. Seeing you here taught me you're adult now. You're needed, and you're valued, and you're loved. Those are wondrous gifts, sweetling. I can't let you throw them away." Tears spilled down her cheeks and her smile quivered, but her blue eyes were steady.

"She is right," Weiryn said gruffly. "The mortals need you, as you do them." He offered the bow and quiver to her. "Since you lost the one you had."

Slowly, feeling numb, Daine accepted the gift. The bow changed subtly, until it fitted her strength and grip exactly, as the last bow Weiryn had given her had done.

"Veralidaine, do you choose?" boomed Mithros. "Diamondflame, take your grandchild in hand!"

*—Skysong, come here,—*ordered her grandsire. Kitten obeyed, still muttering.

"Our daughter is going home," Sarra told the gods, chin high, "to the mortal realms."

Mithros looked at Daine. "Is it so?"

The girl nodded.

"Then I return you—" began the Sun Lord.

*—No,—*said Diamondflame, cutting Mithros off.—*We shall take her back. Sometimes those whom the gods return to other realms—how shall I put it?—they go astray. What a pity it would be if she entered the realms of Chaos, or of death, by mistake. Better not to take chances. Come, Veralidaine.—*

She thought the blue dragon was being unfair. Still, another dragon ride sounded wonderful, and it would give her a brief rest before she plunged back into mopping up Ozorne's army.

Sarra hugged Daine tightly, then kissed her cheeks. "The fall equinox isn't far off," she said. "We'll come to you then."

She stepped back to let Weiryn hug his daughter. "I am glad that you were able to visit us, Veralidaine. Try not to lose that bow."

"I'll try, Da." She knelt to bring herself closer to Broad Foot and the badger. "Thank you," she told them, running a hand over the duck-mole's springy fur and scratching the badger's ears. "You helped save Tortall, both of you."

"It was the least we could do for the friend who tricked Uusoae into the open," Broad Foot replied. "G'day, then, Weiryn's daughter. We'll meet again, I know." Silvery fire condensed around his form. Inside it, he grew smaller, and smaller, until he was gone.

Daine lifted Gold-streak from the badger's wide back and kissed the blot. "What will become of you darkings now?" she asked.

Gold-streak rubbed its head against her cheek. "Dragons invite us to Dragonlands. Darkings go there for now. We must think of what we will become."

"Good luck to you, then," she said.

"We will always remember you," Gold-streak told her. It trickled over to Wingstar to climb onto the dragon's back.

"Badger," Daine said, tears filling her eyes. "I s'pose you're done with me, now that I'm grown and know my da and all."

He thrust a cold, wet nose into the hollow at the base of her throat.

She flinched. Even after he backed away, the sense of coldness remained. Touching the spot, the girl felt a chilly metal curve, its base wrapped in silver wire, attached to a chain. Lifting the claw, she saw that it had been cleaned so thoroughly that there was nothing to remind her of the use she'd made of it. "You left that where it might have been lost," the badger remarked, dark eyes glittering with amusement.

Daine buried her face in his heavy fur, holding him tightly. "Thank you," she whispered, voice cracking. "I'll never take it off again."

"I will check on you often, to be sure you keep your promise. You aren't rid of *me* so easily, my kit." Rearing slightly, he nudged the claw with his nose. "Ozorne always underestimated you. It was a lesson he never seemed to learn."

*—Come,—*ordered Diamondflame. Kitten was already tucked into the circle of his forepaws and talons, safe within the great dragon's hold.—*Gods annoy me.—*

"As dragons annoy us," snapped the Graveyard Hag. She winked at Daine. "Good to see you again, dearie."

"I bet," muttered the girl. Giving the badger a last hug, she climbed onto Diamondflame's back, tucking her skirts so that she could sit astride the dragon's neck. She looked at Sarra once more. "Ma? Can you do something for me?"

Sarra came to the dragon's side. "If I can."

"Can I see you as the Green Lady? Just once?"

Sarra laughed; Weiryn grinned. Light, gold and soft, gathered around Daine's ma. She grew taller. A simple green cotton dress, heavily decorated with embroideries in complex designs, fluttered around her body in a wind that Daine couldn't feel. There was a sheer green veil over Sarra's face and hair; it too fluttered and moved as if windblown. Looking at her, Daine felt comfort and hope.

"You're beautiful, Ma," she said quietly. "I love you."

Sarra raised her veil. "I love you too, sweet."

*—Stand back,—*warned Diamondflame. He opened his great wings, and took flight.

# ⤙ EPILOGUE ⤚

When they glided out of the clouds, Port Legann lay below. On the sea, a few ships still burned. Yamani vessels herded those they had captured into the reopened harbor. All around the city the land was tattered, scorched, and frayed. Everywhere lay the dead. Groups roamed the battlefields, gathering the wounded and the dead, giving the death stroke to dying animals, or scavenging weapons and valuables.

On level ground before the north gate, tables had been placed. On one side, Daine saw enemy leaders—nobles of the Copper Isles, Carthaki renegades—well guarded by royal troops. Opposite them were King Jonathan, reunited and handfast with Queen Thayet, Lord Imrah, the Yamani admiral who had commanded the ten ships that had mopped up the enemy fleet, Onua and her big dog Tahoi, and the mage Harailt. Papers were strewn over the wooden tables, and scribes stood by, heating wax for the seals that would be fixed to each document.

Close by his monarchs, Sir Raoul was perched on a camp stool. A healer examined deep cuts in his scalp and left arm as the big knight tried not to flinch. In the distance, Daine saw her Rider friend Evin and Sarge helping to lift the wounded into wagons that would carry them into the city.

Diamondflame landed on a clear space in the battlefield, Wingstar behind him. Freed of her grandfather's hold, Kitten trotted around to his side, whistling and clucking. Daine looked where her dragonet pointed, and saw a tall, thin, reptilian creature race toward them from the north gate, his tail draped like a train over one long arm. Hard on his heels galloped her small, shaggy gray pony. A broken rope that trailed behind Cloud showed how she had managed to get out of the stables, where she'd stayed since Daine first came to Legann.

Tkaa halted and nodded to the dragons as Daine put her bow and quiver on a nearby tree stump. That done, she threw her arms around Cloud's neck. In mind speech she told the mare everything that had happened, while Cloud lipped her sleeve.

I'm glad you came back, the mare said when she was done. I don't have the patience to train a new rider anymore.

Daine laughed, and straightened. "You *never* had patience with any rider, *including* me!"

Tahoi beat Onua in the run to greet them. Rearing on his hind legs, the dog planted his paws on Daine's shoulders and proceeded to wash her face.

"No—no, Tahoi, that's sweet, but really, I'm practically almost clean!" Holding his paws, Daine backed the dog up until he said that he would be good and not wash her. She released him. He lunged, ran his tongue from her chin to her forehead, then sat, tail pounding the dry earth.

"Very funny," muttered Daine, and wiped her face.

Onua gave her a quick, tight hug. "Ozorne?" she asked, examining the girl for any sign of injury.

"Dead," replied Daine, flushing at the memory. "Just as dead as I could make him without dragging him before the Black God myself. Numair?"

"No one knows" was the quiet reply. "The magic-sign of his duel with Hadensra vanished a while back, but no one's had a chance to go that way to check on him. What in the name of the Goddess happened? There was a—a sound, and the next instant, at least half of the immortals disappeared from the battlefield. Just—vanished!"

"It's a long story," Daine told her friend. "Ask Big Blue to tell it to you." She pointed to Diamondflame, then grabbed her skirt with one hand and mounted Cloud. "I'm going after Numair."

—*Big Blue?*—echoed Kitten's grandfather.—*Hm. An interesting nickname.*—

Onua grabbed Cloud's mane, and was almost bitten for her pains. "Daine, there may be enemy soldiers out that way, still. Wait for a cleanup squad—"

Without needing a word from Daine, Cloud walked over to the tree stump. Daine grabbed her father's bow and quiver, and smiled at K'mir. "It isn't me who has to be wary of them," she said gently. "They'd best be afraid of *me*." She nudged Cloud, who set off at a trot.

She was glad that her mare knew where she wanted to go. Exhaustion, banished temporarily while she wore Gainel's coat, was gnawing at her. She prayed that her words to Onua weren't vainglory, and that she'd be able to use her bow if necessary. It would be too embarrassing to have survived all this, only to be cut down by a straggler determined to make one last kill before he surrendered or escaped.

Watching where she placed her hooves, Cloud picked her way through bodies and equipment for war. The giant wooden barriers made to deter jumping horses had been pulled aside, opening gaps in their line. Pony and rider passed the wooden towers, now black and crumbling after their encounter with dragonfire, and rode through a break in the low earthen wall.

The ground sloped, leading to the camp beside the river. Here the destruction was complete. Tents and goods had been destroyed, burned, or stolen. The bodies of those who had defended, not run, lay everywhere.

The red-and-black globe of magics had not come from the camp, but from upriver. Daine gripped trembling hands in Cloud's mane and prayed as they turned right, following the water east.

Deep gashes were torn from the earth. The shallow river was half blocked by stones and what looked like a yard-long bank of earth-colored glass. Already the water was carving a new path around the obstruction. Steam drifted in the hollows under the trees.

"Whoever you are, if you're here to kill me, you'll need to do it while I remain prone," a familiar voice said nearby. "Have the decency to be quick about it, so I can get back to my rest."

Daine tumbled off Cloud's back, trying to see where he was. "What I've got in mind isn't near so quick as killing!"

There was a long silence; her heart twisted within her chest. Then she heard a cracked whisper: *"Daine?"* Under the long, drooping branches of a nearby willow, a dark figure lurched to its feet.

She ran to Numair, slamming into him with enough force to drive him back against the willow's trunk. "That *hurt*," he gasped. Before she could apologize, he was kissing her nose, her cheeks, her forehead, her lips. She kissed him back. They came up for air, then kissed again, their hands checking each other's bodies, for serious injury as well as simply for the joy of touch.

They came up for air several more times before they had calmed down enough to let each other go—although Numair kept his grip on Daine's hands. "Will you marry me?"

She grinned up at him. "Maybe someday," she replied, eyes dancing. "But only if you're very, very good."

"What if I'm very, very bad?" he whispered, the heat in his voice making her shiver agreeably. He gathered her into his arms and eased his mouth over hers, caressing her lips with his, teasing, until all she could do was hang in his grip.

"Still maybe someday," she replied finally, when she could do more than simply gasp. "But you're welcome to try and convince me to make it sooner."

This is as lovely as colts frisking in the sun, Cloud remarked from outside the screen of willow branches, but you're going to have company. Kitten is bringing Tkaa and Onua here.

Daine giggled and told Numair what the pony had said.

"Then by all means, let us totter down to meet them," said the man with a sigh. "I will resume persuading you in regard to matrimony at another time, when we've rested, and eaten, and had baths."

Daine slung his arm around her shoulders. She was tired, but she could feel him trembling as well. From the grayness of his skin, his battle had cost him a great deal. "So that Inar Hadensra was a hard fight?"

Numair dug his free hand into his shirt pocket and produced a ruby globe: the dead mage's eye. "The hardest. I believe I'll retire and return to juggling for a living." He tossed the ruby into the river. "I could support us with juggling, if you were to marry me."

"We'll see," she said.

"I take it Uusoae was acting though Ozorne?" Numair asked quietly.

Daine nodded. "I'll tell you all of it later. It will take a bit of telling."

There were Stormwings overhead. They descended from behind the cover of the clouds in a spiraling pattern, feathers blazing where they reflected the sun. By the time Tkaa, Kitten, Onua, and Tahoi met Daine and Numair and brought them to the north gate of Port Legann, the Stormwings were at work on the bodies of the fallen. Watching them from a distance, Daine realized that it might be just as well if she told only a few, trusted friends that she had spoken for the Stormwings' right to stay in the mortal realms. Somehow, she had the idea that not everyone would understand.

Tamora Pierce has nineteen fantasy novels for teenagers in print world-wide in English, German, Swedish, and Danish, and audio books in Danish and English, with two more—*Shatterglass* and *Trickster's Choice*, the first book in a new Tortallan series—to appear in 2003. *Alanna: The First Adventure* is her first published book and the foundation of the Tortallan quartets: Song of the Lioness, The Immortals, and The Protector of the Small. *Alanna* received an Author's Citation by the New Jersey Institute of Technology's Seventeenth Annual New Jersey Writers Conference and was on the Recommended Fantasy list of the Preconference on Genres of the Young Adult Services Division of the American Library Association, June 1991. Her other publications include short stories, articles, and her two Circle of Magic quartets. She was also an actor and writer for a radio drama and comedy production company in the 1980s and recently resumed her voice actor's motley for Bruce Coville's Full Cast Audio book company. Tammy has been a housemother, a social worker, a secretary, and an agent's assistant. She lives in New York with her Spouse-Creature, technoweenie Tim Liebe, three cats, two parakeets, and wildlife rescued from the park.